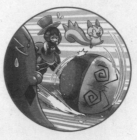

Message from
Hidenori Kusaka

Pokémon Adventures has reached its 25th anniversary. Twenty-five years—that's a quarter of a century, a very long time. I have aged that much as well, and so have the readers! I'm sure many of you have grown up and started working. But when I'm playing *Pokémon*, I can return to the old days, when I was young. *Pokémon* is such a unique work that can be both old and new.

Message from
Satoshi Yamamoto

I worked on Adventure 46 while repeatedly listening to *Chimamire no Hato* (The Bloody Pidgeon) by Itsutsu no Akai Fusen.

Hidenori Kusaka is the writer for *Pokémon Adventures*. Running continuously for over 25 years, *Pokémon Adventures* is the only manga series to completely cover all the *Pokémon* games and has become one of the most popular series of all time. In addition to writing manga, he also edits children's books and plans mixed-media projects for Shogakukan's children's magazines. He uses the Pokémon Electrode as his author portrait.

Satoshi Yamamoto is the artist for *Pokémon Adventures*, which he began working on in 2001, starting with volume 10. Yamamoto launched his manga career in 1993 with the horror-action title *Kimen Senshi*, which ran in Shogakukan's *Weekly Shonen Sunday* magazine, followed by the series *Kaze no Denshosha*. Yamamoto's favorite manga creators/artists include FUJIKO F FUJIO (*Doraemon*), Yukinobu Hoshino (*2001 Nights*), and Katsuhiro Otomo (*Akira*). He loves films, monsters, detective novels, and punk rock music. He uses the Pokémon Swalot as his artist portrait.

Pokémon™

Adventures X·Y

Story by
Hidenori Kusaka

Art by
Satoshi Yamamoto

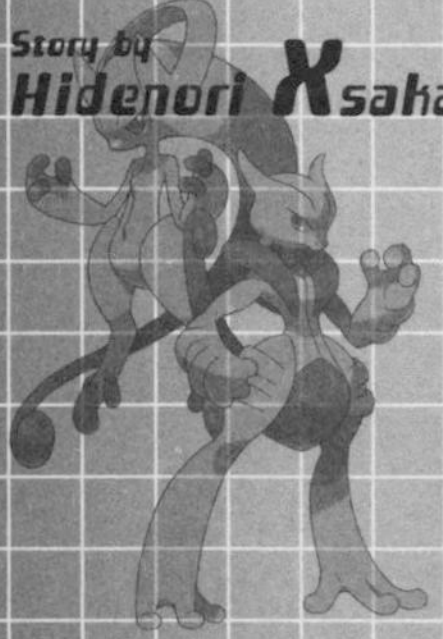

6
VOLUME SIX

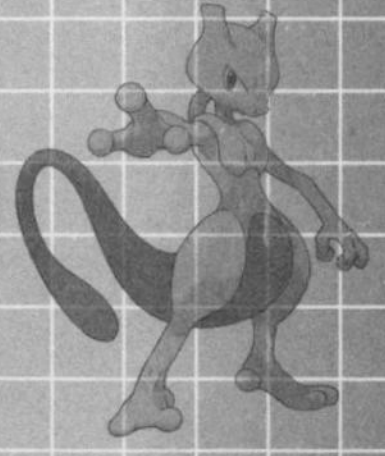

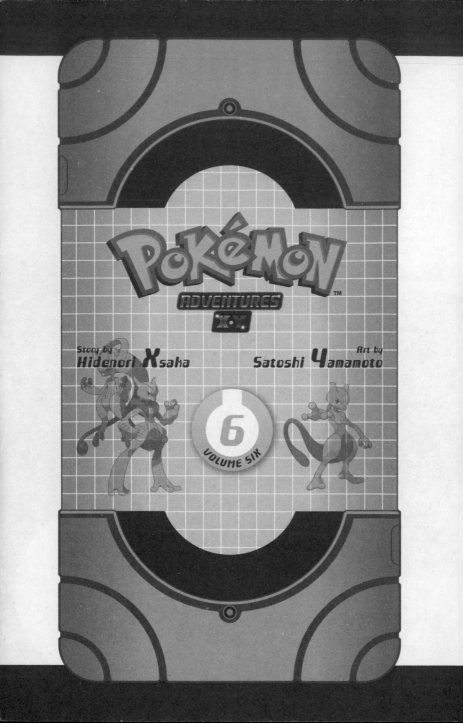

The Story Thus Far...

A story about young people entrusted with Pokédexes by the world's leading Pokémon researchers. Together with their Pokémon, they travel, do battle, and evolve!

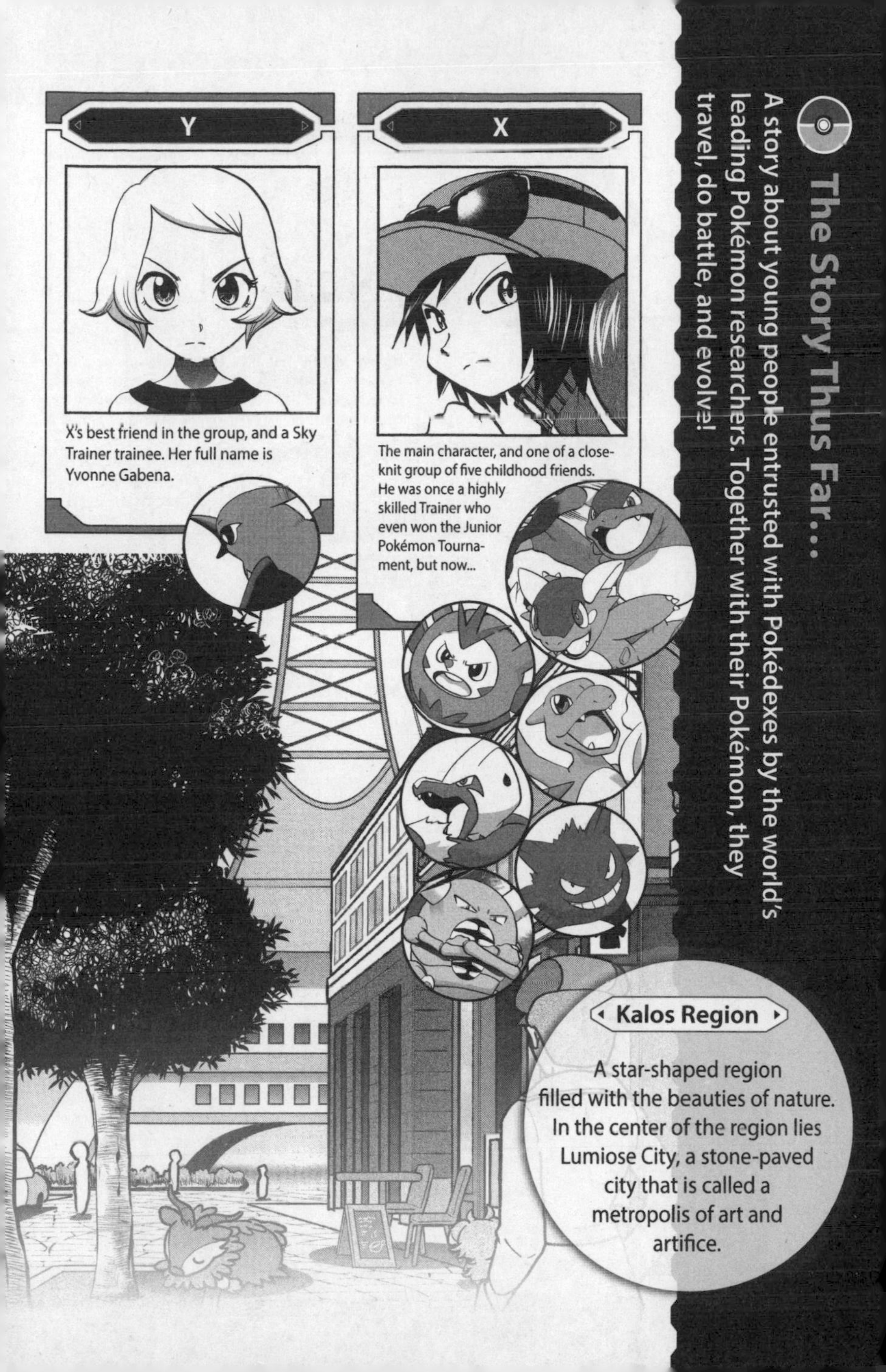

X
Y

X

The main character, and one of a close-knit group of five childhood friends. He was once a highly skilled Trainer who even won the Junior Pokémon Tournament, but now...

Y

X's best friend in the group, and a Sky Trainer trainee. Her full name is Yvonne Gabena.

Kalos Region

A star-shaped region filled with the beauties of nature. In the center of the region lies Lumiose City, a stone-paved city that is called a metropolis of art and artifice.

THE STORY THUS FAR

The Kalos region, Vaniville Town—four close childhood friends are trying to get the reclusive X out of his room when the Legendary Pokémon Yveltal and Xerneas suddenly appear. Then they are all attacked by a mysterious group wearing red suits who try to steal the Mega Ring that X wears on his arm like a bracelet. Now X's team is complete! They learn about the current where-abouts of Lysandre and prepare for the final battle. X and his friends are headed for the Pokémon Village—but Xerosic has been waiting for them. Trevor and the others fall for Malamar's hypnosis trap. Meanwhile, Blaine is in a hurry to meet Mewtwo...

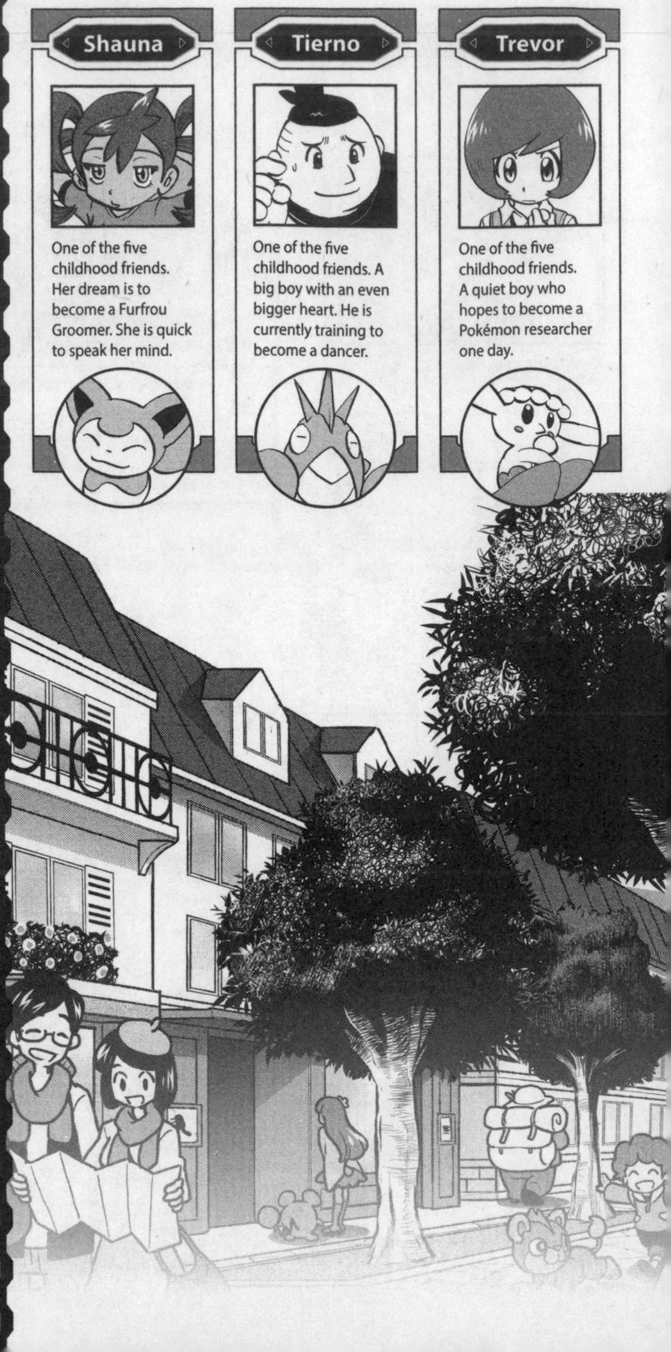
Shauna
One of the five childhood friends. Her dream is to become a Furfrou Groomer. She is quick to speak her mind.
Tierno
One of the five childhood friends. A big boy with an even bigger heart. He is currently training to become a dancer.
Trevor
One of the five childhood friends. A quiet boy who hopes to become a Pokémon researcher one day.

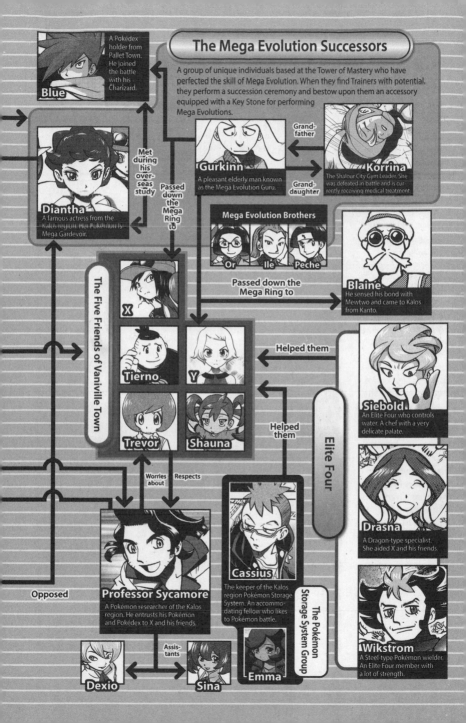

The Mega Evolution Successors

A group of unique individuals based at the Tower of Mastery who have perfected the skill of Mega Evolution. When they find Trainers with potential, they perform a succession ceremony and bestow upon them an accessory equipped with a Key Stone for performing Mega Evolutions.

Blue
A Pokédex holder from Pallet Town. He joined the battle with his Charizard.

Gurkinn
A pleasant elderly man known as the Mega Evolution Guru.

Grandfather

Granddaughter

Korrina
The Shalour City Gym Leader. She was defeated in battle and is currently receiving medical treatment.

Diantha
A famous actress from the Kalos region. Her Pokémon is Mega Gardevoir.

Met during his overseas study

Passed down the Mega Ring to

Mega Evolution Brothers

Or | **Ile** | **Peche**

Passed down the Mega Ring to

Blaine
He sensed his bond with Mewtwo and came to Kalos from Kanto.

The Five Friends of Vaniville Town

X

Tierno

Y

Trevor

Shauna

Helped them

Helped them

Elite Four

Siebold
An Elite Four who controls water. A chef with a very delicate palate.

Drasna
A Dragon-type specialist. She aided X and his friends.

Wikstrom
A Steel-type Pokémon wielder. An Elite Four member with a lot of strength.

Worries about

Respects

Cassius
The keeper of the Kalos region Pokémon Storage System. An accommodating fellow who likes to Pokémon battle.

Professor Sycamore
A Pokémon researcher of the Kalos region. He entrusts his Pokémon and Pokédex to X and his friends.

Opposed

The Pokémon Storage System Group

Emma

Dexio

Assistants

Sina

Character Connection Chart

Track the connections between the people revolving around X.

Attacked

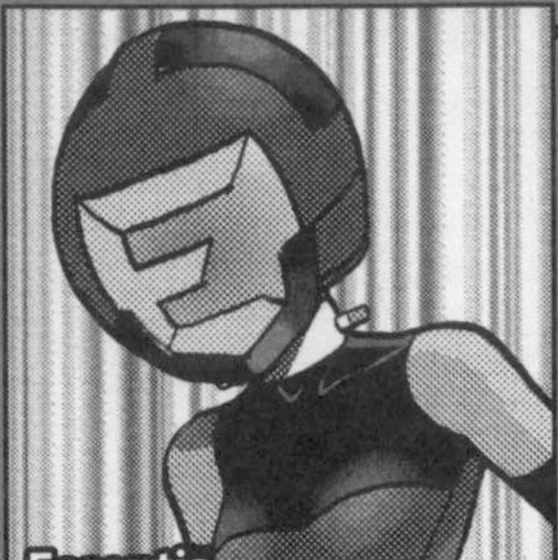

Essentia

A mysterious Trainer who wears an Expansion Suit.

Developed

Obeys

Team Flare

The devious members of this scheming organization are identifiable by their red uniforms and have been wreaking havoc on the Kalos region. Their goal is to capture the legendary Pokémon Yveltal and Xerneas, and because of that their paths cross with X and his friends.

Old friends

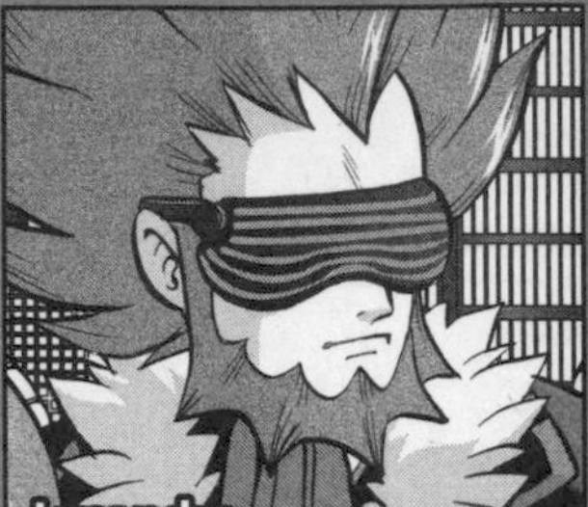

Lysandre

The developer of the Holo Caster. He has a reputation for charitable acts but is also secretly the boss of Team Flare.

Enemies

Trusts

Loyal

Support

Regrets supporting him

Team Flare's Scientific Team

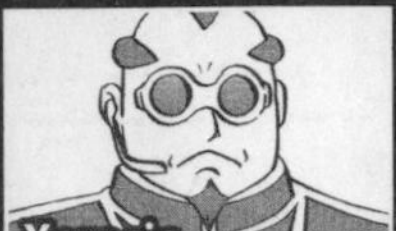

Xerosic

Member of Unit A. The only male member of the team, he is in charge of handling and developing Team Flare's gadgets.

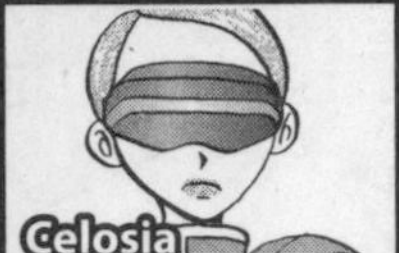

Celosia

Member of Unit A. A vengeful woman who somehow always bounces back from failure.

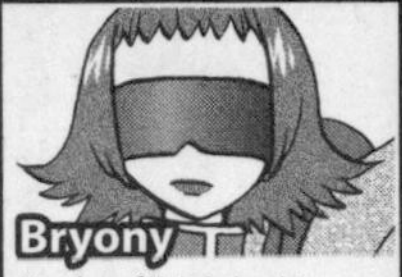

Bryony

Member of Unit A. A quiet bookworm and military scientist who studies battles.

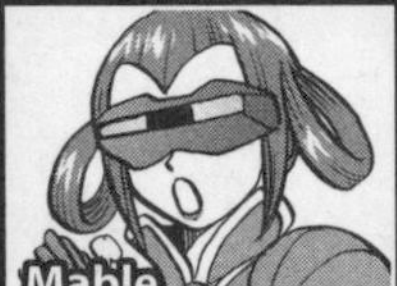

Mable

Member of Unit B. Outspoken and emotional.

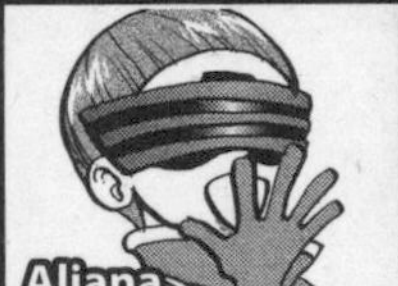

Aliana

Member of Unit B. Charged with obtaining the Mega Ring.

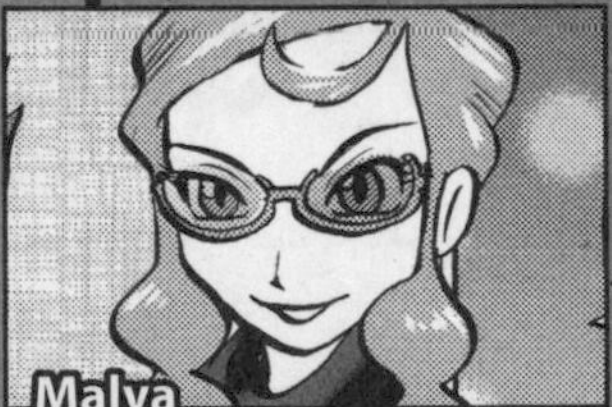

Malva

A member of the Kalos Elite Four who is actually a member of Team Flare. She usually works as a news reporter and takes advantage of the mass media.

Comes up with strategies for their schemes

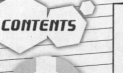

POKÉMON ADVENTURES — the 12th Chapter

twelfth

X·Y

CONTENTS

6
VOLUME SIX

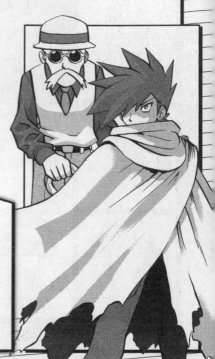

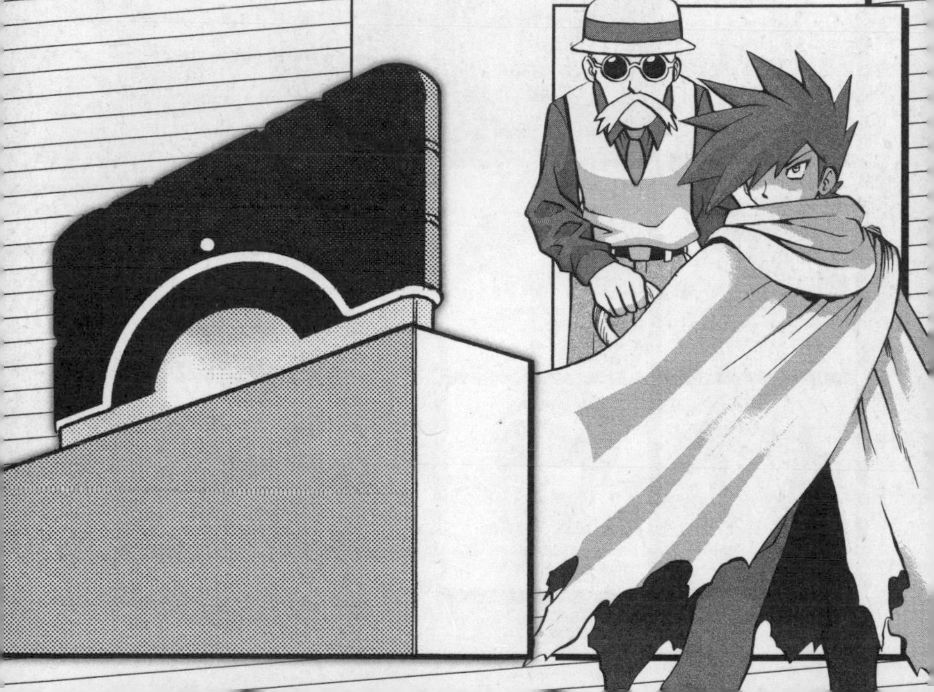

Adventure #40
Chesnaught Protects

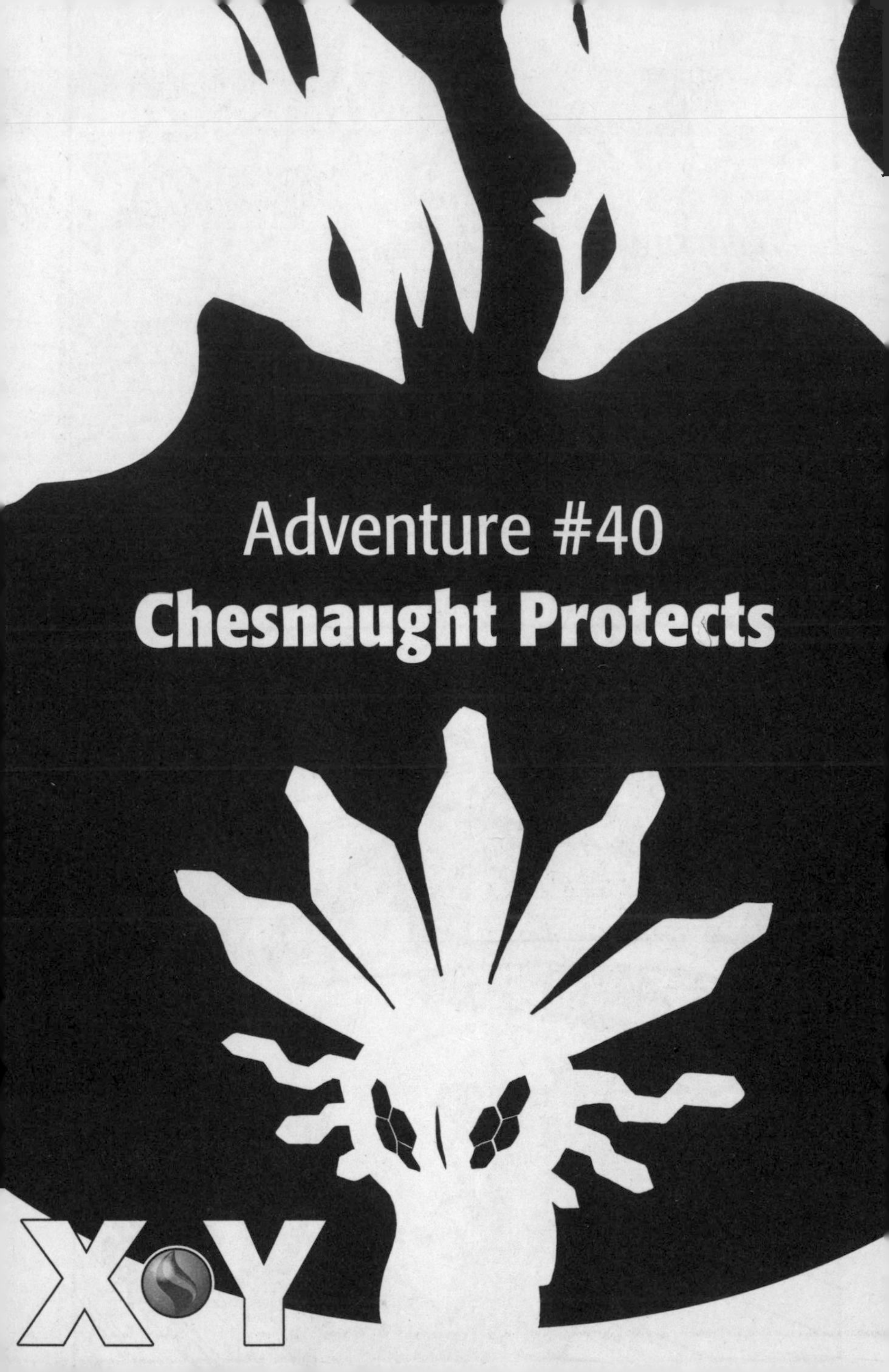

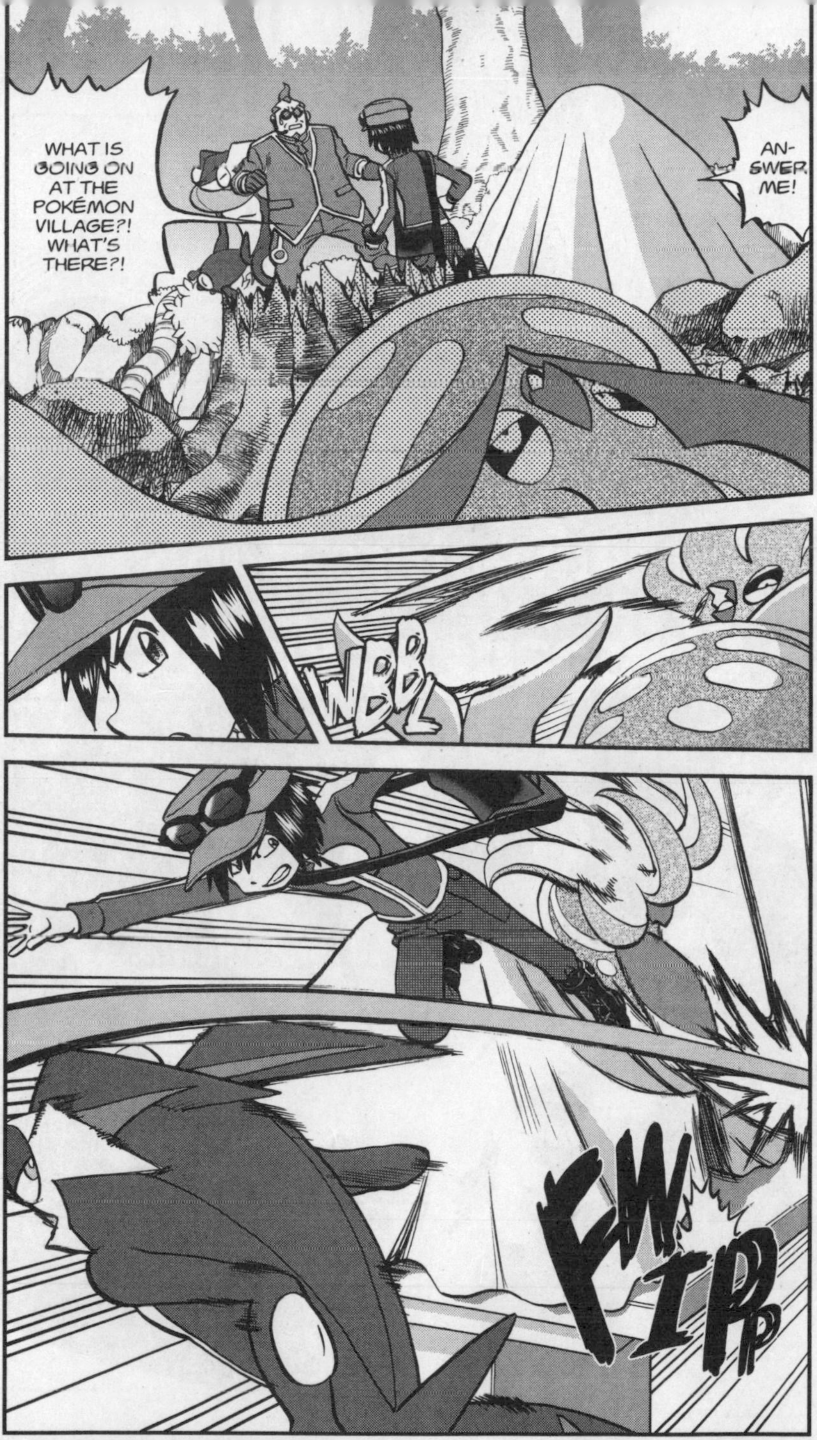
WHAT IS GOING ON AT THE POKÉMON VILLAGE?! WHAT'S THERE?!
AN-SWER ME!
WBBL
FWIPP

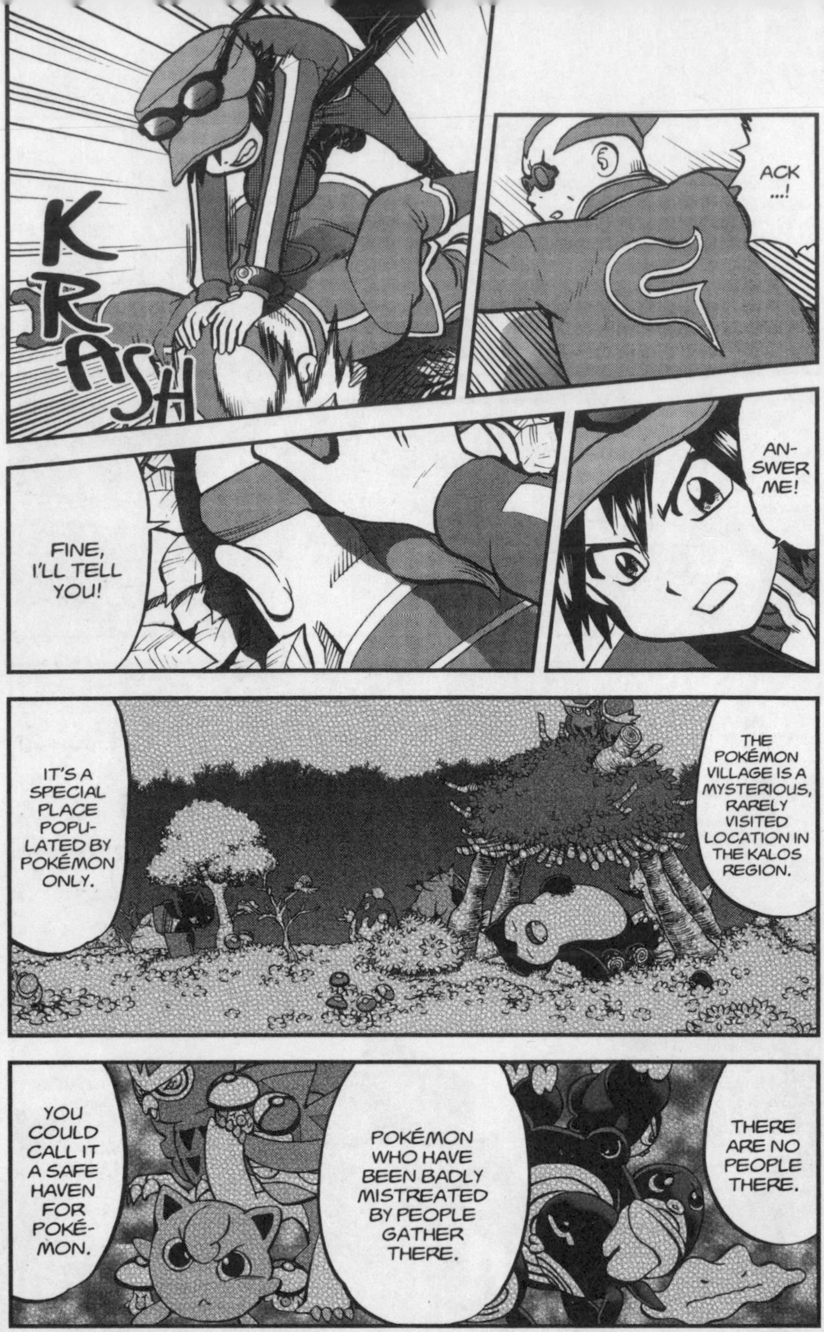
ACK ...!
KRASH
AN-SWER ME!
FINE, I'LL TELL YOU!
THE POKÉMON VILLAGE IS A MYSTERIOUS, RARELY VISITED LOCATION IN THE KALOS REGION.
IT'S A SPECIAL PLACE POPU-LATED BY POKÉMON ONLY.
THERE ARE NO PEOPLE THERE.
POKÉMON WHO HAVE BEEN BADLY MISTREATED BY PEOPLE GATHER THERE.
YOU COULD CALL IT A SAFE HAVEN FOR POKÉ-MON.

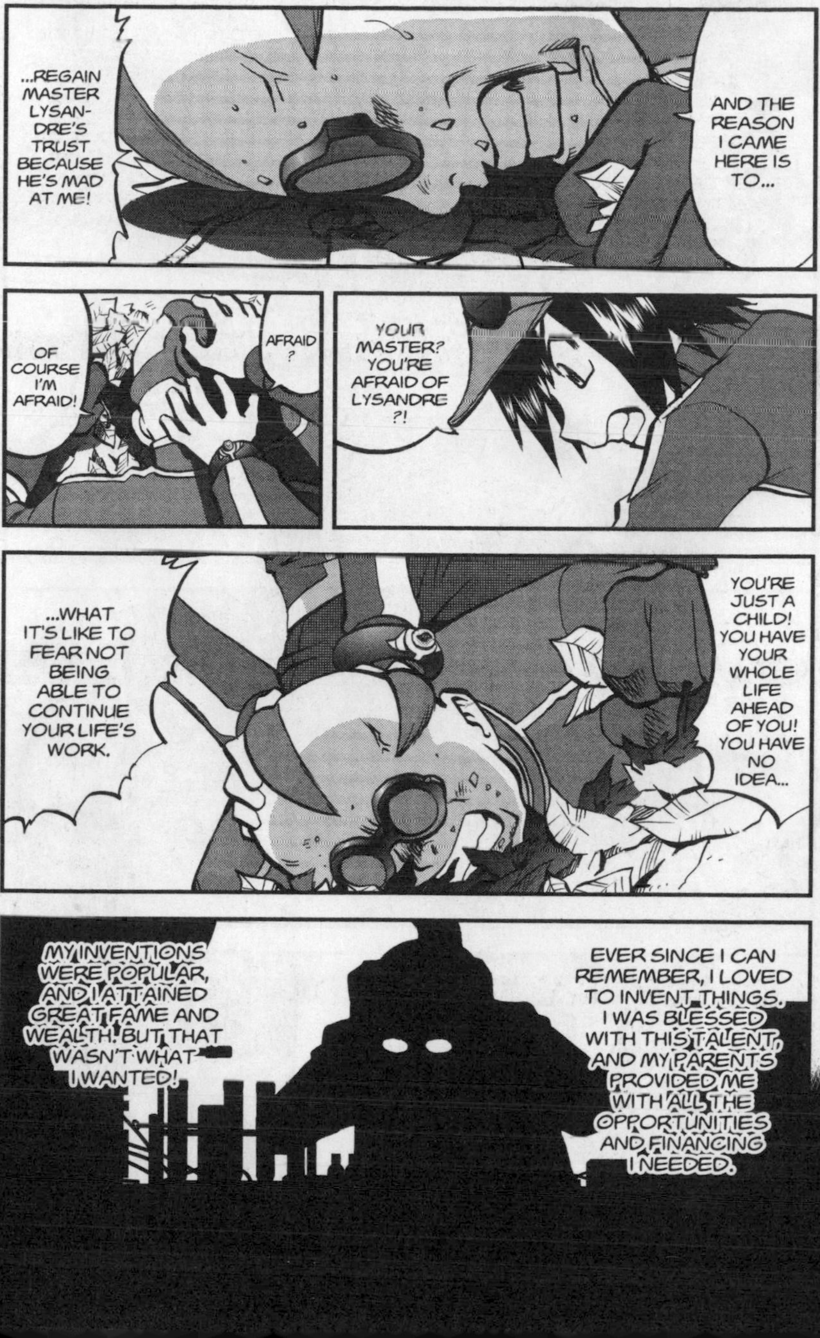
AND THE REASON I CAME HERE IS TO...
...REGAIN MASTER LYSANDRE'S TRUST BECAUSE HE'S MAD AT ME!
YOUR MASTER? YOU'RE AFRAID OF LYSANDRE?!
AFRAID?
OF COURSE I'M AFRAID!
YOU'RE JUST A CHILD! YOU HAVE YOUR WHOLE LIFE AHEAD OF YOU! YOU HAVE NO IDEA...
...WHAT IT'S LIKE TO FEAR NOT BEING ABLE TO CONTINUE YOUR LIFE'S WORK.
EVER SINCE I CAN REMEMBER, I LOVED TO INVENT THINGS. I WAS BLESSED WITH THIS TALENT, AND MY PARENTS PROVIDED ME WITH ALL THE OPPORTUNITIES AND FINANCING I NEEDED.
MY INVENTIONS WERE POPULAR, AND I ATTAINED GREAT FAME AND WEALTH. BUT THAT WASN'T WHAT I WANTED!

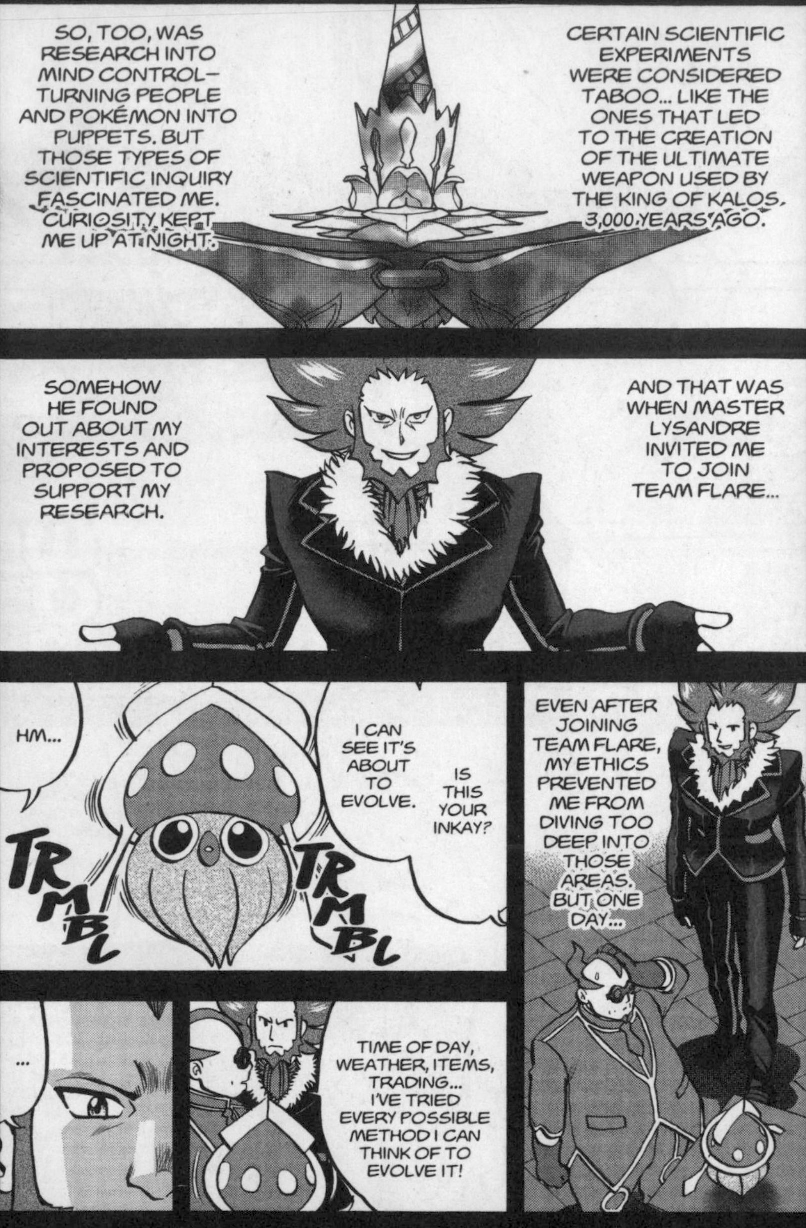
CERTAIN SCIENTIFIC EXPERIMENTS WERE CONSIDERED TABOO... LIKE THE ONES THAT LED TO THE CREATION OF THE ULTIMATE WEAPON USED BY THE KING OF KALOS, 3,000 YEARS AGO.
SO, TOO, WAS RESEARCH INTO MIND CONTROL—TURNING PEOPLE AND POKÉMON INTO PUPPETS. BUT THOSE TYPES OF SCIENTIFIC INQUIRY FASCINATED ME. CURIOSITY KEPT ME UP AT NIGHT.
AND THAT WAS WHEN MASTER LYSANDRE INVITED ME TO JOIN TEAM FLARE...
SOMEHOW HE FOUND OUT ABOUT MY INTERESTS AND PROPOSED TO SUPPORT MY RESEARCH.
EVEN AFTER JOINING TEAM FLARE, MY ETHICS PREVENTED ME FROM DIVING TOO DEEP INTO THOSE AREAS. BUT ONE DAY...
IS THIS YOUR INKAY?
I CAN SEE IT'S ABOUT TO EVOLVE.
HM...
TRMBL
TRMBL
TIME OF DAY, WEATHER, ITEMS, TRADING... I'VE TRIED EVERY POSSIBLE METHOD I CAN THINK OF TO EVOLVE IT!
...

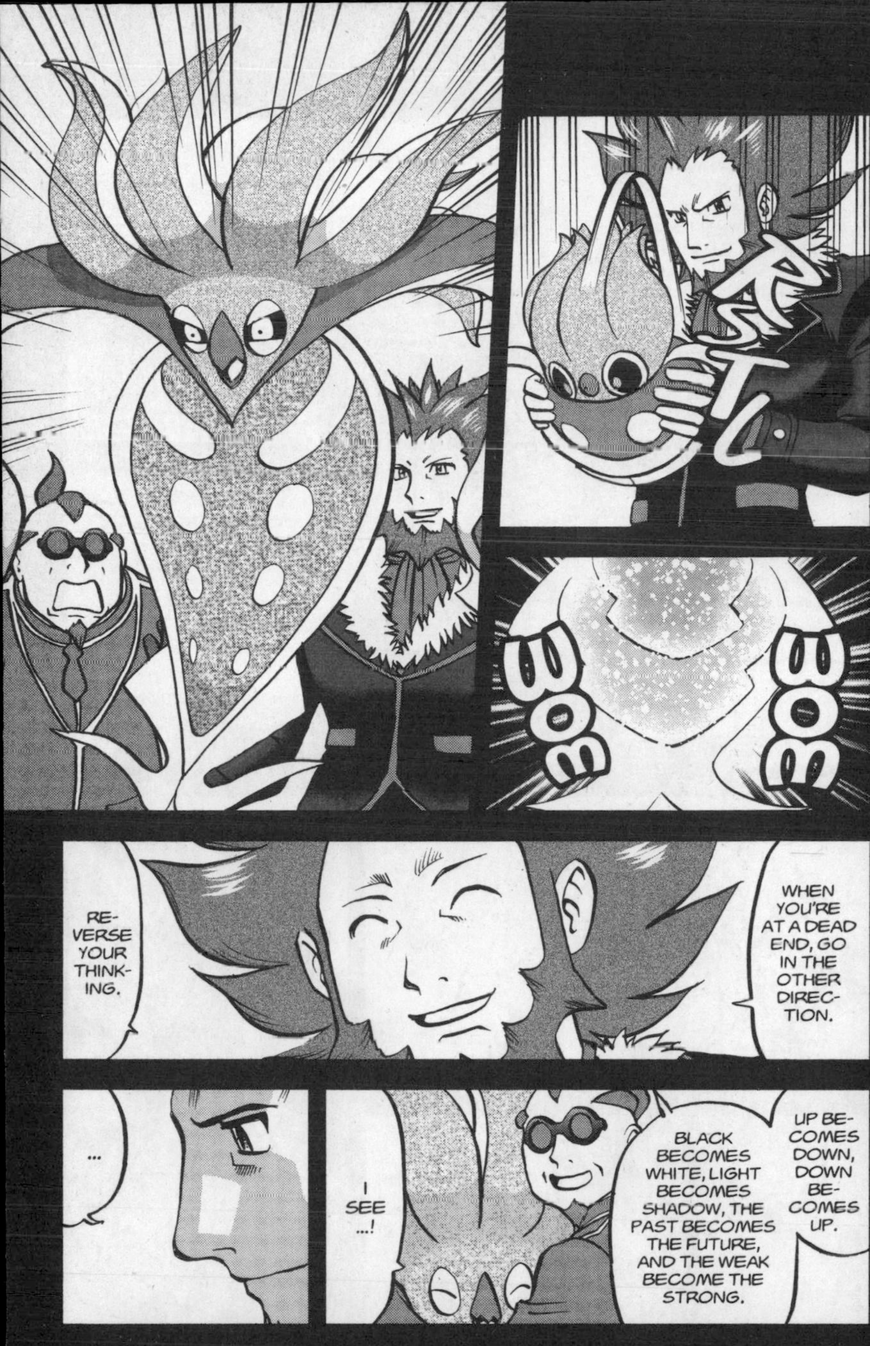

RSTL
BOOM
BOOM
WHEN YOU'RE AT A DEAD END, GO IN THE OTHER DIRECTION.
REVERSE YOUR THINKING.
UP BECOMES DOWN, DOWN BECOMES UP.
BLACK BECOMES WHITE, LIGHT BECOMES SHADOW, THE PAST BECOMES THE FUTURE, AND THE WEAK BECOME THE STRONG.
I SEE ...!
...

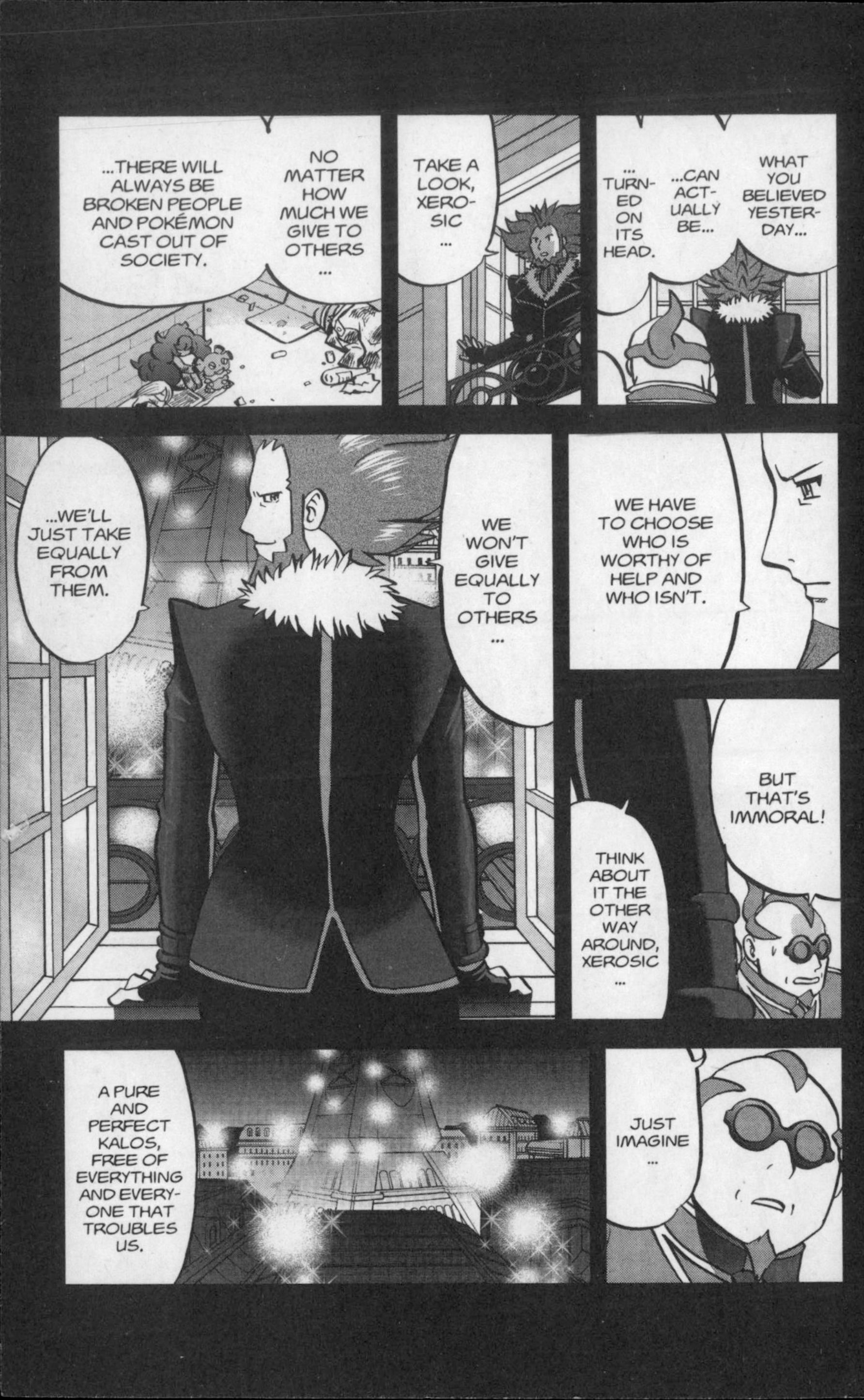
WHAT YOU BELIEVED YESTER-DAY...
...CAN ACT-UALLY BE...
...TURN-ED ON ITS HEAD.
TAKE A LOOK, XERO-SIC...
NO MATTER HOW MUCH WE GIVE TO OTHERS...
...THERE WILL ALWAYS BE BROKEN PEOPLE AND POKÉMON CAST OUT OF SOCIETY.
WE HAVE TO CHOOSE WHO IS WORTHY OF HELP AND WHO ISN'T.
BUT THAT'S IMMORAL!
THINK ABOUT IT THE OTHER WAY AROUND, XEROSIC...
WE WON'T GIVE EQUALLY TO OTHERS...
...WE'LL JUST TAKE EQUALLY FROM THEM.
JUST IMAGINE...
A PURE AND PERFECT KALOS, FREE OF EVERYTHING AND EVERY-ONE THAT TROUBLES US.

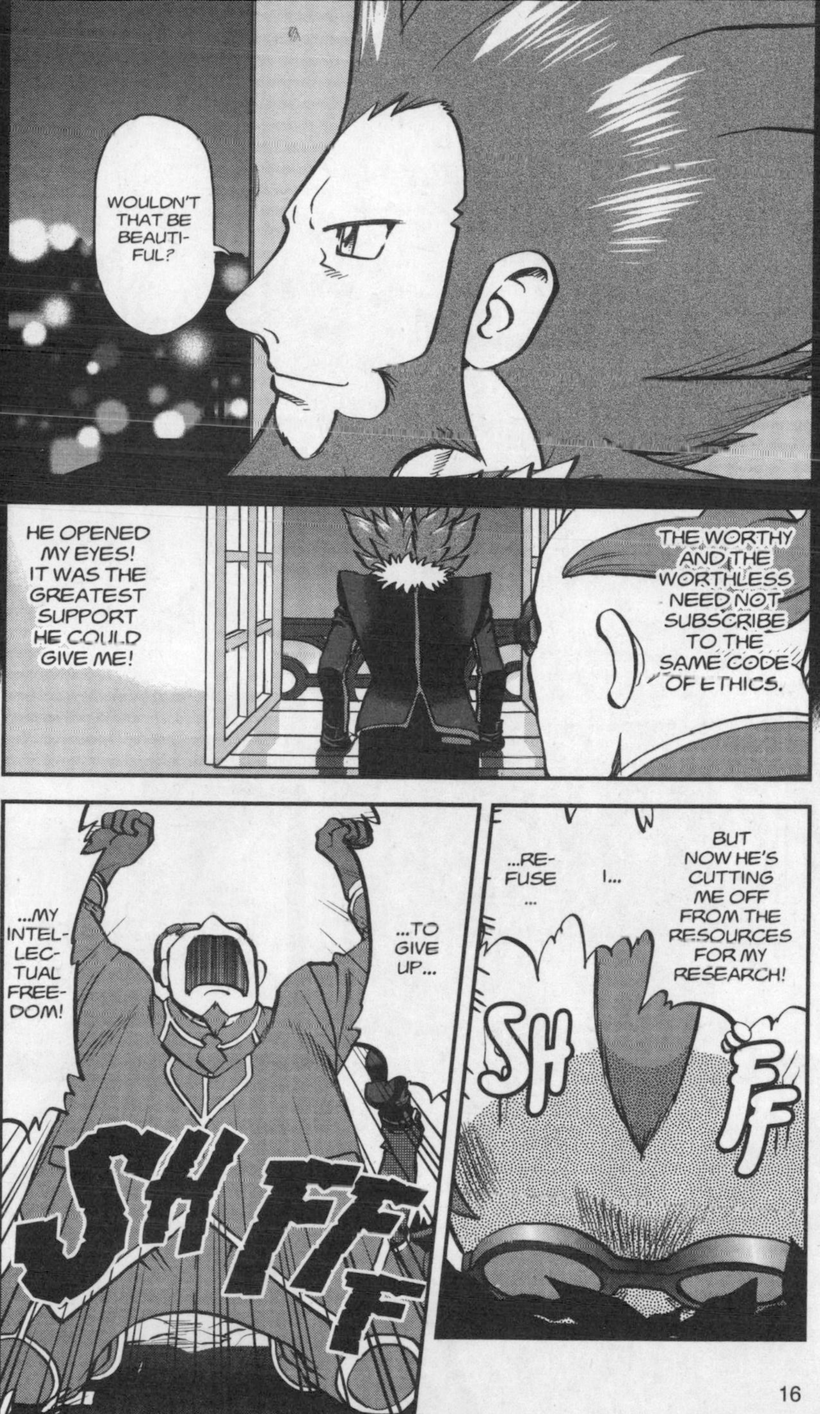
WOULDN'T THAT BE BEAUTI-FUL?
THE WORTHY AND THE WORTHLESS NEED NOT SUBSCRIBE TO THE SAME CODE OF ETHICS.
HE OPENED MY EYES! IT WAS THE GREATEST SUPPORT HE COULD GIVE ME!
BUT NOW HE'S CUTTING ME OFF FROM THE RESOURCES FOR MY RESEARCH!
I...
...RE-FUSE ...
SHFF
...TO GIVE UP...
...MY INTEL-LEC-TUAL FREE-DOM!
SHFFF

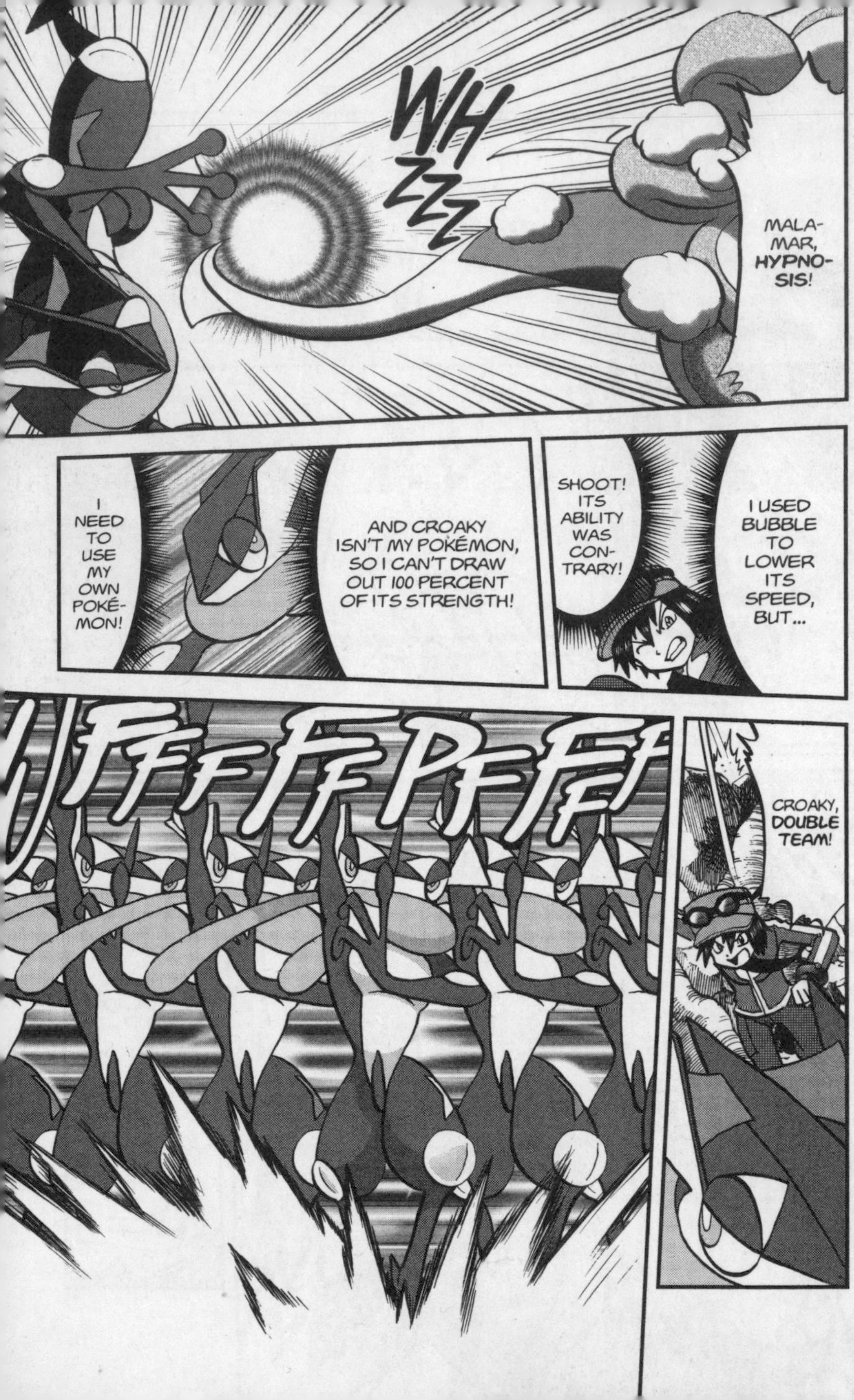
MALA-MAR, HYPNO-SIS!
WHZZZ
I USED BUBBLE TO LOWER ITS SPEED, BUT...
SHOOT! ITS ABILITY WAS CON-TRARY!
AND CROAKY ISN'T MY POKÉMON, SO I CAN'T DRAW OUT 100 PERCENT OF ITS STRENGTH!
I NEED TO USE MY OWN POKÉ-MON!
CROAKY, DOUBLE TEAM!

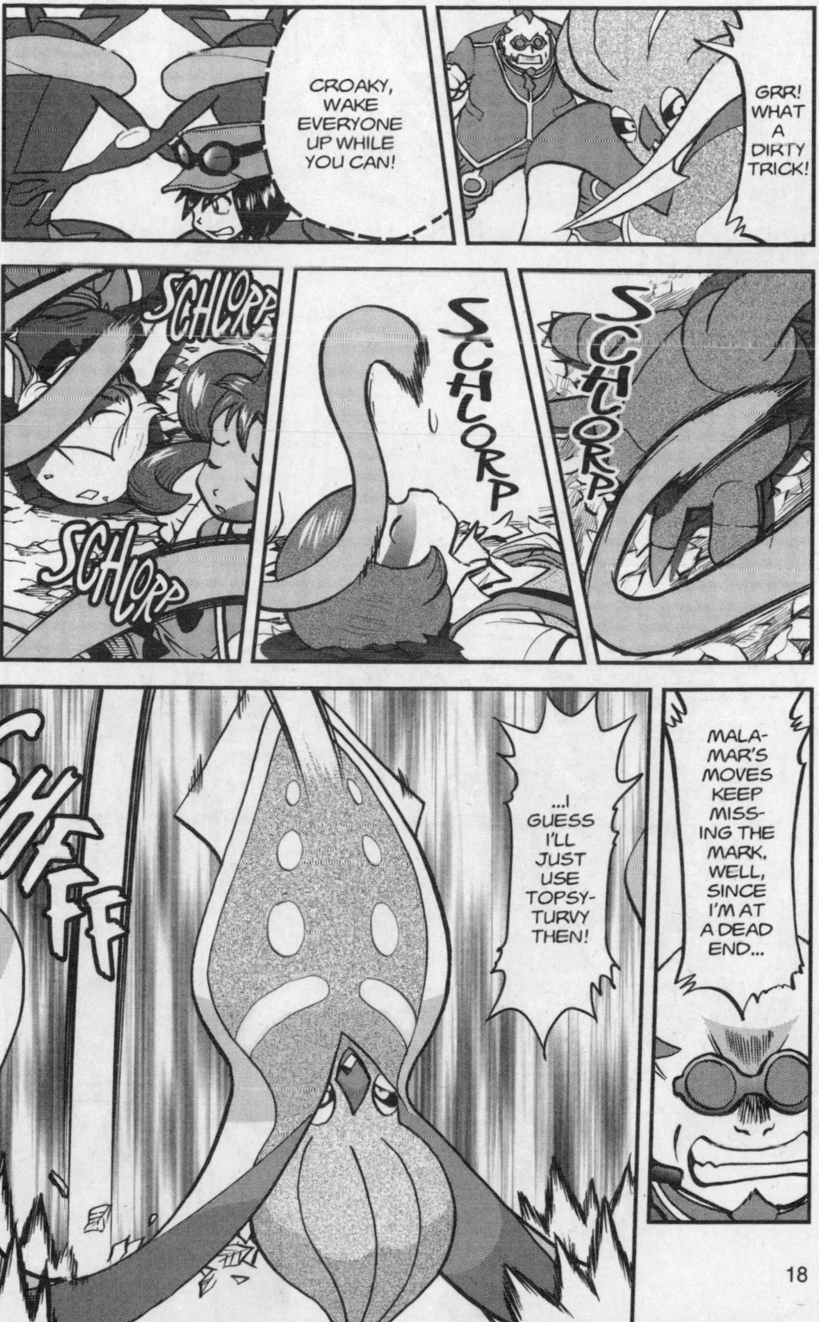
GRR! WHAT A DIRTY TRICK!
CROAKY, WAKE EVERYONE UP WHILE YOU CAN!
SCHLORP
SCHLORP
SCHLORP
SCHLORP
MALA-MAR'S MOVES KEEP MISS-ING THE MARK. WELL, SINCE I'M AT A DEAD END...
...I GUESS I'LL JUST USE TOPSY-TURVY THEN!
SHFFF

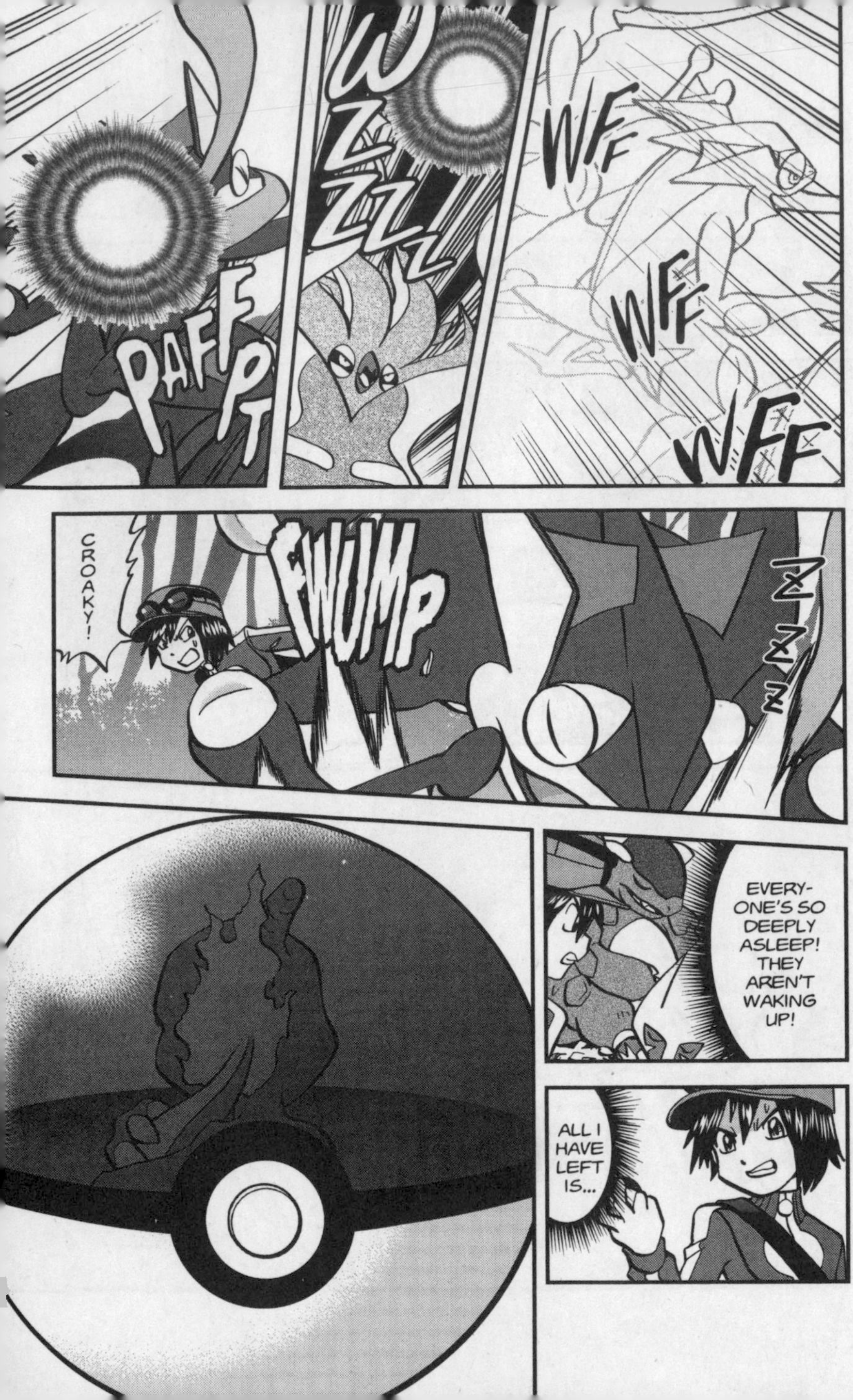
WFF
WFF
WFF
WZZZZZ
PAFFPT
ZZZZ
FWUMP
CROAKY!
EVERYONE'S SO DEEPLY ASLEEP! THEY AREN'T WAKING UP!
ALL I HAVE LEFT IS...

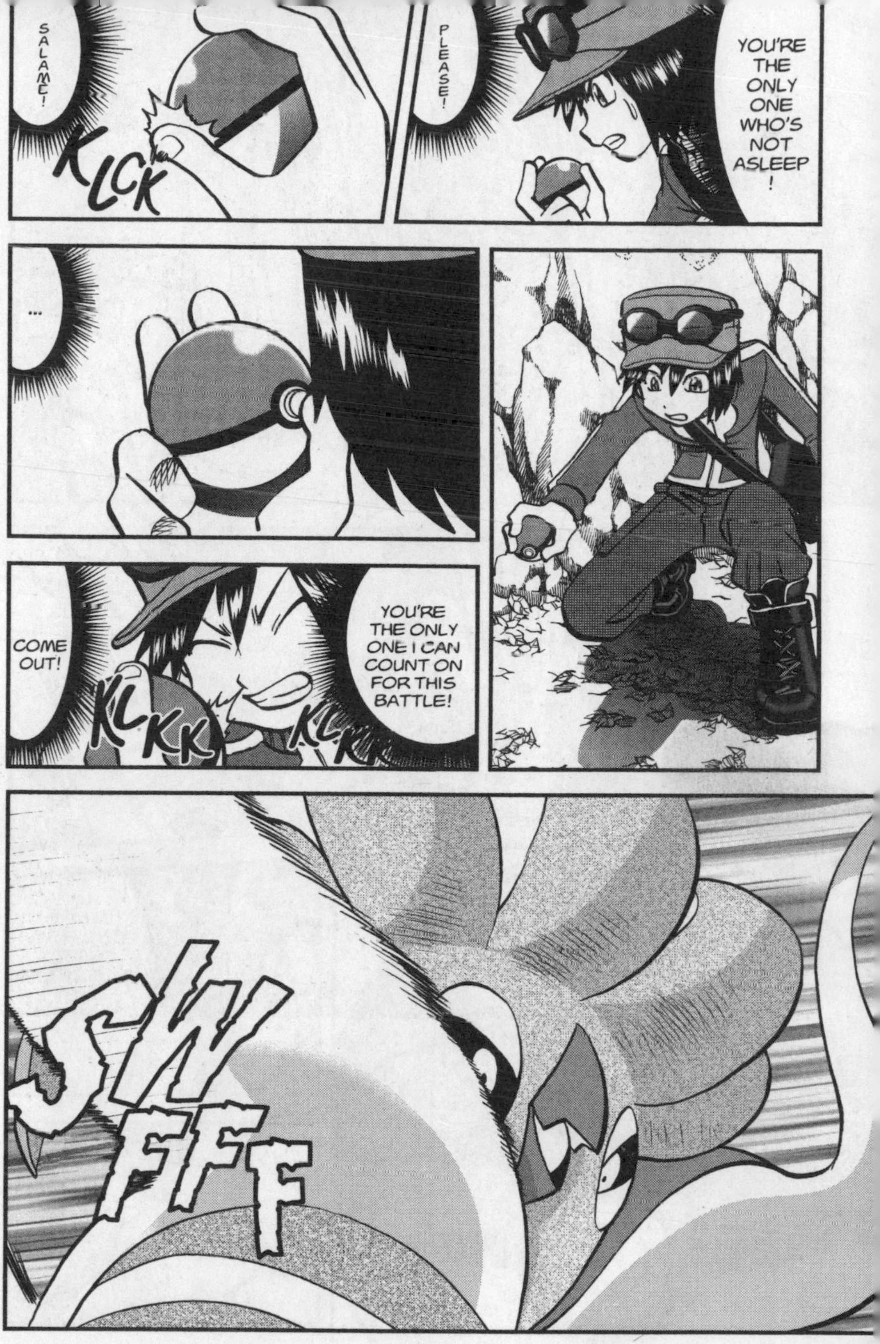
YOU'RE THE ONLY ONE WHO'S NOT ASLEEP!
PLEASE!
SALAME!
KLCK
...
YOU'RE THE ONLY ONE I CAN COUNT ON FOR THIS BATTLE!
COME OUT!
KLKK
KLKK
SWFFF

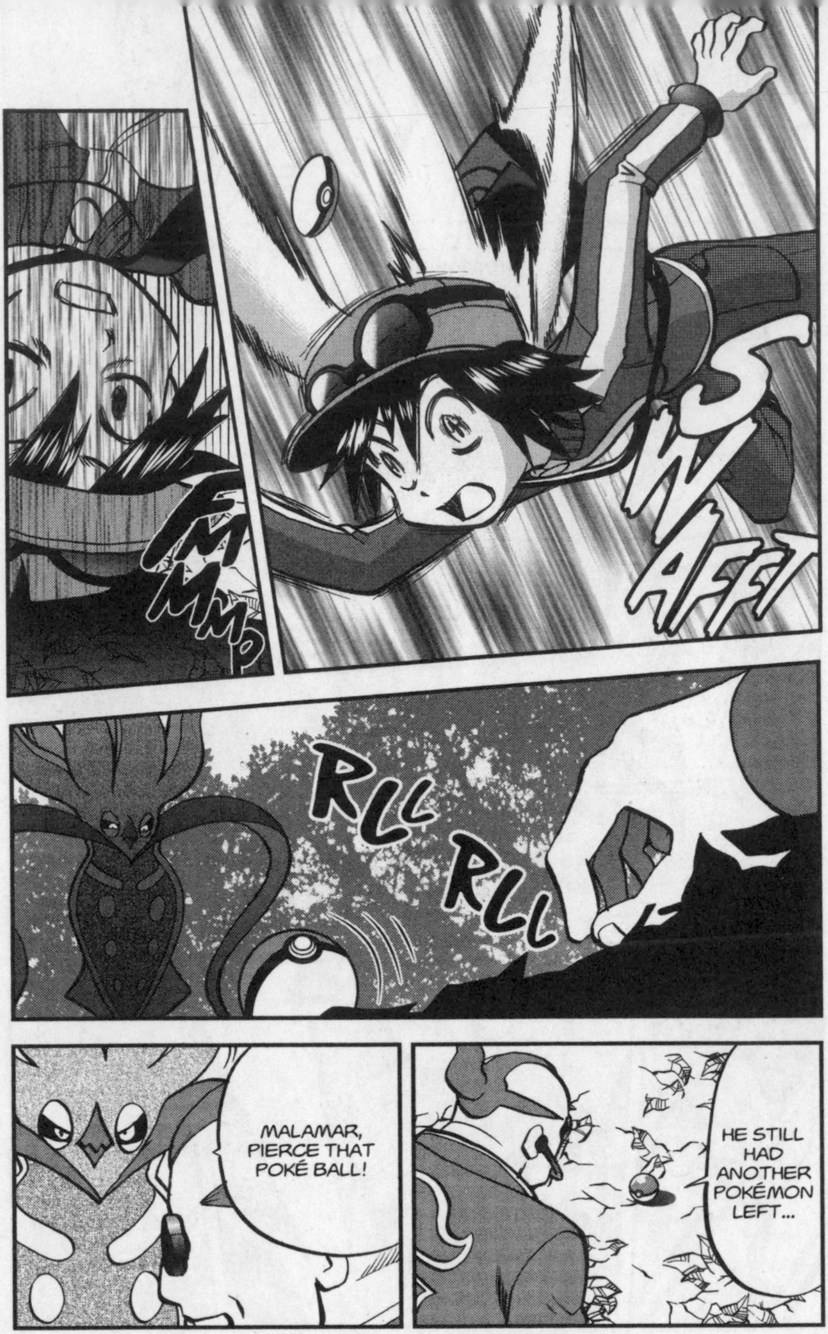
SWAFFT
FMMMP
RLL RLL
HE STILL HAD ANOTHER POKÉMON LEFT...
MALAMAR, PIERCE THAT POKÉ BALL!

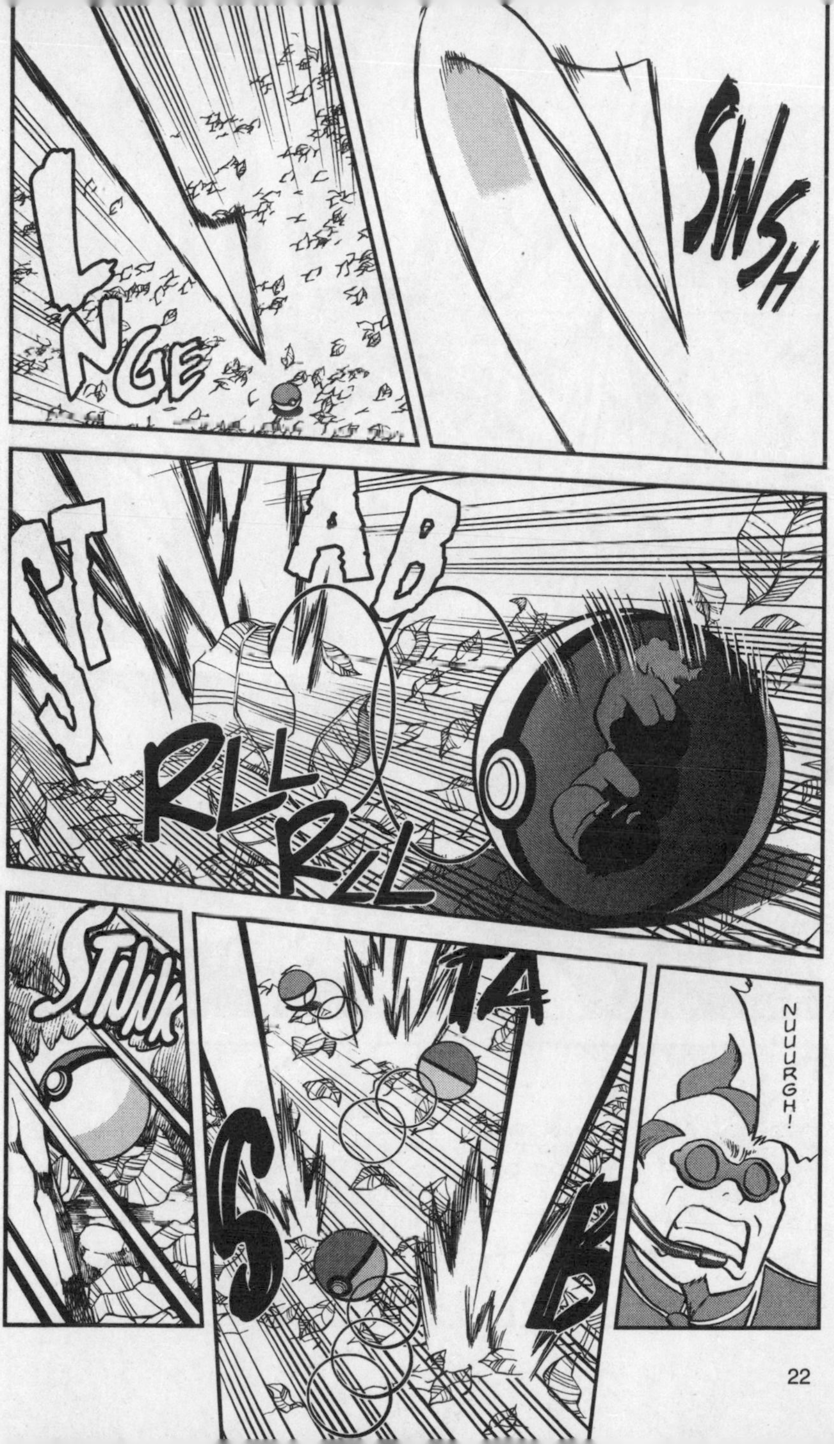
SWSH
NGE
STAB
RLL RLL
NUUURGH!
TA
S
B
STUNK

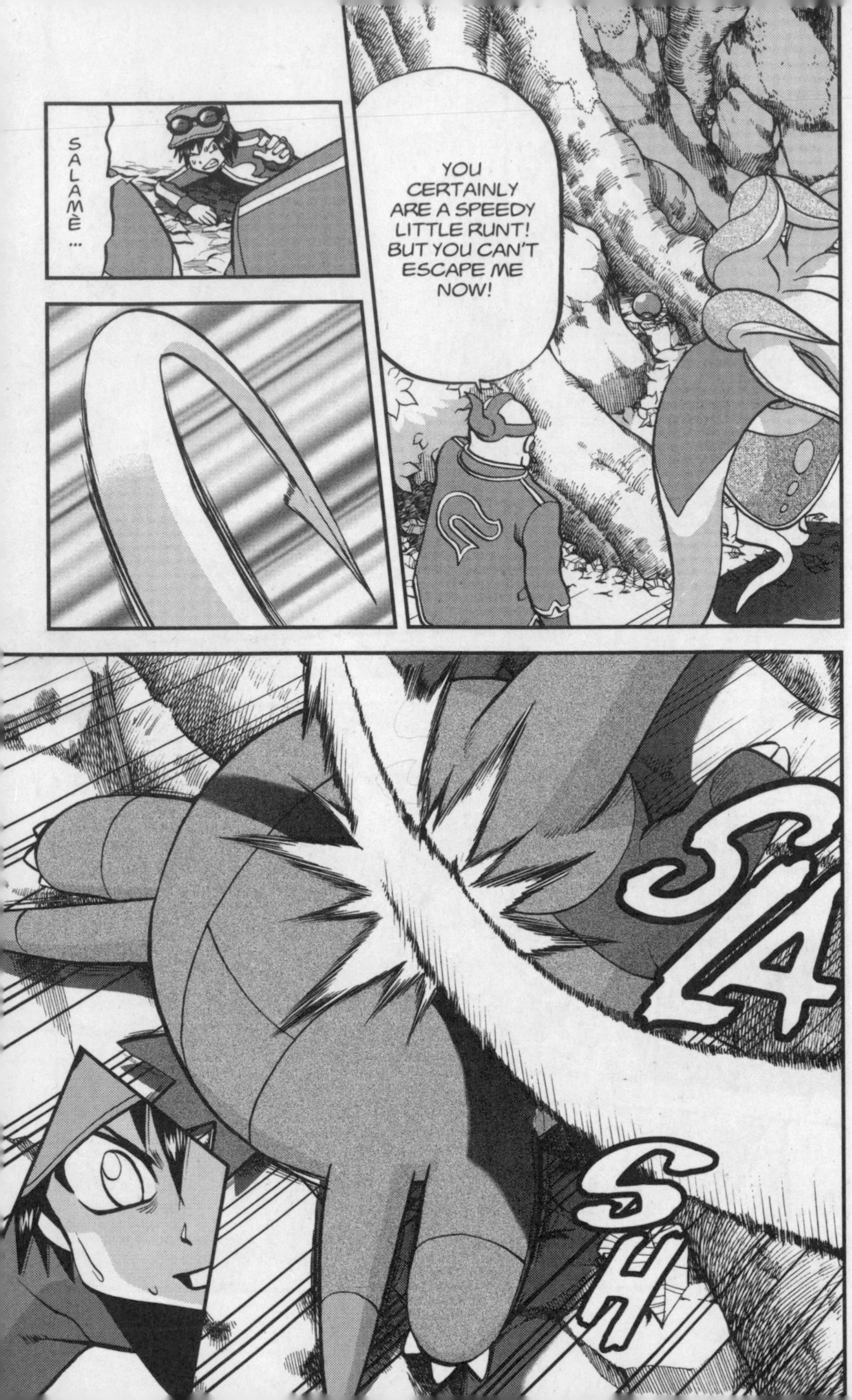
YOU CERTAINLY ARE A SPEEDY LITTLE RUNT! BUT YOU CAN'T ESCAPE ME NOW!
SALAMÈ...
SLA
SH

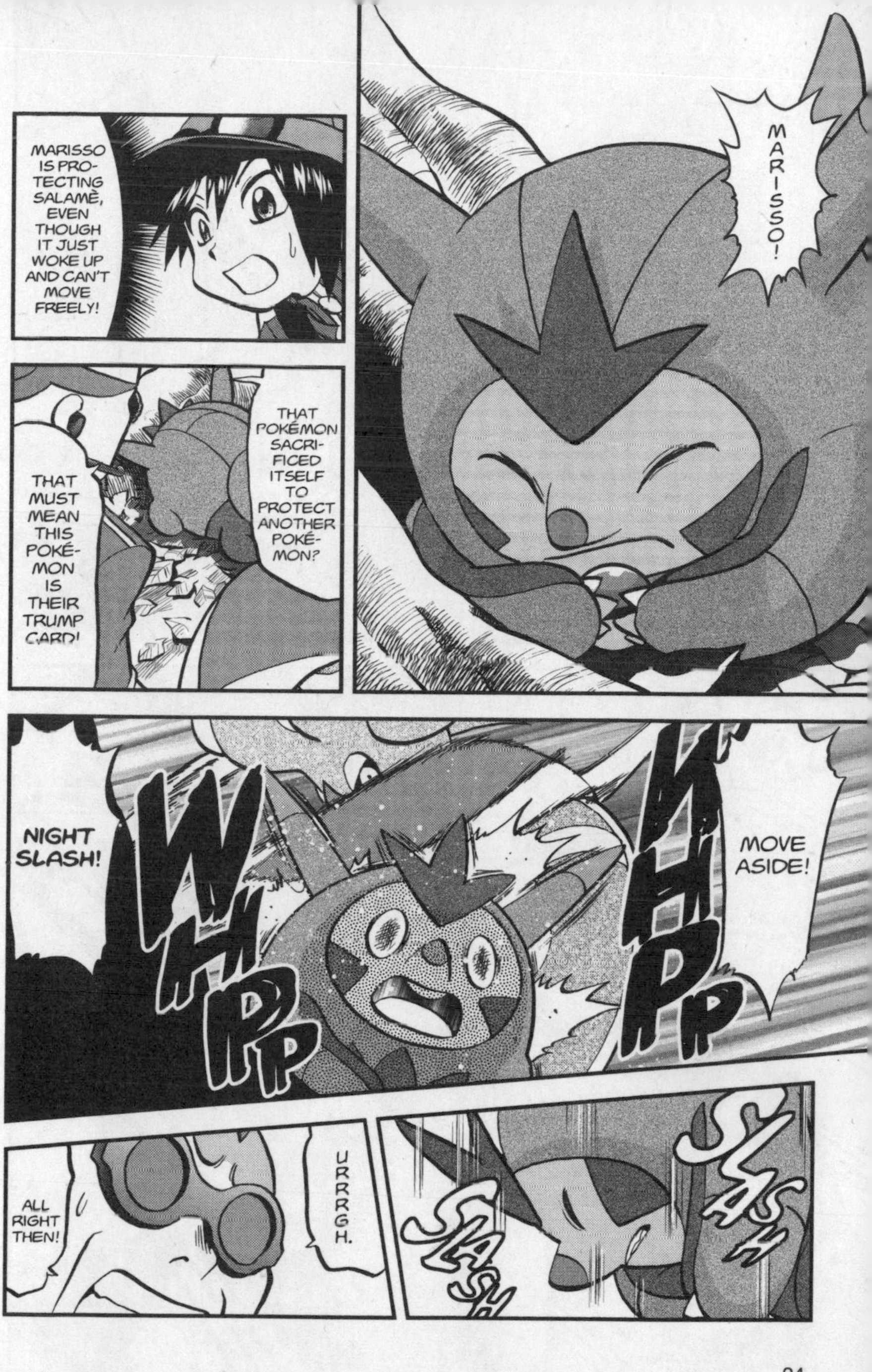
MARISSO!
MARISSO IS PROTECTING SALAMÈ, EVEN THOUGH IT JUST WOKE UP AND CAN'T MOVE FREELY!
THAT POKÉMON SACRIFICED ITSELF TO PROTECT ANOTHER POKÉMON?
THAT MUST MEAN THIS POKÉMON IS THEIR TRUMP CARD!
MOVE ASIDE!
WHIPP
WHIPP
NIGHT SLASH!
SLASH
SLASH
URRRGH.
ALL RIGHT THEN!

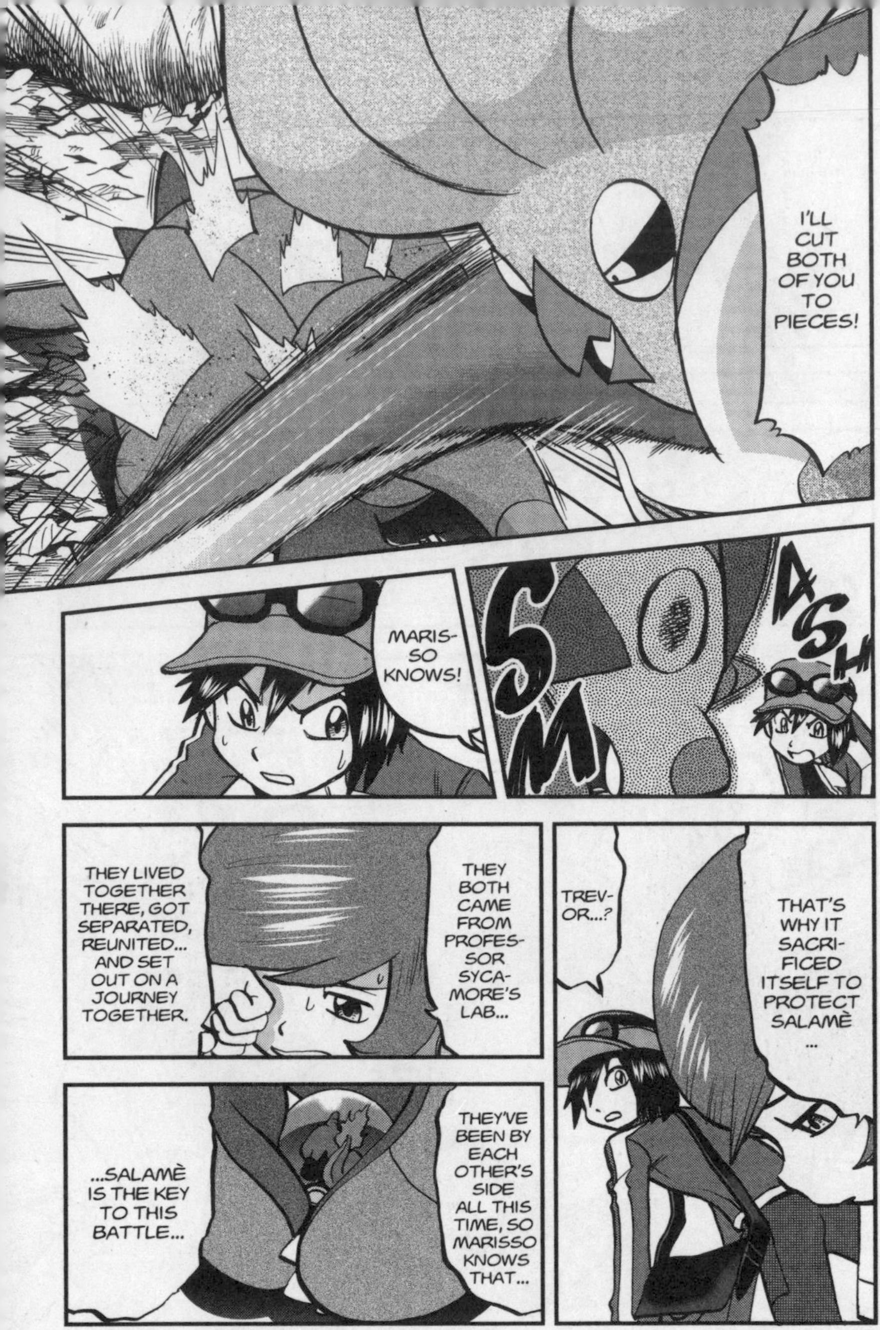
I'LL CUT BOTH OF YOU TO PIECES!
SMASH
MARIS-SO KNOWS!
THAT'S WHY IT SACRI-FICED ITSELF TO PROTECT SALAMÈ ...
TREV-OR...?
THEY BOTH CAME FROM PROFES-SOR SYCA-MORE'S LAB...
THEY LIVED TOGETHER THERE, GOT SEPARATED, REUNITED... AND SET OUT ON A JOURNEY TOGETHER.
THEY'VE BEEN BY EACH OTHER'S SIDE ALL THIS TIME, SO MARISSO KNOWS THAT...
...SALAMÈ IS THE KEY TO THIS BATTLE...

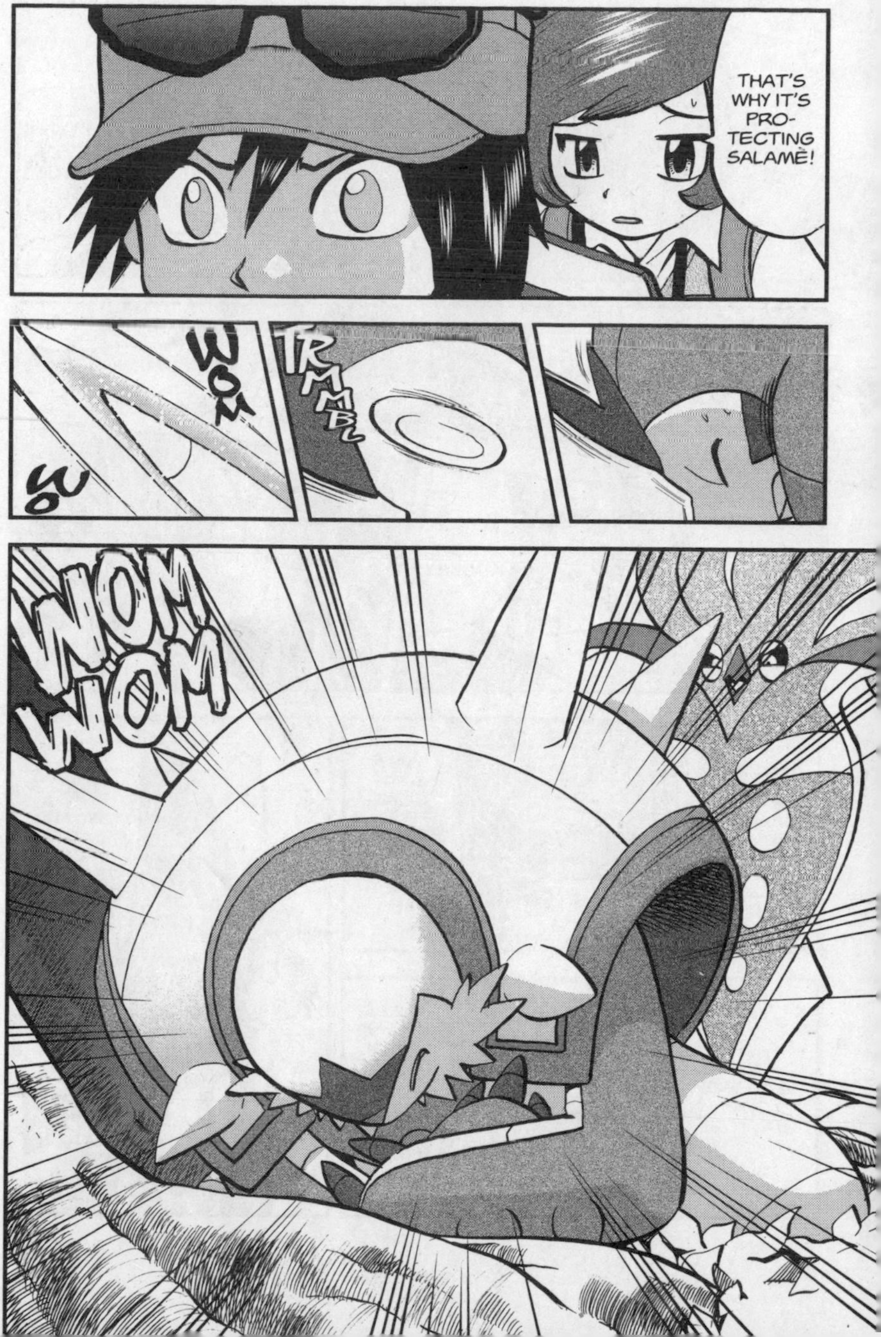
THAT'S WHY IT'S PRO-TECTING SALAMÈ!
TRMMBL
WOM
WO
WOM WOM

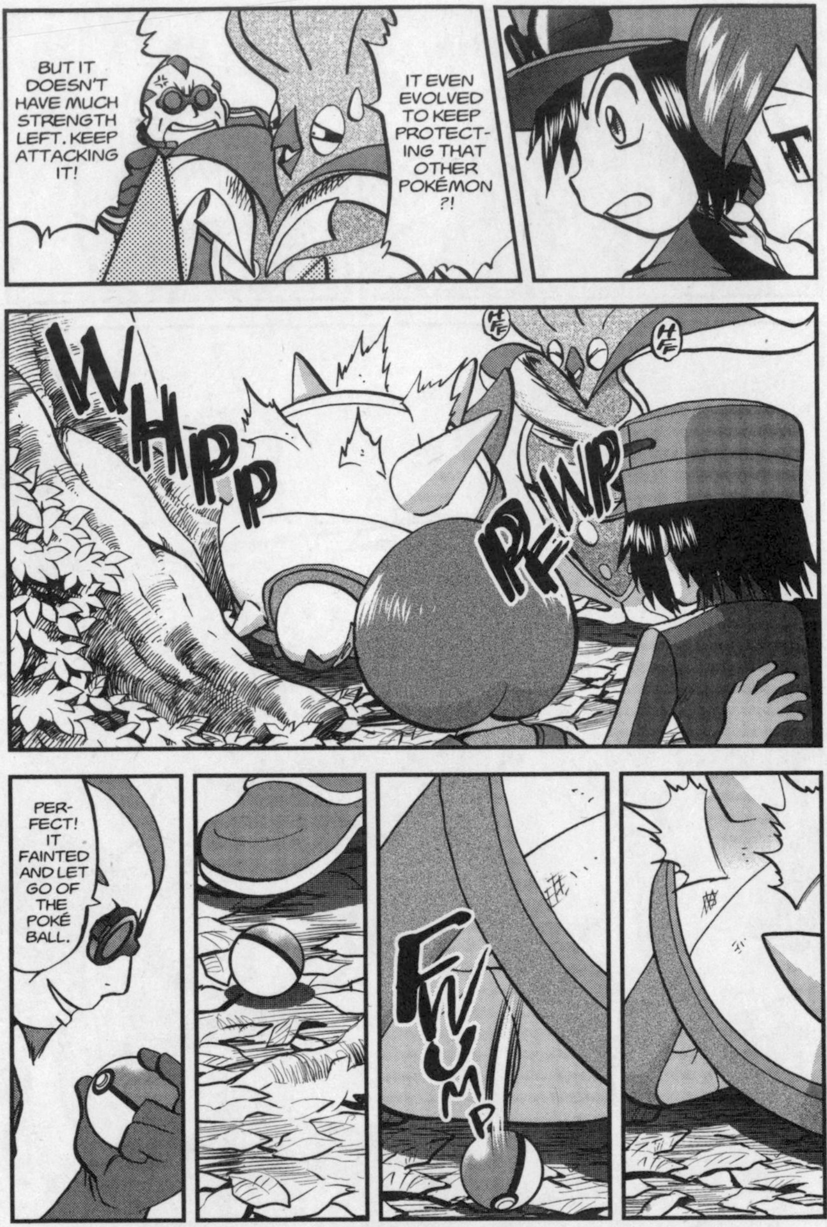
IT EVEN EVOLVED TO KEEP PROTECTING THAT OTHER POKÉMON?!
BUT IT DOESN'T HAVE MUCH STRENGTH LEFT. KEEP ATTACKING IT!
HF
HF
WHPP
PFWP
FWUMP
PERFECT! IT FAINTED AND LET GO OF THE POKÉ BALL.

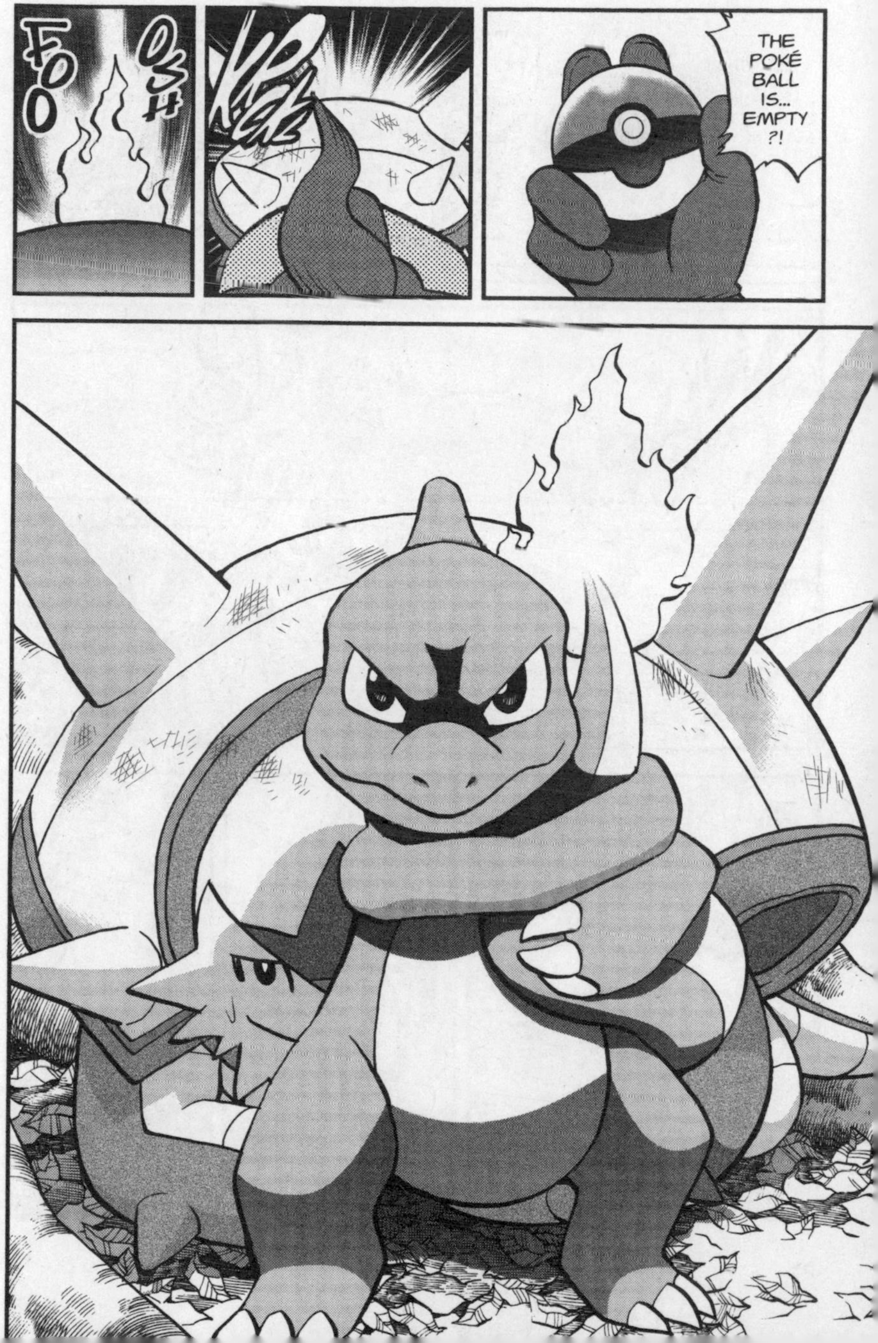
THE POKÉ BALL IS... EMPTY ?!
FOOOSH

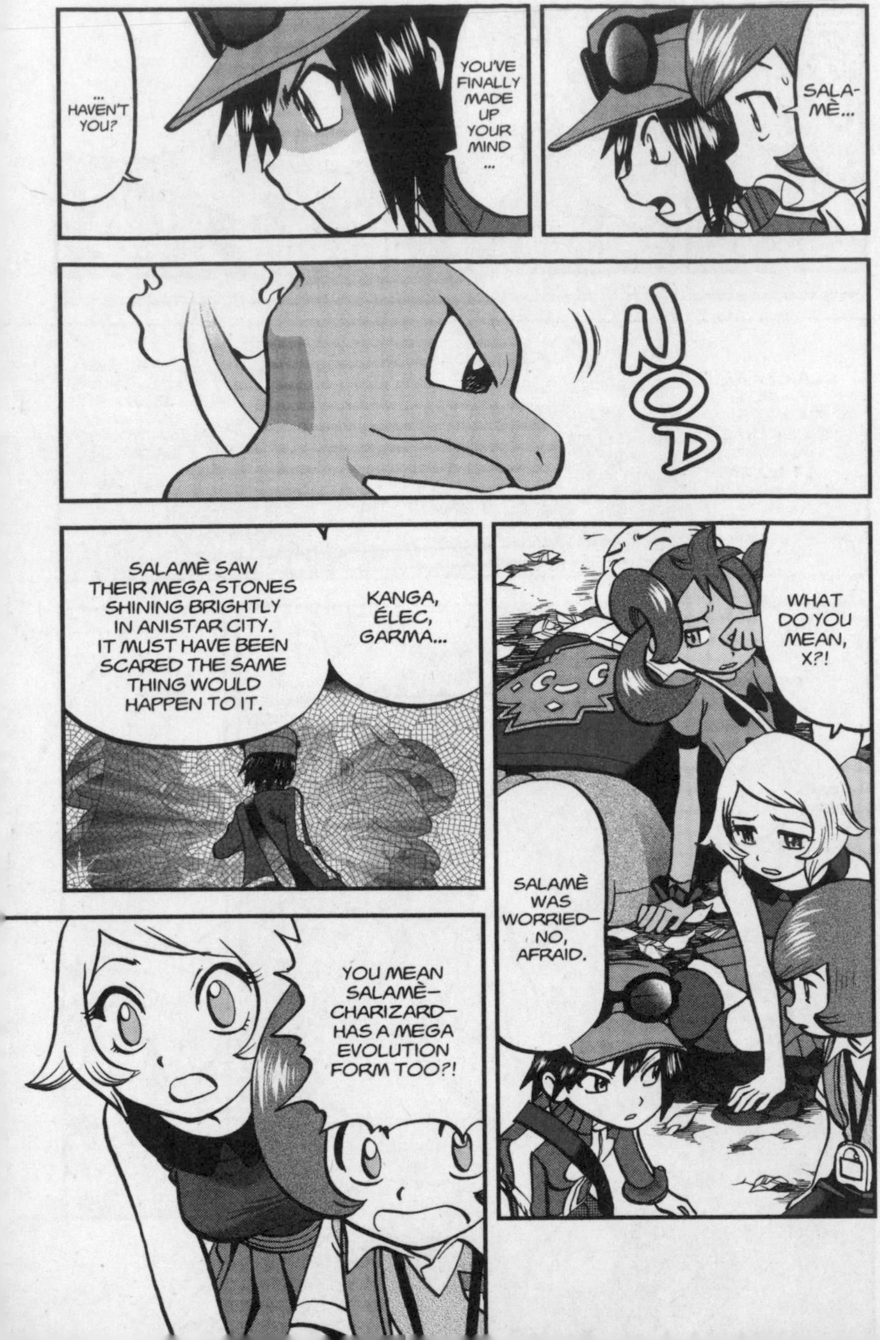
SALA-MÈ...
YOU'VE FINALLY MADE UP YOUR MIND ...
... HAVEN'T YOU?
NOD
WHAT DO YOU MEAN, X?!
SALAMÈ WAS WORRIED— NO, AFRAID.
KANGA, ÉLEC, GARMA...
SALAMÈ SAW THEIR MEGA STONES SHINING BRIGHTLY IN ANISTAR CITY. IT MUST HAVE BEEN SCARED THE SAME THING WOULD HAPPEN TO IT.
YOU MEAN SALAMÈ— CHARIZARD— HAS A MEGA EVOLUTION FORM TOO?!

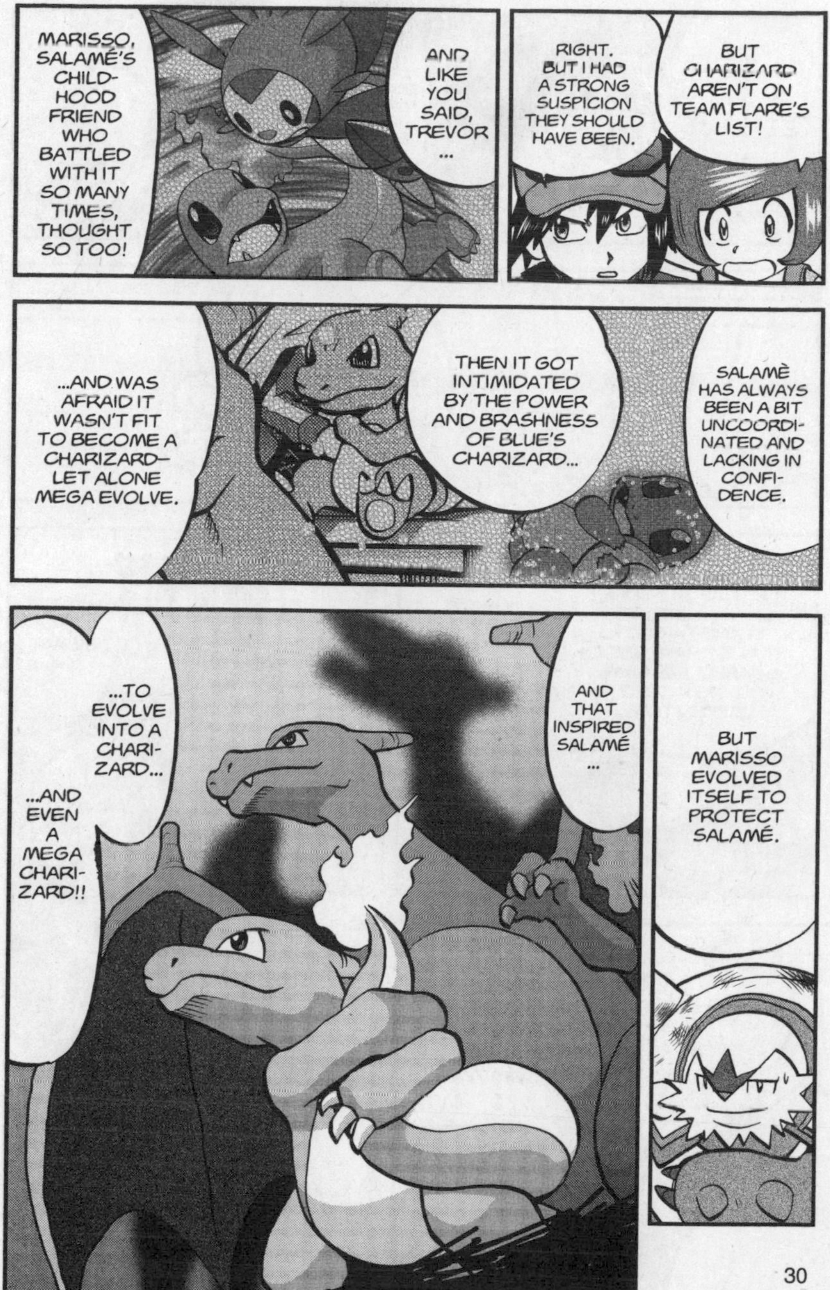
BUT CHARIZARD AREN'T ON TEAM FLARE'S LIST!
RIGHT. BUT I HAD A STRONG SUSPICION THEY SHOULD HAVE BEEN.
AND LIKE YOU SAID, TREVOR...
MARISSO, SALAMÉ'S CHILDHOOD FRIEND WHO BATTLED WITH IT SO MANY TIMES, THOUGHT SO TOO!
SALAMÈ HAS ALWAYS BEEN A BIT UNCOORDINATED AND LACKING IN CONFIDENCE.
THEN IT GOT INTIMIDATED BY THE POWER AND BRASHNESS OF BLUE'S CHARIZARD...
...AND WAS AFRAID IT WASN'T FIT TO BECOME A CHARIZARD—LET ALONE MEGA EVOLVE.
BUT MARISSO EVOLVED ITSELF TO PROTECT SALAMÉ.
AND THAT INSPIRED SALAMÉ...
...TO EVOLVE INTO A CHARIZARD...
...AND EVEN A MEGA CHARIZARD!!

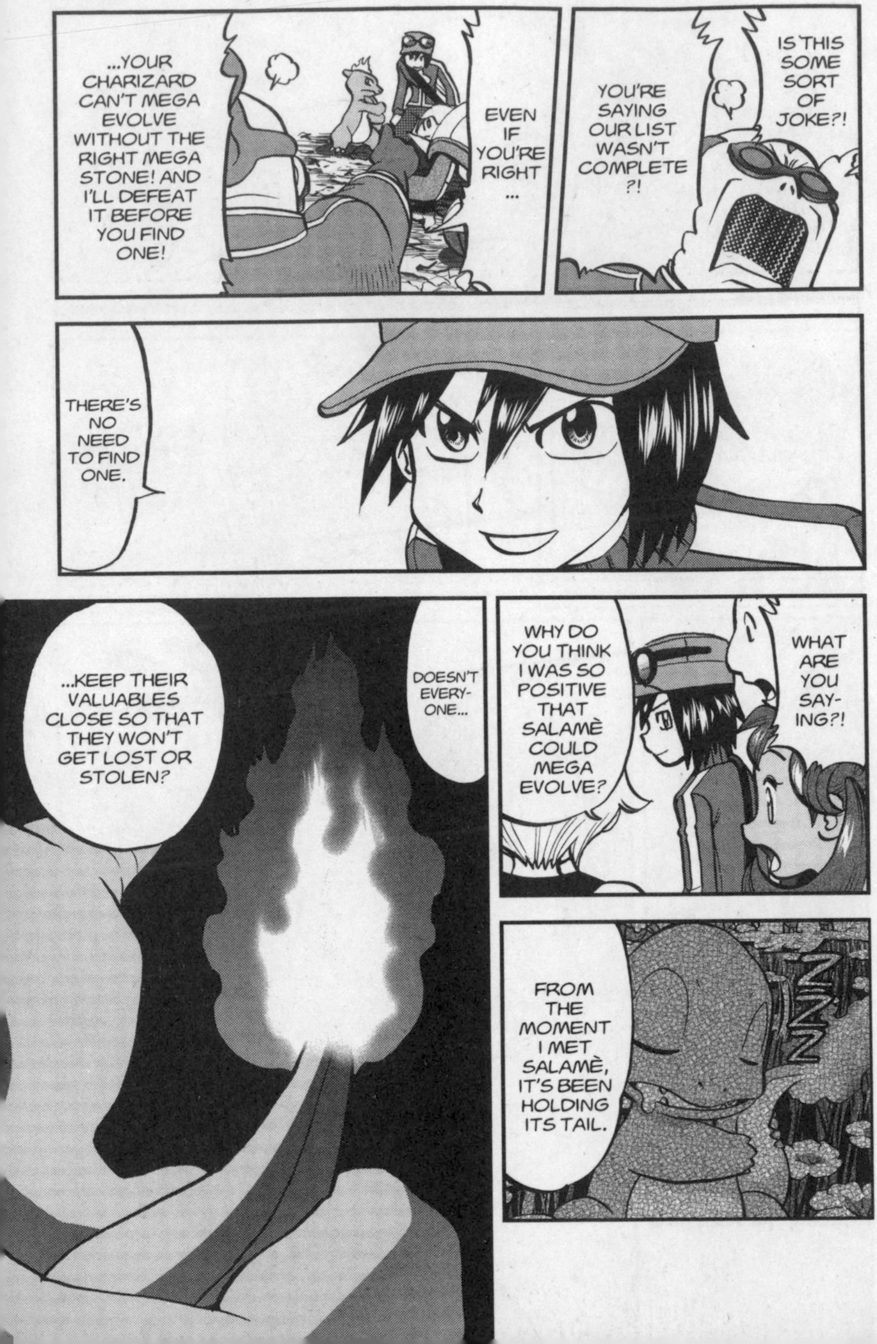
IS THIS SOME SORT OF JOKE?!
YOU'RE SAYING OUR LIST WASN'T COMPLETE ?!
EVEN IF YOU'RE RIGHT ...
...YOUR CHARIZARD CAN'T MEGA EVOLVE WITHOUT THE RIGHT MEGA STONE! AND I'LL DEFEAT IT BEFORE YOU FIND ONE!
THERE'S NO NEED TO FIND ONE.
WHAT ARE YOU SAY-ING?!
WHY DO YOU THINK I WAS SO POSITIVE THAT SALAMÈ COULD MEGA EVOLVE?
FROM THE MOMENT I MET SALAMÈ, IT'S BEEN HOLDING ITS TAIL.
DOESN'T EVERY-ONE...
...KEEP THEIR VALUABLES CLOSE SO THAT THEY WON'T GET LOST OR STOLEN?

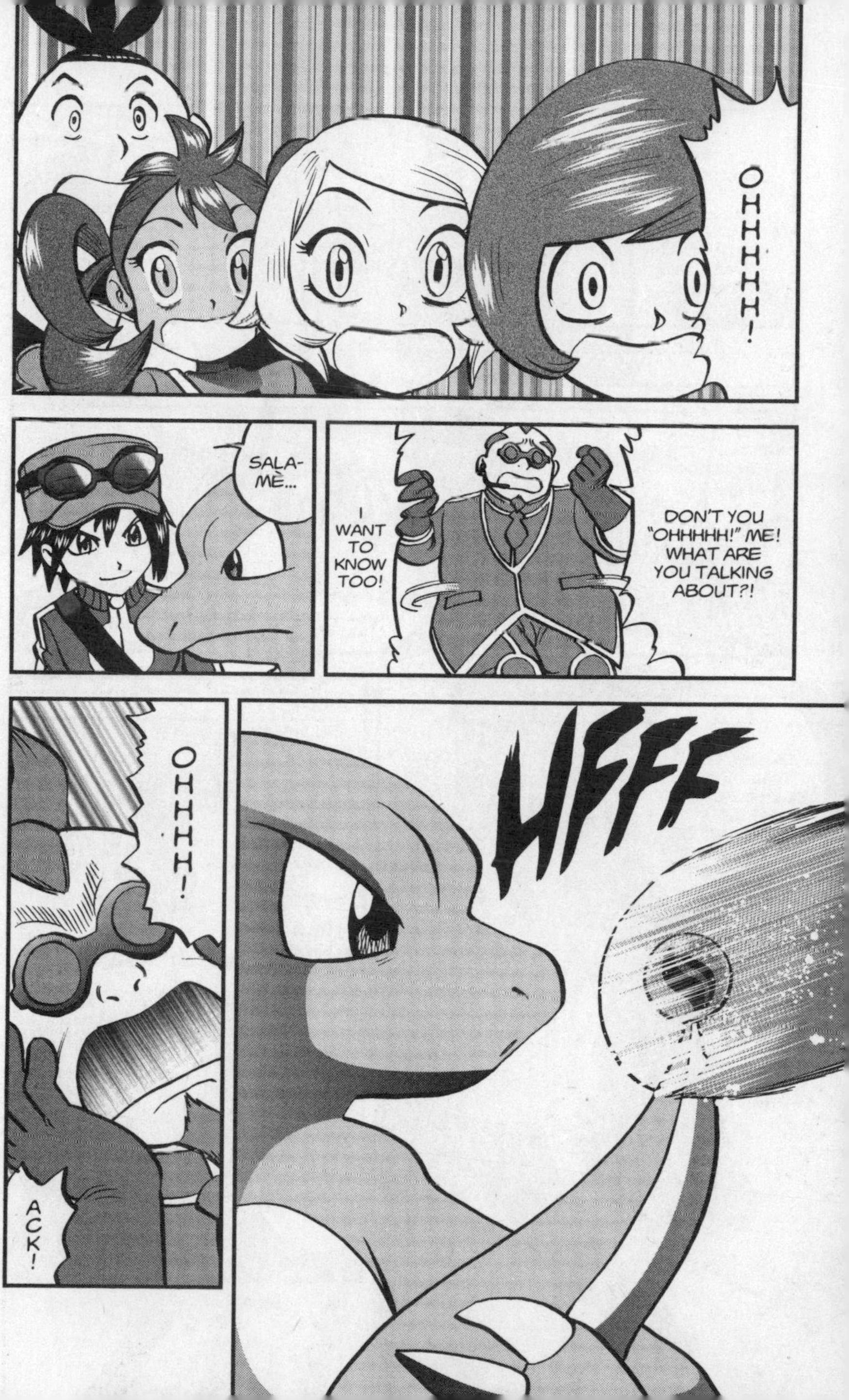
OHHHHH!
DON'T YOU "OHHHHH!" ME! WHAT ARE YOU TALKING ABOUT?!
I WANT TO KNOW TOO!
SALA-MÈ...
WFFF
OHHHH!
ACK!

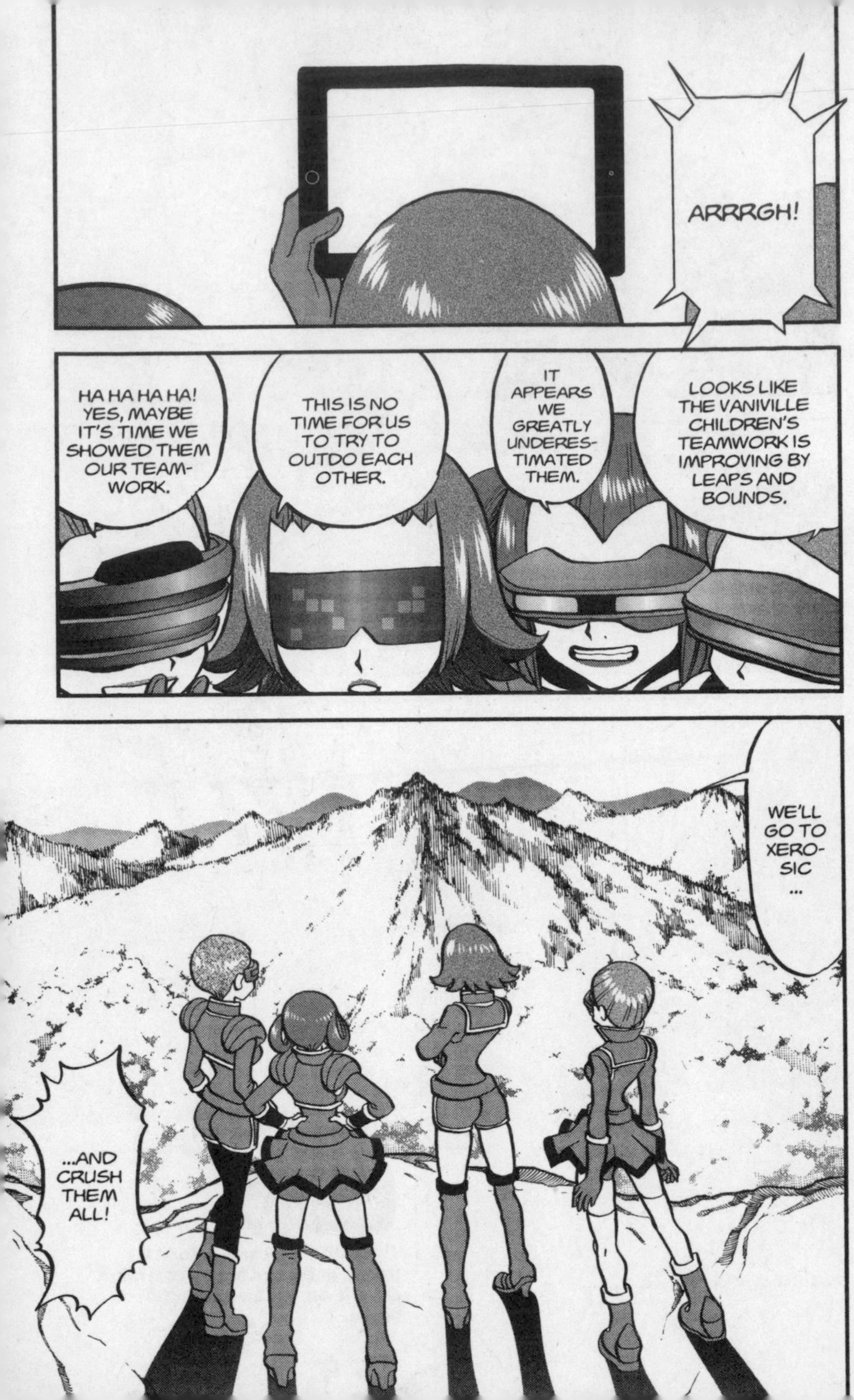
ARRRGH!
LOOKS LIKE THE VANIVILLE CHILDREN'S TEAMWORK IS IMPROVING BY LEAPS AND BOUNDS.
IT APPEARS WE GREATLY UNDERES-TIMATED THEM.
THIS IS NO TIME FOR US TO TRY TO OUTDO EACH OTHER.
HA HA HA HA! YES, MAYBE IT'S TIME WE SHOWED THEM OUR TEAM-WORK.
WE'LL GO TO XERO-SIC ...
...AND CRUSH THEM ALL!

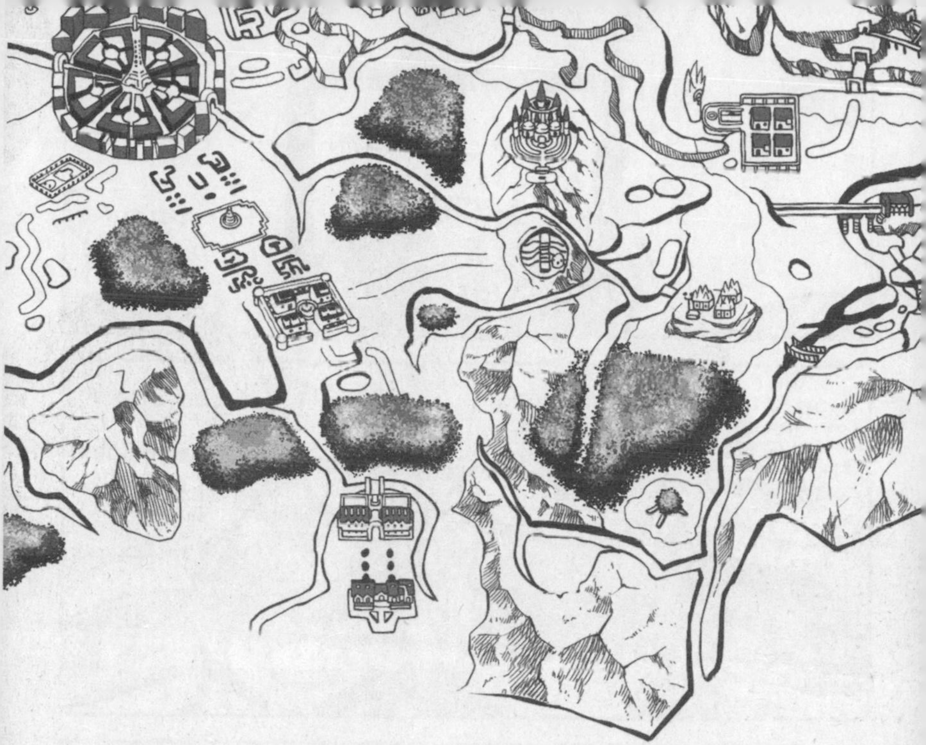

Current Location

Route 18
Vallée Étroite Way

This path is best known for its trolley, once used for the coal mine, and the curious Inverse Battle house.

Adventure #41
Charizard Transforms

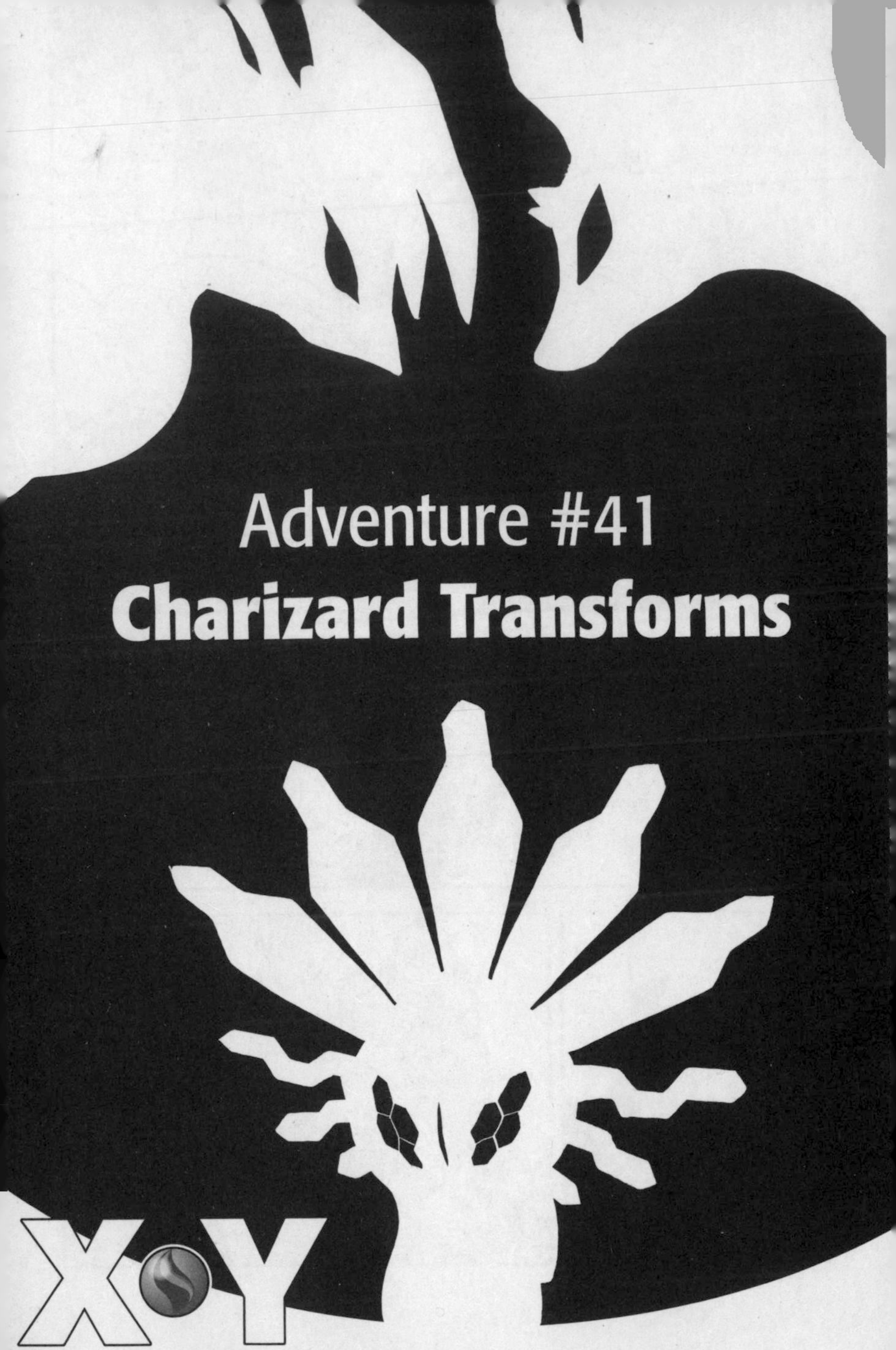

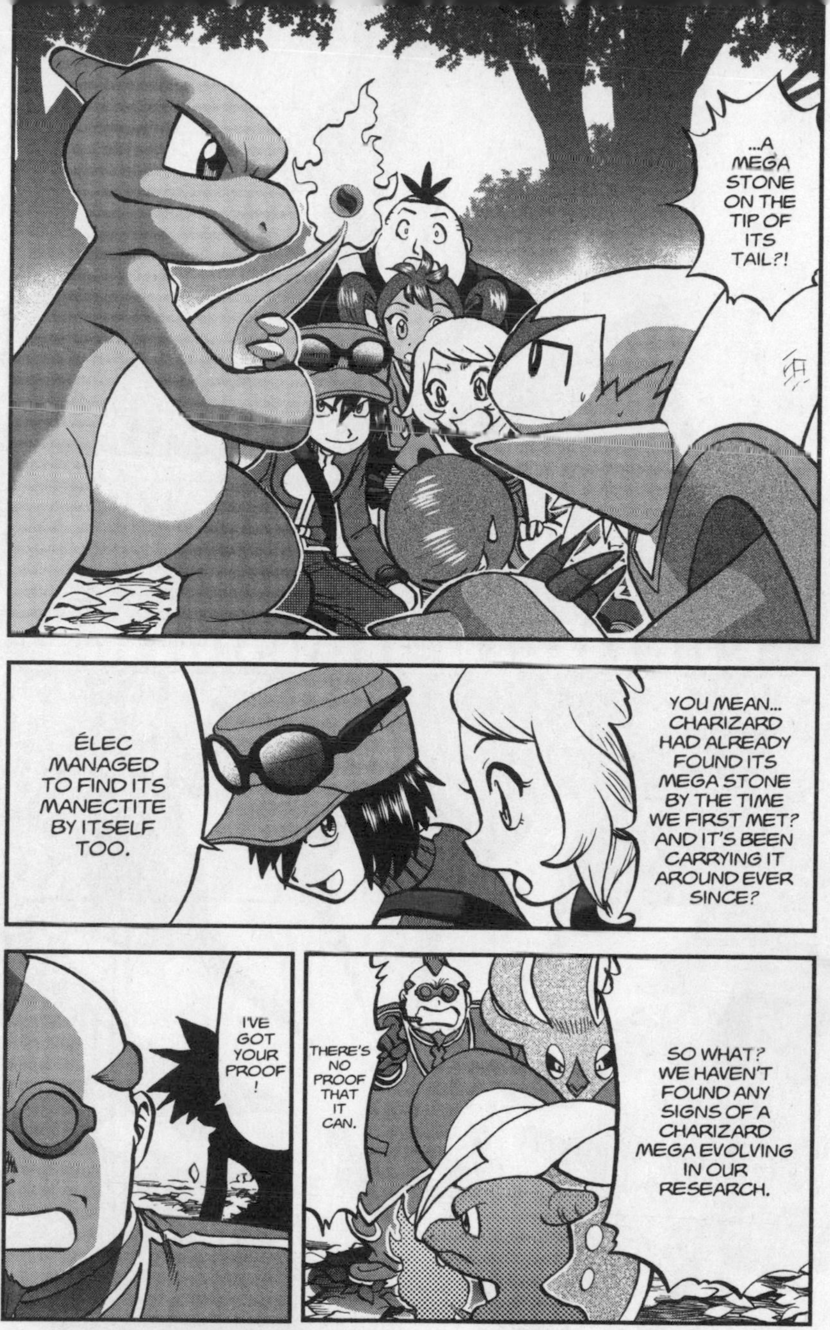
...A MEGA STONE ON THE TIP OF ITS TAIL?!
YOU MEAN... CHARIZARD HAD ALREADY FOUND ITS MEGA STONE BY THE TIME WE FIRST MET? AND IT'S BEEN CARRYING IT AROUND EVER SINCE?
ÉLEC MANAGED TO FIND ITS MANECTITE BY ITSELF TOO.
SO WHAT? WE HAVEN'T FOUND ANY SIGNS OF A CHARIZARD MEGA EVOLVING IN OUR RESEARCH.
THERE'S NO PROOF THAT IT CAN.
I'VE GOT YOUR PROOF!

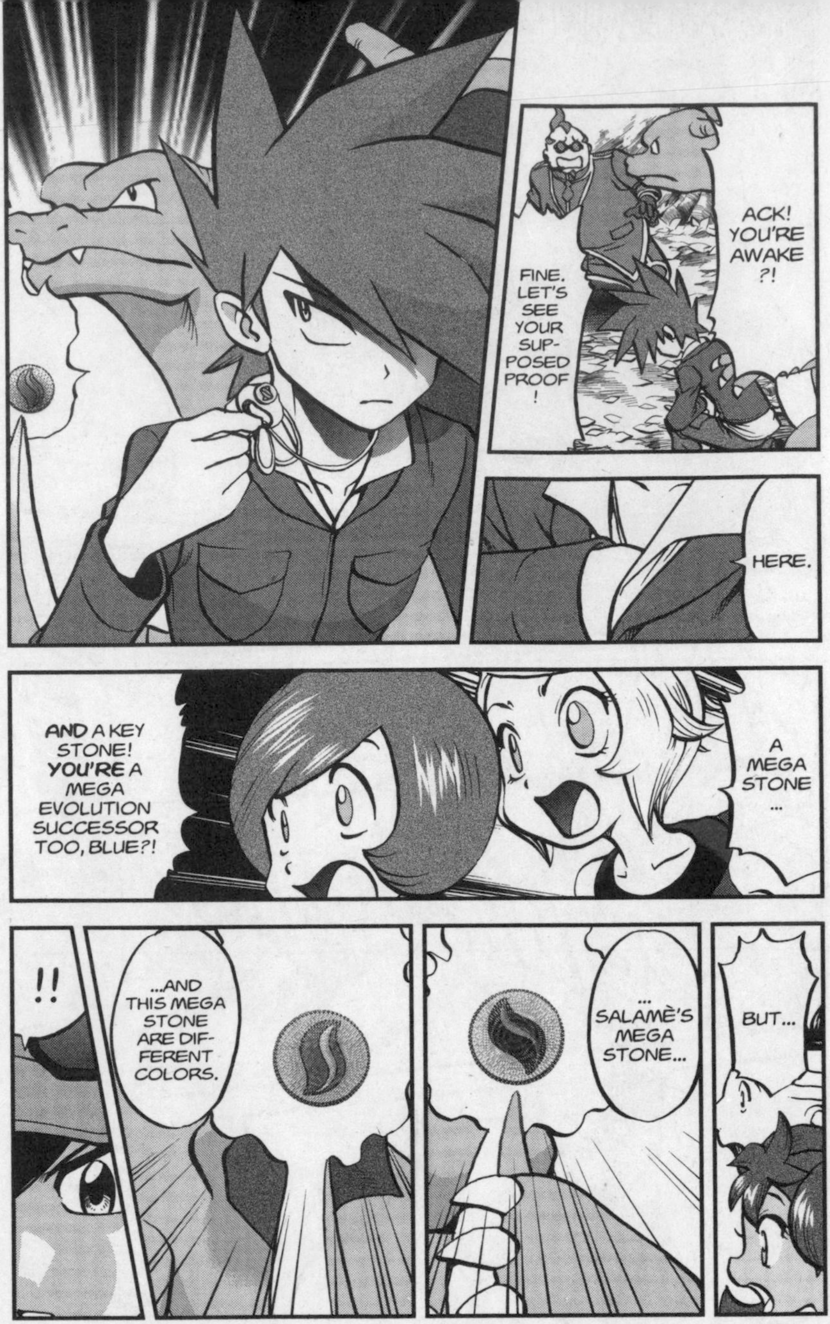
ACK! YOU'RE AWAKE?!
FINE. LET'S SEE YOUR SUPPOSED PROOF!
HERE.
A MEGA STONE...
AND A KEY STONE! YOU'RE A MEGA EVOLUTION SUCCESSOR TOO, BLUE?!
BUT...
... SALAMÈ'S MEGA STONE...
...AND THIS MEGA STONE ARE DIFFERENT COLORS.
!!

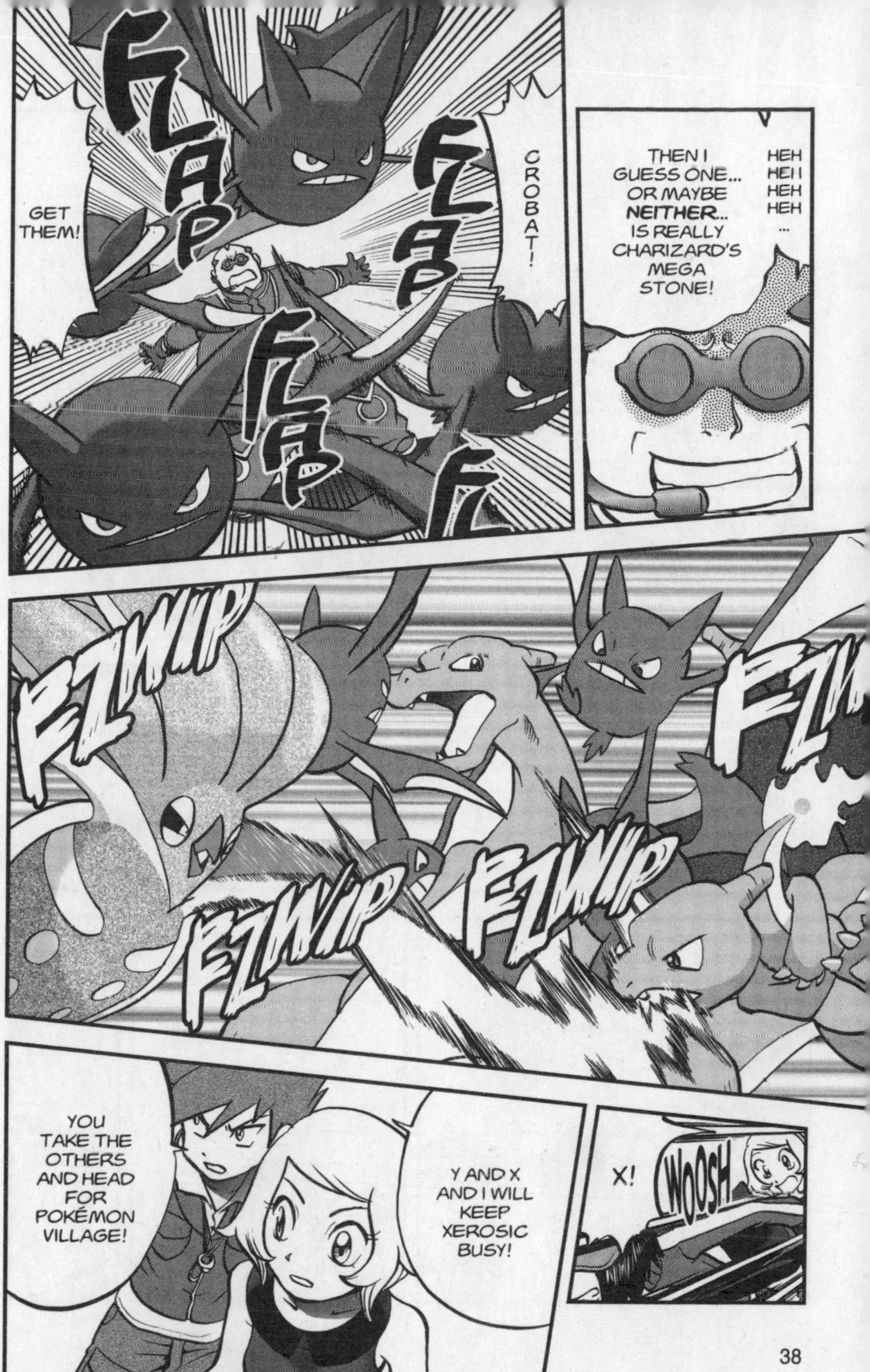
HEH HEH HEH HEH ...
THEN I GUESS ONE... OR MAYBE **NEITHER**... IS REALLY CHARIZARD'S MEGA STONE!
CROBAT!
FLAP
FLAP
FLAP
FL
GET THEM!
FZWIP
FZWIP
FZWIP
FZWIP
WOOSH
X!
Y AND X AND I WILL KEEP XEROSIC BUSY!
YOU TAKE THE OTHERS AND HEAD FOR POKÉMON VILLAGE!

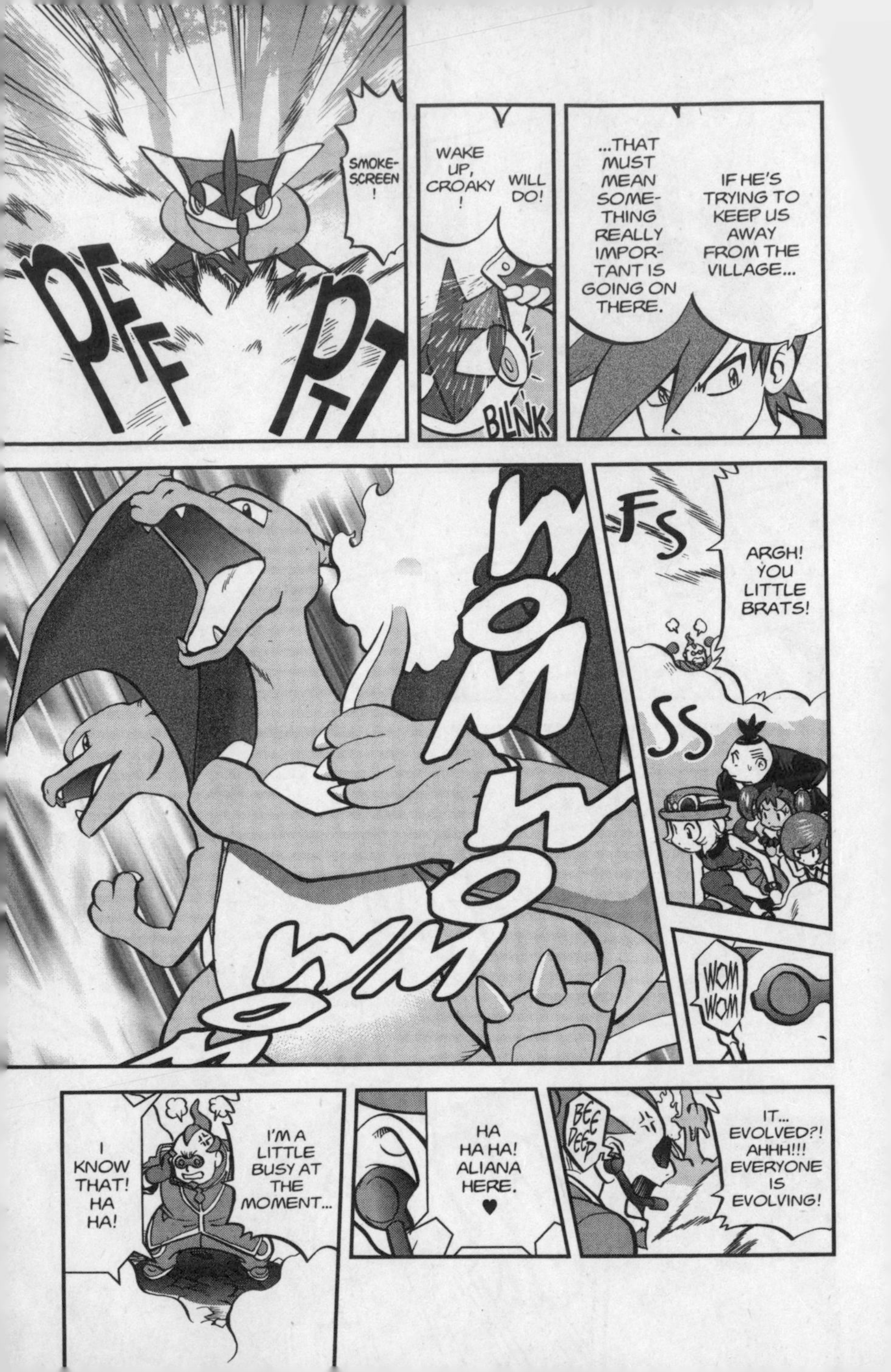
IF HE'S TRYING TO KEEP US AWAY FROM THE VILLAGE...
...THAT MUST MEAN SOMETHING REALLY IMPORTANT IS GOING ON THERE.
WAKE UP, CROAKY!
WILL DO!
BLINK
SMOKE-SCREEN!
PFFFT
FS
ARGH! YOU LITTLE BRATS!
SS
WOM WOM
WOMWOMWOM
BEE DEEP
IT... EVOLVED?! AHHH!!! EVERYONE IS EVOLVING!
HA HA HA! ALIANA HERE. ♥
I'M A LITTLE BUSY AT THE MOMENT...
I KNOW THAT! HA HA!

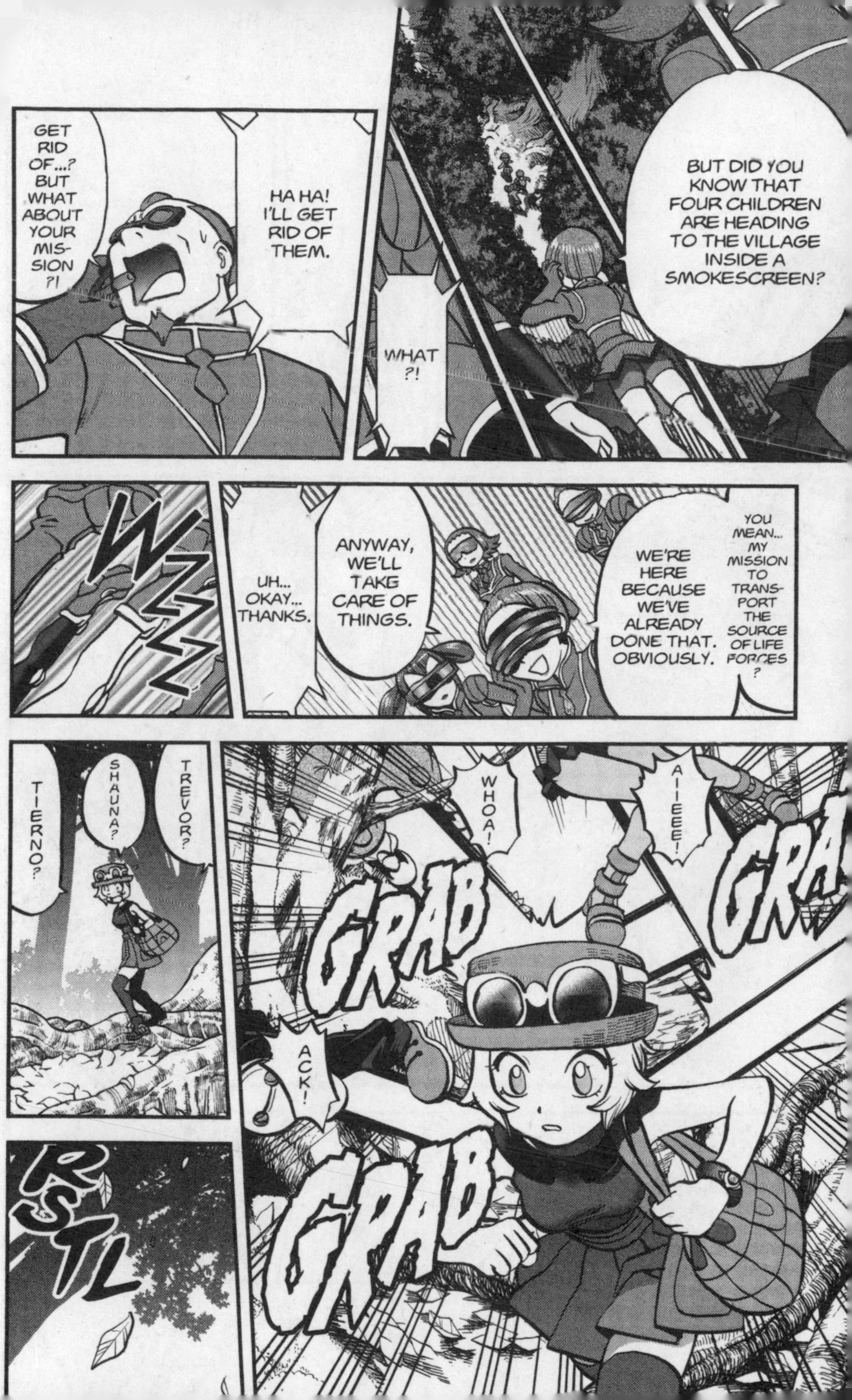
BUT DID YOU KNOW THAT FOUR CHILDREN ARE HEADING TO THE VILLAGE INSIDE A SMOKESCREEN?
WHAT ?!
HA HA! I'LL GET RID OF THEM.
GET RID OF...? BUT WHAT ABOUT YOUR MIS-SION ?!
YOU MEAN... MY MISSION TO TRANS-PORT THE SOURCE OF LIFE FORCES ?
WE'RE HERE BECAUSE WE'VE ALREADY DONE THAT. OBVIOUSLY.
ANYWAY, WE'LL TAKE CARE OF THINGS.
UH... OKAY... THANKS.
WZZZ
AIIEEE!
WHOA!
GRAB
GRAB
ACK!
GRAB
TREVOR?
SHAUNA?
TIERNO?
RSTL

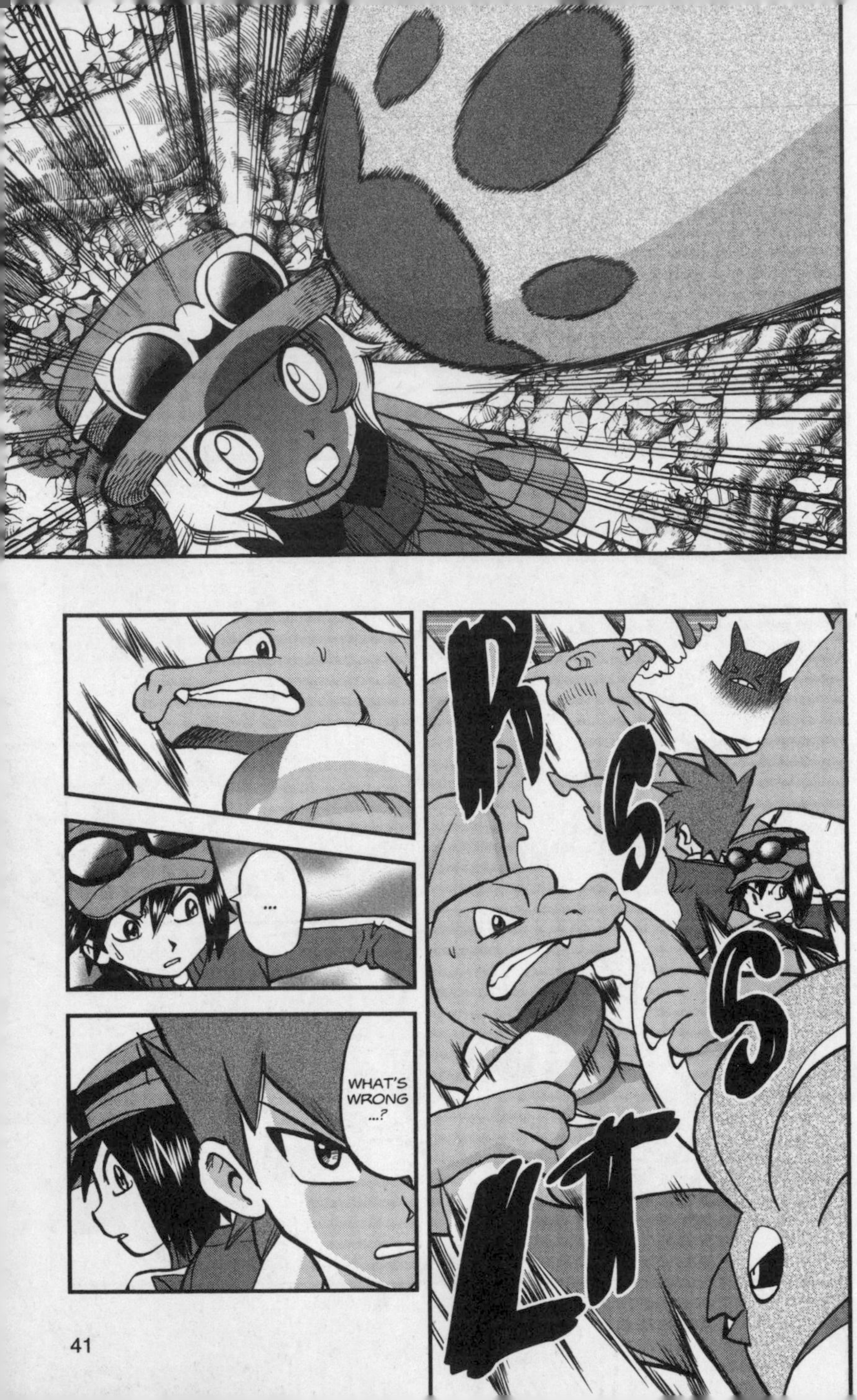
...
WHAT'S WRONG ...?

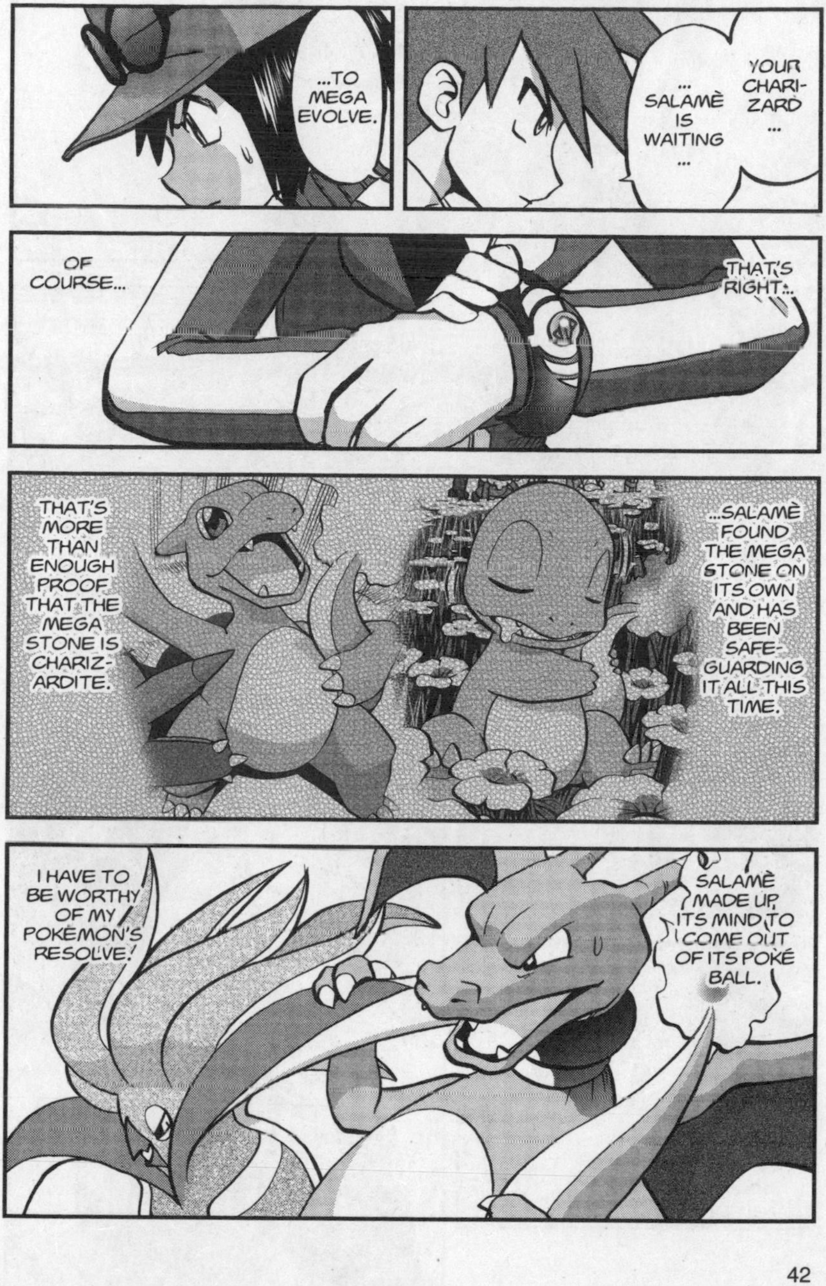
YOUR CHARIZARD ...
... SALAMÈ IS WAITING ...
...TO MEGA EVOLVE.
THAT'S RIGHT...
OF COURSE...
...SALAMÈ FOUND THE MEGA STONE ON ITS OWN AND HAS BEEN SAFEGUARDING IT ALL THIS TIME.
THAT'S MORE THAN ENOUGH PROOF THAT THE MEGA STONE IS CHARIZARDITE.
SALAMÈ MADE UP ITS MIND TO COME OUT OF ITS POKÉ BALL.
I HAVE TO BE WORTHY OF MY POKÉMON'S RESOLVE!

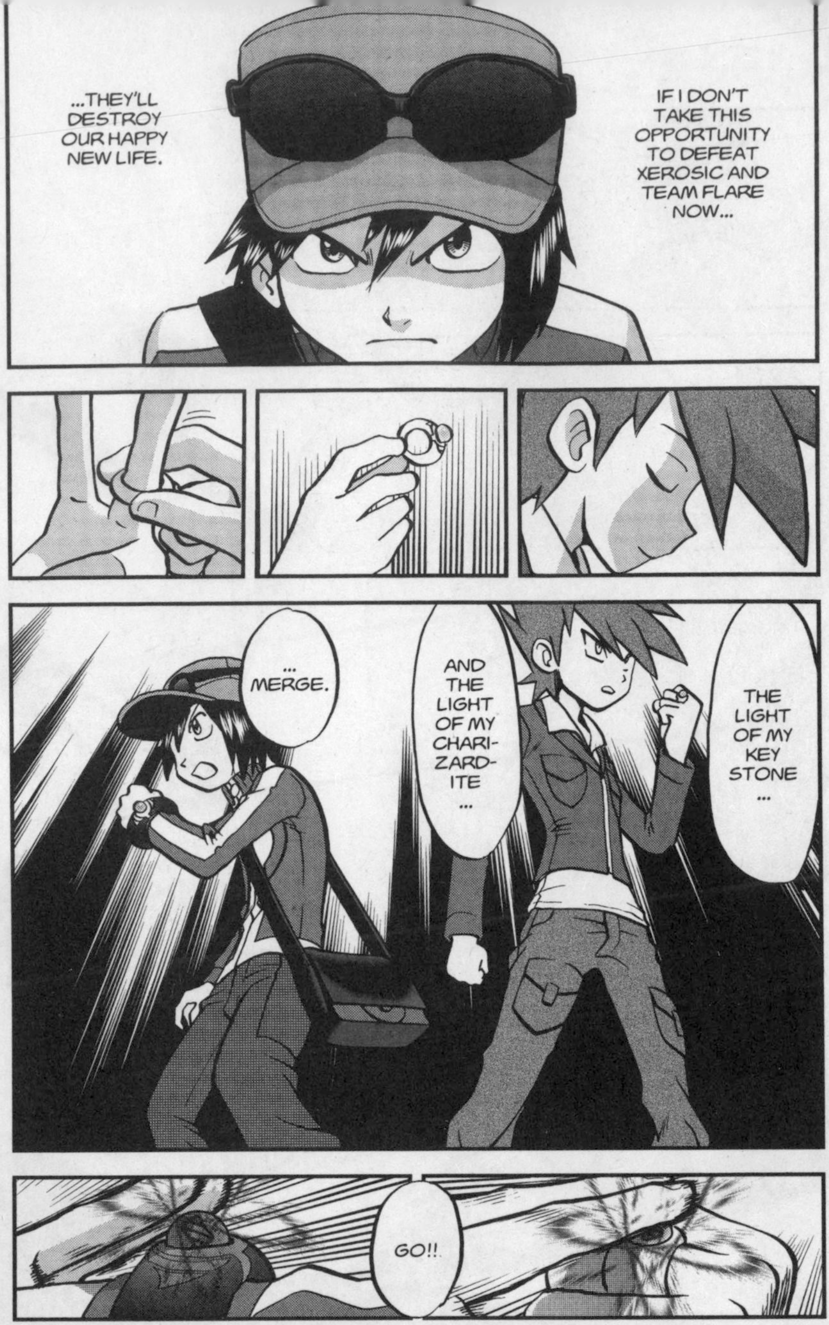
IF I DON'T TAKE THIS OPPORTUNITY TO DEFEAT XEROSIC AND TEAM FLARE NOW...
...THEY'LL DESTROY OUR HAPPY NEW LIFE.
THE LIGHT OF MY KEY STONE ...
AND THE LIGHT OF MY CHARIZARDITE ...
... MERGE.
GO!!

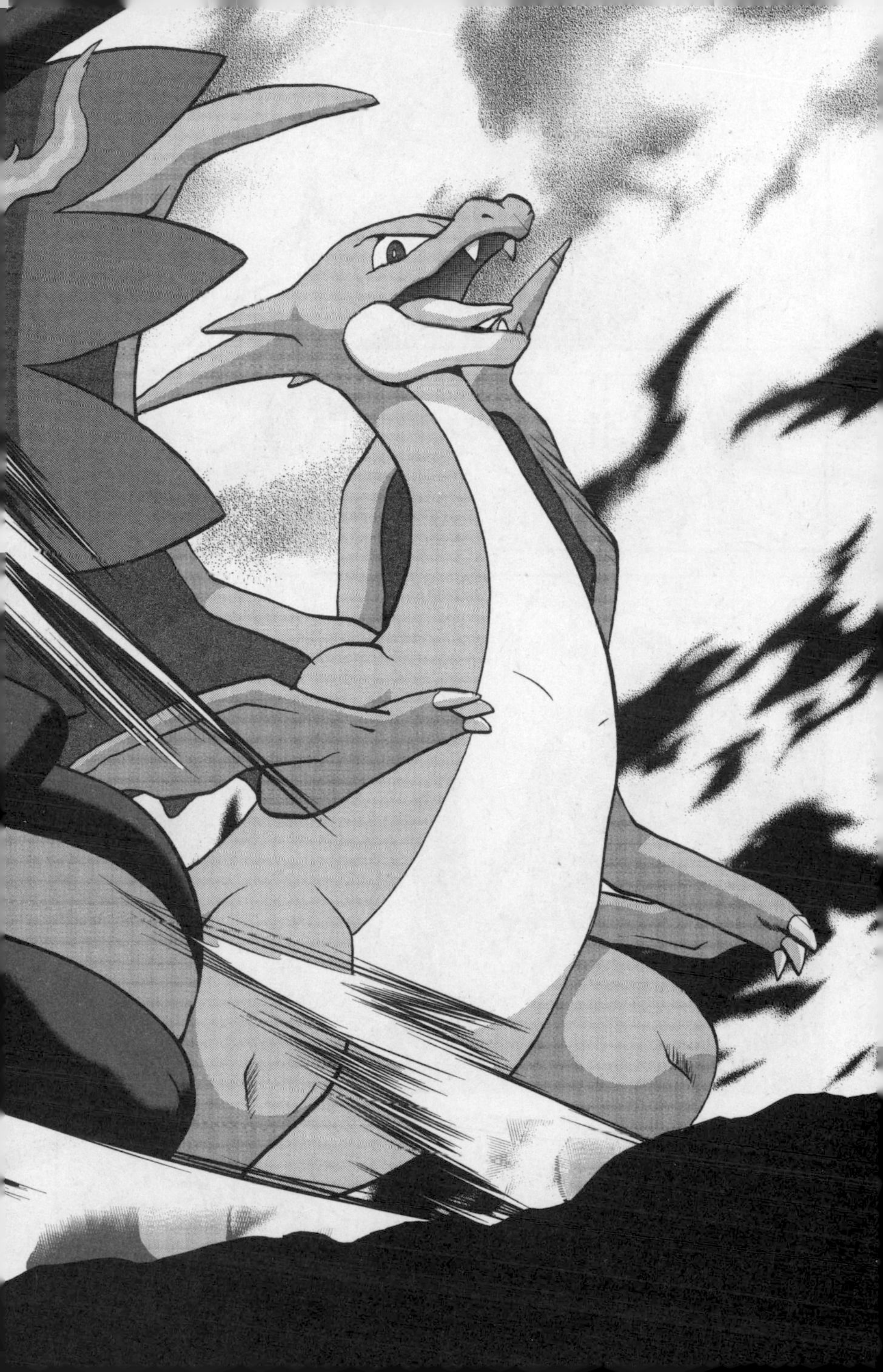

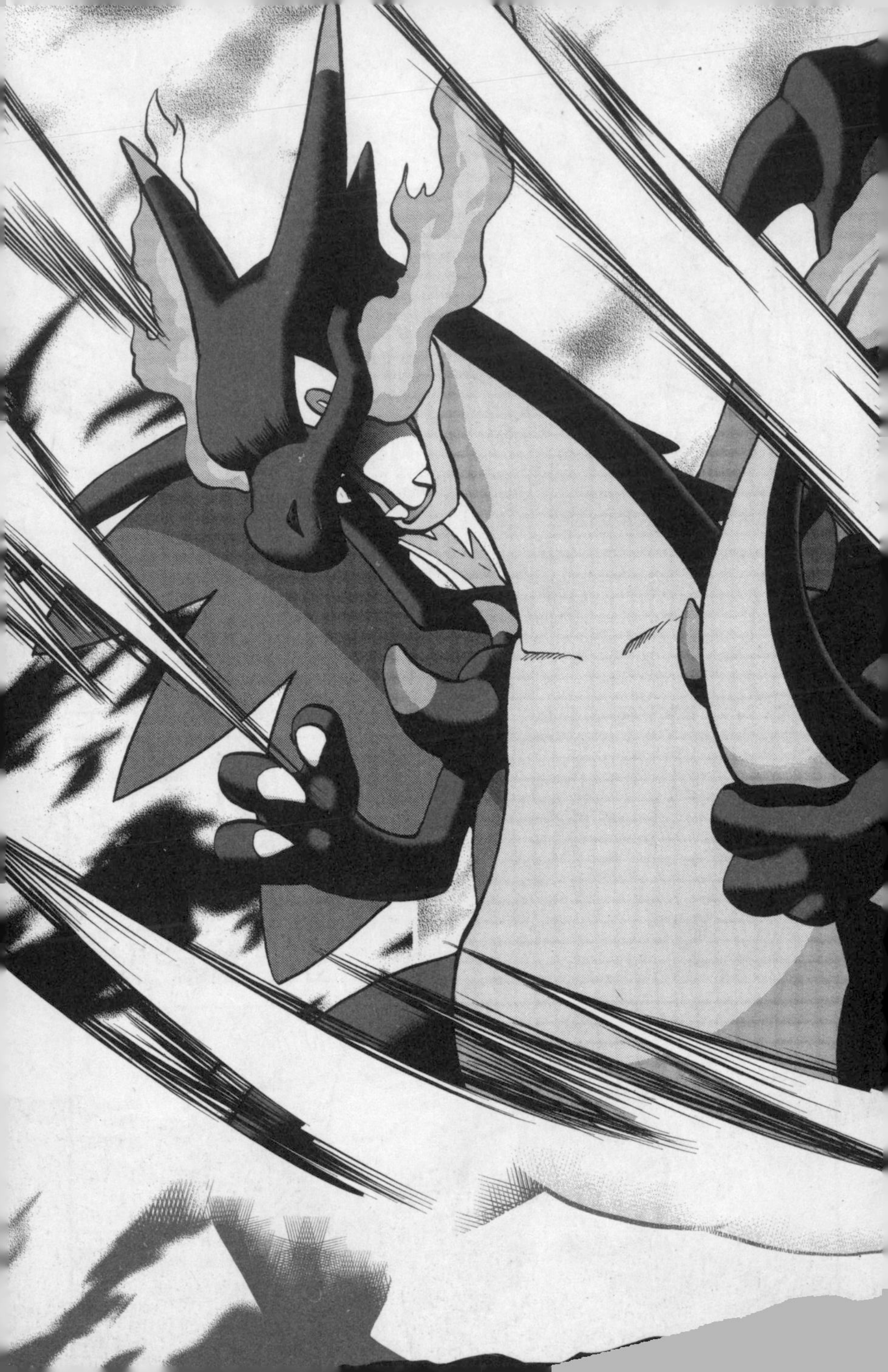

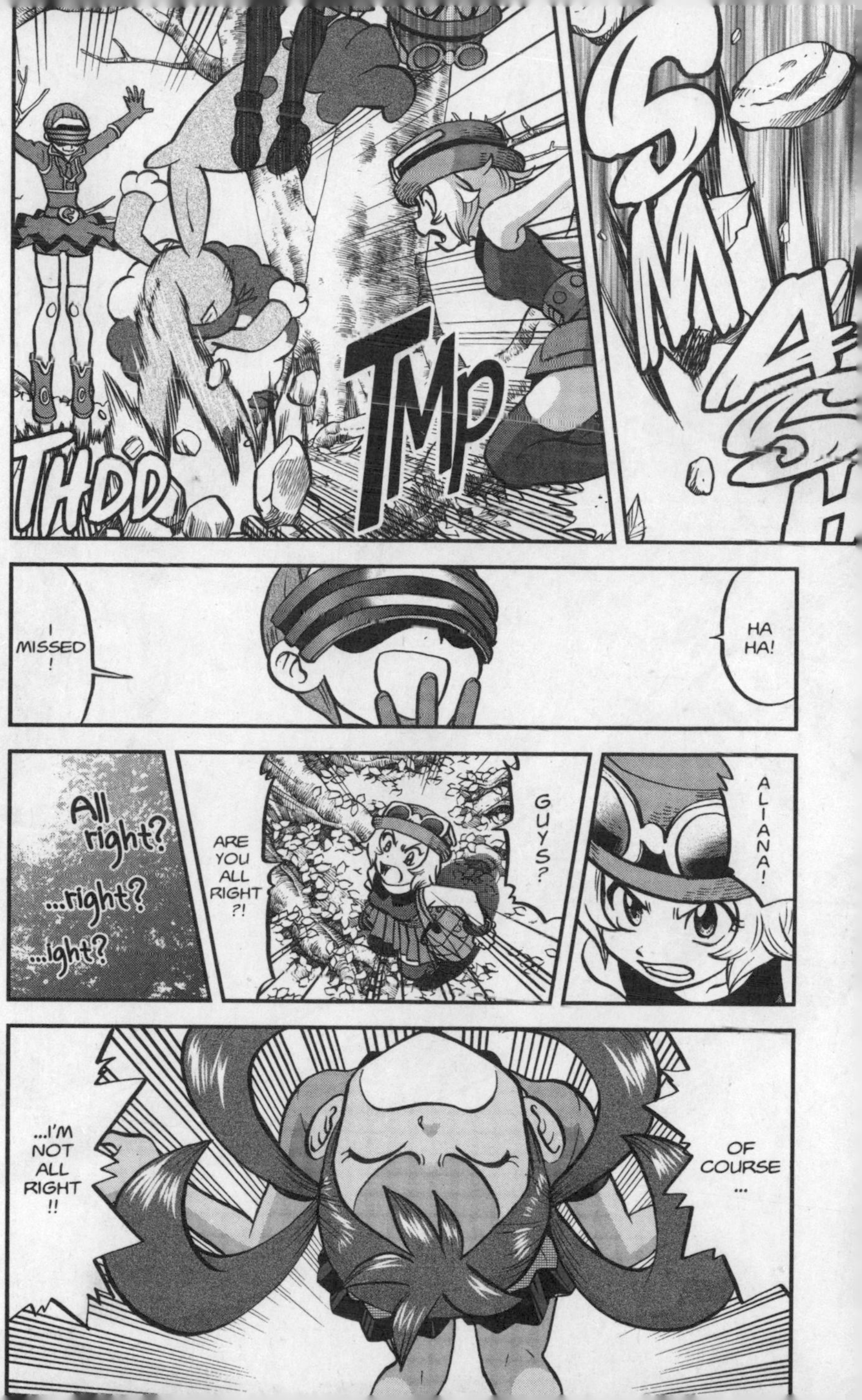
SMASH
TMP
THDD
HA HA!
I MISSED!
ALIANA!
GUYS?
ARE YOU ALL RIGHT?!
All right?
...right?
...ight?
OF COURSE...
...I'M NOT ALL RIGHT!!

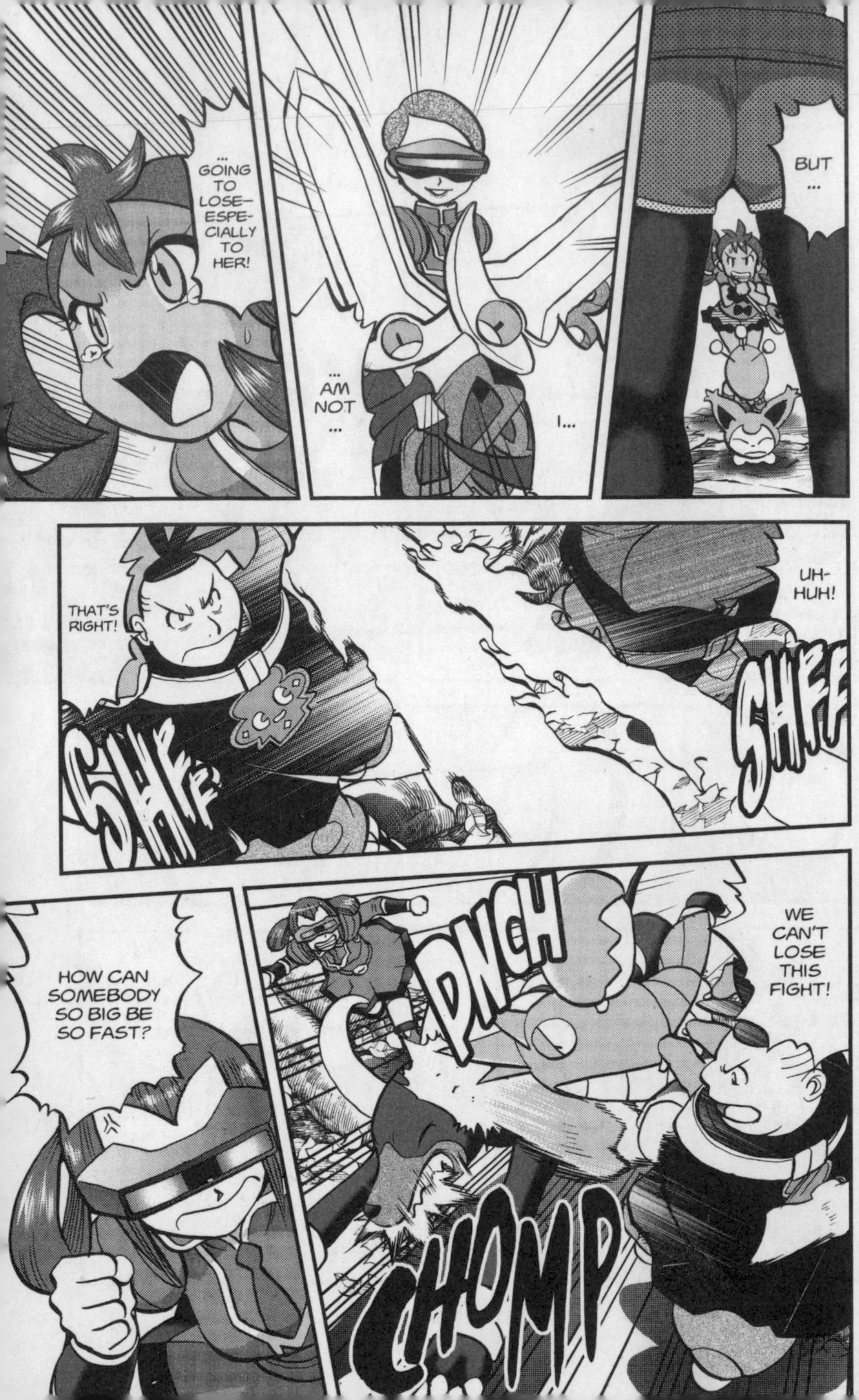
BUT ...
I...
... AM NOT ...
... GOING TO LOSE— ESPECIALLY TO HER!
UH-HUH!
SHFF
THAT'S RIGHT!
SHFF
WE CAN'T LOSE THIS FIGHT!
PNCH
CHOMP
HOW CAN SOMEBODY SO BIG BE SO FAST?

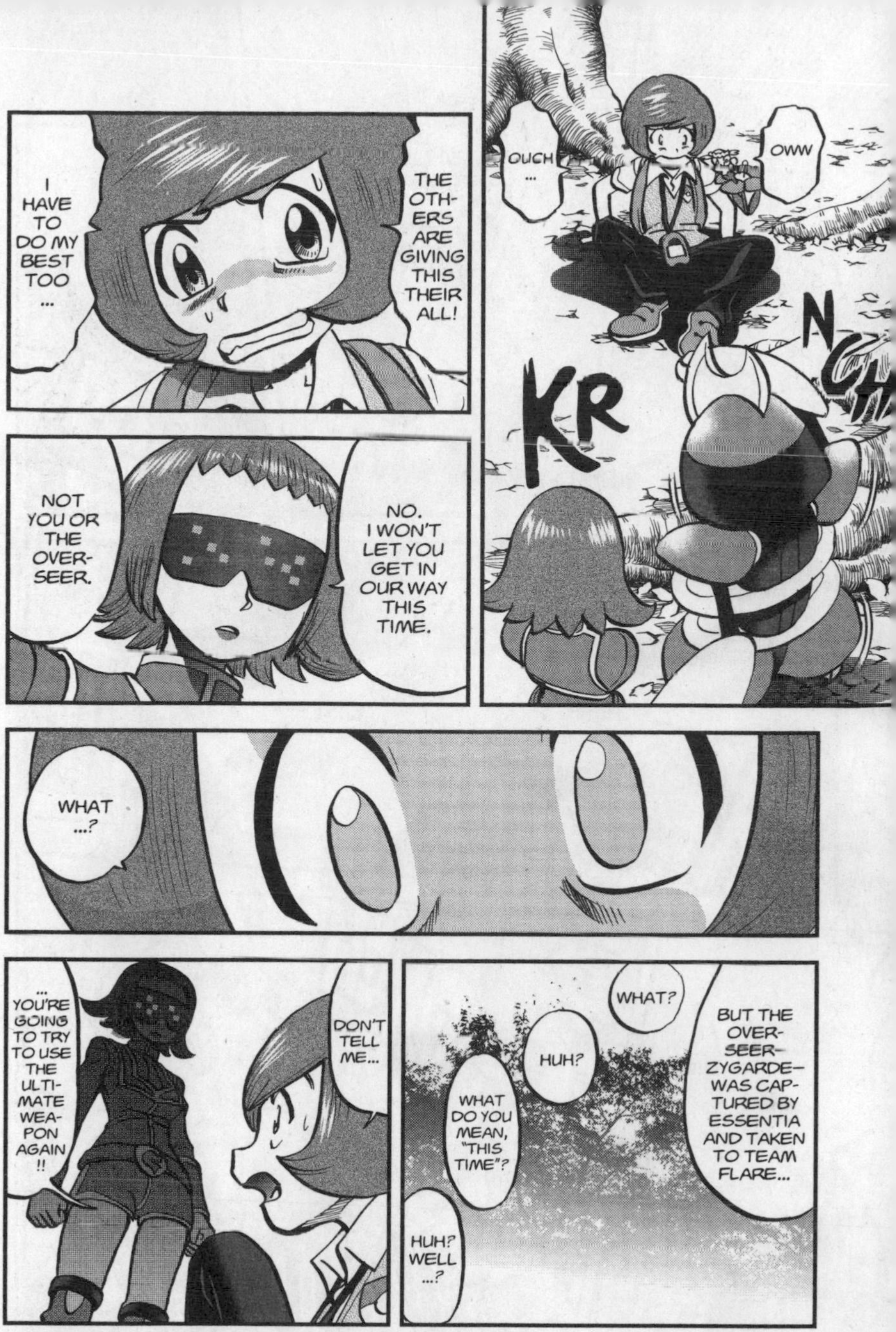
OWW
OUCH ...
KRNCH
THE OTHERS ARE GIVING THIS THEIR ALL!
I HAVE TO DO MY BEST TOO ...
NO. I WON'T LET YOU GET IN OUR WAY THIS TIME.
NOT YOU OR THE OVERSEER.
WHAT ...?
BUT THE OVERSEER—ZYGARDE—WAS CAPTURED BY ESSENTIA AND TAKEN TO TEAM FLARE...
WHAT?
HUH?
WHAT DO YOU MEAN, "THIS TIME"?
HUH? WELL ...?
DON'T TELL ME...
... YOU'RE GOING TO TRY TO USE THE ULTIMATE WEAPON AGAIN !!

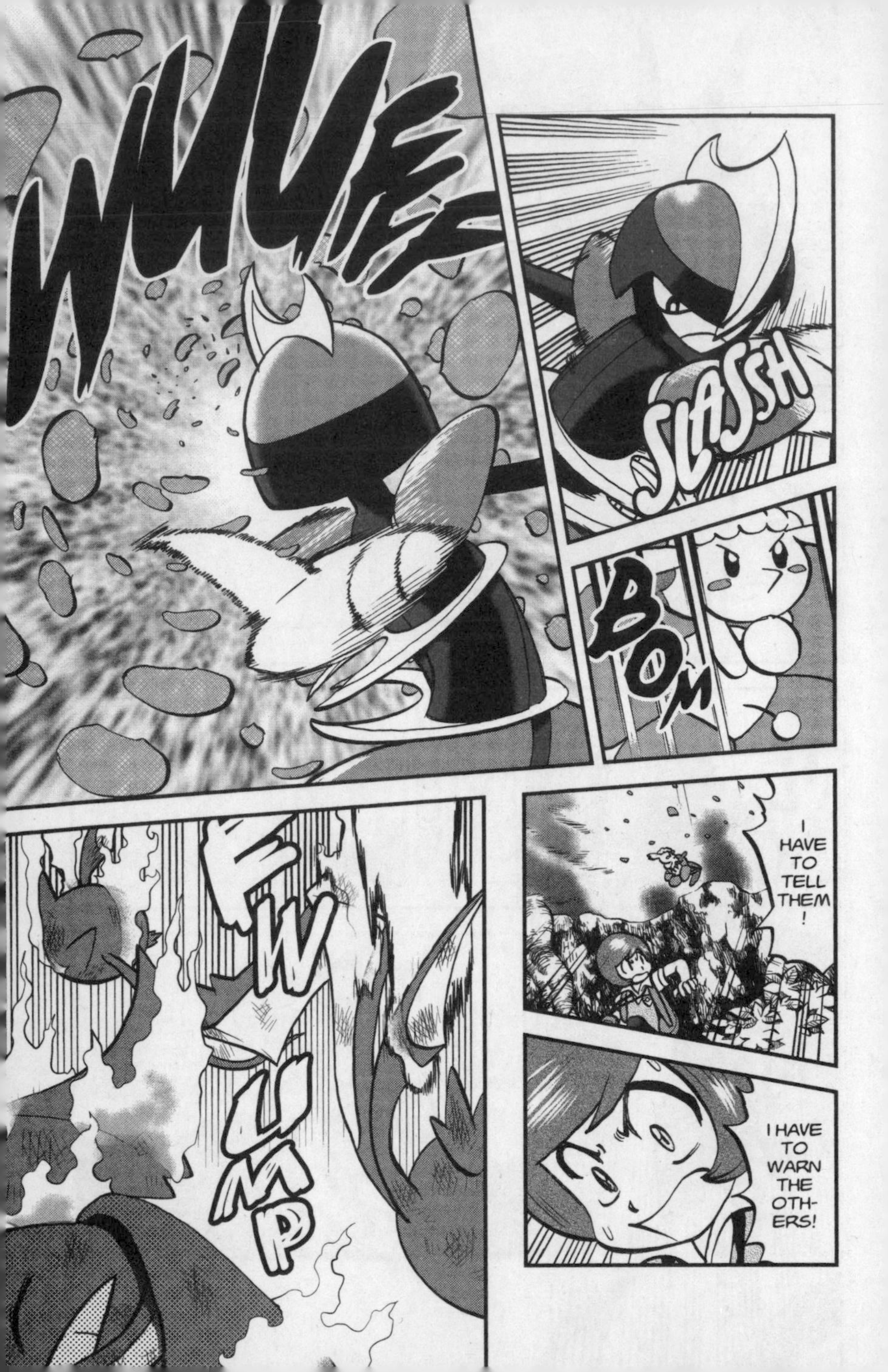
SLASSH
BOM
I HAVE TO TELL THEM!
I HAVE TO WARN THE OTHERS!

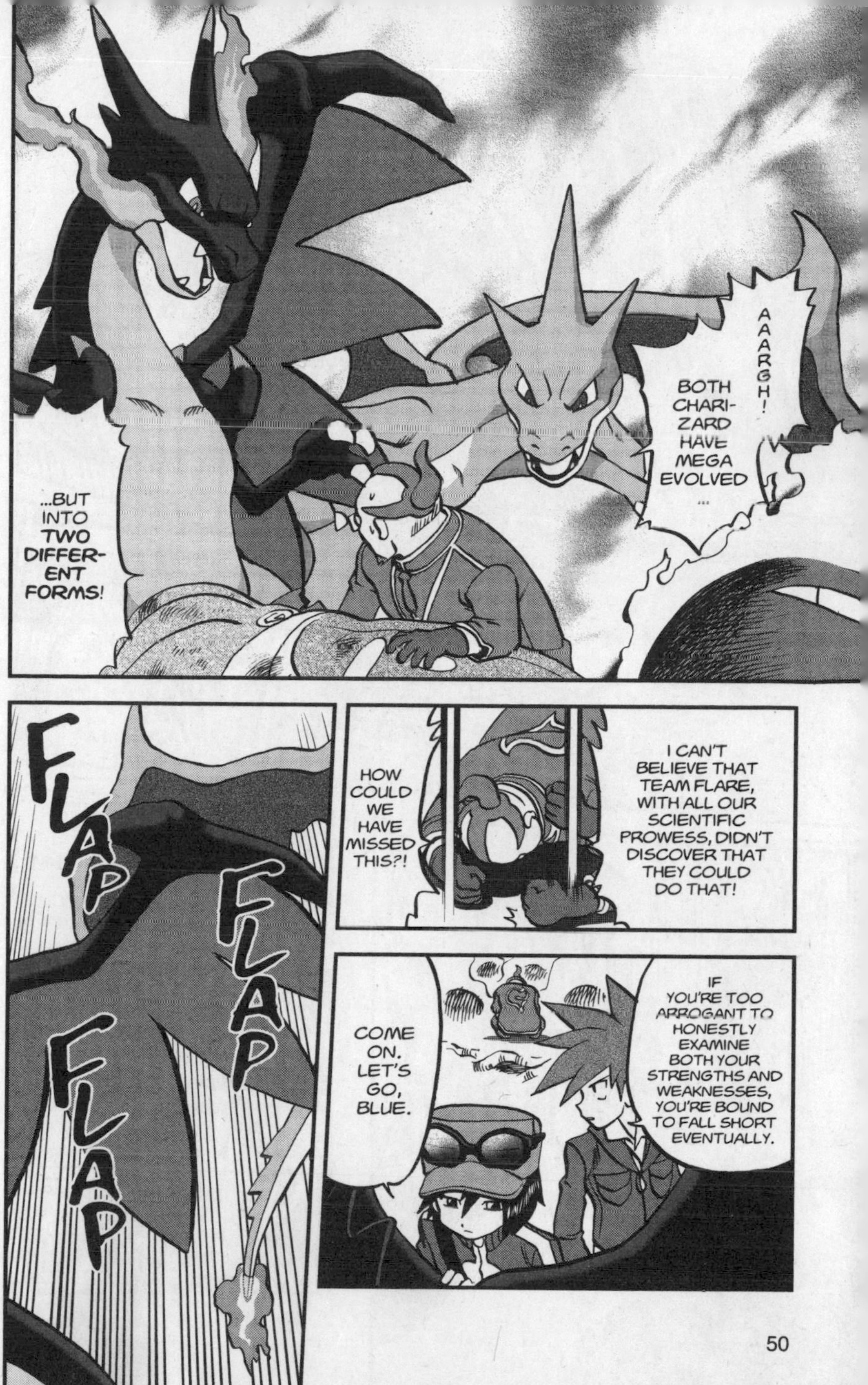

AAAARGH! BOTH CHARIZARD HAVE MEGA EVOLVED...
...BUT INTO TWO DIFFERENT FORMS!
I CAN'T BELIEVE THAT TEAM FLARE, WITH ALL OUR SCIENTIFIC PROWESS, DIDN'T DISCOVER THAT THEY COULD DO THAT!
HOW COULD WE HAVE MISSED THIS?!
IF YOU'RE TOO ARROGANT TO HONESTLY EXAMINE BOTH YOUR STRENGTHS AND WEAKNESSES, YOU'RE BOUND TO FALL SHORT EVENTUALLY.
COME ON. LET'S GO, BLUE.
FLAP
FLAP
FLAP

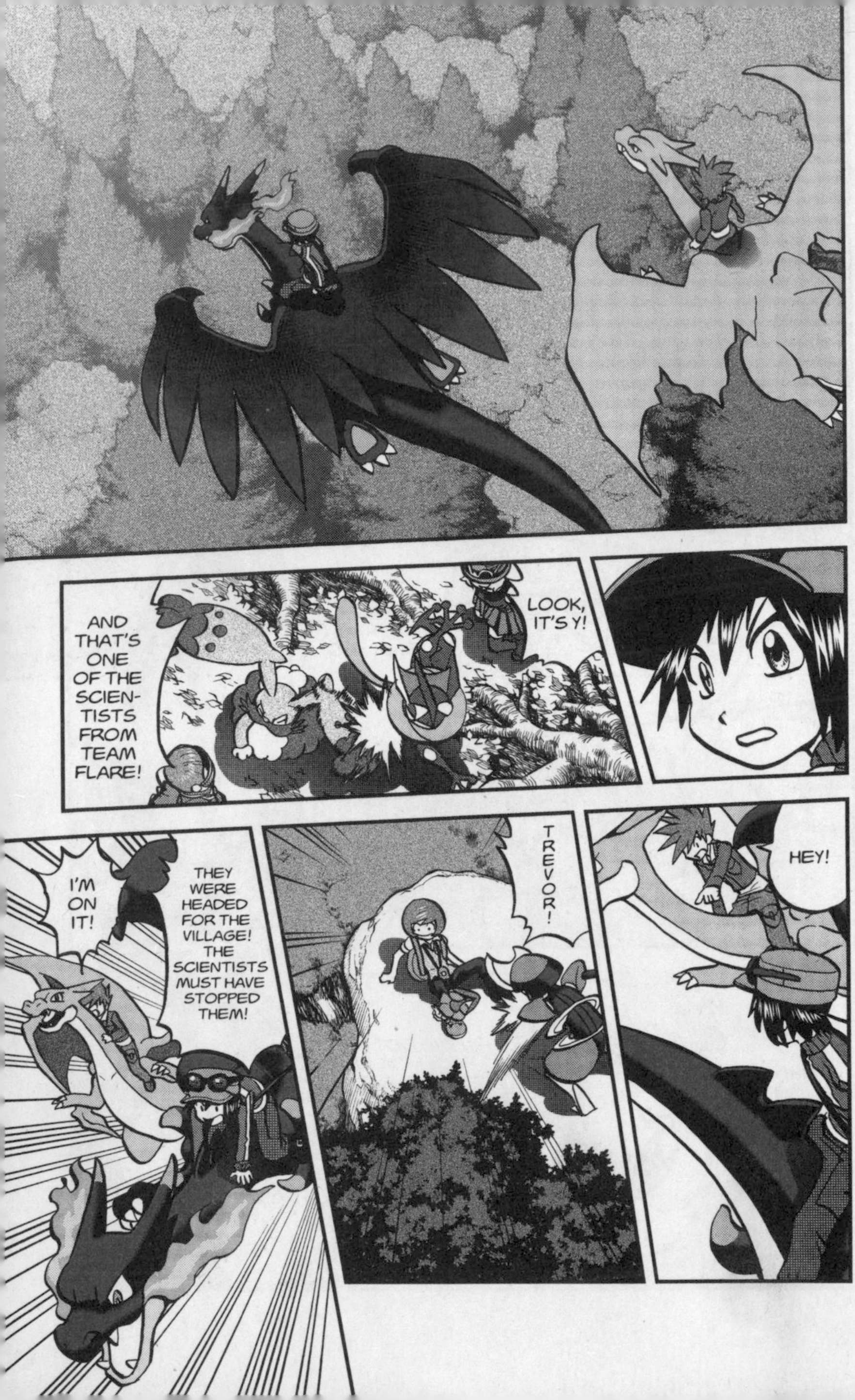
LOOK, IT'S Y!
AND THAT'S ONE OF THE SCIENTISTS FROM TEAM FLARE!
HEY!
TREVOR!
THEY WERE HEADED FOR THE VILLAGE! THE SCIENTISTS MUST HAVE STOPPED THEM!
I'M ON IT!

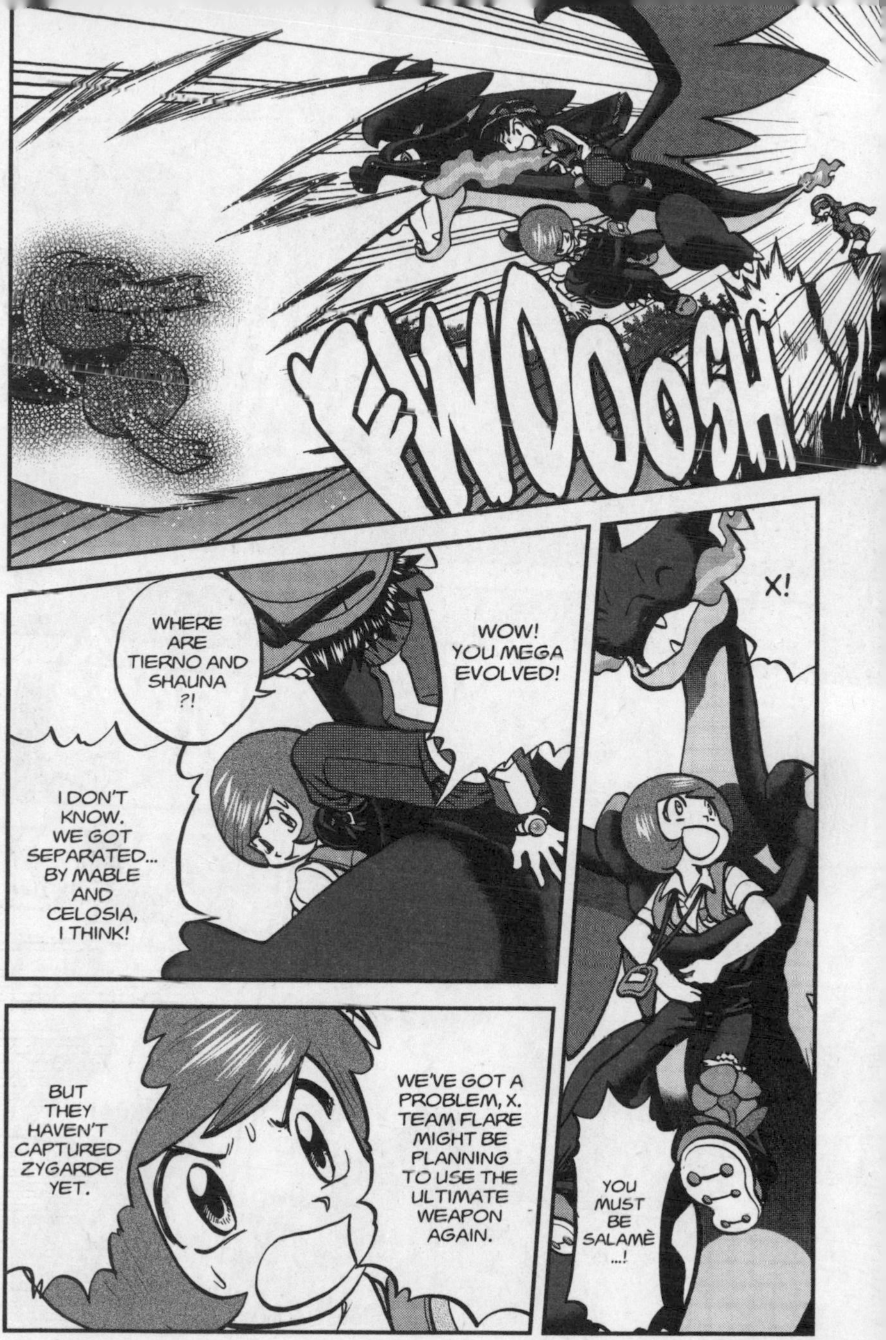
FWOOOSH
X!
YOU MUST BE SALAMÈ ...!
WOW! YOU MEGA EVOLVED!
WHERE ARE TIERNO AND SHAUNA ?!
I DON'T KNOW. WE GOT SEPARATED... BY MABLE AND CELOSIA, I THINK!
WE'VE GOT A PROBLEM, X. TEAM FLARE MIGHT BE PLANNING TO USE THE ULTIMATE WEAPON AGAIN.
BUT THEY HAVEN'T CAPTURED ZYGARDE YET.

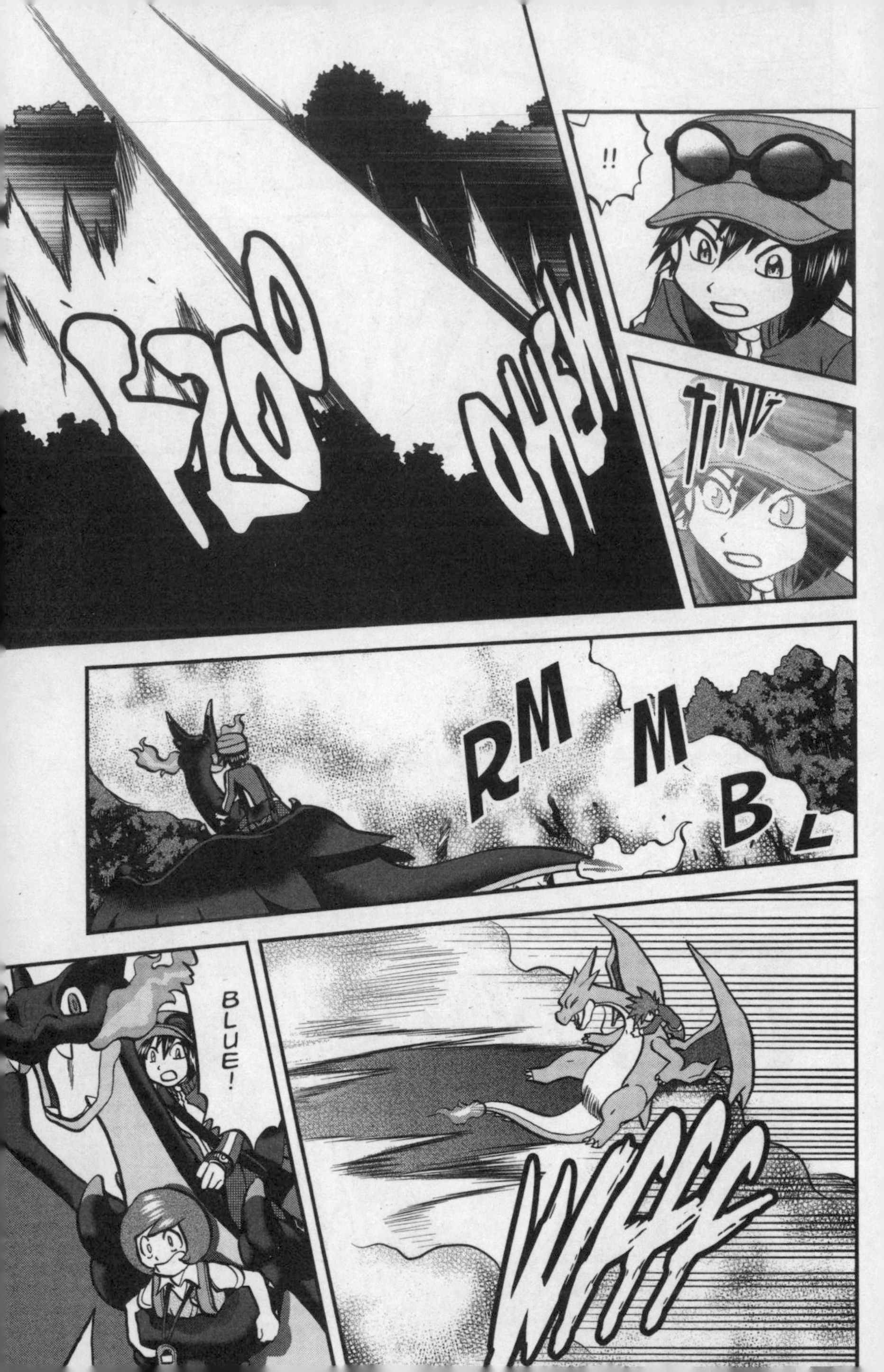
!!
RMMBL
BLUE!

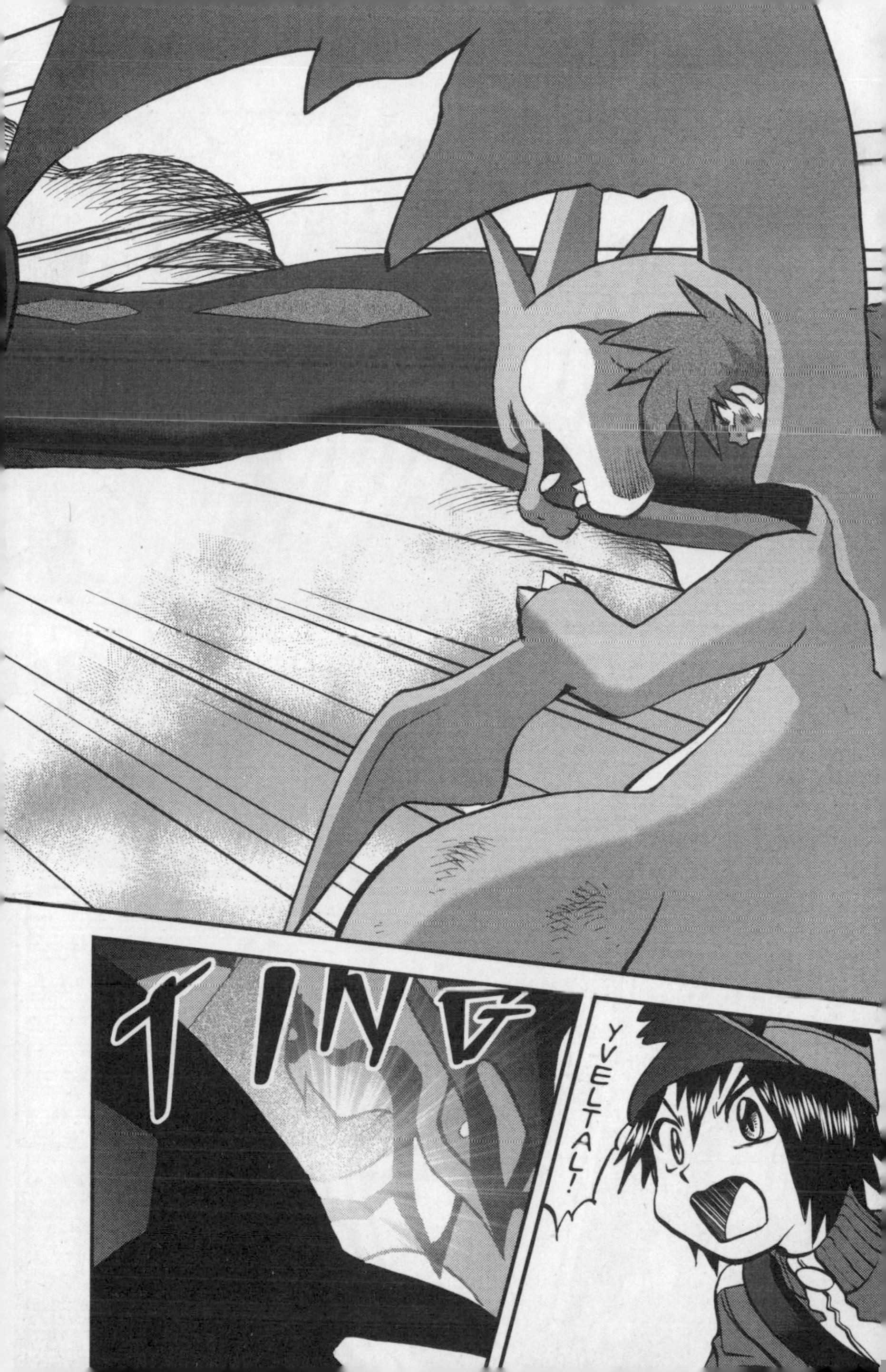
YVELTAL!
TING

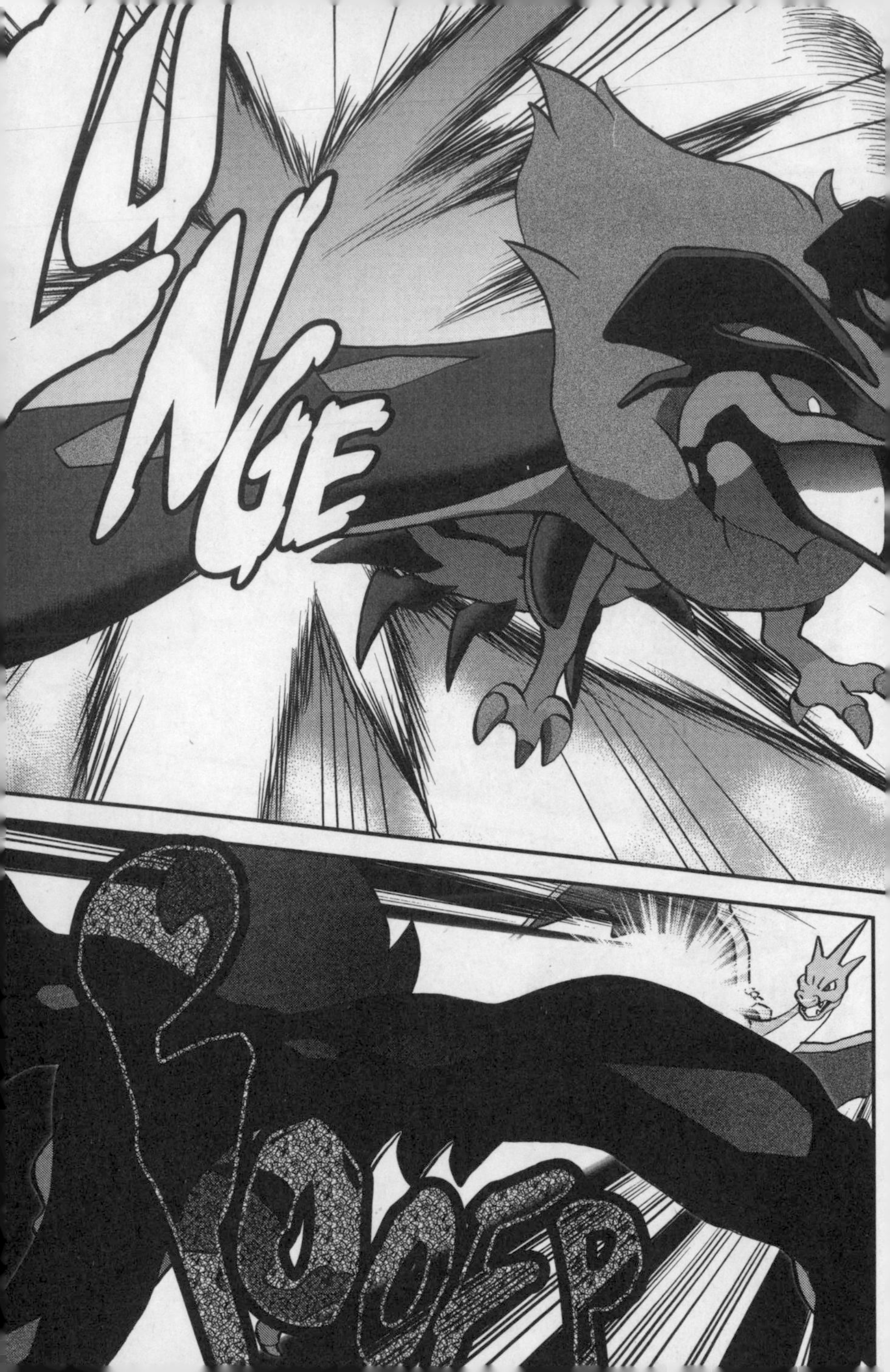
NGE

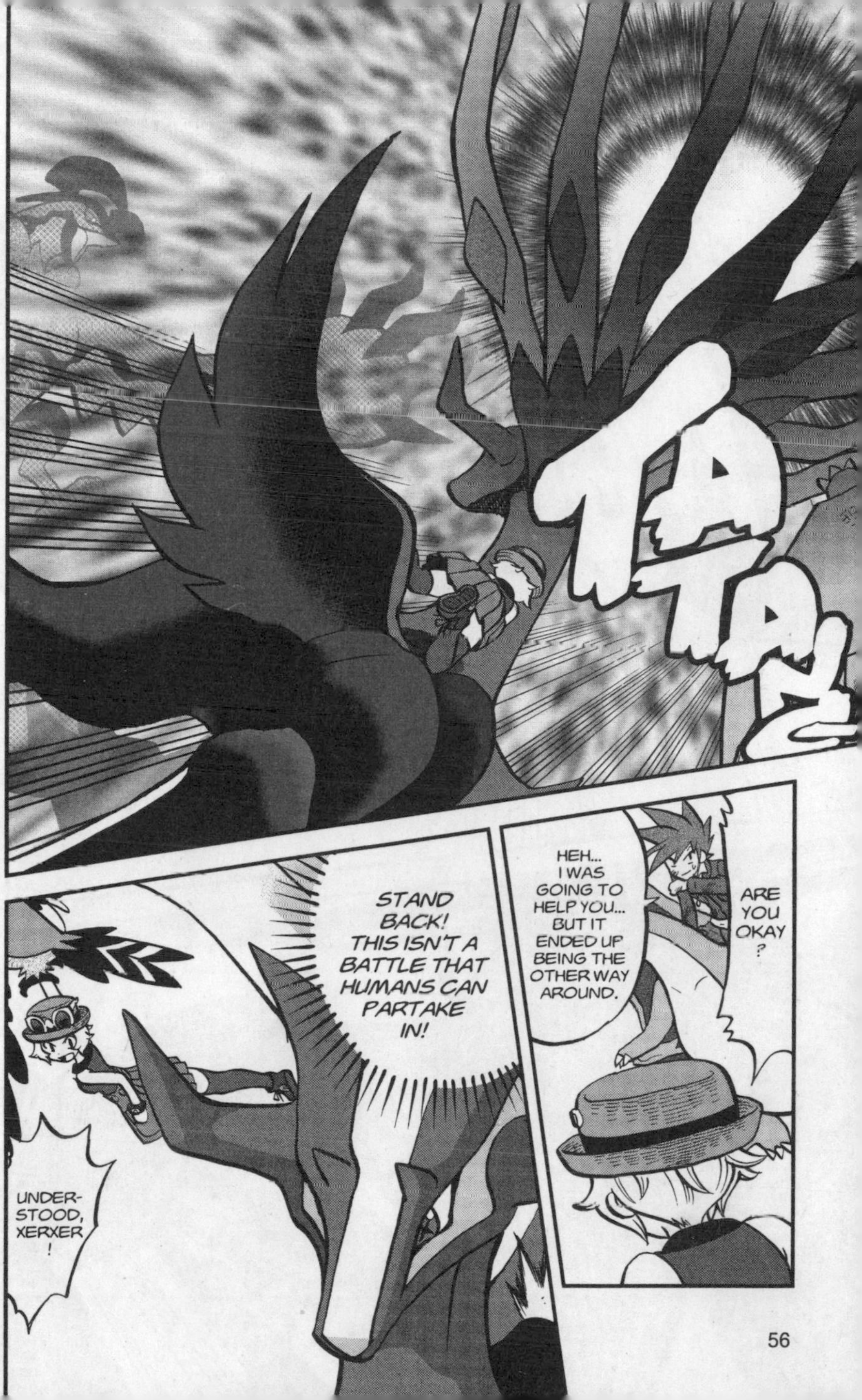
TA TA
ARE YOU OKAY?
HEH... I WAS GOING TO HELP YOU... BUT IT ENDED UP BEING THE OTHER WAY AROUND.
STAND BACK! THIS ISN'T A BATTLE THAT HUMANS CAN PARTAKE IN!
UNDER-STOOD, XERXER!

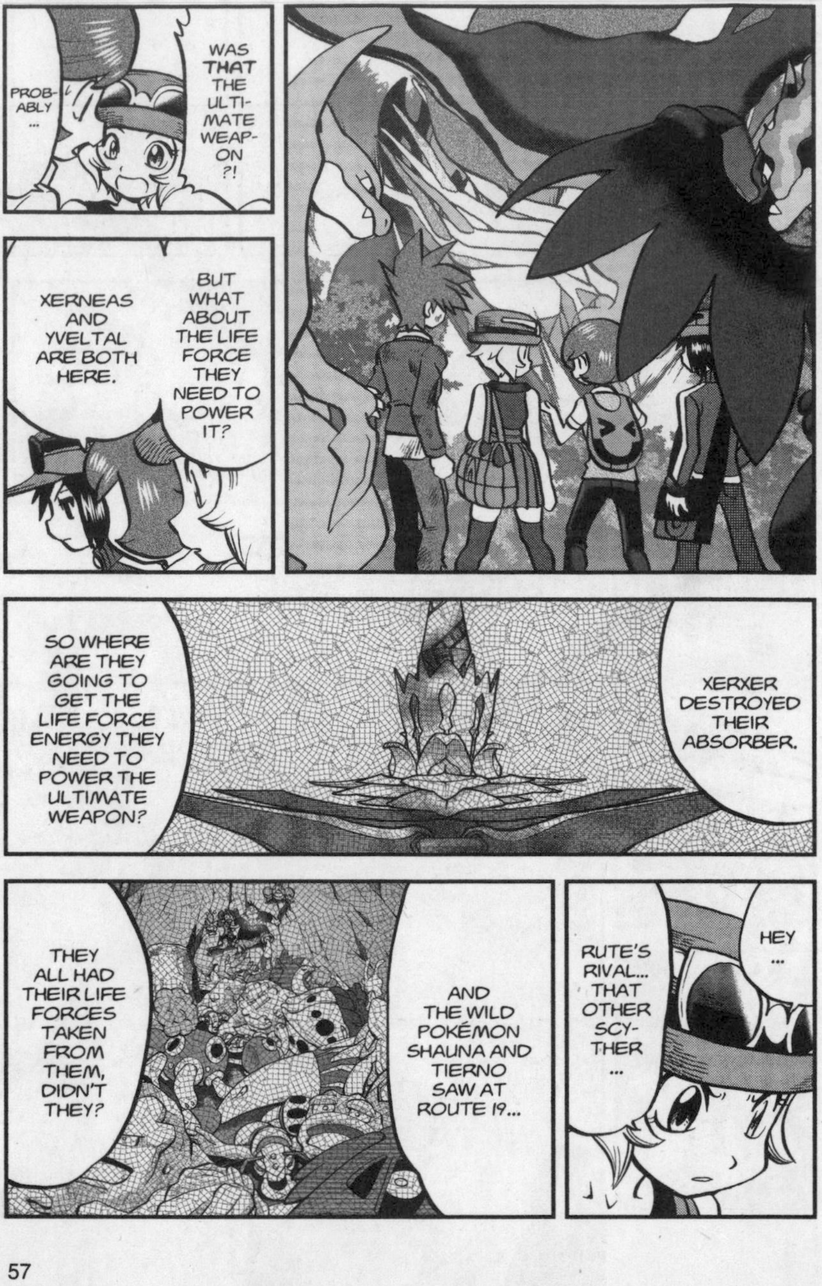
WAS THAT THE ULTIMATE WEAPON?!
PROBABLY...
XERNEAS AND YVELTAL ARE BOTH HERE.
BUT WHAT ABOUT THE LIFE FORCE THEY NEED TO POWER IT?
XERXER DESTROYED THEIR ABSORBER.
SO WHERE ARE THEY GOING TO GET THE LIFE FORCE ENERGY THEY NEED TO POWER THE ULTIMATE WEAPON?
HEY...
RUTE'S RIVAL... THAT OTHER SCYTHER...
AND THE WILD POKÉMON SHAUNA AND TIERNO SAW AT ROUTE 19...
THEY ALL HAD THEIR LIFE FORCES TAKEN FROM THEM, DIDN'T THEY?

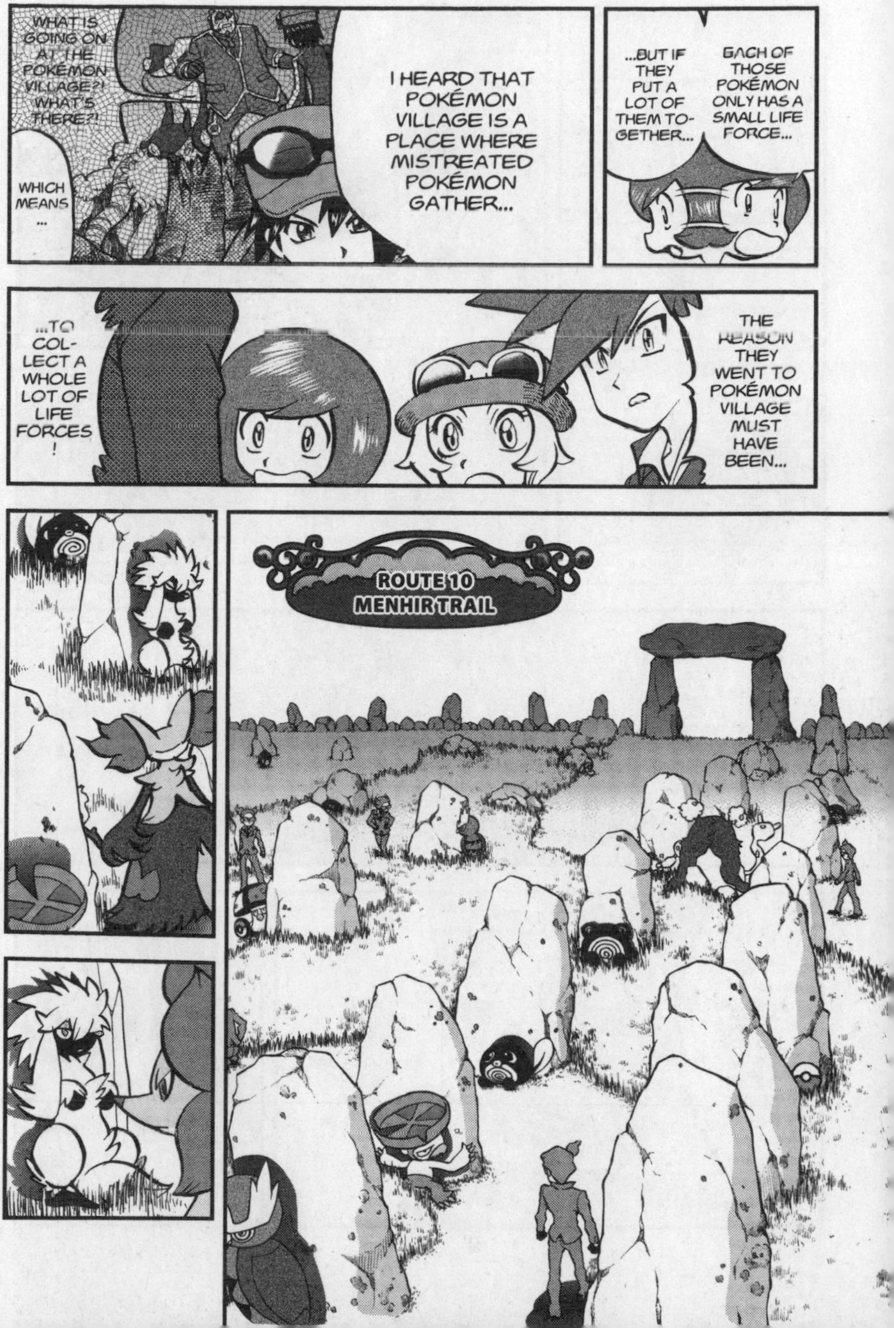
EACH OF THOSE POKÉMON ONLY HAS A SMALL LIFE FORCE...
...BUT IF THEY PUT A LOT OF THEM TOGETHER...
I HEARD THAT POKÉMON VILLAGE IS A PLACE WHERE MISTREATED POKÉMON GATHER...
WHAT IS GOING ON AT THE POKÉMON VILLAGE?! WHAT'S THERE?!
WHICH MEANS...
THE REASON THEY WENT TO POKÉMON VILLAGE MUST HAVE BEEN...
...TO COLLECT A WHOLE LOT OF LIFE FORCES!
ROUTE 10
MENHIR TRAIL

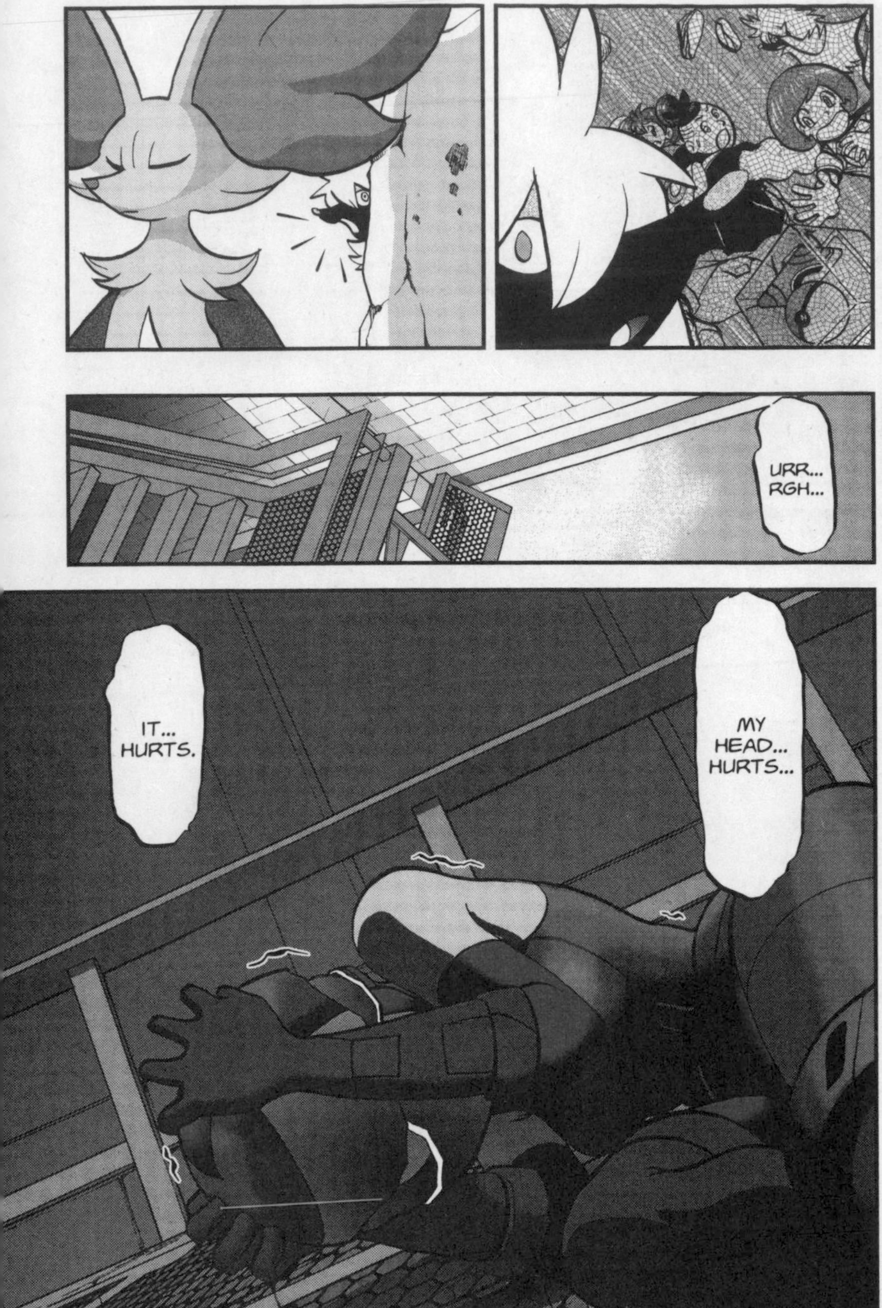
URR... RGH...
MY HEAD... HURTS...
IT... HURTS.

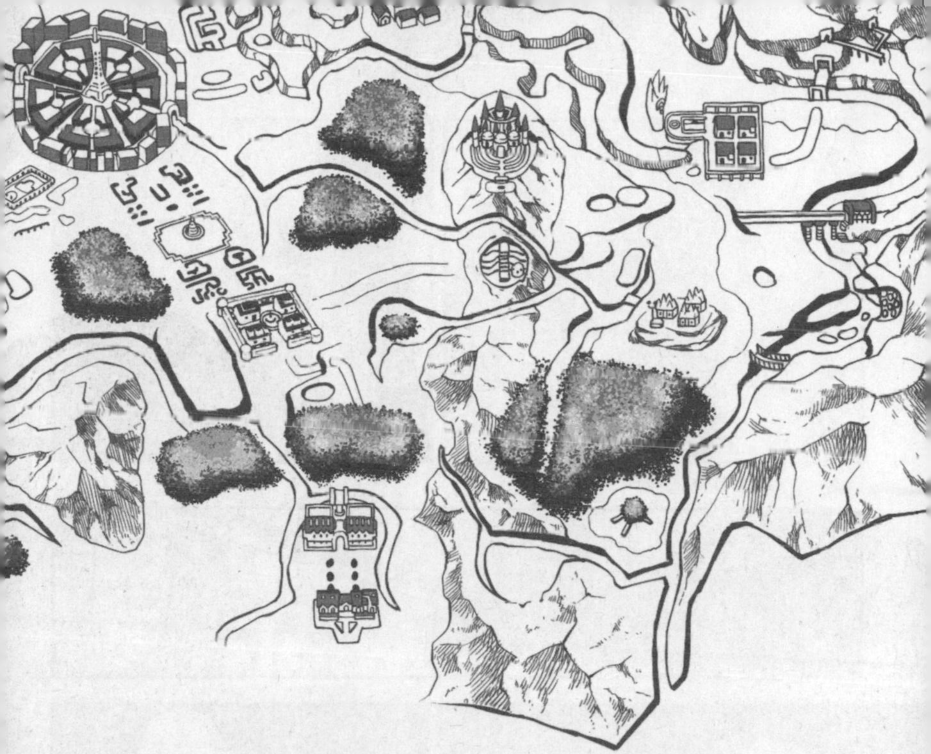

Current Location

Route 18
Vallée Étroite Way

This path is best known for its trolley, once used for the coal mine, and the curious Inverse Battle House.

Adventure #42
Yveltal Steals

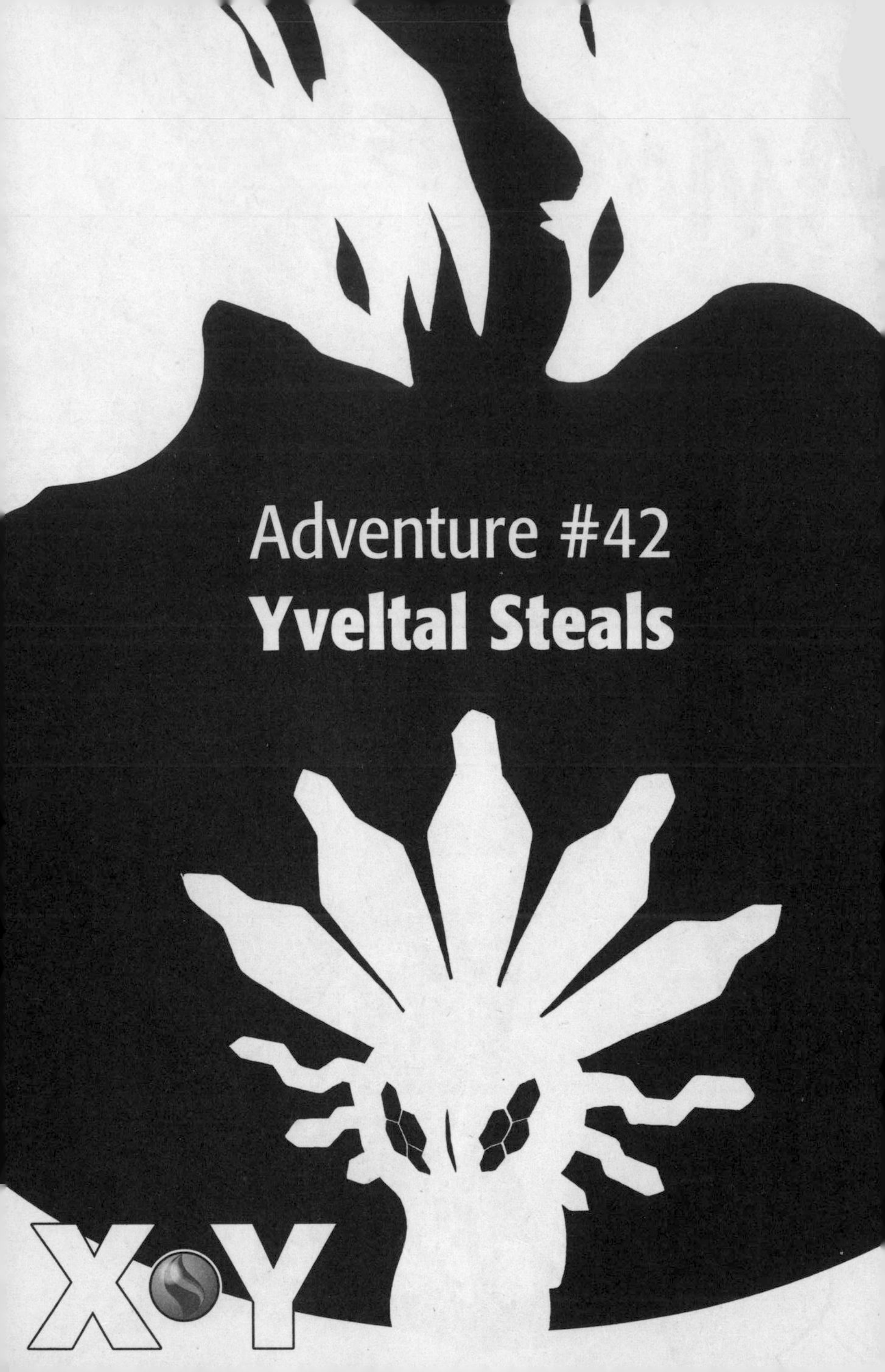

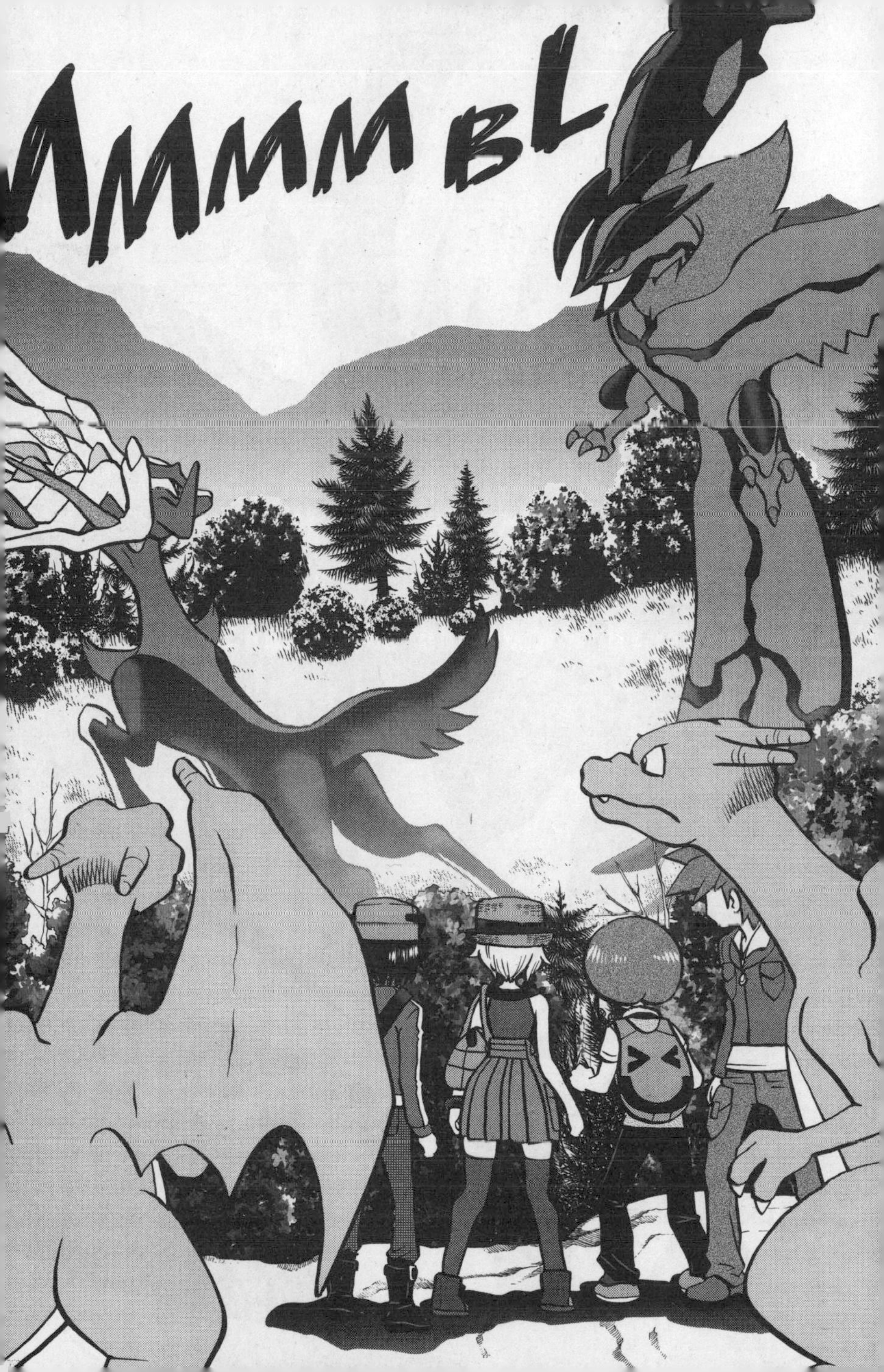
MMMMBL

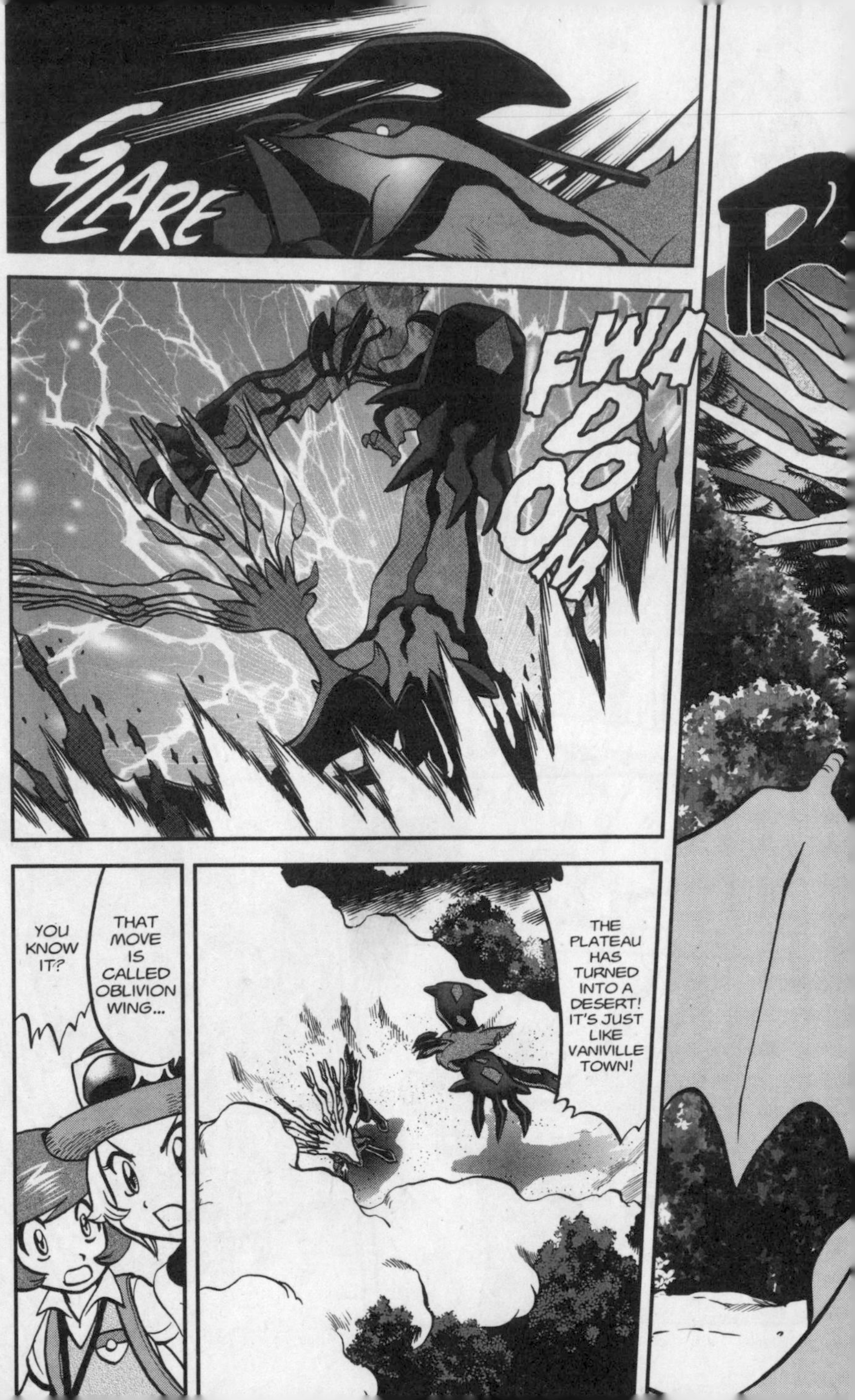
GLARE
FWADOOOM
THE PLATEAU HAS TURNED INTO A DESERT! IT'S JUST LIKE VANIVILLE TOWN!
THAT MOVE IS CALLED OBLIVION WING...
YOU KNOW IT?

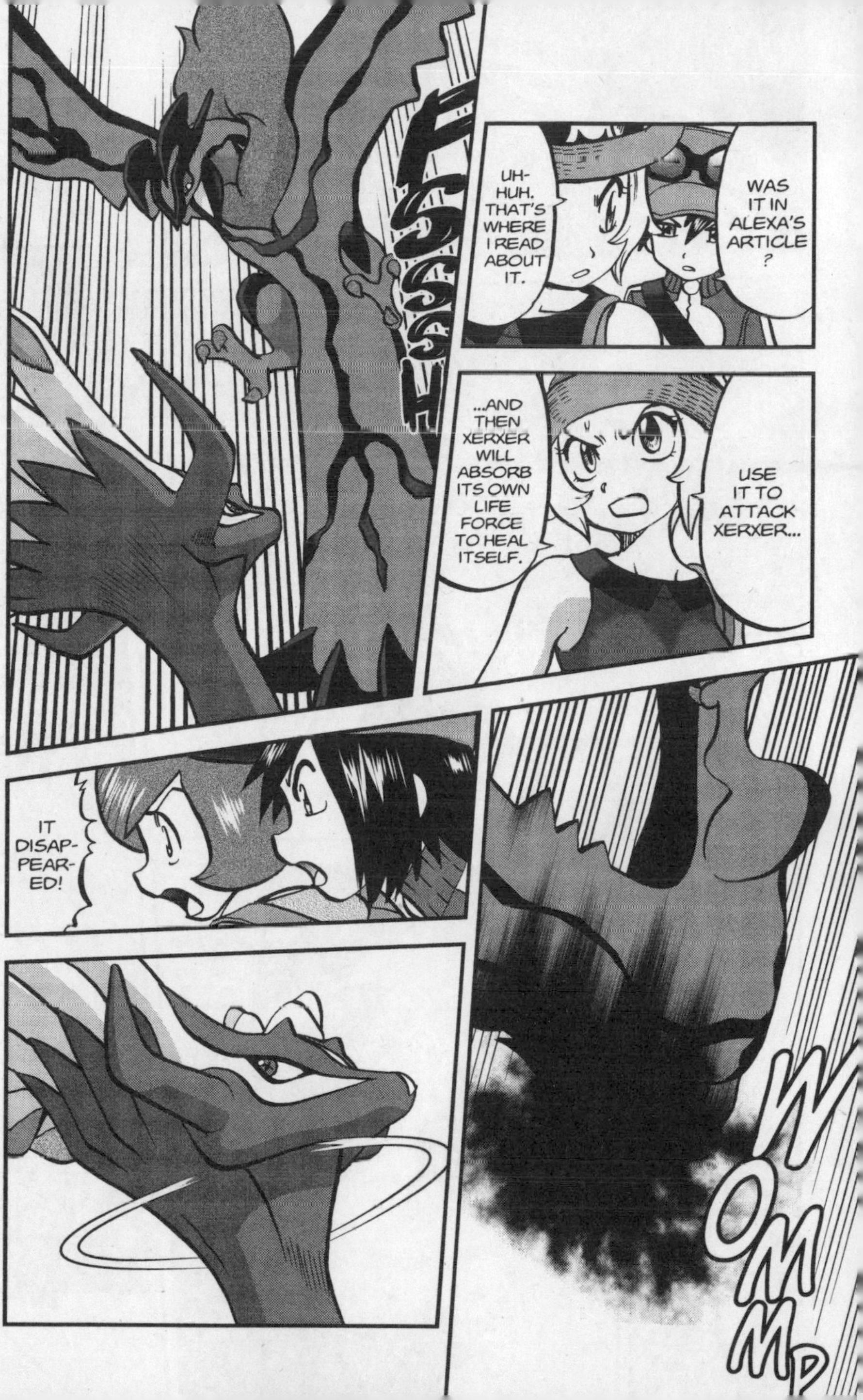
WAS IT IN ALEXA'S ARTICLE?
UH-HUH. THAT'S WHERE I READ ABOUT IT.
USE IT TO ATTACK XERXER...
...AND THEN XERXER WILL ABSORB ITS OWN LIFE FORCE TO HEAL ITSELF.
IT DISAPPEARED!

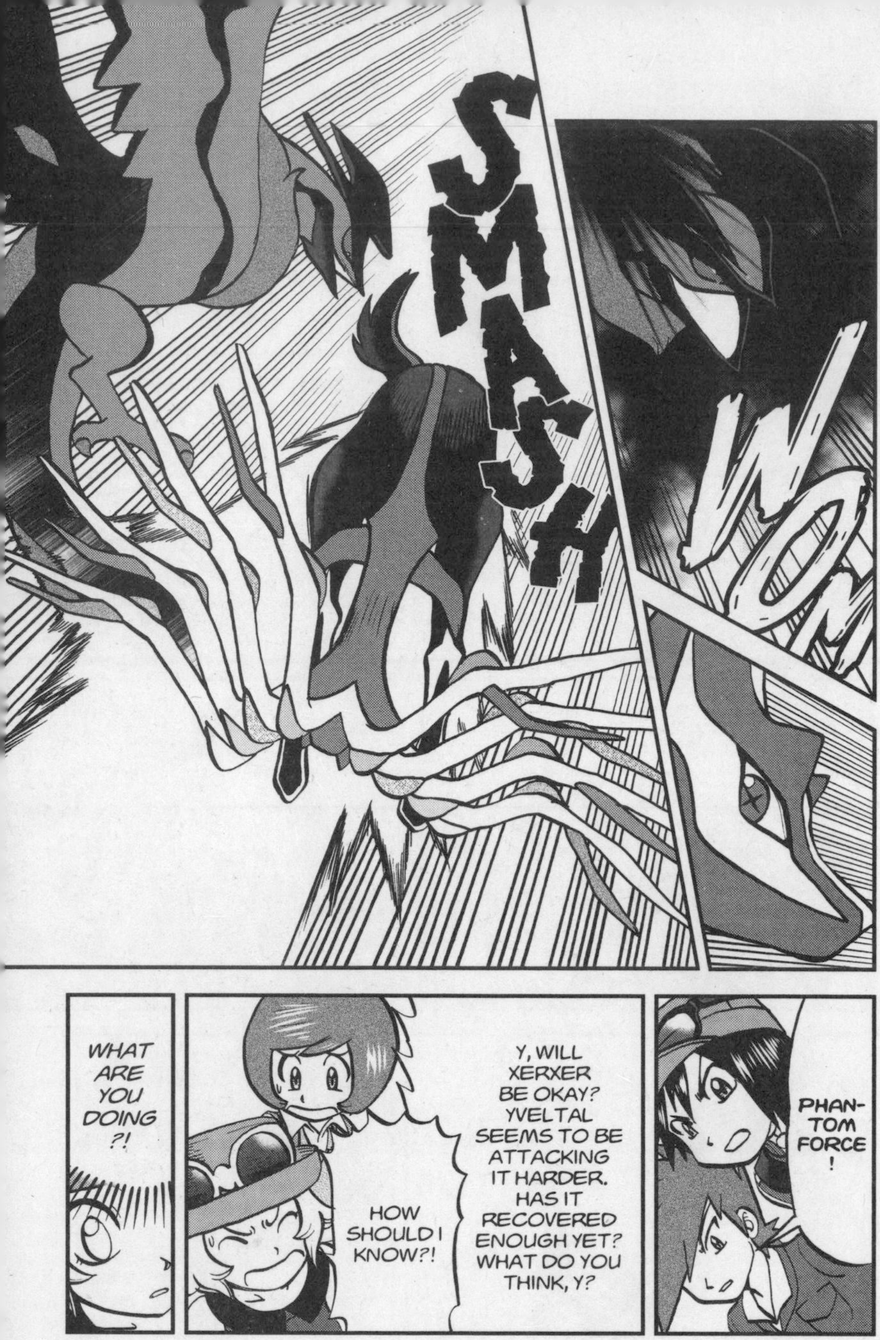
WOM
SMASH
PHANTOM FORCE!
Y, WILL XERXER BE OKAY? YVELTAL SEEMS TO BE ATTACKING IT HARDER. HAS IT RECOVERED ENOUGH YET? WHAT DO YOU THINK, Y?
HOW SHOULD I KNOW?!
WHAT ARE YOU DOING?!

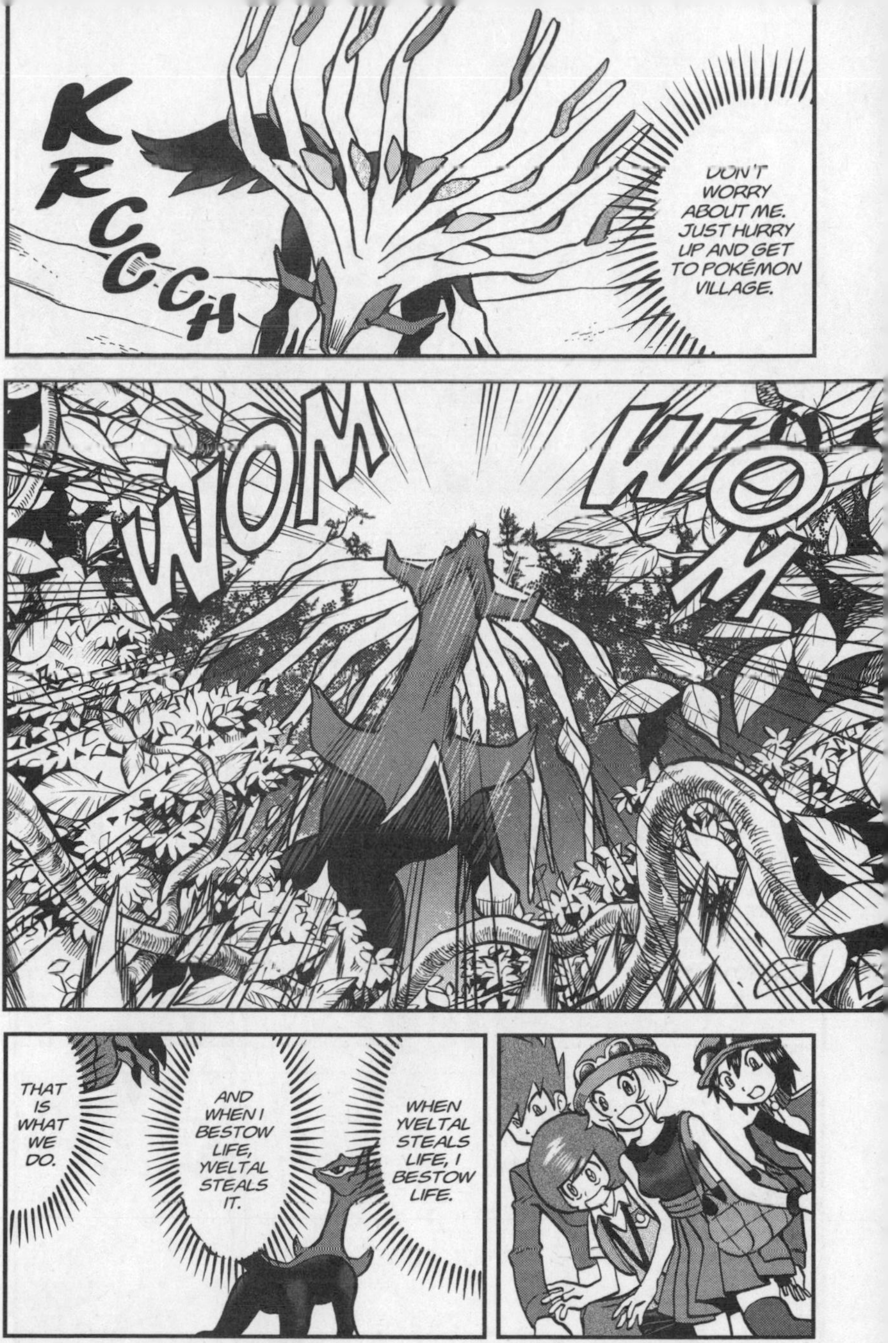
DON'T WORRY ABOUT ME. JUST HURRY UP AND GET TO POKÉMON VILLAGE.
KRCCCH
WOM
WOM
WHEN YVELTAL STEALS LIFE, I BESTOW LIFE.
AND WHEN I BESTOW LIFE, YVELTAL STEALS IT.
THAT IS WHAT WE DO.

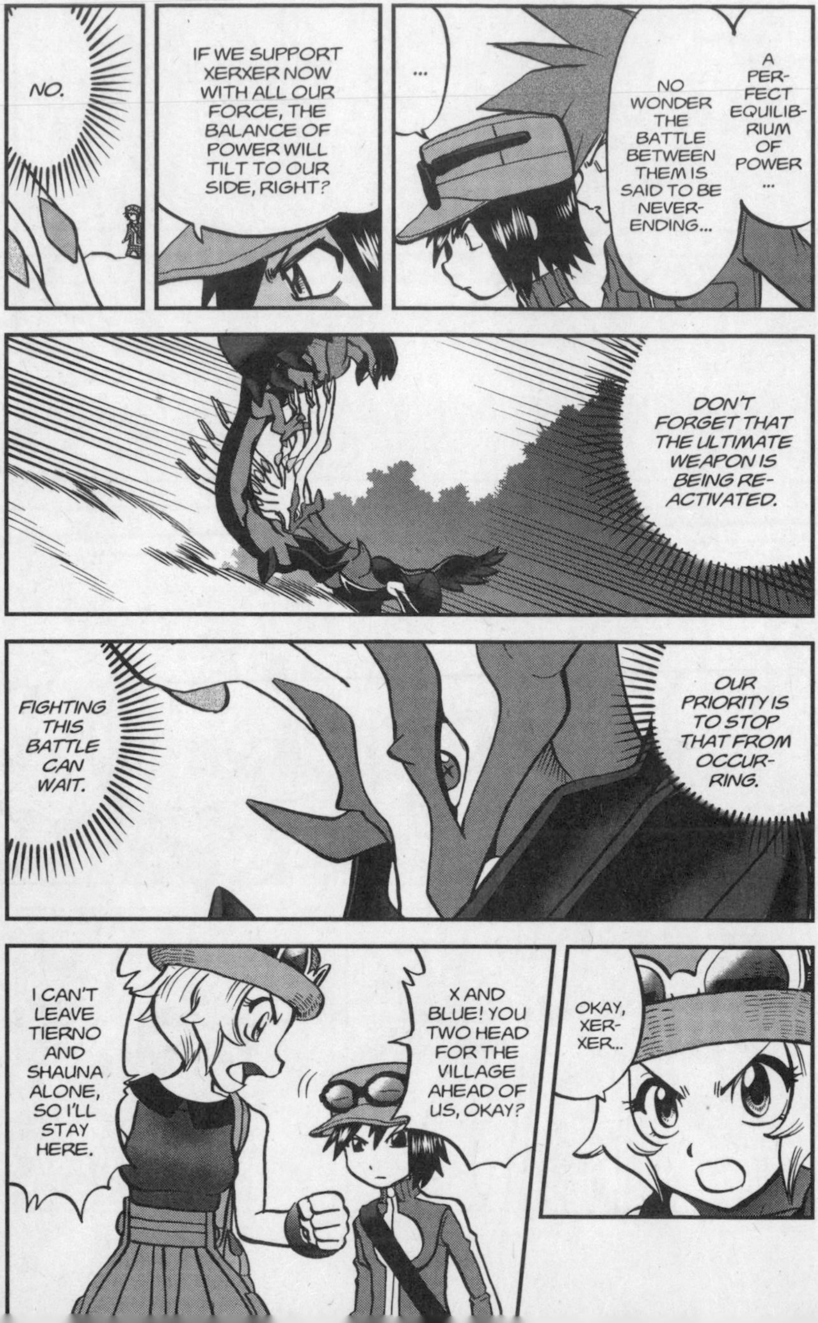
A PER-FECT EQUILIB-RIUM OF POWER ...
NO WONDER THE BATTLE BETWEEN THEM IS SAID TO BE NEVER-ENDING...
...
IF WE SUPPORT XERXER NOW WITH ALL OUR FORCE, THE BALANCE OF POWER WILL TILT TO OUR SIDE, RIGHT?
NO.
DON'T FORGET THAT THE ULTIMATE WEAPON IS BEING RE-ACTIVATED.
OUR PRIORITY IS TO STOP THAT FROM OCCUR-RING.
FIGHTING THIS BATTLE CAN WAIT.
OKAY, XER-XER...
X AND BLUE! YOU TWO HEAD FOR THE VILLAGE AHEAD OF US, OKAY?
I CAN'T LEAVE TIERNO AND SHAUNA ALONE, SO I'LL STAY HERE.

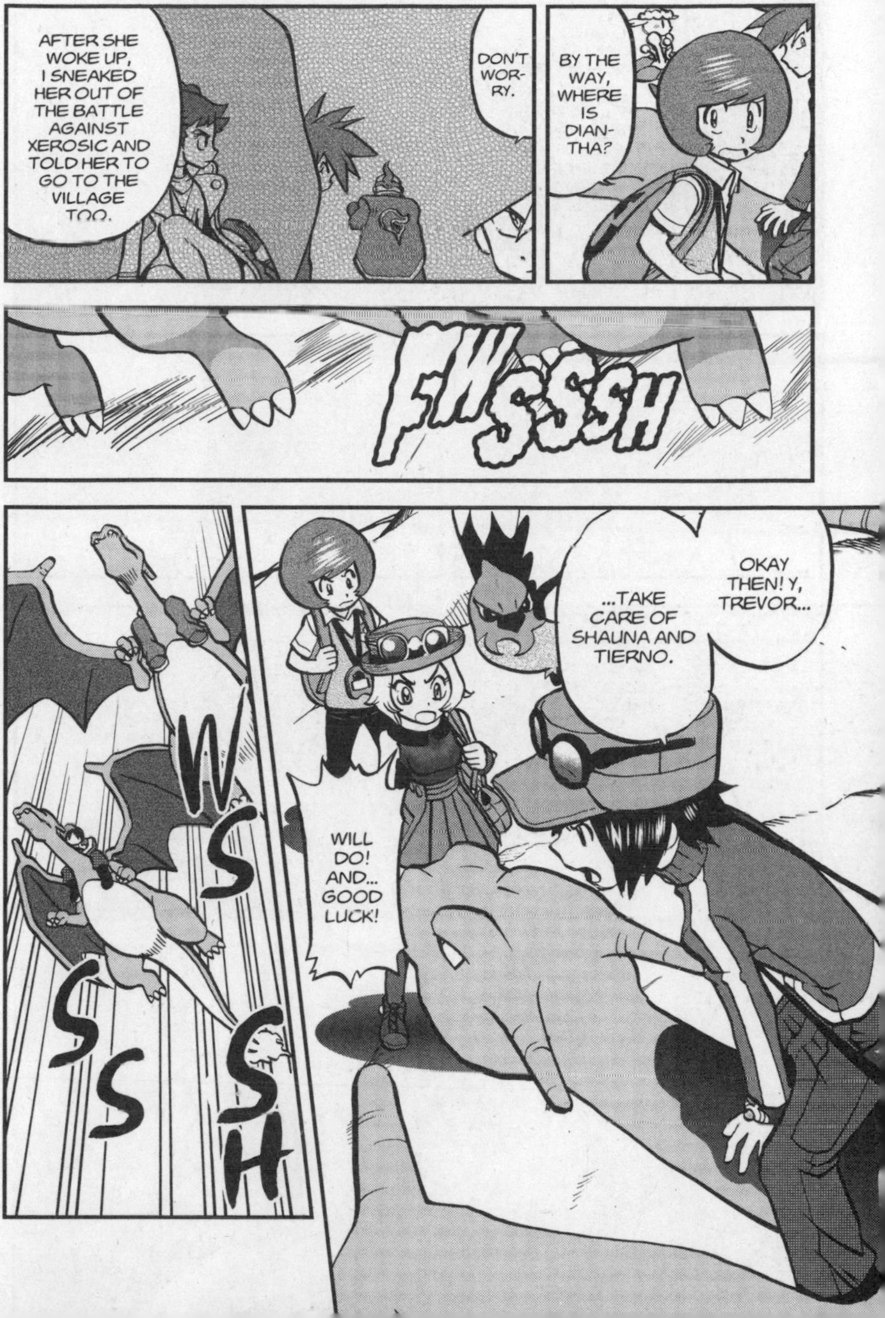
BY THE WAY, WHERE IS DIANTHA?
DON'T WORRY.
AFTER SHE WOKE UP, I SNEAKED HER OUT OF THE BATTLE AGAINST XEROSIC AND TOLD HER TO GO TO THE VILLAGE TOO.
FWSSSH
OKAY THEN! Y, TREVOR...
...TAKE CARE OF SHAUNA AND TIERNO.
WILL DO! AND... GOOD LUCK!
WSSSSH

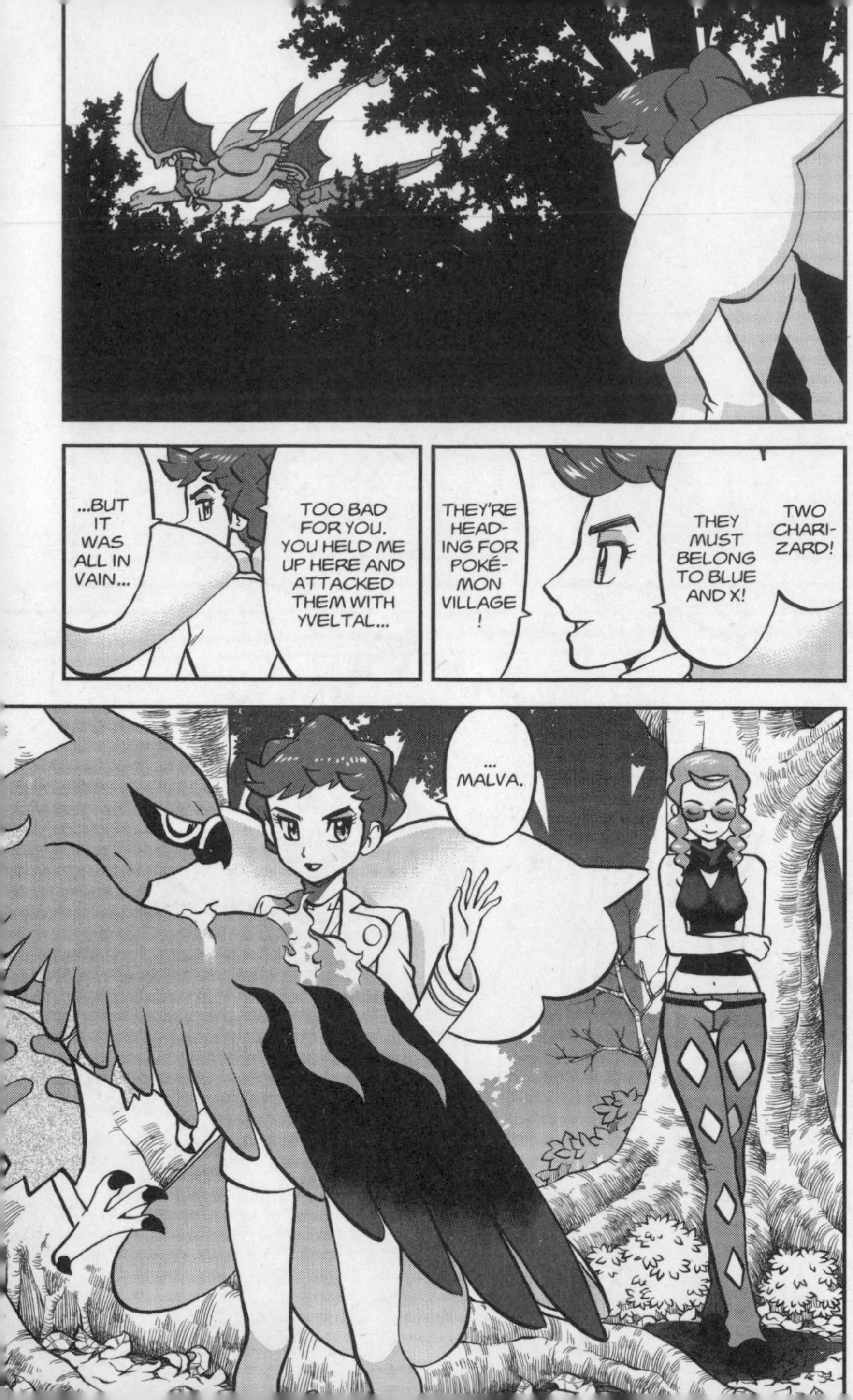
TWO CHARIZARD!
THEY MUST BELONG TO BLUE AND X!
THEY'RE HEADING FOR POKÉMON VILLAGE!
TOO BAD FOR YOU. YOU HELD ME UP HERE AND ATTACKED THEM WITH YVELTAL...
...BUT IT WAS ALL IN VAIN...
... MALVA.

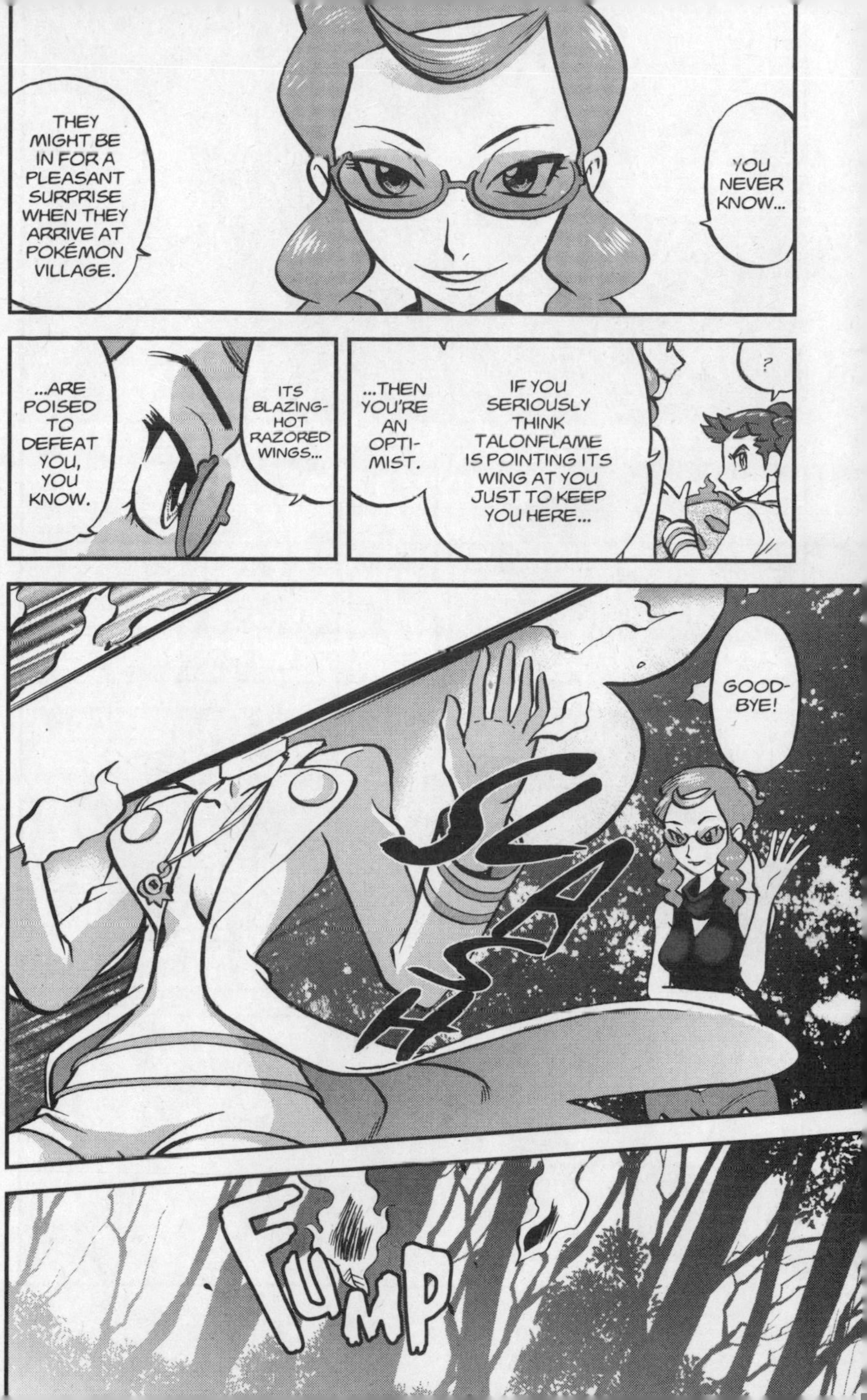
YOU NEVER KNOW...
THEY MIGHT BE IN FOR A PLEASANT SURPRISE WHEN THEY ARRIVE AT POKÉMON VILLAGE.
?
IF YOU SERIOUSLY THINK TALONFLAME IS POINTING ITS WING AT YOU JUST TO KEEP YOU HERE...
...THEN YOU'RE AN OPTI-MIST.
ITS BLAZING-HOT RAZORED WINGS...
...ARE POISED TO DEFEAT YOU, YOU KNOW.
GOOD-BYE!
SLASH
FUMP

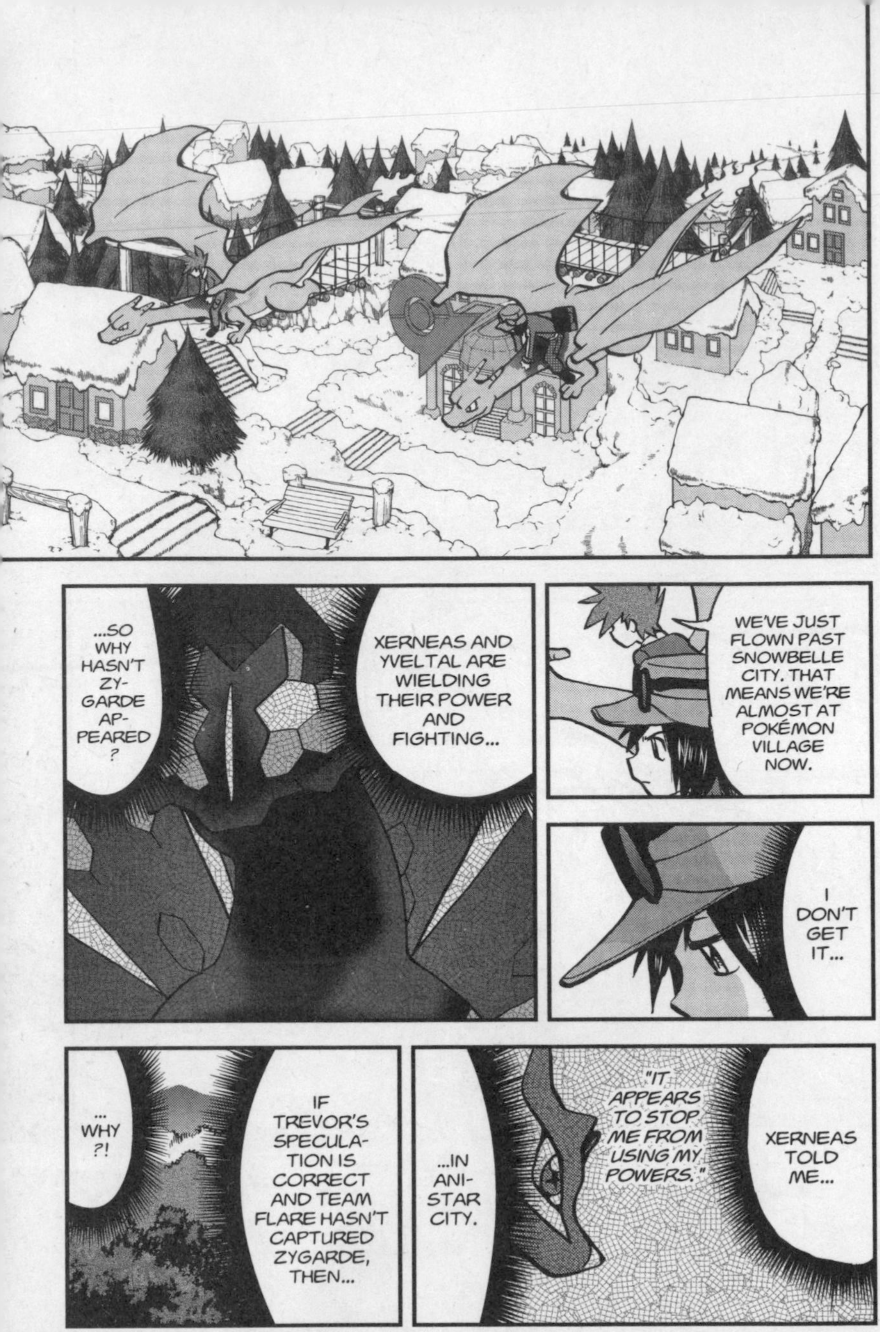
WE'VE JUST FLOWN PAST SNOWBELLE CITY. THAT MEANS WE'RE ALMOST AT POKÉMON VILLAGE NOW.
I DON'T GET IT...
XERNEAS AND YVELTAL ARE WIELDING THEIR POWER AND FIGHTING...
...SO WHY HASN'T ZYGARDE APPEARED?
XERNEAS TOLD ME...
"IT APPEARS TO STOP ME FROM USING MY POWERS."
...IN ANISTAR CITY.
IF TREVOR'S SPECULATION IS CORRECT AND TEAM FLARE HASN'T CAPTURED ZYGARDE, THEN...
...WHY?!

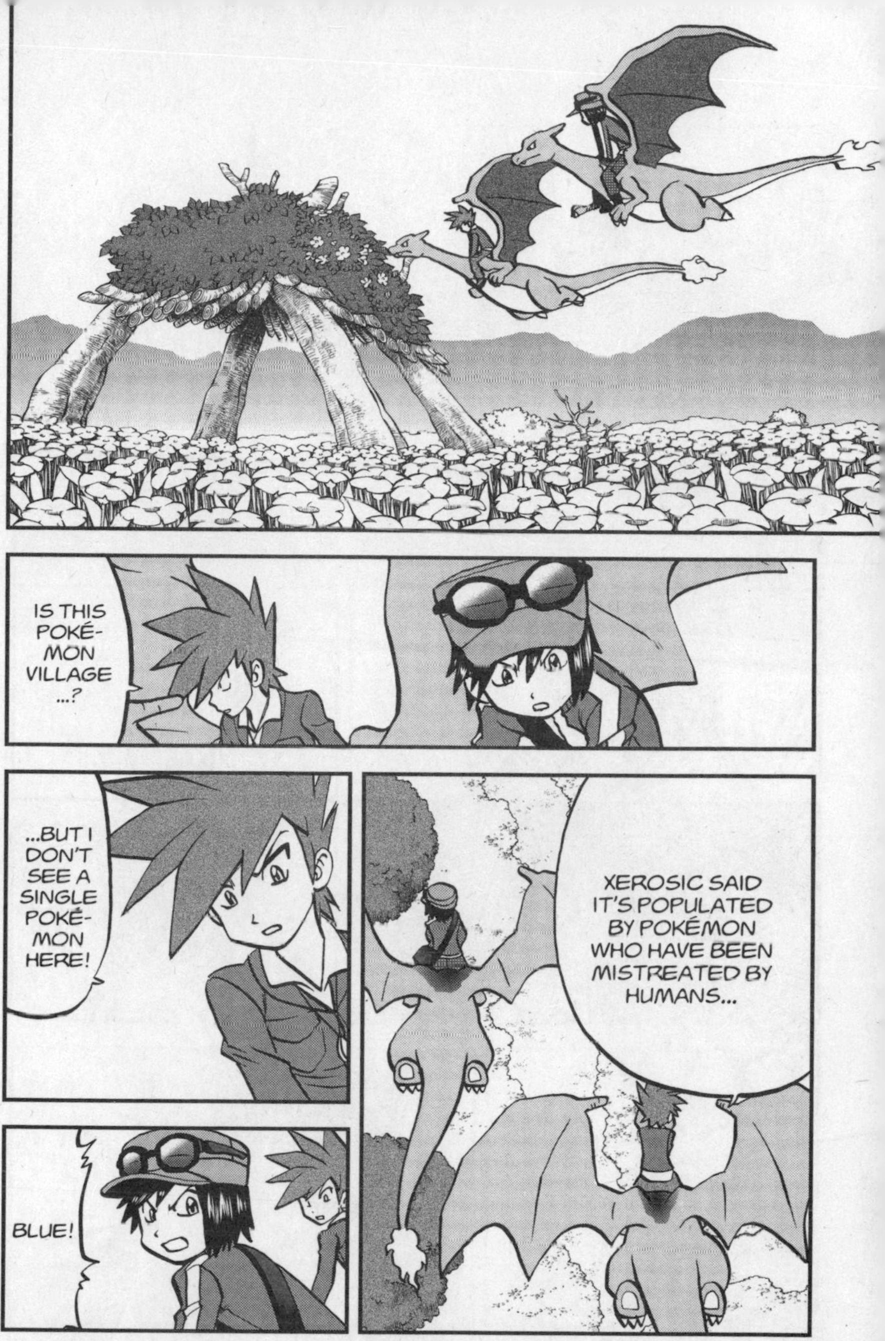
IS THIS POKÉ-MON VILLAGE ...?
XEROSIC SAID IT'S POPULATED BY POKÉMON WHO HAVE BEEN MISTREATED BY HUMANS...
...BUT I DON'T SEE A SINGLE POKÉ-MON HERE!
BLUE!

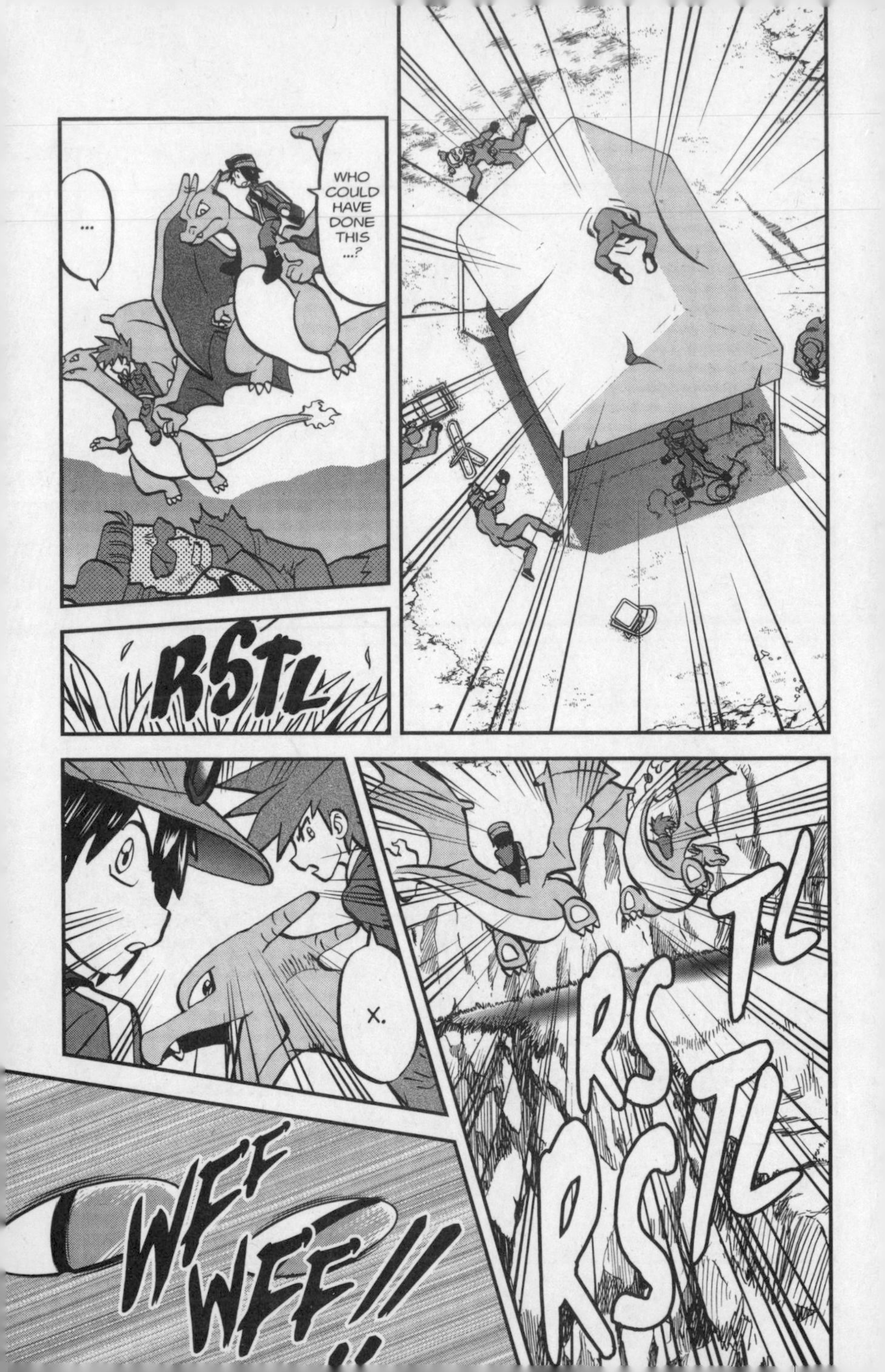
WHO COULD HAVE DONE THIS ...?
...
RSTL
RSTL
RSTL
X.
WFF WFF!!

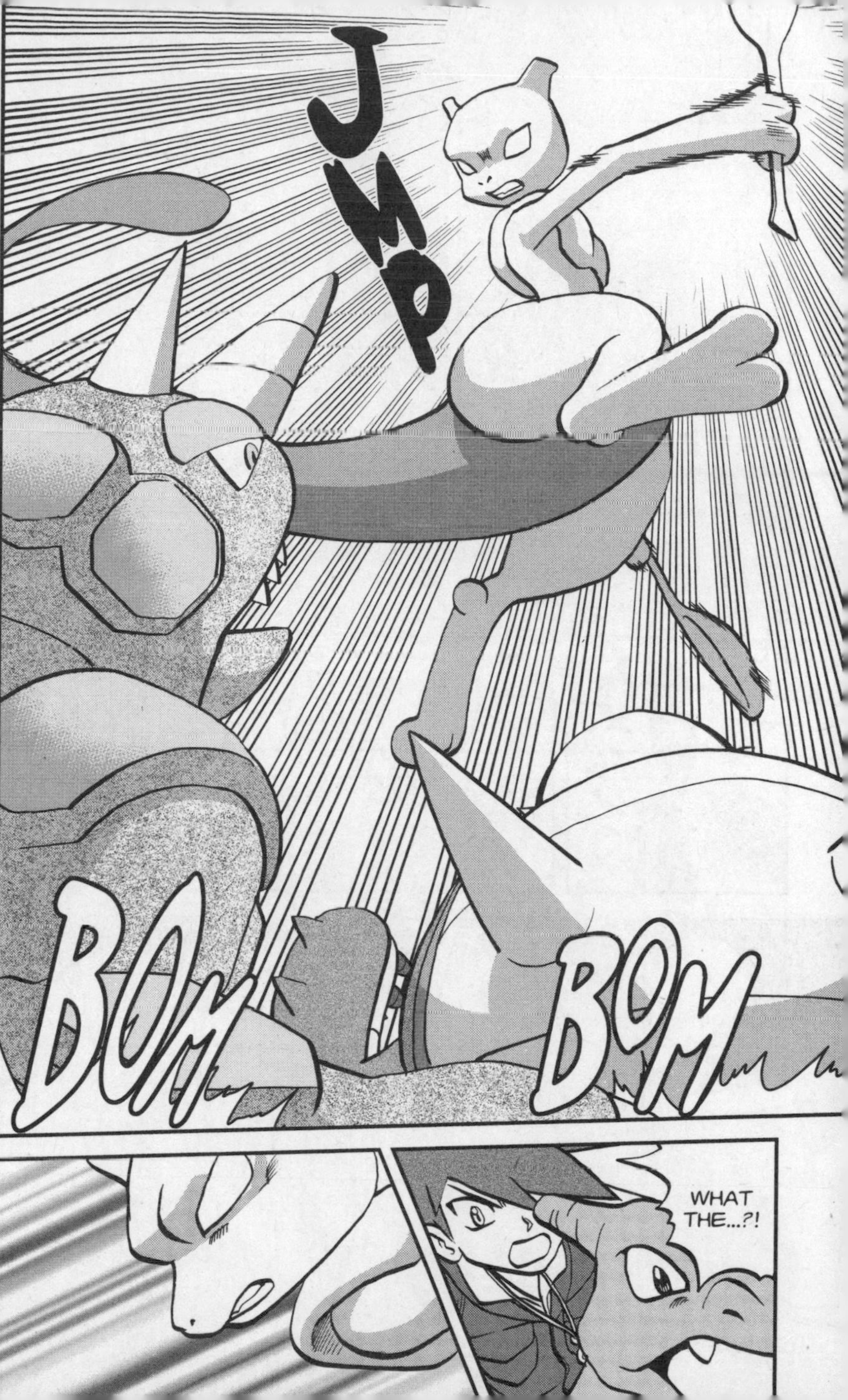
JMP
BOM
BOM
WHAT THE...?!

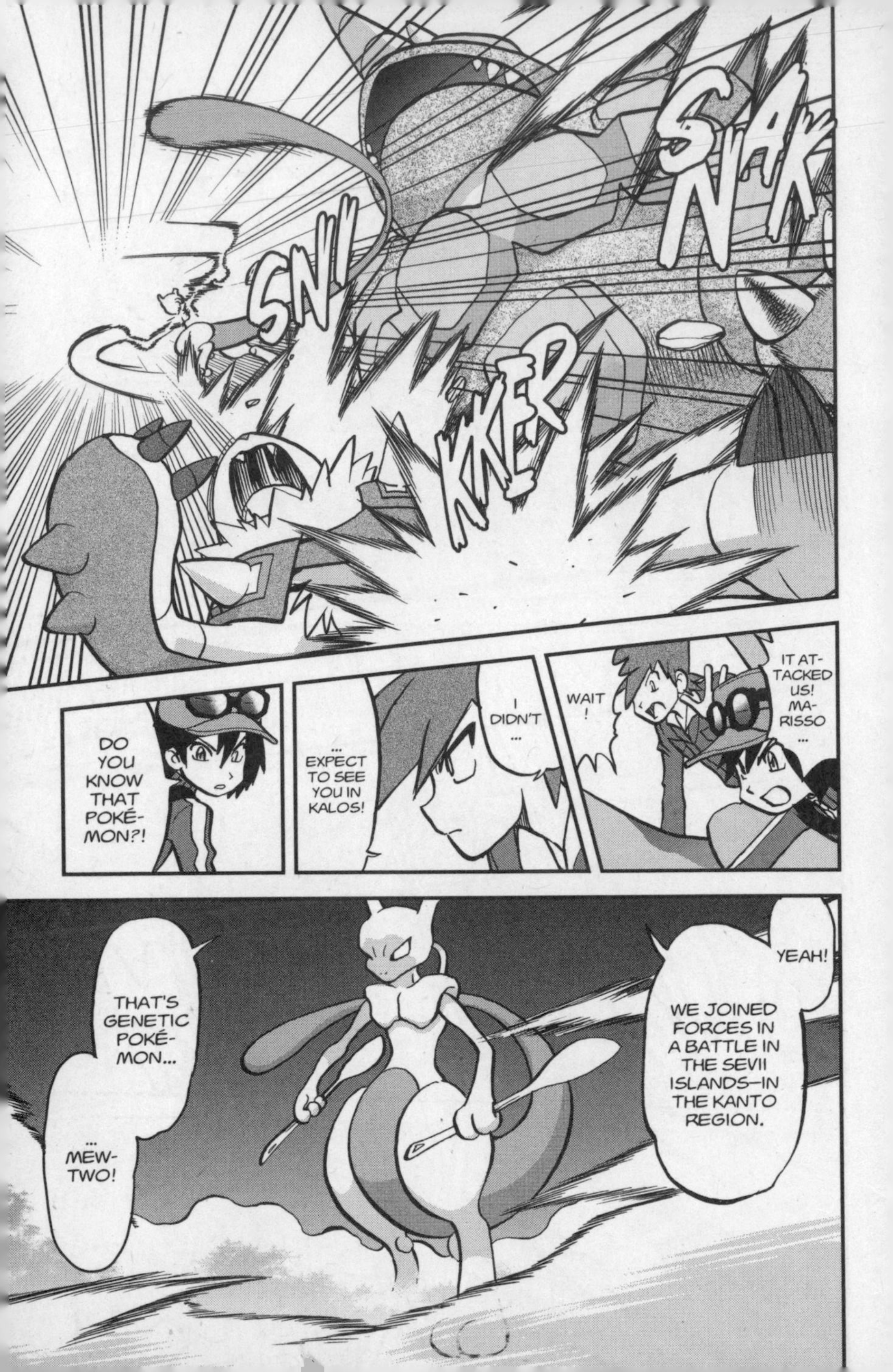
SNAK
SNIKKER
IT ATTACKED US! MARISSO...
WAIT!
I DIDN'T...
...EXPECT TO SEE YOU IN KALOS!
DO YOU KNOW THAT POKÉMON?!
YEAH!
WE JOINED FORCES IN A BATTLE IN THE SEVII ISLANDS—IN THE KANTO REGION.
THAT'S GENETIC POKÉMON...
...MEWTWO!

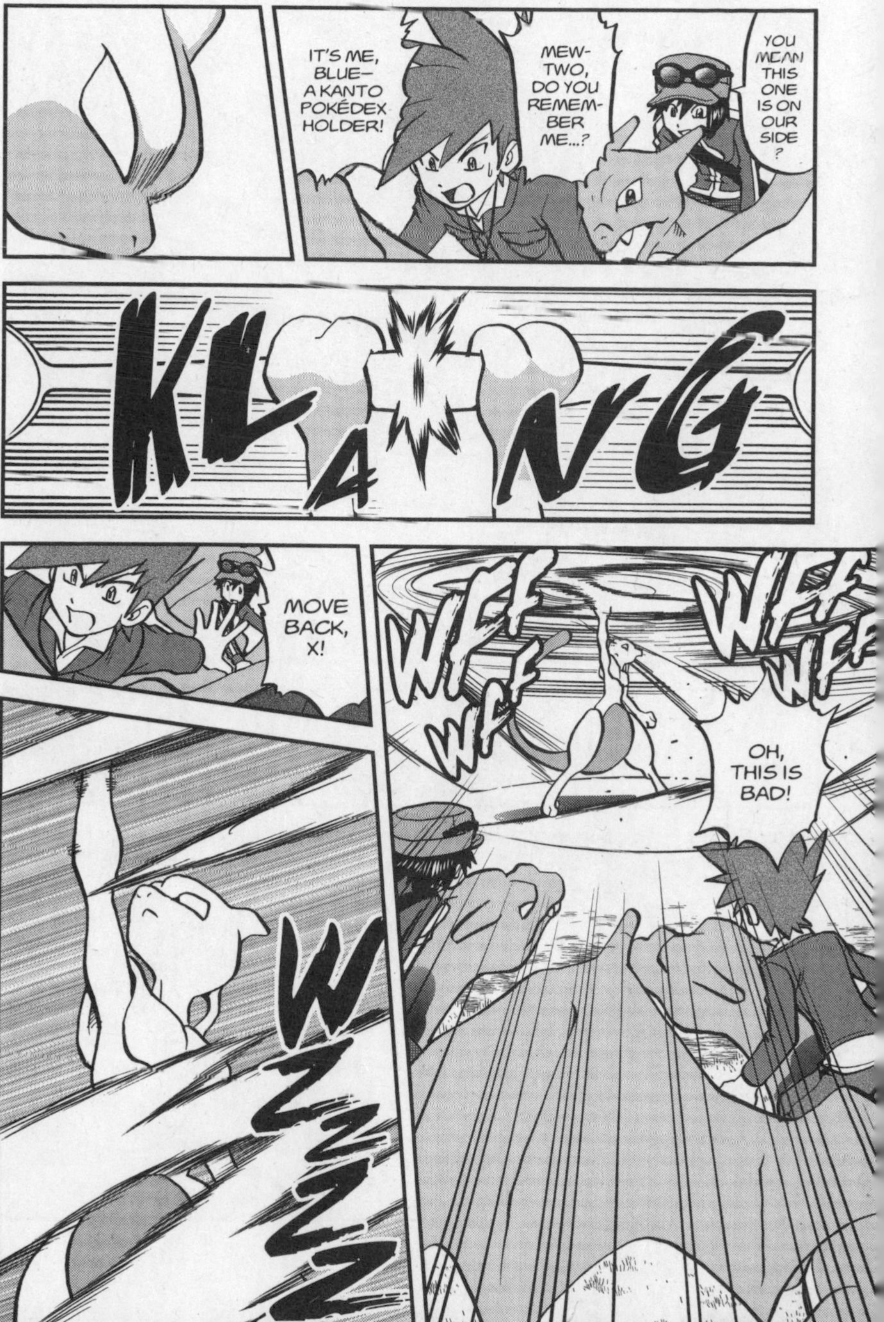
YOU MEAN THIS ONE IS ON OUR SIDE?
MEW-TWO, DO YOU REMEMBER ME...?
IT'S ME, BLUE—A KANTO POKÉDEX HOLDER!
KLANG
WFF WFF
WFF WFF
OH, THIS IS BAD!
MOVE BACK, X!

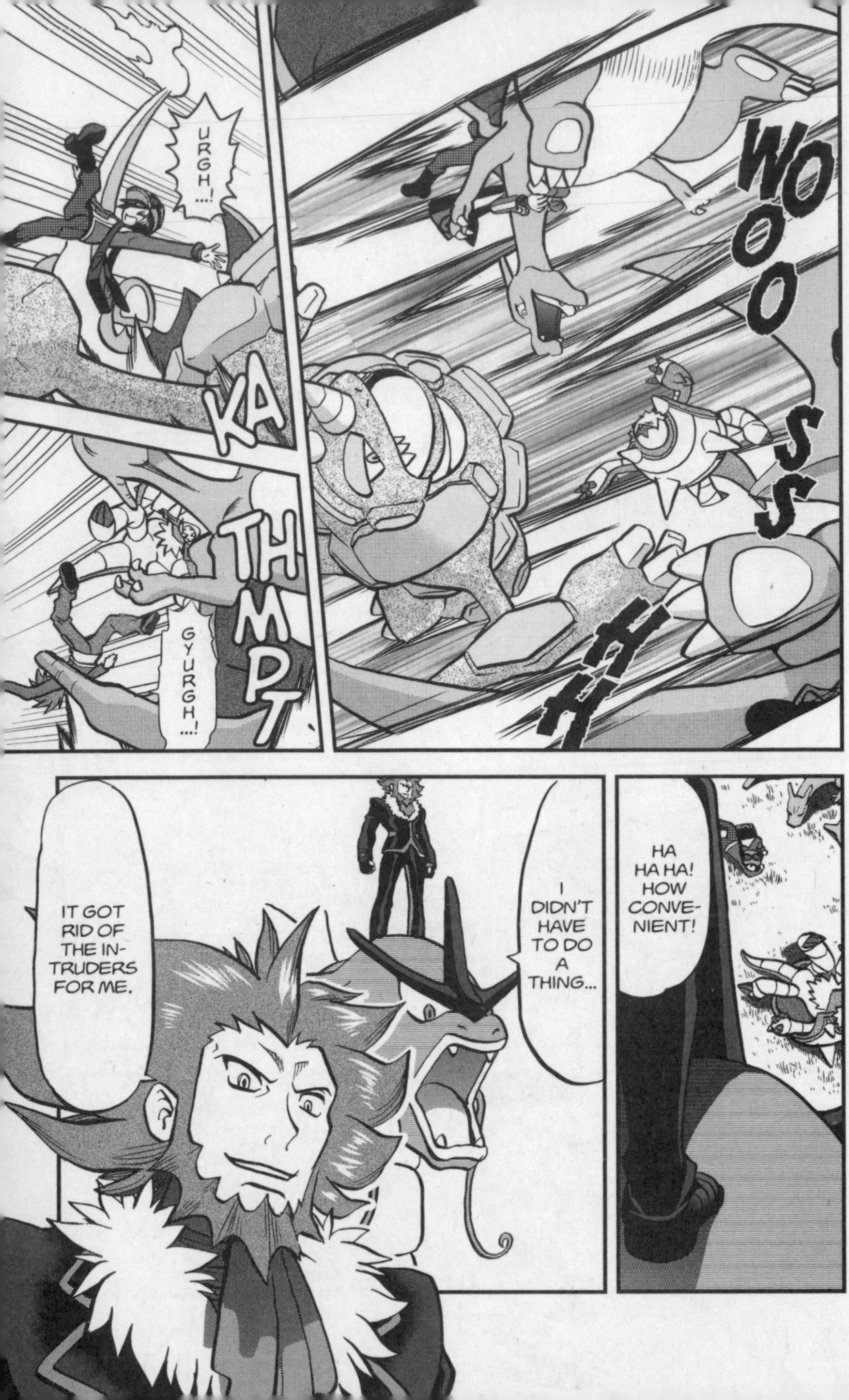
WOOOSSH
URGH...!
KA
THMPT
GYURGH...!
HA HA HA! HOW CONVENIENT!
I DIDN'T HAVE TO DO A THING...
IT GOT RID OF THE INTRUDERS FOR ME.

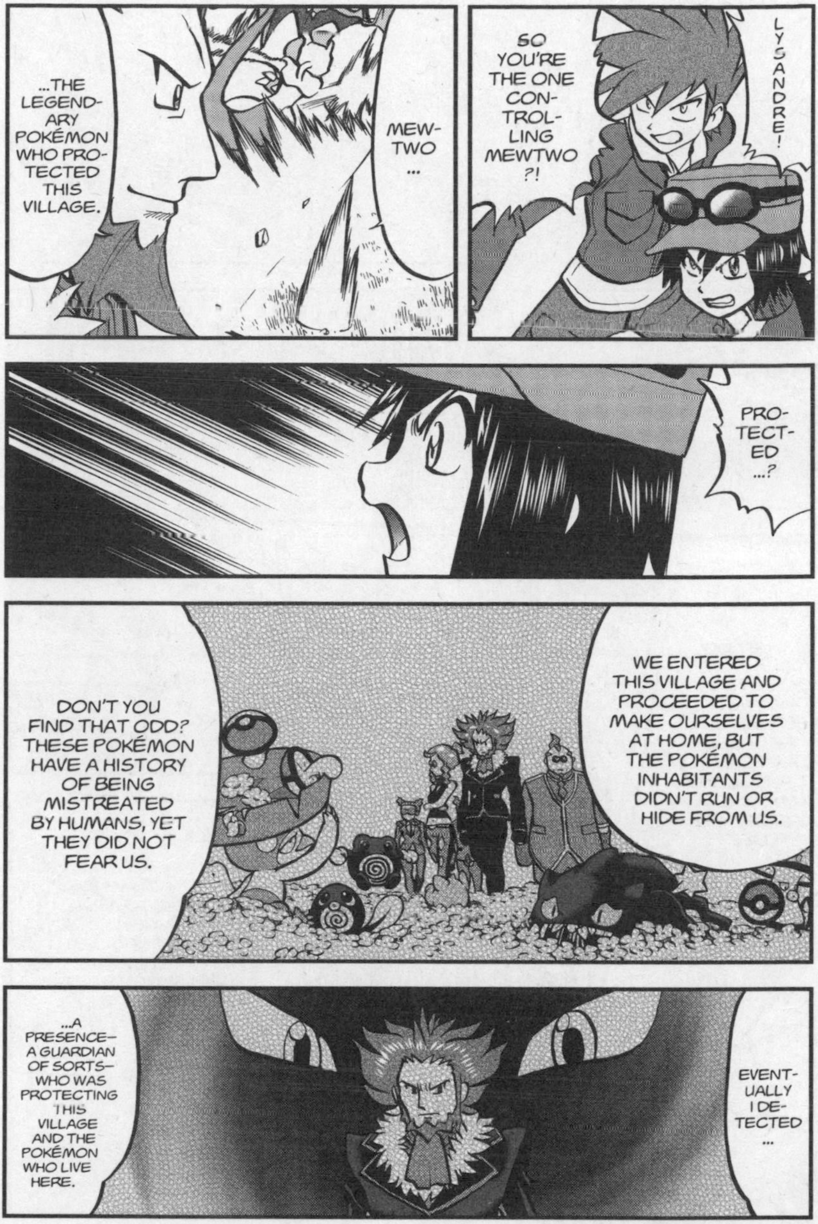
LYSANDRE!
SO YOU'RE THE ONE CONTROLLING MEWTWO?!
MEW-TWO...
...THE LEGENDARY POKÉMON WHO PROTECTED THIS VILLAGE.
PROTECTED...?
WE ENTERED THIS VILLAGE AND PROCEEDED TO MAKE OURSELVES AT HOME, BUT THE POKÉMON INHABITANTS DIDN'T RUN OR HIDE FROM US.
DON'T YOU FIND THAT ODD? THESE POKÉMON HAVE A HISTORY OF BEING MISTREATED BY HUMANS, YET THEY DID NOT FEAR US.
EVENTUALLY I DETECTED...
...A PRESENCE—A GUARDIAN OF SORTS—WHO WAS PROTECTING THIS VILLAGE AND THE POKÉMON WHO LIVE HERE.

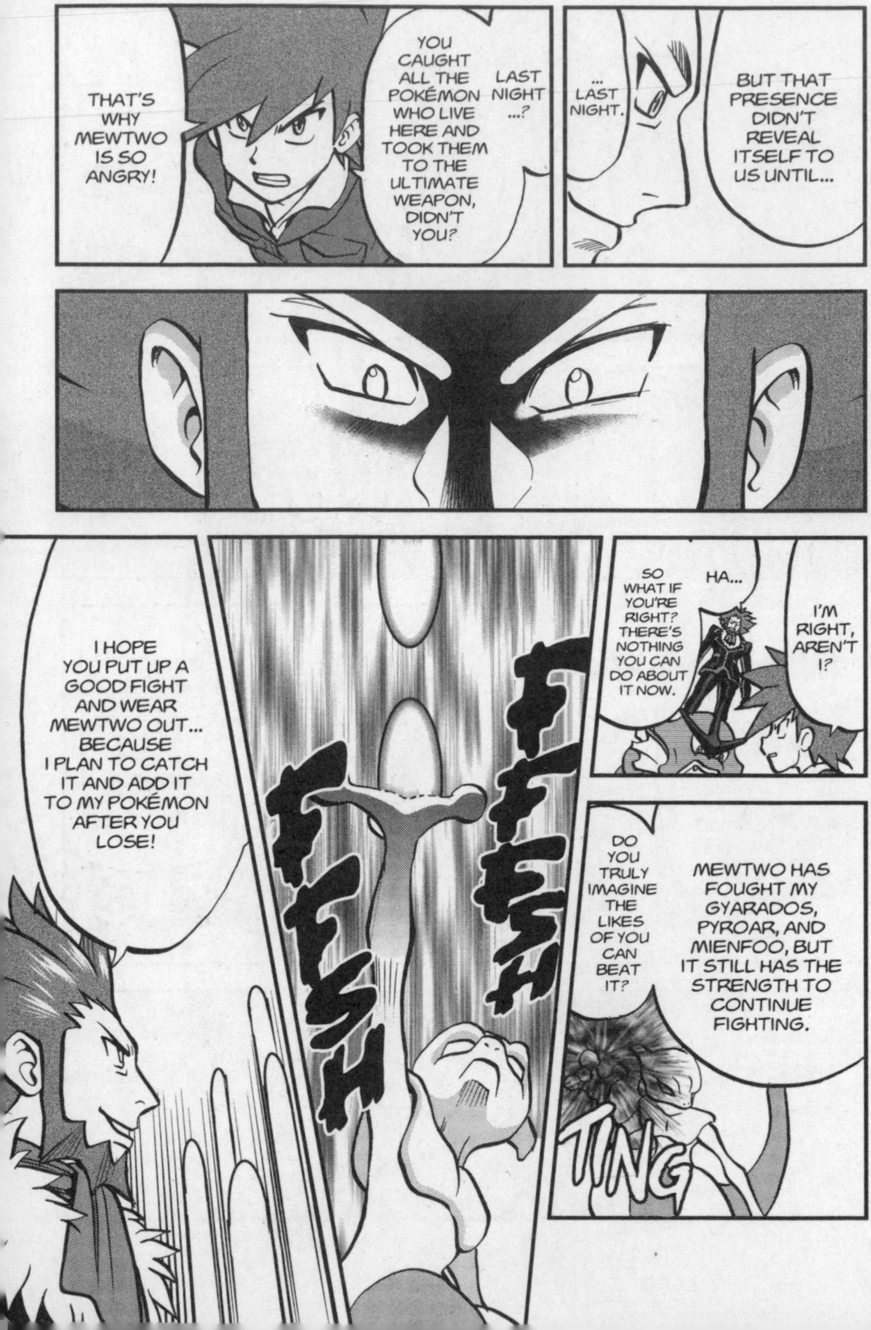
BUT THAT PRESENCE DIDN'T REVEAL ITSELF TO US UNTIL...
... LAST NIGHT.
LAST NIGHT ...?
YOU CAUGHT ALL THE POKÉMON WHO LIVE HERE AND TOOK THEM TO THE ULTIMATE WEAPON, DIDN'T YOU?
THAT'S WHY MEWTWO IS SO ANGRY!
I'M RIGHT, AREN'T I?
HA...
SO WHAT IF YOU'RE RIGHT? THERE'S NOTHING YOU CAN DO ABOUT IT NOW.
MEWTWO HAS FOUGHT MY GYARADOS, PYROAR, AND MIENFOO, BUT IT STILL HAS THE STRENGTH TO CONTINUE FIGHTING.
DO YOU TRULY IMAGINE THE LIKES OF YOU CAN BEAT IT?
TING
FESH
FESH
I HOPE YOU PUT UP A GOOD FIGHT AND WEAR MEWTWO OUT... BECAUSE I PLAN TO CATCH IT AND ADD IT TO MY POKÉMON AFTER YOU LOSE!

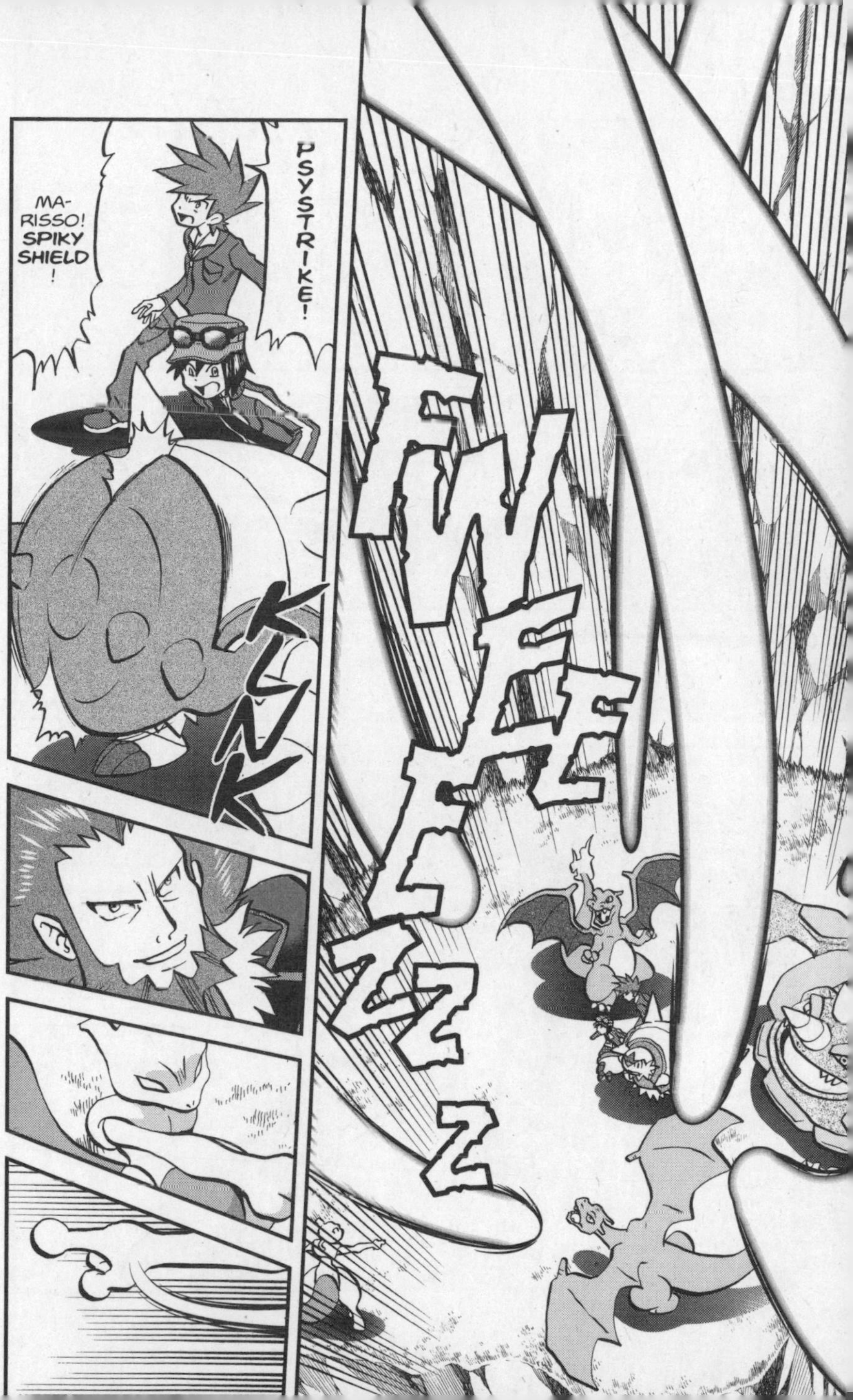
FWEEEZZZ
PSYSTRIKE!
MA-RISSO! SPIKY SHIELD!
KLINK

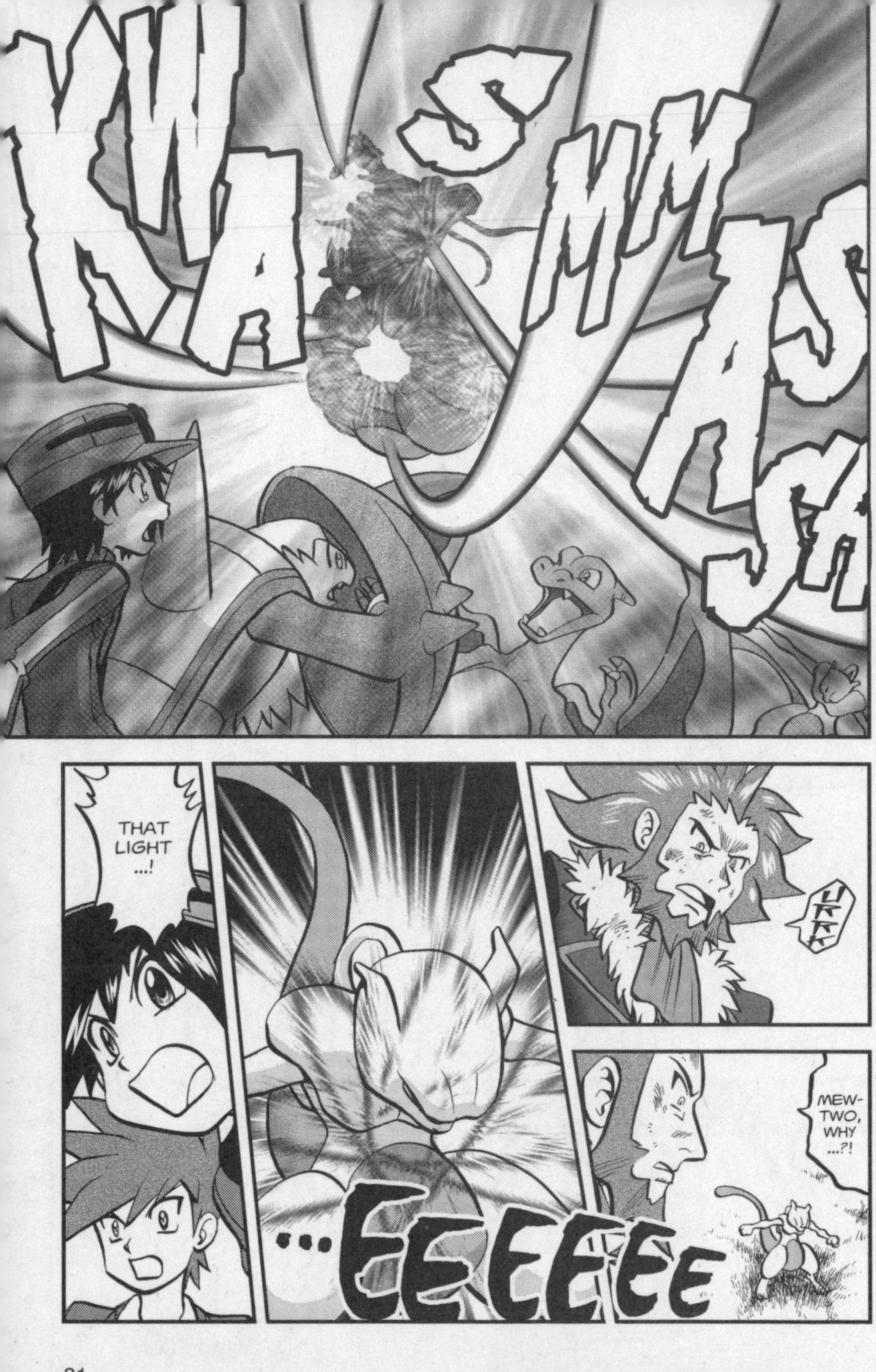
KWA
SMMAS
AS
URRK
MEW-TWO, WHY ...?!
...EEEEEE
THAT LIGHT ...!

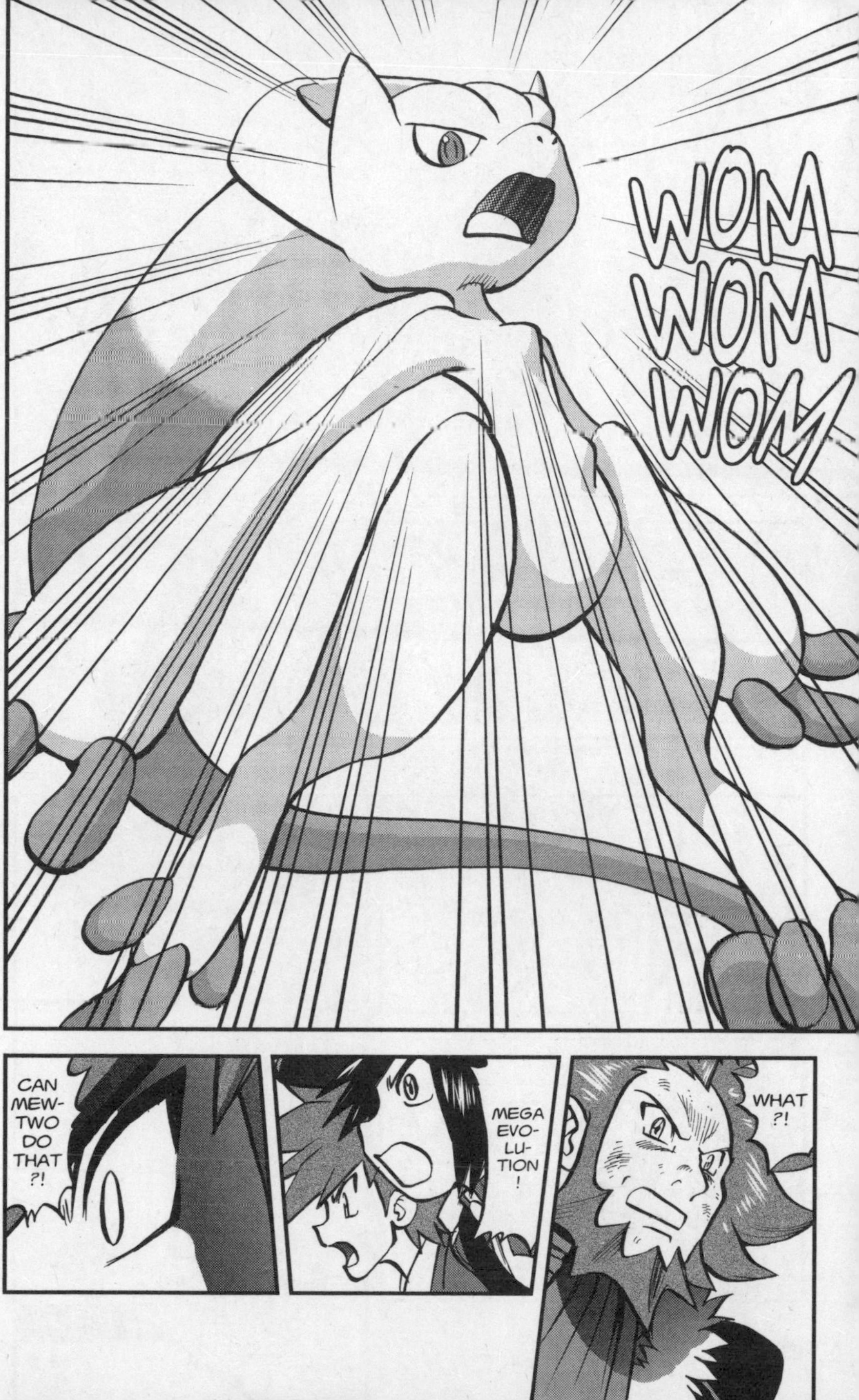
WOM WOM WOM
WHAT?!
MEGA EVOLUTION!
CAN MEWTWO DO THAT?!

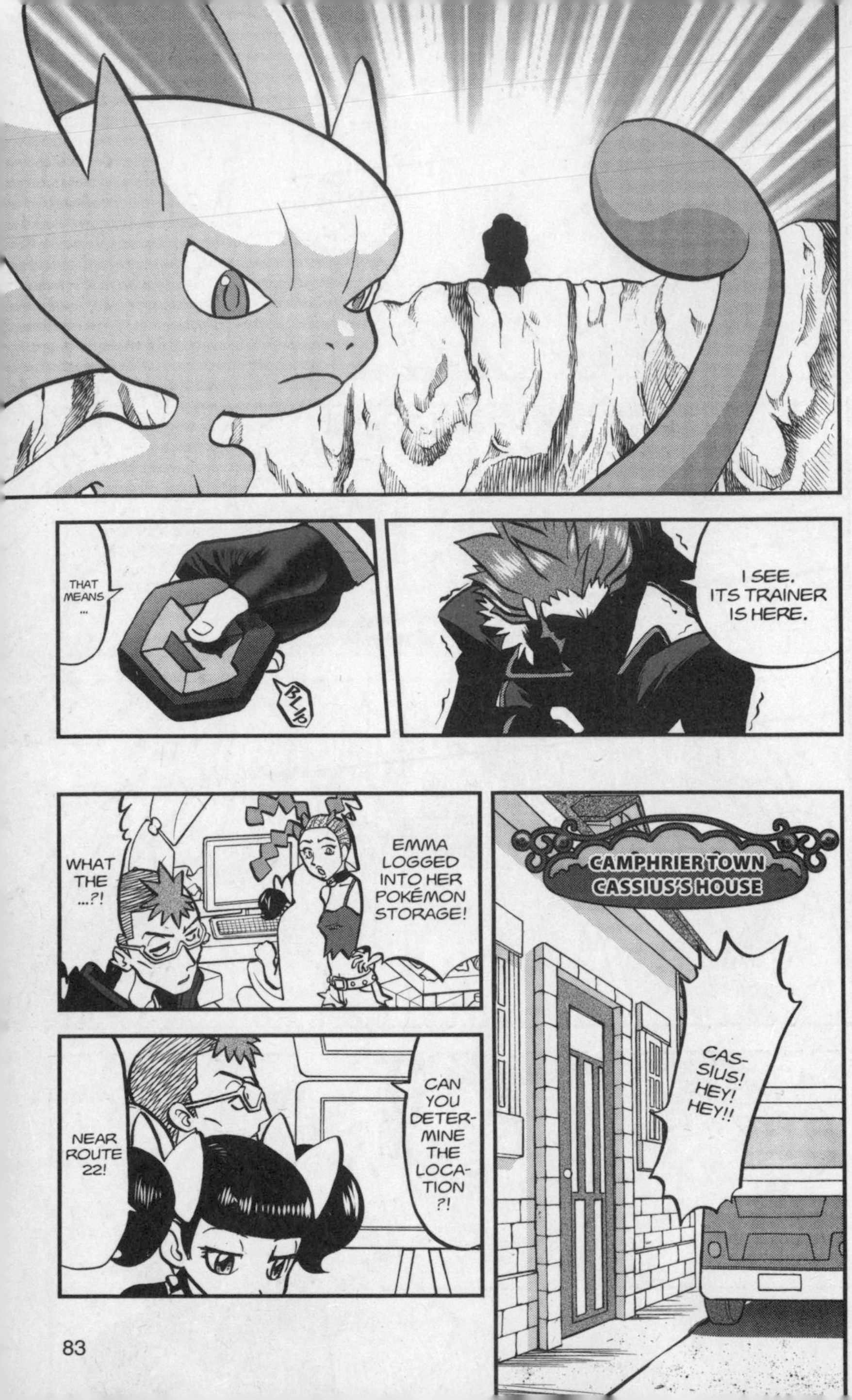
I SEE. ITS TRAINER IS HERE.
THAT MEANS ...
BLIP
CAMPHRIER TOWN CASSIUS'S HOUSE
CASSIUS! HEY! HEY!!
EMMA LOGGED INTO HER POKÉMON STORAGE!
WHAT THE ...?!
CAN YOU DETERMINE THE LOCATION ?!
NEAR ROUTE 22!

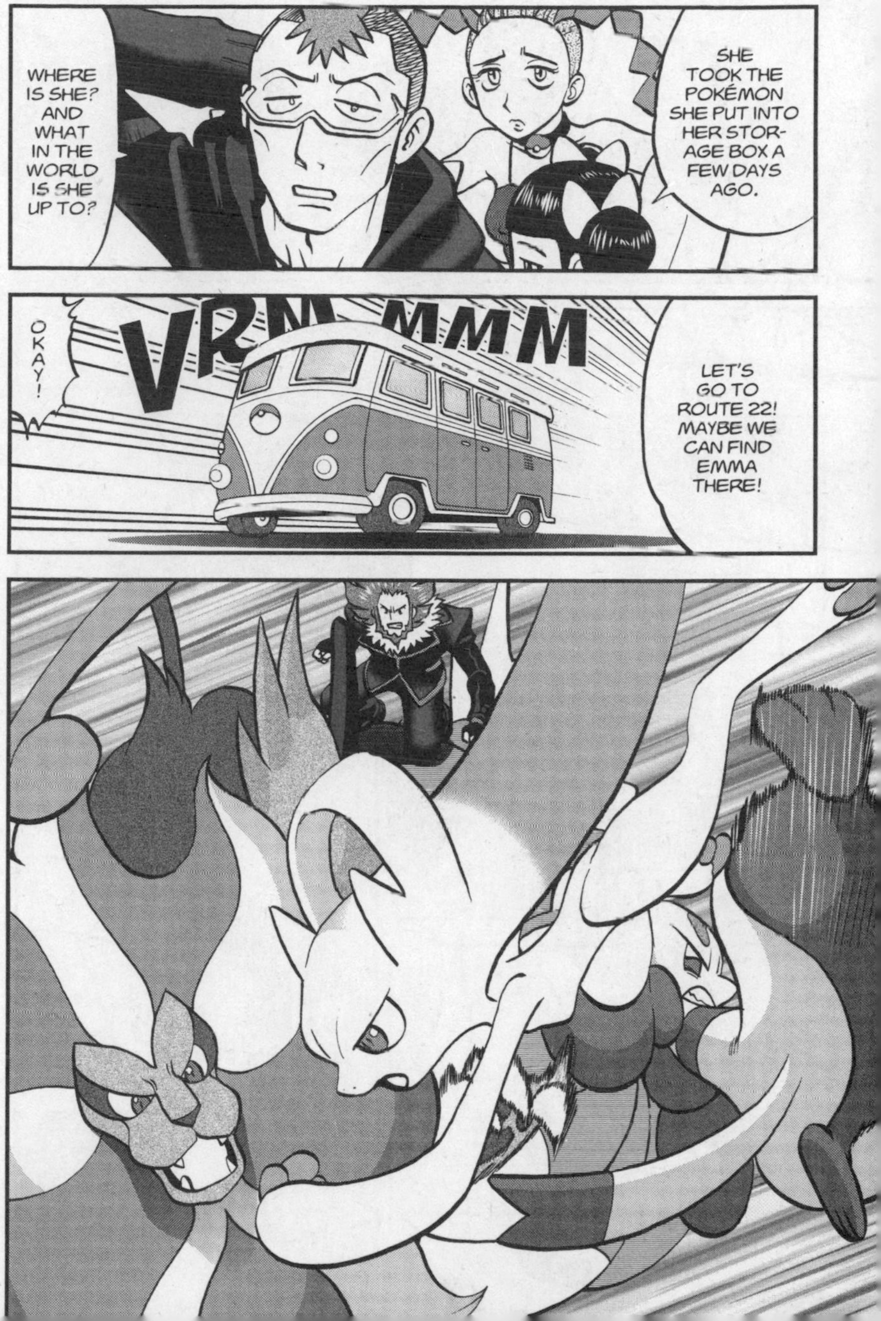
SHE TOOK THE POKÉMON SHE PUT INTO HER STORAGE BOX A FEW DAYS AGO.
WHERE IS SHE? AND WHAT IN THE WORLD IS SHE UP TO?
LET'S GO TO ROUTE 22! MAYBE WE CAN FIND EMMA THERE!
VRM MMMM
OKAY!

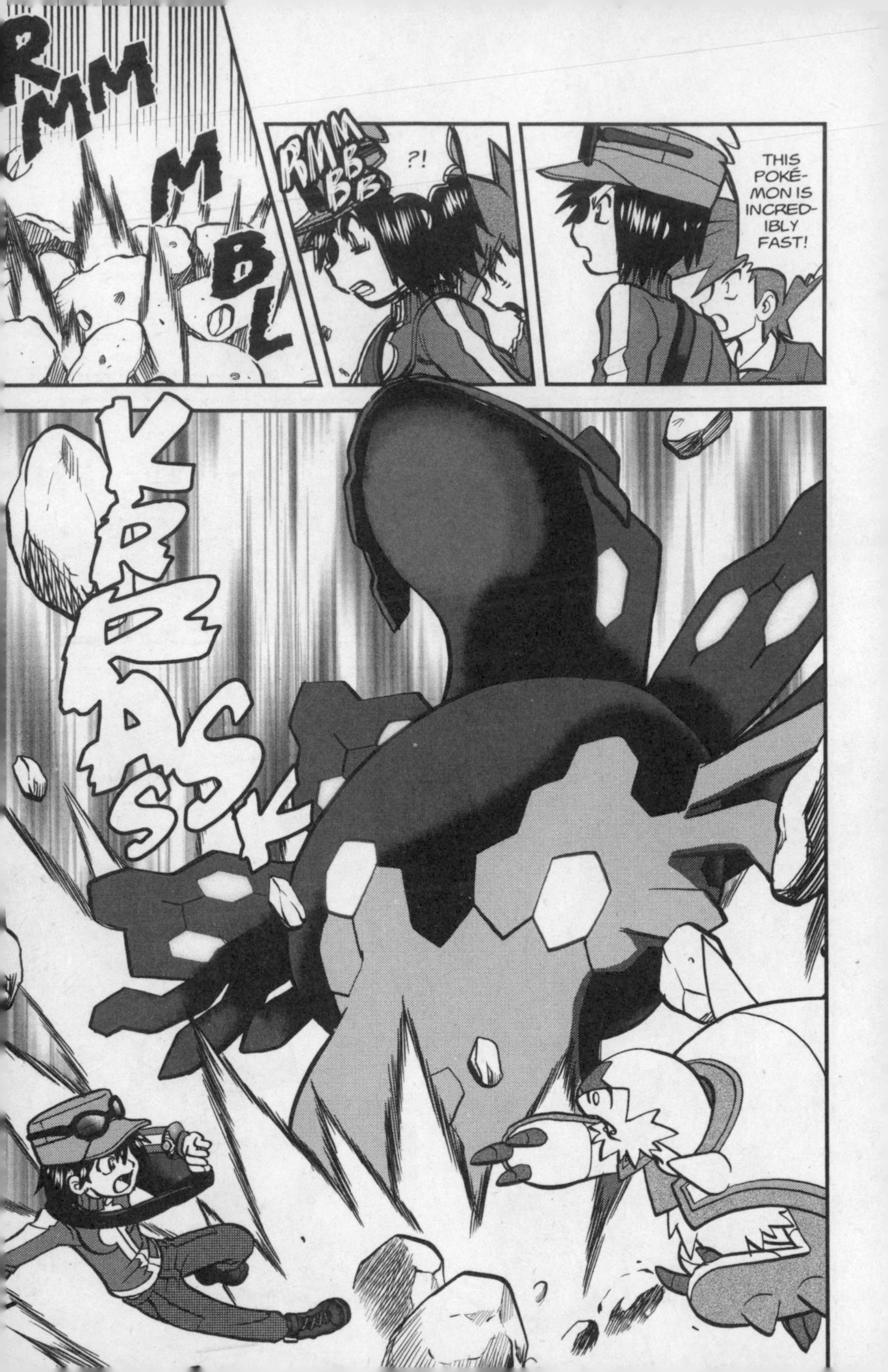
THIS POKÉMON IS INCREDIBLY FAST!
RMMBBB
?!
RMMMBL
KREASSCK

Adventure #43
Mewtwo Angered

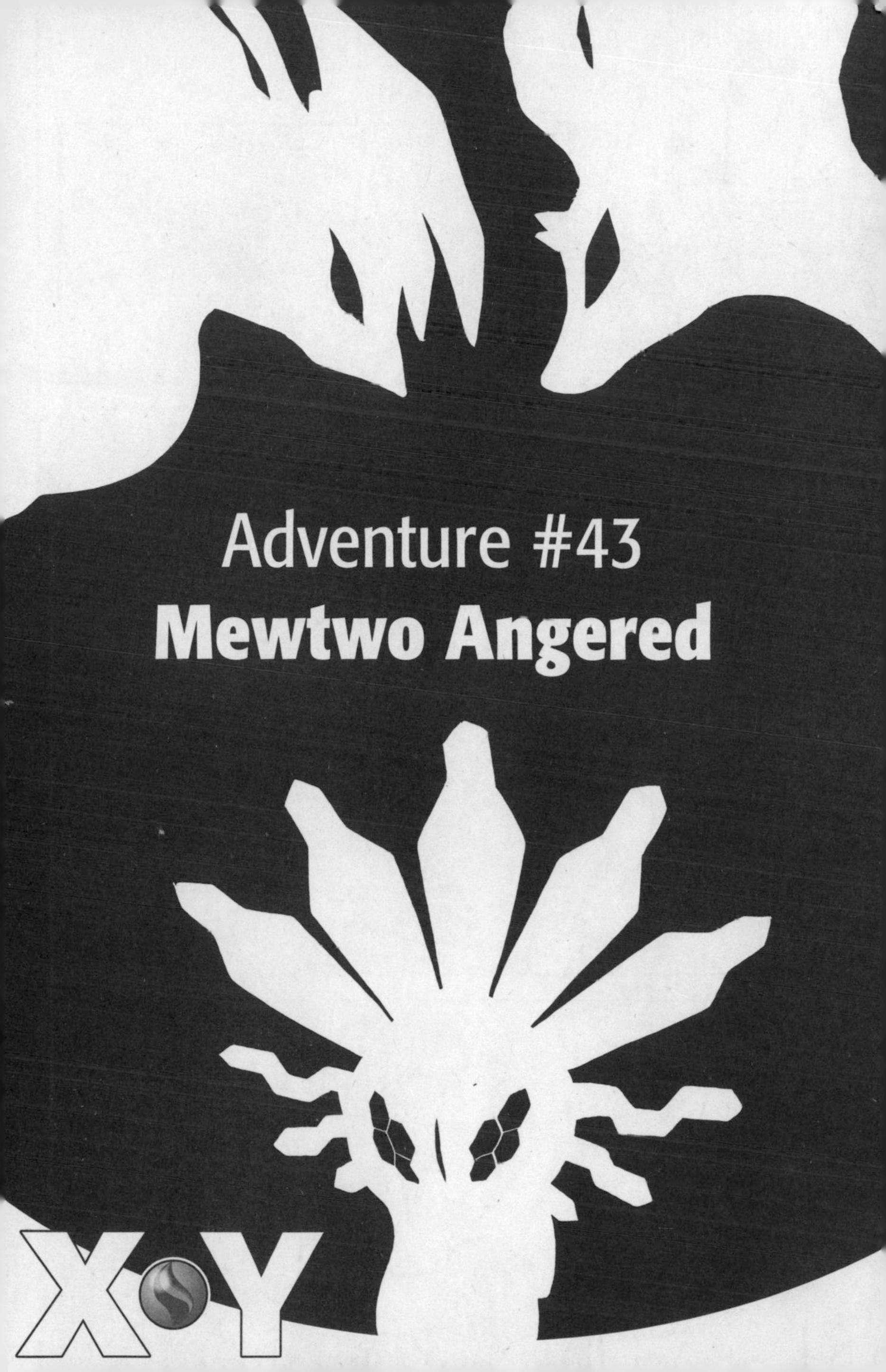

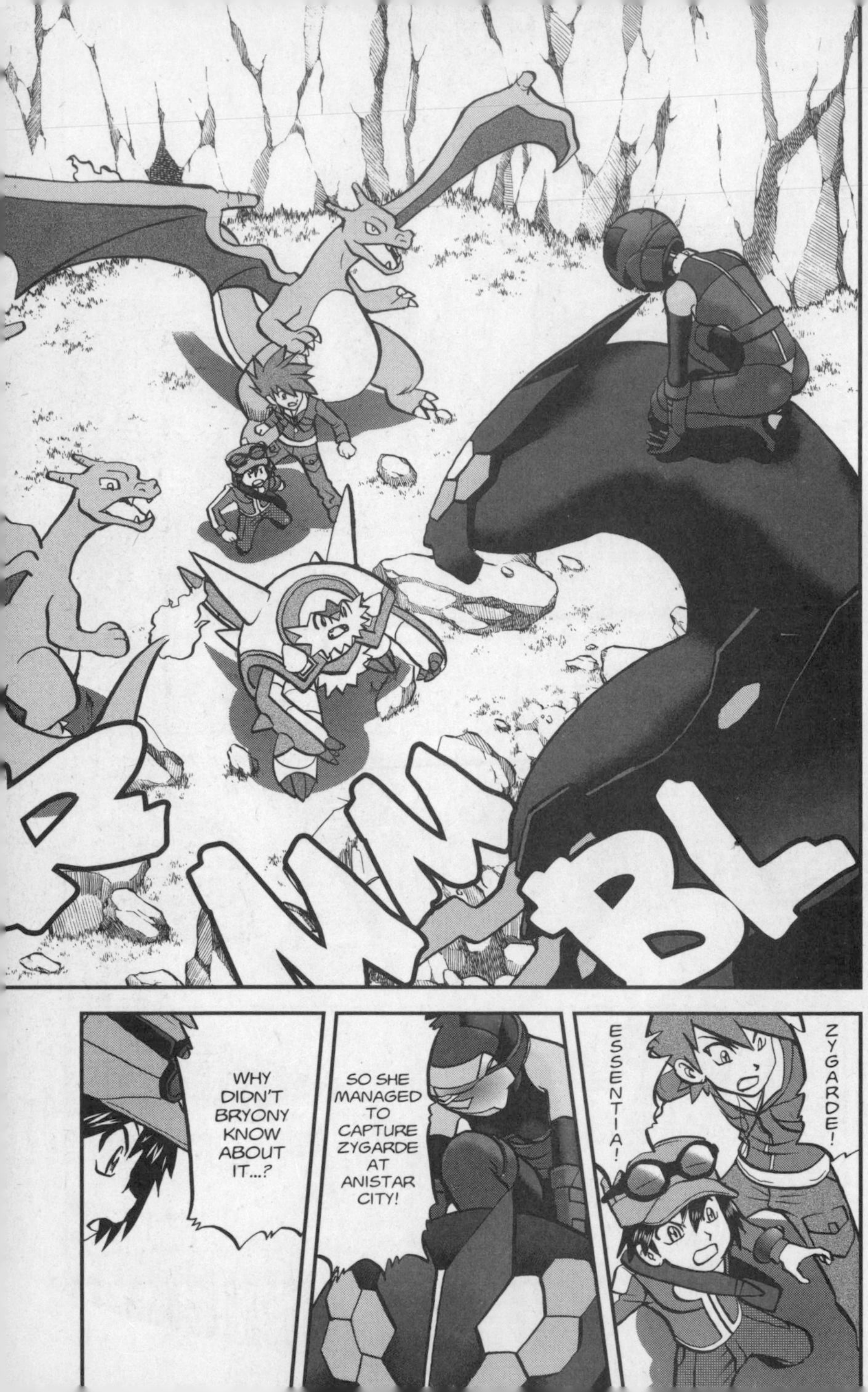
ZYGARDE!
ESSENTIA!
SO SHE MANAGED TO CAPTURE ZYGARDE AT ANISTAR CITY!
WHY DIDN'T BRYONY KNOW ABOUT IT...?

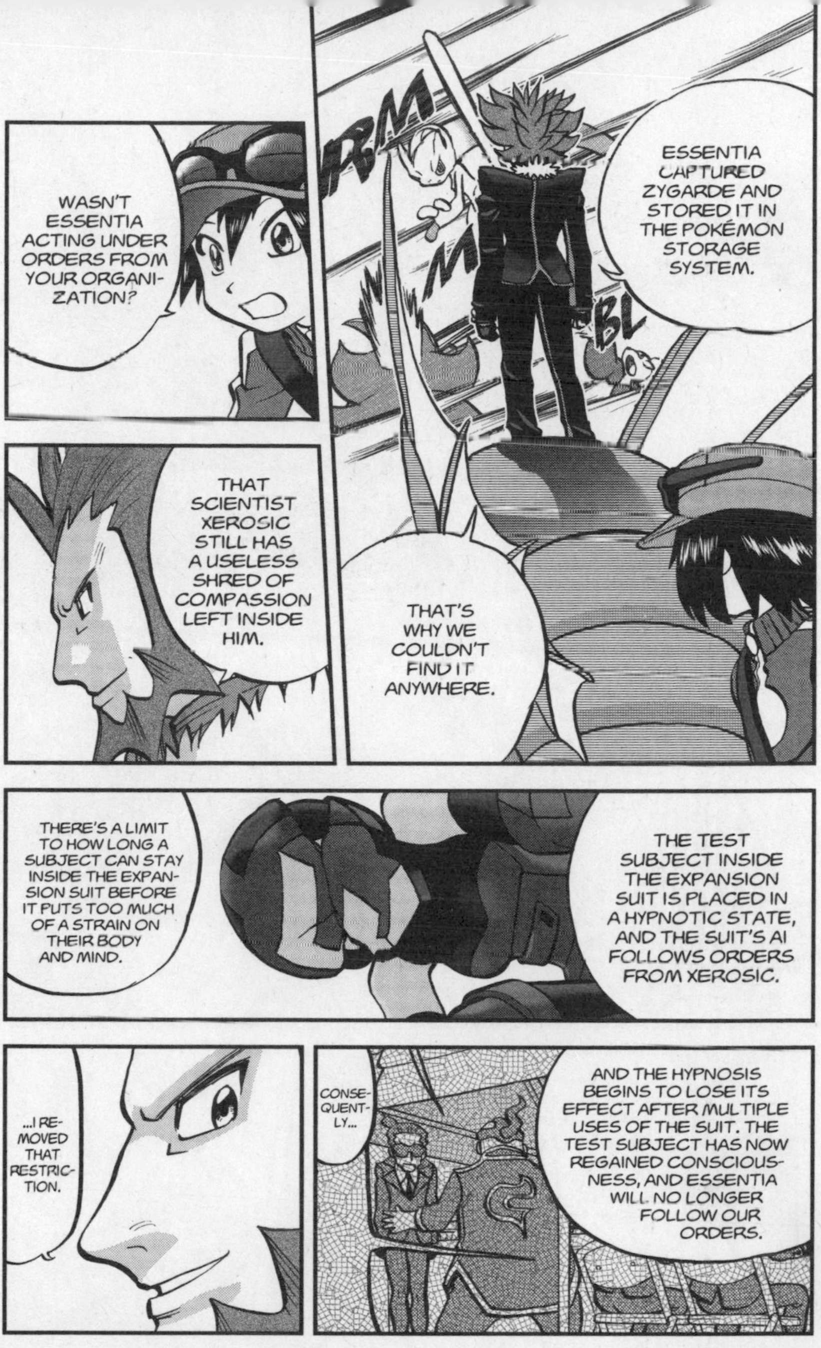
ESSENTIA CAPTURED ZYGARDE AND STORED IT IN THE POKÉMON STORAGE SYSTEM.
THAT'S WHY WE COULDN'T FIND IT ANYWHERE.
WASN'T ESSENTIA ACTING UNDER ORDERS FROM YOUR ORGANI-ZATION?
THAT SCIENTIST XEROSIC STILL HAS A USELESS SHRED OF COMPASSION LEFT INSIDE HIM.
THE TEST SUBJECT INSIDE THE EXPANSION SUIT IS PLACED IN A HYPNOTIC STATE, AND THE SUIT'S AI FOLLOWS ORDERS FROM XEROSIC.
THERE'S A LIMIT TO HOW LONG A SUBJECT CAN STAY INSIDE THE EXPAN-SION SUIT BEFORE IT PUTS TOO MUCH OF A STRAIN ON THEIR BODY AND MIND.
CONSE-QUENT-LY...
AND THE HYPNOSIS BEGINS TO LOSE ITS EFFECT AFTER MULTIPLE USES OF THE SUIT. THE TEST SUBJECT HAS NOW REGAINED CONSCIOUS-NESS, AND ESSENTIA WILL NO LONGER FOLLOW OUR ORDERS.
...I RE-MOVED THAT RESTRIC-TION.

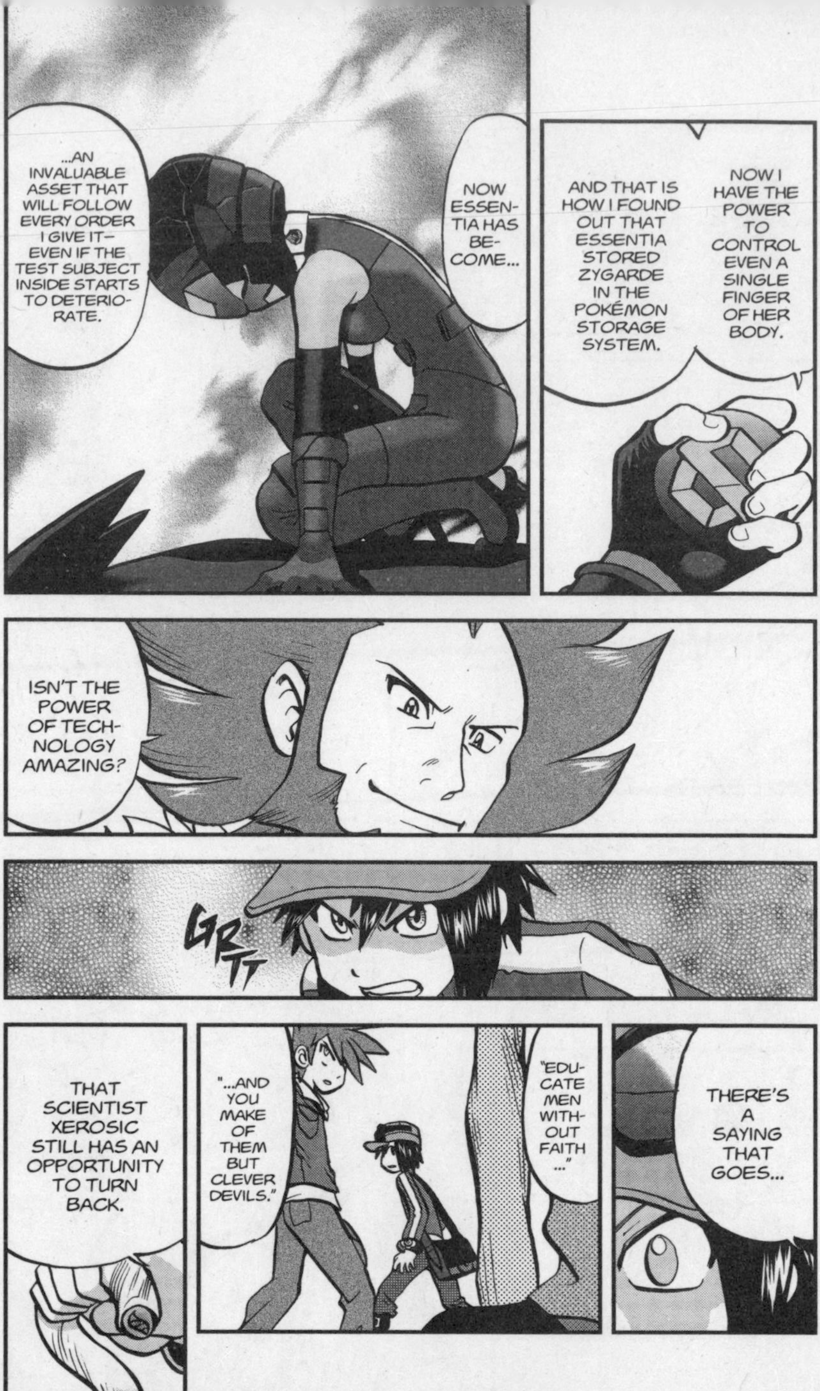
NOW I HAVE THE POWER TO CONTROL EVEN A SINGLE FINGER OF HER BODY.
AND THAT IS HOW I FOUND OUT THAT ESSENTIA STORED ZYGARDE IN THE POKÉMON STORAGE SYSTEM.
NOW ESSENTIA HAS BECOME...
...AN INVALUABLE ASSET THAT WILL FOLLOW EVERY ORDER I GIVE IT—EVEN IF THE TEST SUBJECT INSIDE STARTS TO DETERIORATE.
ISN'T THE POWER OF TECHNOLOGY AMAZING?
GRTT
THERE'S A SAYING THAT GOES...
"EDUCATE MEN WITHOUT FAITH..."
"...AND YOU MAKE OF THEM BUT CLEVER DEVILS."
THAT SCIENTIST XEROSIC STILL HAS AN OPPORTUNITY TO TURN BACK.

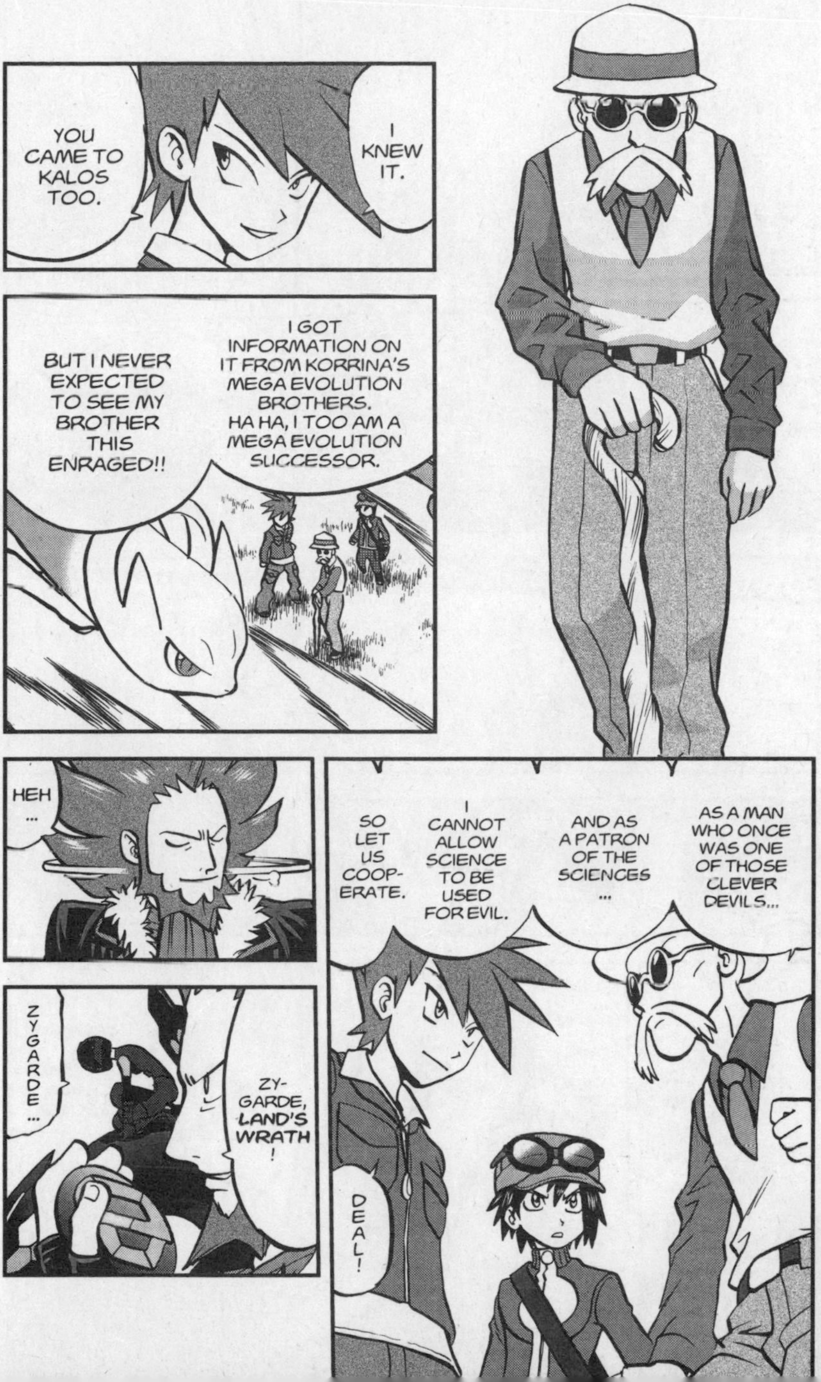
I KNEW IT.
YOU CAME TO KALOS TOO.
I GOT INFORMATION ON IT FROM KORRINA'S MEGA EVOLUTION BROTHERS. HA HA, I TOO AM A MEGA EVOLUTION SUCCESSOR.
BUT I NEVER EXPECTED TO SEE MY BROTHER THIS ENRAGED!!
AS A MAN WHO ONCE WAS ONE OF THOSE CLEVER DEVILS...
AND AS A PATRON OF THE SCIENCES ...
I CANNOT ALLOW SCIENCE TO BE USED FOR EVIL.
SO LET US COOP-ERATE.
DEAL!
HEH ...
ZY-GARDE, LAND'S WRATH!
ZYGARDE ...

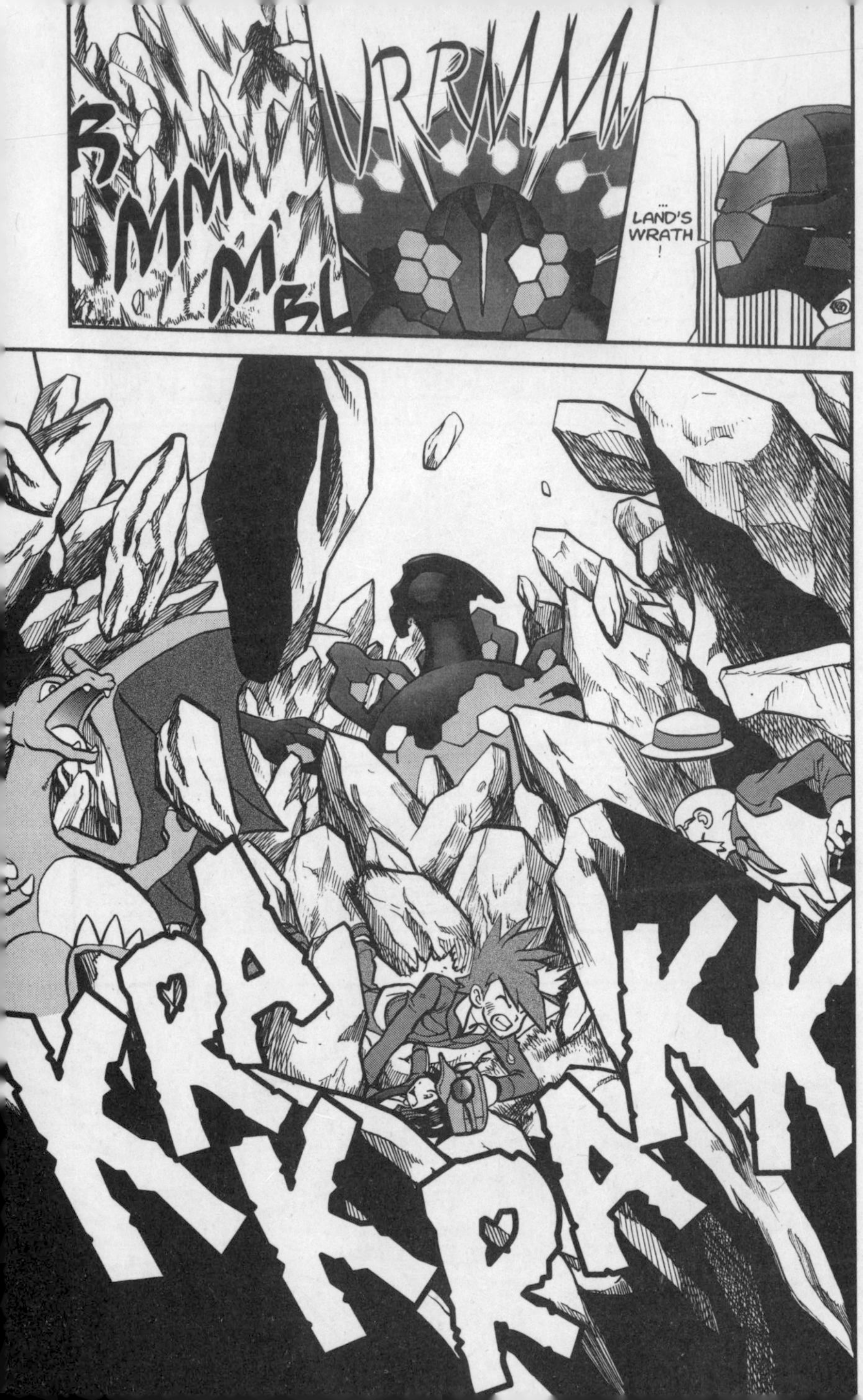
... LAND'S WRATH !
VRRMMM
BRMMMMBL

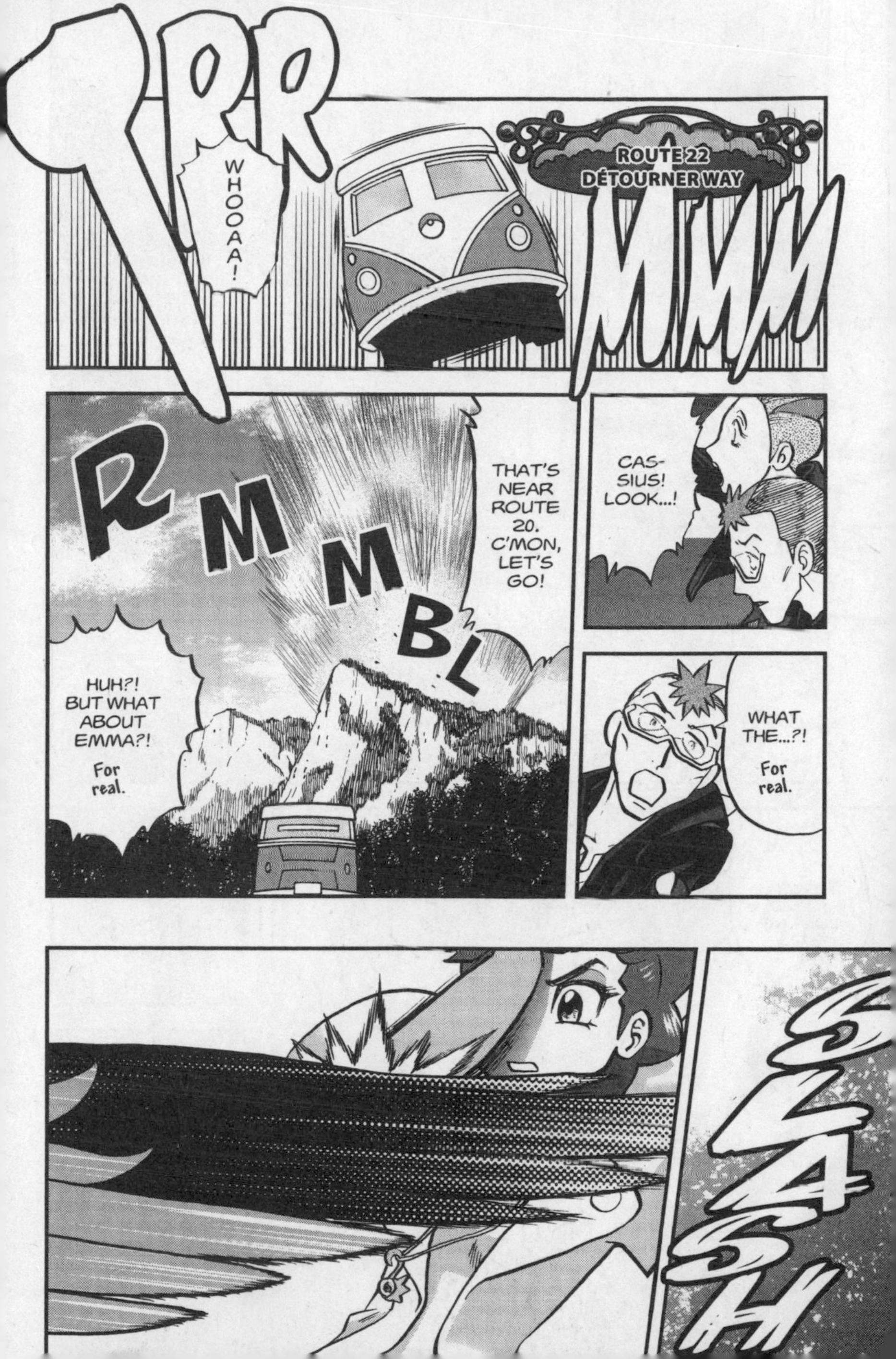
ROUTE 22 DÉTOURNER WAY
VRR
MMMM
WHOOOAA!
CAS-SIUS! LOOK...!
WHAT THE...?! For real.
THAT'S NEAR ROUTE 20. C'MON, LET'S GO!
RMMBL
HUH?! BUT WHAT ABOUT EMMA?! For real.
SLASH

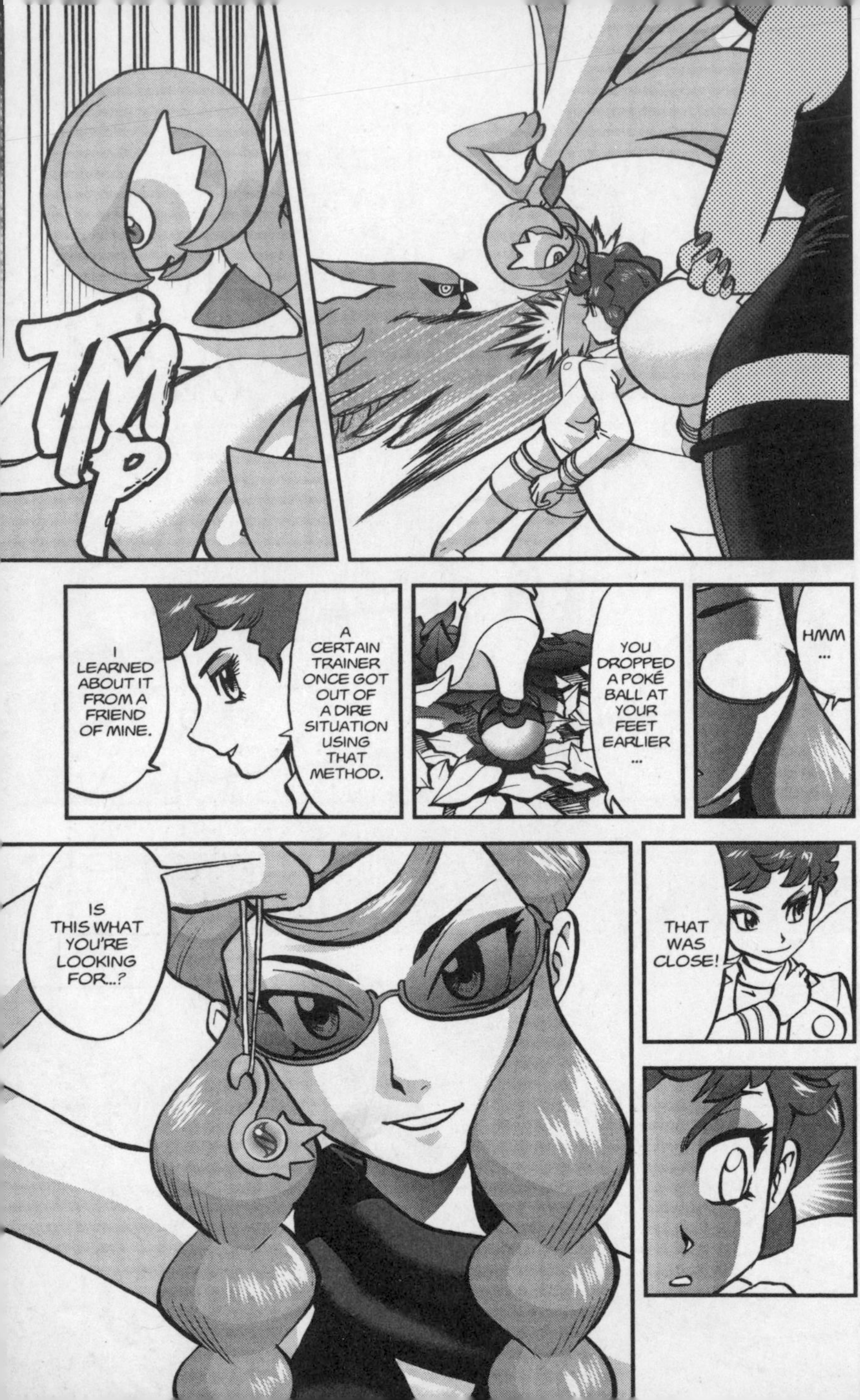
TMP
HMM ...
YOU DROPPED A POKÉ BALL AT YOUR FEET EARLIER ...
A CERTAIN TRAINER ONCE GOT OUT OF A DIRE SITUATION USING THAT METHOD.
I LEARNED ABOUT IT FROM A FRIEND OF MINE.
THAT WAS CLOSE!
IS THIS WHAT YOU'RE LOOKING FOR...?

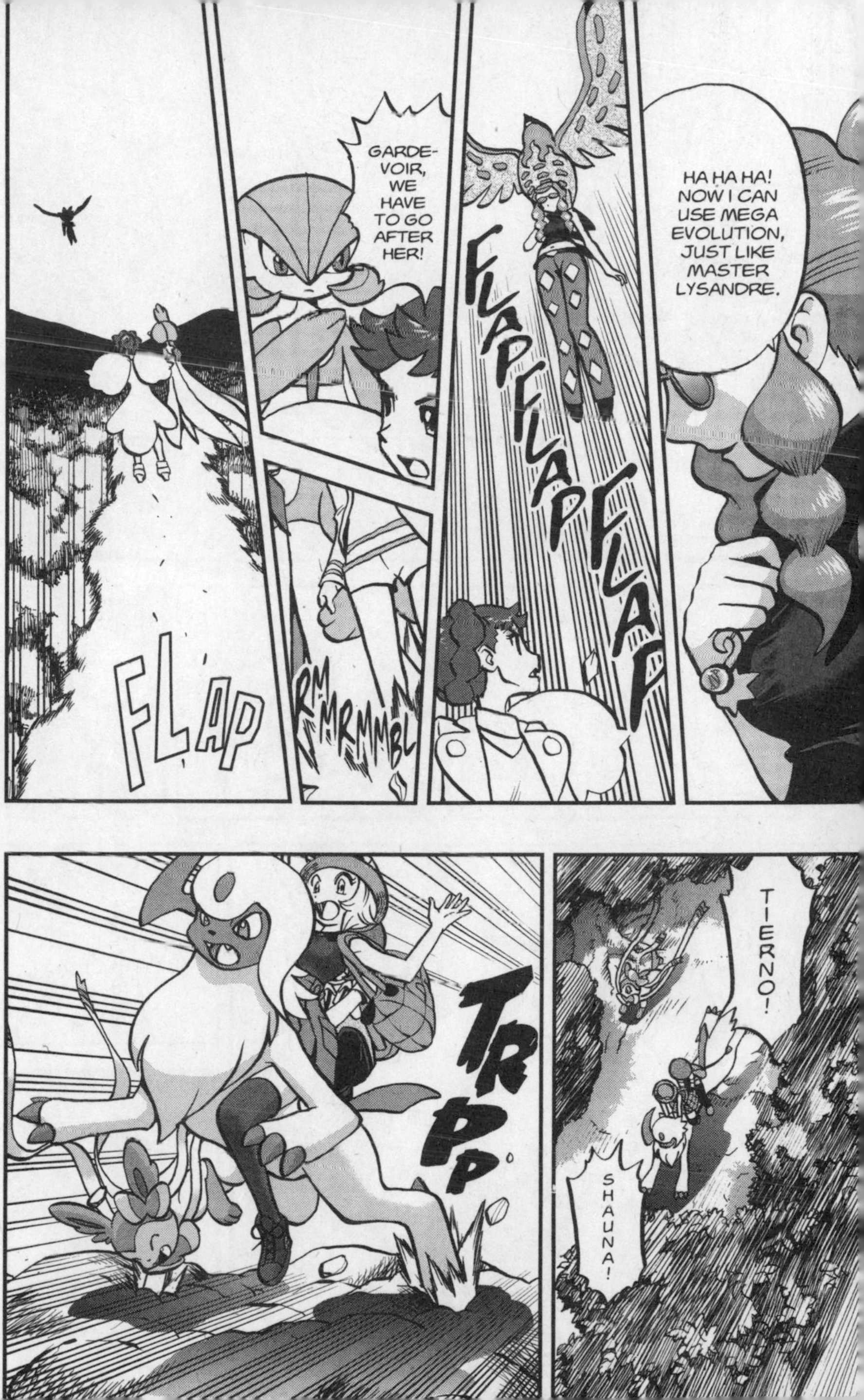
HA HA HA! NOW I CAN USE MEGA EVOLUTION, JUST LIKE MASTER LYSANDRE.
FLAP FLAP FLAP FLAP
GARDE-VOIR, WE HAVE TO GO AFTER HER!
RMMRMMMBL
FLAP
TIERNO!
SHAUNA!
TRPP

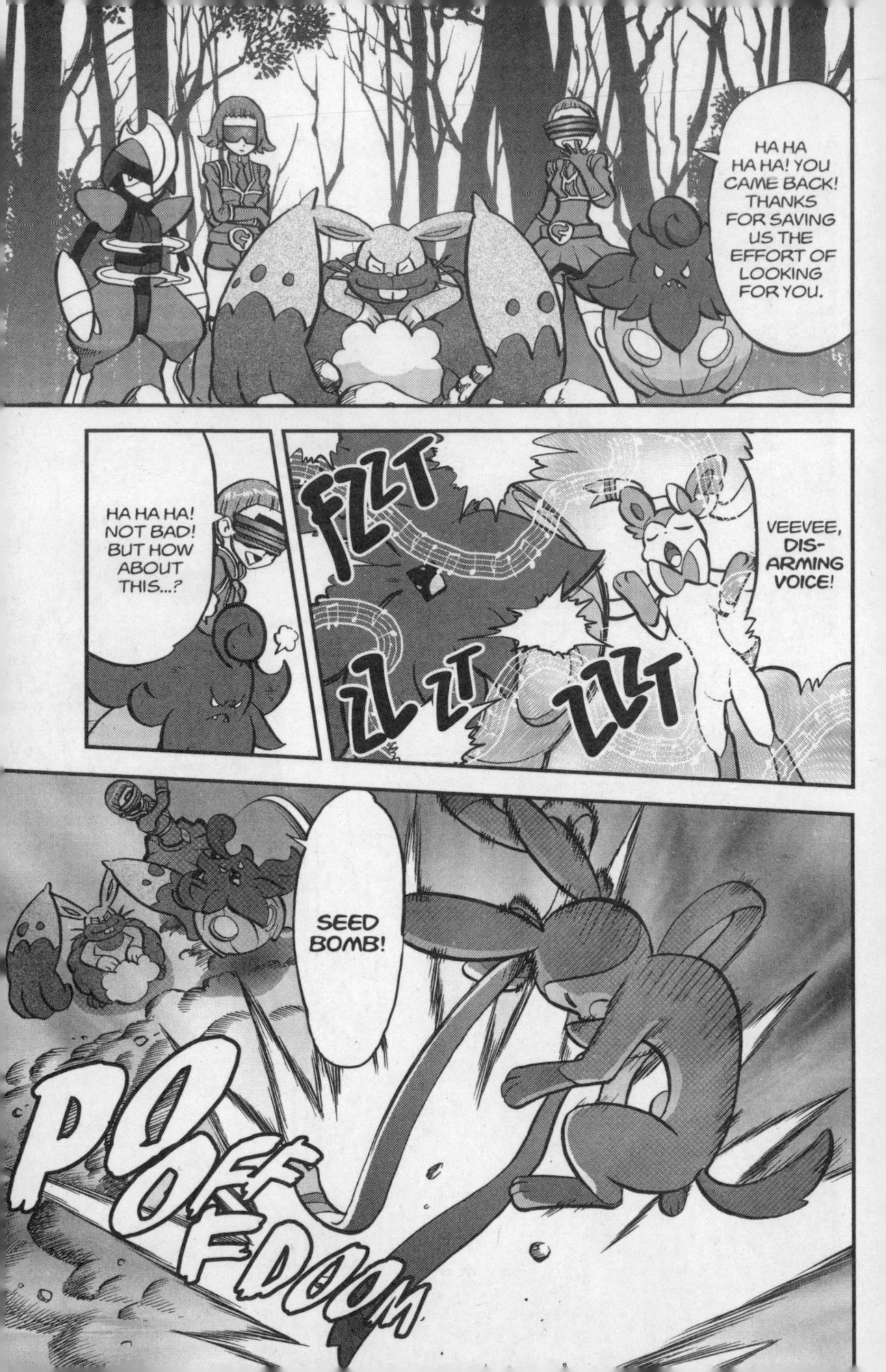
HA HA HA HA! YOU CAME BACK! THANKS FOR SAVING US THE EFFORT OF LOOKING FOR YOU.
VEEVEE, DIS-ARMING VOICE!
FZZT
ZZZT
ZZZT
HA HA HA! NOT BAD! BUT HOW ABOUT THIS...?
SEED BOMB!
POOF OF DOOM

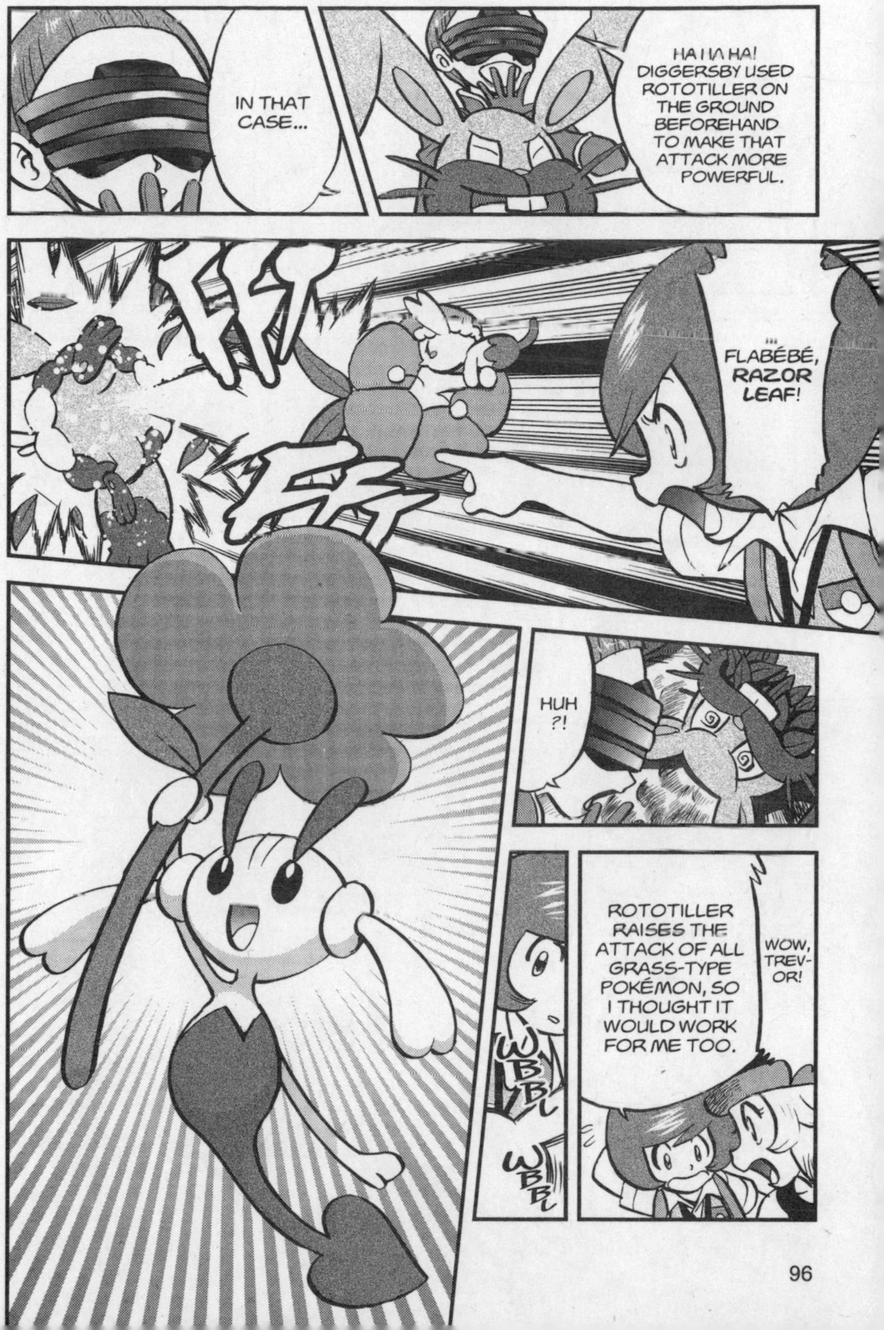
HA HA HA! DIGGERSBY USED ROTOTILLER ON THE GROUND BEFOREHAND TO MAKE THAT ATTACK MORE POWERFUL.
IN THAT CASE...
... FLABÉBÉ, RAZOR LEAF!
HUH ?!
ROTOTILLER RAISES THE ATTACK OF ALL GRASS-TYPE POKÉMON, SO I THOUGHT IT WOULD WORK FOR ME TOO.
WOW, TREV-OR!
WBBL
WBBL

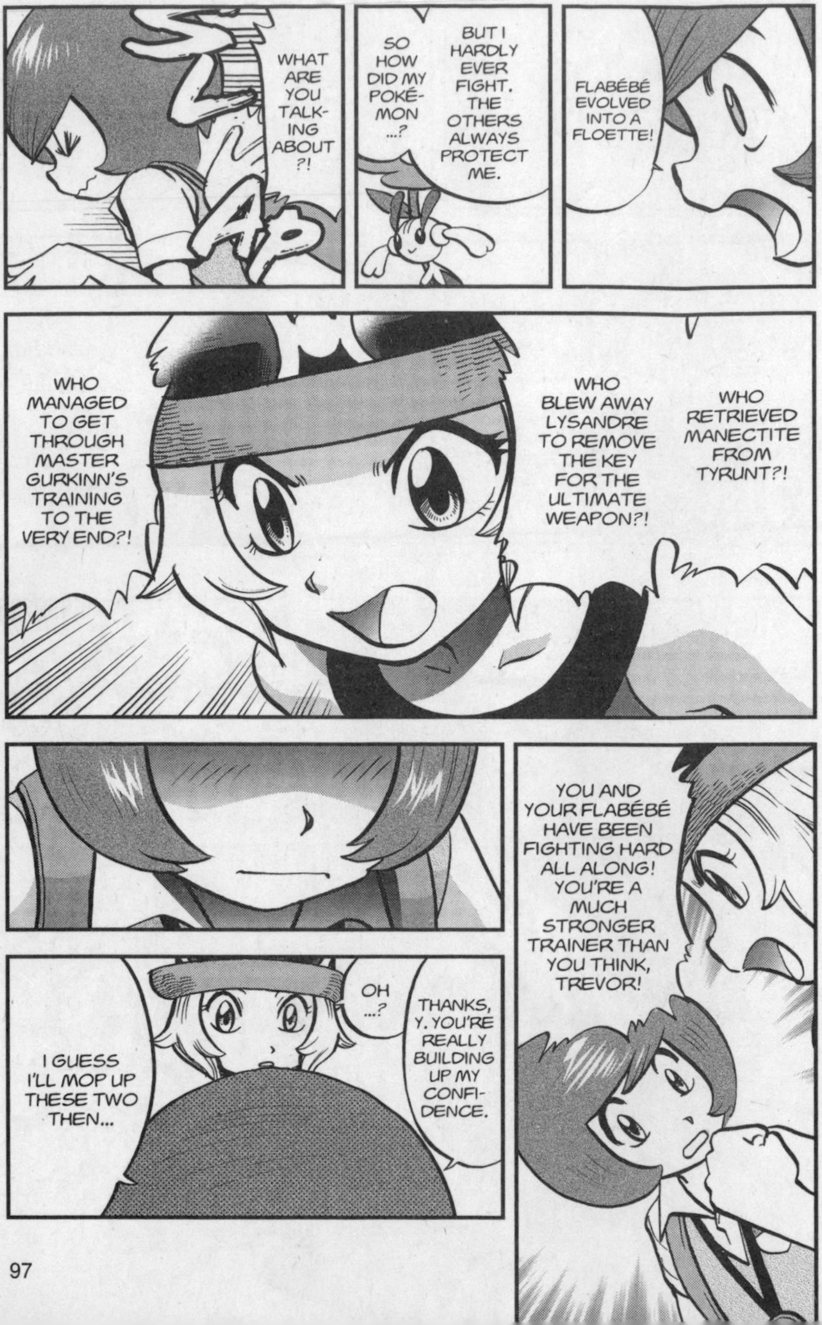
FLABÉBÉ EVOLVED INTO A FLOETTE!
BUT I HARDLY EVER FIGHT. THE OTHERS ALWAYS PROTECT ME.
SO HOW DID MY POKÉ-MON ...?
WHAT ARE YOU TALK-ING ABOUT ?!
AP
WHO RETRIEVED MANECTITE FROM TYRUNT?!
WHO BLEW AWAY LYSANDRE TO REMOVE THE KEY FOR THE ULTIMATE WEAPON?!
WHO MANAGED TO GET THROUGH MASTER GURKINN'S TRAINING TO THE VERY END?!
YOU AND YOUR FLABÉBÉ HAVE BEEN FIGHTING HARD ALL ALONG! YOU'RE A MUCH STRONGER TRAINER THAN YOU THINK, TREVOR!
THANKS, Y. YOU'RE REALLY BUILDING UP MY CONFI-DENCE.
OH ...?
I GUESS I'LL MOP UP THESE TWO THEN...

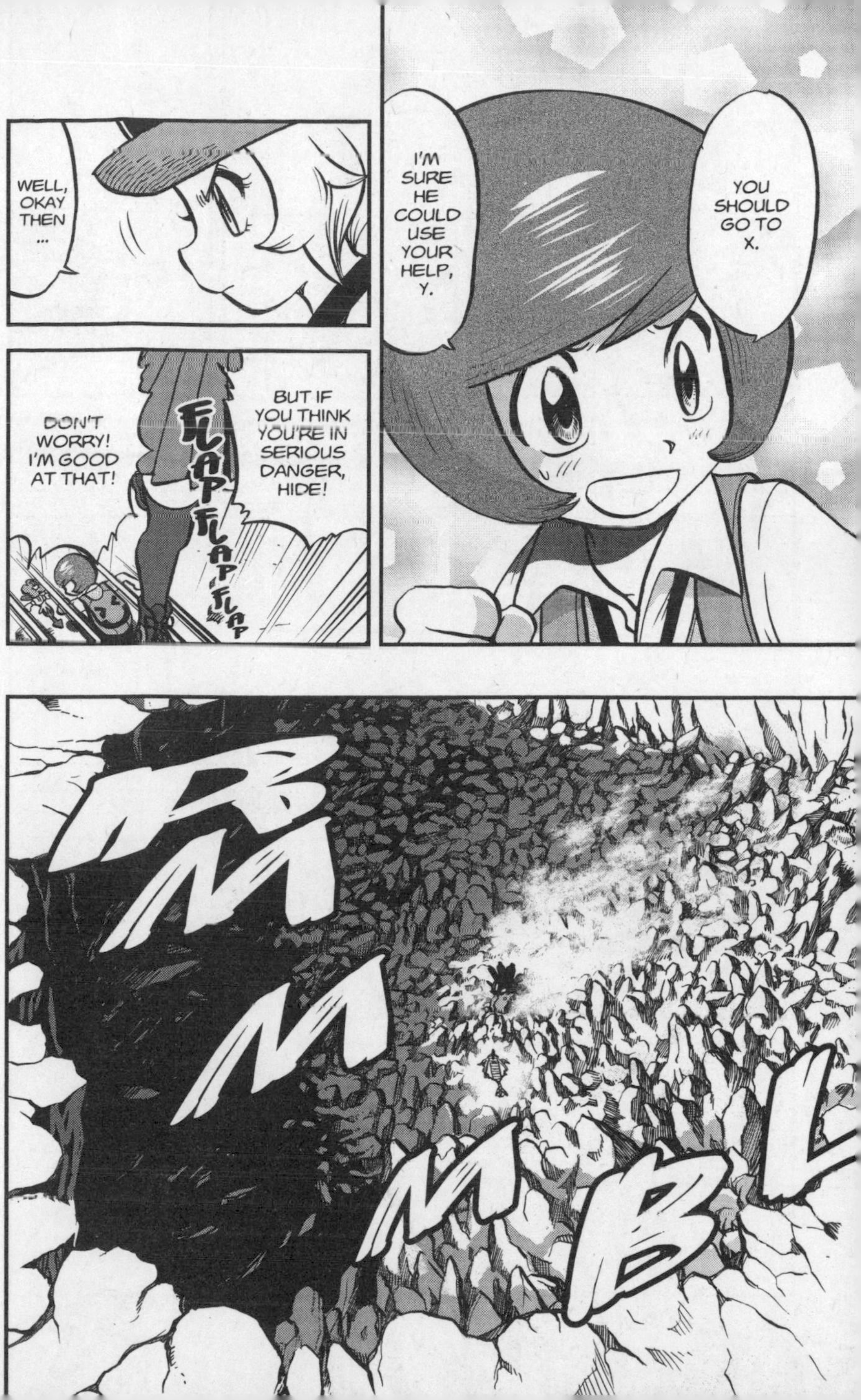
YOU SHOULD GO TO X.
I'M SURE HE COULD USE YOUR HELP, Y.
WELL, OKAY THEN ...
BUT IF YOU THINK YOU'RE IN SERIOUS DANGER, HIDE!
DON'T WORRY! I'M GOOD AT THAT!
FLAP FLAP FLAP FLAP
RMMMMB

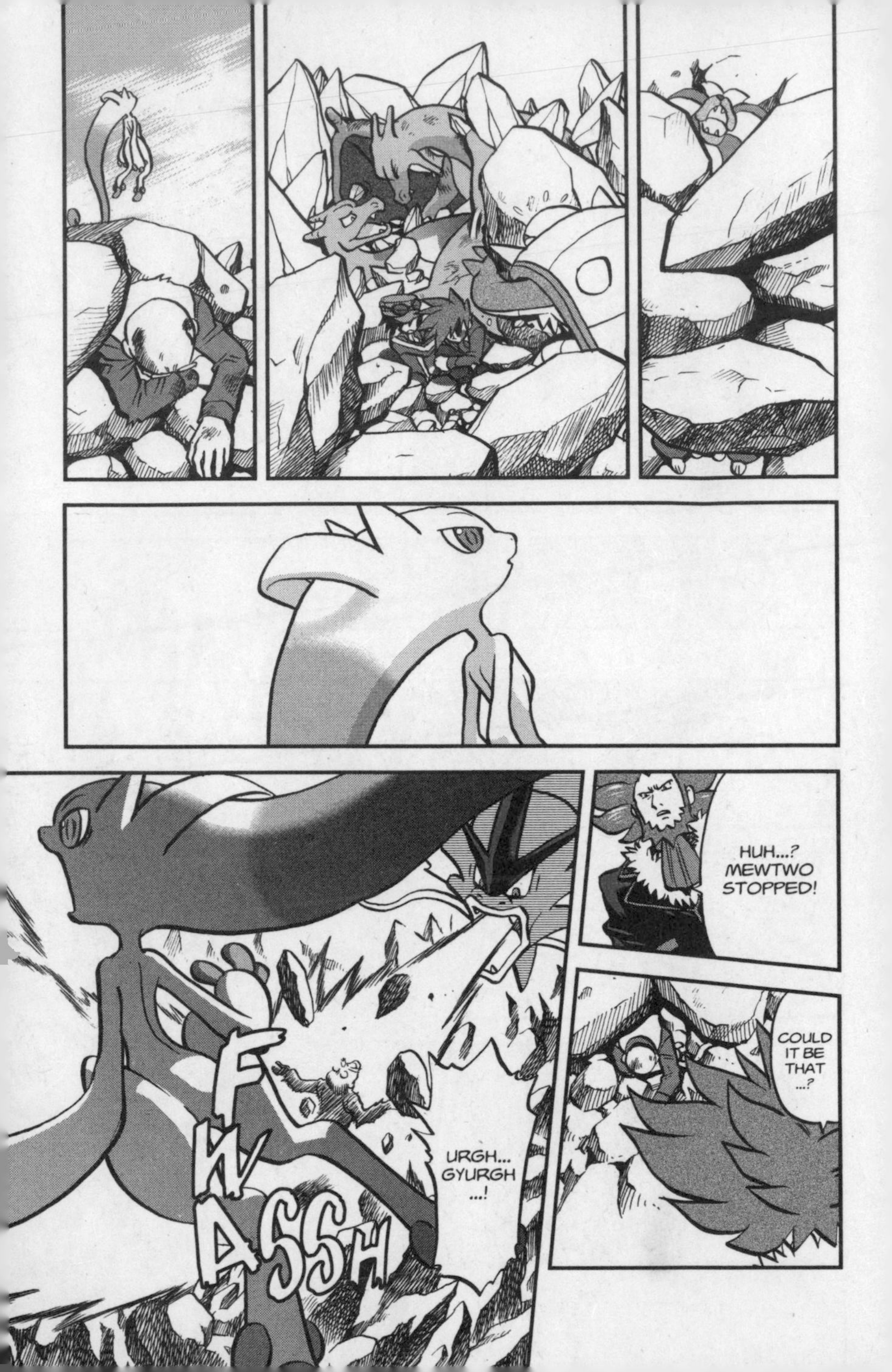
HUH...? MEWTWO STOPPED!
COULD IT BE THAT ...?
URGH... GYURGH ...!
FWASSH

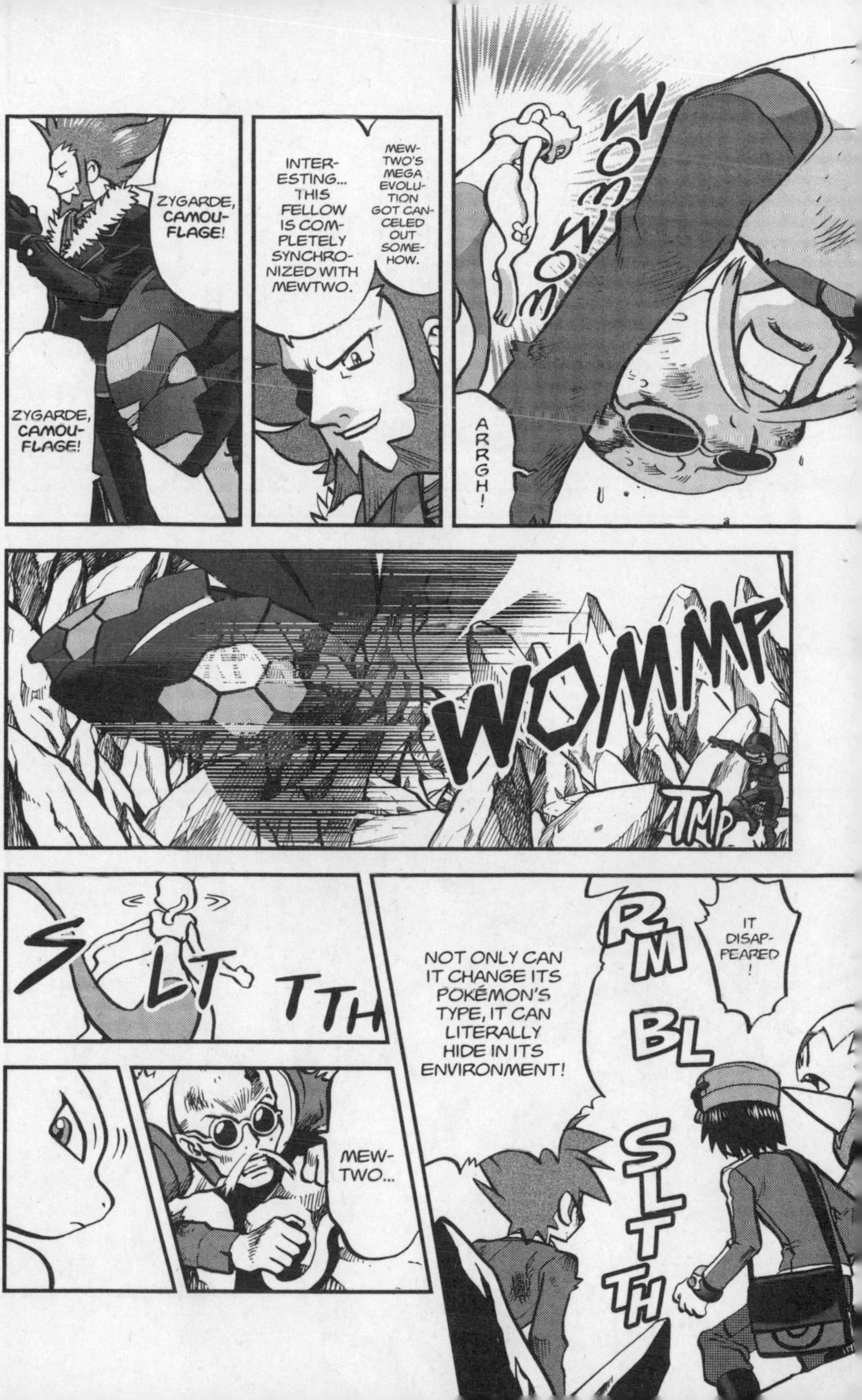
WOMWOMWOM
ARRGH!
MEW-TWO'S MEGA EVOLUTION GOT CANCELED OUT SOME-HOW.
INTER-ESTING... THIS FELLOW IS COM-PLETELY SYNCHRO-NIZED WITH MEWTWO.
ZYGARDE, CAMOU-FLAGE!
ZYGARDE, CAMOU-FLAGE!
WOMMP
TMP
IT DISAP-PEARED!
RM BL
SLTTH
NOT ONLY CAN IT CHANGE ITS POKÉMON'S TYPE, IT CAN LITERALLY HIDE IN ITS ENVIRONMENT!
SLT TTH
MEW-TWO...

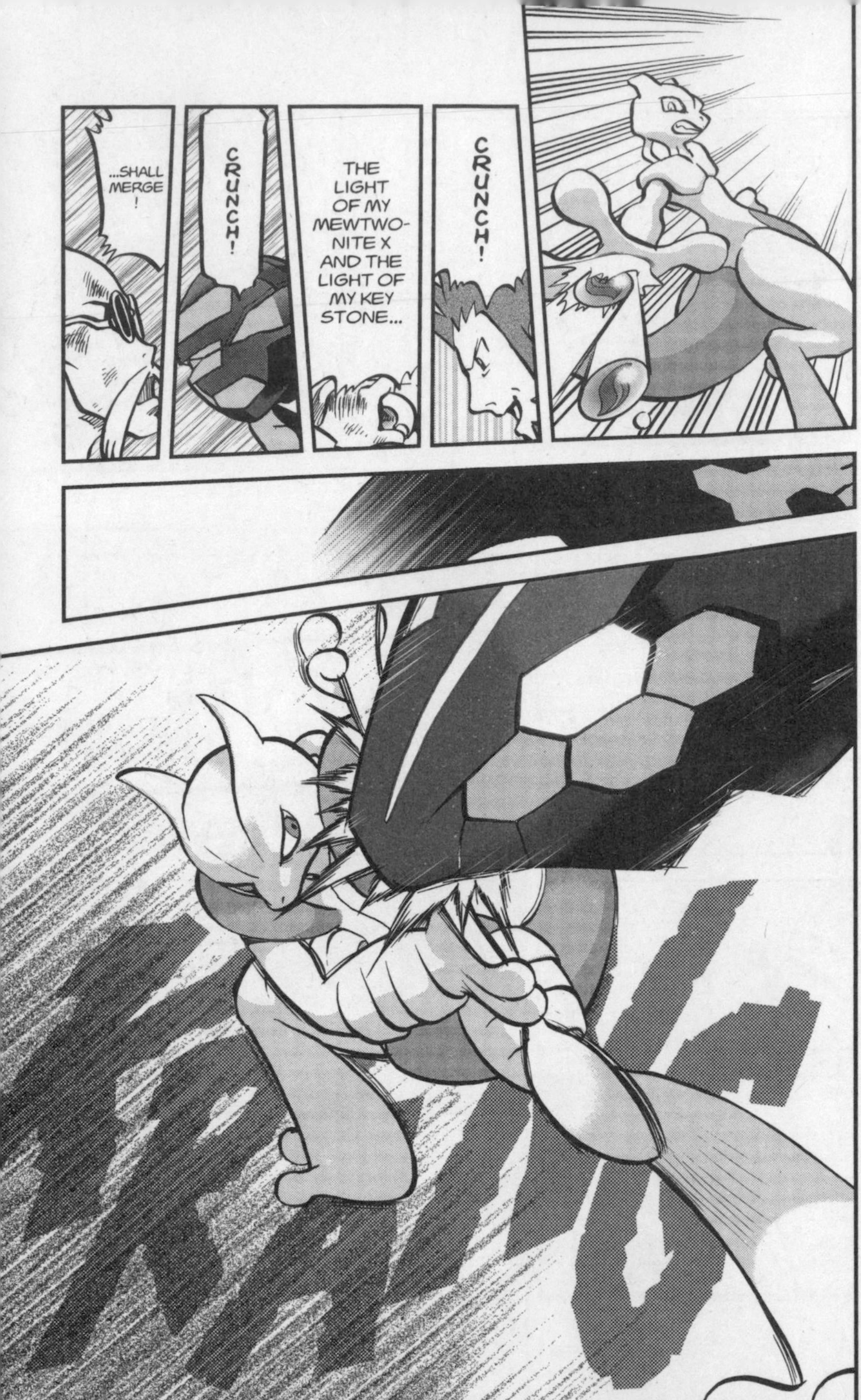
CRUNCH!
THE LIGHT OF MY MEWTWO-NITE X AND THE LIGHT OF MY KEY STONE...
CRUNCH!
...SHALL MERGE!

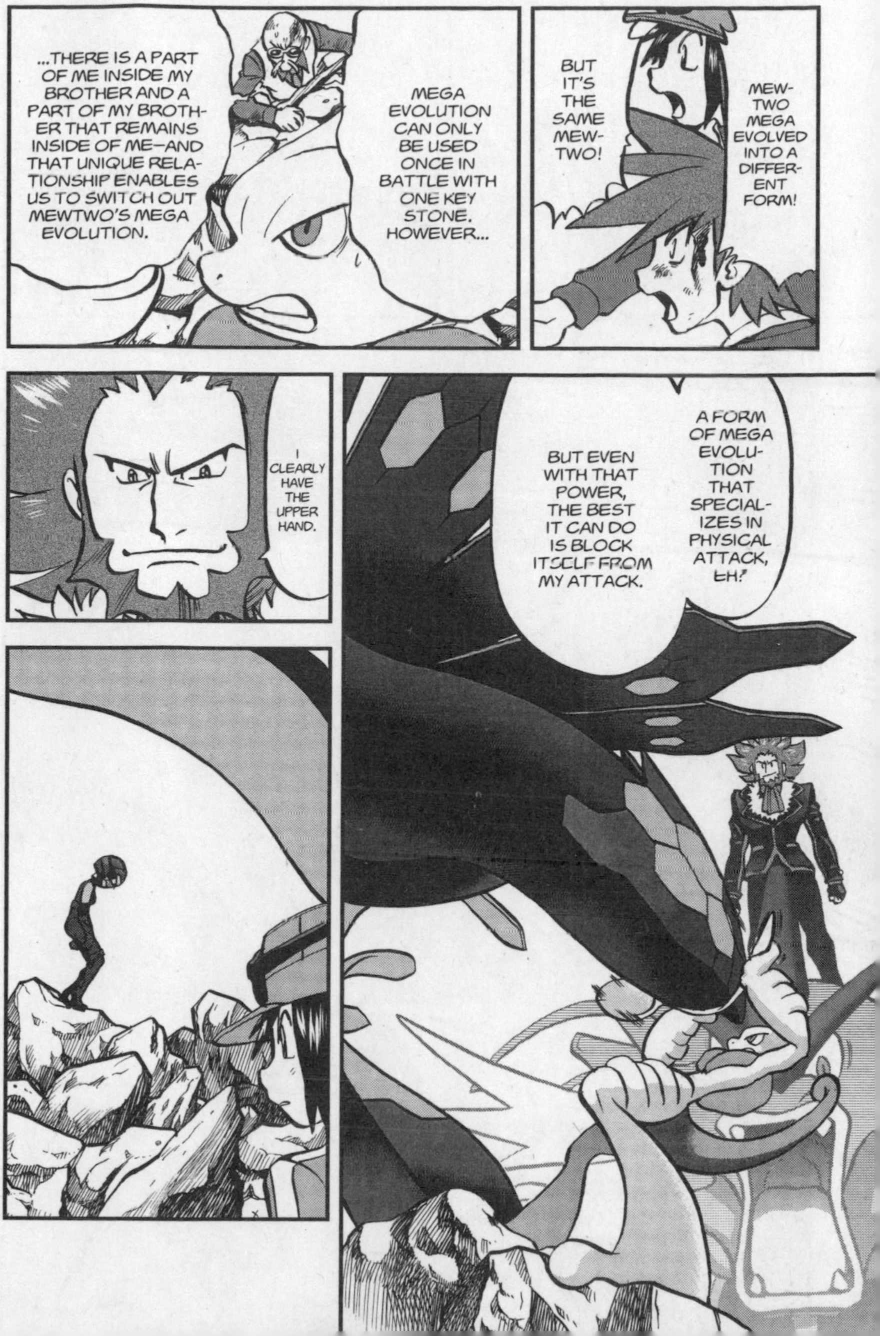
MEW-TWO MEGA EVOLVED INTO A DIFFERENT FORM!
BUT IT'S THE SAME MEW-TWO!
MEGA EVOLUTION CAN ONLY BE USED ONCE IN BATTLE WITH ONE KEY STONE. HOWEVER...
...THERE IS A PART OF ME INSIDE MY BROTHER AND A PART OF MY BROTHER THAT REMAINS INSIDE OF ME—AND THAT UNIQUE RELATIONSHIP ENABLES US TO SWITCH OUT MEWTWO'S MEGA EVOLUTION.
A FORM OF MEGA EVOLUTION THAT SPECIALIZES IN PHYSICAL ATTACK, EH?
BUT EVEN WITH THAT POWER, THE BEST IT CAN DO IS BLOCK ITSELF FROM MY ATTACK.
I CLEARLY HAVE THE UPPER HAND.

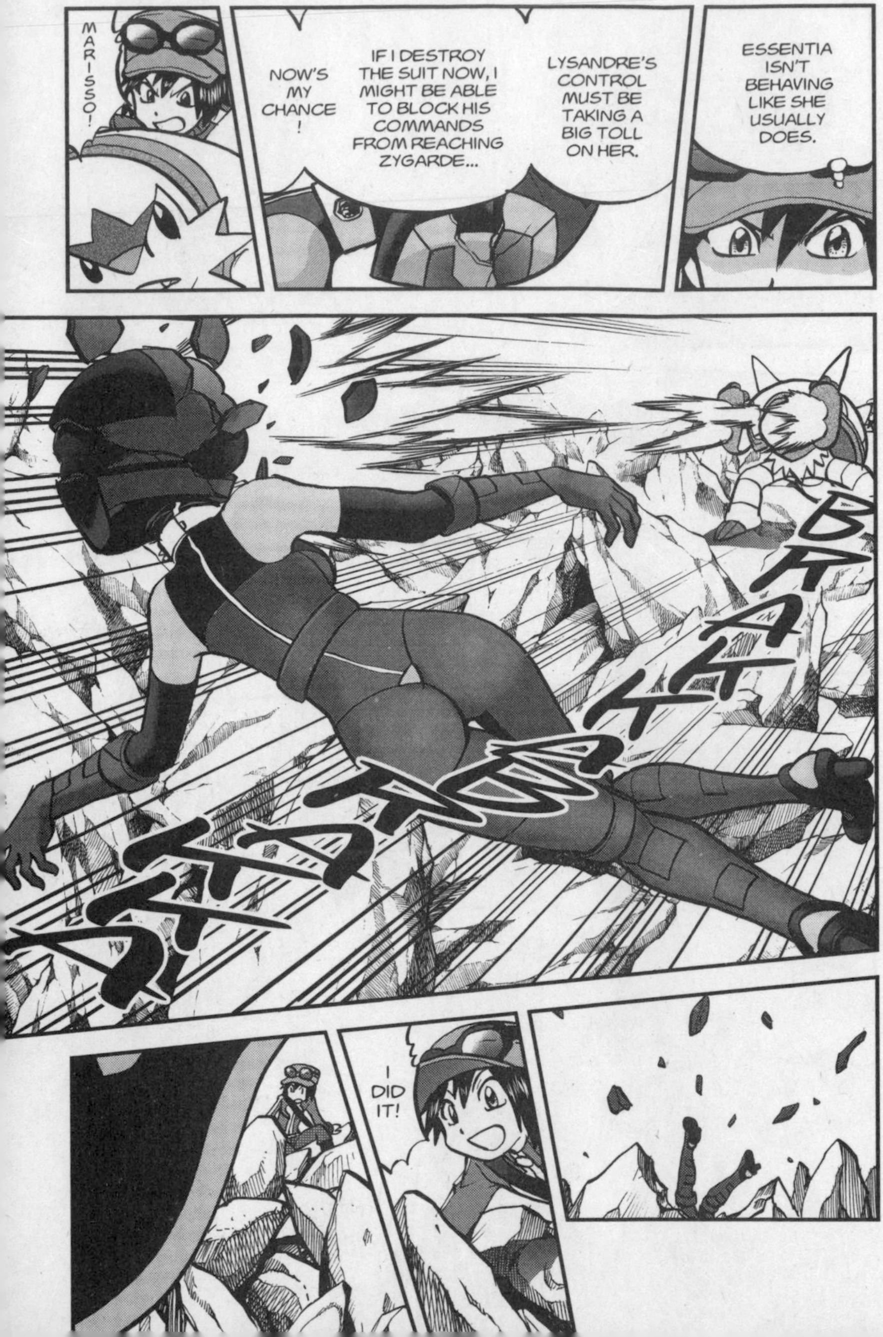
ESSENTIA ISN'T BEHAVING LIKE SHE USUALLY DOES.
LYSANDRE'S CONTROL MUST BE TAKING A BIG TOLL ON HER.
IF I DESTROY THE SUIT NOW, I MIGHT BE ABLE TO BLOCK HIS COMMANDS FROM REACHING ZYGARDE...
NOW'S MY CHANCE!
MARISSO!
I DID IT!

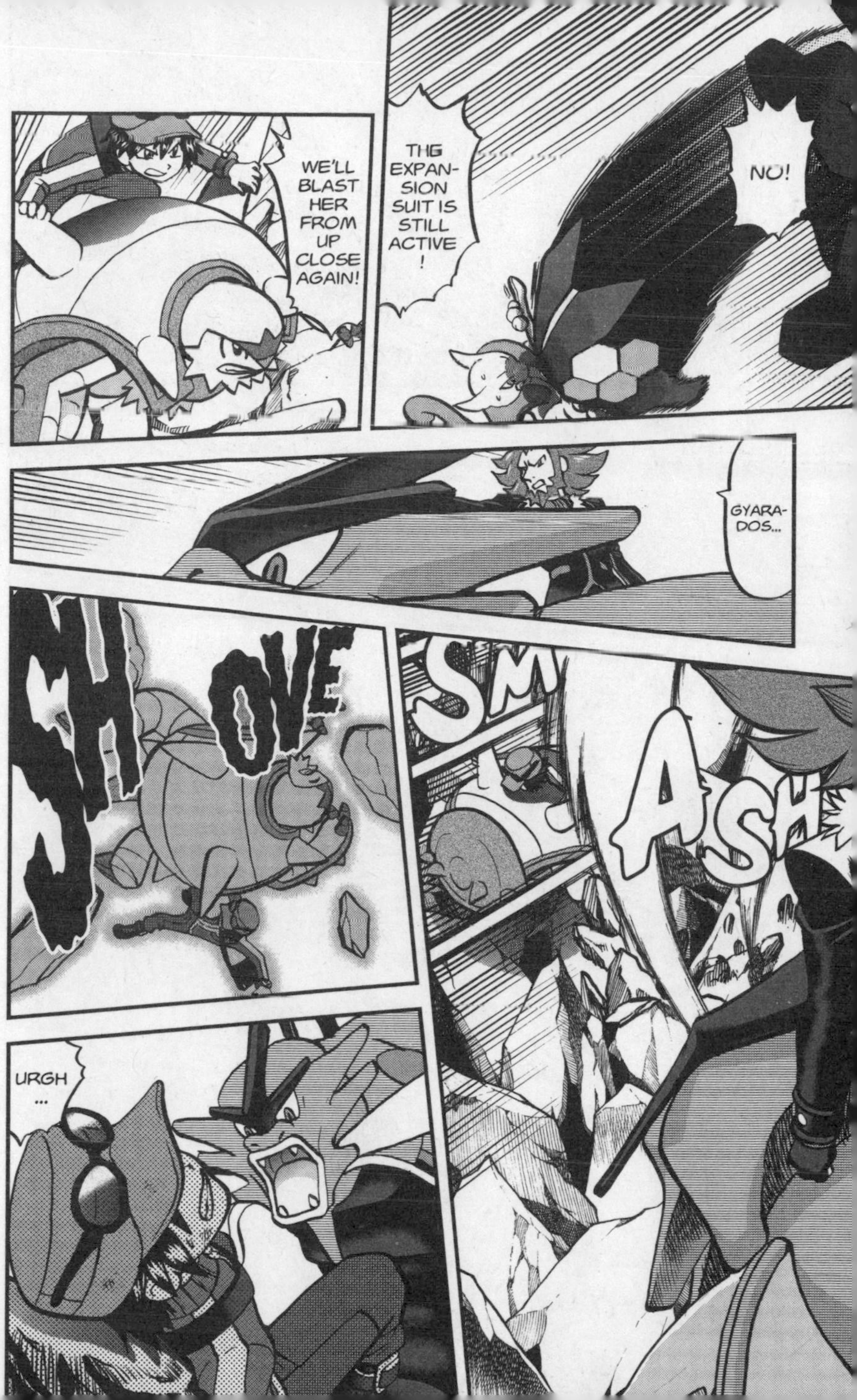
NO!
THE EXPANSION SUIT IS STILL ACTIVE!
WE'LL BLAST HER FROM UP CLOSE AGAIN!
GYARADOS...
SMASH
SHOVE
URGH...

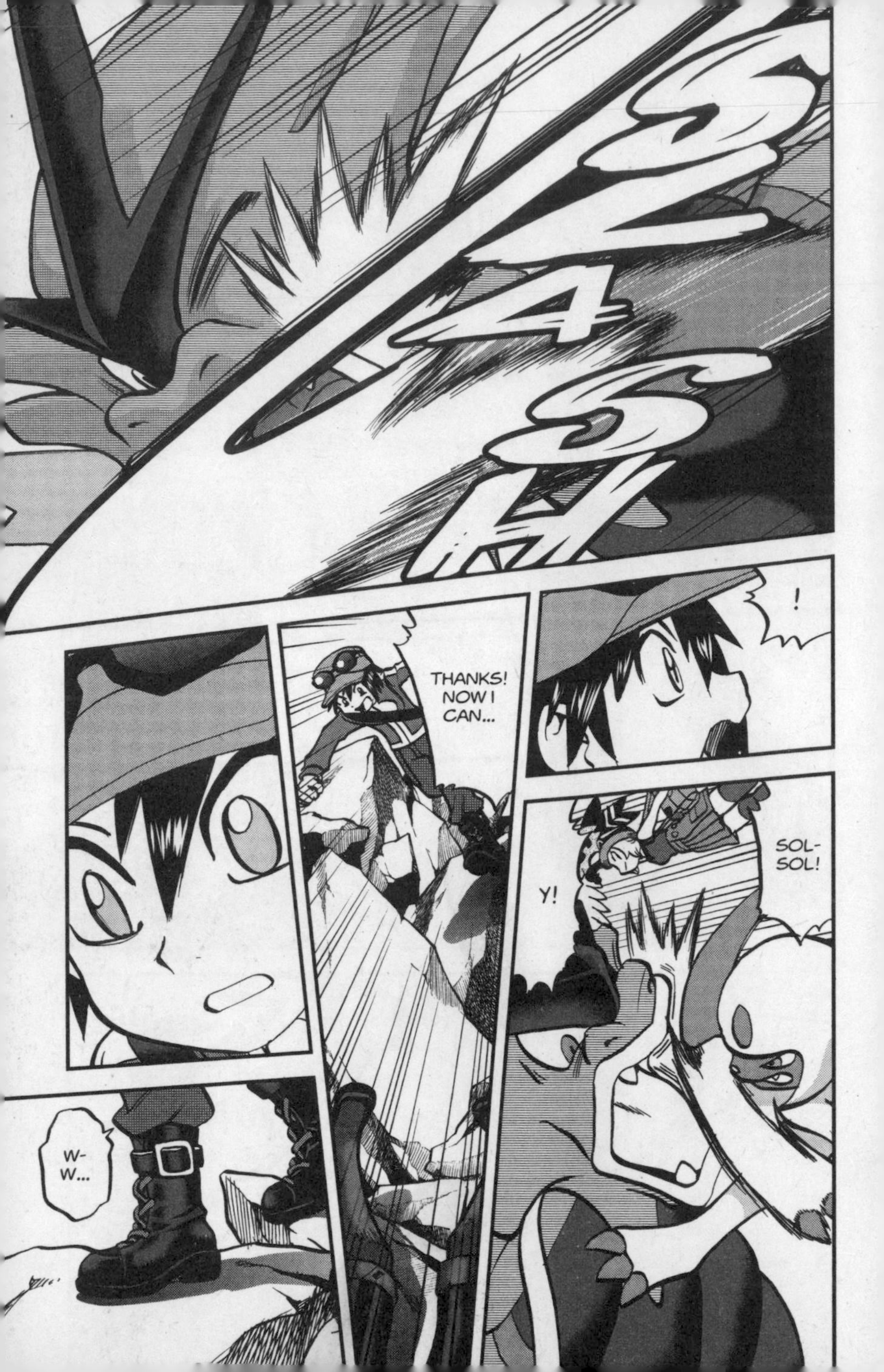
SLASH
!
SOL-SOL!
Y!
THANKS! NOW I CAN...
W- W...

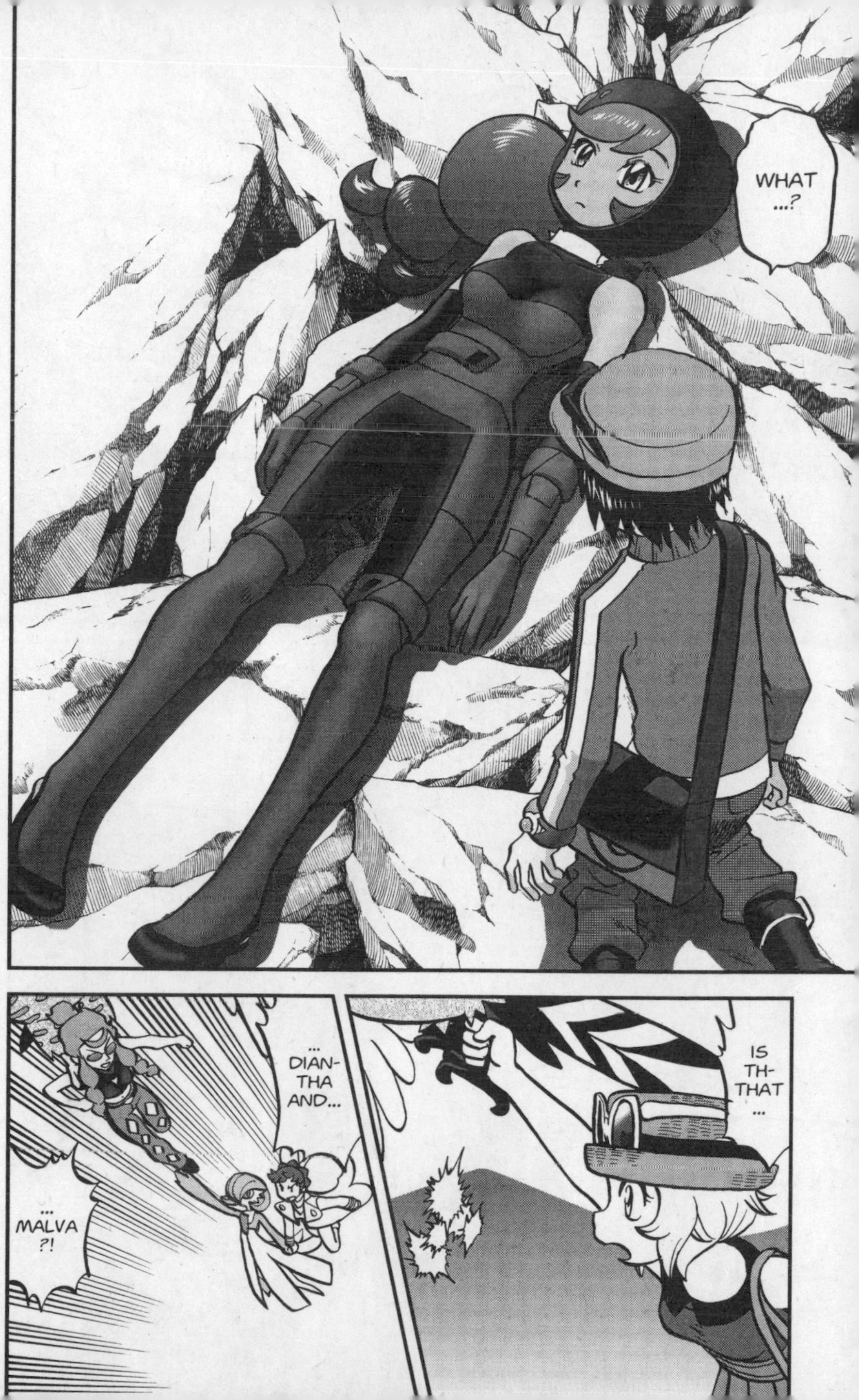
WHAT ...?
IS TH-THAT ...
... DIAN-THA AND...
... MALVA ?!

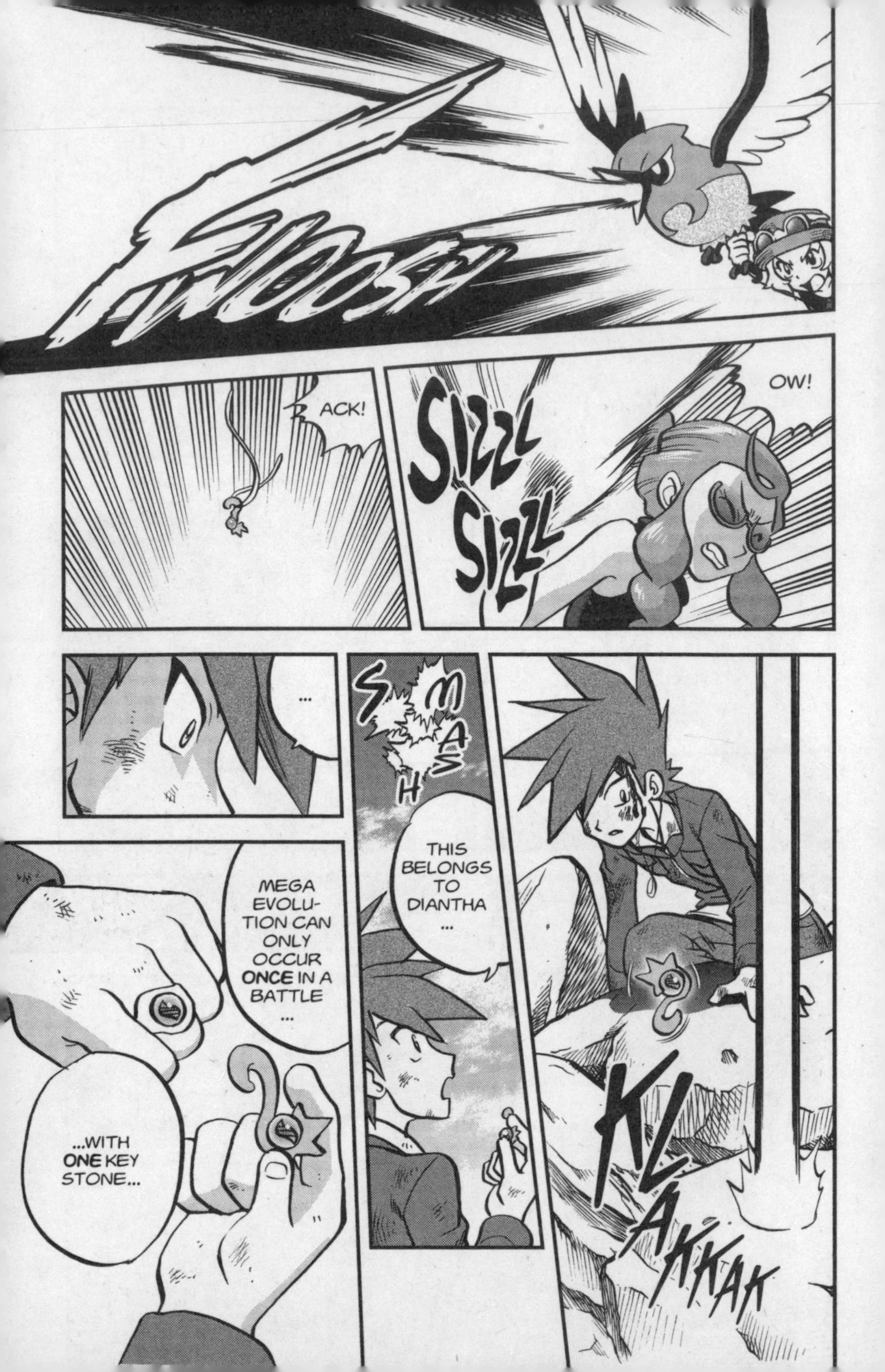
WHOOSH
OW!
SIZZL SIZZL
ACK!
KLAKKAK
SMASH
THIS BELONGS TO DIANTHA ...
...
MEGA EVOLUTION CAN ONLY OCCUR ONCE IN A BATTLE ...
...WITH ONE KEY STONE...

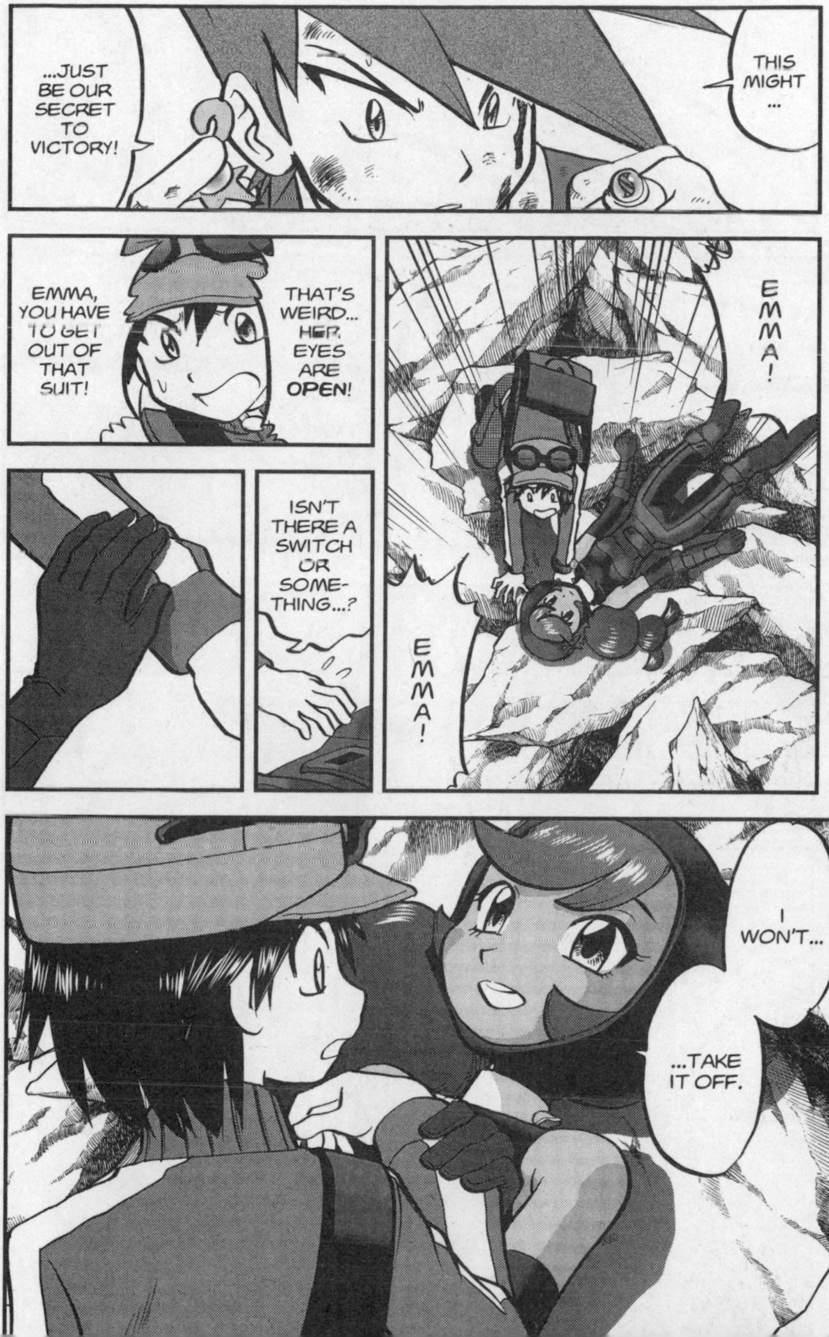
THIS MIGHT ...
...JUST BE OUR SECRET TO VICTORY!
EMMA!
EMMA!
THAT'S WEIRD... HER EYES ARE OPEN!
EMMA, YOU HAVE TO GET OUT OF THAT SUIT!
ISN'T THERE A SWITCH OR SOME-THING...?
I WON'T...
...TAKE IT OFF.

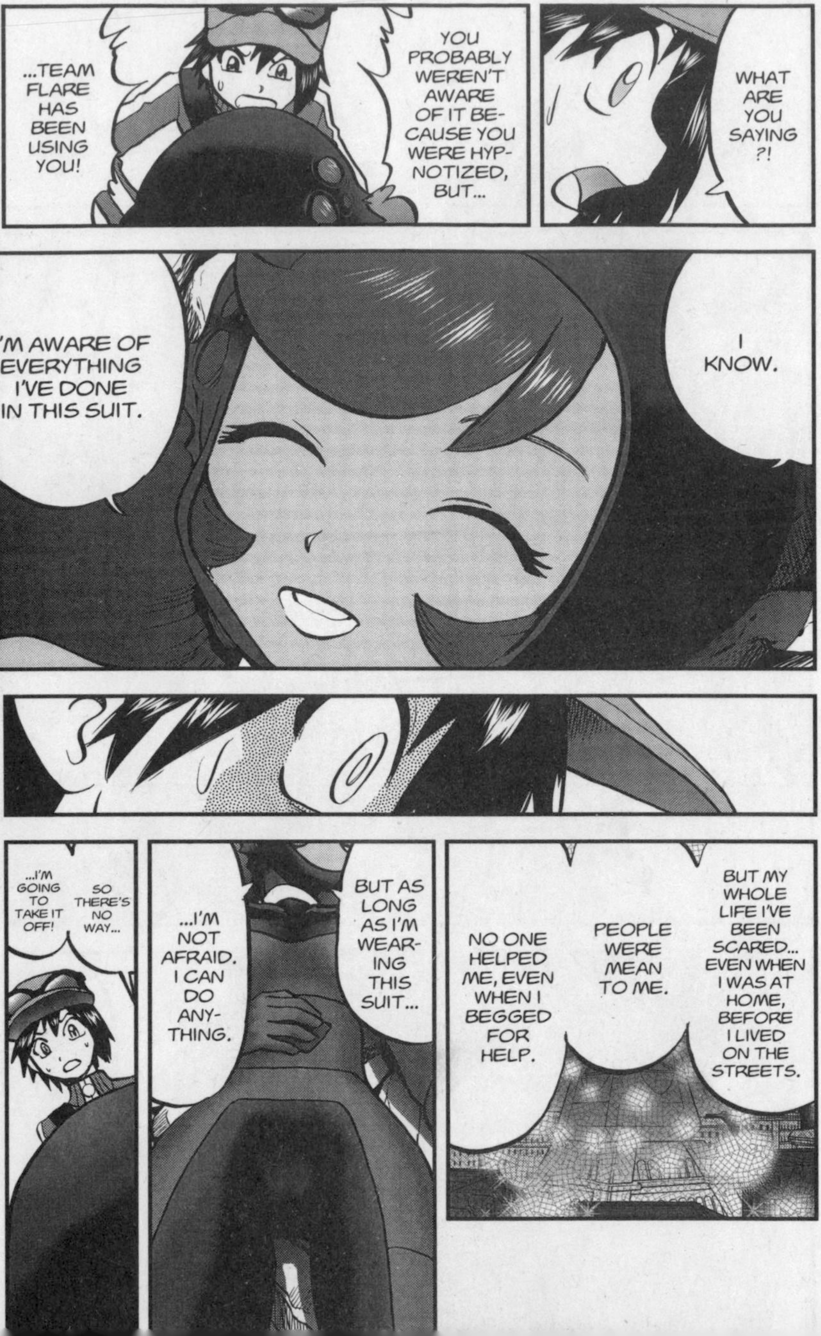
WHAT ARE YOU SAYING?!
YOU PROBABLY WEREN'T AWARE OF IT BECAUSE YOU WERE HYPNOTIZED, BUT...
...TEAM FLARE HAS BEEN USING YOU!
I KNOW.
I'M AWARE OF EVERYTHING I'VE DONE IN THIS SUIT.
BUT MY WHOLE LIFE I'VE BEEN SCARED... EVEN WHEN I WAS AT HOME, BEFORE I LIVED ON THE STREETS.
PEOPLE WERE MEAN TO ME.
NO ONE HELPED ME, EVEN WHEN I BEGGED FOR HELP.
BUT AS LONG AS I'M WEARING THIS SUIT...
...I'M NOT AFRAID. I CAN DO ANYTHING.
SO THERE'S NO WAY...
...I'M GOING TO TAKE IT OFF!

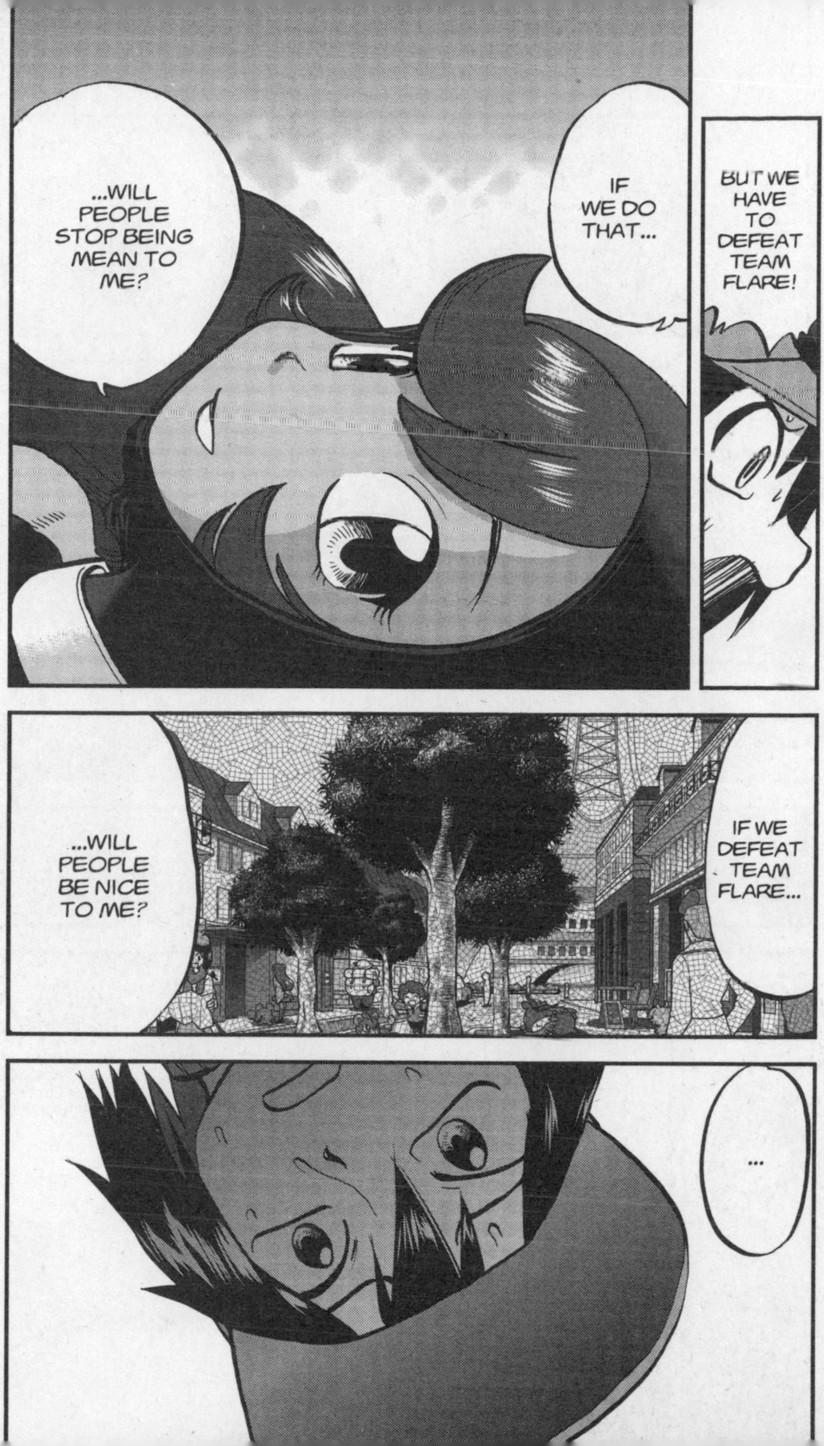
BUT WE HAVE TO DEFEAT TEAM FLARE!
IF WE DO THAT...
...WILL PEOPLE STOP BEING MEAN TO ME?
IF WE DEFEAT TEAM FLARE...
...WILL PEOPLE BE NICE TO ME?
...

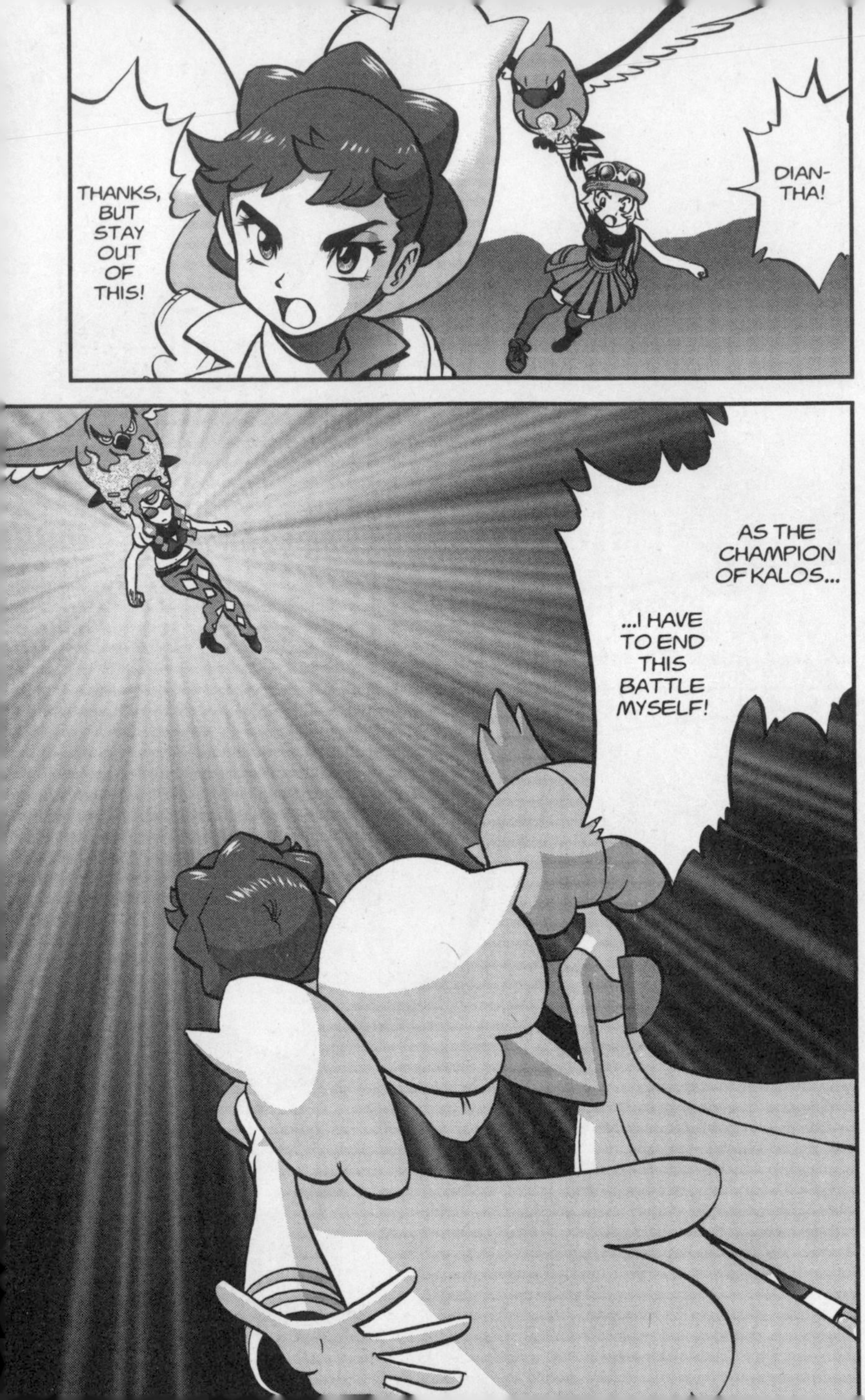
DIAN-
THA!
THANKS, BUT STAY OUT OF THIS!
AS THE CHAMPION OF KALOS...
...I HAVE TO END THIS BATTLE MYSELF!

Adventure #44

Zygarde Agitated

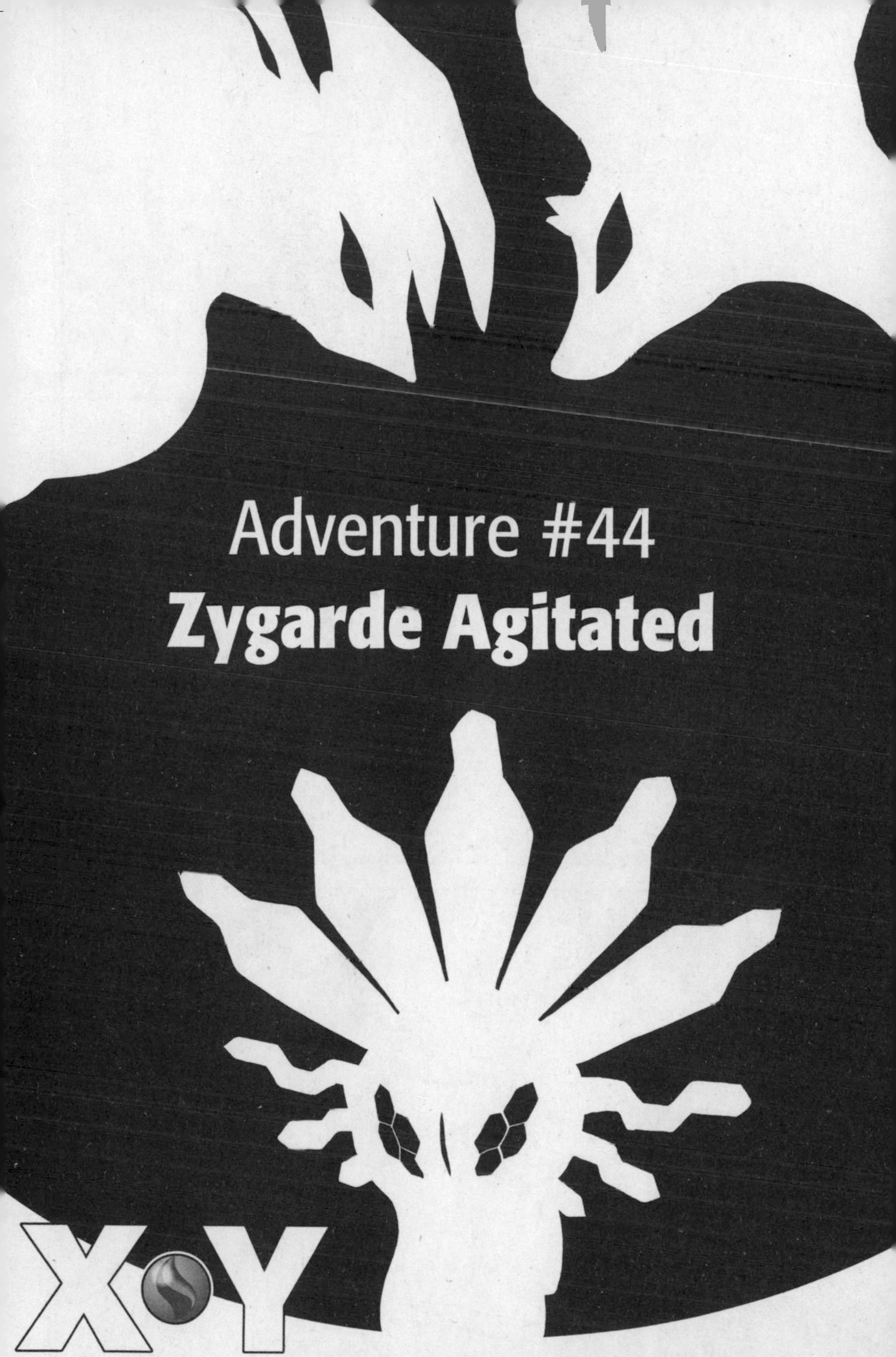

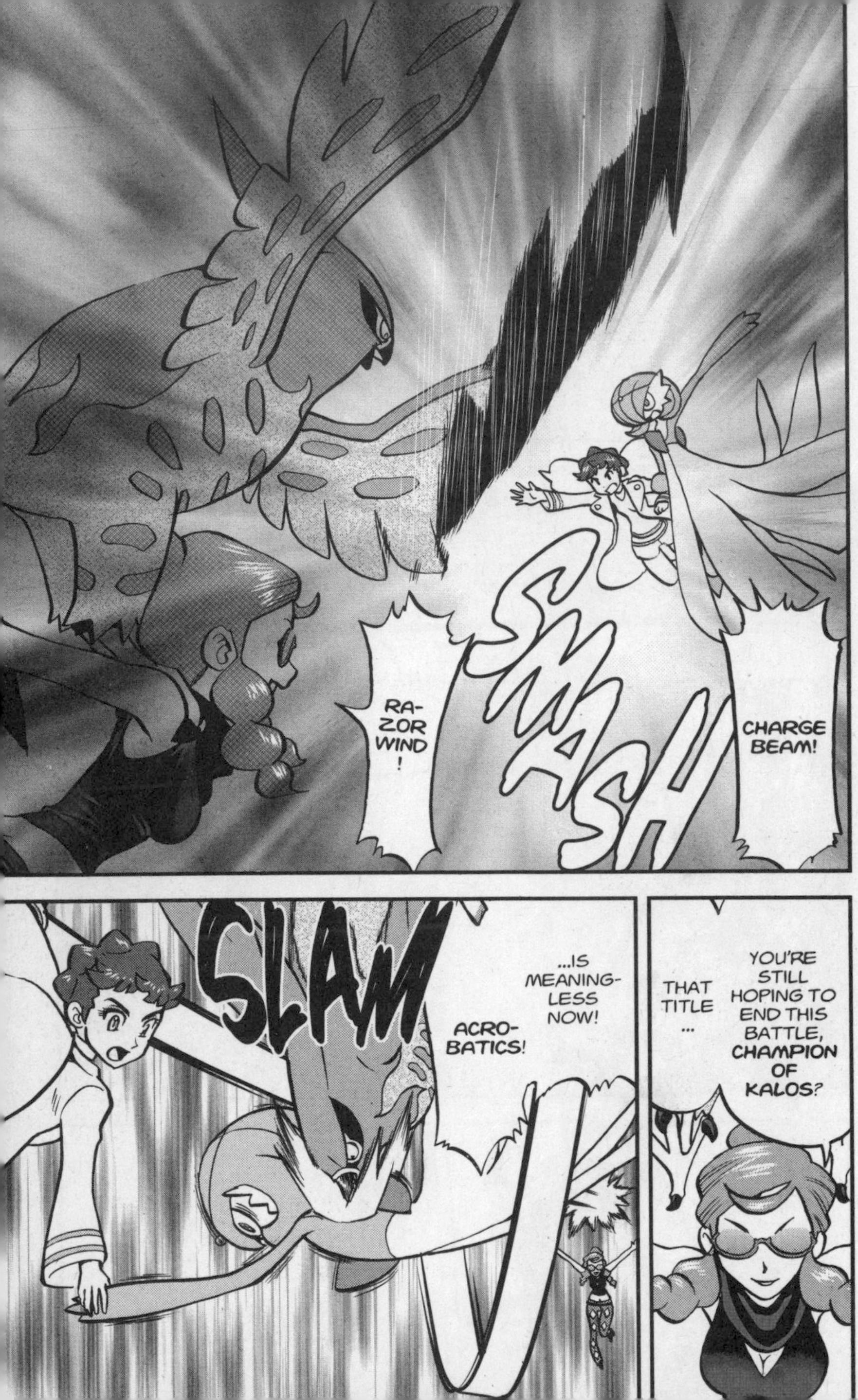
CHARGE BEAM!
SMASH
RA-ZOR WIND!
YOU'RE STILL HOPING TO END THIS BATTLE, **CHAMPION OF KALOS?**
THAT TITLE...
...IS MEANING-LESS NOW!
ACRO-BATICS!
SLAM

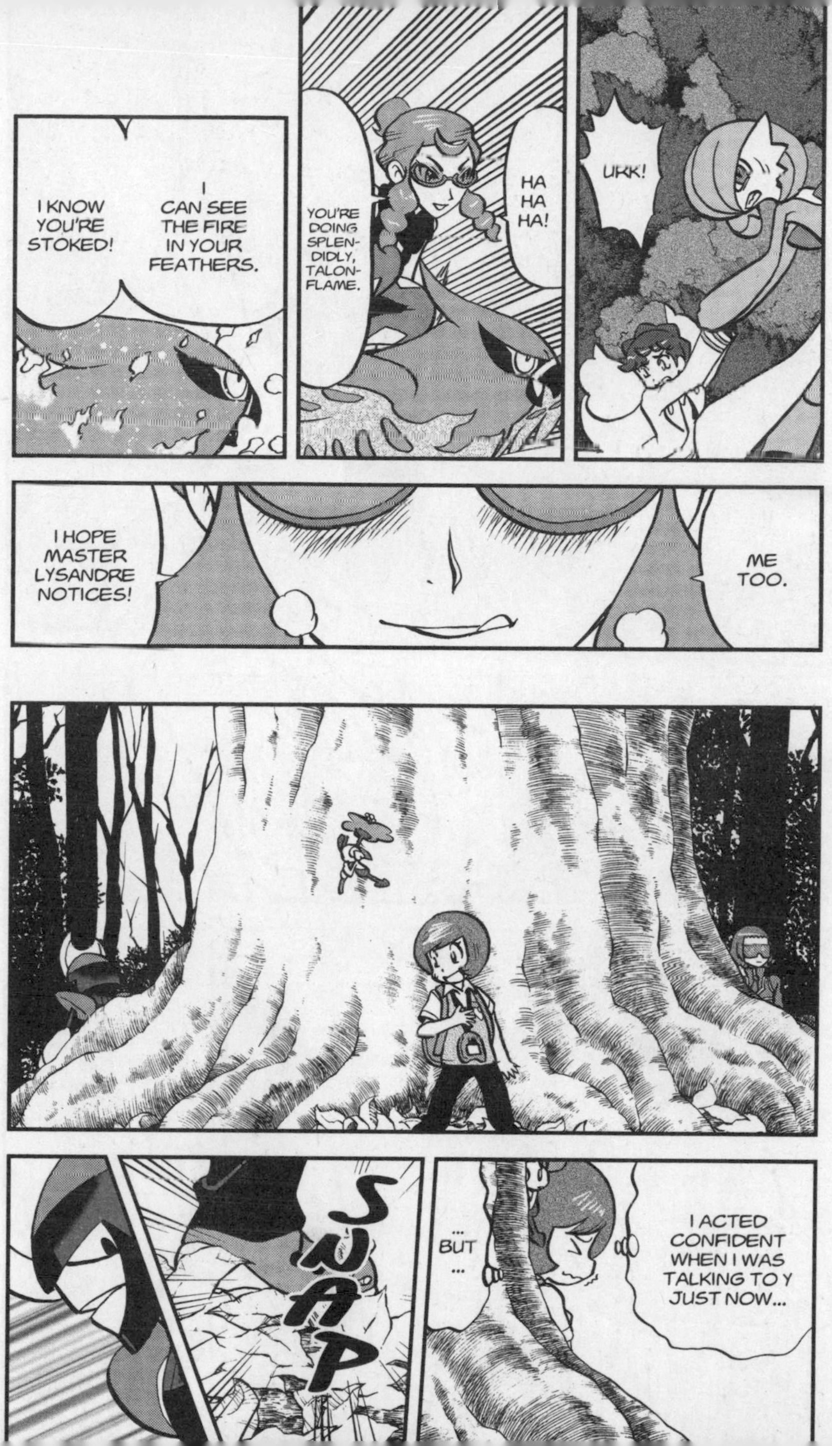
UKK!
HA HA HA!
YOU'RE DOING SPLEN-DIDLY, TALON-FLAME.
I CAN SEE THE FIRE IN YOUR FEATHERS.
I KNOW YOU'RE STOKED!
ME TOO.
I HOPE MASTER LYSANDRE NOTICES!
I ACTED CONFIDENT WHEN I WAS TALKING TO Y JUST NOW...
...BUT...
SNAP

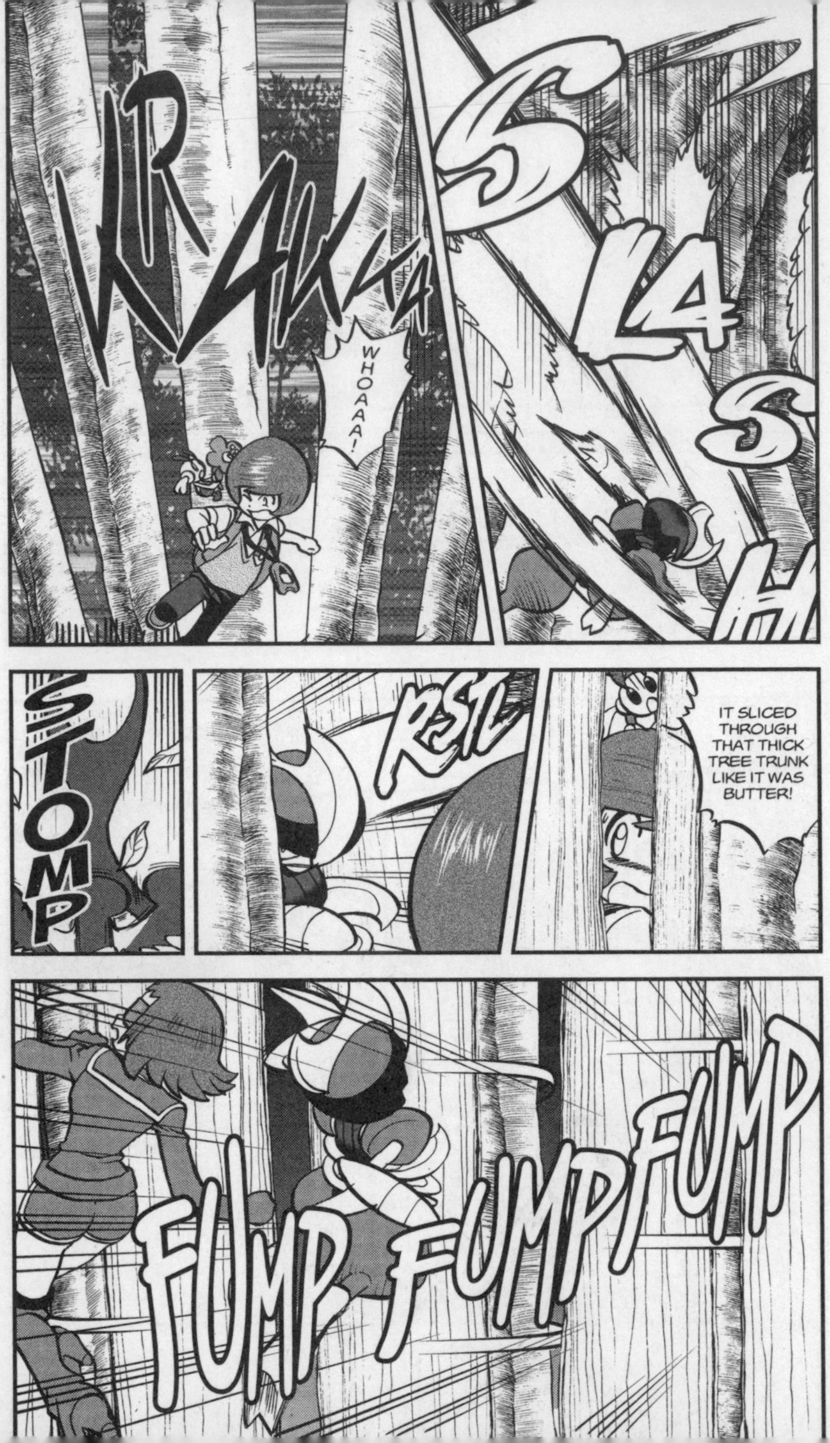
SLASH
WRAKKA
WHOAAA!
IT SLICED THROUGH THAT THICK TREE TRUNK LIKE IT WAS BUTTER!
RSTL
STOMP
FUMP FUMP FUMP

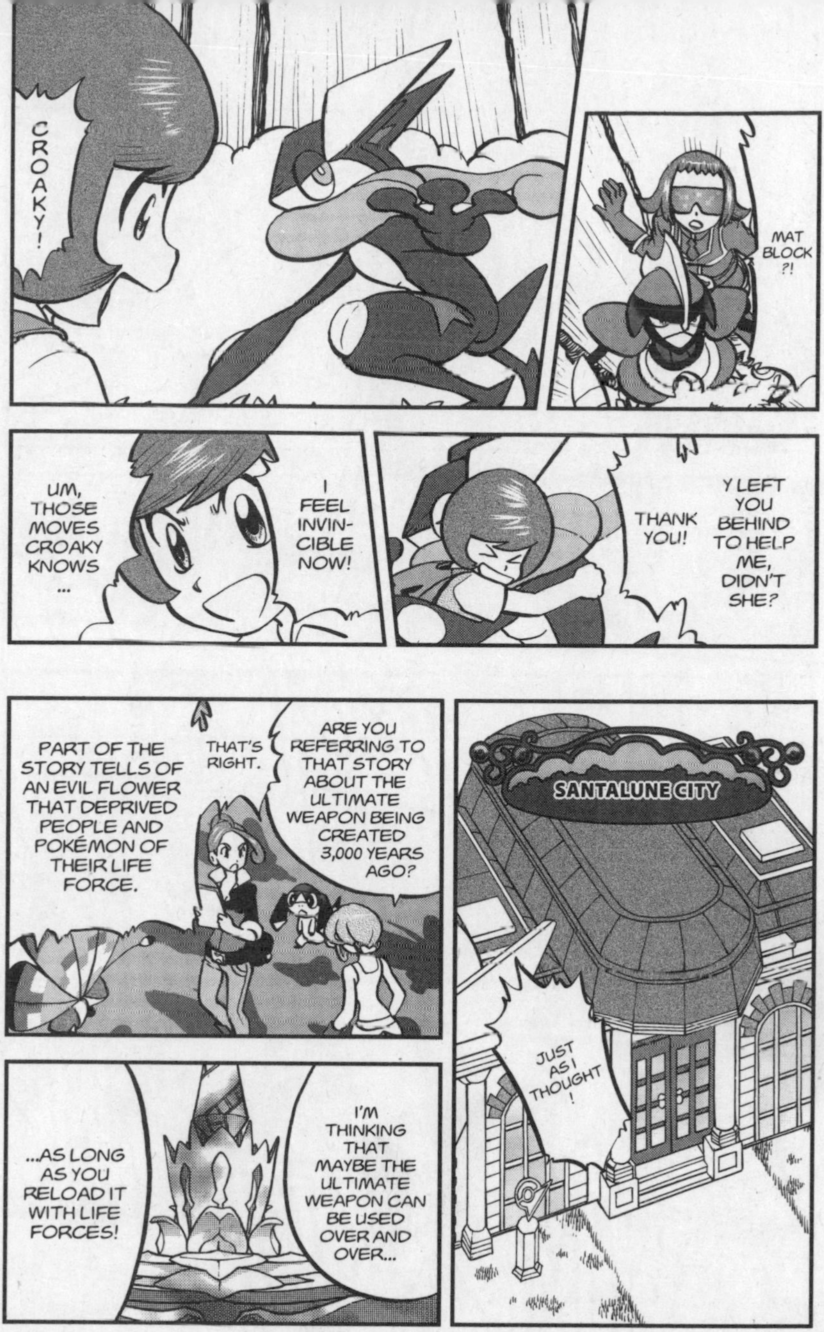
MAT BLOCK ?!
CROAKY!
Y LEFT YOU BEHIND TO HELP ME, DIDN'T SHE?
THANK YOU!
I FEEL INVIN-CIBLE NOW!
UM, THOSE MOVES CROAKY KNOWS ...
SANTALUNE CITY
JUST AS I THOUGHT !
ARE YOU REFERRING TO THAT STORY ABOUT THE ULTIMATE WEAPON BEING CREATED 3,000 YEARS AGO?
THAT'S RIGHT.
PART OF THE STORY TELLS OF AN EVIL FLOWER THAT DEPRIVED PEOPLE AND POKÉMON OF THEIR LIFE FORCE.
I'M THINKING THAT MAYBE THE ULTIMATE WEAPON CAN BE USED OVER AND OVER...
...AS LONG AS YOU RELOAD IT WITH LIFE FORCES!

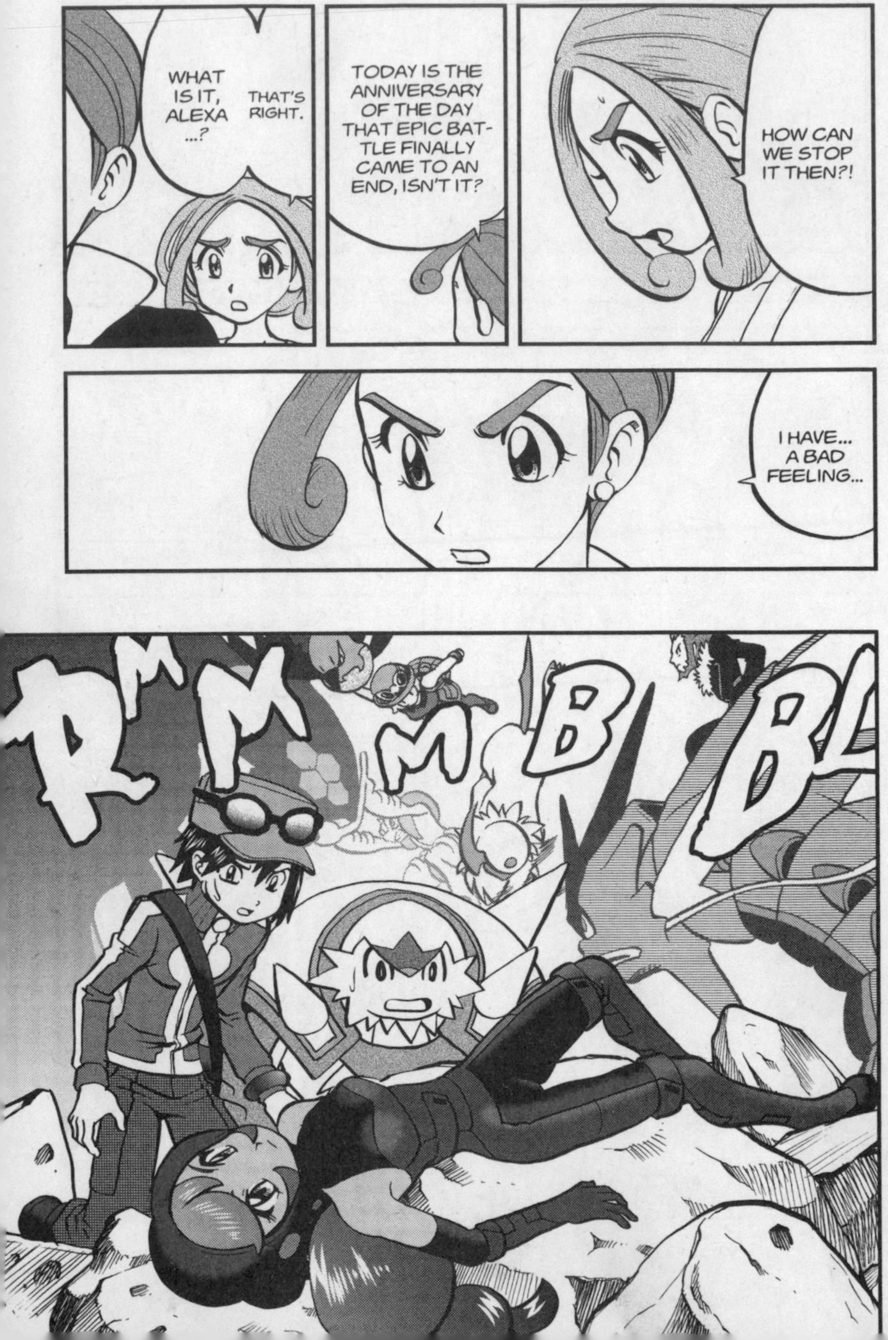
HOW CAN WE STOP IT THEN?!
TODAY IS THE ANNIVERSARY OF THE DAY THAT EPIC BATTLE FINALLY CAME TO AN END, ISN'T IT?
THAT'S RIGHT.
WHAT IS IT, ALEXA ...?
I HAVE... A BAD FEELING...

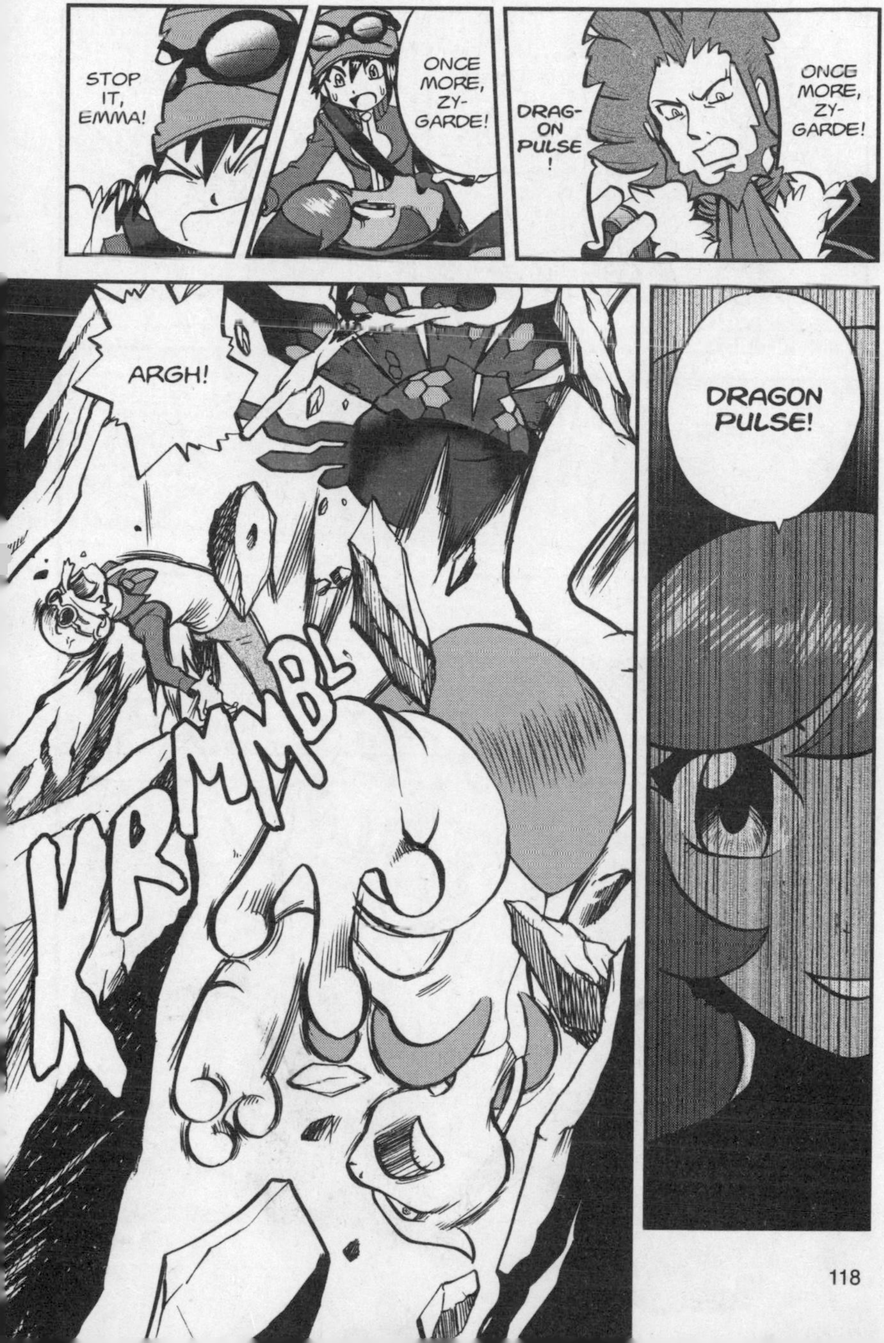
ONCE MORE, ZY-GARDE!
DRAG-ON PULSE!
ONCE MORE, ZY-GARDE!
STOP IT, EMMA!
DRAGON PULSE!
ARGH!
KRMMBL

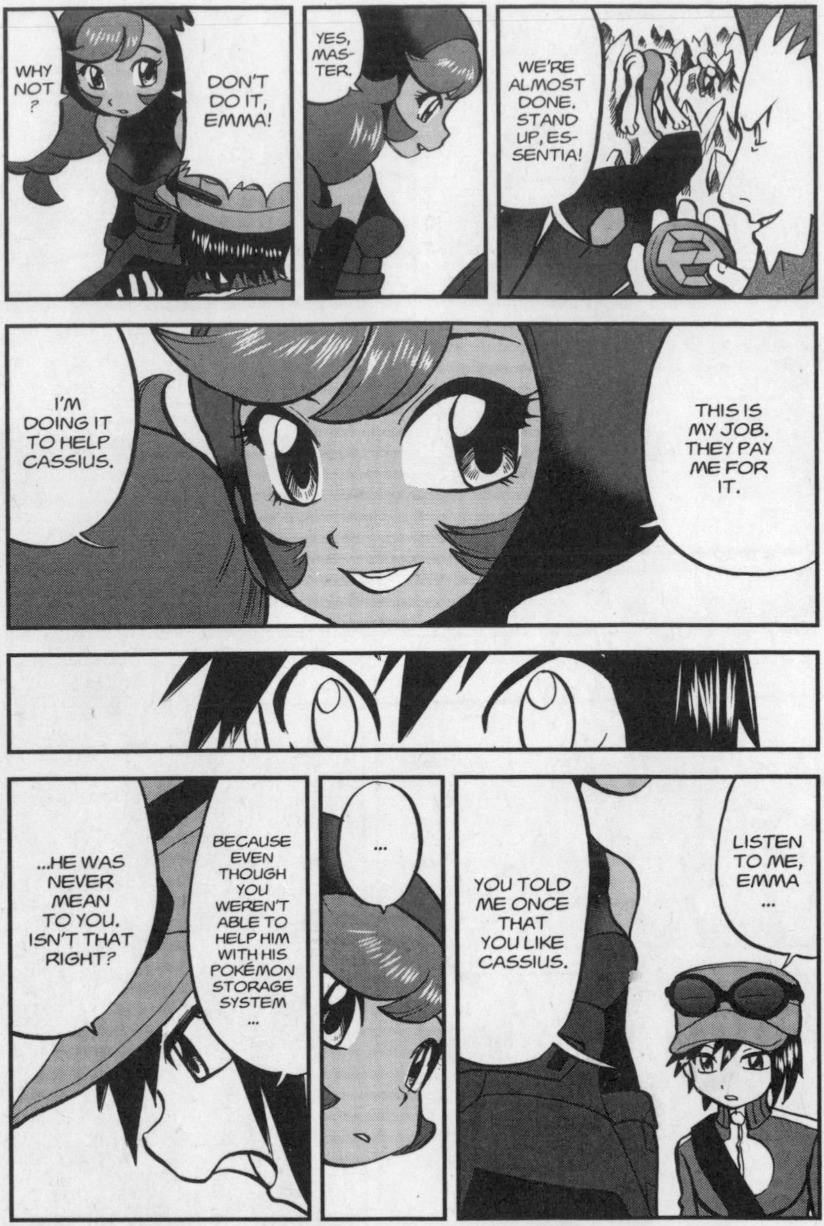

WE'RE ALMOST DONE. STAND UP, ES-SENTIA!
YES, MAS-TER.
DON'T DO IT, EMMA!
WHY NOT ?
THIS IS MY JOB. THEY PAY ME FOR IT.
I'M DOING IT TO HELP CASSIUS.
LISTEN TO ME, EMMA ...
YOU TOLD ME ONCE THAT YOU LIKE CASSIUS.
...
BECAUSE EVEN THOUGH YOU WEREN'T ABLE TO HELP HIM WITH HIS POKÉMON STORAGE SYSTEM ...
...HE WAS NEVER MEAN TO YOU. ISN'T THAT RIGHT?

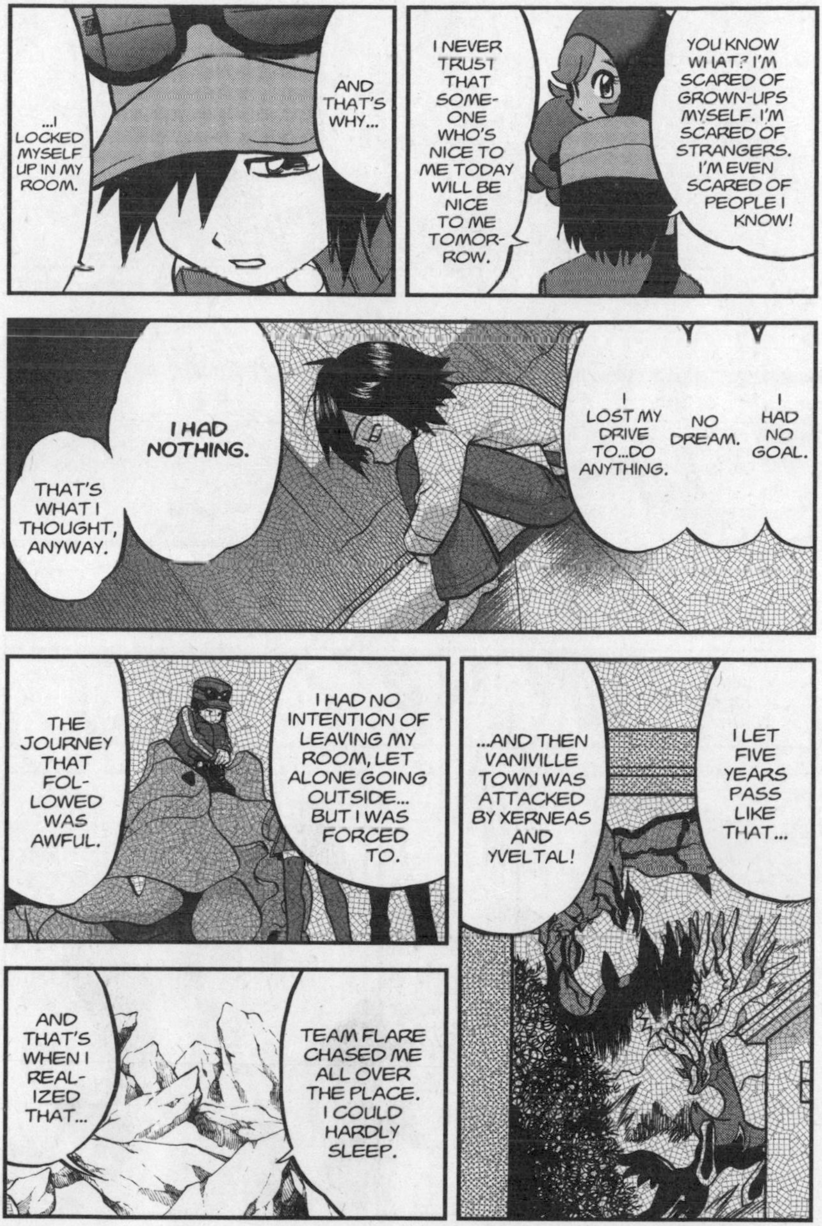
YOU KNOW WHAT? I'M SCARED OF GROWN-UPS MYSELF. I'M SCARED OF STRANGERS. I'M EVEN SCARED OF PEOPLE I KNOW!
I NEVER TRUST THAT SOMEONE WHO'S NICE TO ME TODAY WILL BE NICE TO ME TOMORROW.
AND THAT'S WHY...
...I LOCKED MYSELF UP IN MY ROOM.
I HAD NO GOAL.
NO DREAM.
I LOST MY DRIVE TO...DO ANYTHING.
I HAD NOTHING.
THAT'S WHAT I THOUGHT, ANYWAY.
I LET FIVE YEARS PASS LIKE THAT...
...AND THEN VANIVILLE TOWN WAS ATTACKED BY XERNEAS AND YVELTAL!
I HAD NO INTENTION OF LEAVING MY ROOM, LET ALONE GOING OUTSIDE... BUT I WAS FORCED TO.
THE JOURNEY THAT FOLLOWED WAS AWFUL.
TEAM FLARE CHASED ME ALL OVER THE PLACE. I COULD HARDLY SLEEP.
AND THAT'S WHEN I REALIZED THAT...

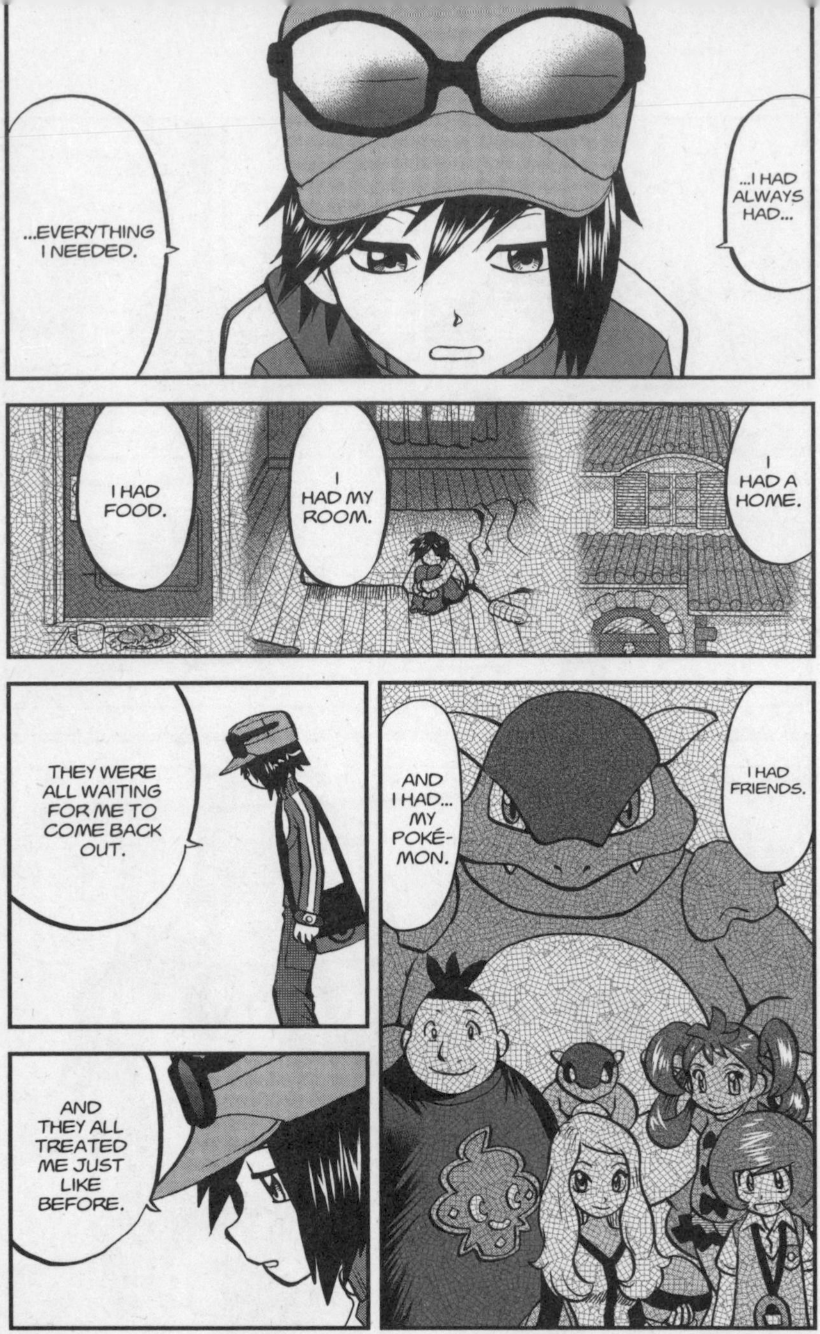
...I HAD ALWAYS HAD...
...EVERYTHING I NEEDED.
I HAD A HOME.
I HAD MY ROOM.
I HAD FOOD.
I HAD FRIENDS.
AND I HAD... MY POKÉMON.
THEY WERE ALL WAITING FOR ME TO COME BACK OUT.
AND THEY ALL TREATED ME JUST LIKE BEFORE.

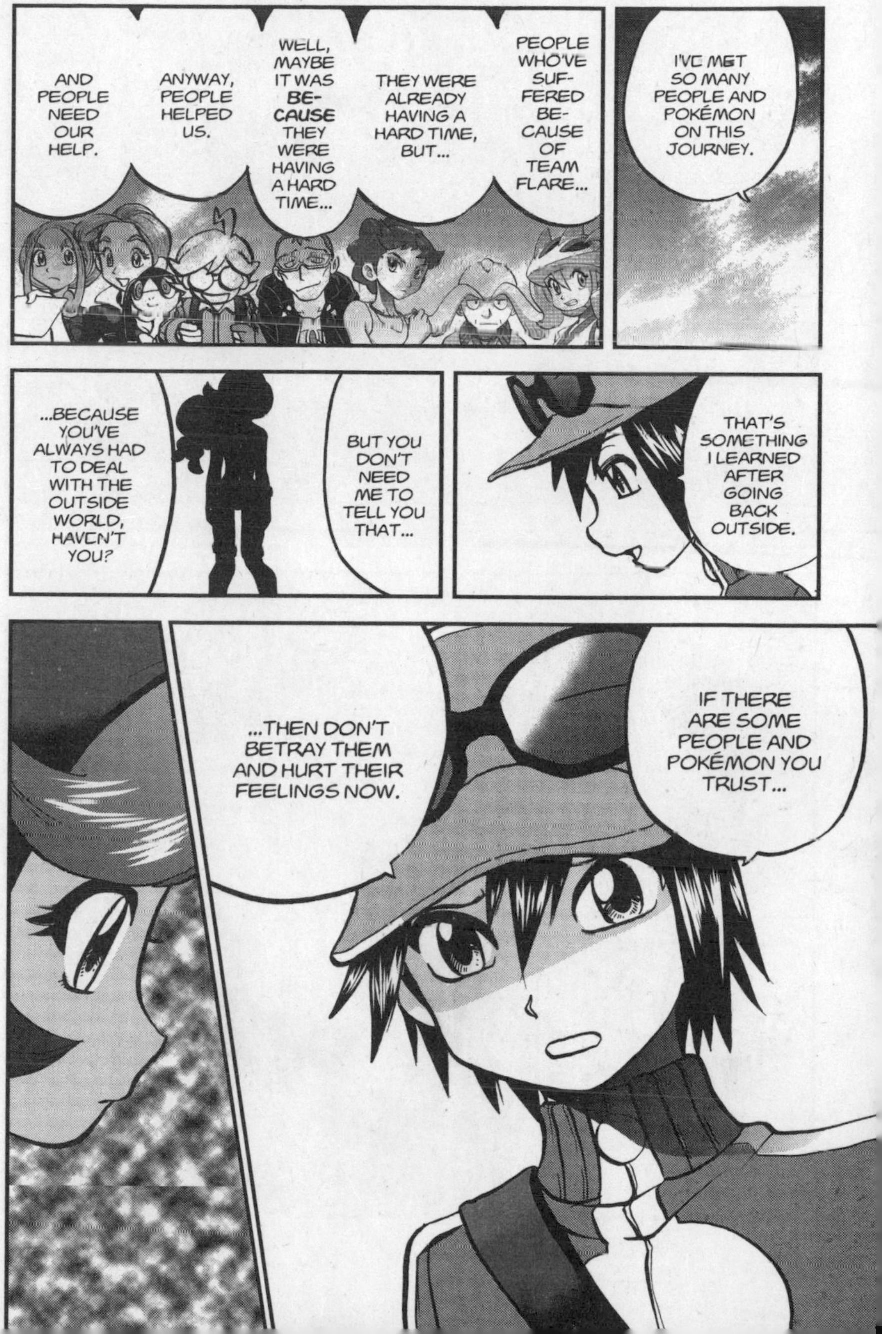
I'VE MET SO MANY PEOPLE AND POKÉMON ON THIS JOURNEY.
PEOPLE WHO'VE SUFFERED BECAUSE OF TEAM FLARE...
THEY WERE ALREADY HAVING A HARD TIME, BUT...
WELL, MAYBE IT WAS **BECAUSE** THEY WERE HAVING A HARD TIME...
ANYWAY, PEOPLE HELPED US.
AND PEOPLE NEED OUR HELP.
THAT'S SOMETHING I LEARNED AFTER GOING BACK OUTSIDE.
BUT YOU DON'T NEED ME TO TELL YOU THAT...
...BECAUSE YOU'VE ALWAYS HAD TO DEAL WITH THE OUTSIDE WORLD, HAVEN'T YOU?
IF THERE ARE SOME PEOPLE AND POKÉMON YOU TRUST...
...THEN DON'T BETRAY THEM AND HURT THEIR FEELINGS NOW.

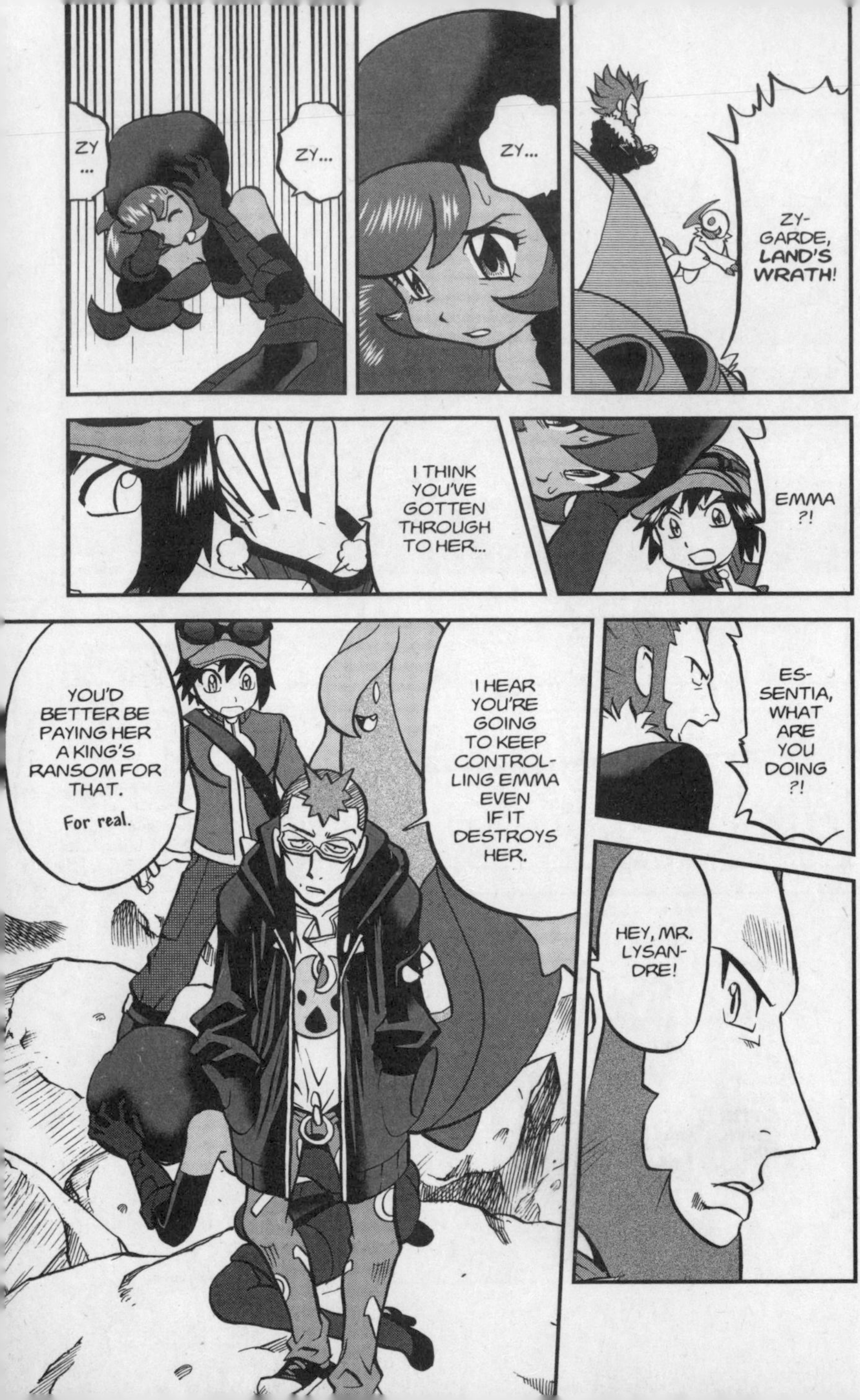
ZY-GARDE, LAND'S WRATH!
ZY...
ZY...
ZY ...
EMMA ?!
I THINK YOU'VE GOTTEN THROUGH TO HER...
ES-SENTIA, WHAT ARE YOU DOING ?!
HEY, MR. LYSANDRE!
I HEAR YOU'RE GOING TO KEEP CONTROL-LING EMMA EVEN IF IT DESTROYS HER.
YOU'D BETTER BE PAYING HER A KING'S RANSOM FOR THAT.
For real.

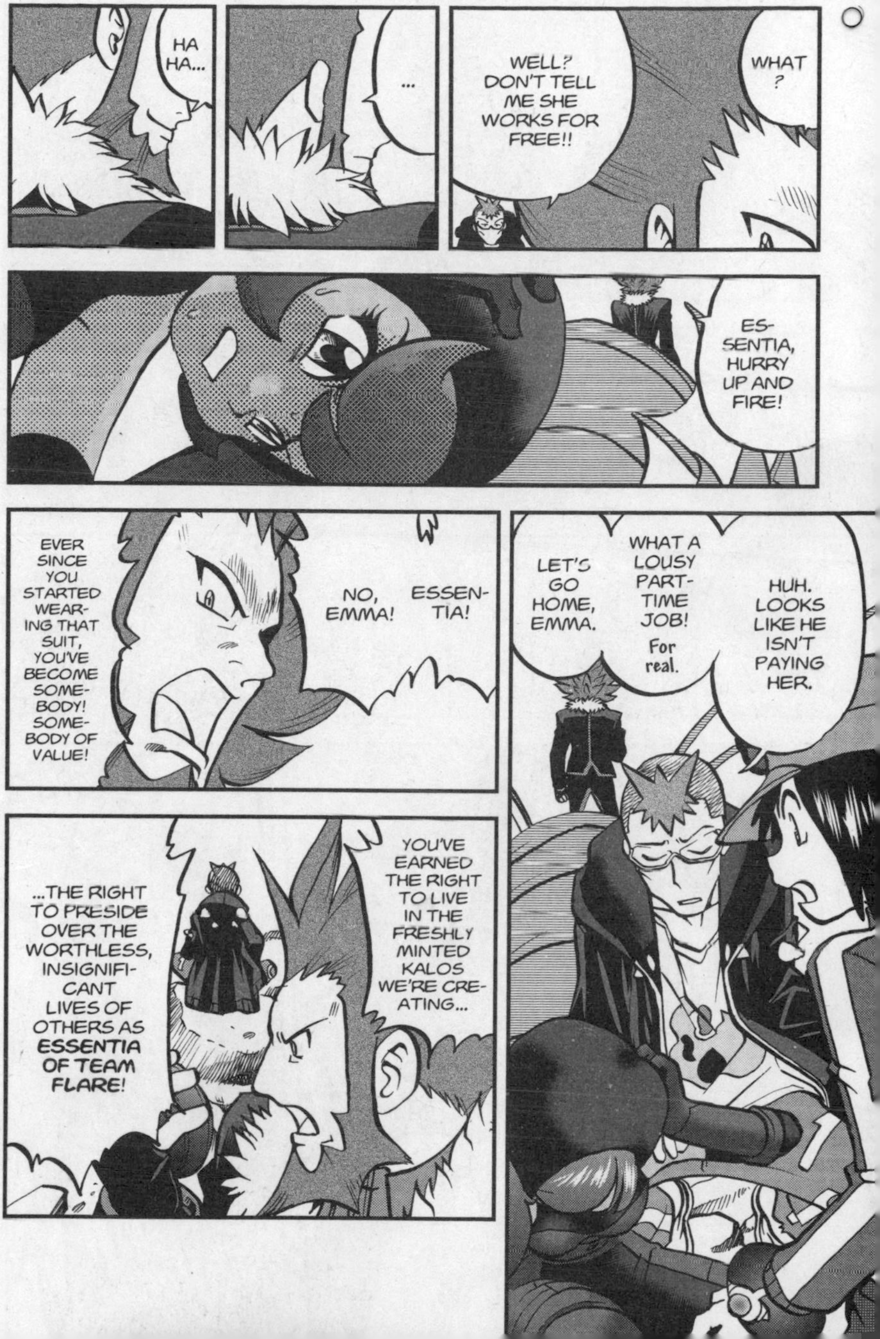
WHAT ?
WELL? DON'T TELL ME SHE WORKS FOR FREE!!
...
HA HA...
ES-SENTIA, HURRY UP AND FIRE!
HUH. LOOKS LIKE HE ISN'T PAYING HER.
WHAT A LOUSY PART-TIME JOB!
For real.
LET'S GO HOME, EMMA.
ESSEN-TIA!
NO, EMMA!
EVER SINCE YOU STARTED WEAR-ING THAT SUIT, YOU'VE BECOME SOME-BODY! SOME-BODY OF VALUE!
YOU'VE EARNED THE RIGHT TO LIVE IN THE FRESHLY MINTED KALOS WE'RE CRE-ATING...
...THE RIGHT TO PRESIDE OVER THE WORTHLESS, INSIGNIFI-CANT LIVES OF OTHERS AS **ESSENTIA OF TEAM FLARE**!

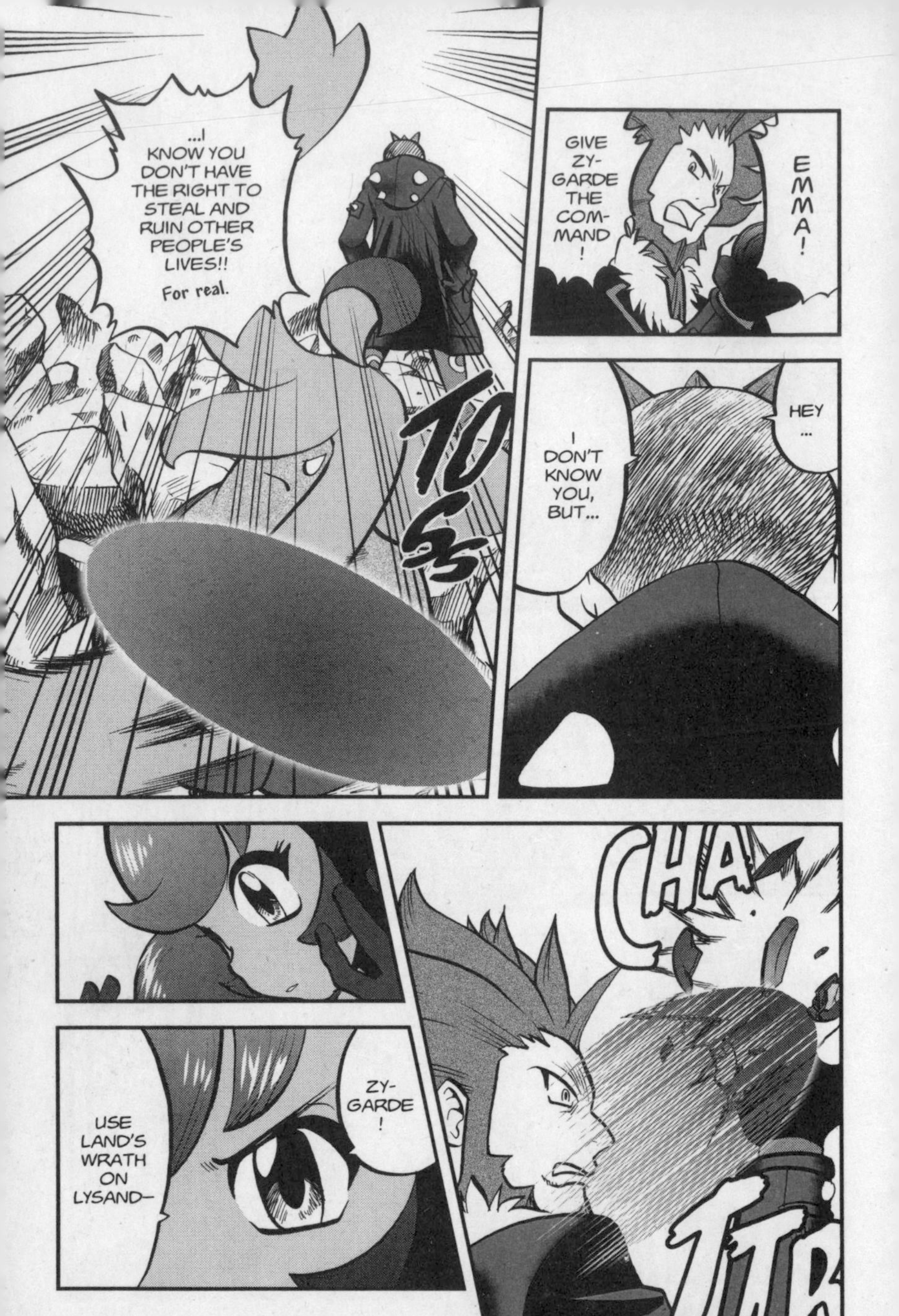
EMMA!
GIVE ZYGARDE THE COMMAND!
HEY...
I DON'T KNOW YOU, BUT...
...I KNOW YOU DON'T HAVE THE RIGHT TO STEAL AND RUIN OTHER PEOPLE'S LIVES!!
For real.
TOSS
CHA
TTR
ZYGARDE!
USE LAND'S WRATH ON LYSAND—

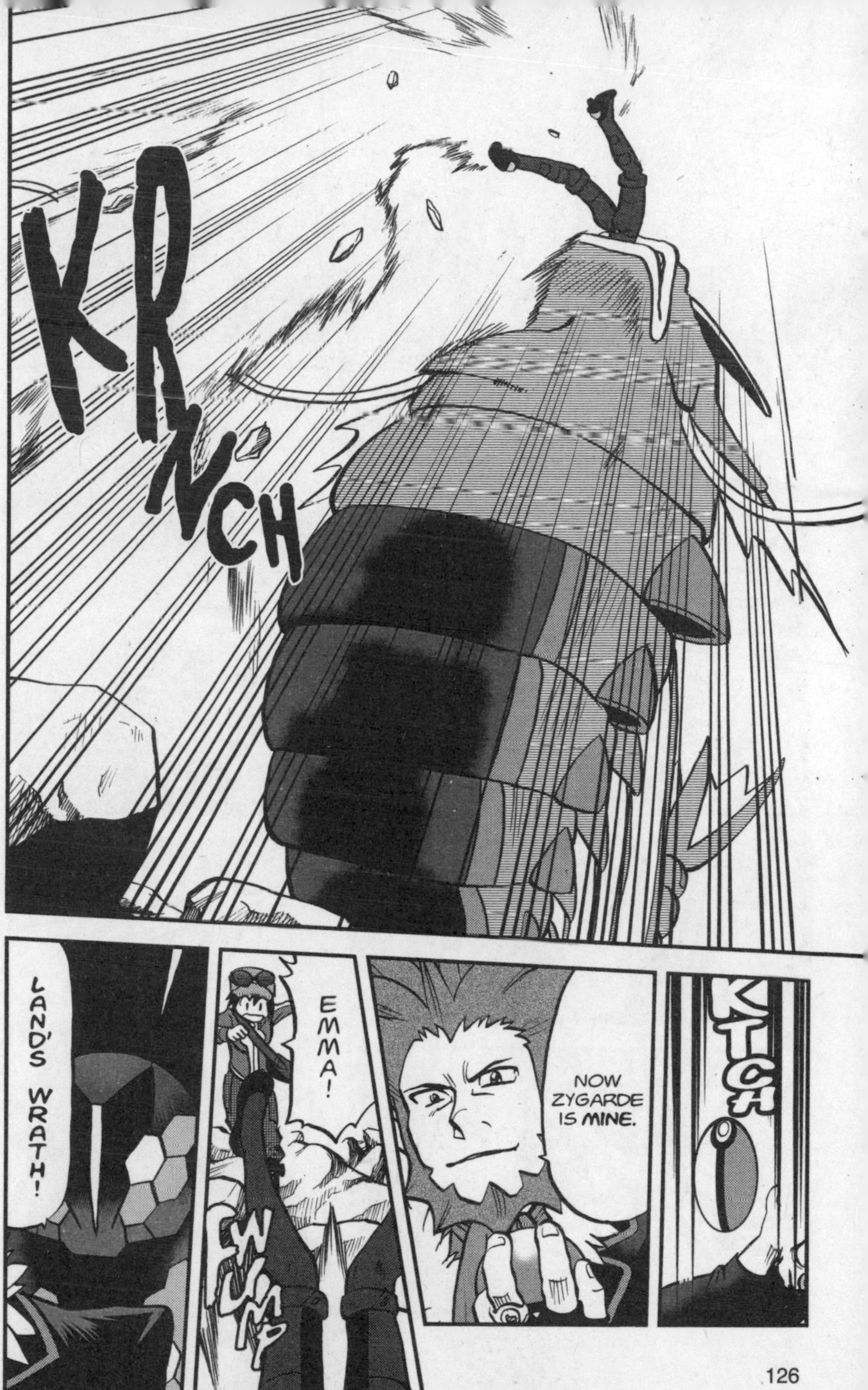
KRNCH
KTCH
NOW ZYGARDE IS MINE.
EMMA!
WUMP
LAND'S WRATH!

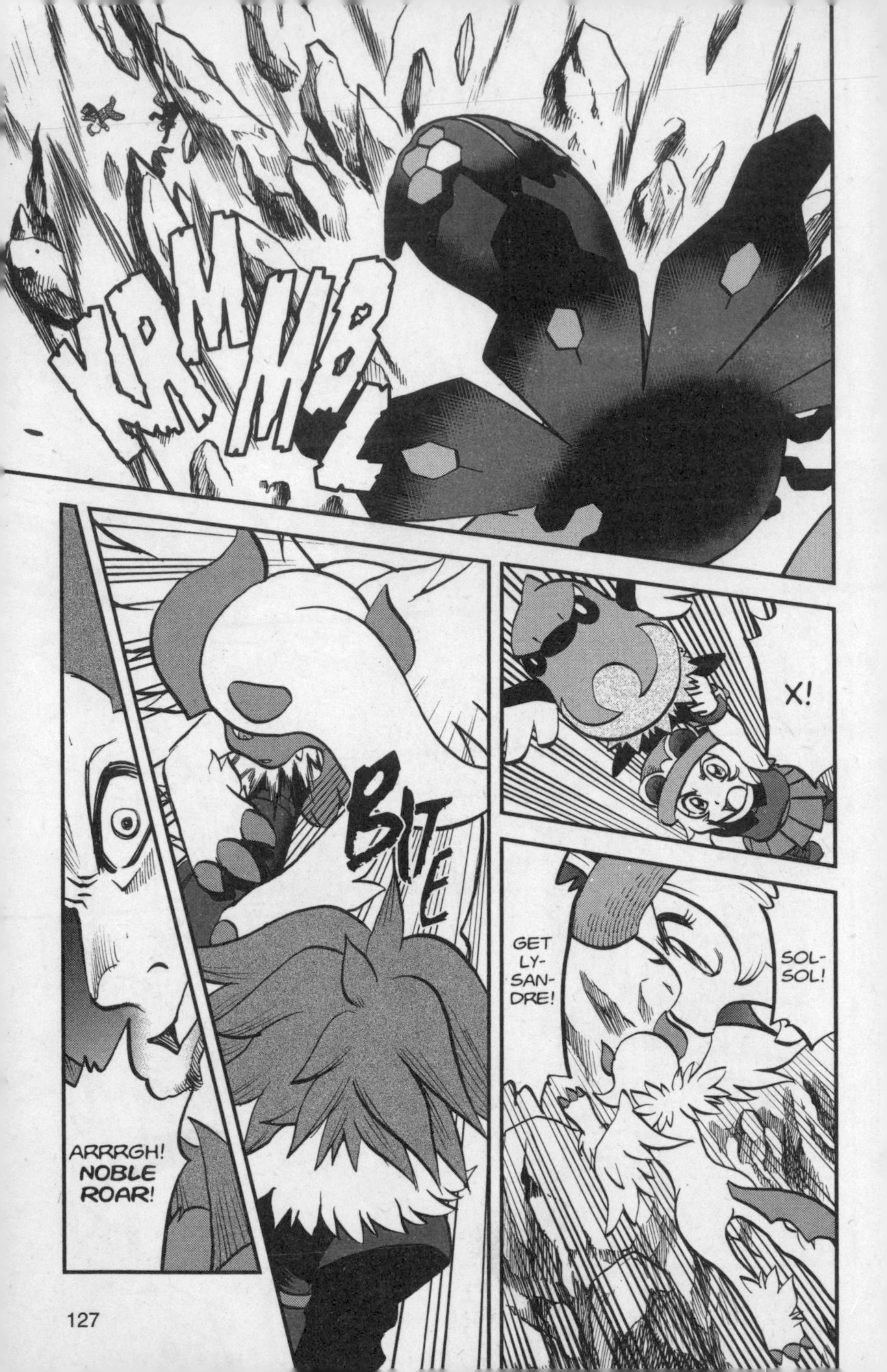
X!
SOL-SOL!
GET LY-SAN-DRE!
BITE
ARRRGH! NOBLE ROAR!

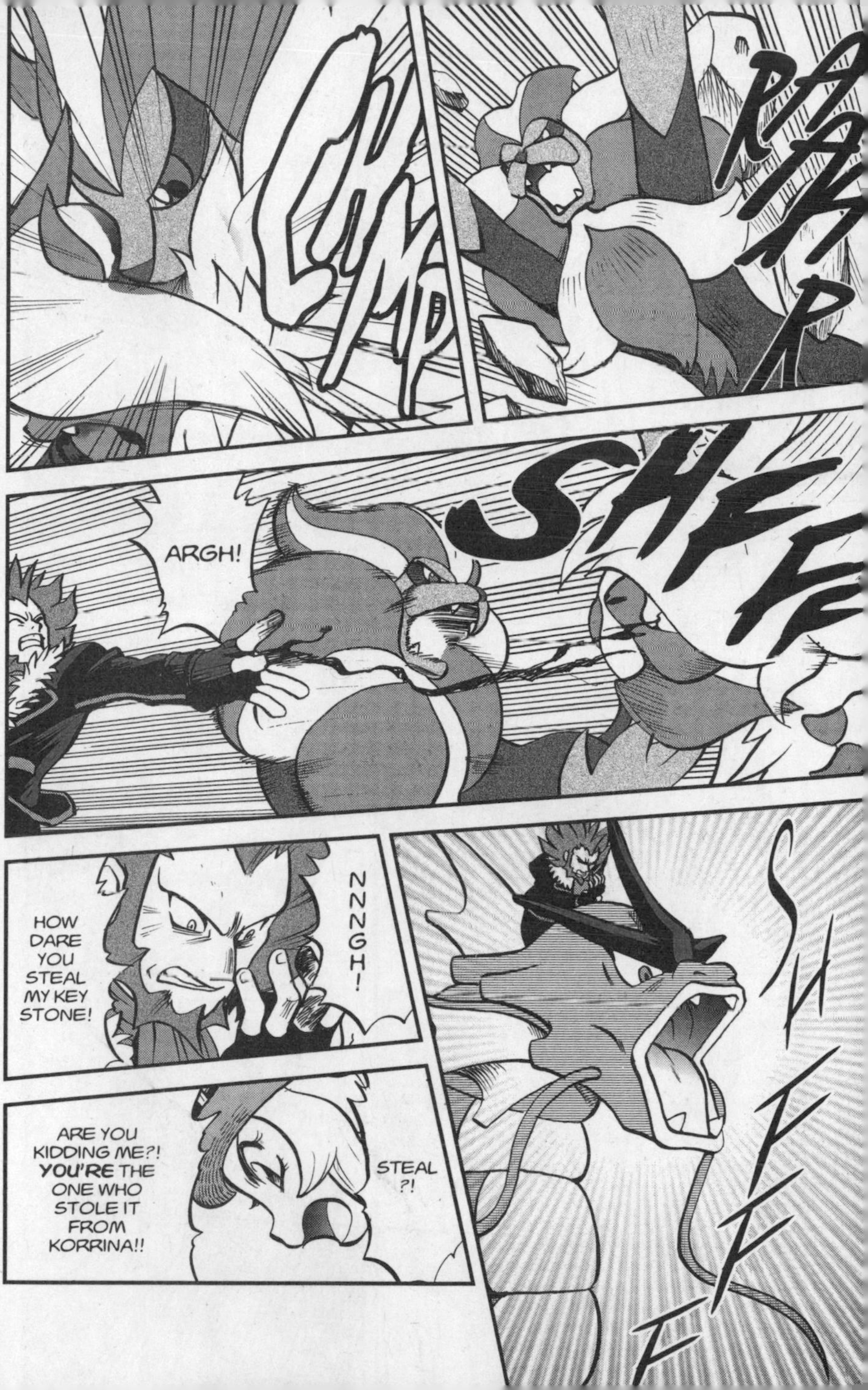
CHOMP
SHFF
ARGH!
NNNGH!
HOW DARE YOU STEAL MY KEY STONE!
STEAL?!
ARE YOU KIDDING ME?! **YOU'RE** THE ONE WHO STOLE IT FROM KORRINA!!

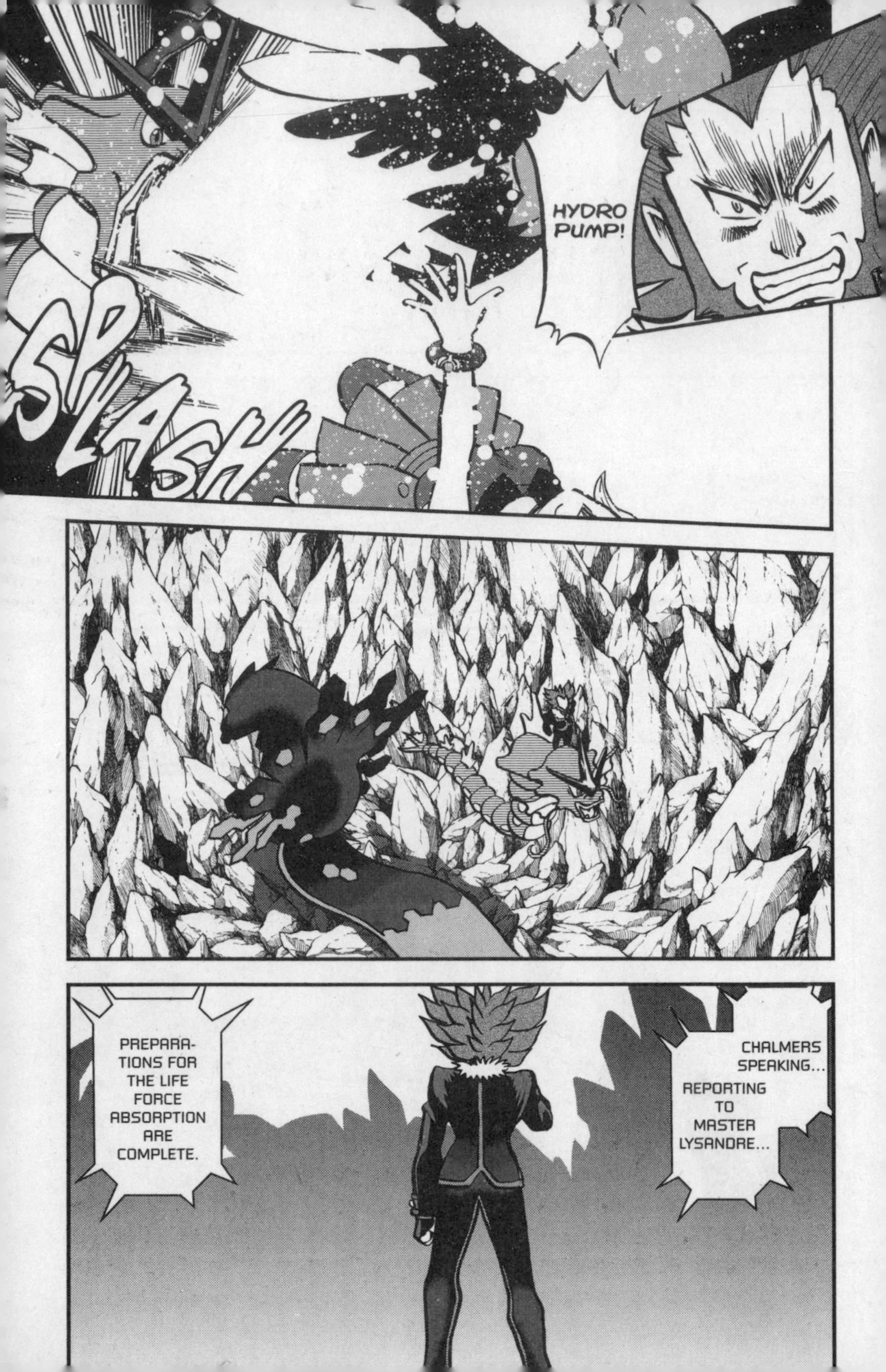
HYDRO PUMP!
SPLASH
CHALMERS SPEAKING... REPORTING TO MASTER LYSANDRE...
PREPARATIONS FOR THE LIFE FORCE ABSORPTION ARE COMPLETE.

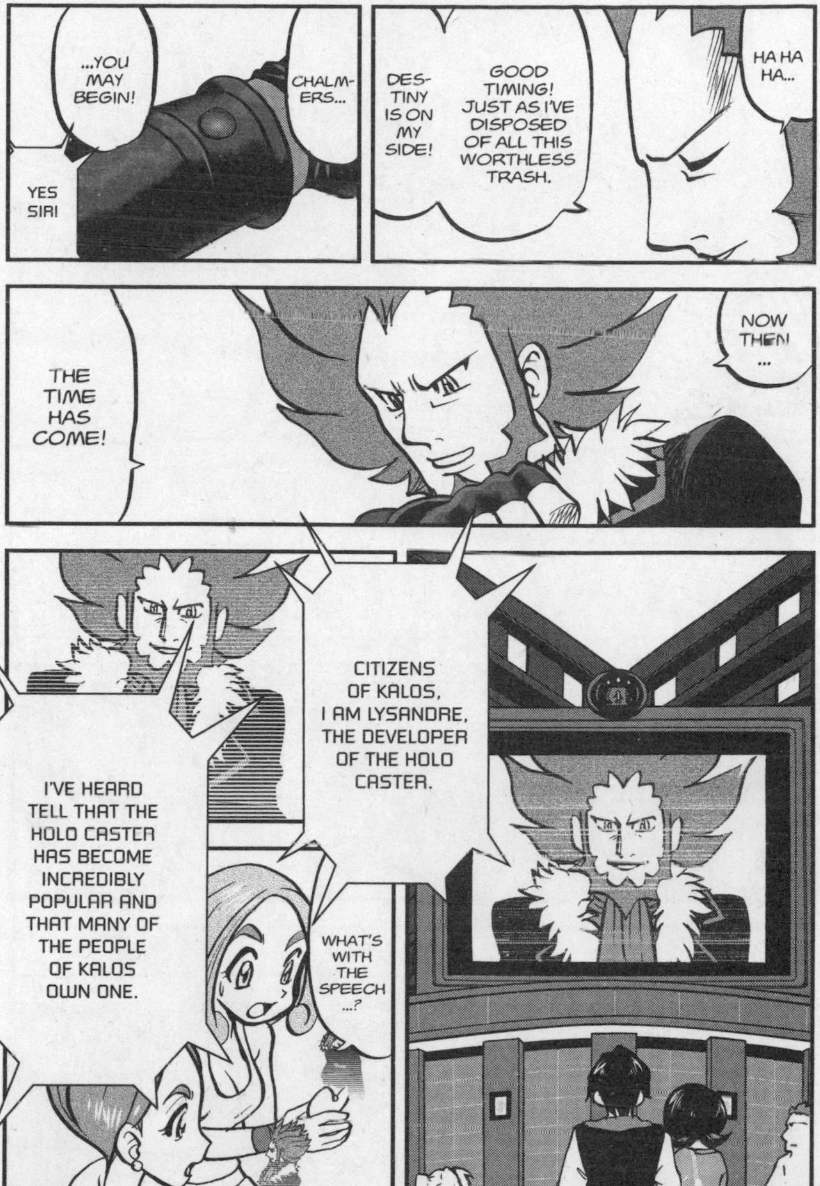
HA HA HA...
GOOD TIMING! JUST AS I'VE DISPOSED OF ALL THIS WORTHLESS TRASH.
DES-TINY IS ON MY SIDE!
CHALM-ERS...
...YOU MAY BEGIN!
YES SIR!
NOW THEN! ...
THE TIME HAS COME!
CITIZENS OF KALOS, I AM LYSANDRE, THE DEVELOPER OF THE HOLO CASTER.
I'VE HEARD TELL THAT THE HOLO CASTER HAS BECOME INCREDIBLY POPULAR AND THAT MANY OF THE PEOPLE OF KALOS OWN ONE.
WHAT'S WITH THE SPEECH ...?

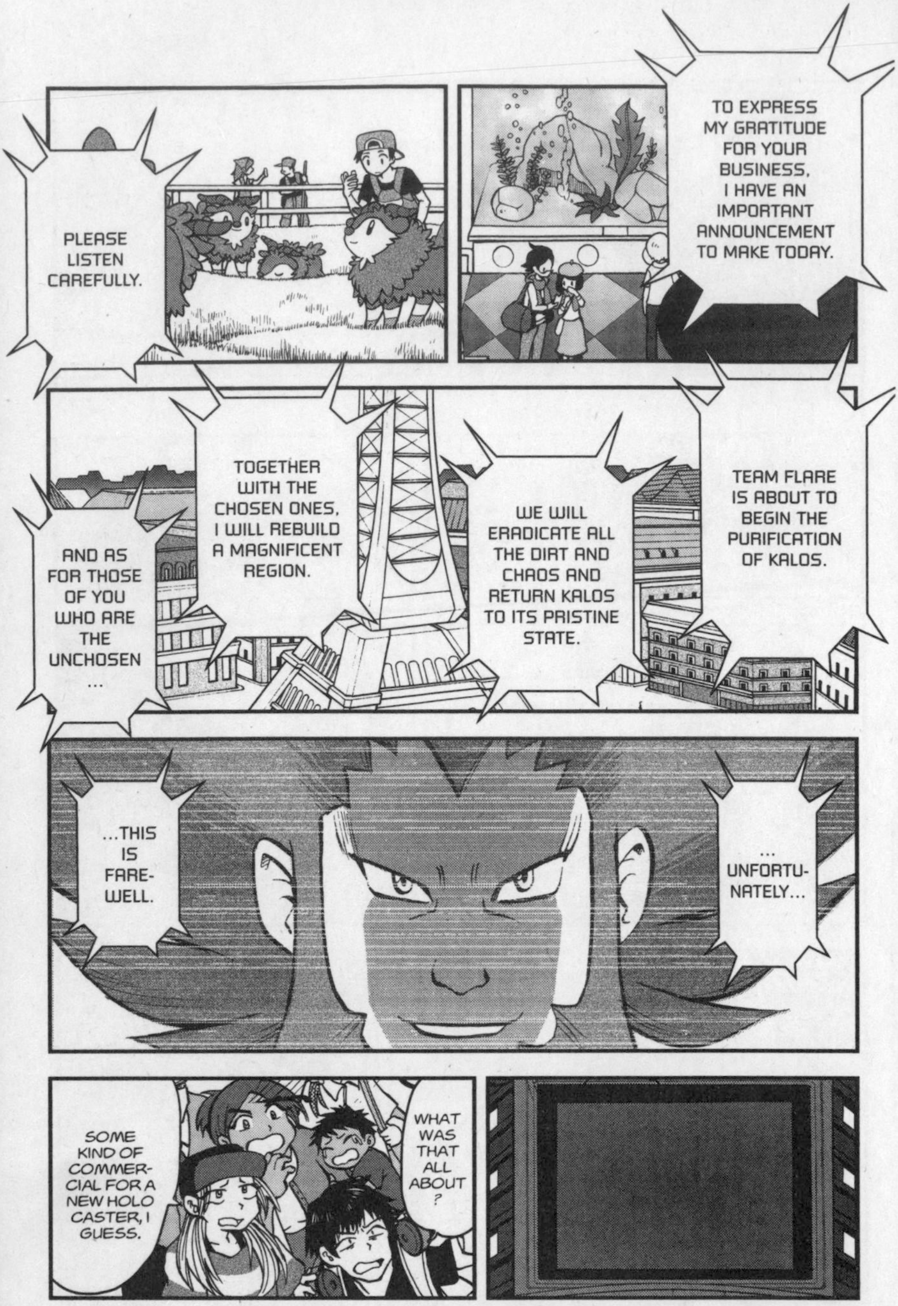
TO EXPRESS MY GRATITUDE FOR YOUR BUSINESS, I HAVE AN IMPORTANT ANNOUNCEMENT TO MAKE TODAY.
PLEASE LISTEN CAREFULLY.
TEAM FLARE IS ABOUT TO BEGIN THE PURIFICATION OF KALOS.
WE WILL ERADICATE ALL THE DIRT AND CHAOS AND RETURN KALOS TO ITS PRISTINE STATE.
TOGETHER WITH THE CHOSEN ONES, I WILL REBUILD A MAGNIFICENT REGION.
AND AS FOR THOSE OF YOU WHO ARE THE UNCHOSEN ...
... UNFORTU-NATELY...
...THIS IS FARE-WELL.
WHAT WAS THAT ALL ABOUT ?
SOME KIND OF COMMER-CIAL FOR A NEW HOLO CASTER, I GUESS.

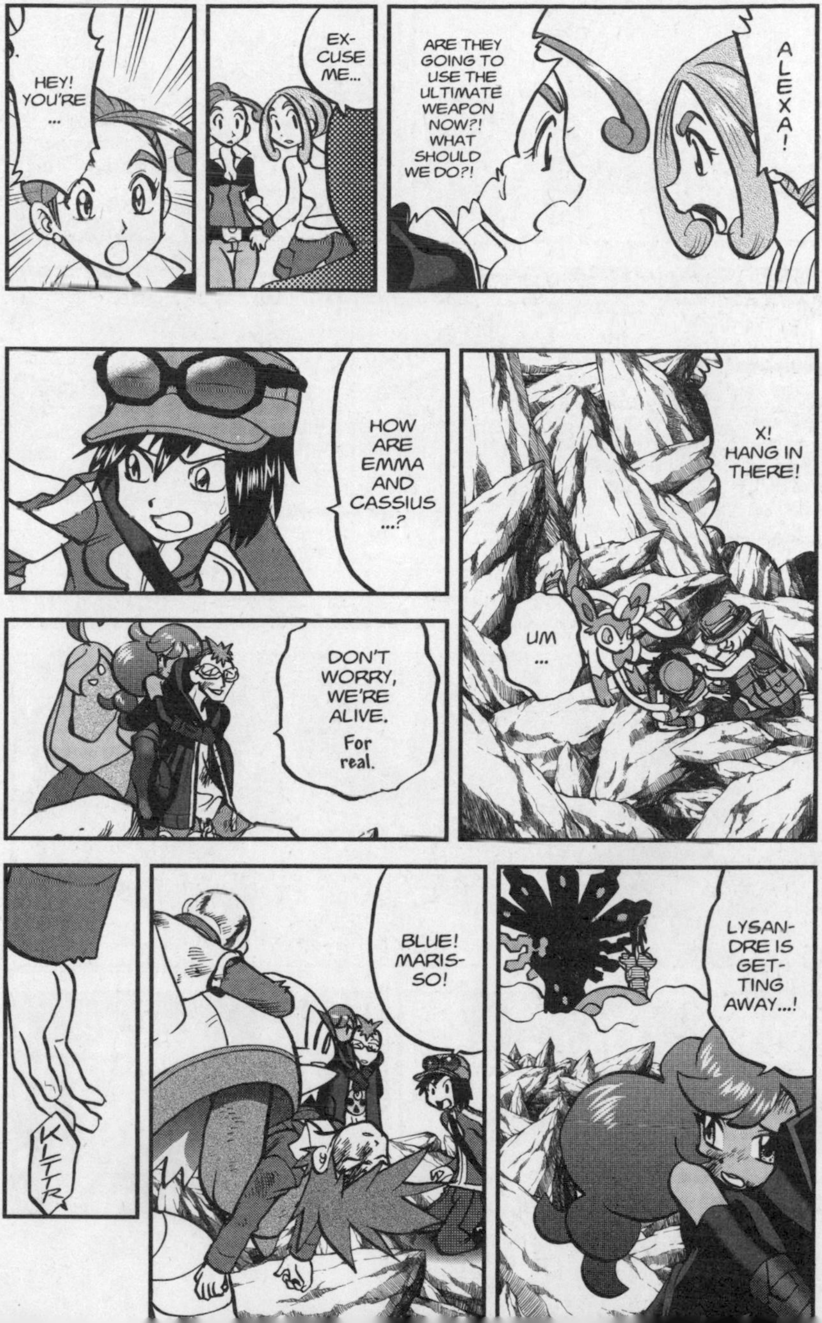
ALEXA!
ARE THEY GOING TO USE THE ULTIMATE WEAPON NOW?! WHAT SHOULD WE DO?!
EX-CUSE ME...
HEY! YOU'RE ...
X! HANG IN THERE!
UM ...
HOW ARE EMMA AND CASSIUS ...?
DON'T WORRY, WE'RE ALIVE. For real.
LYSAN-DRE IS GET-TING AWAY...!
BLUE! MARIS-SO!
KLTTR

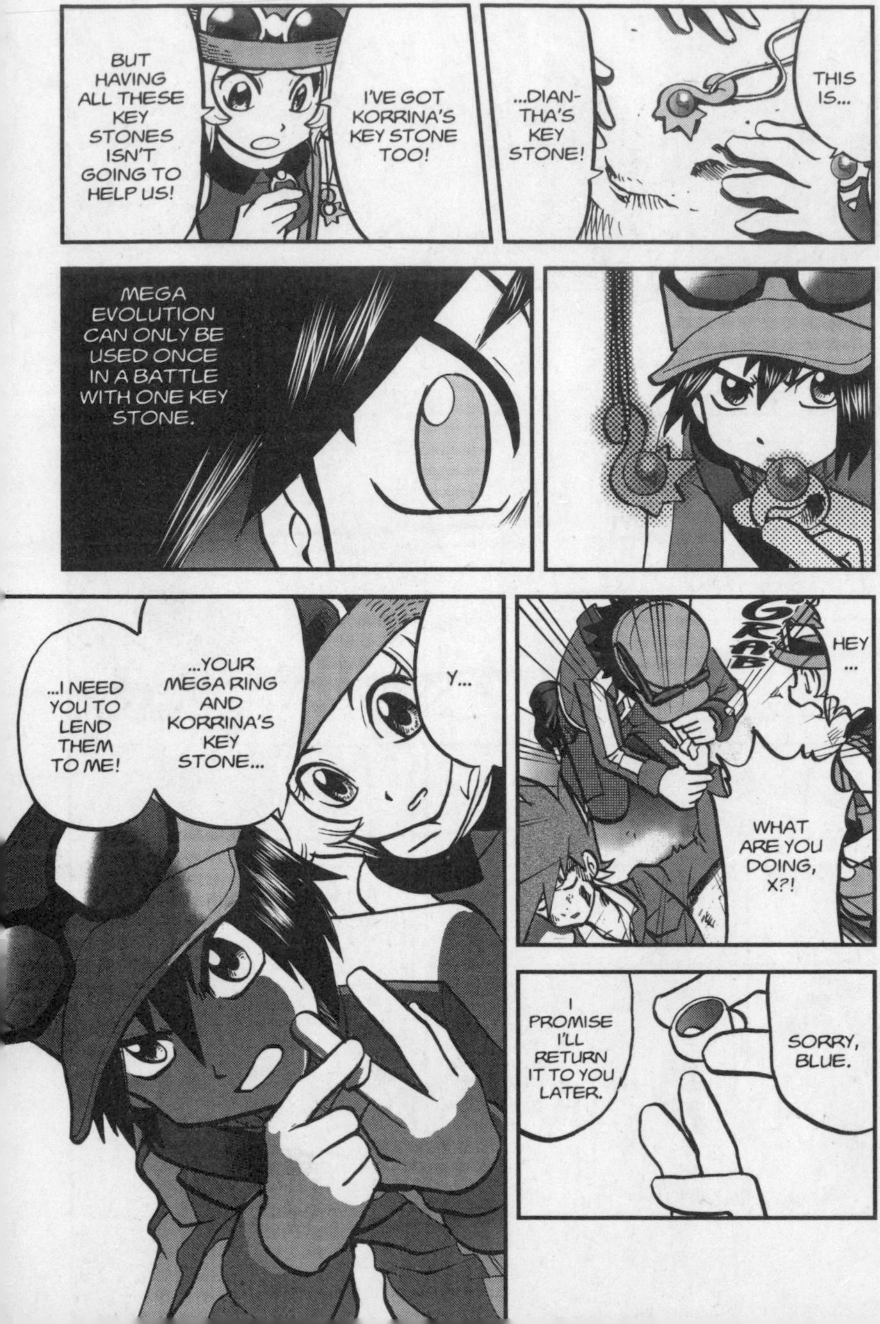
THIS IS...
...DIANTHA'S KEY STONE!
I'VE GOT KORRINA'S KEY STONE TOO!
BUT HAVING ALL THESE KEY STONES ISN'T GOING TO HELP US!
MEGA EVOLUTION CAN ONLY BE USED ONCE IN A BATTLE WITH ONE KEY STONE.
GRAB
HEY...
WHAT ARE YOU DOING, X?!
SORRY, BLUE.
I PROMISE I'LL RETURN IT TO YOU LATER.
Y...
...YOUR MEGA RING AND KORRINA'S KEY STONE...
...I NEED YOU TO LEND THEM TO ME!

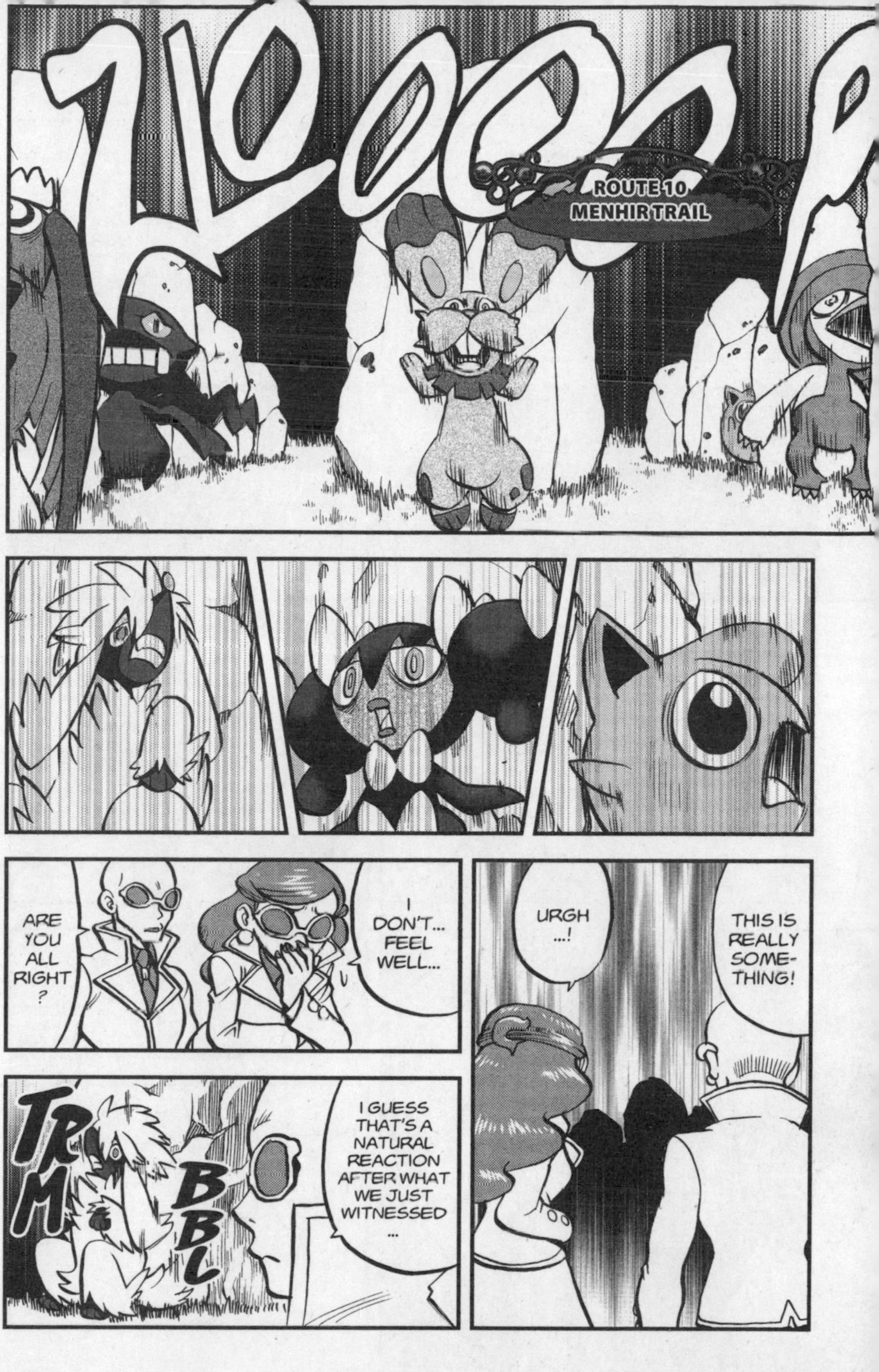
ROUTE 10
MENHIR TRAIL
THIS IS REALLY SOME-THING!
URGH...!
I DON'T... FEEL WELL...
ARE YOU ALL RIGHT?
I GUESS THAT'S A NATURAL REACTION AFTER WHAT WE JUST WITNESSED...
BBL
TRM

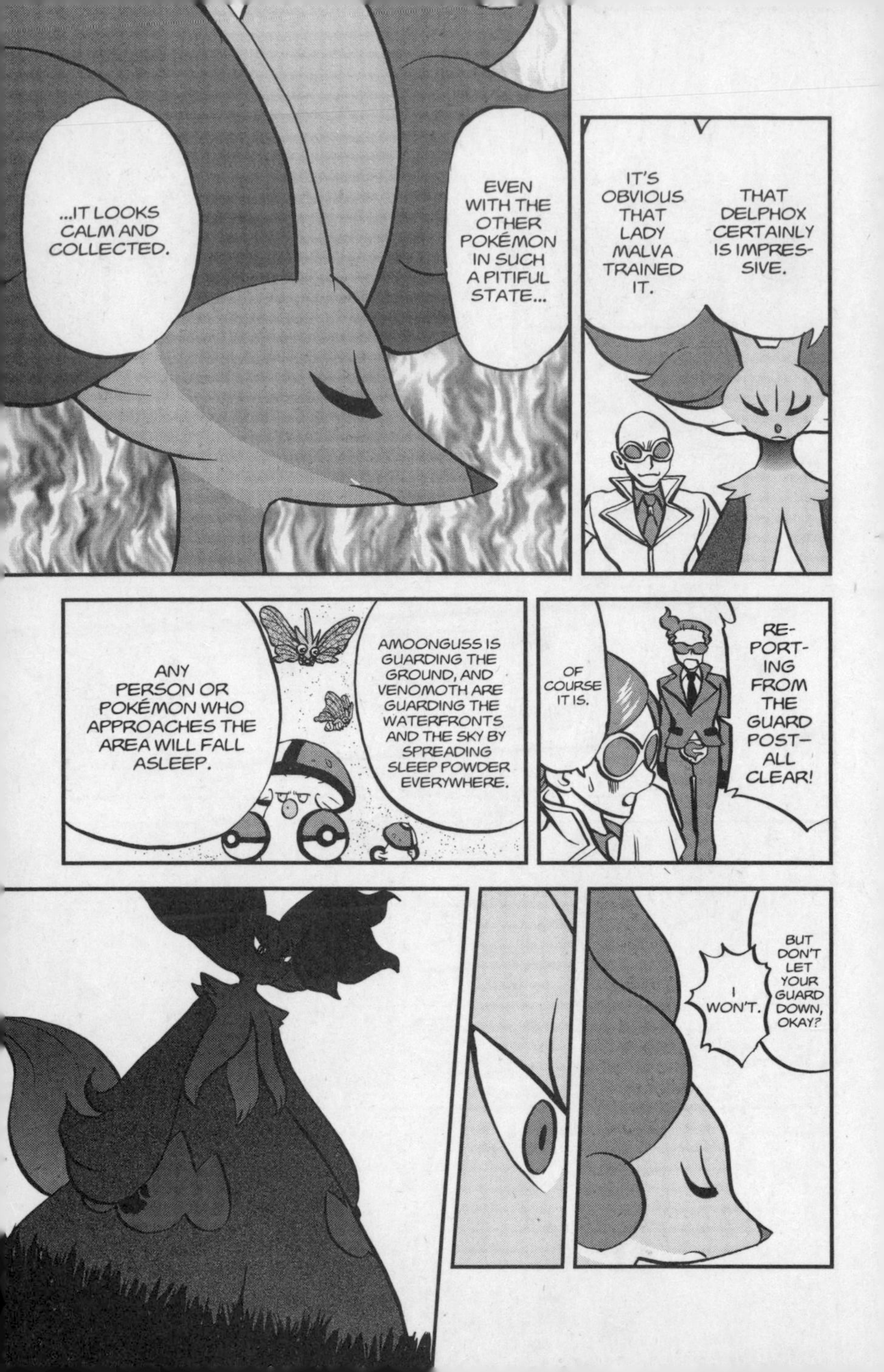
THAT DELPHOX CERTAINLY IS IMPRESSIVE.
IT'S OBVIOUS THAT LADY MALVA TRAINED IT.
EVEN WITH THE OTHER POKÉMON IN SUCH A PITIFUL STATE...
...IT LOOKS CALM AND COLLECTED.
REPORTING FROM THE GUARD POST—ALL CLEAR!
OF COURSE IT IS.
AMOONGUSS IS GUARDING THE GROUND, AND VENOMOTH ARE GUARDING THE WATERFRONTS AND THE SKY BY SPREADING SLEEP POWDER EVERYWHERE.
ANY PERSON OR POKÉMON WHO APPROACHES THE AREA WILL FALL ASLEEP.
BUT DON'T LET YOUR GUARD DOWN, OKAY?
I WON'T.

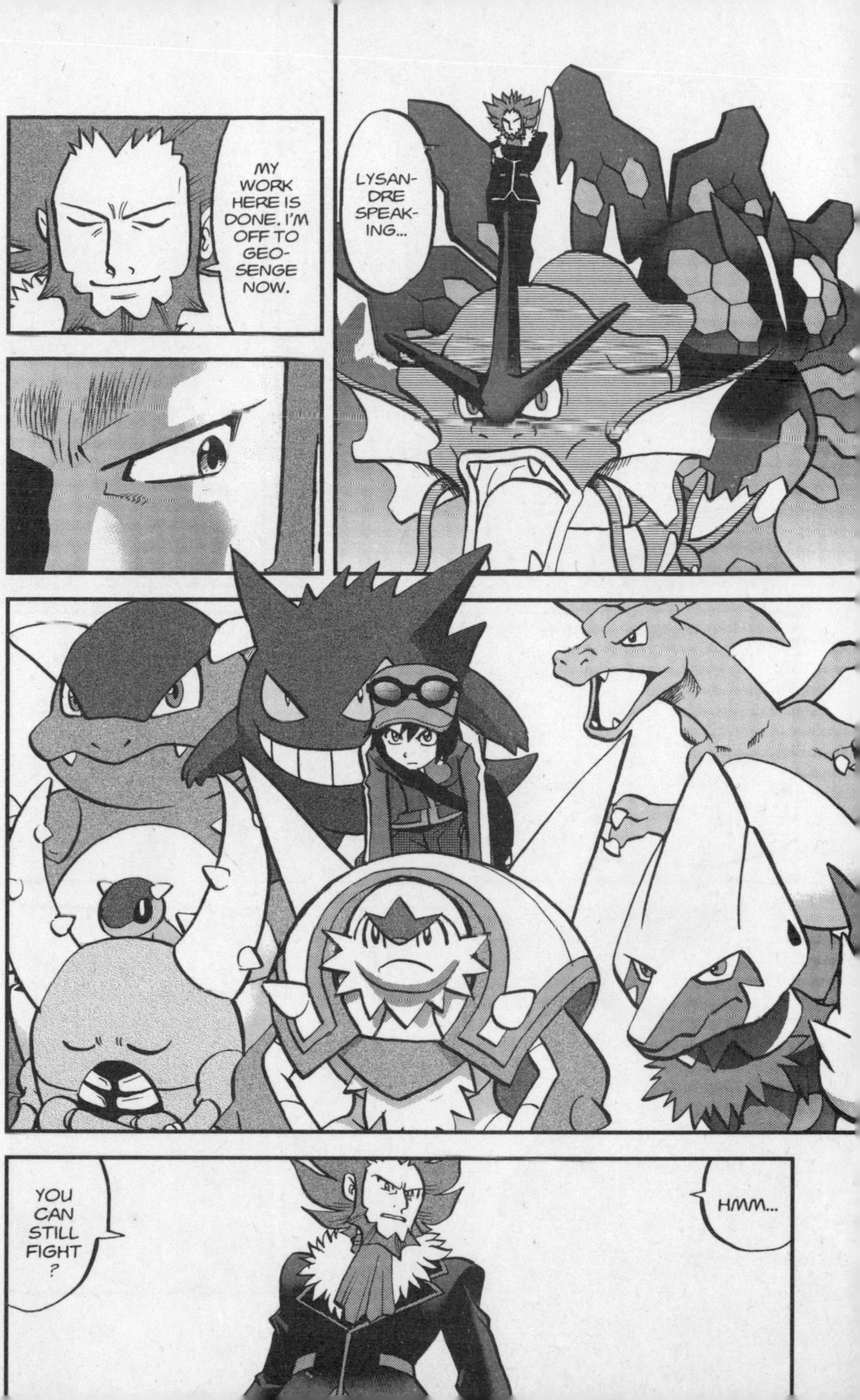
LYSAN-DRE SPEAK-ING...
MY WORK HERE IS DONE. I'M OFF TO GEO-SENGE NOW.
HMM...
YOU CAN STILL FIGHT?

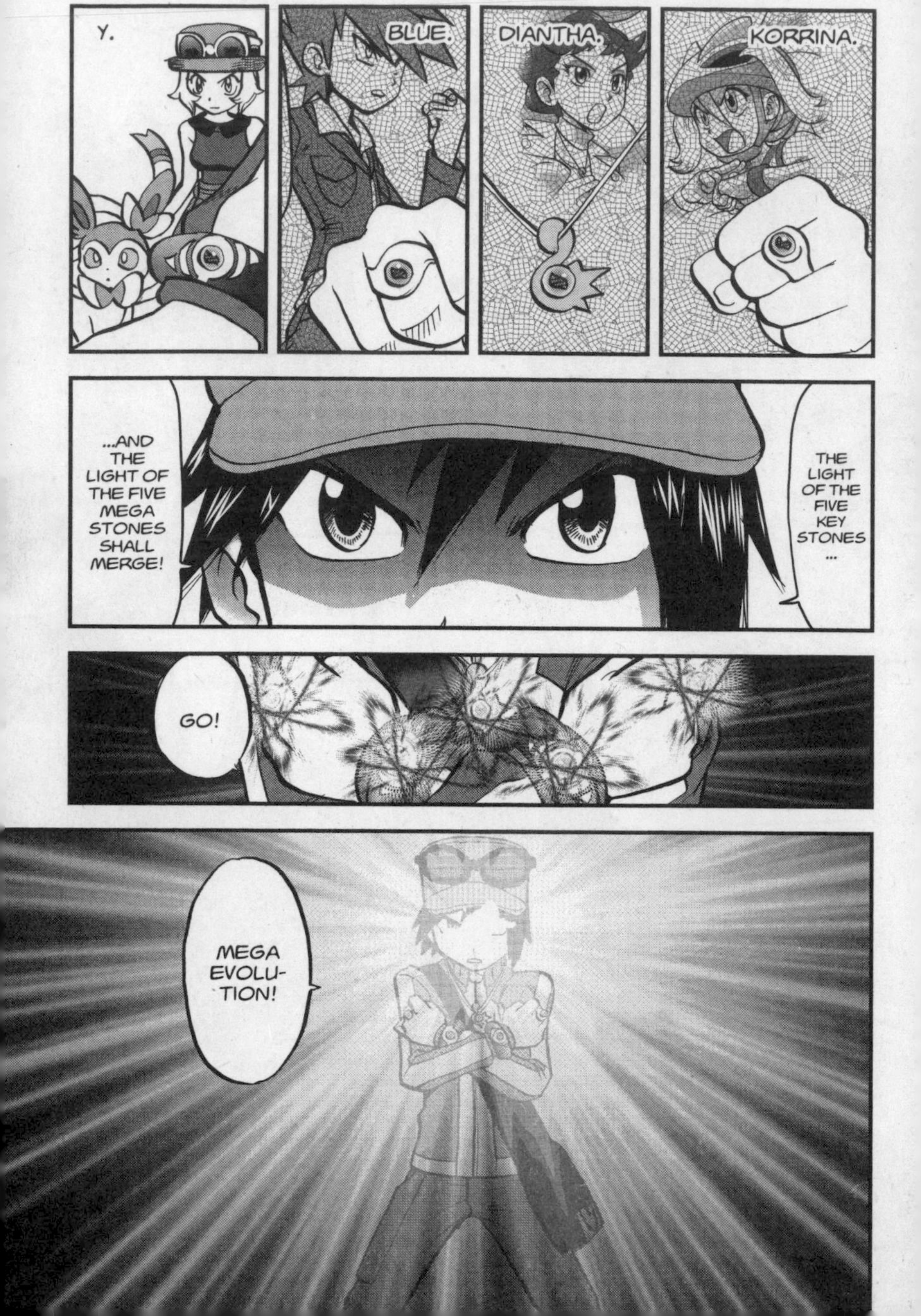
KORRINA.
DIANTHA.
BLUE.
Y.
THE LIGHT OF THE FIVE KEY STONES...
...AND THE LIGHT OF THE FIVE MEGA STONES SHALL MERGE!
GO!
MEGA EVOLU-TION!

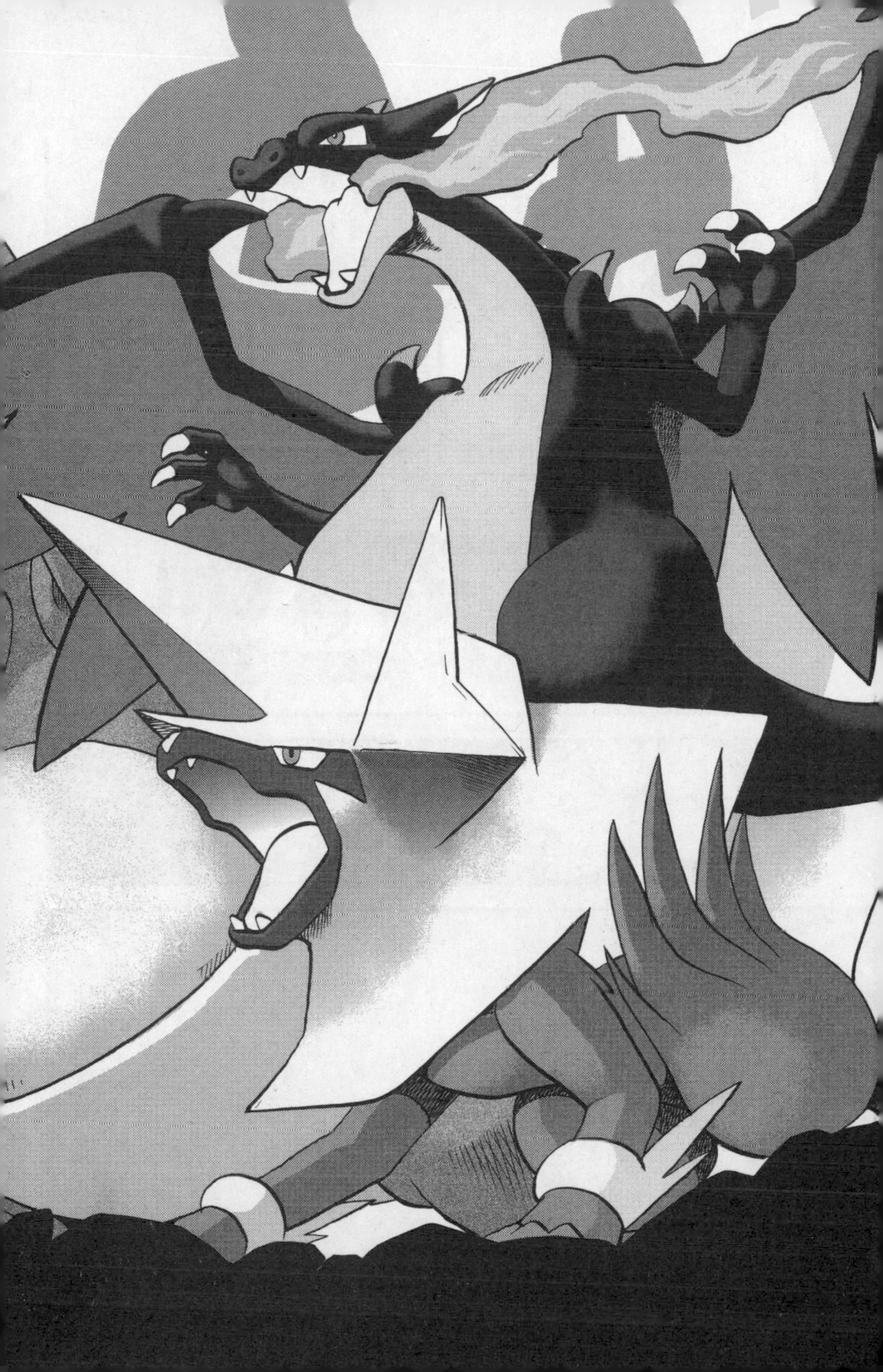

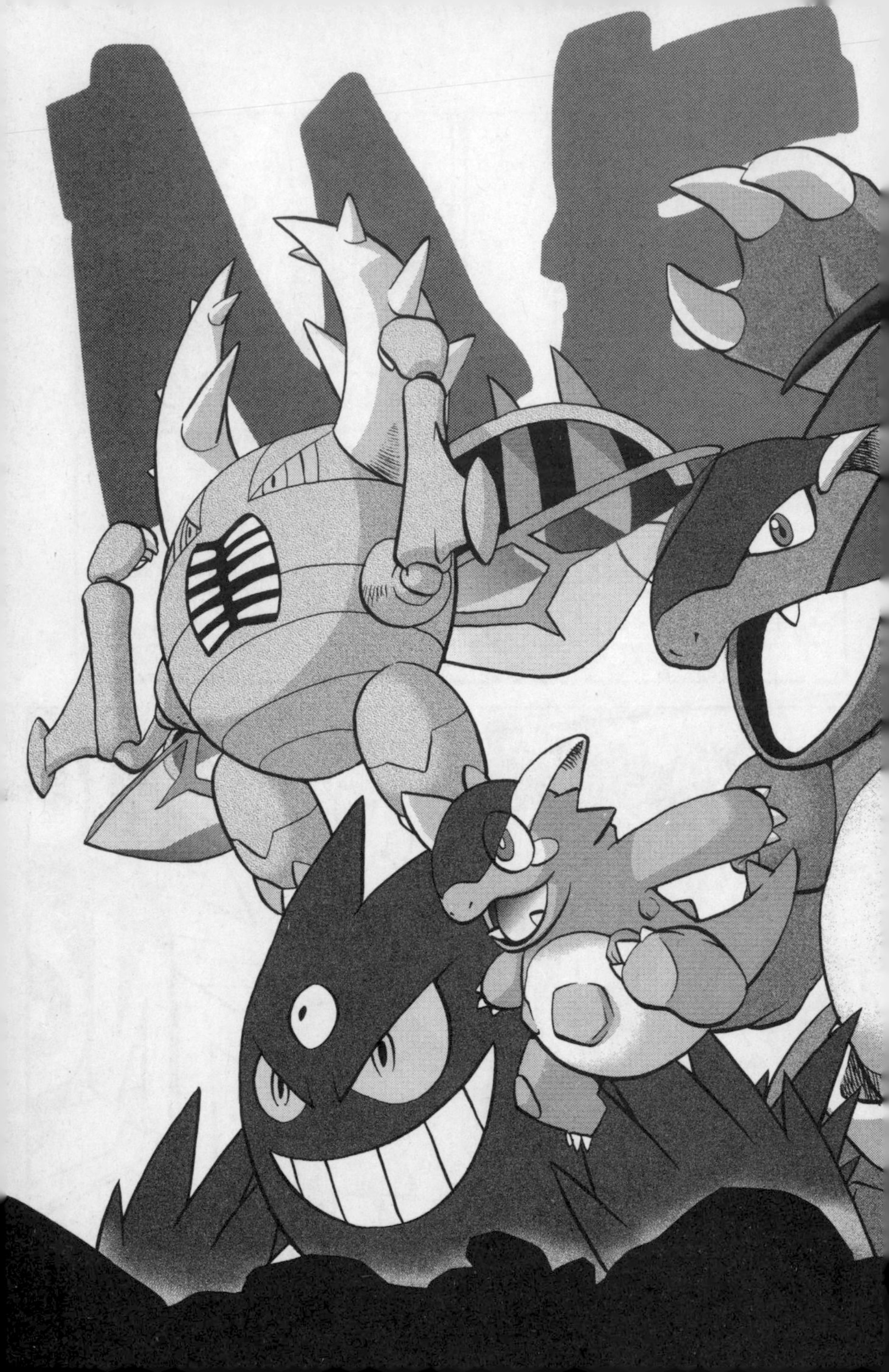

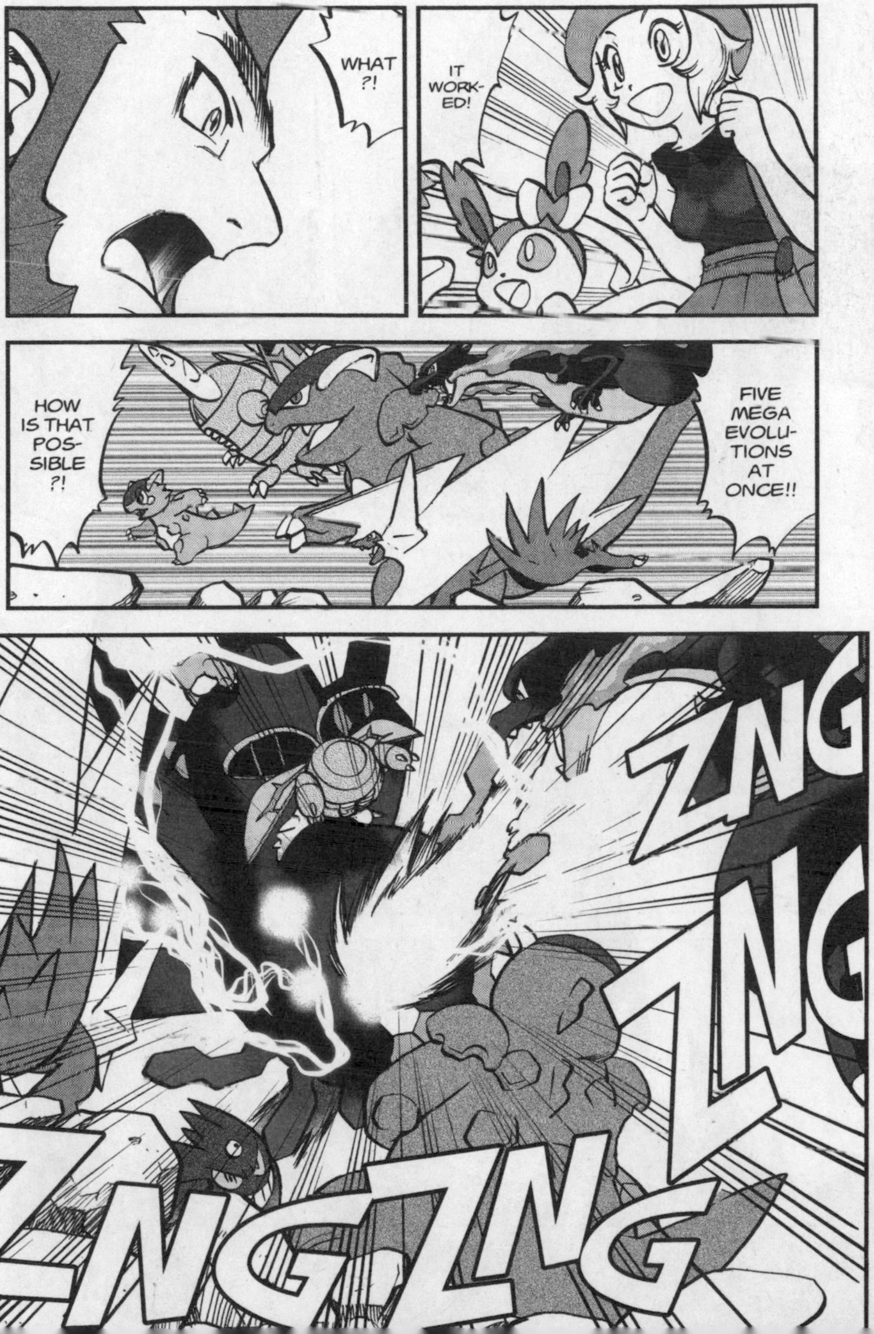
IT WORKED!
WHAT?!
FIVE MEGA EVOLUTIONS AT ONCE!!
HOW IS THAT POSSIBLE?!
ZNG
ZNG
ZNG
ZNG

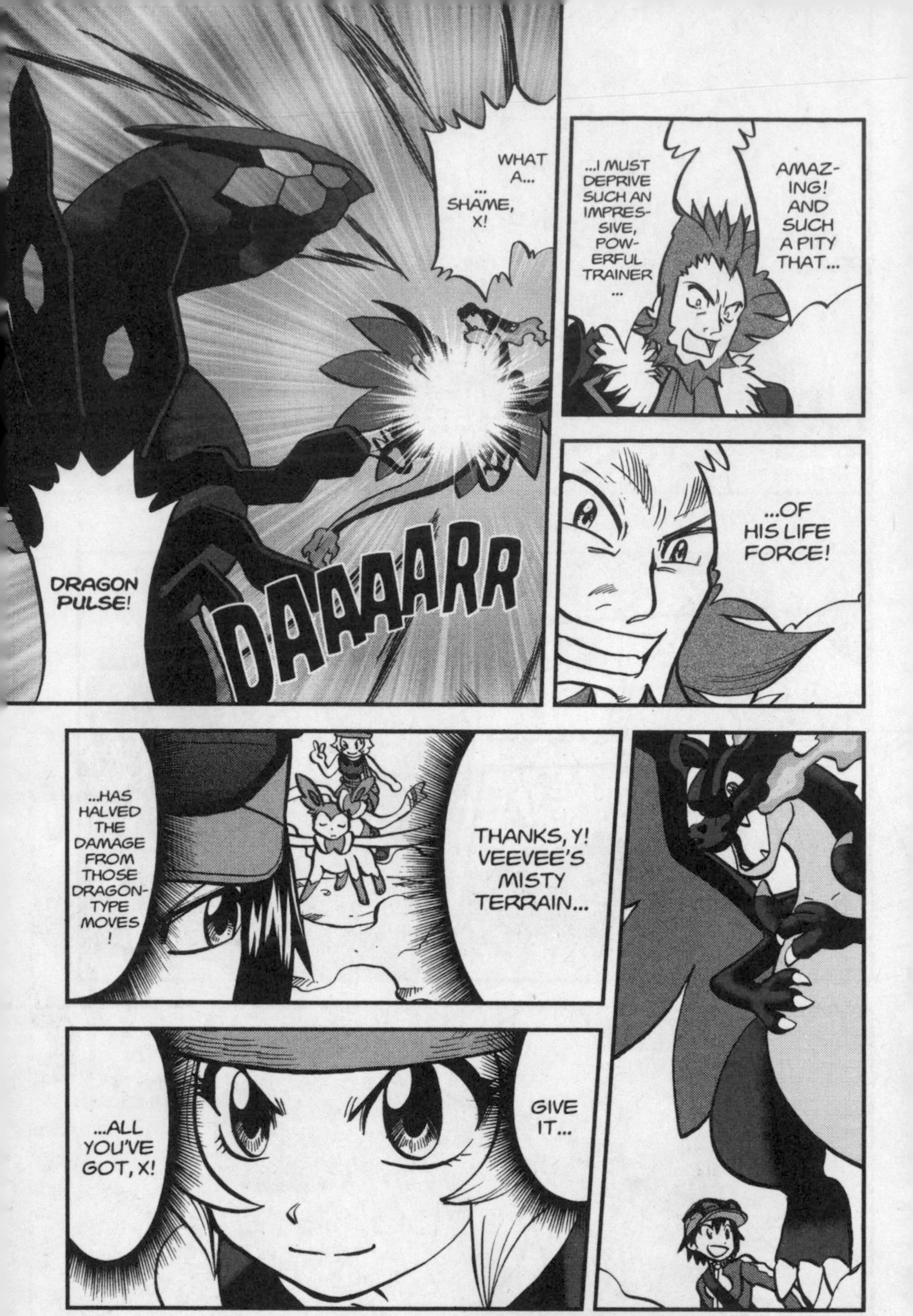
AMAZ-ING! AND SUCH A PITY THAT...
...I MUST DEPRIVE SUCH AN IMPRESSIVE, POWERFUL TRAINER...
...OF HIS LIFE FORCE!
WHAT A... ... SHAME, X!
DRAGON PULSE!
DAAAAARR
THANKS, Y! VEEVEE'S MISTY TERRAIN...
...HAS HALVED THE DAMAGE FROM THOSE DRAGON-TYPE MOVES!
GIVE IT...
...ALL YOU'VE GOT, X!

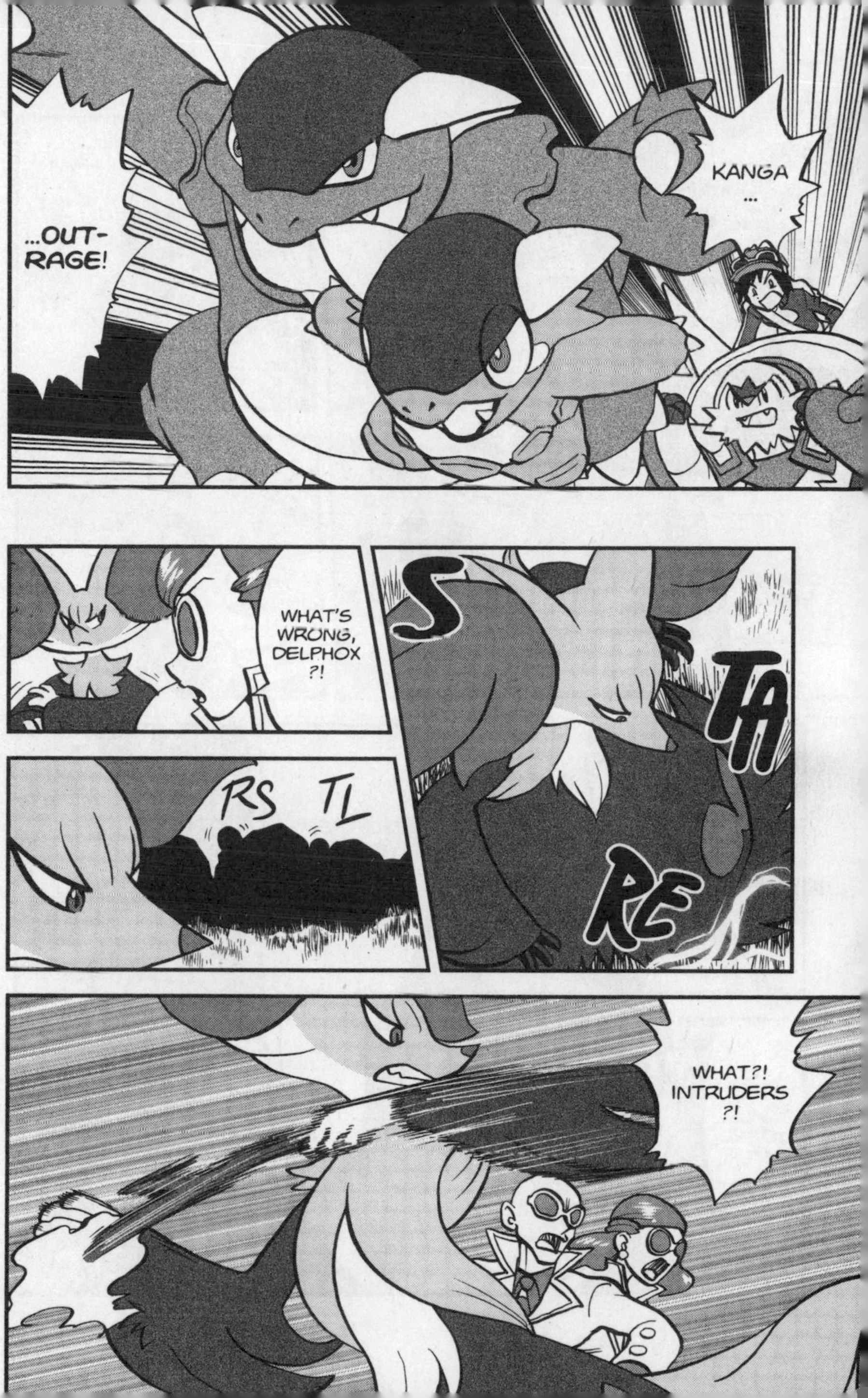
KANGA ...
...OUT-RAGE!
S
TA
RE
WHAT'S WRONG, DELPHOX?!
RS TL
WHAT?! INTRUDERS?!

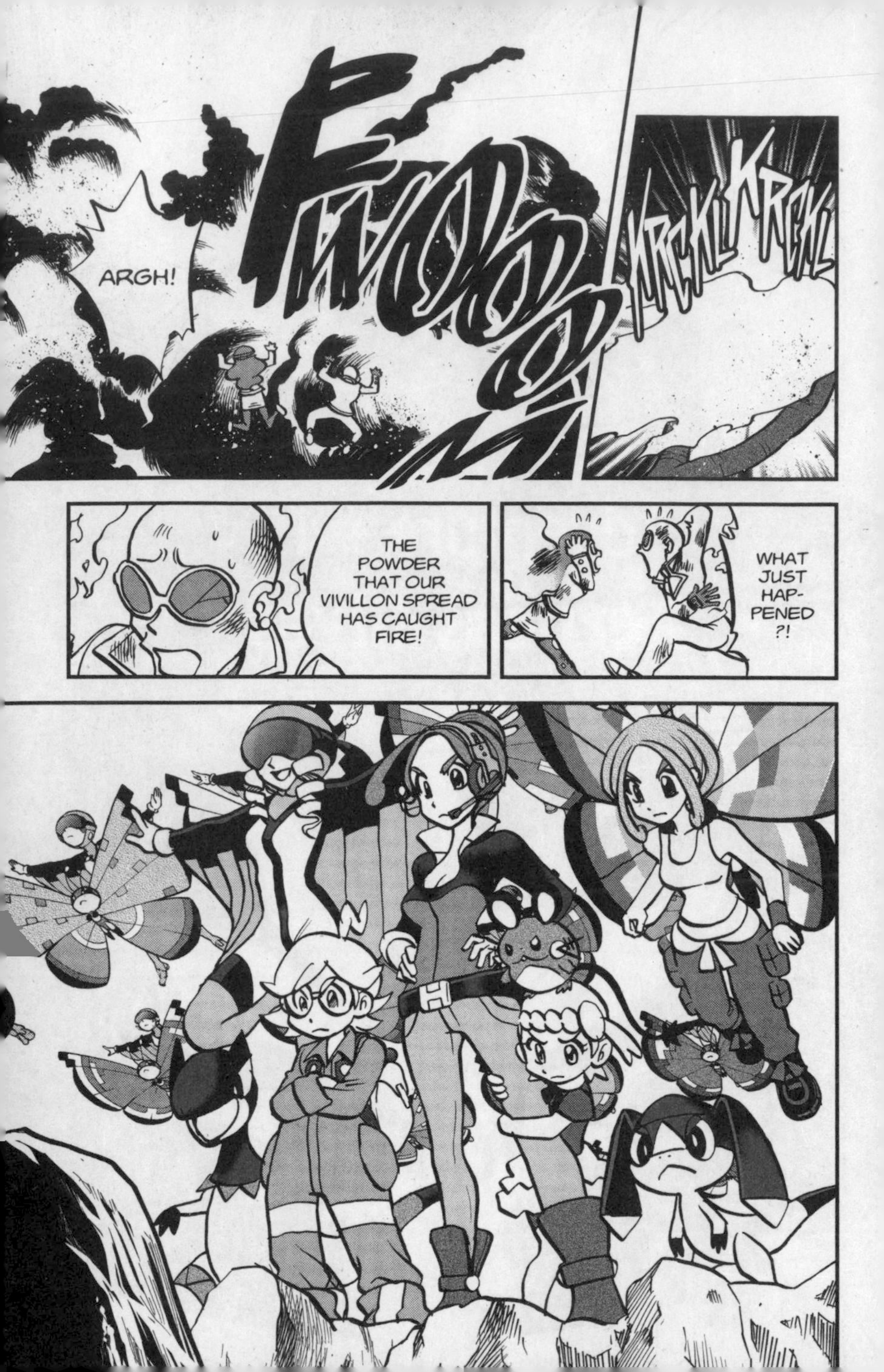
KRCKL KRCKL
ARGH!
WHAT JUST HAP-PENED?!
THE POWDER THAT OUR VIVILLON SPREAD HAS CAUGHT FIRE!

Adventure #45
Xerneas Gives

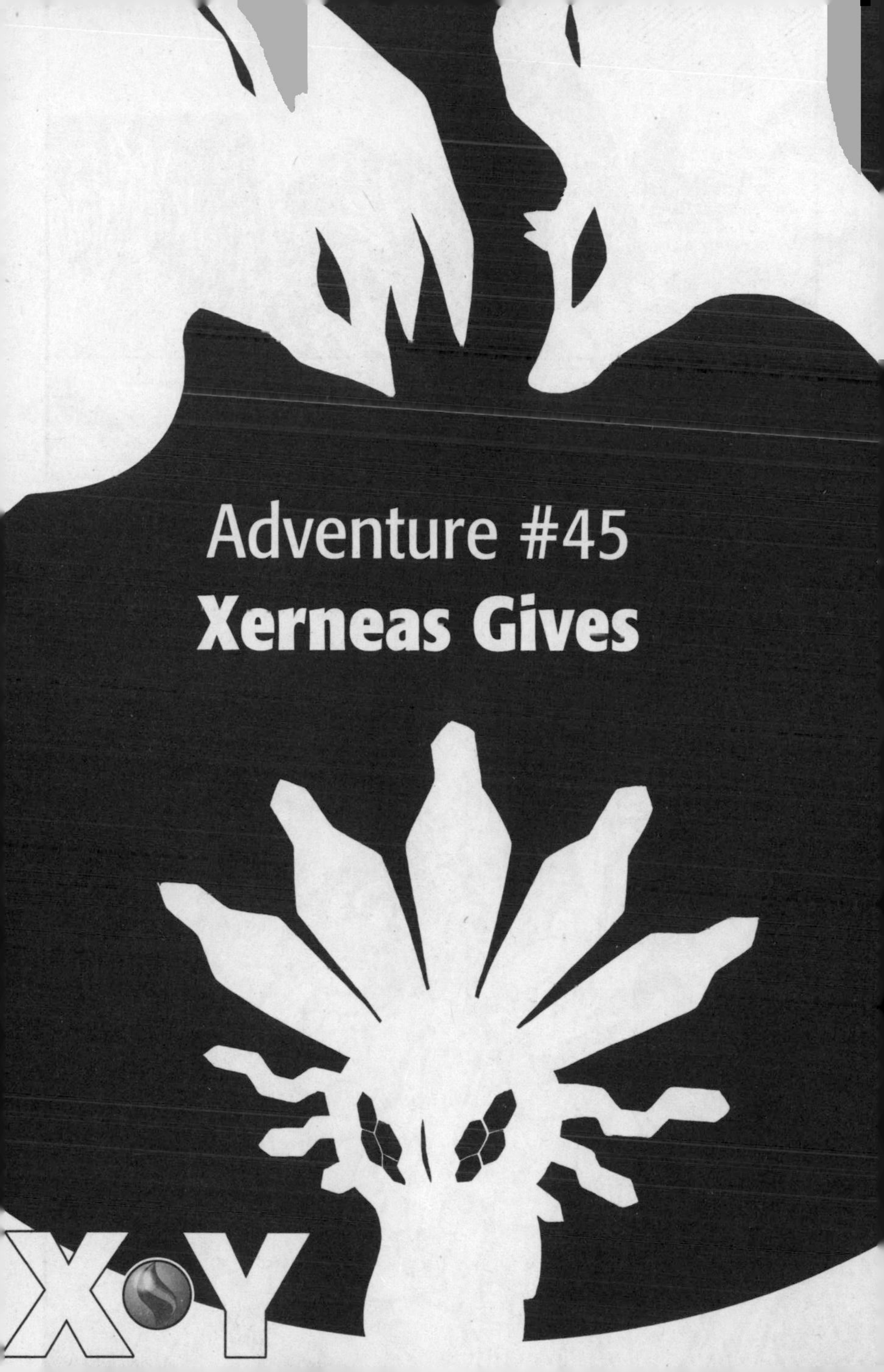

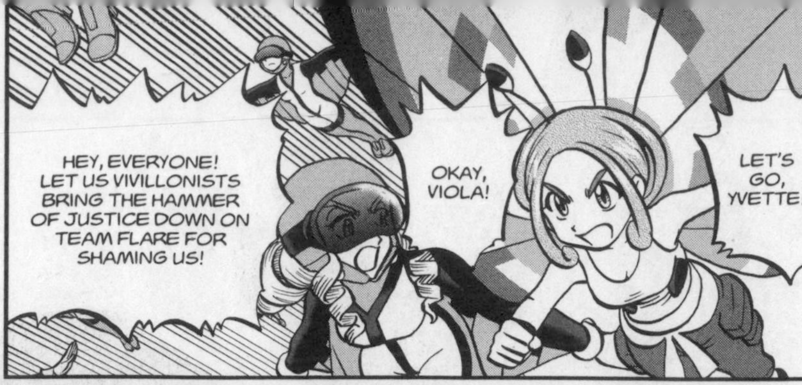
LET'S GO, YVETTE!
OKAY, VIOLA!
HEY, EVERYONE! LET US VIVILLONISTS BRING THE HAMMER OF JUSTICE DOWN ON TEAM FLARE FOR SHAMING US!

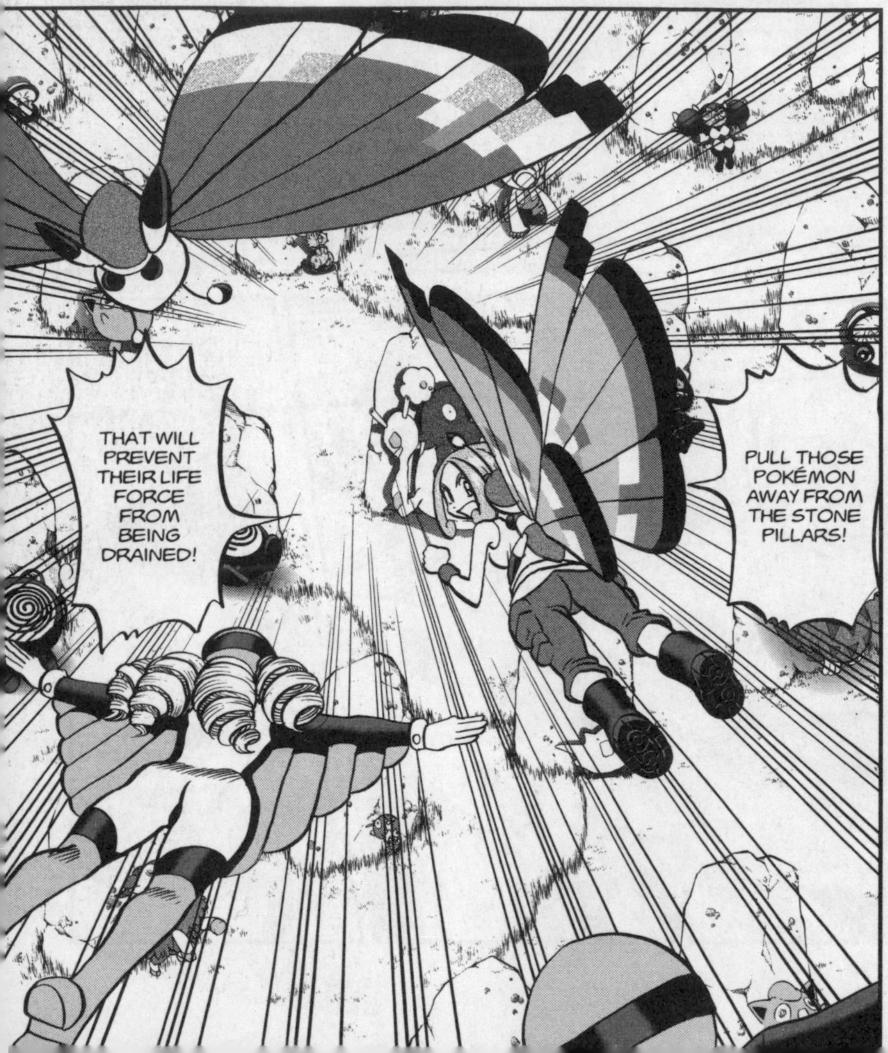
PULL THOSE POKÉMON AWAY FROM THE STONE PILLARS!
THAT WILL PREVENT THEIR LIFE FORCE FROM BEING DRAINED!

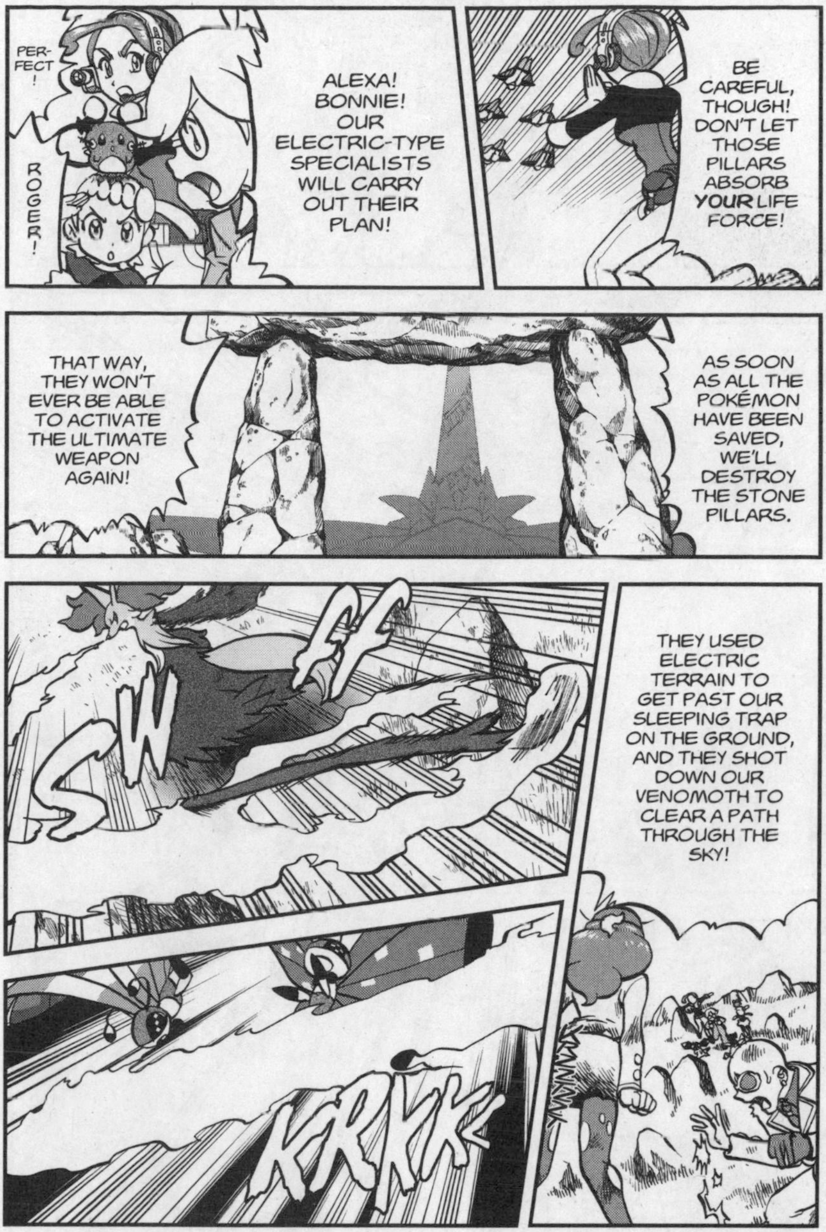
BE CAREFUL, THOUGH! DON'T LET THOSE PILLARS ABSORB YOUR LIFE FORCE!
ALEXA! BONNIE! OUR ELECTRIC-TYPE SPECIALISTS WILL CARRY OUT THEIR PLAN!
PER-FECT!
ROGER!
AS SOON AS ALL THE POKÉMON HAVE BEEN SAVED, WE'LL DESTROY THE STONE PILLARS.
THAT WAY, THEY WON'T EVER BE ABLE TO ACTIVATE THE ULTIMATE WEAPON AGAIN!
THEY USED ELECTRIC TERRAIN TO GET PAST OUR SLEEPING TRAP ON THE GROUND, AND THEY SHOT DOWN OUR VENOMOTH TO CLEAR A PATH THROUGH THE SKY!
SWFF
KRKK

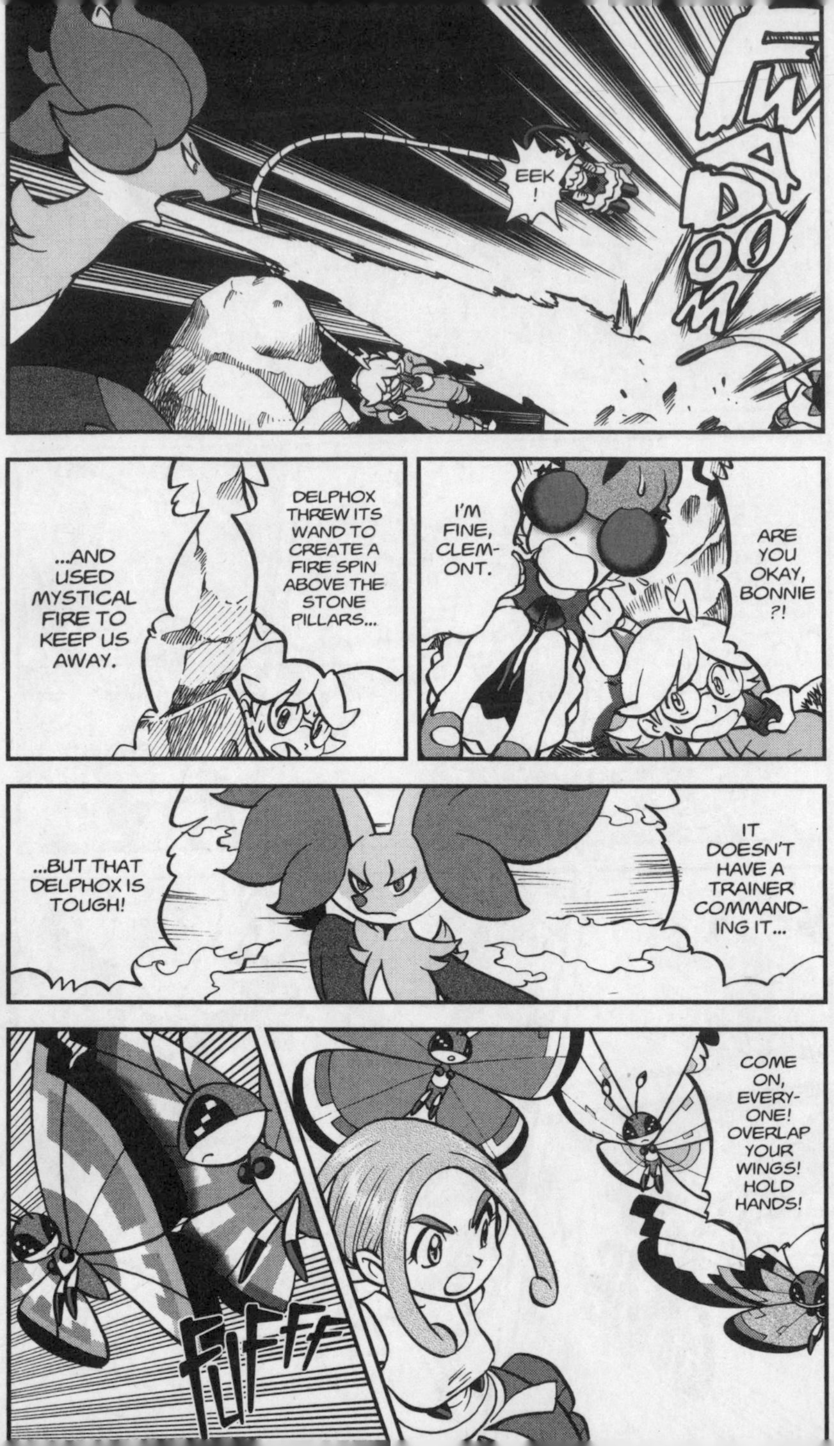
FWADOOM
EEK!
ARE YOU OKAY, BONNIE?!
I'M FINE, CLEMONT.
DELPHOX THREW ITS WAND TO CREATE A FIRE SPIN ABOVE THE STONE PILLARS...
...AND USED MYSTICAL FIRE TO KEEP US AWAY.
IT DOESN'T HAVE A TRAINER COMMANDING IT...
...BUT THAT DELPHOX IS TOUGH!
COME ON, EVERYONE! OVERLAP YOUR WINGS! HOLD HANDS!
FUFFF

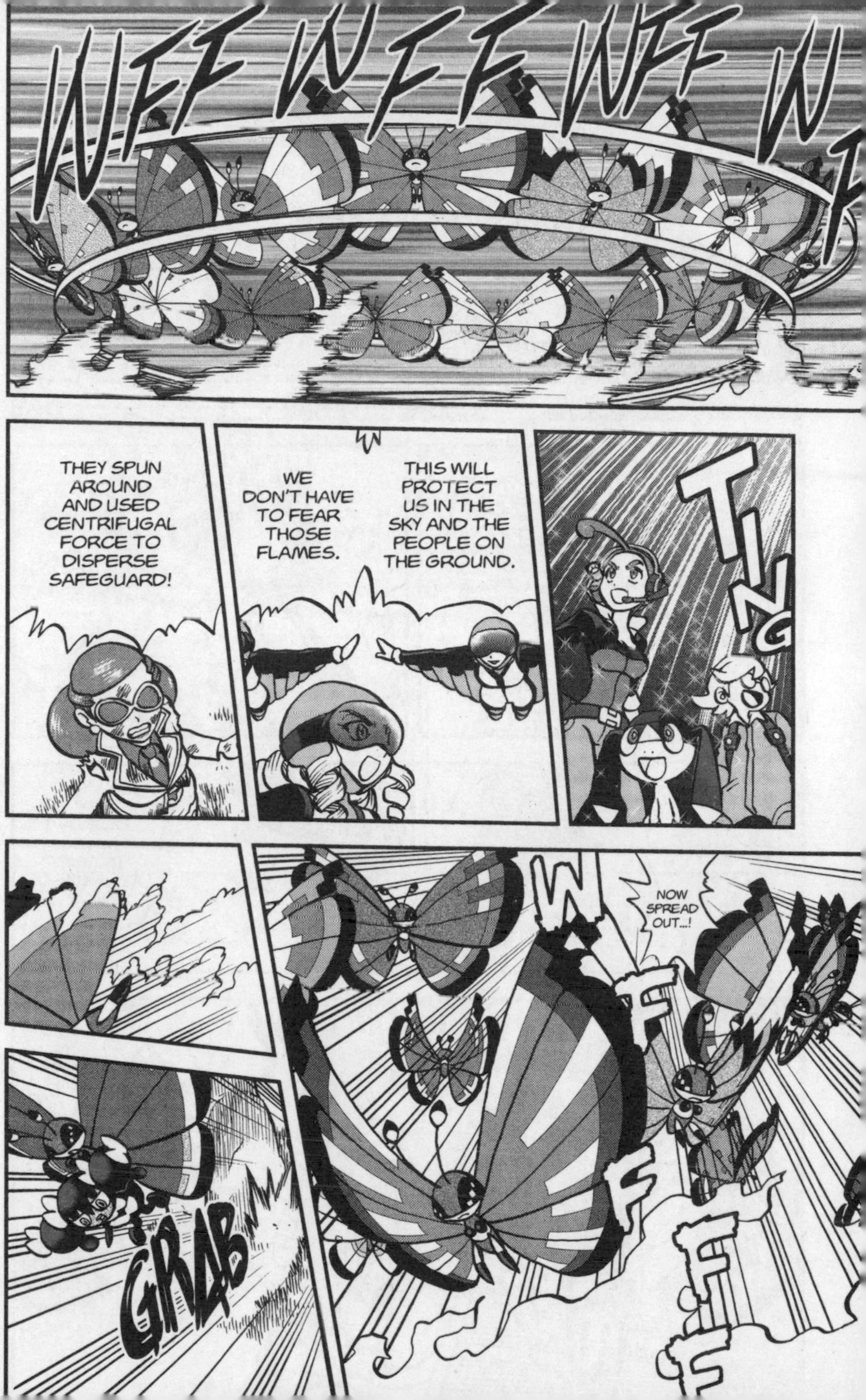
WFF WFF WFF WF
TING
THIS WILL PROTECT US IN THE SKY AND THE PEOPLE ON THE GROUND.
WE DON'T HAVE TO FEAR THOSE FLAMES.
THEY SPUN AROUND AND USED CENTRIFUGAL FORCE TO DISPERSE SAFEGUARD!
NOW SPREAD OUT...!
WFF
FFF
GRAB

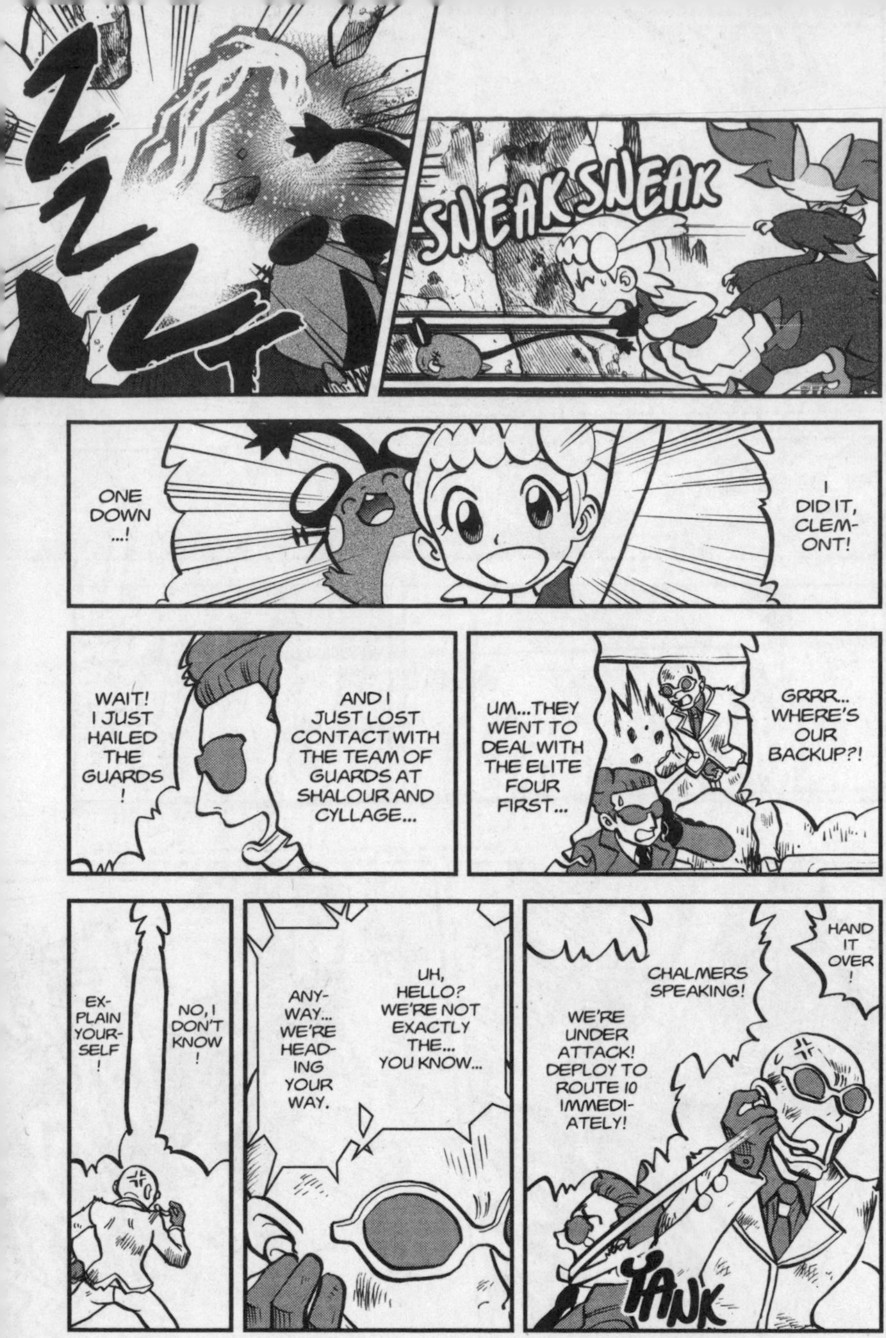
SNEAKSNEAK
I DID IT, CLEMONT!
ONE DOWN...!
GRRR... WHERE'S OUR BACKUP?!
UM...THEY WENT TO DEAL WITH THE ELITE FOUR FIRST...
AND I JUST LOST CONTACT WITH THE TEAM OF GUARDS AT SHALOUR AND CYLLAGE...
WAIT! I JUST HAILED THE GUARDS!
HAND IT OVER!
CHALMERS SPEAKING!
WE'RE UNDER ATTACK! DEPLOY TO ROUTE 10 IMMEDIATELY!
YANK
UH, HELLO? WE'RE NOT EXACTLY THE... YOU KNOW...
ANYWAY... WE'RE HEADING YOUR WAY.
NO, I DON'T KNOW!
EXPLAIN YOURSELF!

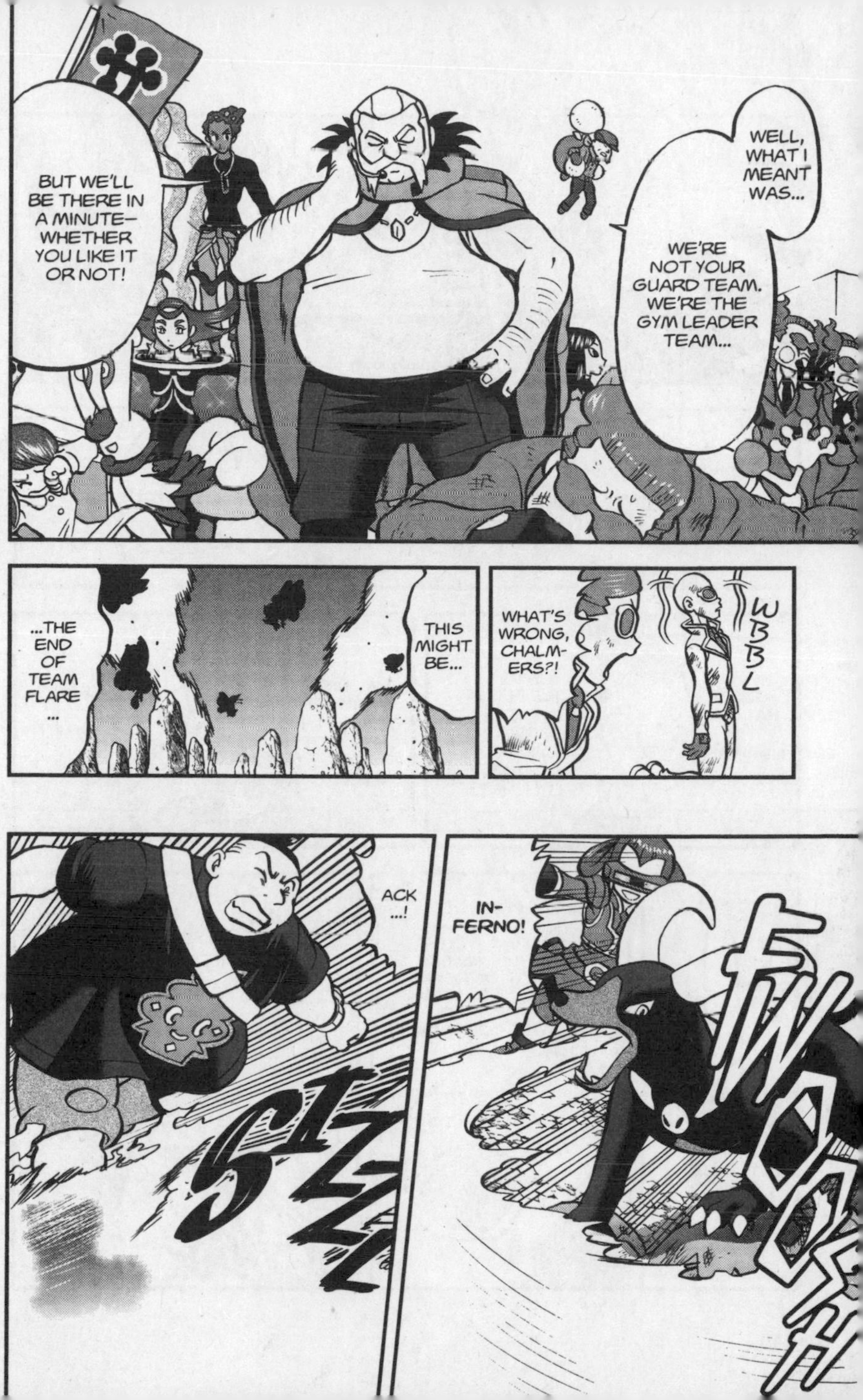
WELL, WHAT I MEANT WAS...
WE'RE NOT YOUR GUARD TEAM. WE'RE THE GYM LEADER TEAM...
BUT WE'LL BE THERE IN A MINUTE—WHETHER YOU LIKE IT OR NOT!
WBBL
WHAT'S WRONG, CHALMERS?!
THIS MIGHT BE...
...THE END OF TEAM FLARE...
IN-FERNO!
FWOOSH
ACK ...!
SIZZ

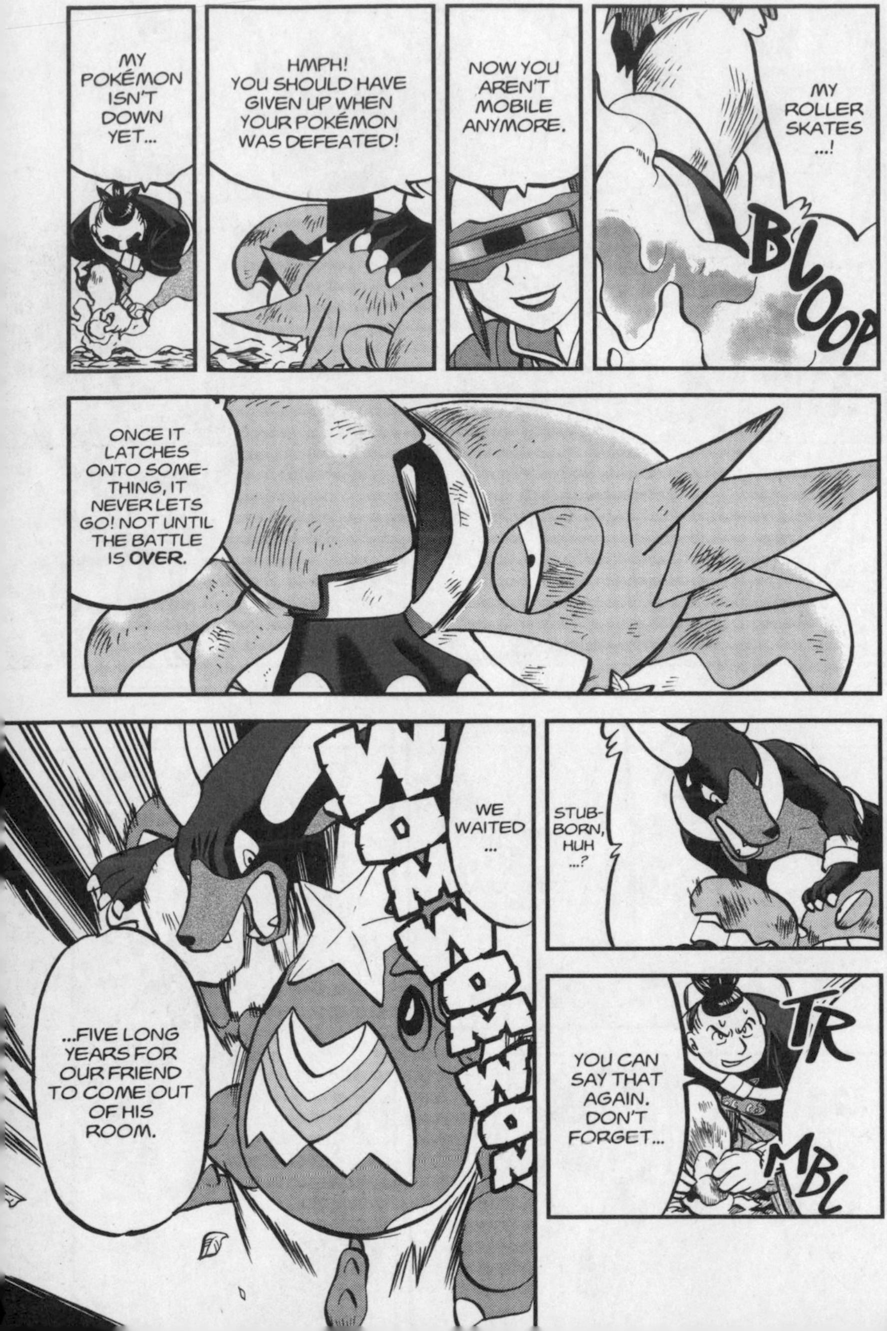
MY ROLLER SKATES ...!
BLOOP
NOW YOU AREN'T MOBILE ANYMORE.
HMPH! YOU SHOULD HAVE GIVEN UP WHEN YOUR POKÉMON WAS DEFEATED!
MY POKÉMON ISN'T DOWN YET...
ONCE IT LATCHES ONTO SOME-THING, IT NEVER LETS GO! NOT UNTIL THE BATTLE IS **OVER**.
STUB-BORN, HUH ...?
YOU CAN SAY THAT AGAIN. DON'T FORGET...
TR
MBL
WE WAITED ...
WOMWOMWOM
...FIVE LONG YEARS FOR OUR FRIEND TO COME OUT OF HIS ROOM.

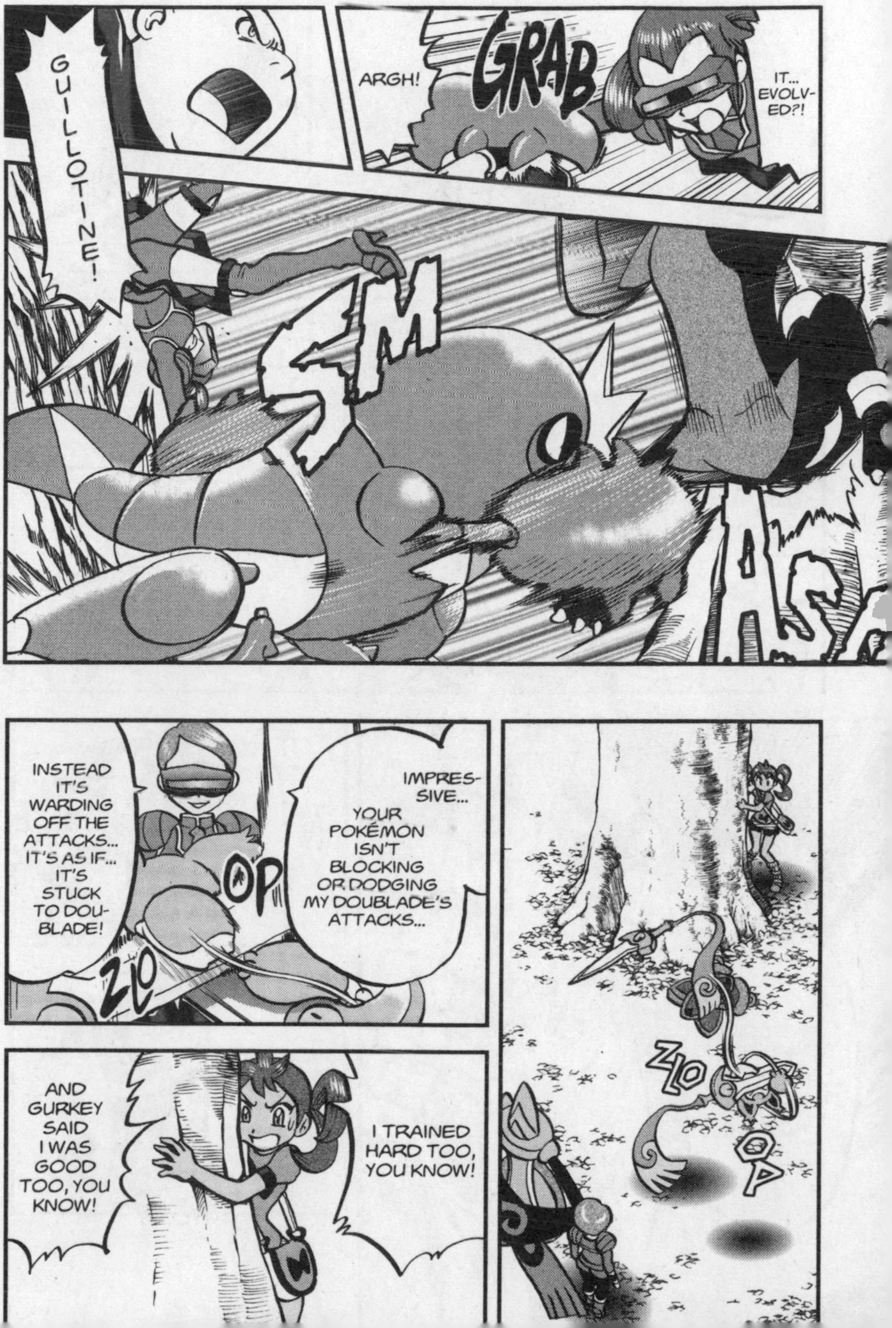
IT... EVOLV-ED?!
GRAB
ARGH!
GUILLOTINE!
SM
AS
ZLO
OP
IMPRES-SIVE...
YOUR POKÉMON ISN'T BLOCKING OR DODGING MY DOUBLADE'S ATTACKS...
INSTEAD IT'S WARDING OFF THE ATTACKS... IT'S AS IF... IT'S STUCK TO DOU-BLADE!
OP
ZLO
I TRAINED HARD TOO, YOU KNOW!
AND GURKEY SAID I WAS GOOD TOO, YOU KNOW!

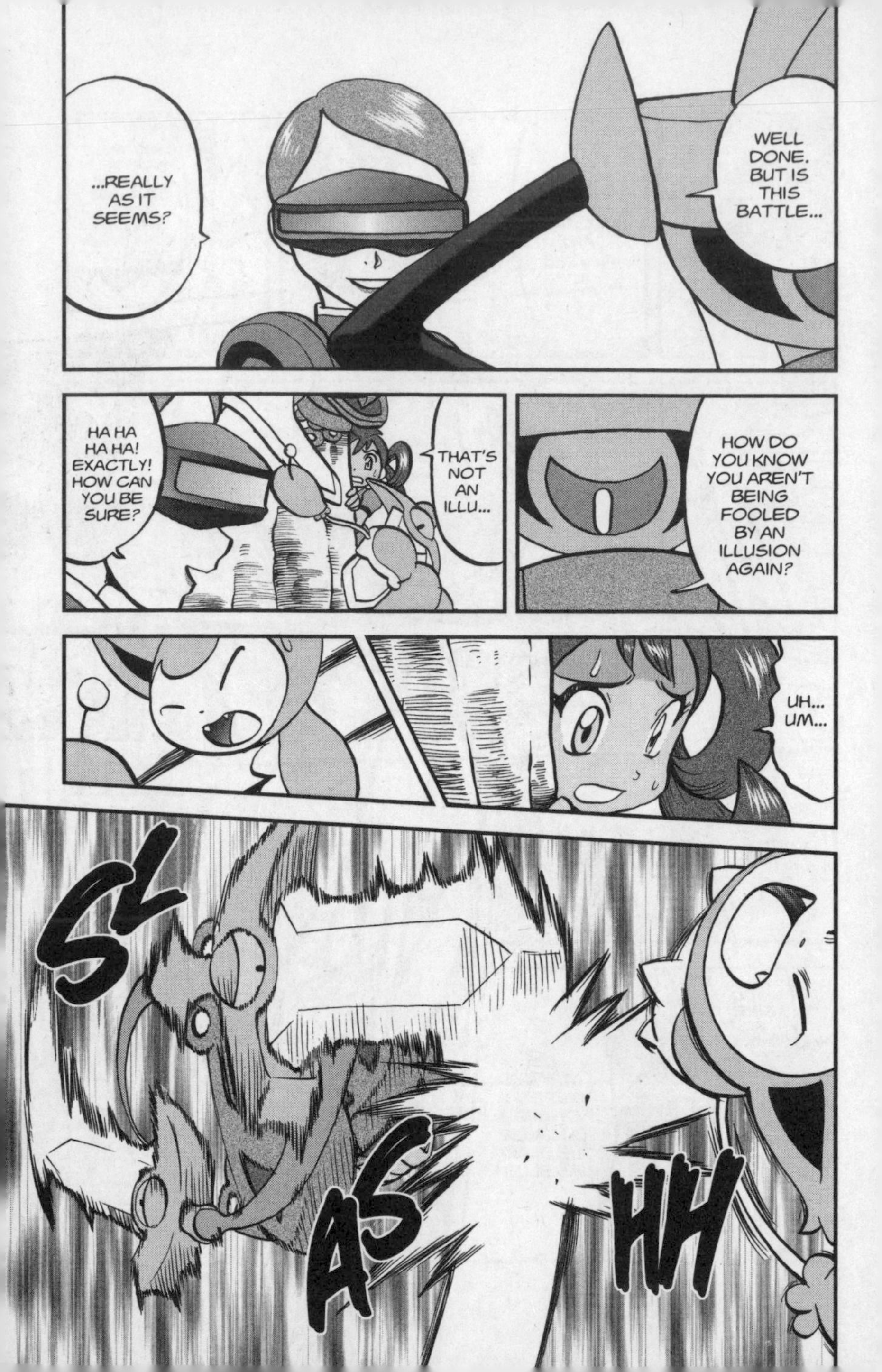
WELL DONE. BUT IS THIS BATTLE...
...REALLY AS IT SEEMS?
HOW DO YOU KNOW YOU AREN'T BEING FOOLED BY AN ILLUSION AGAIN?
THAT'S NOT AN ILLU...
HA HA HA HA! EXACTLY! HOW CAN YOU BE SURE?
UH... UM...
SLASHH

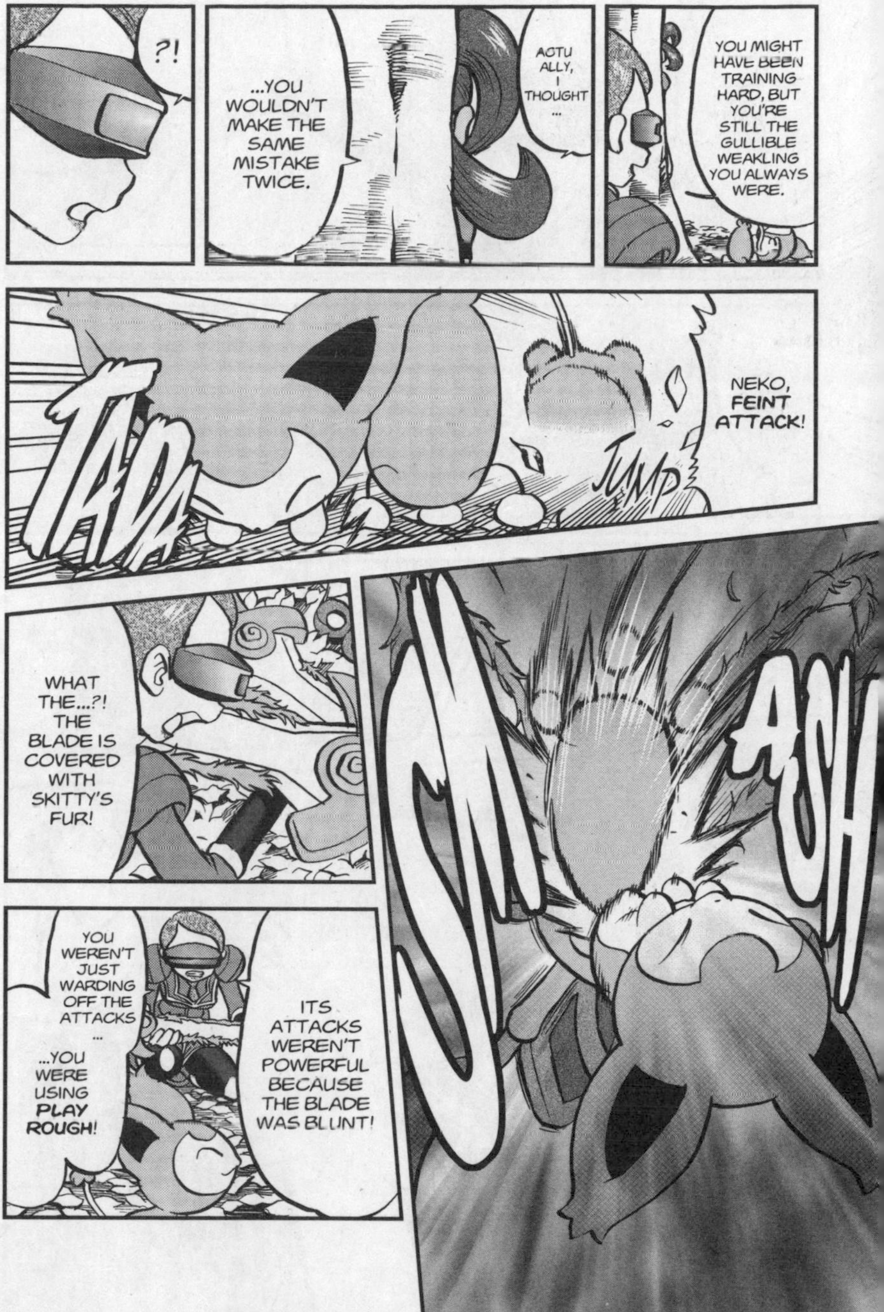
YOU MIGHT HAVE BEEN TRAINING HARD, BUT YOU'RE STILL THE GULLIBLE WEAKLING YOU ALWAYS WERE.
ACTU ALLY, I THOUGHT ...
...YOU WOULDN'T MAKE THE SAME MISTAKE TWICE.
?!
NEKO, **FEINT ATTACK**!
JUMP
TADA
SMASH
WHAT THE...?! THE BLADE IS COVERED WITH SKITTY'S FUR!
ITS ATTACKS WEREN'T POWERFUL BECAUSE THE BLADE WAS BLUNT!
YOU WEREN'T JUST WARDING OFF THE ATTACKS ...
...YOU WERE USING **PLAY ROUGH**!

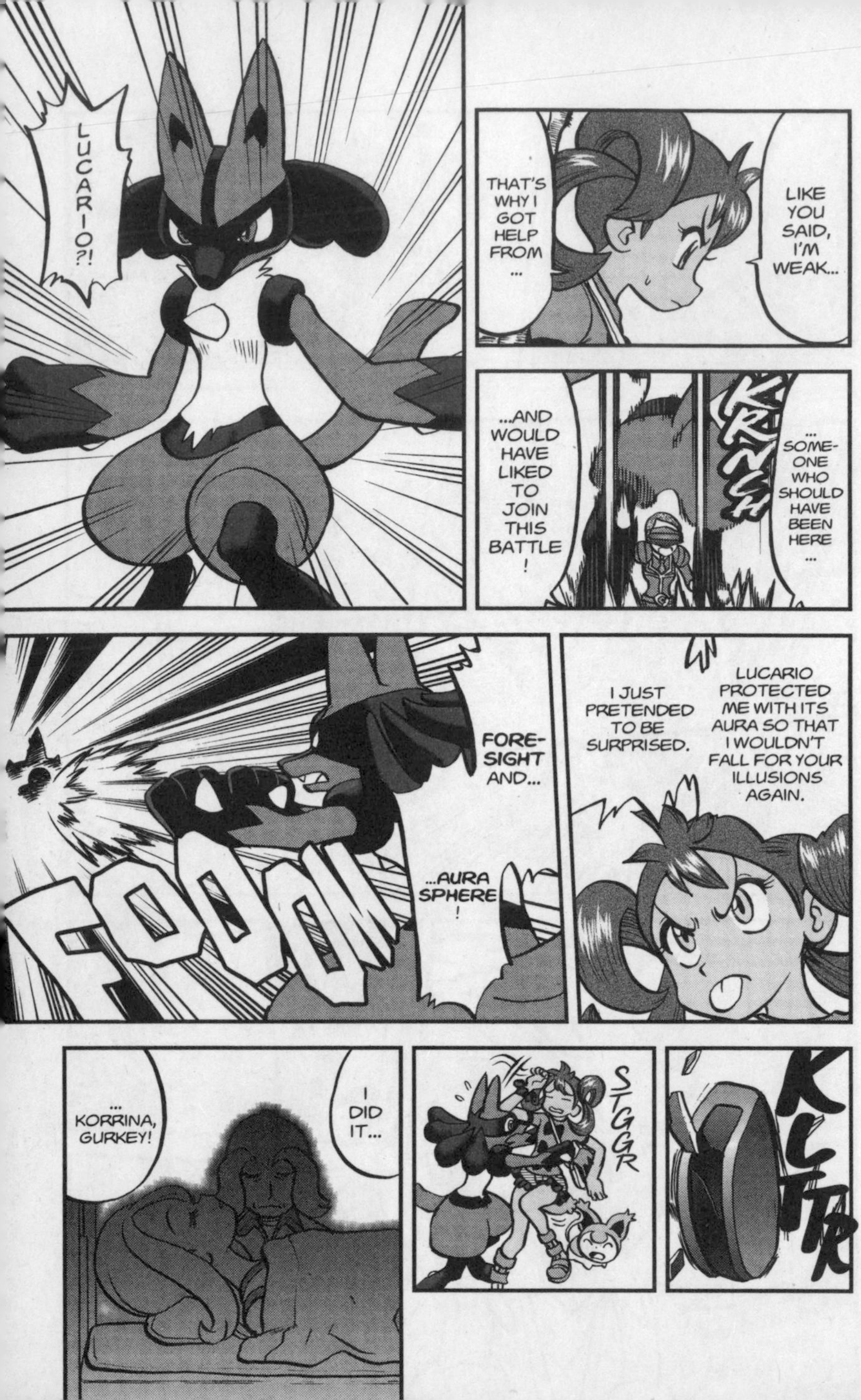
LIKE YOU SAID, I'M WEAK...
THAT'S WHY I GOT HELP FROM ...
... SOMEONE WHO SHOULD HAVE BEEN HERE ...
KRNCH
...AND WOULD HAVE LIKED TO JOIN THIS BATTLE !
LUCARIO?!
LUCARIO PROTECTED ME WITH ITS AURA SO THAT I WOULDN'T FALL FOR YOUR ILLUSIONS AGAIN.
I JUST PRETENDED TO BE SURPRISED.
FORESIGHT AND...
...AURA SPHERE !
FOOOM
KLTTR
STGGR
I DID IT...
... KORRINA, GURKEY!

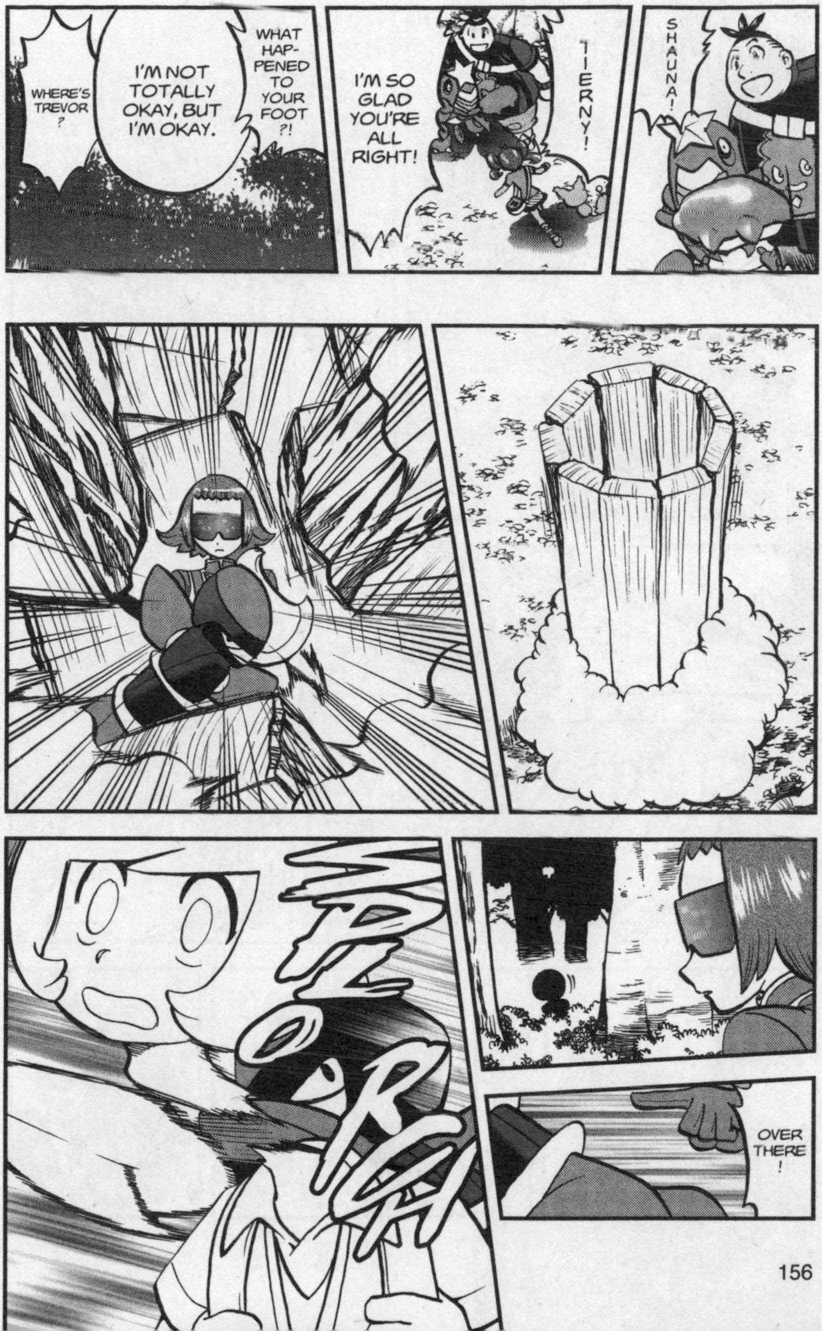
SHAUNA!
TIERNY!
I'M SO GLAD YOU'RE ALL RIGHT!
WHAT HAPPENED TO YOUR FOOT?!
I'M NOT TOTALLY OKAY, BUT I'M OKAY.
WHERE'S TREVOR?
OVER THERE!

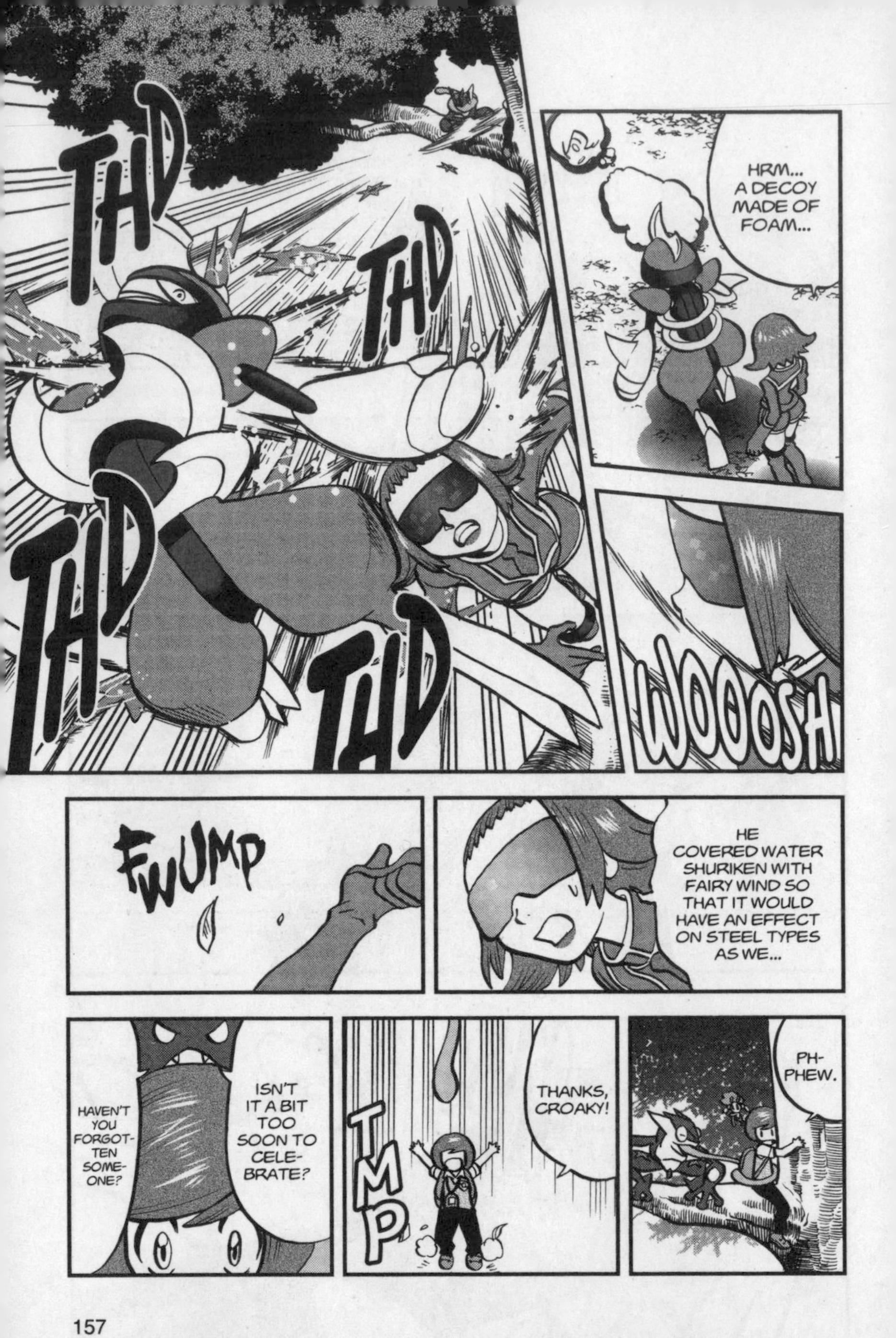
HRM... A DECOY MADE OF FOAM...
WOOOSH
THD
THD
THD
THD
HE COVERED WATER SHURIKEN WITH FAIRY WIND SO THAT IT WOULD HAVE AN EFFECT ON STEEL TYPES AS WE...
FWUMP
PH-PHEW.
THANKS, CROAKY!
TMP
ISN'T IT A BIT TOO SOON TO CELEBRATE?
HAVEN'T YOU FORGOTTEN SOMEONE?

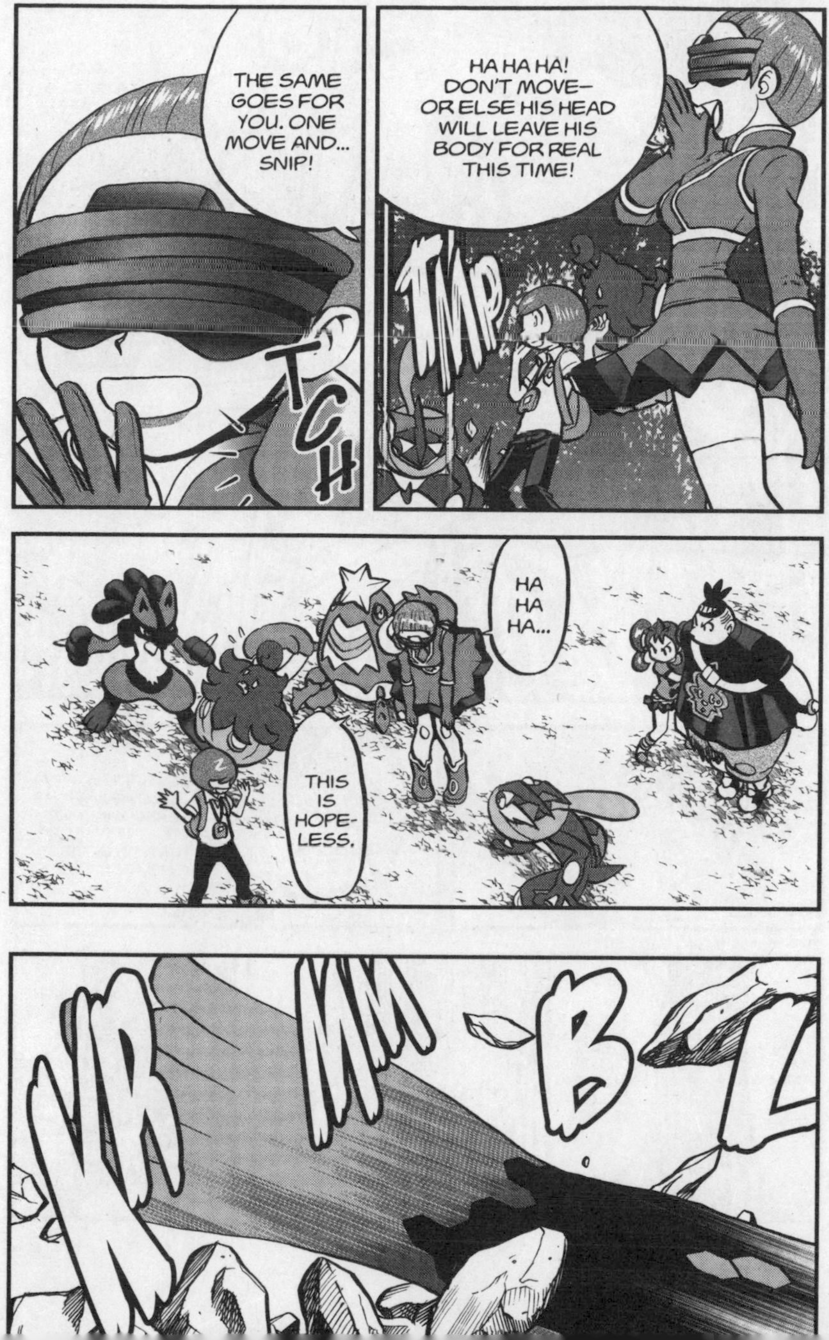
HA HA HA! DON'T MOVE— OR ELSE HIS HEAD WILL LEAVE HIS BODY FOR REAL THIS TIME!
TMP
THE SAME GOES FOR YOU. ONE MOVE AND... SNIP!
TCH
HA HA HA...
THIS IS HOPE-LESS.
VRMM-B

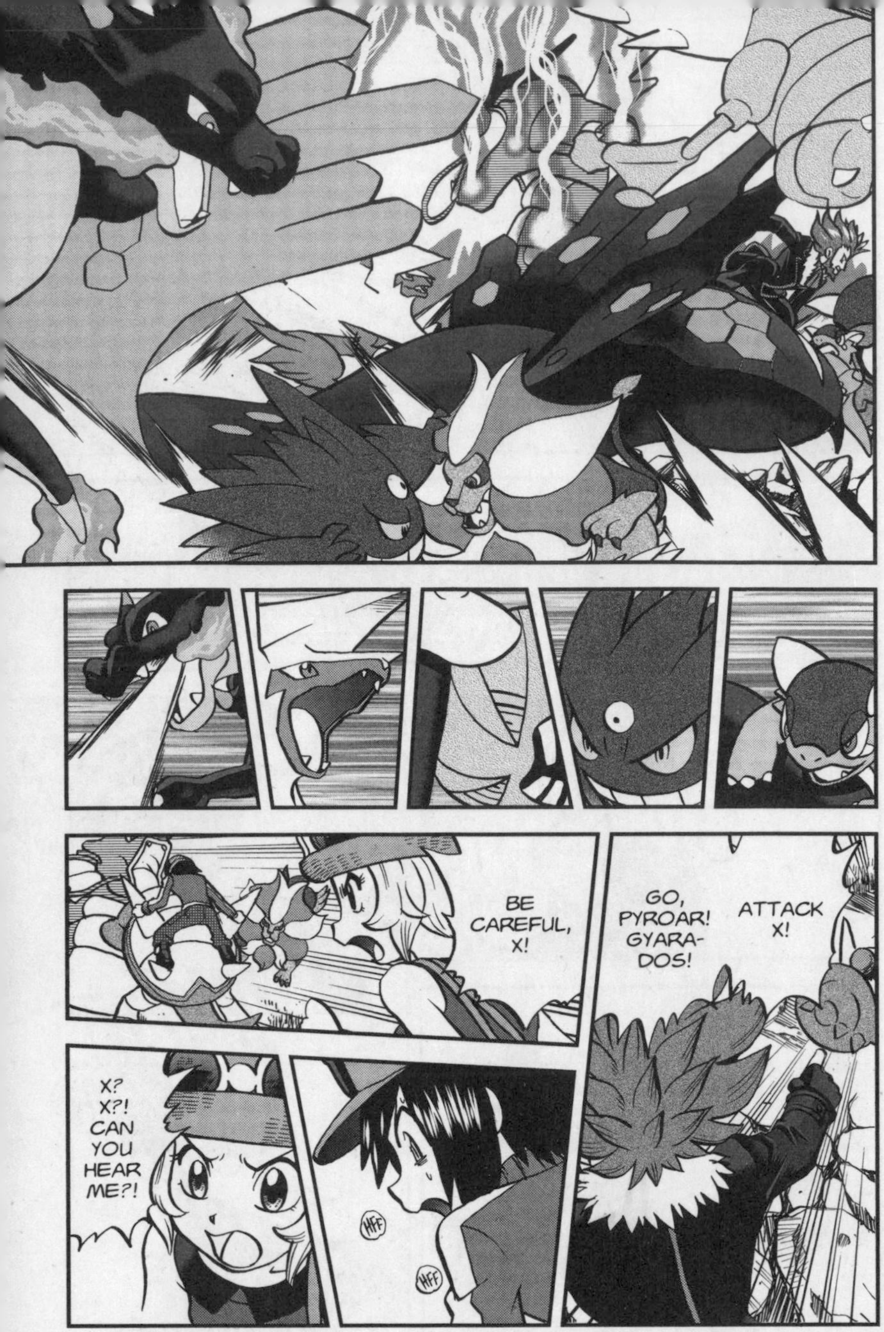
ATTACK X!
GO, PYROAR! GYARA-DOS!
BE CAREFUL, X!
HFF
HFF
X? X?! CAN YOU HEAR ME?!

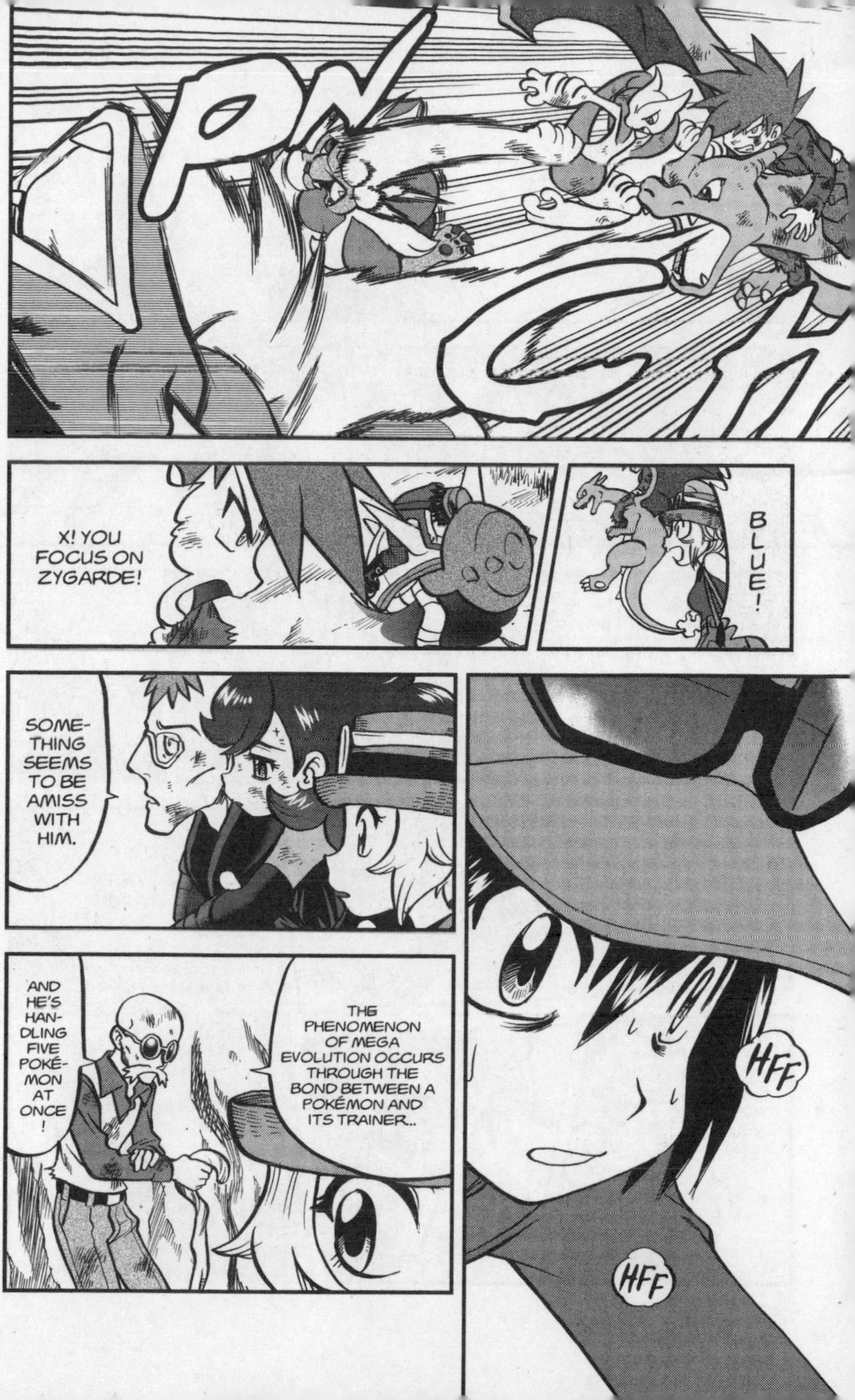
BLUE!
X! YOU FOCUS ON ZYGARDE!
HFF
HFF
SOMETHING SEEMS TO BE AMISS WITH HIM.
THE PHENOMENON OF MEGA EVOLUTION OCCURS THROUGH THE BOND BETWEEN A POKÉMON AND ITS TRAINER...
AND HE'S HANDLING FIVE POKÉMON AT ONCE!

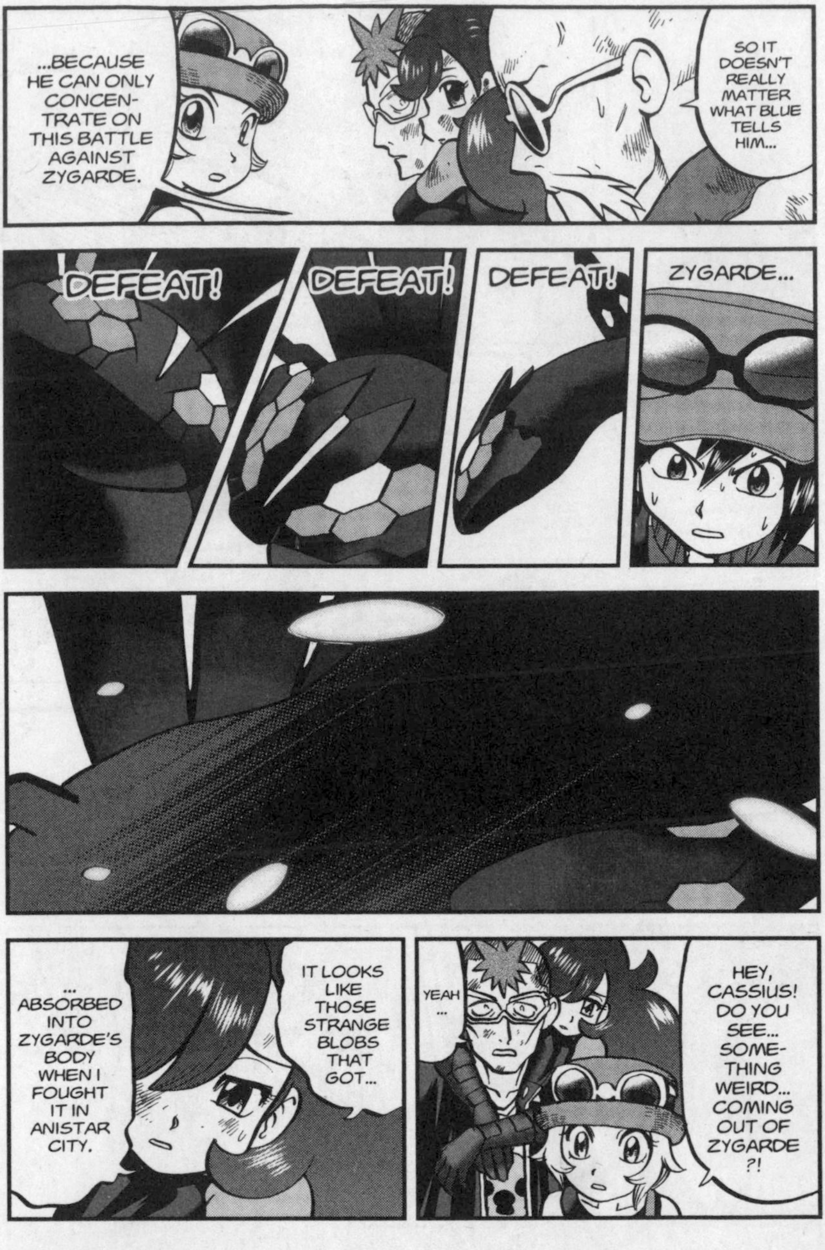
SO IT DOESN'T REALLY MATTER WHAT BLUE TELLS HIM...
...BECAUSE HE CAN ONLY CONCEN-TRATE ON THIS BATTLE AGAINST ZYGARDE.
ZYGARDE...
DEFEAT!
DEFEAT!
DEFEAT!
HEY, CASSIUS! DO YOU SEE... SOME-THING WEIRD... COMING OUT OF ZYGARDE?!
YEAH...
IT LOOKS LIKE THOSE STRANGE BLOBS THAT GOT...
...ABSORBED INTO ZYGARDE'S BODY WHEN I FOUGHT IT IN ANISTAR CITY.

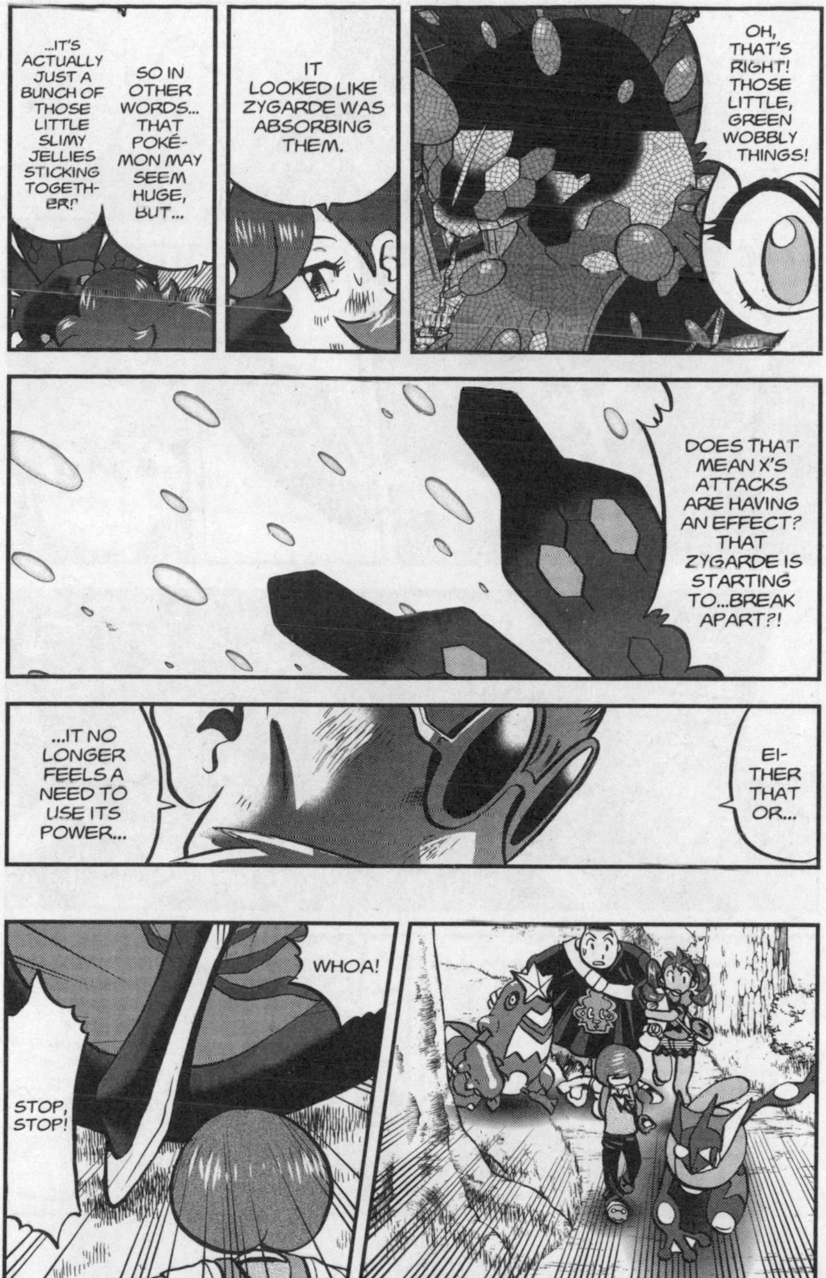
OH, THAT'S RIGHT! THOSE LITTLE, GREEN WOBBLY THINGS!
IT LOOKED LIKE ZYGARDE WAS ABSORBING THEM.
SO IN OTHER WORDS... THAT POKÉMON MAY SEEM HUGE, BUT...
...IT'S ACTUALLY JUST A BUNCH OF THOSE LITTLE SLIMY JELLIES STICKING TOGETHER!
DOES THAT MEAN X'S ATTACKS ARE HAVING AN EFFECT? THAT ZYGARDE IS STARTING TO...BREAK APART?!
EITHER THAT OR...
...IT NO LONGER FEELS A NEED TO USE ITS POWER...
WHOA!
STOP, STOP!

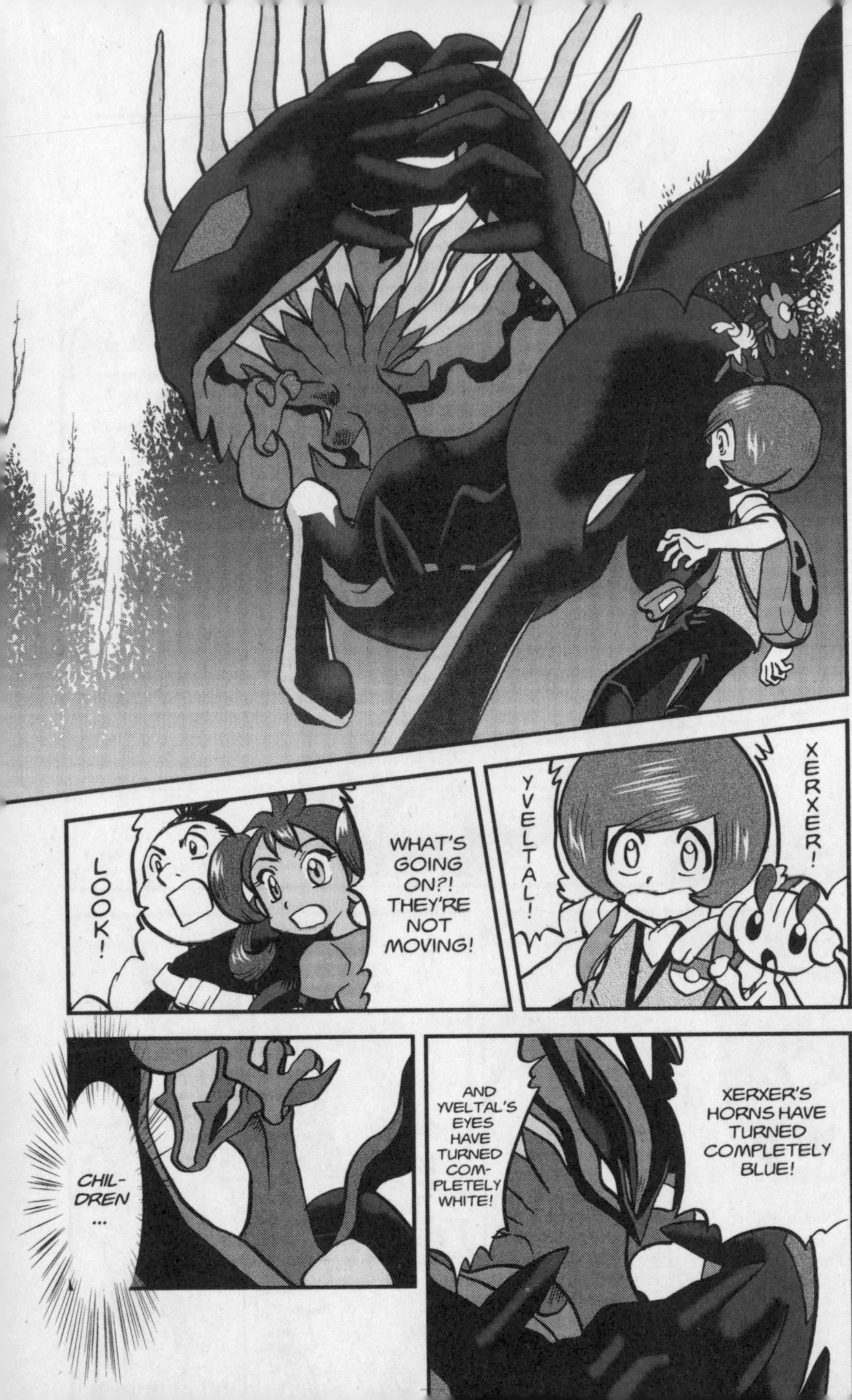
XERXER!
YVELTAL!
WHAT'S GOING ON?! THEY'RE NOT MOVING!
LOOK!
XERXER'S HORNS HAVE TURNED COMPLETELY BLUE!
AND YVELTAL'S EYES HAVE TURNED COM-PLETELY WHITE!
CHIL-DREN ...

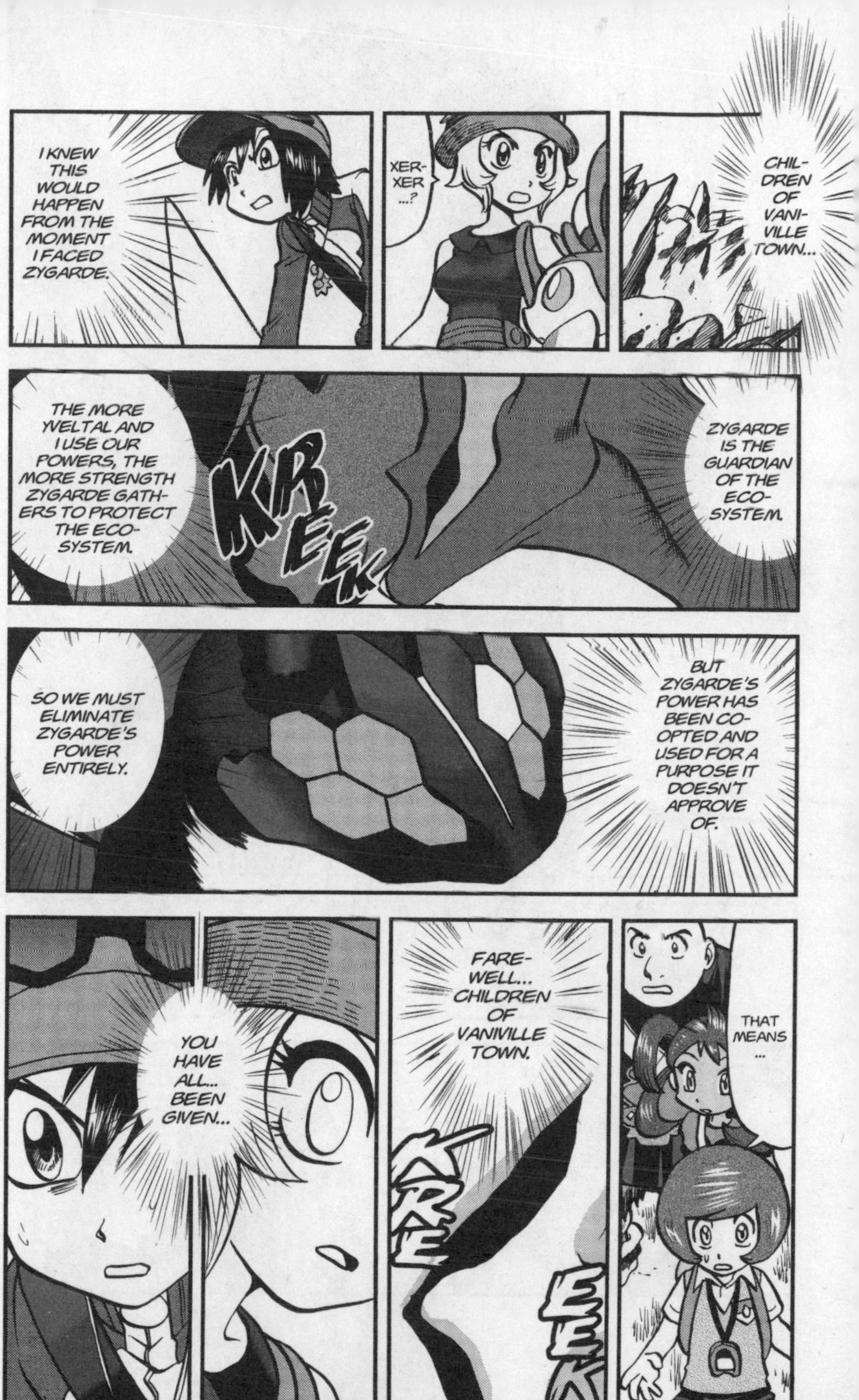
CHIL-DREN OF VANI-VILLE TOWN...
XER-XER ...?
I KNEW THIS WOULD HAPPEN FROM THE MOMENT I FACED ZYGARDE.
ZYGARDE IS THE GUARDIAN OF THE ECO-SYSTEM.
KRREEK
THE MORE YVELTAL AND I USE OUR POWERS, THE MORE STRENGTH ZYGARDE GATH-ERS TO PROTECT THE ECO-SYSTEM.
BUT ZYGARDE'S POWER HAS BEEN CO-OPTED AND USED FOR A PURPOSE IT DOESN'T APPROVE OF.
SO WE MUST ELIMINATE ZYGARDE'S POWER ENTIRELY.
THAT MEANS ...
FARE-WELL... CHILDREN OF VANIVILLE TOWN.
KREEEK
YOU HAVE ALL... BEEN GIVEN...

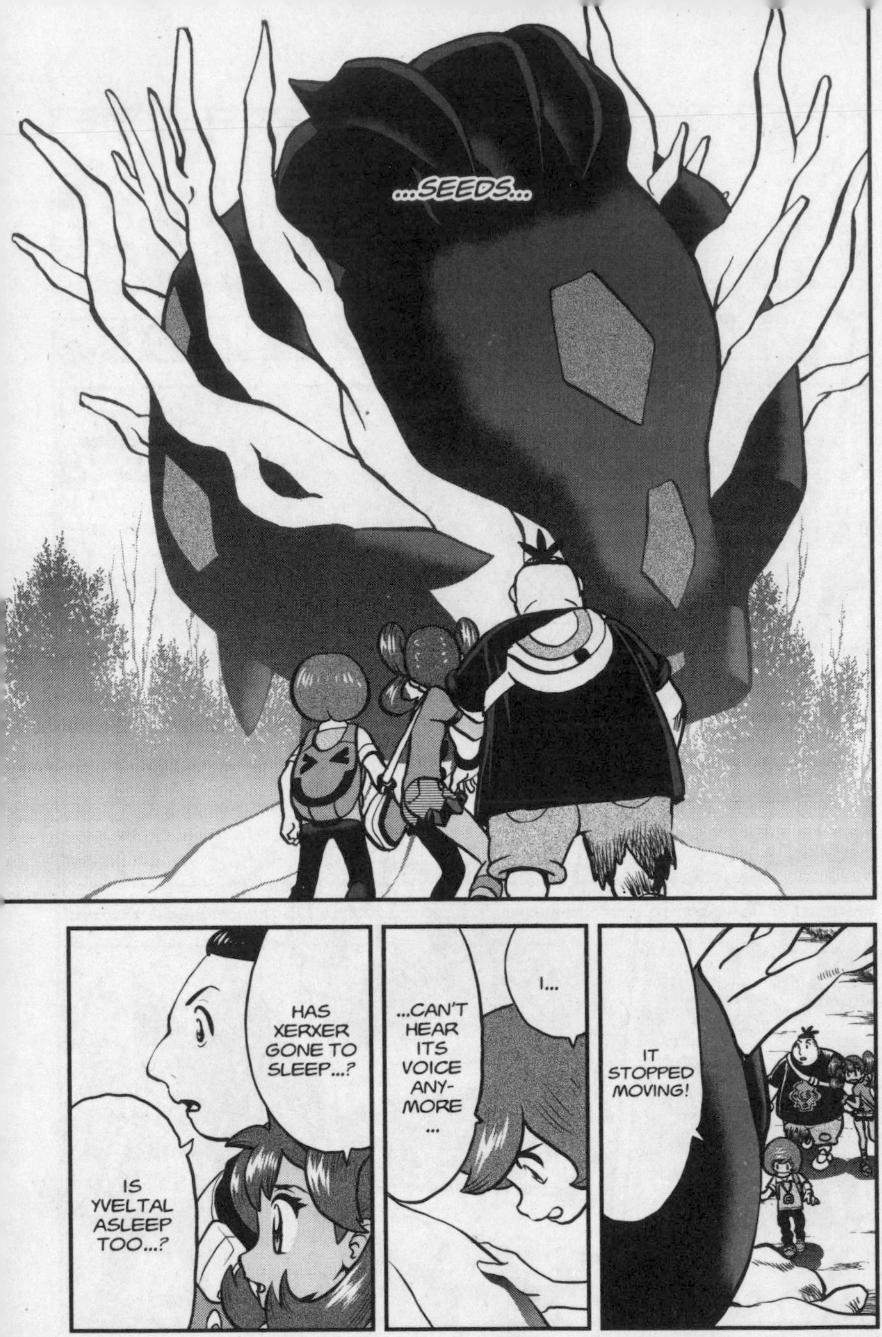
...SEEDS...
IT STOPPED MOVING!
I...
...CAN'T HEAR ITS VOICE ANYMORE ...
HAS XERXER GONE TO SLEEP...?
IS YVELTAL ASLEEP TOO...?

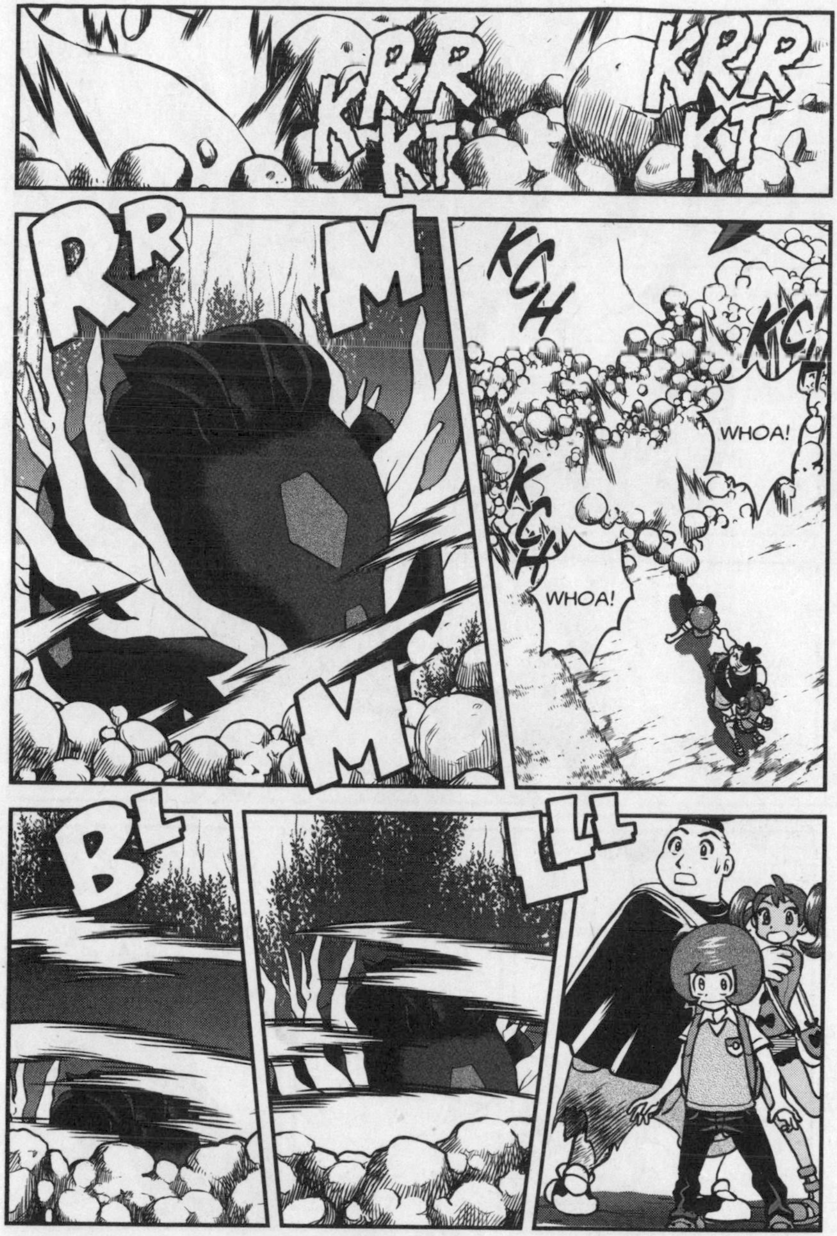
KRR KT
KRR KT
KCH
KCH
WHOA!
WHOA!
RR
M
M
LLL
BL

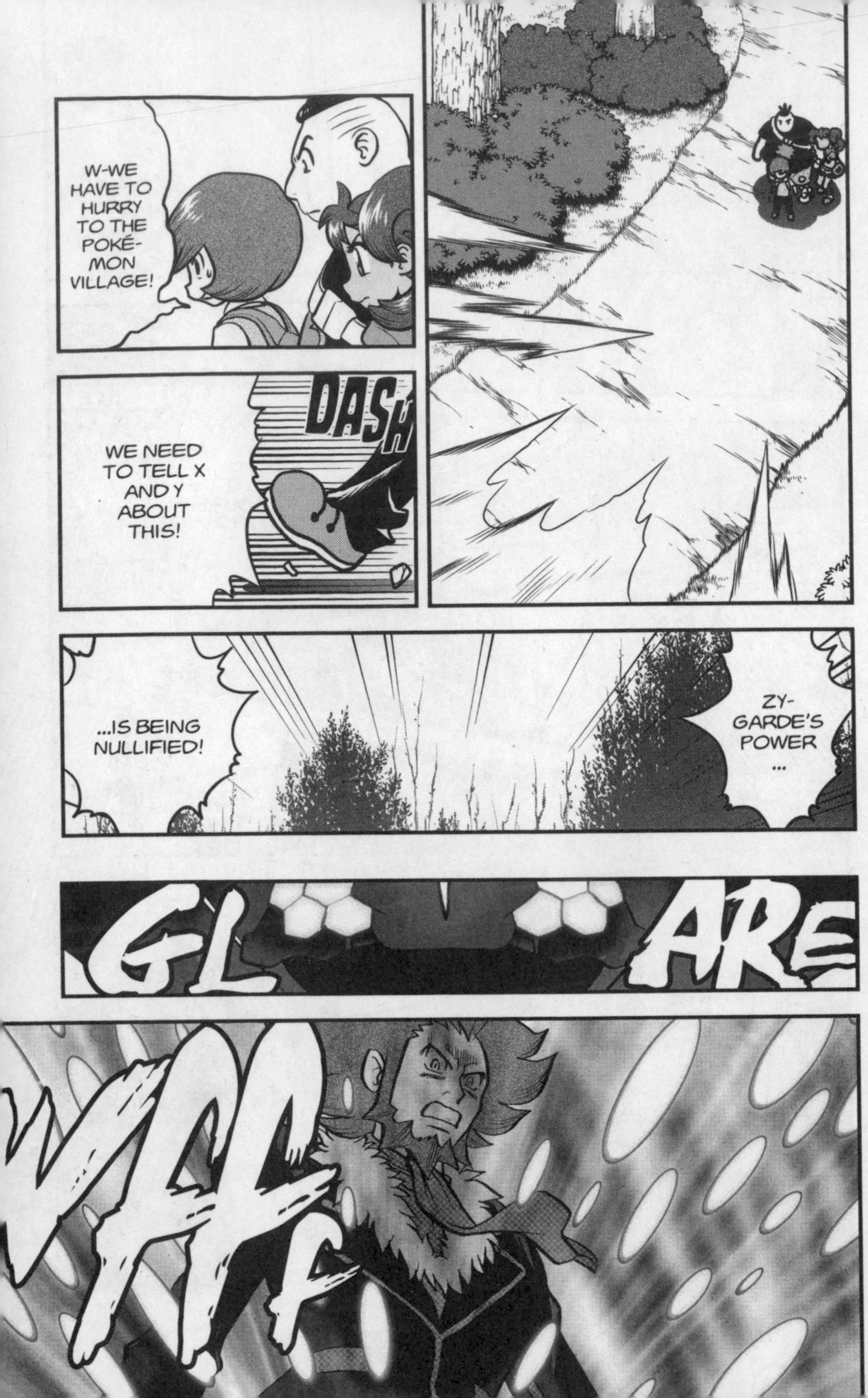
W-WE HAVE TO HURRY TO THE POKÉMON VILLAGE!
DASH
WE NEED TO TELL X AND Y ABOUT THIS!
ZYGARDE'S POWER ...
...IS BEING NULLIFIED!
GLARE

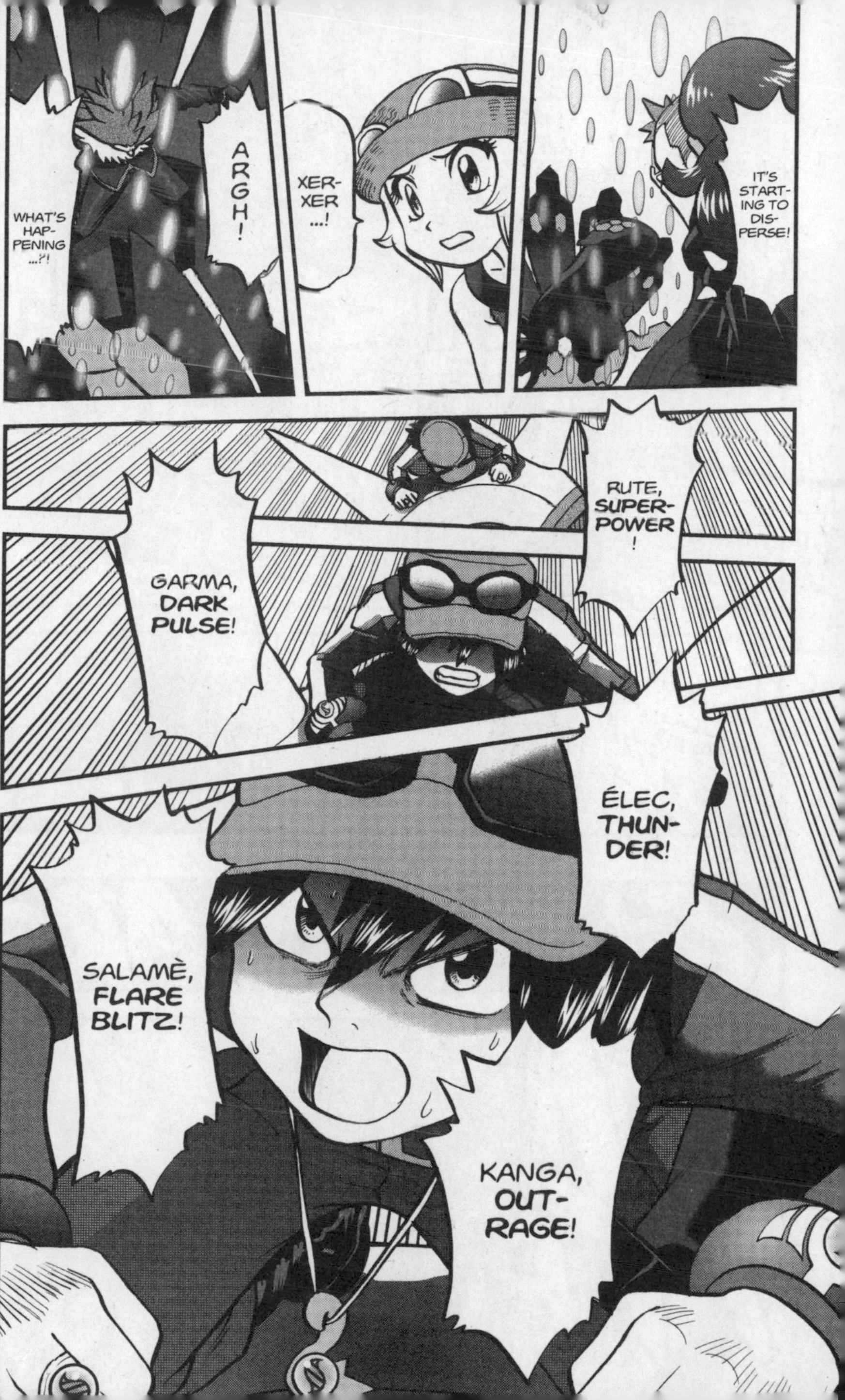
IT'S STARTING TO DISPERSE!
XERXER...!
ARGH!
WHAT'S HAPPENING...?!
RUTE, SUPERPOWER!
GARMA, DARK PULSE!
ÉLEC, THUNDER!
SALAMÈ, FLARE BLITZ!
KANGA, OUTRAGE!

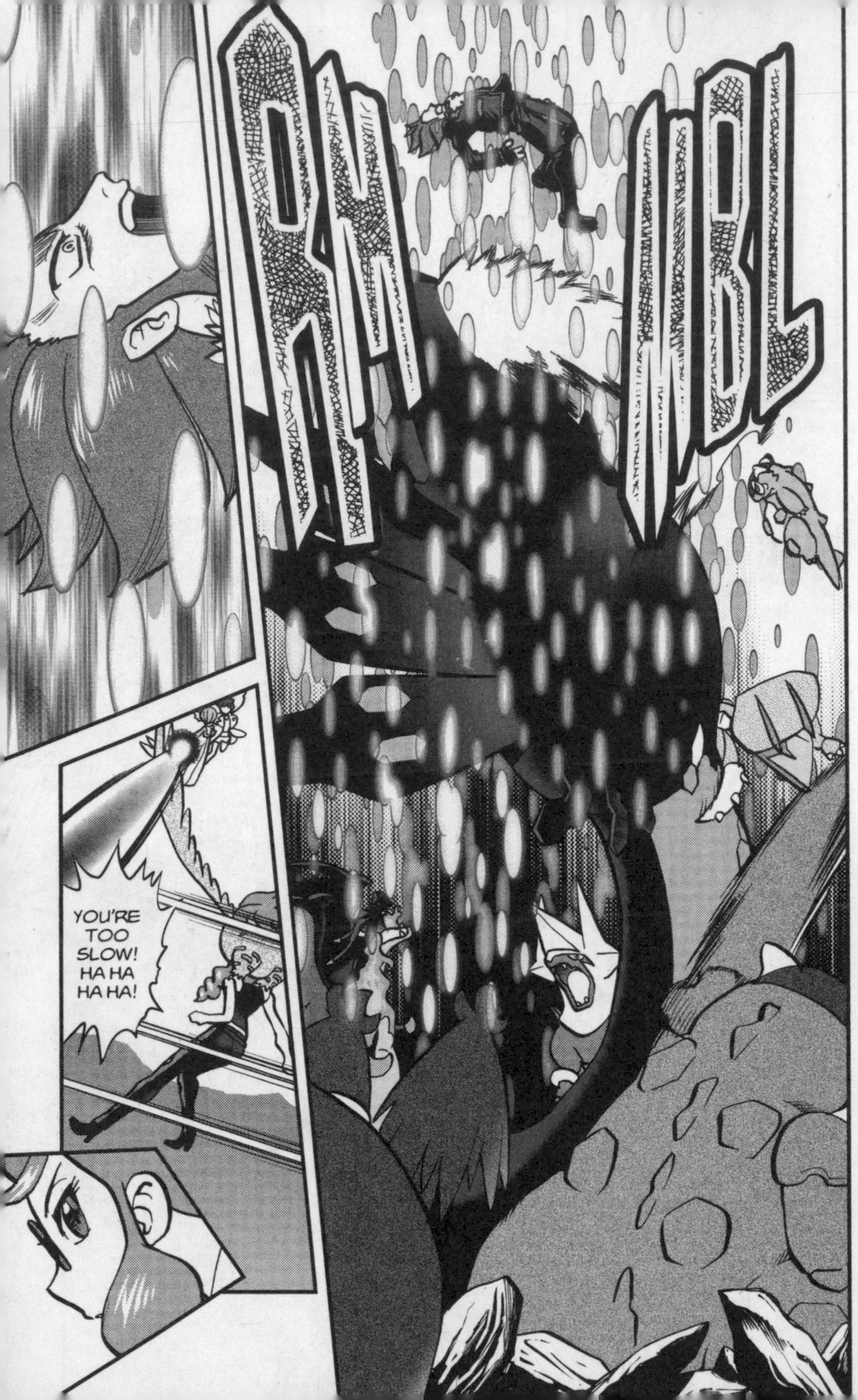
YOU'RE TOO SLOW! HA HA HA HA!

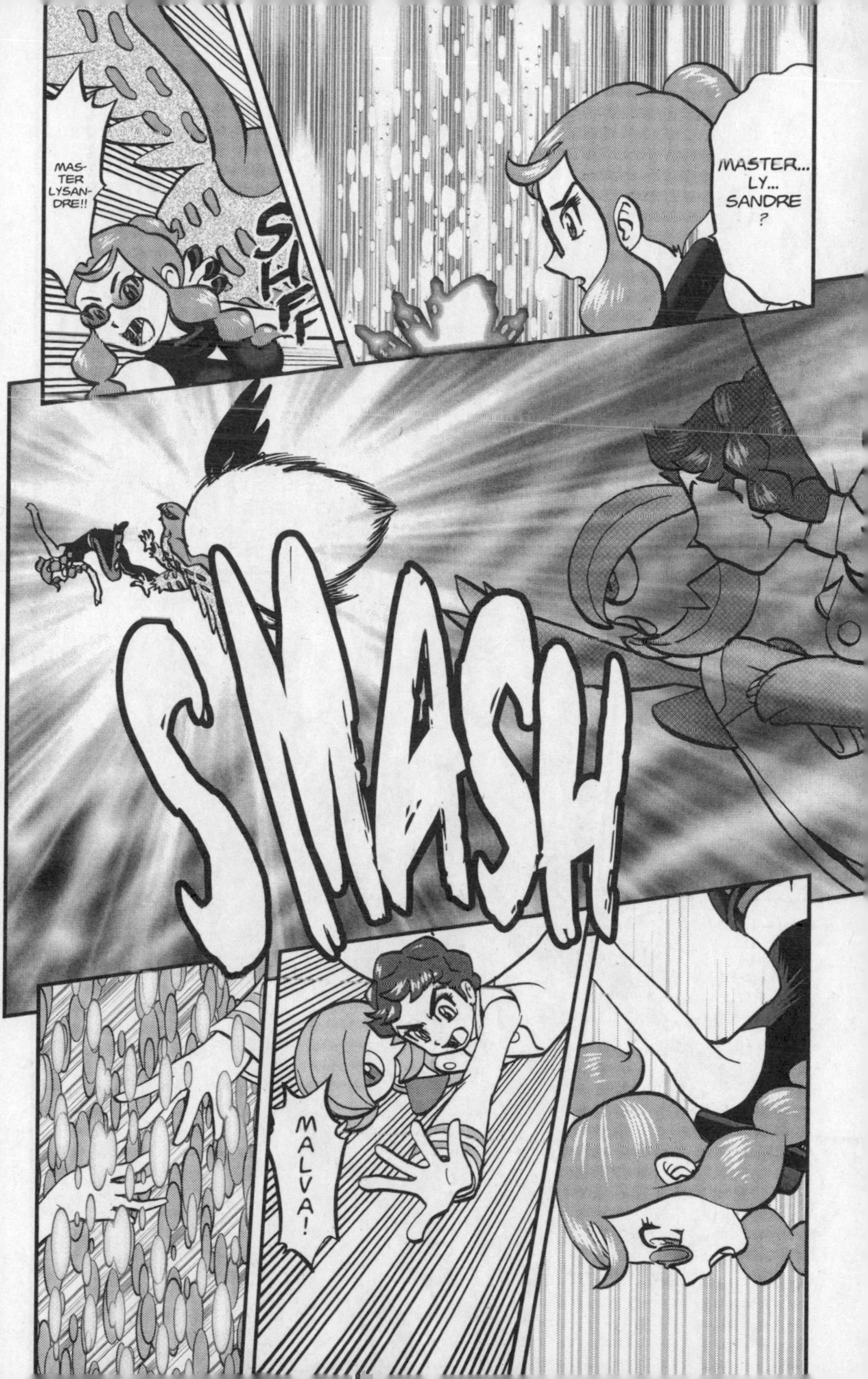
MASTER... LY... SANDRE ?
MAS-TER LYSANDRE!!
SHFF
SMASH
MALVA!

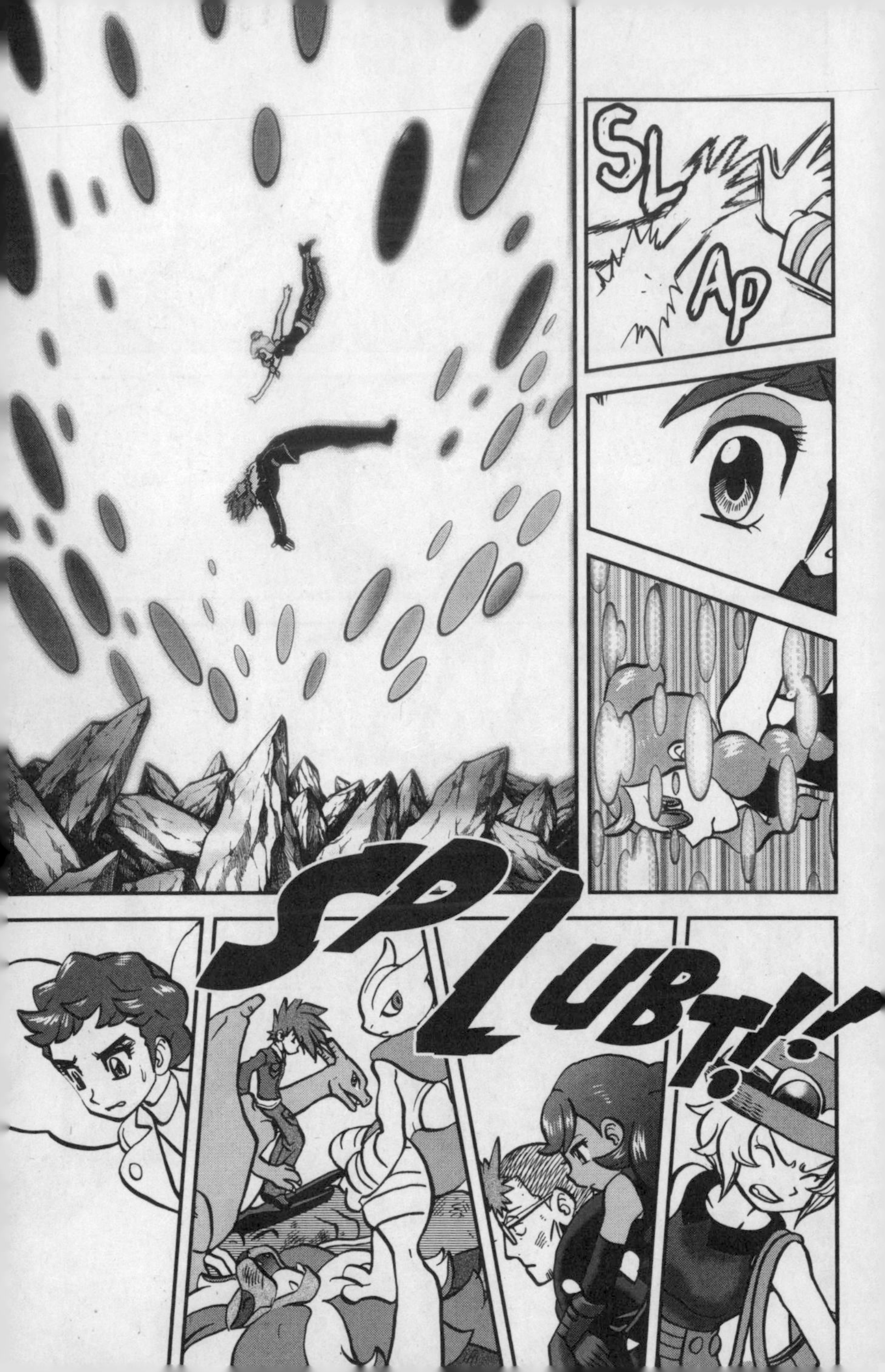
SLAP
SPLUBT!!

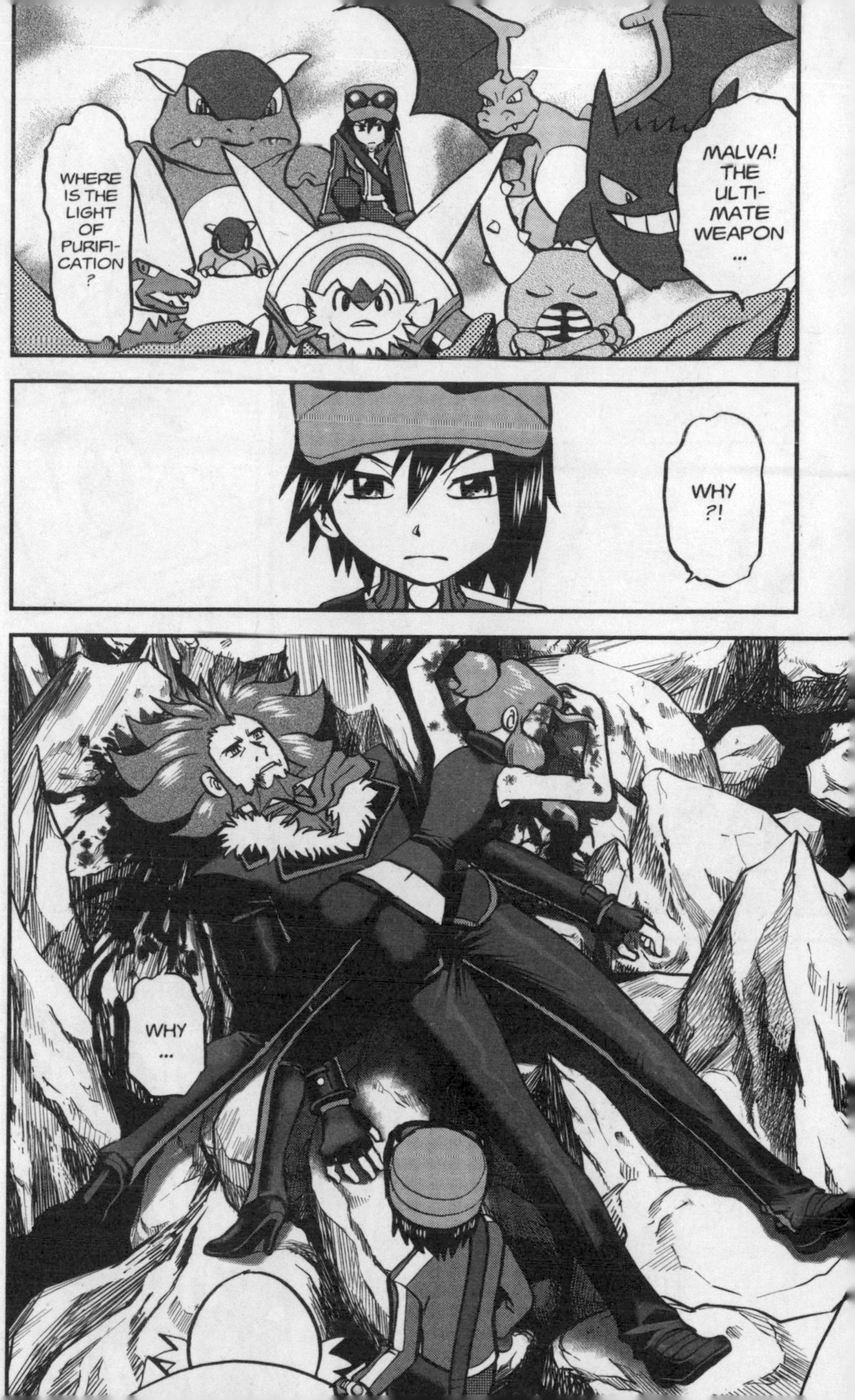
MALVA! THE ULTI-MATE WEAPON ...
WHERE IS THE LIGHT OF PURIFI-CATION ?
WHY ?!
WHY ...

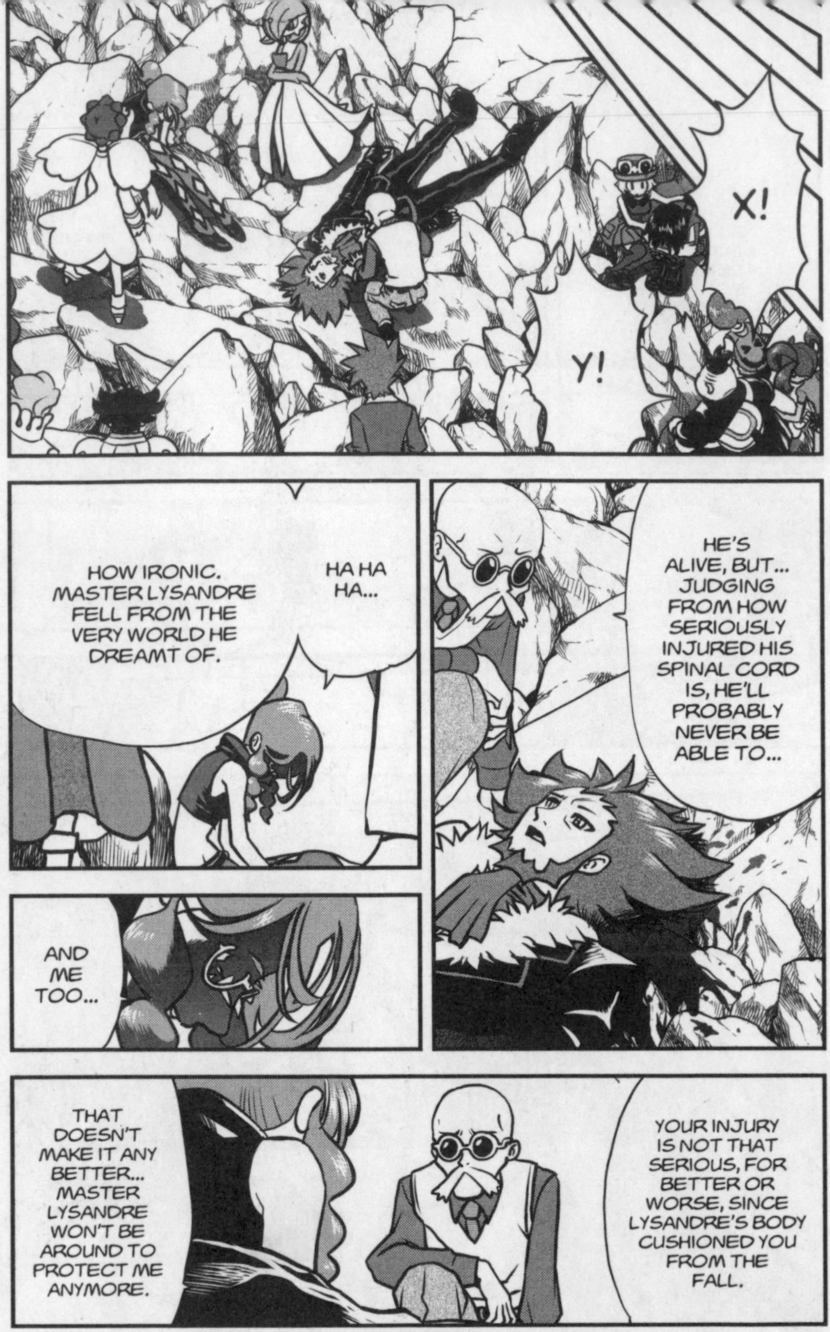
X!
Y!
HE'S ALIVE, BUT... JUDGING FROM HOW SERIOUSLY INJURED HIS SPINAL CORD IS, HE'LL PROBABLY NEVER BE ABLE TO...
HA HA HA...
HOW IRONIC. MASTER LYSANDRE FELL FROM THE VERY WORLD HE DREAMT OF.
AND ME TOO...
YOUR INJURY IS NOT THAT SERIOUS, FOR BETTER OR WORSE, SINCE LYSANDRE'S BODY CUSHIONED YOU FROM THE FALL.
THAT DOESN'T MAKE IT ANY BETTER... MASTER LYSANDRE WON'T BE AROUND TO PROTECT ME ANYMORE.

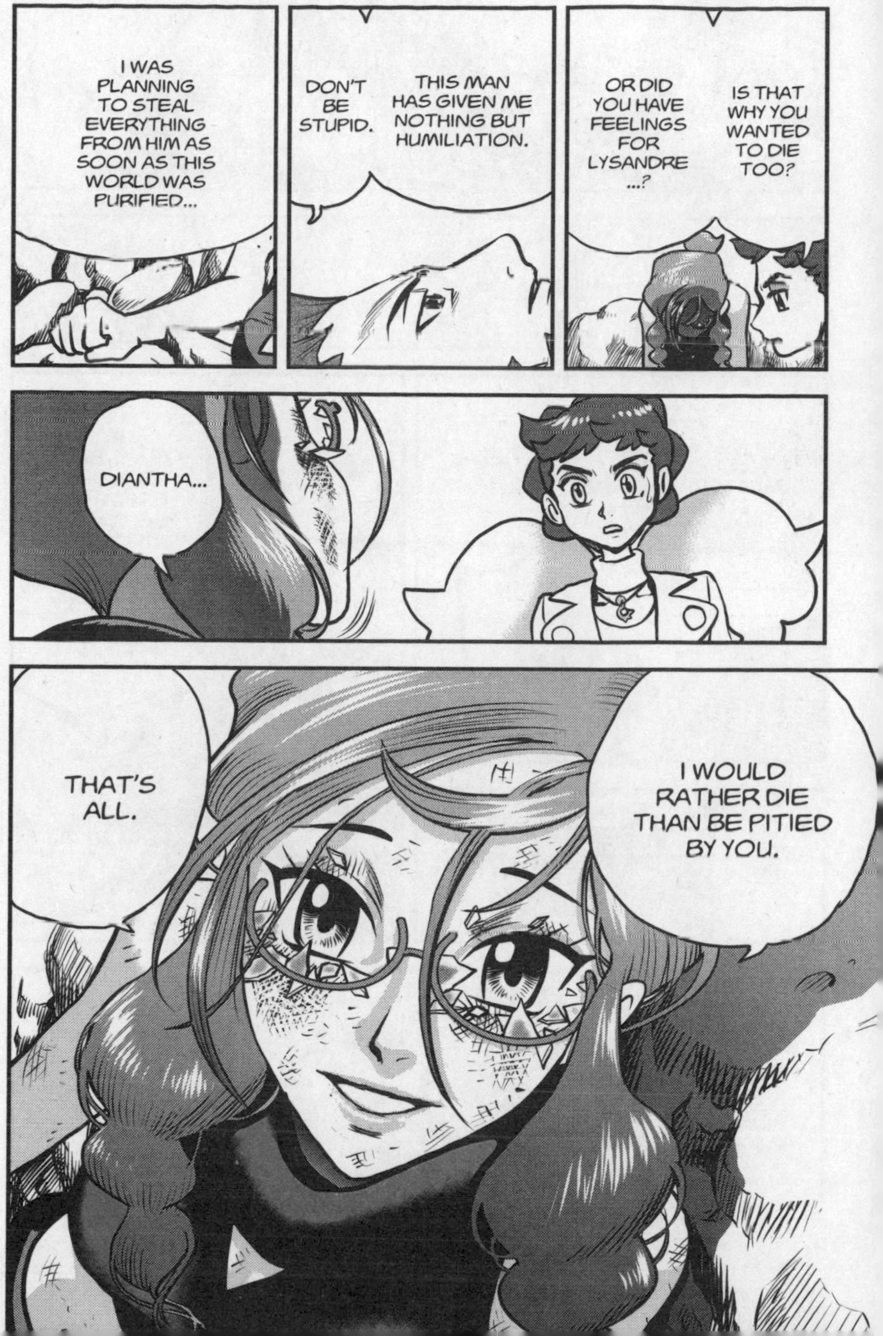
IS THAT WHY YOU WANTED TO DIE TOO?
OR DID YOU HAVE FEELINGS FOR LYSANDRE ...?
THIS MAN HAS GIVEN ME NOTHING BUT HUMILIATION.
DON'T BE STUPID.
I WAS PLANNING TO STEAL EVERYTHING FROM HIM AS SOON AS THIS WORLD WAS PURIFIED...
DIANTHA...
I WOULD RATHER DIE THAN BE PITIED BY YOU.
THAT'S ALL.

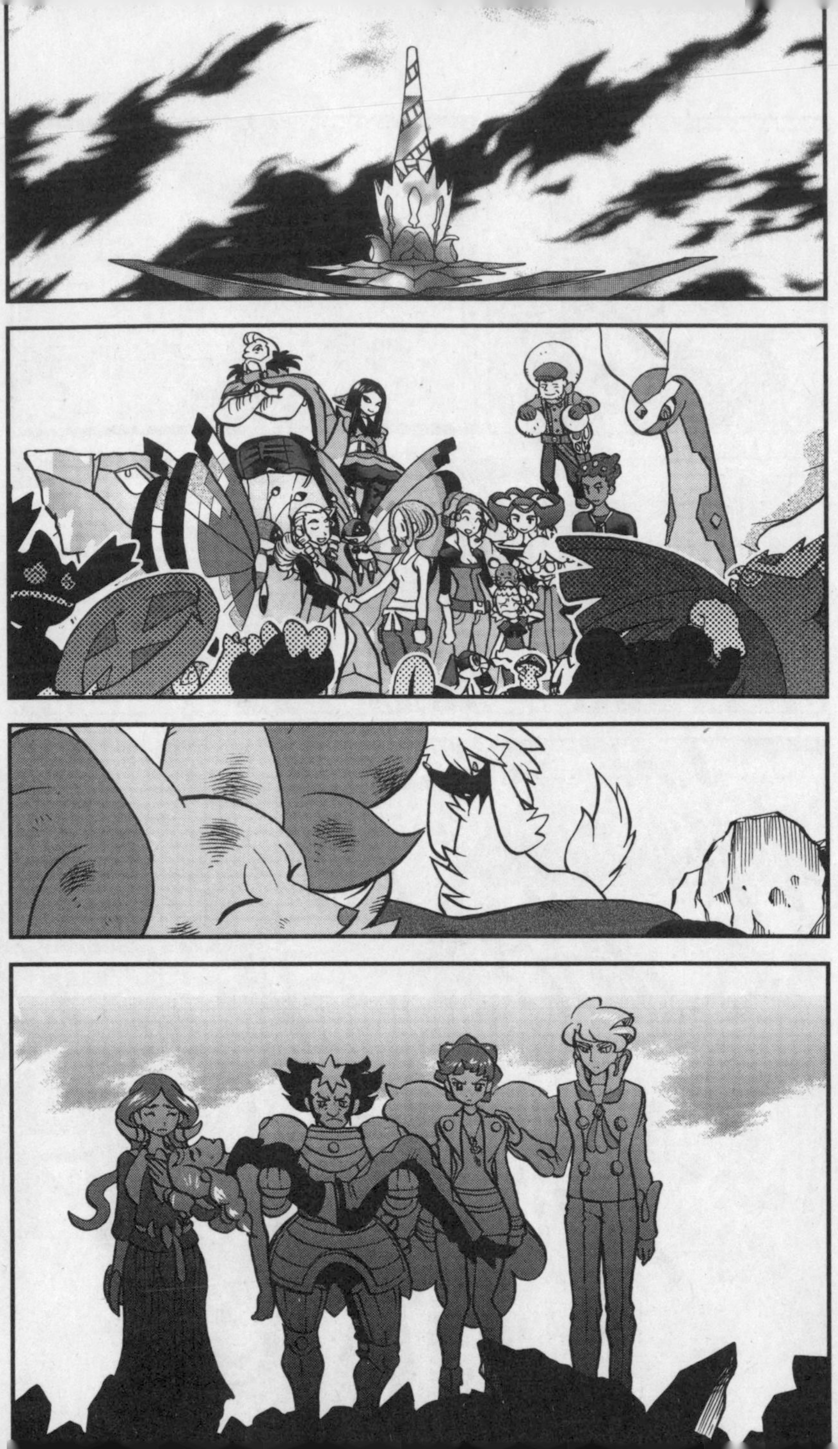

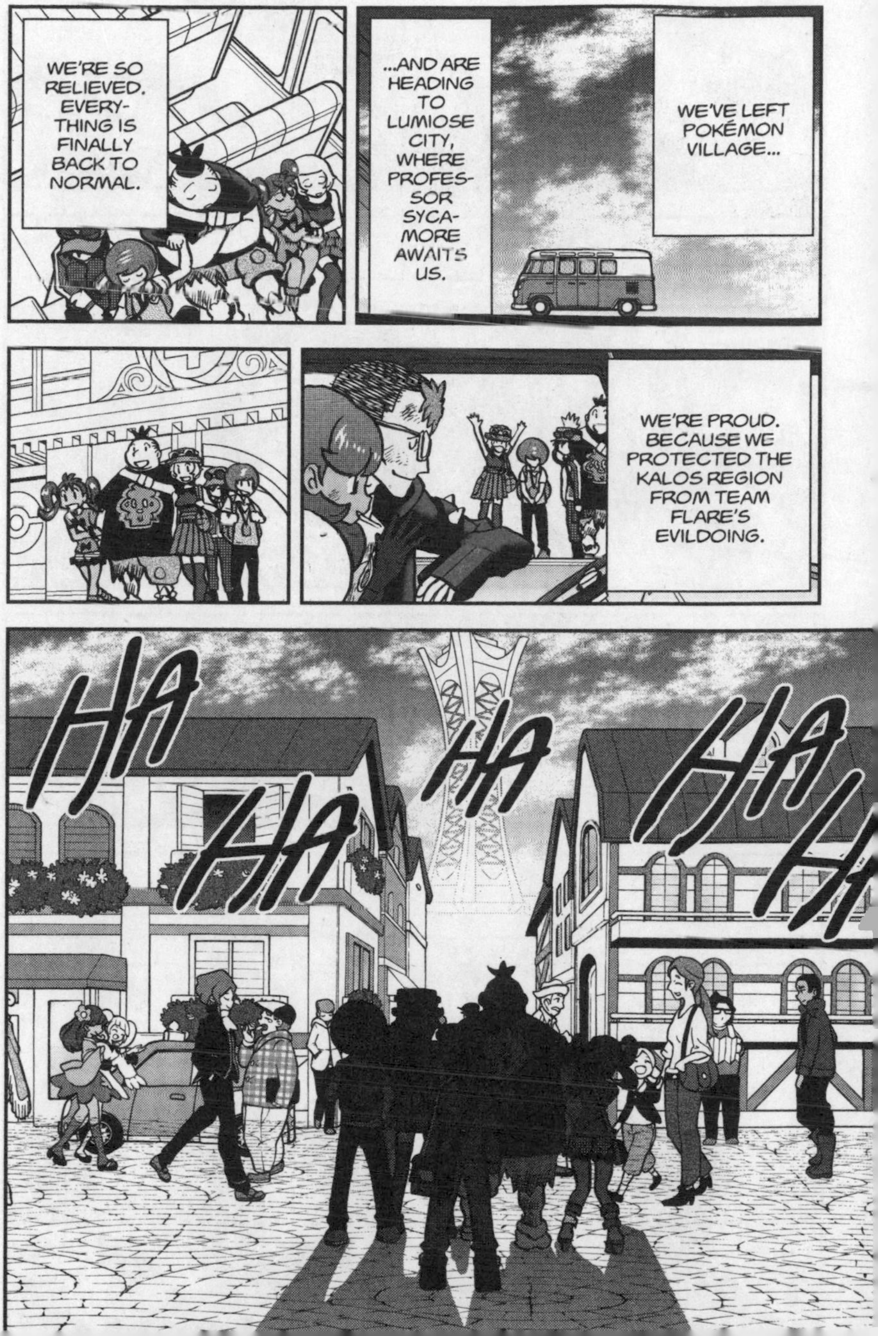
WE'VE LEFT POKÉMON VILLAGE...
...AND ARE HEADING TO LUMIOSE CITY, WHERE PROFESSOR SYCAMORE AWAITS US.
WE'RE SO RELIEVED. EVERYTHING IS FINALLY BACK TO NORMAL.
WE'RE PROUD. BECAUSE WE PROTECTED THE KALOS REGION FROM TEAM FLARE'S EVILDOING.
HA HA
HA
HA HA

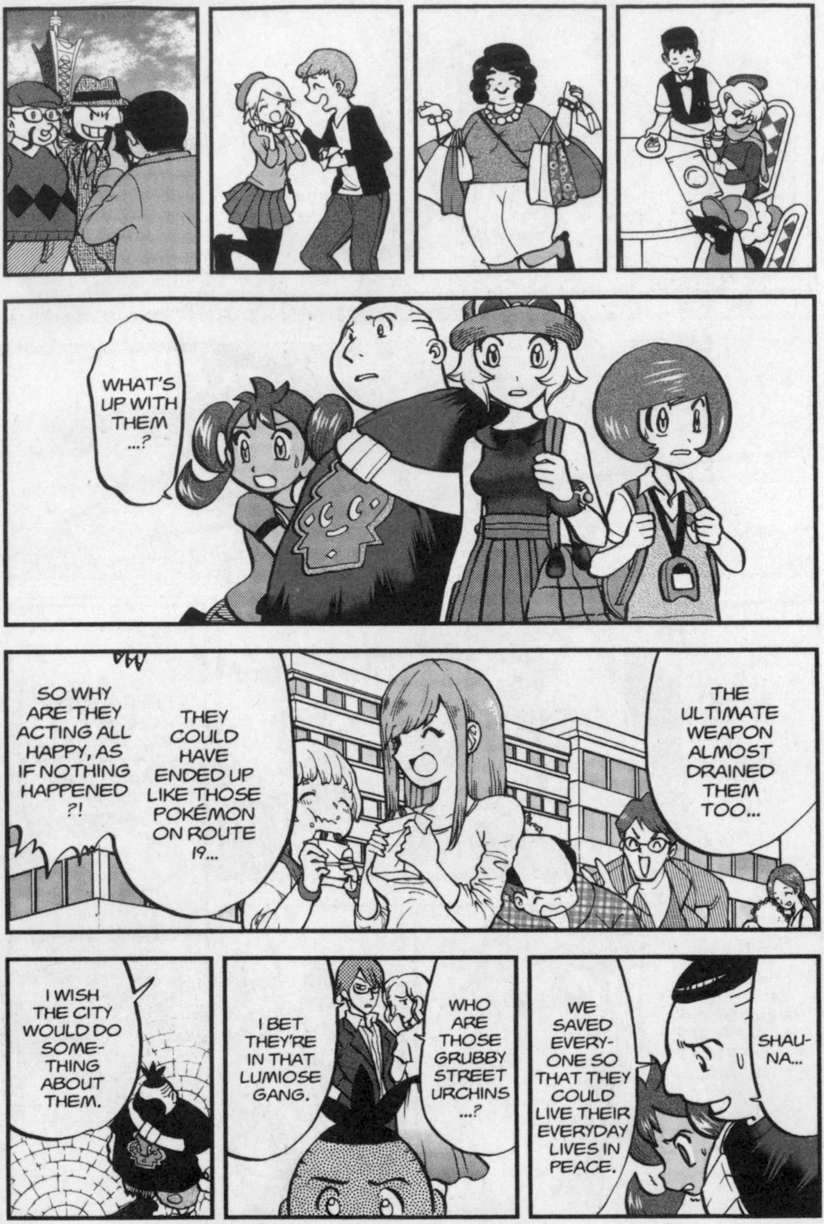
WHAT'S UP WITH THEM ...?
THE ULTIMATE WEAPON ALMOST DRAINED THEM TOO...
THEY COULD HAVE ENDED UP LIKE THOSE POKÉMON ON ROUTE 19...
SO WHY ARE THEY ACTING ALL HAPPY, AS IF NOTHING HAPPENED ?!
SHAU-NA...
WE SAVED EVERY-ONE SO THAT THEY COULD LIVE THEIR EVERYDAY LIVES IN PEACE.
WHO ARE THOSE GRUBBY STREET URCHINS ...?
I BET THEY'RE IN THAT LUMIOSE GANG.
I WISH THE CITY WOULD DO SOME-THING ABOUT THEM.

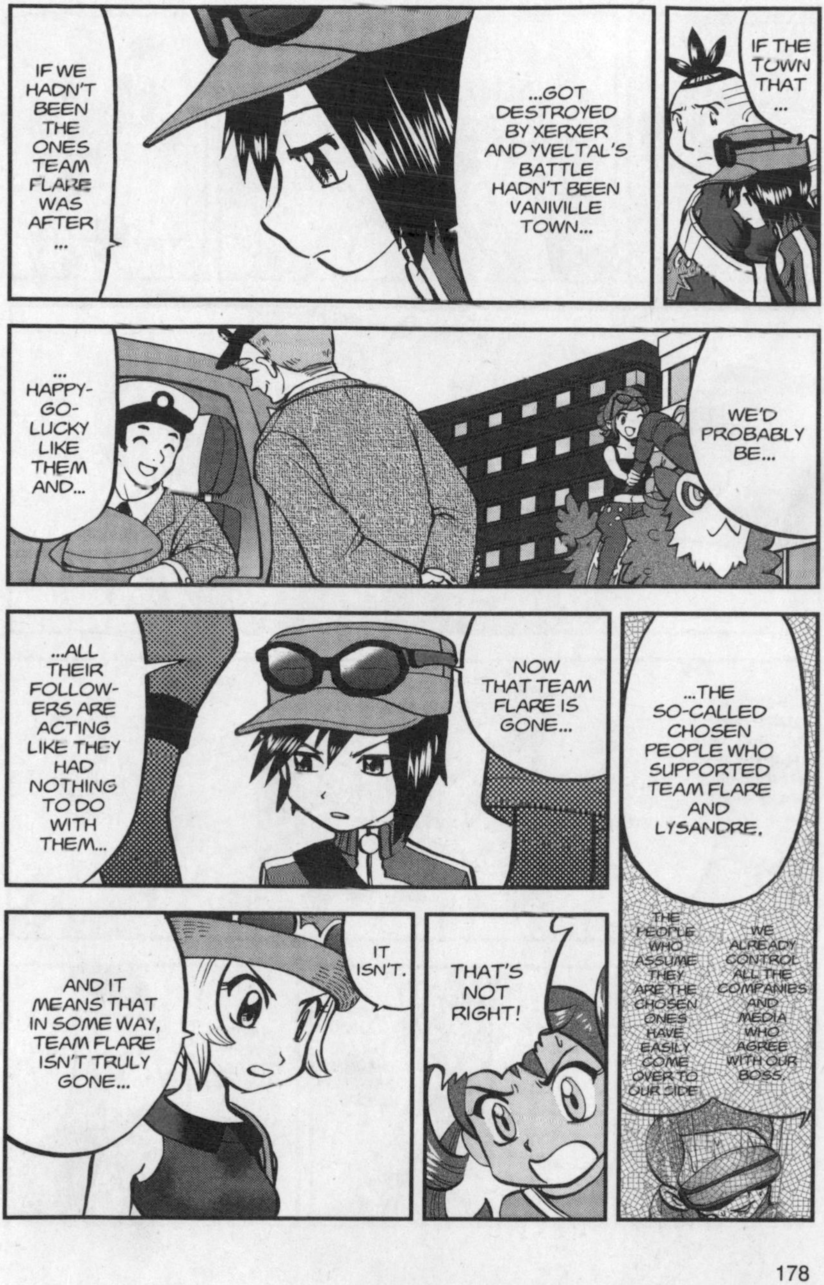
IF THE TOWN THAT ...
...GOT DESTROYED BY XERXER AND YVELTAL'S BATTLE HADN'T BEEN VANIVILLE TOWN...
IF WE HADN'T BEEN THE ONES TEAM FLARE WAS AFTER ...
WE'D PROBABLY BE...
... HAPPY-GO-LUCKY LIKE THEM AND...
...THE SO-CALLED CHOSEN PEOPLE WHO SUPPORTED TEAM FLARE AND LYSANDRE.
WE ALREADY CONTROL ALL THE COMPANIES AND MEDIA WHO AGREE WITH OUR BOSS.
THE PEOPLE WHO ASSUME THEY ARE THE CHOSEN ONES HAVE EASILY COME OVER TO OUR SIDE
NOW THAT TEAM FLARE IS GONE...
...ALL THEIR FOLLOWERS ARE ACTING LIKE THEY HAD NOTHING TO DO WITH THEM...
THAT'S NOT RIGHT!
IT ISN'T.
AND IT MEANS THAT IN SOME WAY, TEAM FLARE ISN'T TRULY GONE...

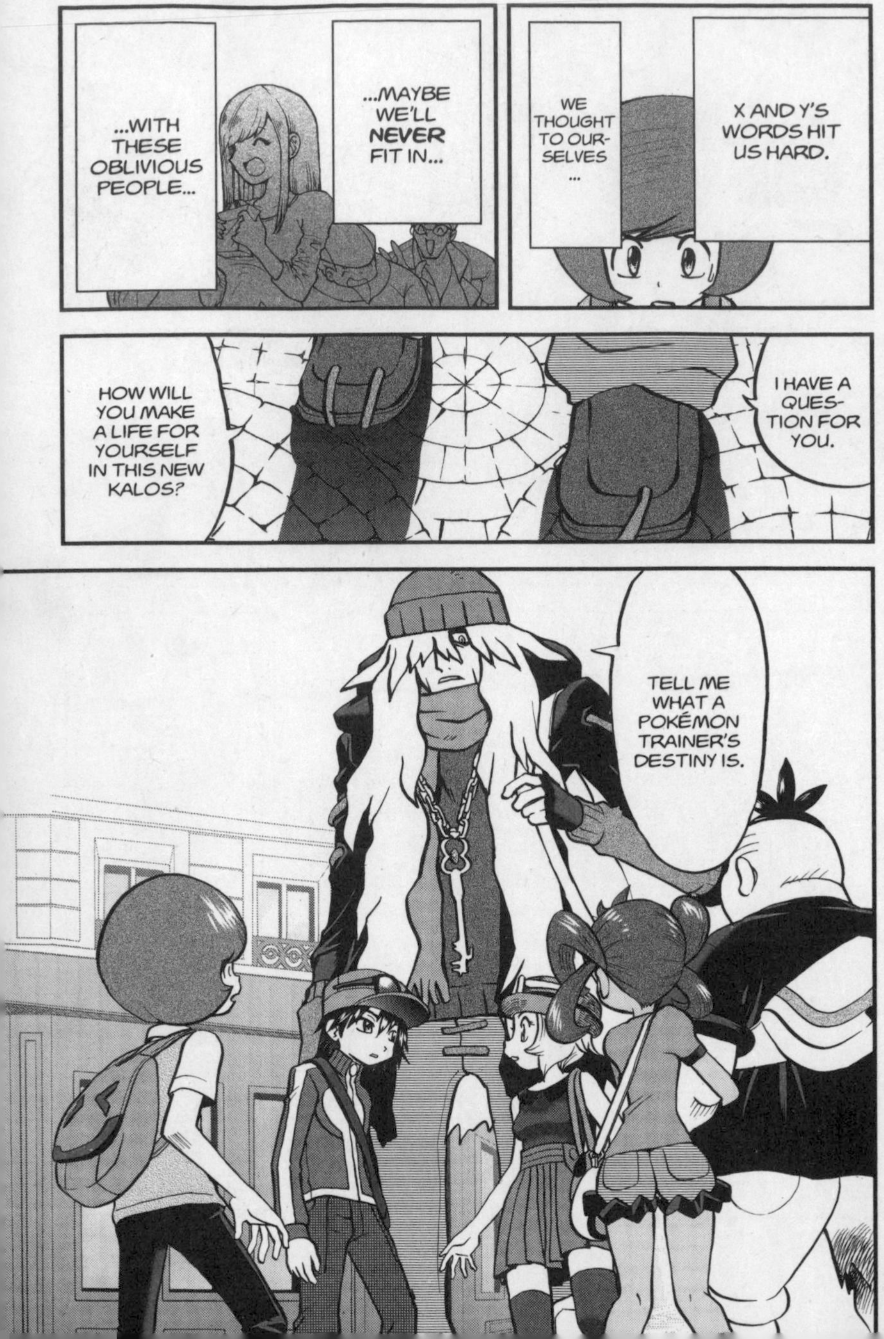
X AND Y'S WORDS HIT US HARD.
WE THOUGHT TO OURSELVES ...
...MAYBE WE'LL **NEVER** FIT IN...
...WITH THESE OBLIVIOUS PEOPLE...
I HAVE A QUESTION FOR YOU.
HOW WILL YOU MAKE A LIFE FOR YOURSELF IN THIS NEW KALOS?
TELL ME WHAT A POKÉMON TRAINER'S DESTINY IS.

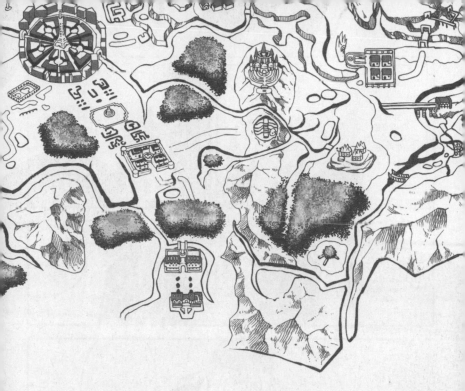

Current Location

Lumiose City

A dazzling metropolis of art and artifice, located in the very heart of the Kalos region.

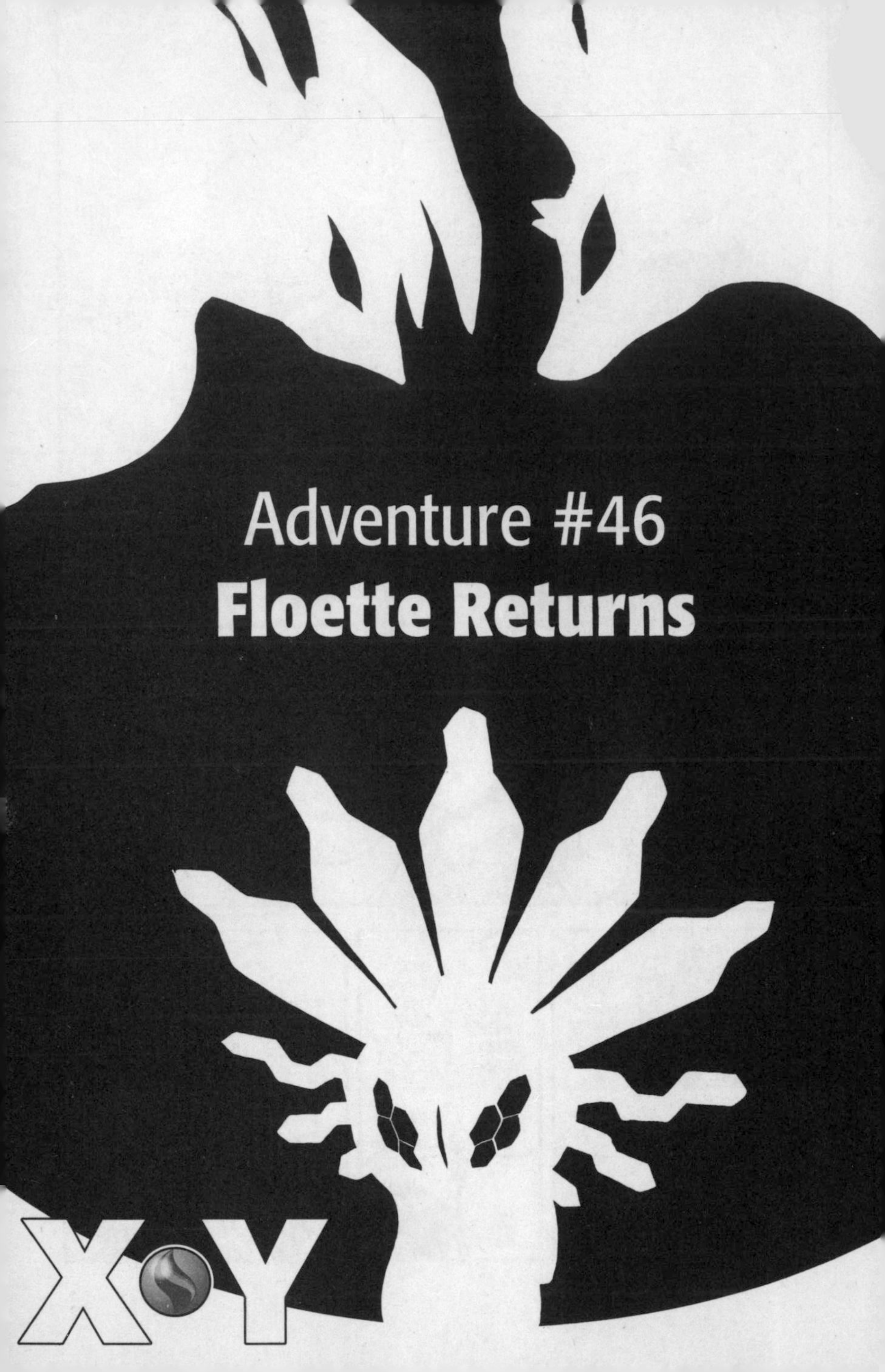

Adventure #46
Floette Returns

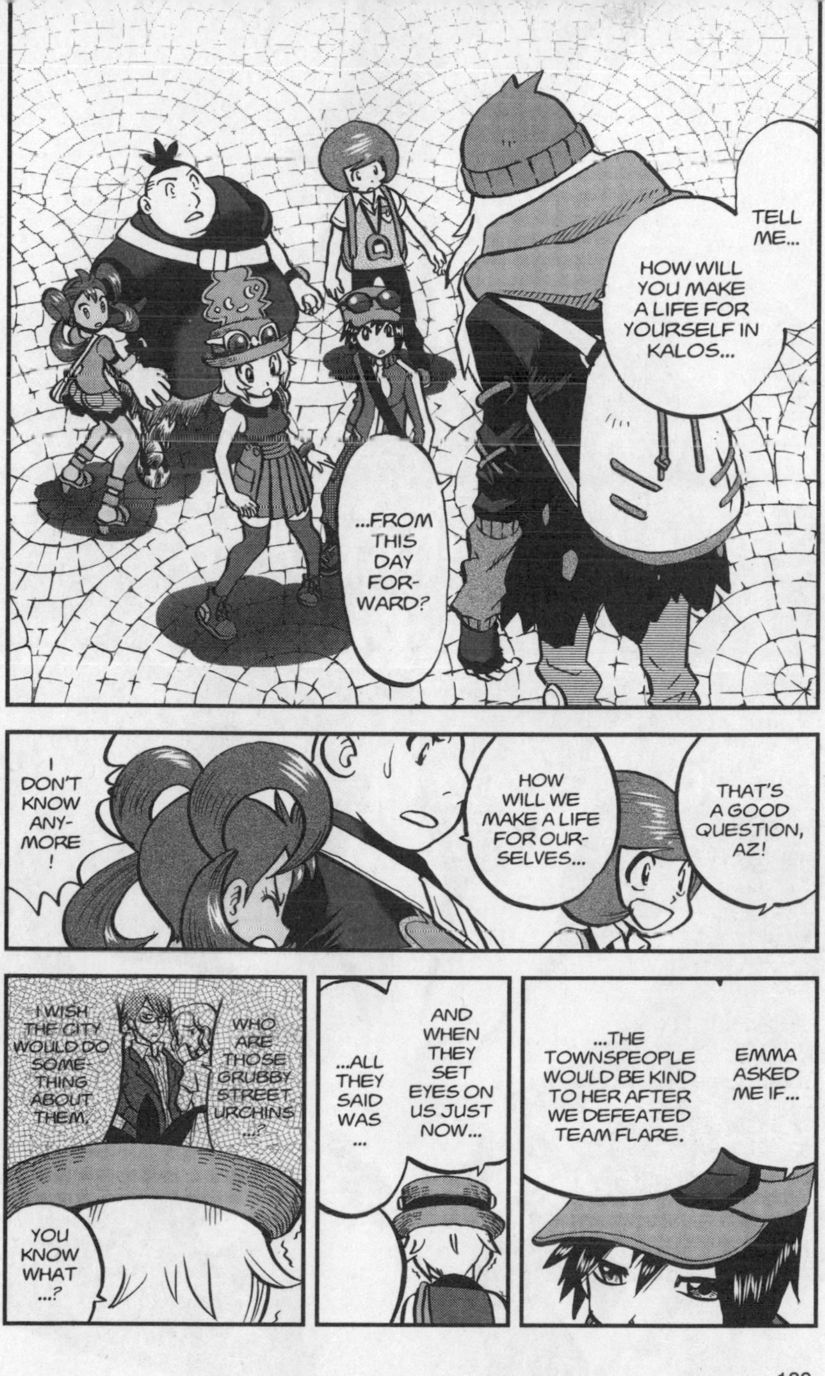
TELL ME... HOW WILL YOU MAKE A LIFE FOR YOURSELF IN KALOS...
...FROM THIS DAY FORWARD?
THAT'S A GOOD QUESTION, AZ!
HOW WILL WE MAKE A LIFE FOR OURSELVES...
I DON'T KNOW ANYMORE!
EMMA ASKED ME IF...
...THE TOWNSPEOPLE WOULD BE KIND TO HER AFTER WE DEFEATED TEAM FLARE.
AND WHEN THEY SET EYES ON US JUST NOW...
...ALL THEY SAID WAS...
WHO ARE THOSE GRUBBY STREET URCHINS...?
I WISH THE CITY WOULD DO SOMETHING ABOUT THEM.
YOU KNOW WHAT...?

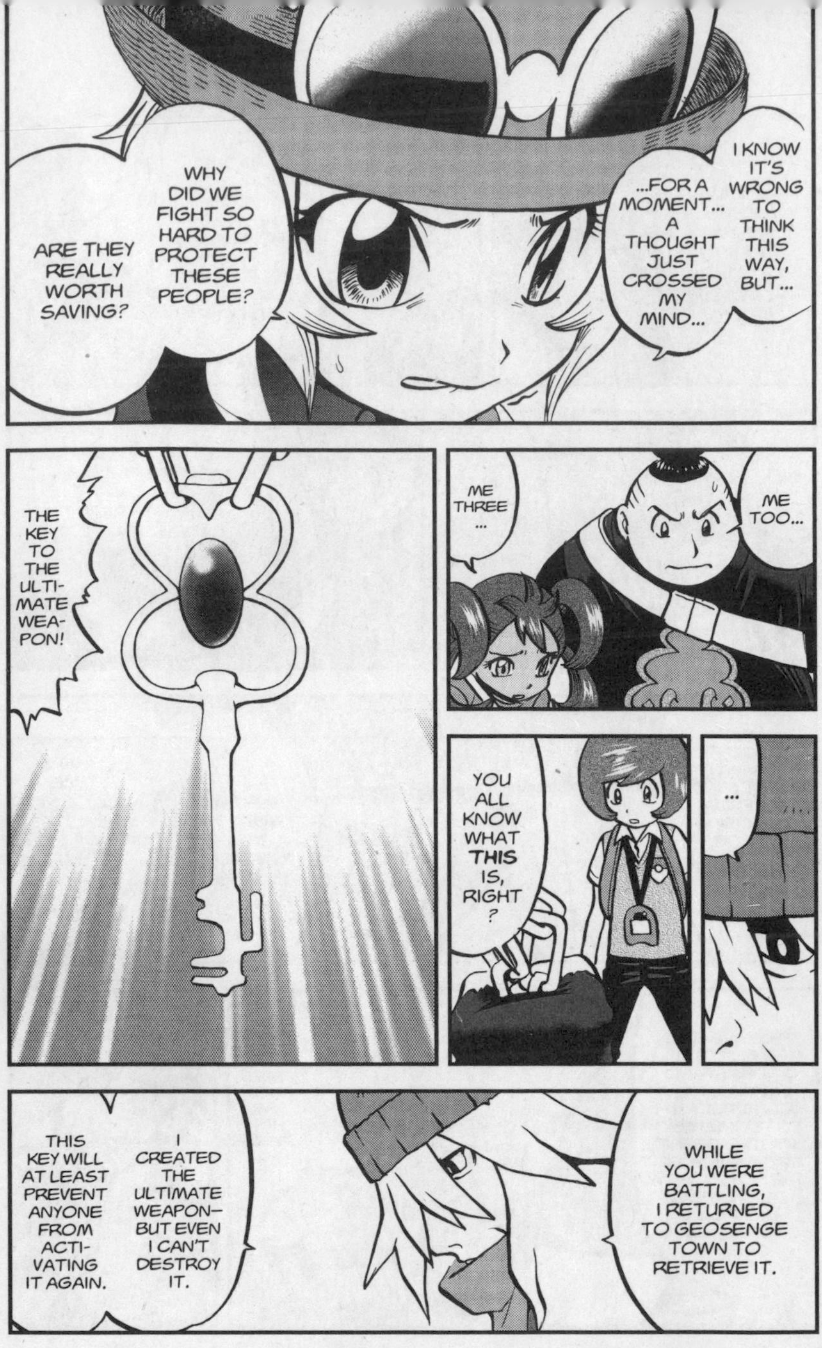
I KNOW IT'S WRONG TO THINK THIS WAY, BUT...
...FOR A MOMENT... A THOUGHT JUST CROSSED MY MIND...
WHY DID WE FIGHT SO HARD TO PROTECT THESE PEOPLE?
ARE THEY REALLY WORTH SAVING?
ME TOO...
ME THREE ...
...
YOU ALL KNOW WHAT **THIS** IS, RIGHT?
THE KEY TO THE ULTIMATE WEAPON!
WHILE YOU WERE BATTLING, I RETURNED TO GEOSENGE TOWN TO RETRIEVE IT.
I CREATED THE ULTIMATE WEAPON—BUT EVEN I CAN'T DESTROY IT.
THIS KEY WILL AT LEAST PREVENT ANYONE FROM ACTIVATING IT AGAIN.

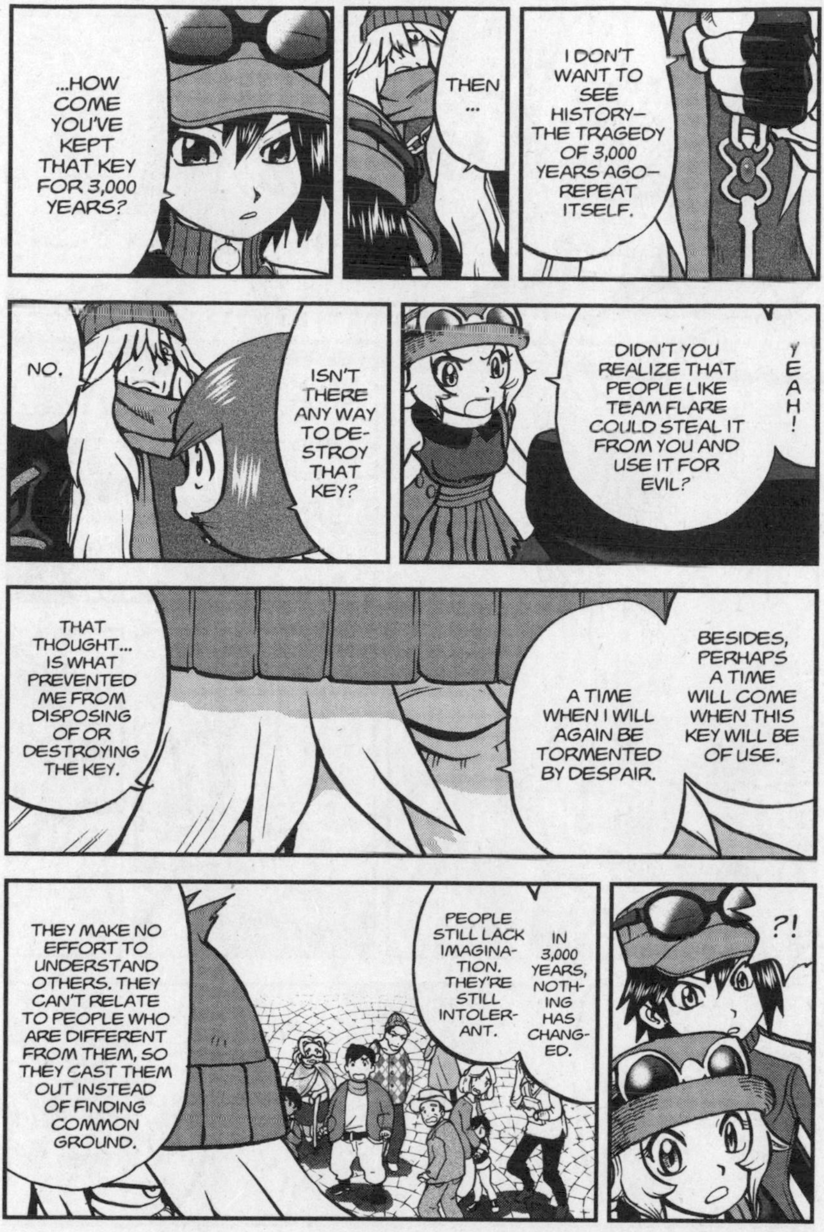
I DON'T WANT TO SEE HISTORY—THE TRAGEDY OF 3,000 YEARS AGO—REPEAT ITSELF.
THEN ...
...HOW COME YOU'VE KEPT THAT KEY FOR 3,000 YEARS?
YEAH!
DIDN'T YOU REALIZE THAT PEOPLE LIKE TEAM FLARE COULD STEAL IT FROM YOU AND USE IT FOR EVIL?
ISN'T THERE ANY WAY TO DESTROY THAT KEY?
NO.
BESIDES, PERHAPS A TIME WILL COME WHEN THIS KEY WILL BE OF USE.
A TIME WHEN I WILL AGAIN BE TORMENTED BY DESPAIR.
THAT THOUGHT... IS WHAT PREVENTED ME FROM DISPOSING OF OR DESTROYING THE KEY.
?!
IN 3,000 YEARS, NOTHING HAS CHANGED.
PEOPLE STILL LACK IMAGINATION. THEY'RE STILL INTOLERANT.
THEY MAKE NO EFFORT TO UNDERSTAND OTHERS. THEY CAN'T RELATE TO PEOPLE WHO ARE DIFFERENT FROM THEM, SO THEY CAST THEM OUT INSTEAD OF FINDING COMMON GROUND.

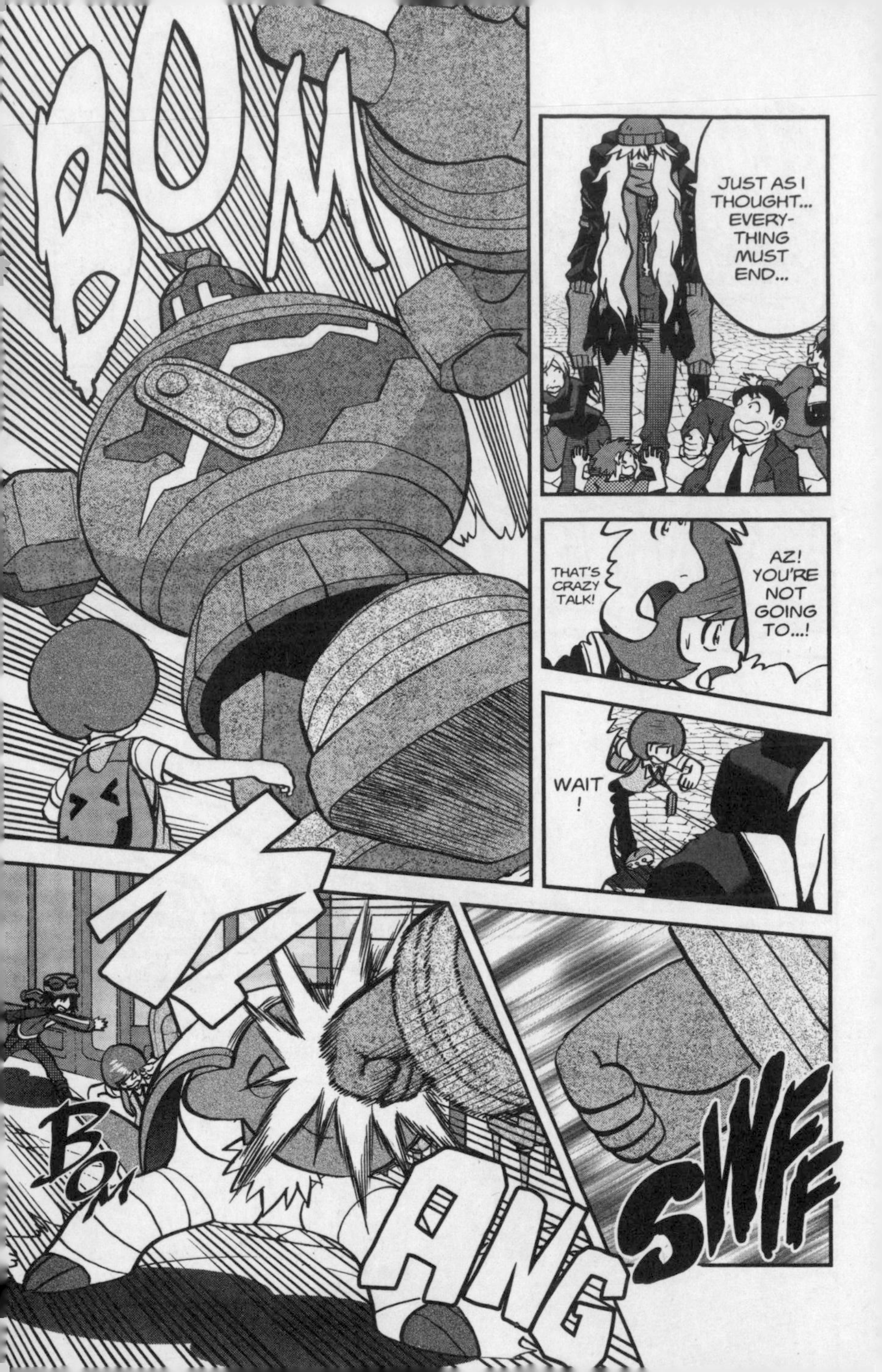
JUST AS I THOUGHT... EVERY-THING MUST END...
AZ! YOU'RE NOT GOING TO...!
THAT'S CRAZY TALK!
WAIT!
BOOM

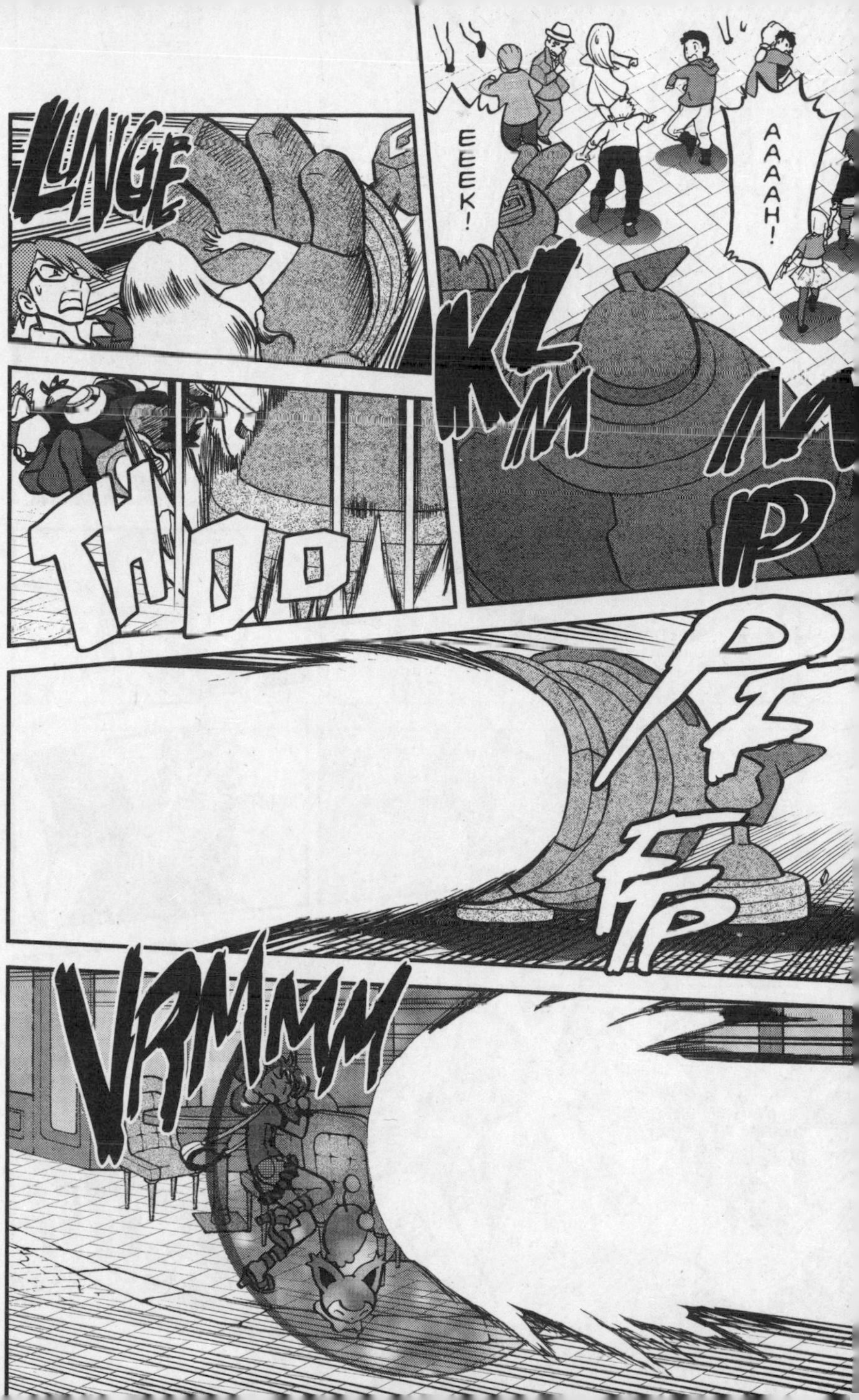
AAAAH!
EEEK!
LUNGE
VRMMM

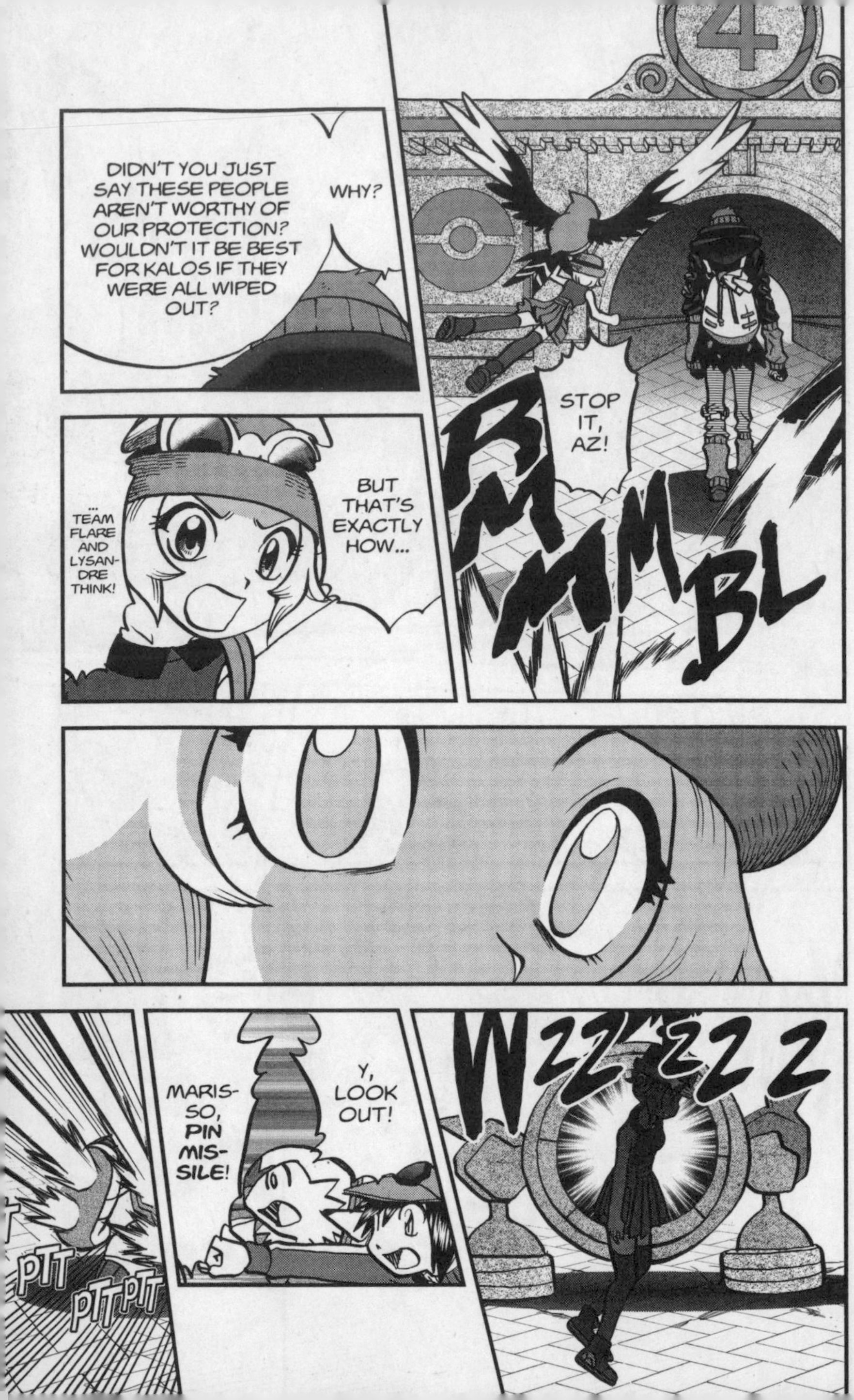
STOP IT, AZ!
RMMMBL
WHY?
DIDN'T YOU JUST SAY THESE PEOPLE AREN'T WORTHY OF OUR PROTECTION? WOULDN'T IT BE BEST FOR KALOS IF THEY WERE ALL WIPED OUT?
BUT THAT'S EXACTLY HOW...
... TEAM FLARE AND LYSANDRE THINK!
WZZZZZ
Y, LOOK OUT!
MARIS-SO, PIN MIS-SILE!
PTT
PTTPTT

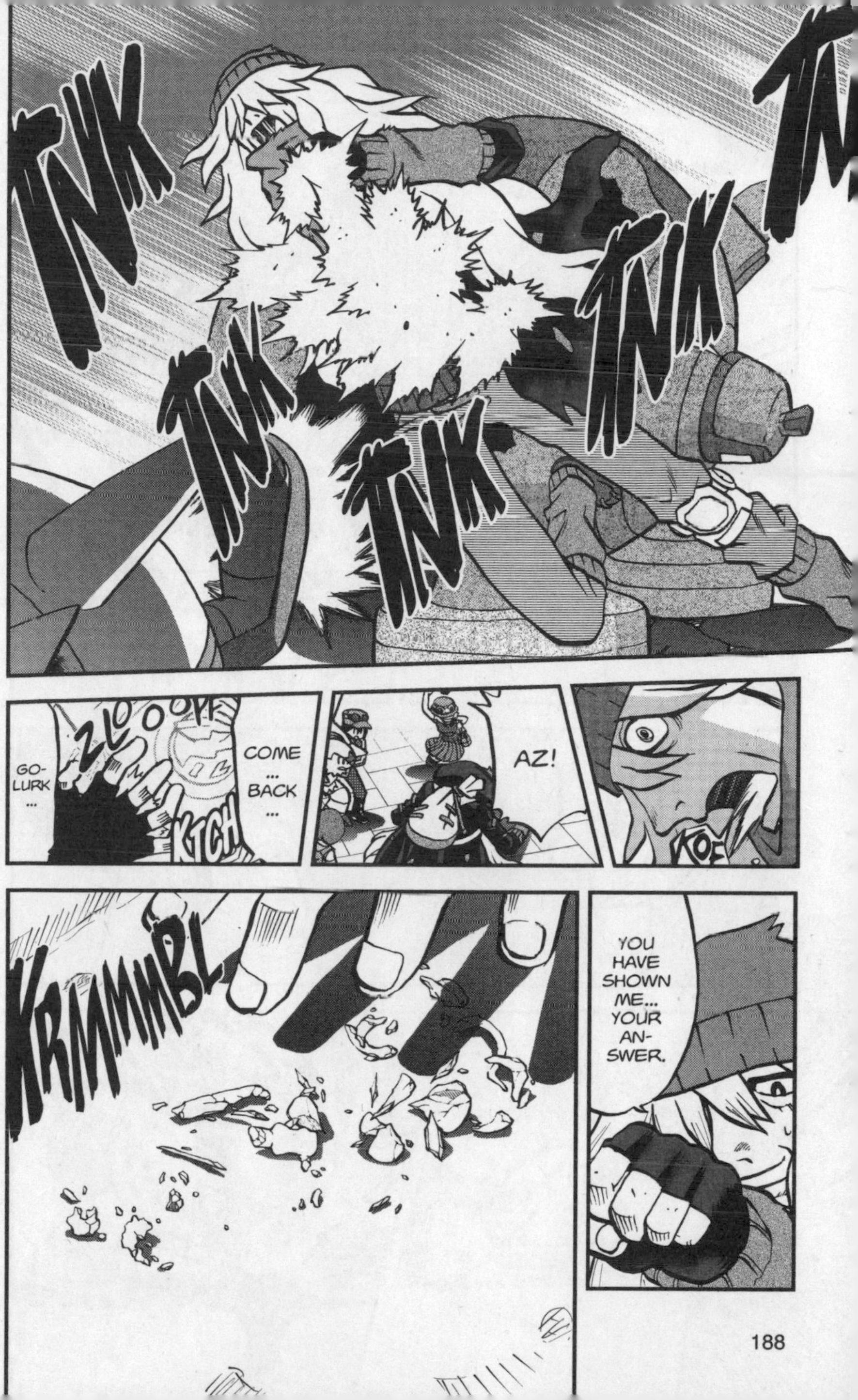

TINK
TINK
TINK
TINK
TINK
KOF
AZ!
COME ... BACK ...
ZLOOOP
GO-LURK ...
KTCH
YOU HAVE SHOWN ME... YOUR ANSWER.
KRMMMBL

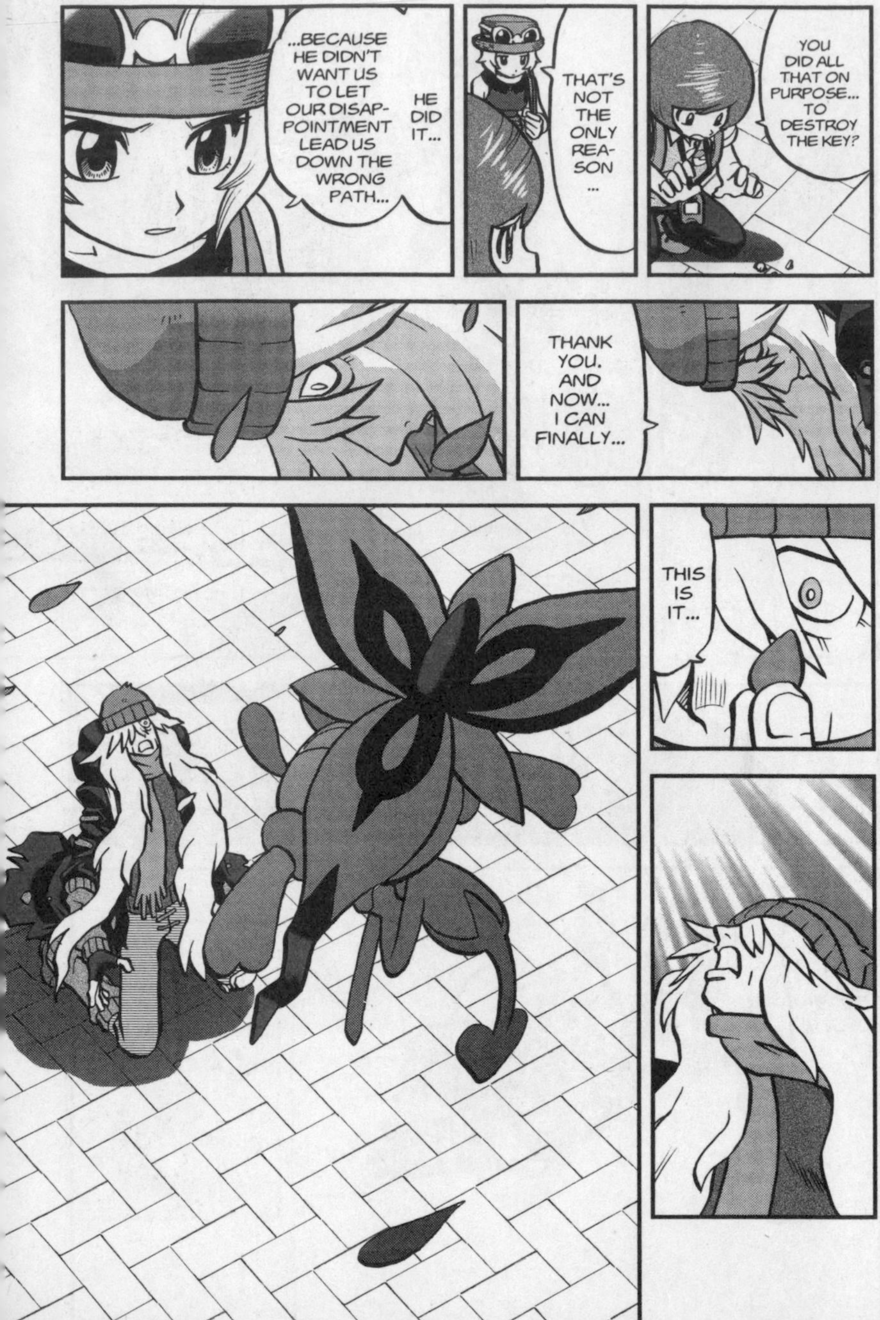
YOU DID ALL THAT ON PURPOSE... TO DESTROY THE KEY?
THAT'S NOT THE ONLY REA-SON ...
HE DID IT...
...BECAUSE HE DIDN'T WANT US TO LET OUR DISAP-POINTMENT LEAD US DOWN THE WRONG PATH...
THANK YOU. AND NOW... I CAN FINALLY...
THIS IS IT...

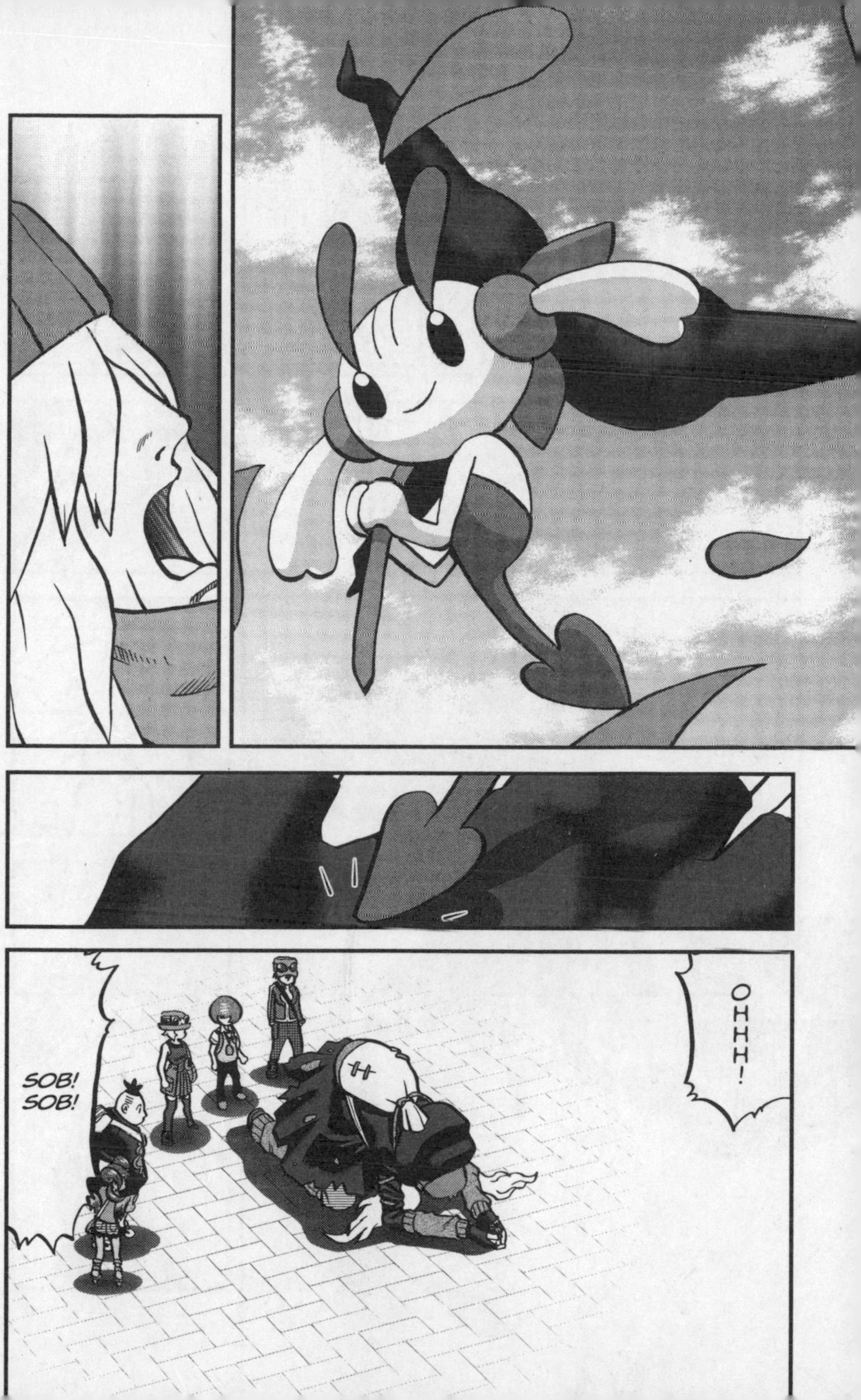
OHHH!
SOB!
SOB!

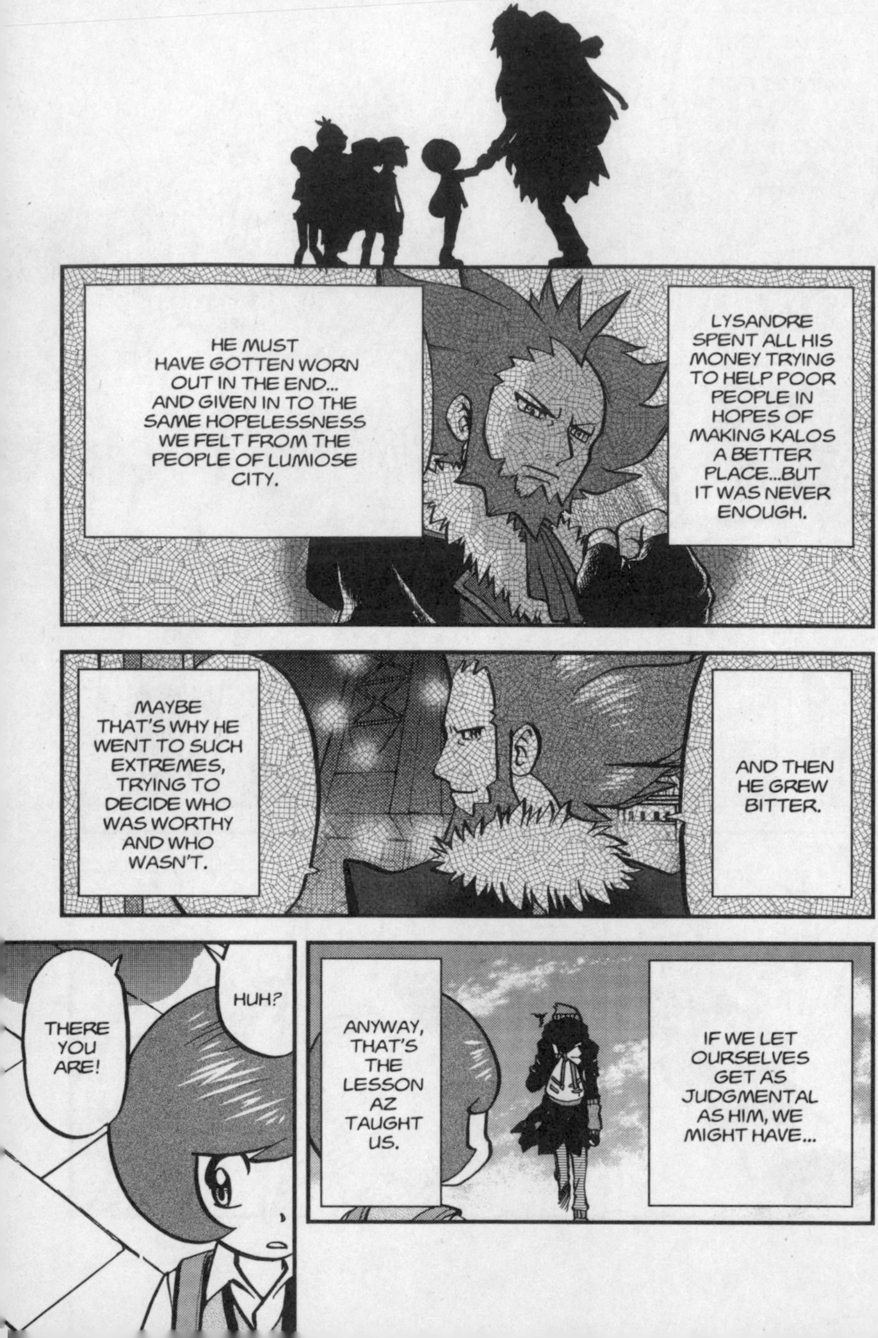
LYSANDRE SPENT ALL HIS MONEY TRYING TO HELP POOR PEOPLE IN HOPES OF MAKING KALOS A BETTER PLACE...BUT IT WAS NEVER ENOUGH.
HE MUST HAVE GOTTEN WORN OUT IN THE END... AND GIVEN IN TO THE SAME HOPELESSNESS WE FELT FROM THE PEOPLE OF LUMIOSE CITY.
AND THEN HE GREW BITTER.
MAYBE THAT'S WHY HE WENT TO SUCH EXTREMES, TRYING TO DECIDE WHO WAS WORTHY AND WHO WASN'T.
IF WE LET OURSELVES GET AS JUDGMENTAL AS HIM, WE MIGHT HAVE...
ANYWAY, THAT'S THE LESSON AZ TAUGHT US.
HUH?
THERE YOU ARE!

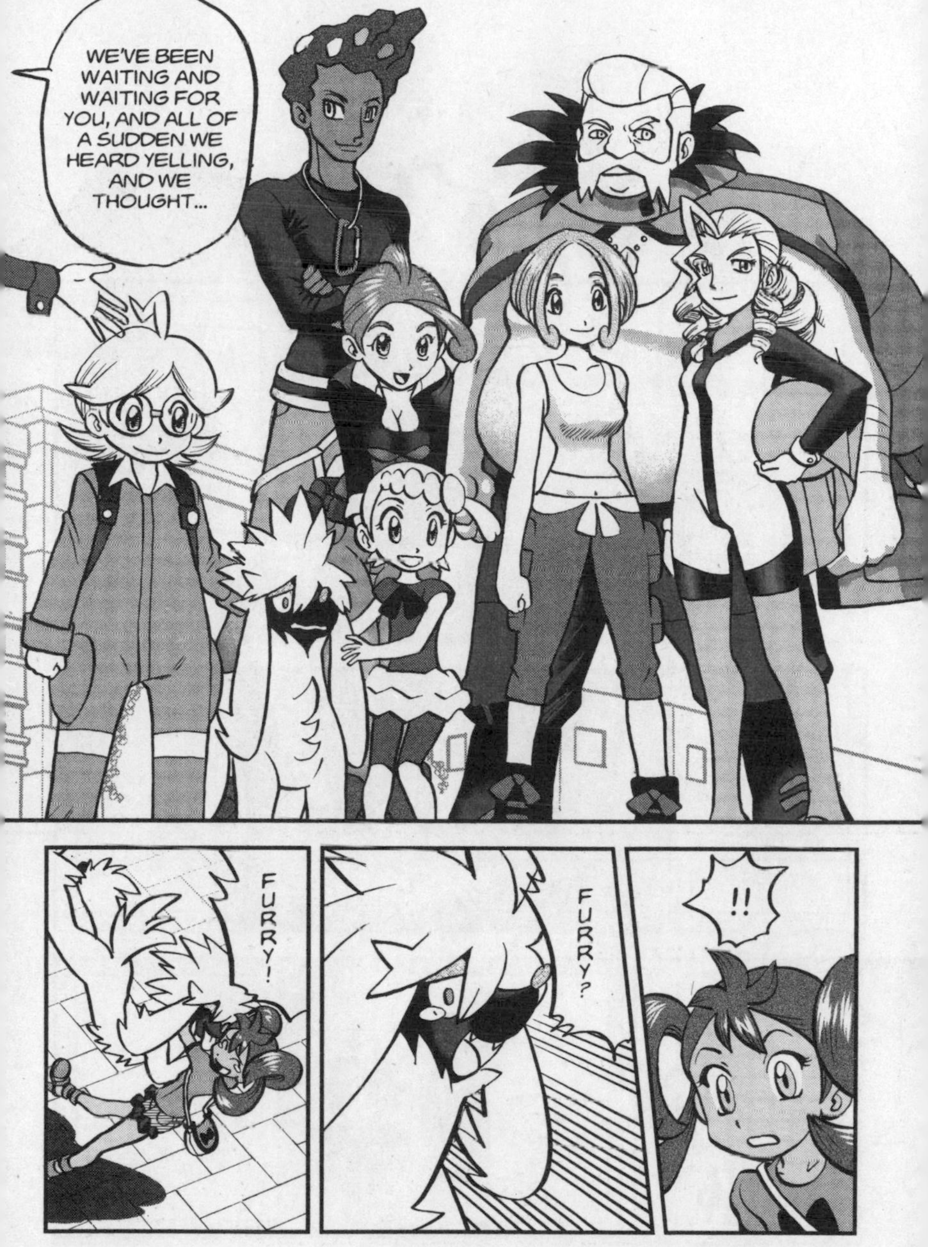
WE'VE BEEN WAITING AND WAITING FOR YOU, AND ALL OF A SUDDEN WE HEARD YELLING, AND WE THOUGHT...
!!
FURRY?
FURRY!

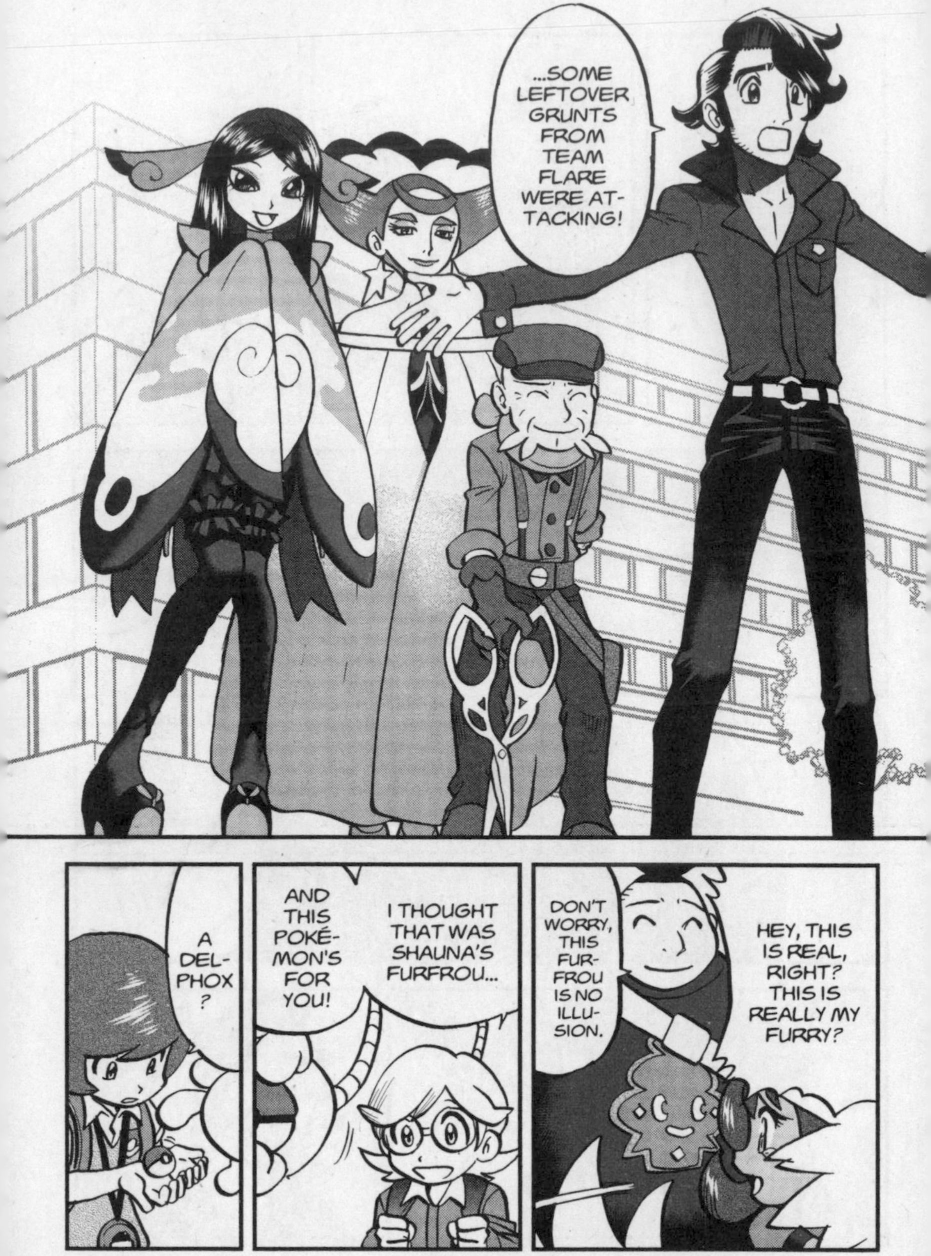
...SOME LEFTOVER GRUNTS FROM TEAM FLARE WERE AT-TACKING!
HEY, THIS IS REAL, RIGHT? THIS IS REALLY MY FURRY?
DON'T WORRY, THIS FUR-FROU IS NO ILLU-SION.
I THOUGHT THAT WAS SHAUNA'S FURFROU...
AND THIS POKÉ-MON'S FOR YOU!
A DEL-PHOX ?

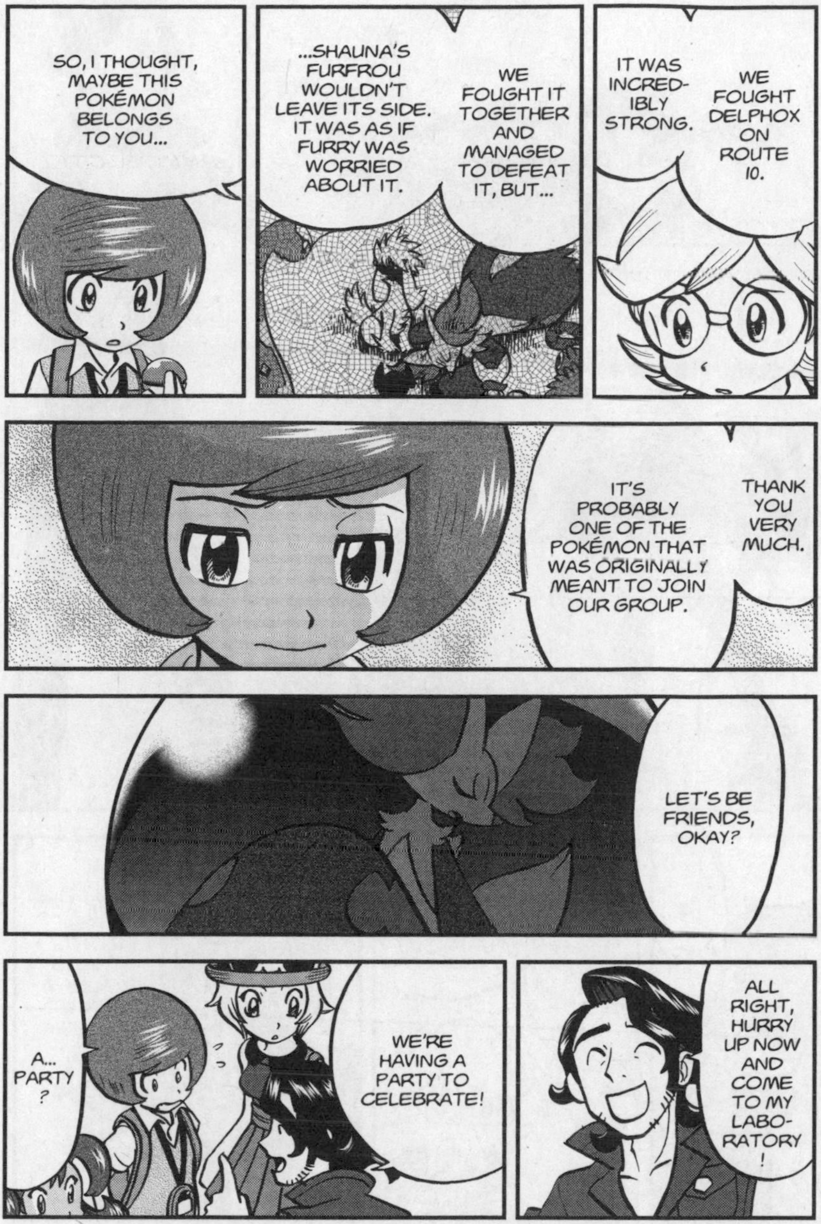
WE FOUGHT DELPHOX ON ROUTE 10.
IT WAS INCRED-IBLY STRONG.
WE FOUGHT IT TOGETHER AND MANAGED TO DEFEAT IT, BUT...
...SHAUNA'S FURFROU WOULDN'T LEAVE ITS SIDE. IT WAS AS IF FURRY WAS WORRIED ABOUT IT.
SO, I THOUGHT, MAYBE THIS POKÉMON BELONGS TO YOU...
THANK YOU VERY MUCH.
IT'S PROBABLY ONE OF THE POKÉMON THAT WAS ORIGINALLY MEANT TO JOIN OUR GROUP.
LET'S BE FRIENDS, OKAY?
ALL RIGHT, HURRY UP NOW AND COME TO MY LABO-RATORY!
WE'RE HAVING A PARTY TO CELEBRATE!
A... PARTY?

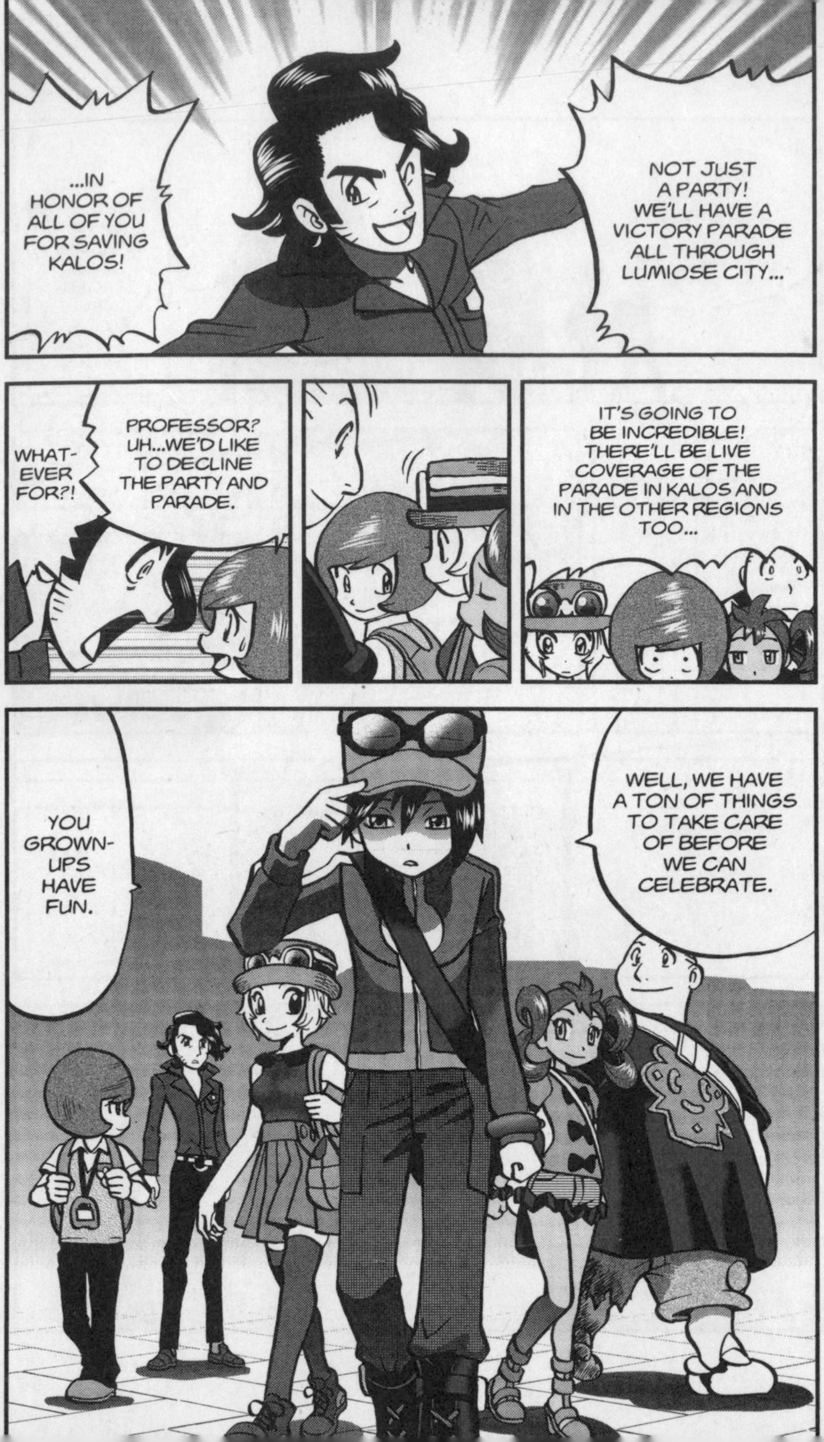
NOT JUST A PARTY! WE'LL HAVE A VICTORY PARADE ALL THROUGH LUMIOSE CITY...
...IN HONOR OF ALL OF YOU FOR SAVING KALOS!
IT'S GOING TO BE INCREDIBLE! THERE'LL BE LIVE COVERAGE OF THE PARADE IN KALOS AND IN THE OTHER REGIONS TOO...
PROFESSOR? UH...WE'D LIKE TO DECLINE THE PARTY AND PARADE.
WHAT-EVER FOR?!
WELL, WE HAVE A TON OF THINGS TO TAKE CARE OF BEFORE WE CAN CELEBRATE.
YOU GROWN-UPS HAVE FUN.

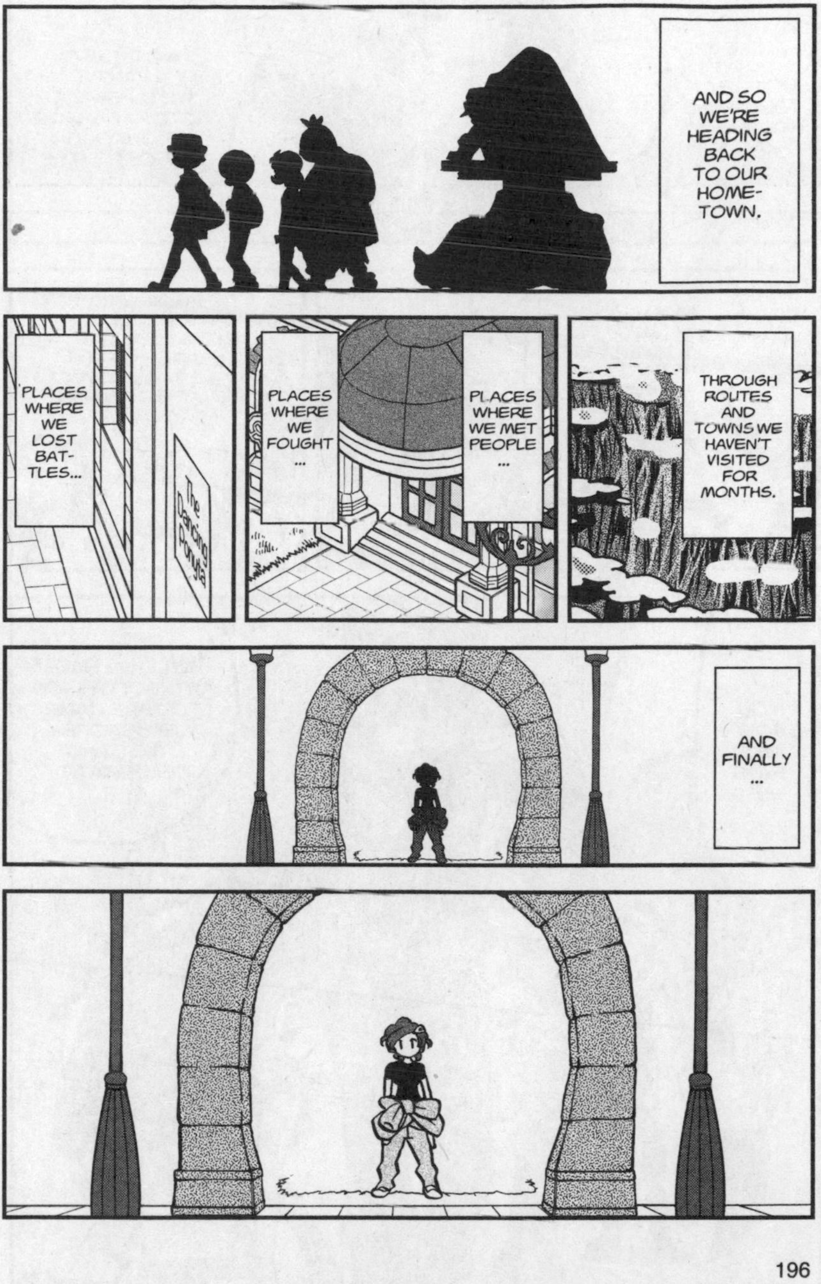
AND SO WE'RE HEADING BACK TO OUR HOME-TOWN.
THROUGH ROUTES AND TOWNS WE HAVEN'T VISITED FOR MONTHS.
PLACES WHERE WE MET PEOPLE ...
PLACES WHERE WE FOUGHT ...
PLACES WHERE WE LOST BAT-TLES...
The Dancing Ponyta
AND FINALLY ...

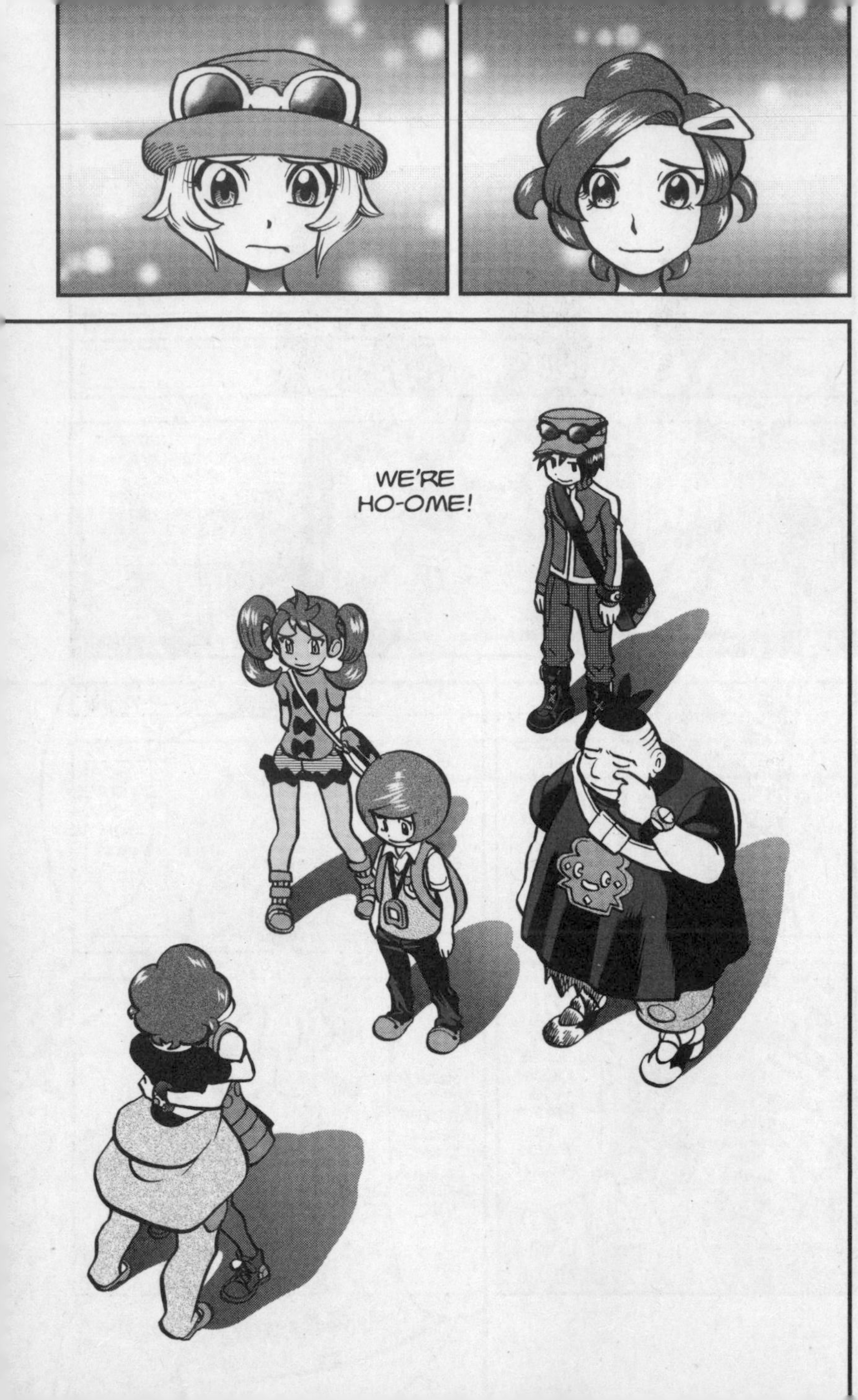
WE'RE HO-OME!

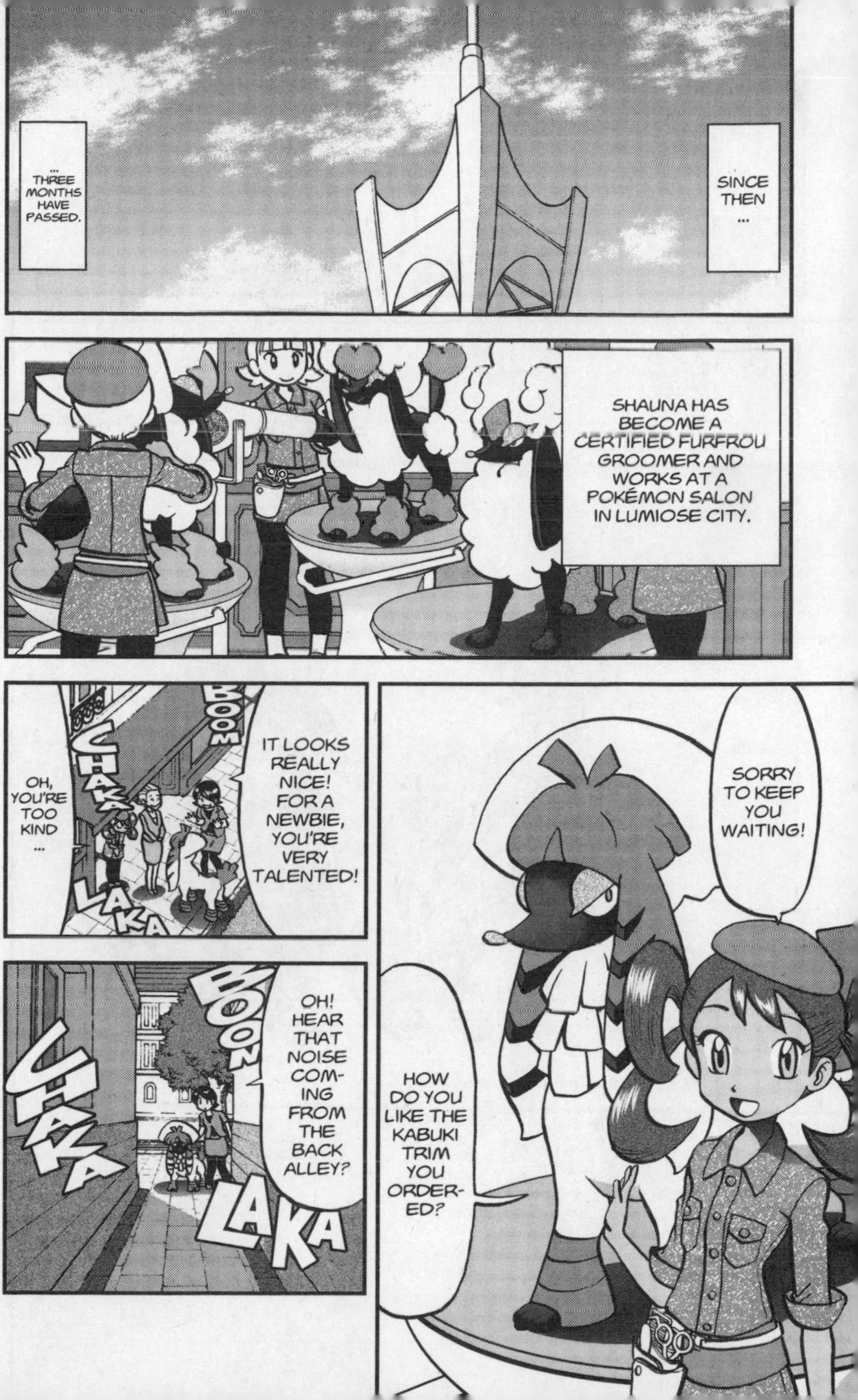
SINCE THEN ...
... THREE MONTHS HAVE PASSED.
SHAUNA HAS BECOME A CERTIFIED FURFROU GROOMER AND WORKS AT A POKÉMON SALON IN LUMIOSE CITY.
SORRY TO KEEP YOU WAITING!
HOW DO YOU LIKE THE KABUKI TRIM YOU ORDERED?
BOOM
IT LOOKS REALLY NICE! FOR A NEWBIE, YOU'RE VERY TALENTED!
OH, YOU'RE TOO KIND ...
CHAKA
LAKA
BOOM
OH! HEAR THAT NOISE COMING FROM THE BACK ALLEY?
CHAKA
LAKA

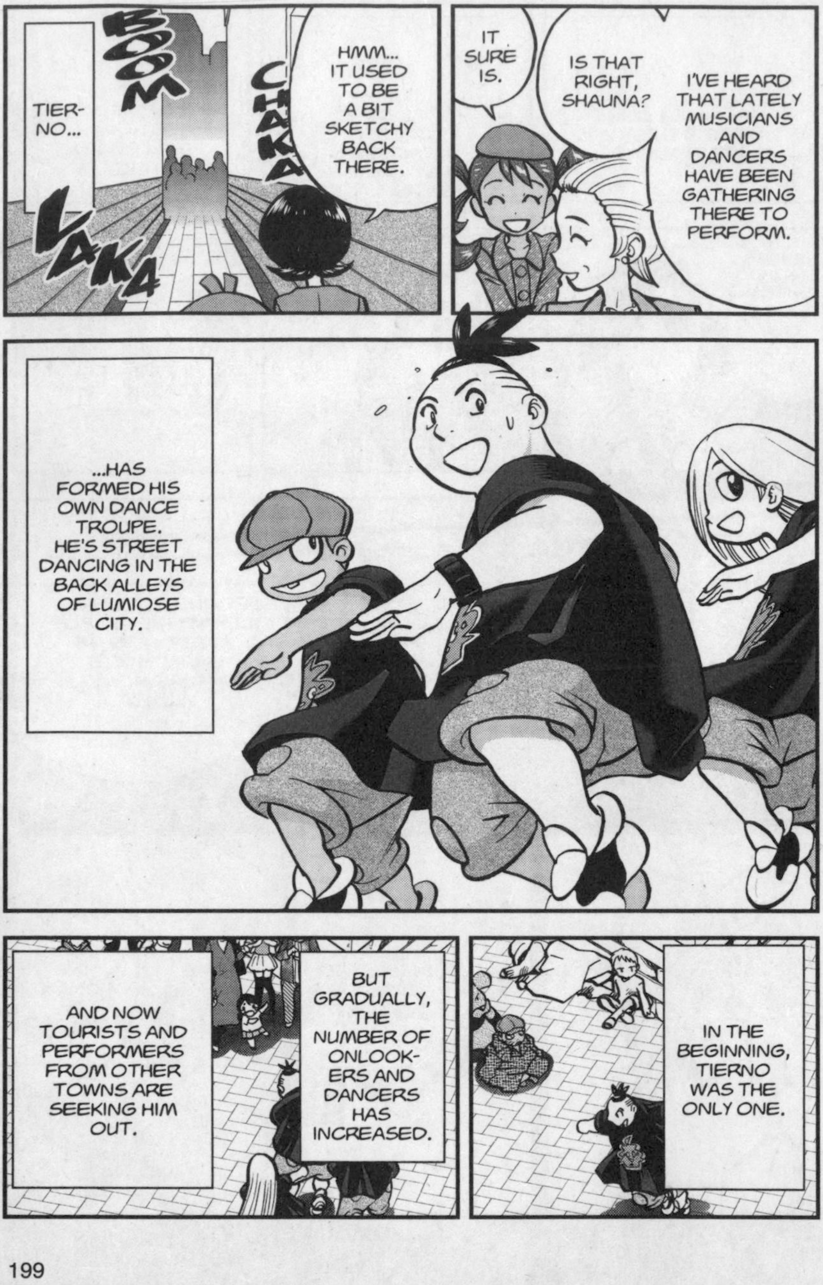
I'VE HEARD THAT LATELY MUSICIANS AND DANCERS HAVE BEEN GATHERING THERE TO PERFORM.
IS THAT RIGHT, SHAUNA?
IT SURE IS.
HMM... IT USED TO BE A BIT SKETCHY BACK THERE.
CHAKA
BOOM
TIER-NO...
LAKA
...HAS FORMED HIS OWN DANCE TROUPE. HE'S STREET DANCING IN THE BACK ALLEYS OF LUMIOSE CITY.
IN THE BEGINNING, TIERNO WAS THE ONLY ONE.
BUT GRADUALLY, THE NUMBER OF ONLOOK-ERS AND DANCERS HAS INCREASED.
AND NOW TOURISTS AND PERFORMERS FROM OTHER TOWNS ARE SEEKING HIM OUT.

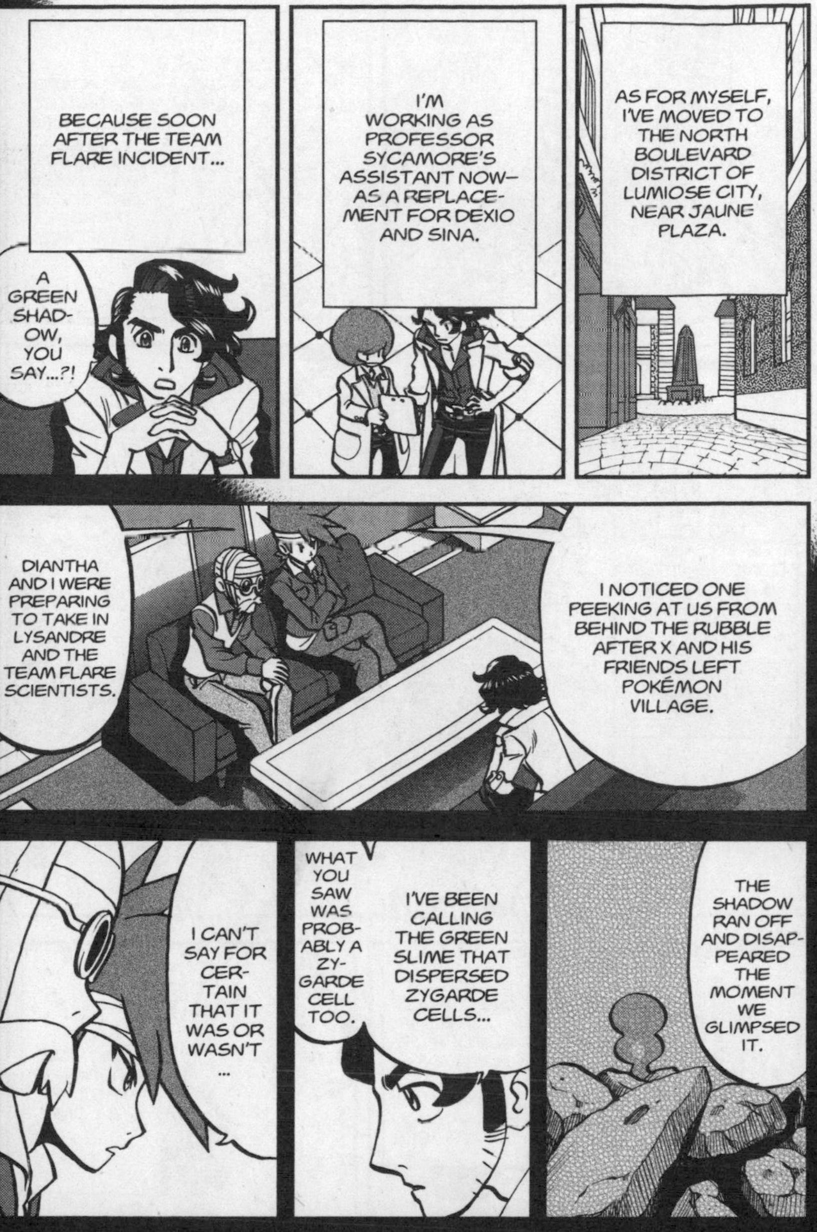

AS FOR MYSELF, I'VE MOVED TO THE NORTH BOULEVARD DISTRICT OF LUMIOSE CITY, NEAR JAUNE PLAZA.
I'M WORKING AS PROFESSOR SYCAMORE'S ASSISTANT NOW—AS A REPLACEMENT FOR DEXIO AND SINA.
BECAUSE SOON AFTER THE TEAM FLARE INCIDENT...
A GREEN SHADOW, YOU SAY...?!
I NOTICED ONE PEEKING AT US FROM BEHIND THE RUBBLE AFTER X AND HIS FRIENDS LEFT POKÉMON VILLAGE.
DIANTHA AND I WERE PREPARING TO TAKE IN LYSANDRE AND THE TEAM FLARE SCIENTISTS.
THE SHADOW RAN OFF AND DISAPPEARED THE MOMENT WE GLIMPSED IT.
I'VE BEEN CALLING THE GREEN SLIME THAT DISPERSED ZYGARDE CELLS...
WHAT YOU SAW WAS PROBABLY A ZYGARDE CELL TOO.
I CAN'T SAY FOR CERTAIN THAT IT WAS OR WASN'T ...

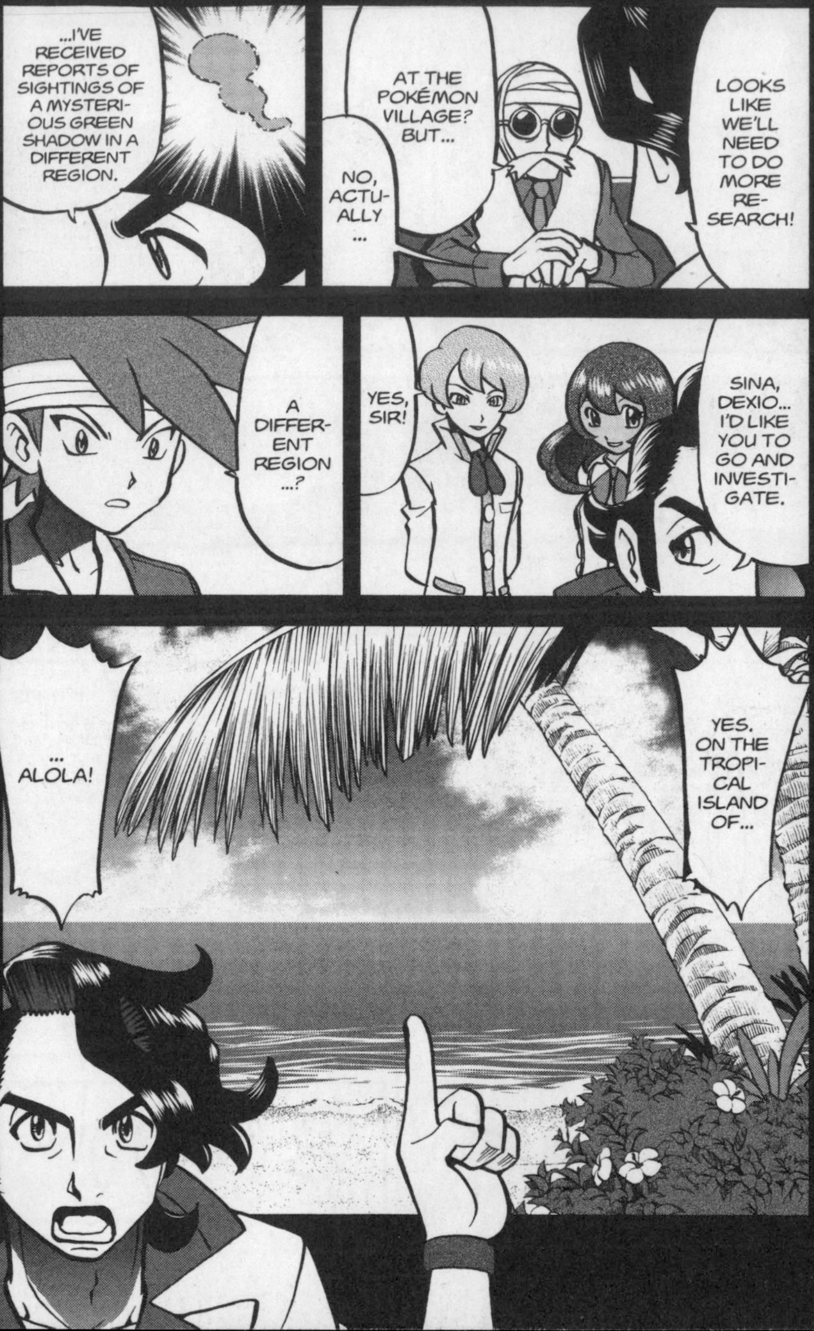
LOOKS LIKE WE'LL NEED TO DO MORE RE-SEARCH!
AT THE POKÉMON VILLAGE? BUT...
NO, ACTU-ALLY...
...I'VE RECEIVED REPORTS OF SIGHTINGS OF A MYSTERI-OUS GREEN SHADOW IN A DIFFERENT REGION.
SINA, DEXIO... I'D LIKE YOU TO GO AND INVESTI-GATE.
YES, SIR!
A DIFFER-ENT REGION...?
YES. ON THE TROPI-CAL ISLAND OF...
... ALOLA!

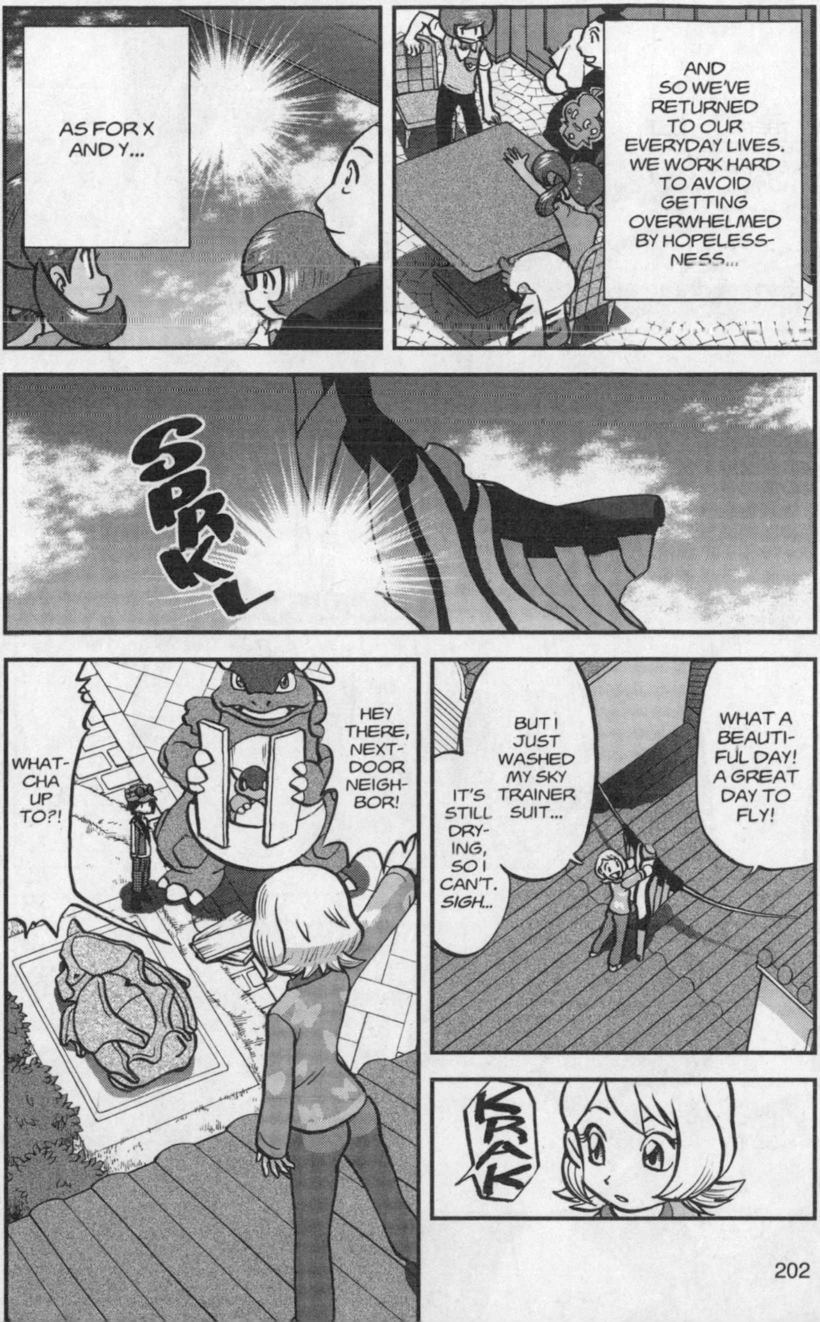
AND SO WE'VE RETURNED TO OUR EVERYDAY LIVES. WE WORK HARD TO AVOID GETTING OVERWHELMED BY HOPELESS-NESS...
AS FOR X AND Y...
SPRKL
WHAT A BEAUTI-FUL DAY! A GREAT DAY TO FLY!
BUT I JUST WASHED MY SKY TRAINER SUIT...
IT'S STILL DRY-ING, SO I CAN'T. SIGH...
KRAK
HEY THERE, NEXT-DOOR NEIGH-BOR!
WHAT-CHA UP TO?!

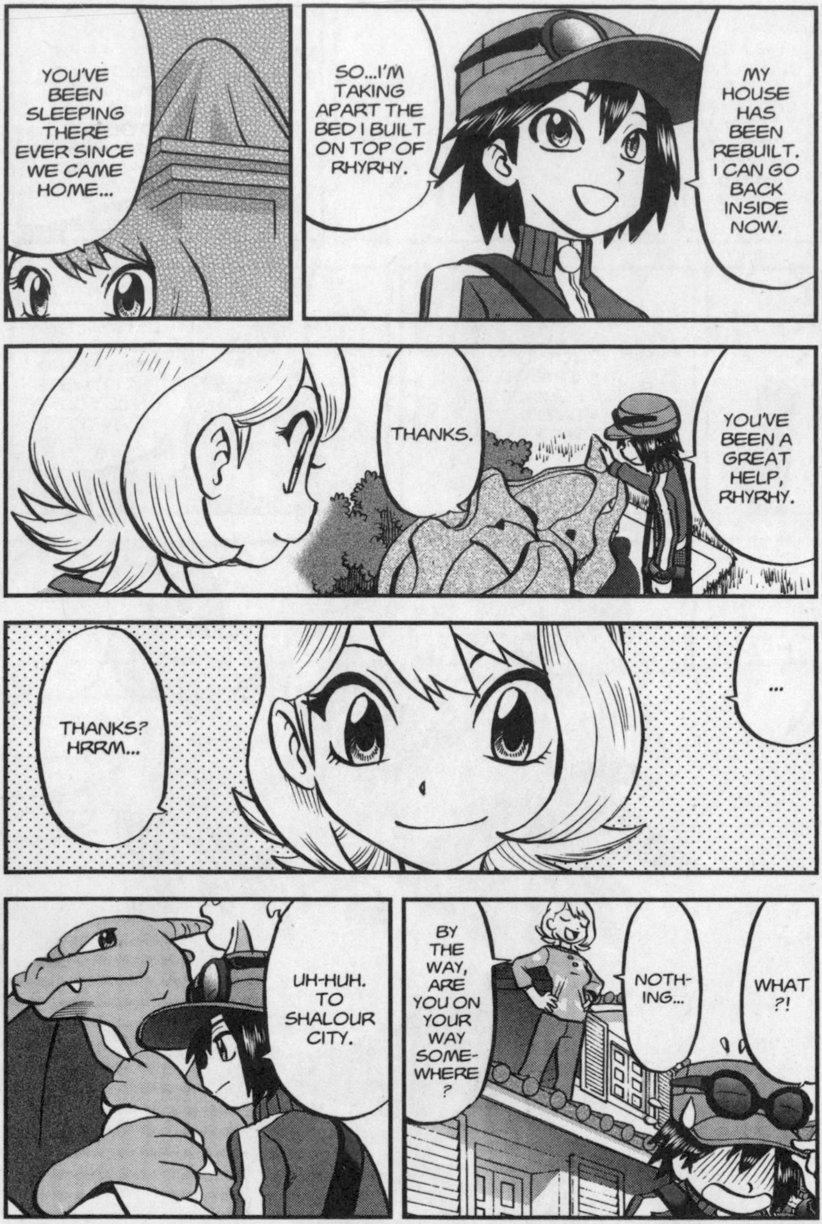
MY HOUSE HAS BEEN REBUILT. I CAN GO BACK INSIDE NOW.
SO...I'M TAKING APART THE BED I BUILT ON TOP OF RHYRHY.
YOU'VE BEEN SLEEPING THERE EVER SINCE WE CAME HOME...
YOU'VE BEEN A GREAT HELP, RHYRHY.
THANKS.
...
THANKS? HRRM...
WHAT?!
NOTH-ING...
BY THE WAY, ARE YOU ON YOUR WAY SOME-WHERE?
UH-HUH. TO SHALOUR CITY.

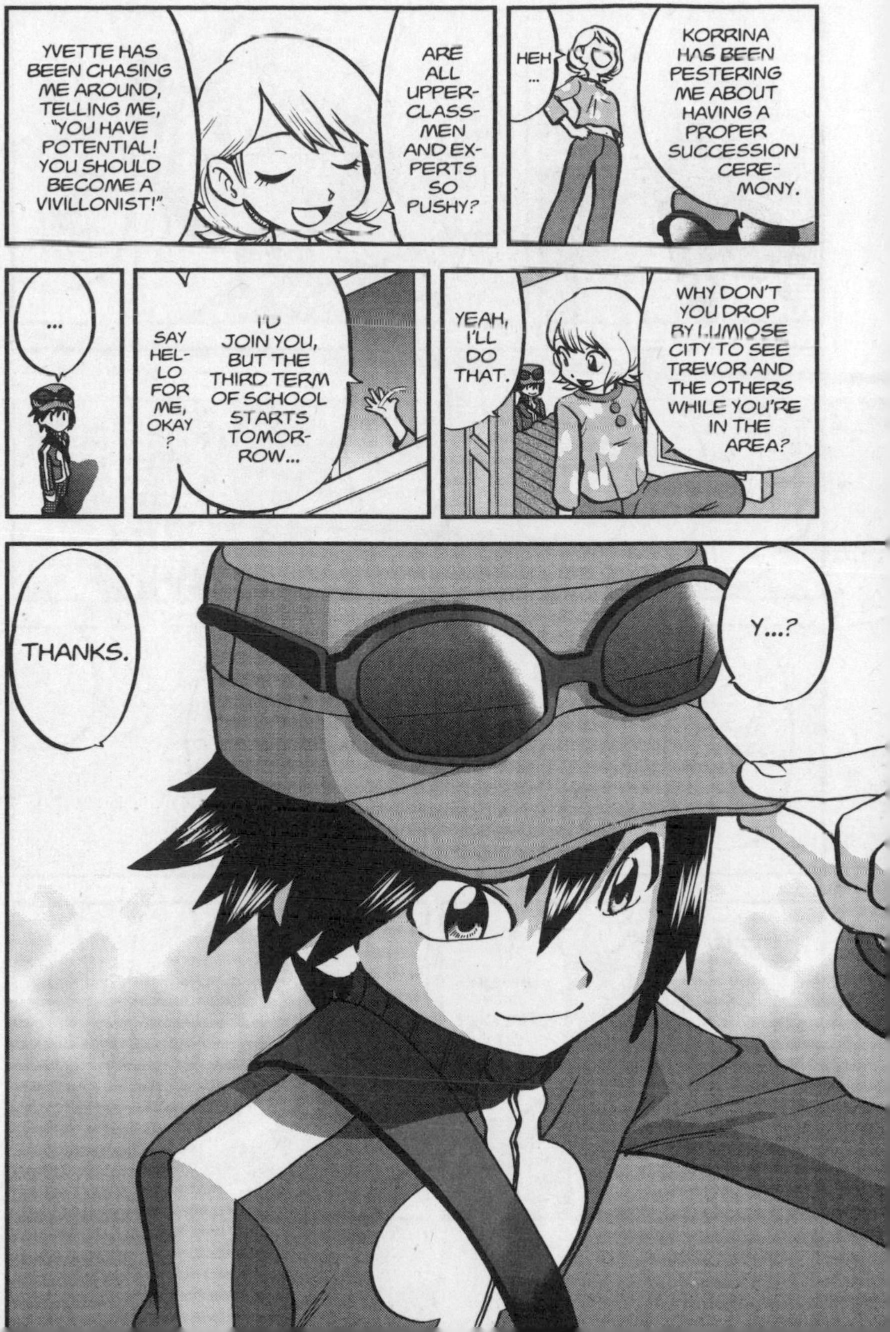
KORRINA HAS BEEN PESTERING ME ABOUT HAVING A PROPER SUCCESSION CEREMONY.
HEH...
ARE ALL UPPERCLASSMEN AND EXPERTS SO PUSHY?
YVETTE HAS BEEN CHASING ME AROUND, TELLING ME, "YOU HAVE POTENTIAL! YOU SHOULD BECOME A VIVILLONIST!"
WHY DON'T YOU DROP BY LUMIOSE CITY TO SEE TREVOR AND THE OTHERS WHILE YOU'RE IN THE AREA?
YEAH, I'LL DO THAT.
I'D JOIN YOU, BUT THE THIRD TERM OF SCHOOL STARTS TOMORROW...
SAY HELLO FOR ME, OKAY?
...
Y...?
THANKS.

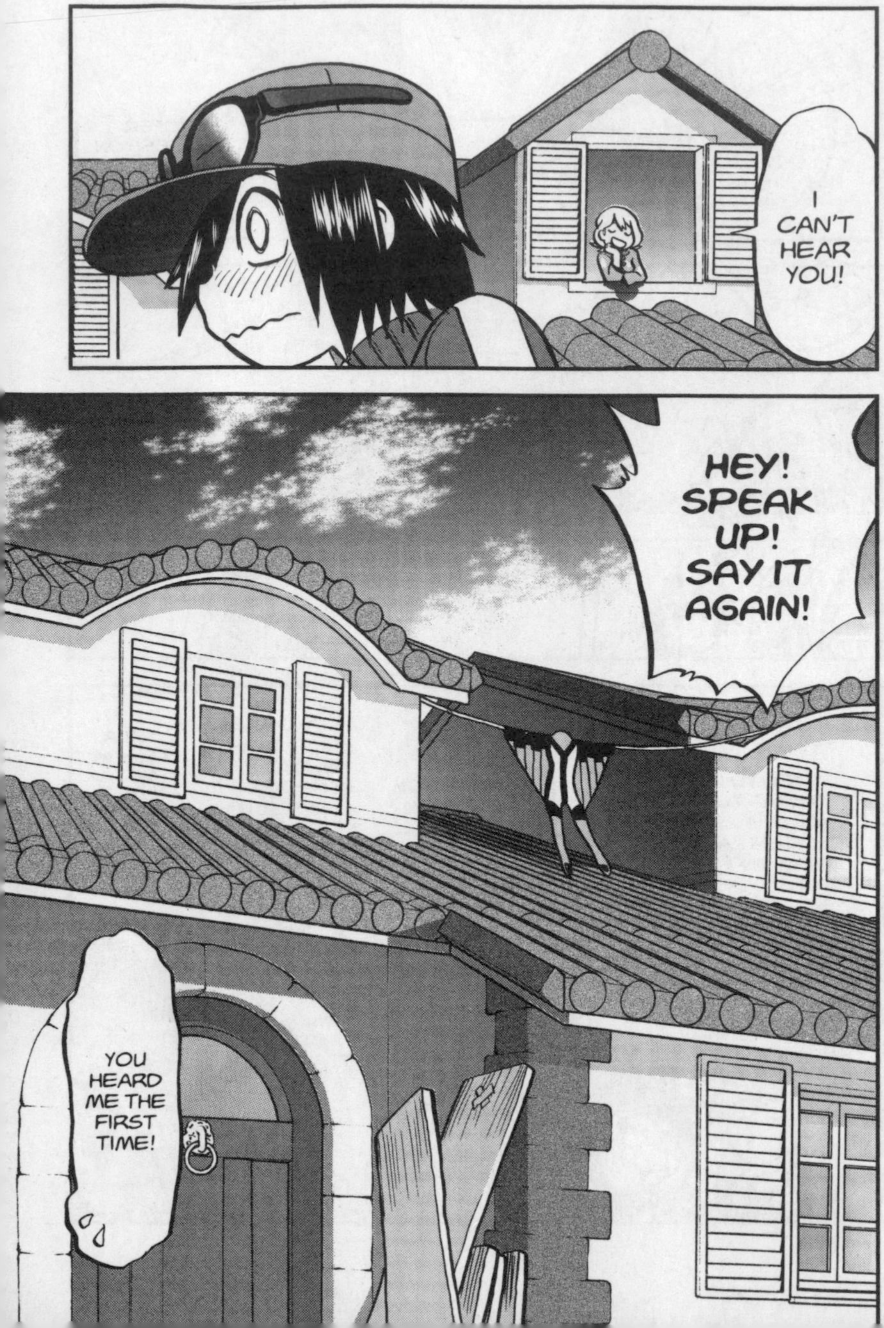
I CAN'T HEAR YOU!
HEY! SPEAK UP! SAY IT AGAIN!
YOU HEARD ME THE FIRST TIME!

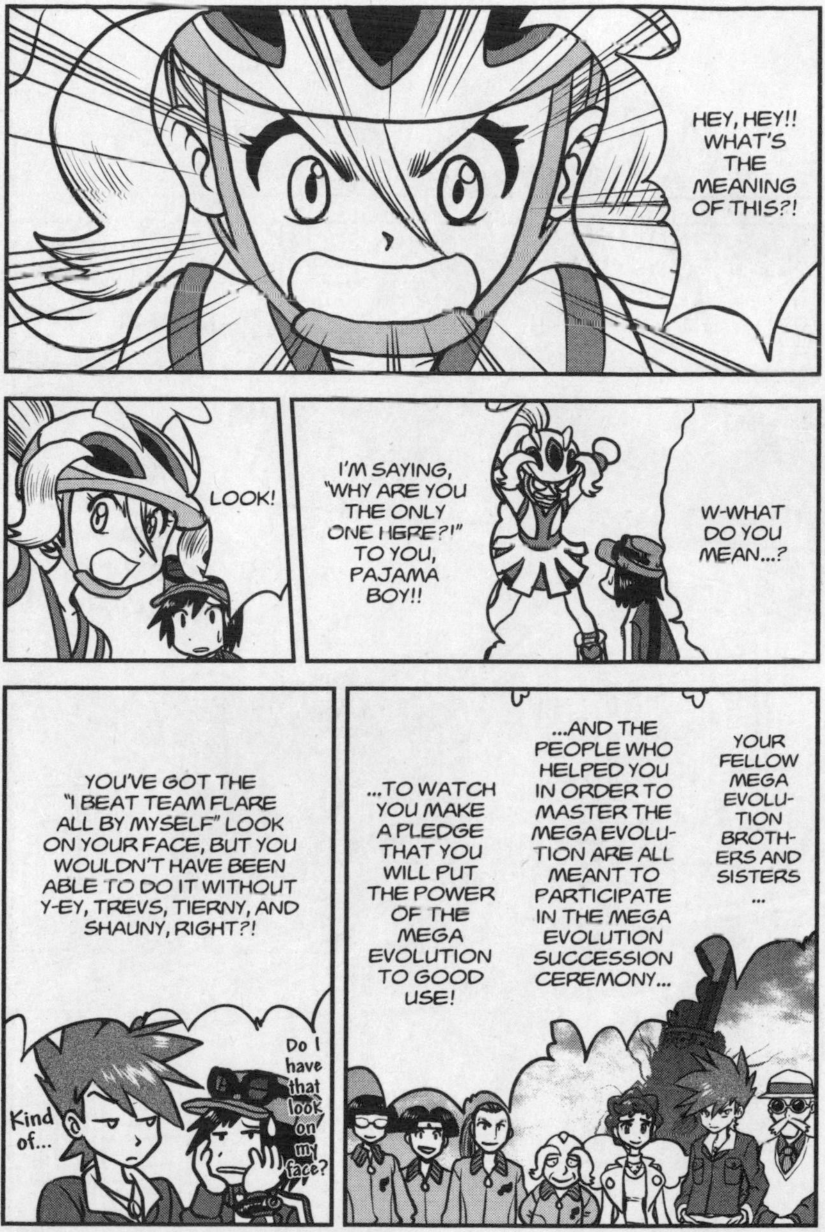
HEY, HEY!! WHAT'S THE MEANING OF THIS?!
W-WHAT DO YOU MEAN...?
I'M SAYING, "WHY ARE YOU THE ONLY ONE HERE?!" TO YOU, PAJAMA BOY!!
LOOK!
YOUR FELLOW MEGA EVOLUTION BROTHERS AND SISTERS...
...AND THE PEOPLE WHO HELPED YOU IN ORDER TO MASTER THE MEGA EVOLUTION ARE ALL MEANT TO PARTICIPATE IN THE MEGA EVOLUTION SUCCESSION CEREMONY...
...TO WATCH YOU MAKE A PLEDGE THAT YOU WILL PUT THE POWER OF THE MEGA EVOLUTION TO GOOD USE!
YOU'VE GOT THE "I BEAT TEAM FLARE ALL BY MYSELF" LOOK ON YOUR FACE, BUT YOU WOULDN'T HAVE BEEN ABLE TO DO IT WITHOUT Y-EY, TREVS, TIERNY, AND SHAUNY, RIGHT?!
Do I have that look on my face?
Kind of...

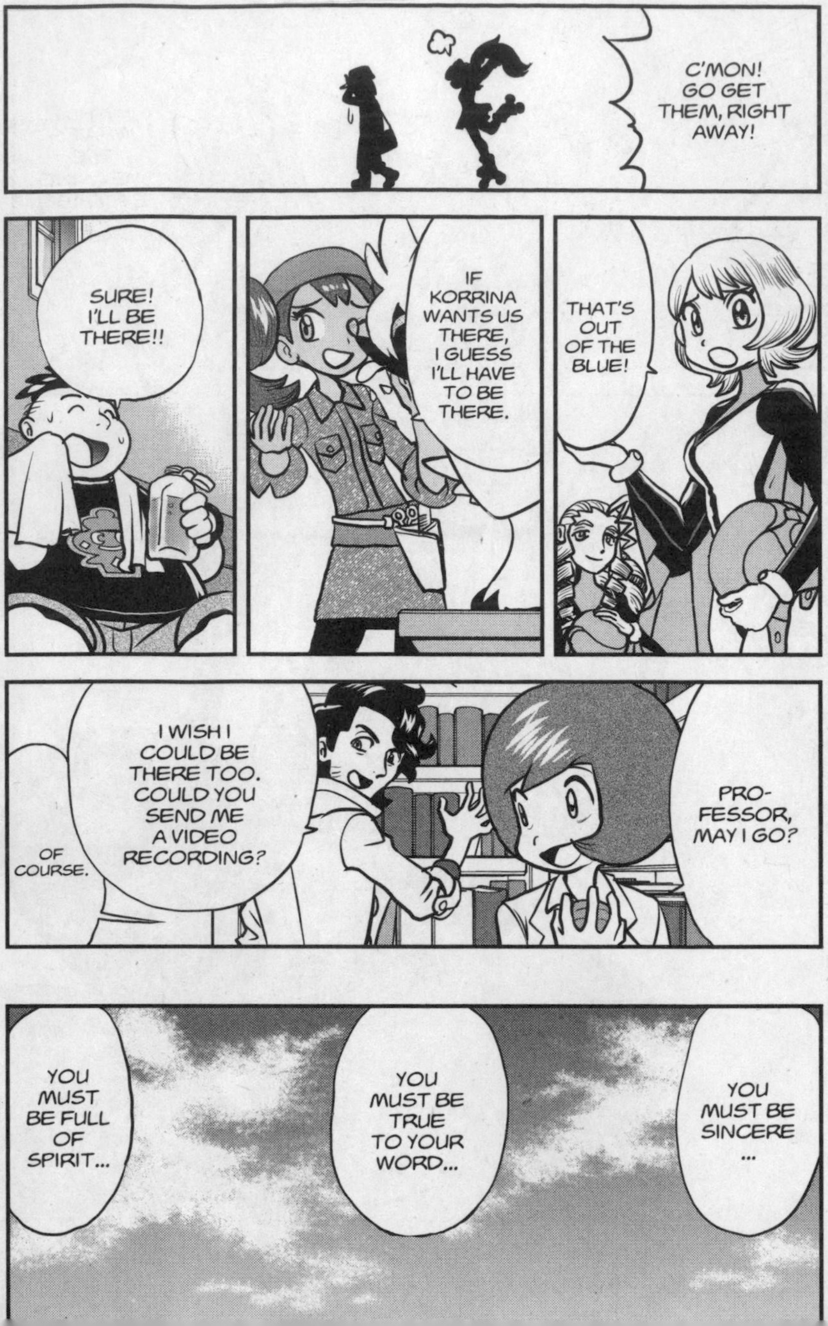
C'MON! GO GET THEM, RIGHT AWAY!
THAT'S OUT OF THE BLUE!
IF KORRINA WANTS US THERE, I GUESS I'LL HAVE TO BE THERE.
SURE! I'LL BE THERE!!
PRO-FESSOR, MAY I GO?
I WISH I COULD BE THERE TOO. COULD YOU SEND ME A VIDEO RECORDING?
OF COURSE.
YOU MUST BE SINCERE ...
YOU MUST BE TRUE TO YOUR WORD...
YOU MUST BE FULL OF SPIRIT...

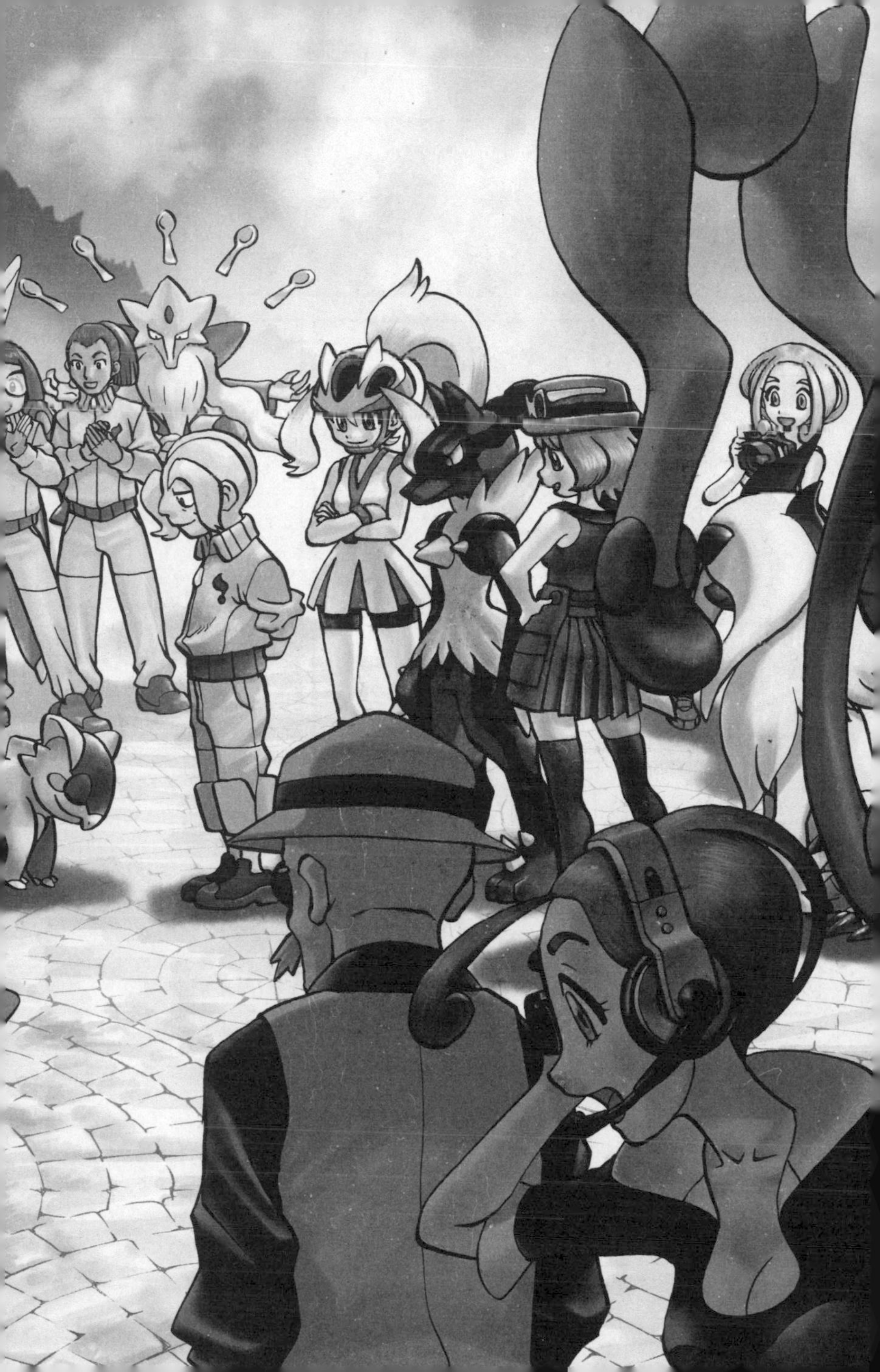

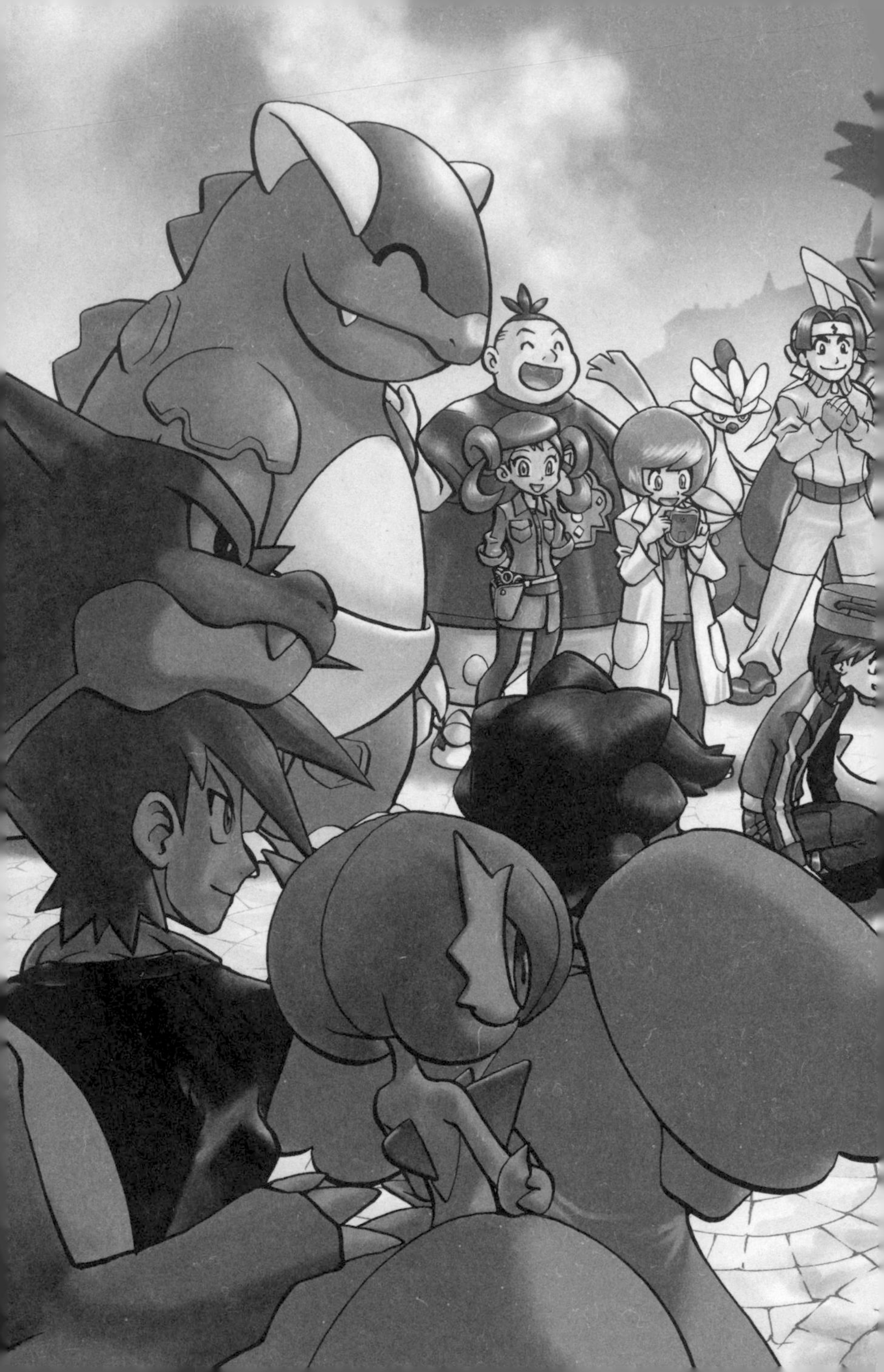

Adventure #47
Magearna Moves

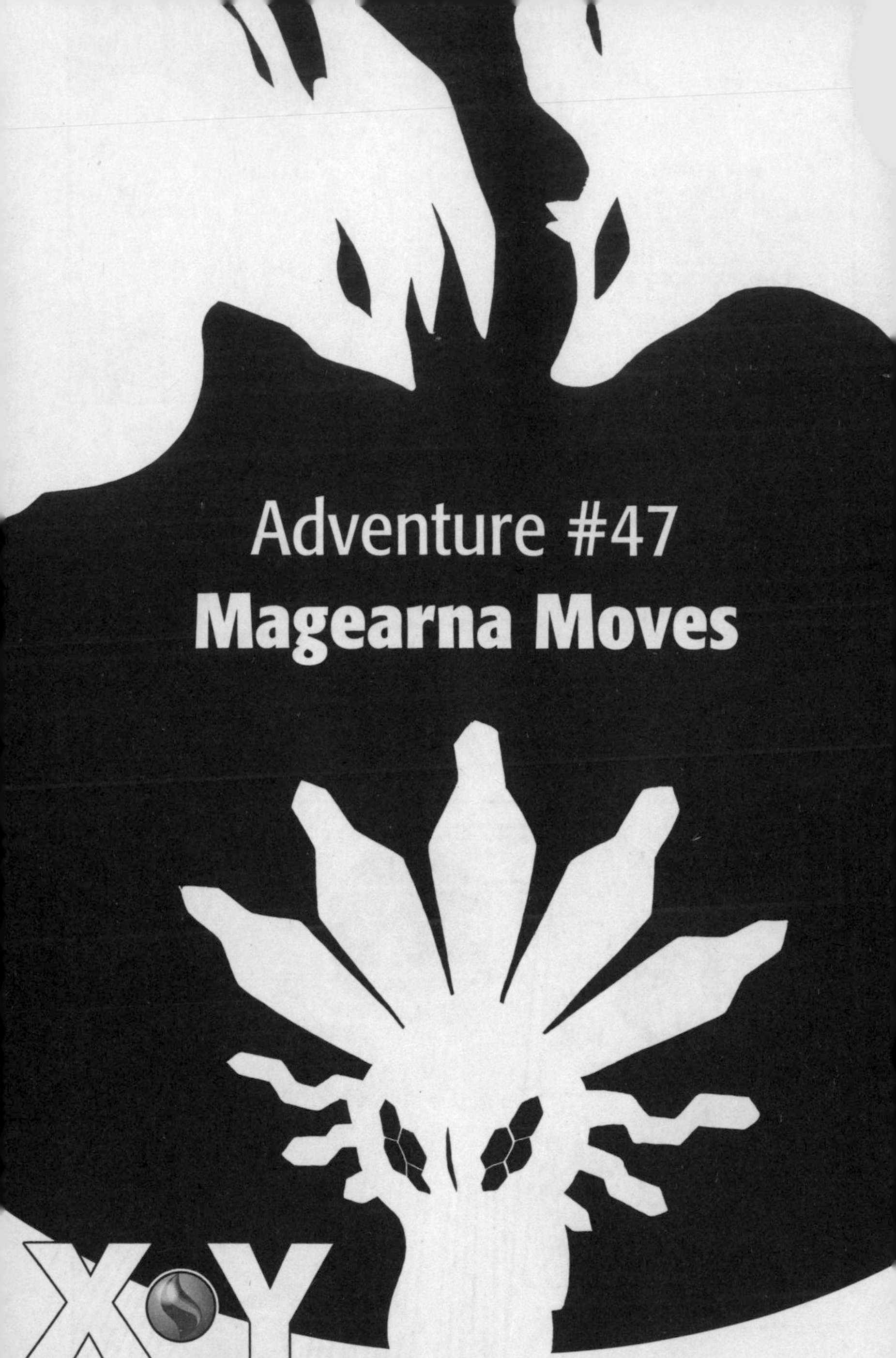

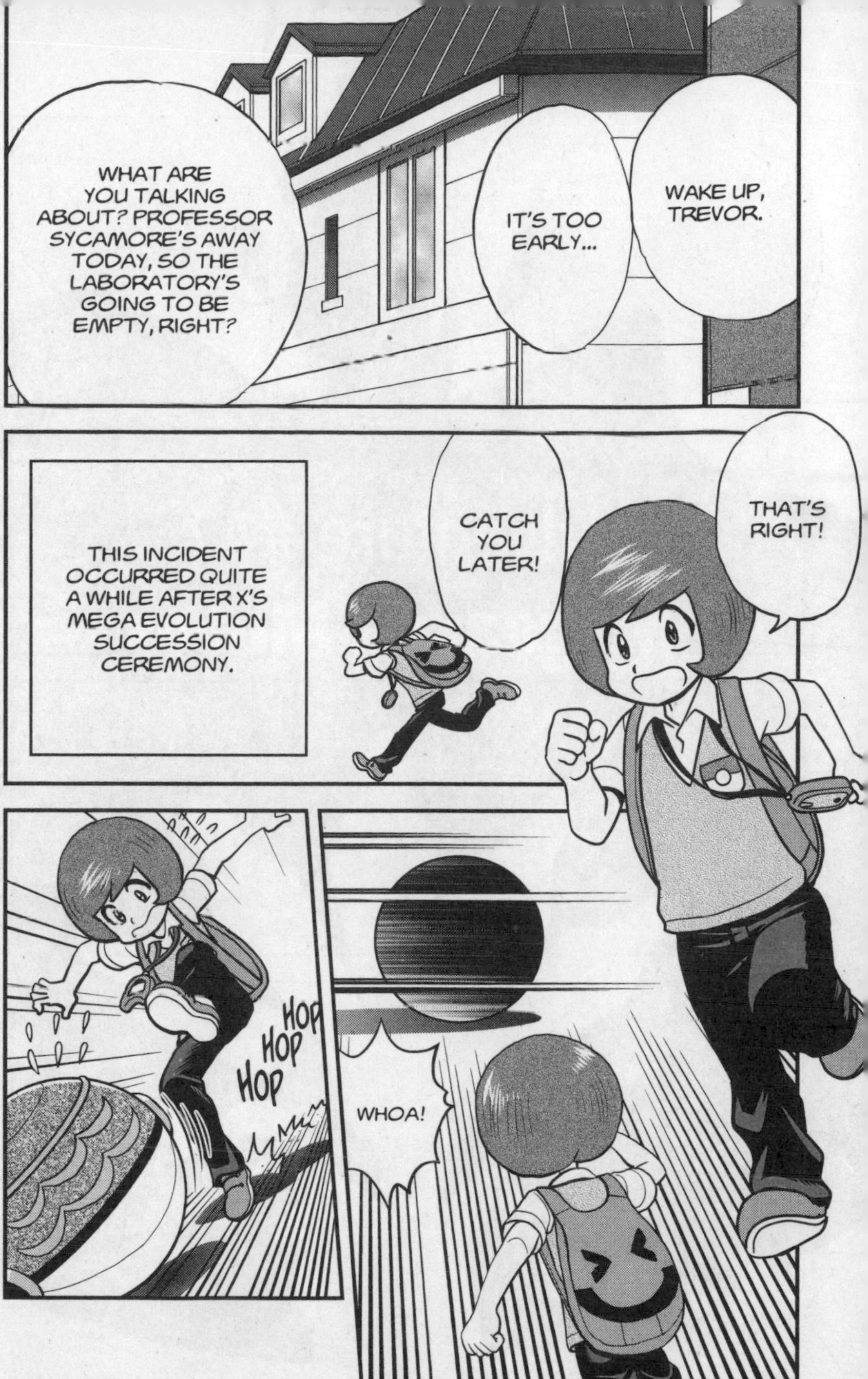
WAKE UP, TREVOR.
IT'S TOO EARLY...
WHAT ARE YOU TALKING ABOUT? PROFESSOR SYCAMORE'S AWAY TODAY, SO THE LABORATORY'S GOING TO BE EMPTY, RIGHT?
THAT'S RIGHT!
CATCH YOU LATER!
THIS INCIDENT OCCURRED QUITE A WHILE AFTER X'S MEGA EVOLUTION SUCCESSION CEREMONY.
WHOA!
HOP
HOP
HOP

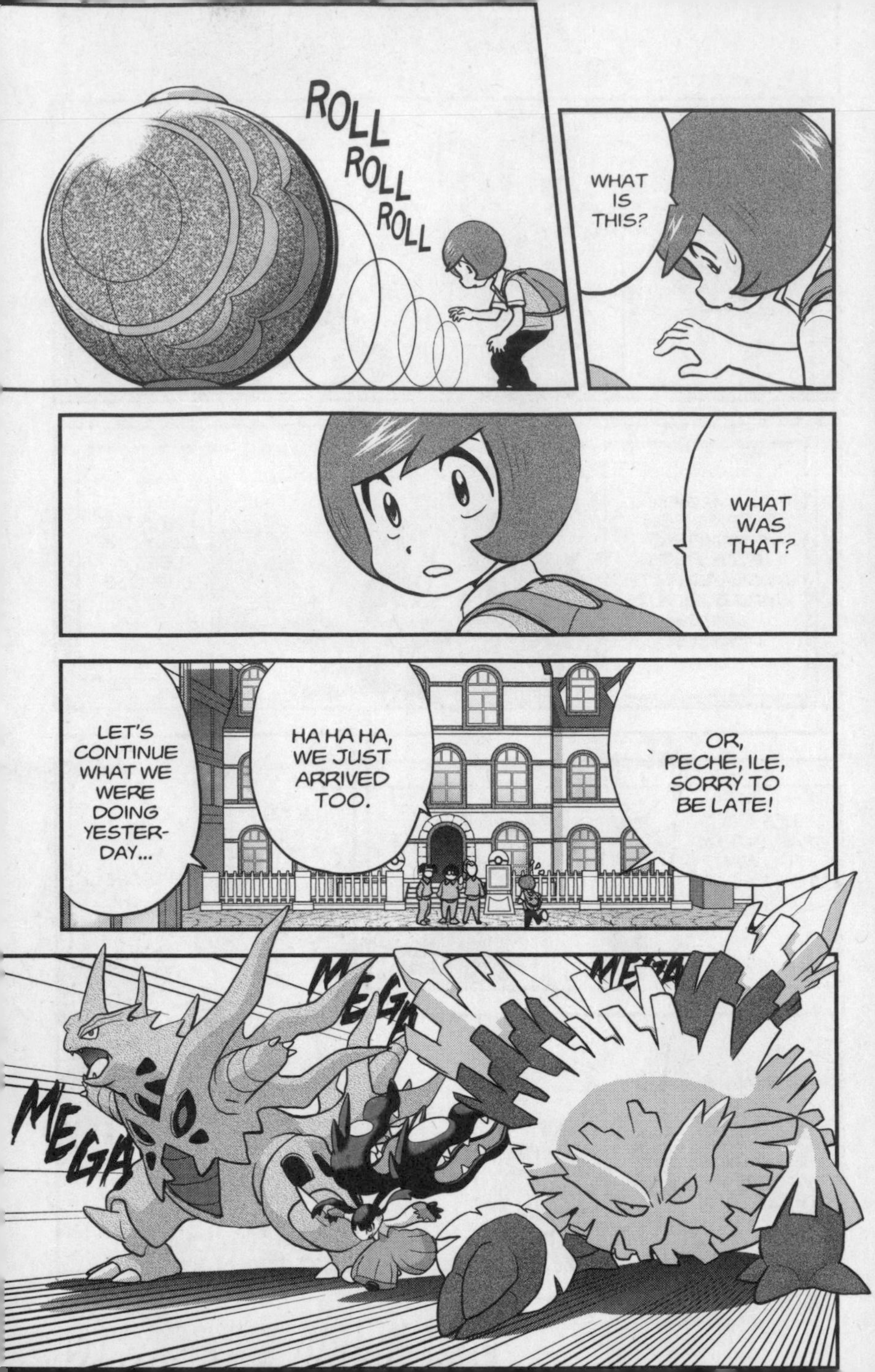
WHAT IS THIS?
ROLL ROLL ROLL
WHAT WAS THAT?
OR, PECHE, ILE, SORRY TO BE LATE!
HA HA HA, WE JUST ARRIVED TOO.
LET'S CONTINUE WHAT WE WERE DOING YESTER-DAY...
MEGA
MEGA
MEGA

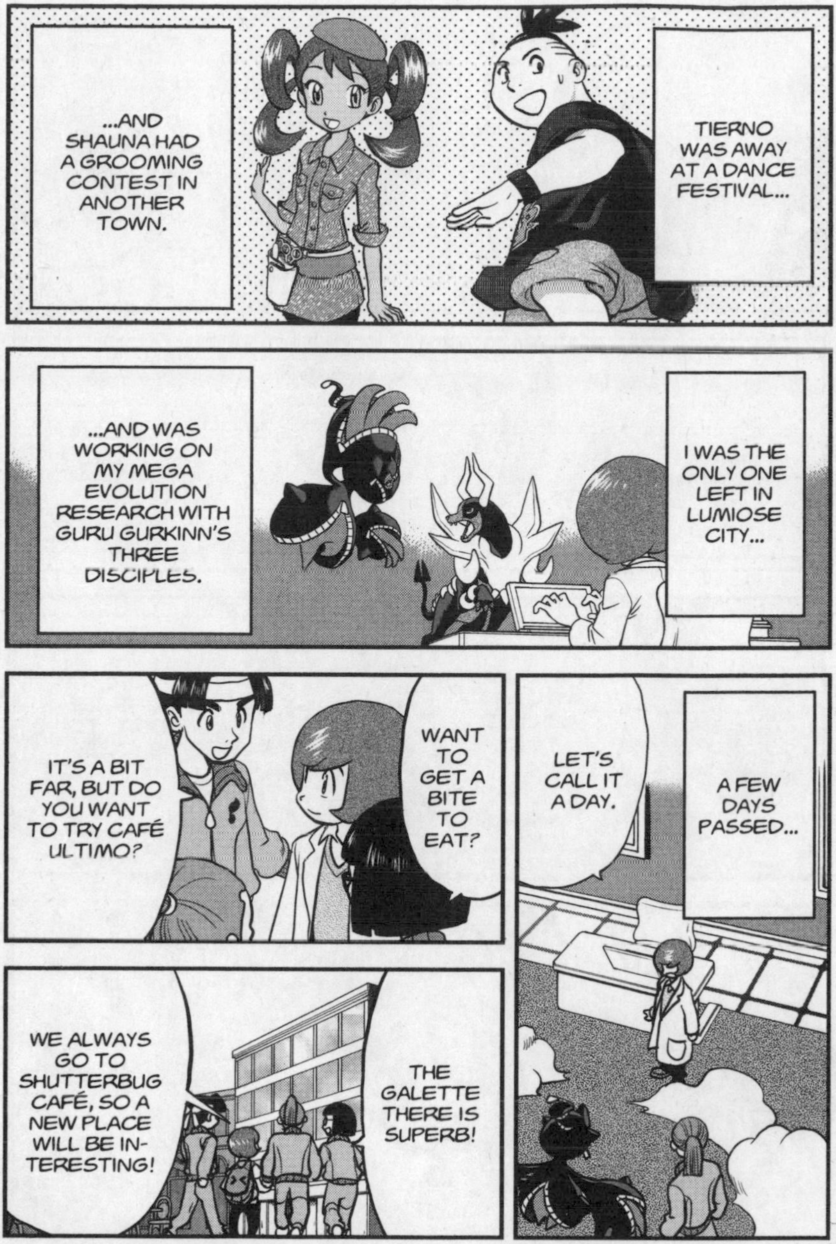
TIERNO WAS AWAY AT A DANCE FESTIVAL...
...AND SHAUNA HAD A GROOMING CONTEST IN ANOTHER TOWN.
I WAS THE ONLY ONE LEFT IN LUMIOSE CITY...
...AND WAS WORKING ON MY MEGA EVOLUTION RESEARCH WITH GURU GURKINN'S THREE DISCIPLES.
A FEW DAYS PASSED...
LET'S CALL IT A DAY.
WANT TO GET A BITE TO EAT?
IT'S A BIT FAR, BUT DO YOU WANT TO TRY CAFÉ ULTIMO?
THE GALETTE THERE IS SUPERB!
WE ALWAYS GO TO SHUTTERBUG CAFÉ, SO A NEW PLACE WILL BE INTERESTING!

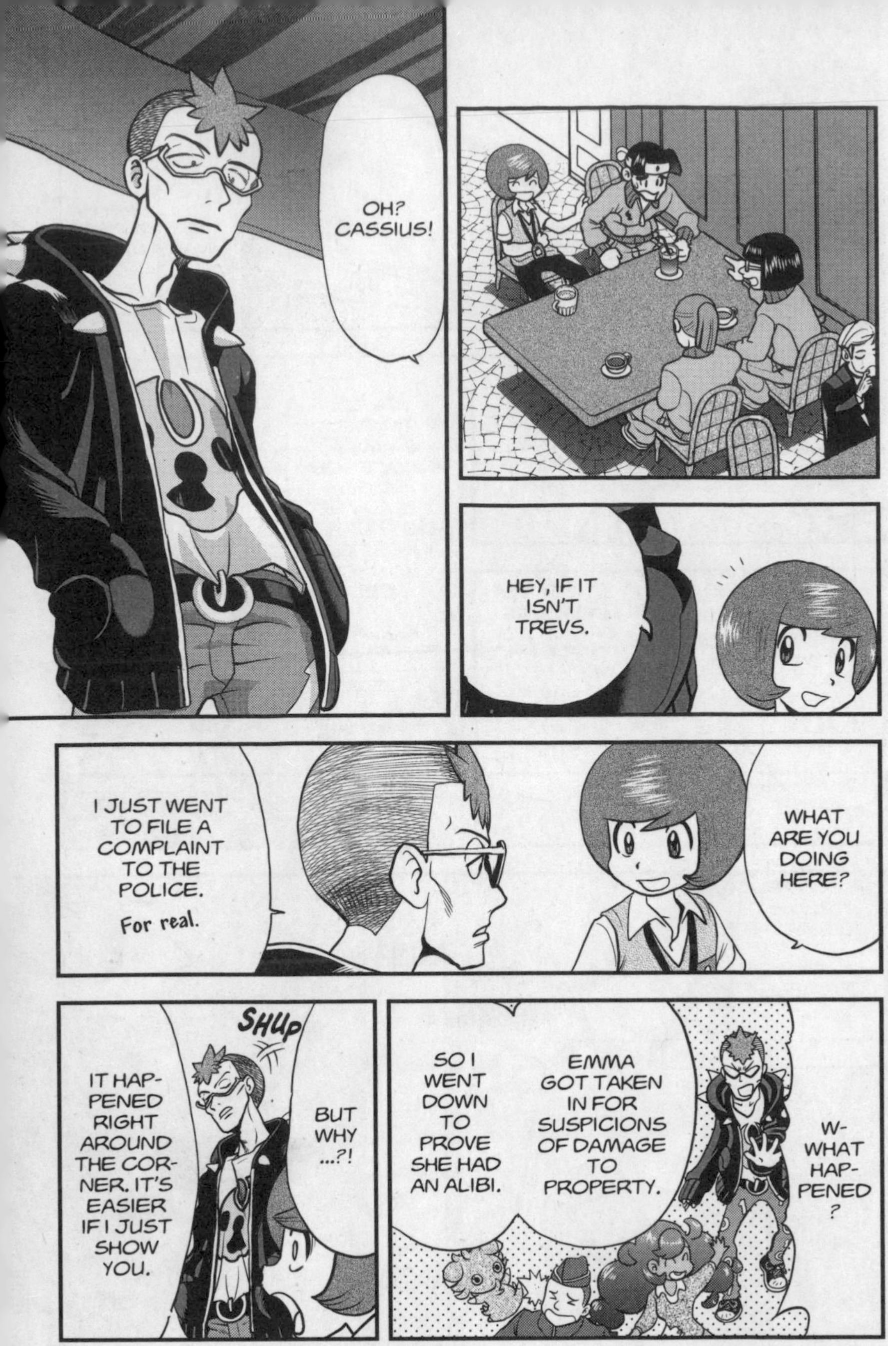
HEY, IF IT ISN'T TREVS.
OH? CASSIUS!
WHAT ARE YOU DOING HERE?
I JUST WENT TO FILE A COMPLAINT TO THE POLICE.
For real.
W-WHAT HAP-PENED?
EMMA GOT TAKEN IN FOR SUSPICIONS OF DAMAGE TO PROPERTY.
SO I WENT DOWN TO PROVE SHE HAD AN ALIBI.
BUT WHY ...?!
SHUP
IT HAP-PENED RIGHT AROUND THE COR-NER. IT'S EASIER IF I JUST SHOW YOU.

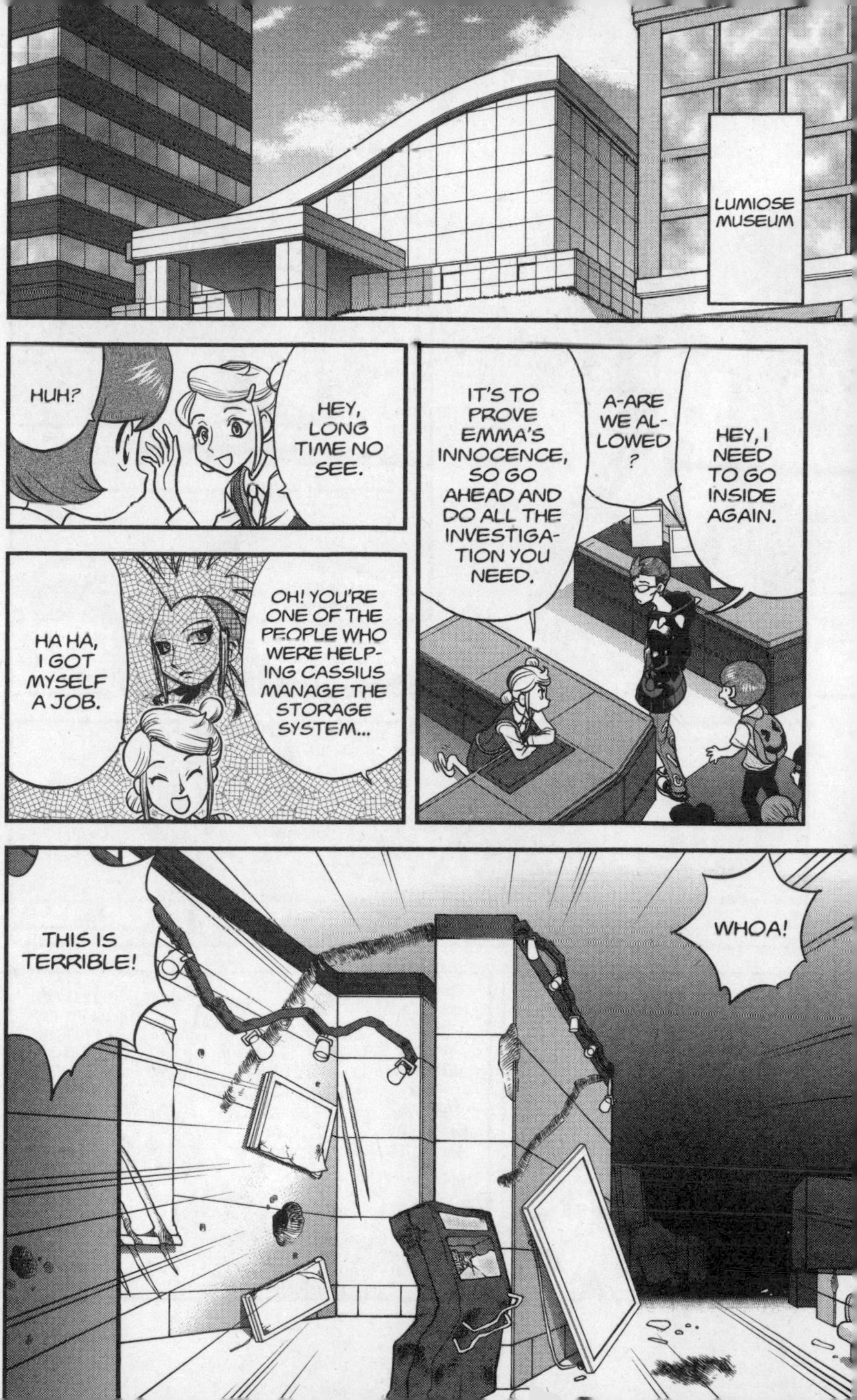
LUMIOSE MUSEUM
HEY, I NEED TO GO INSIDE AGAIN.
A-ARE WE AL-LOWED?
IT'S TO PROVE EMMA'S INNOCENCE, SO GO AHEAD AND DO ALL THE INVESTIGA-TION YOU NEED.
HEY, LONG TIME NO SEE.
HUH?
OH! YOU'RE ONE OF THE PEOPLE WHO WERE HELP-ING CASSIUS MANAGE THE STORAGE SYSTEM...
HA HA, I GOT MYSELF A JOB.
WHOA!
THIS IS TERRIBLE!

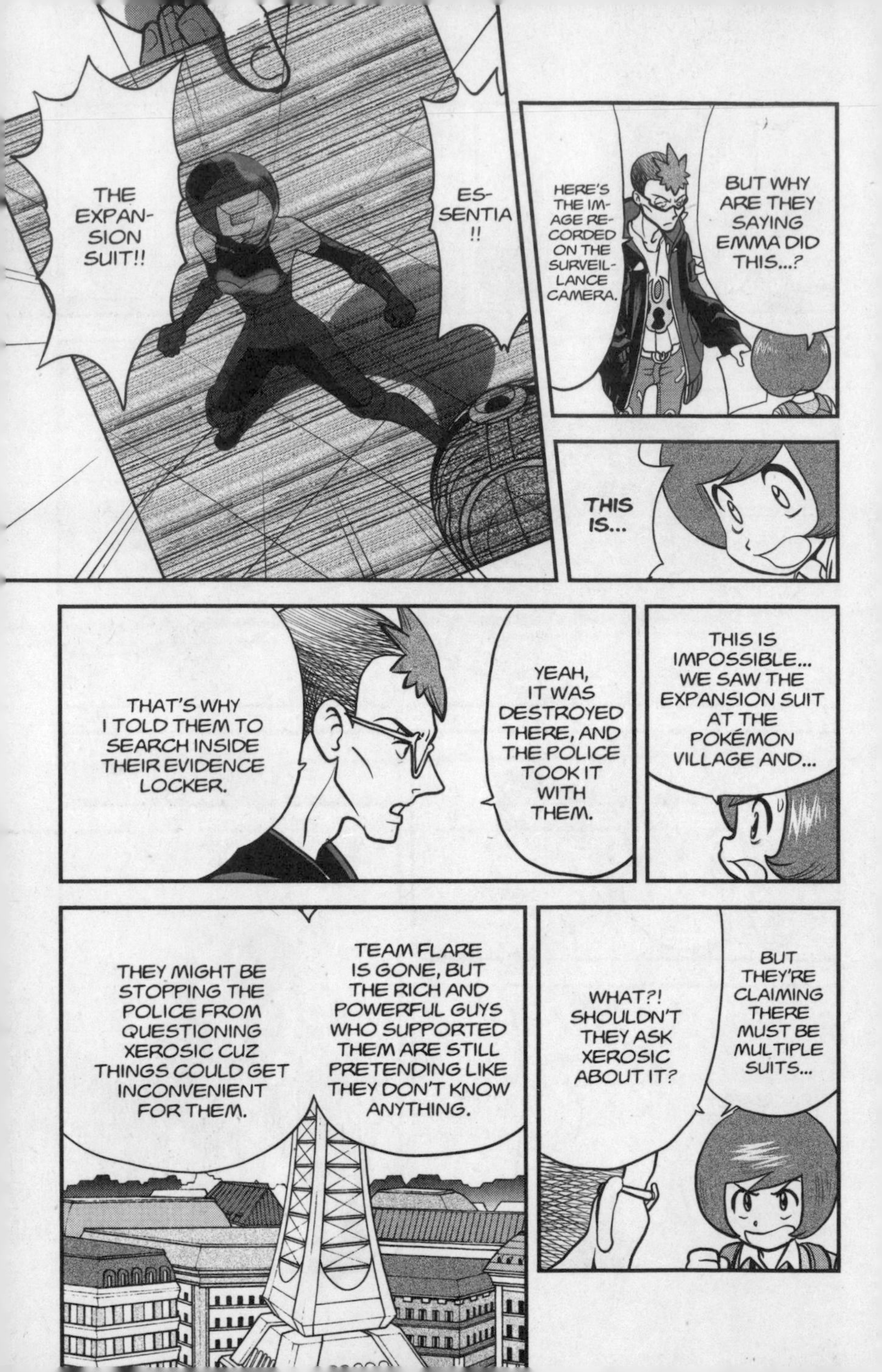
BUT WHY ARE THEY SAYING EMMA DID THIS...?
HERE'S THE IMAGE RECORDED ON THE SURVEILLANCE CAMERA.
THIS IS...
ESSENTIA!!
THE EXPANSION SUIT!!
THIS IS IMPOSSIBLE... WE SAW THE EXPANSION SUIT AT THE POKÉMON VILLAGE AND...
YEAH, IT WAS DESTROYED THERE, AND THE POLICE TOOK IT WITH THEM.
THAT'S WHY I TOLD THEM TO SEARCH INSIDE THEIR EVIDENCE LOCKER.
BUT THEY'RE CLAIMING THERE MUST BE MULTIPLE SUITS...
WHAT?! SHOULDN'T THEY ASK XEROSIC ABOUT IT?
TEAM FLARE IS GONE, BUT THE RICH AND POWERFUL GUYS WHO SUPPORTED THEM ARE STILL PRETENDING LIKE THEY DON'T KNOW ANYTHING.
THEY MIGHT BE STOPPING THE POLICE FROM QUESTIONING XEROSIC CUZ THINGS COULD GET INCONVENIENT FOR THEM.

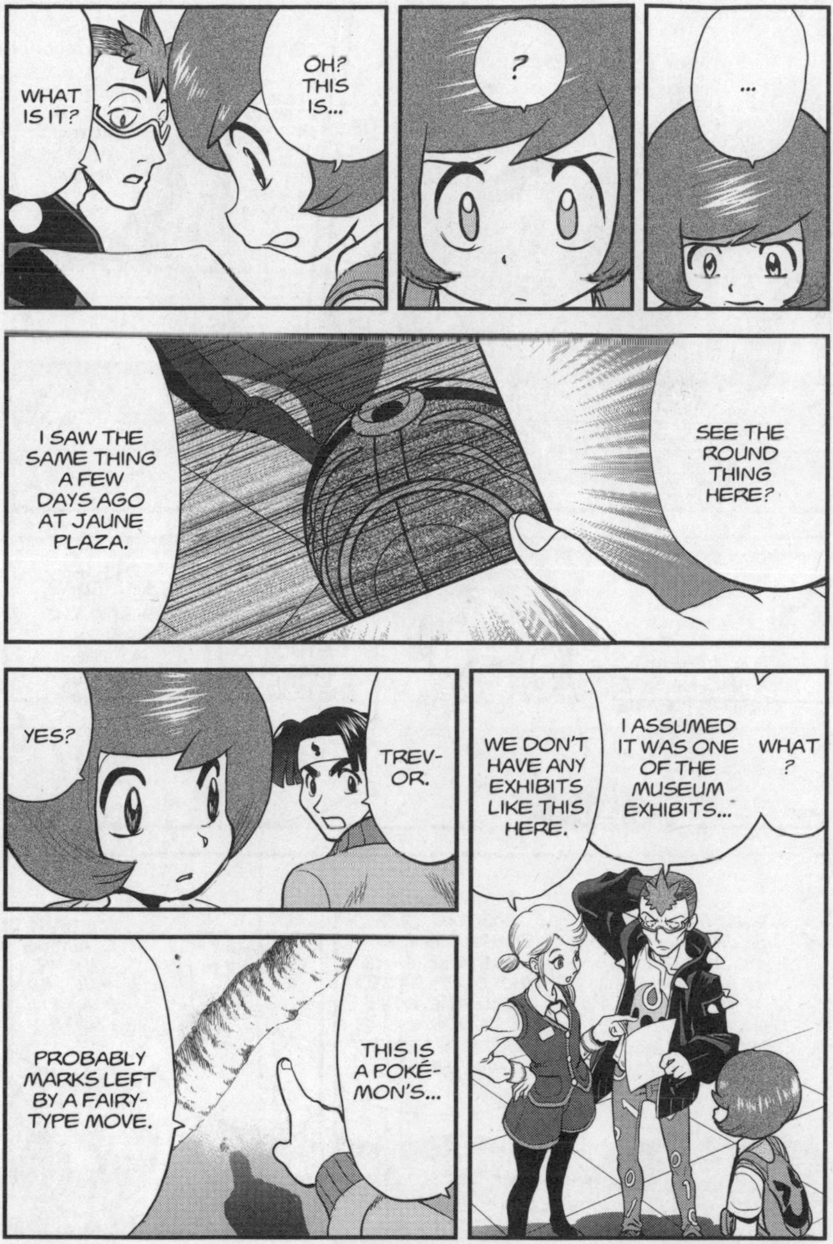
...
?
OH? THIS IS...
WHAT IS IT?
SEE THE ROUND THING HERE?
I SAW THE SAME THING A FEW DAYS AGO AT JAUNE PLAZA.
WHAT?
I ASSUMED IT WAS ONE OF THE MUSEUM EXHIBITS...
WE DON'T HAVE ANY EXHIBITS LIKE THIS HERE.
TREV-OR.
YES?
THIS IS A POKÉMON'S...
PROBABLY MARKS LEFT BY A FAIRY-TYPE MOVE.

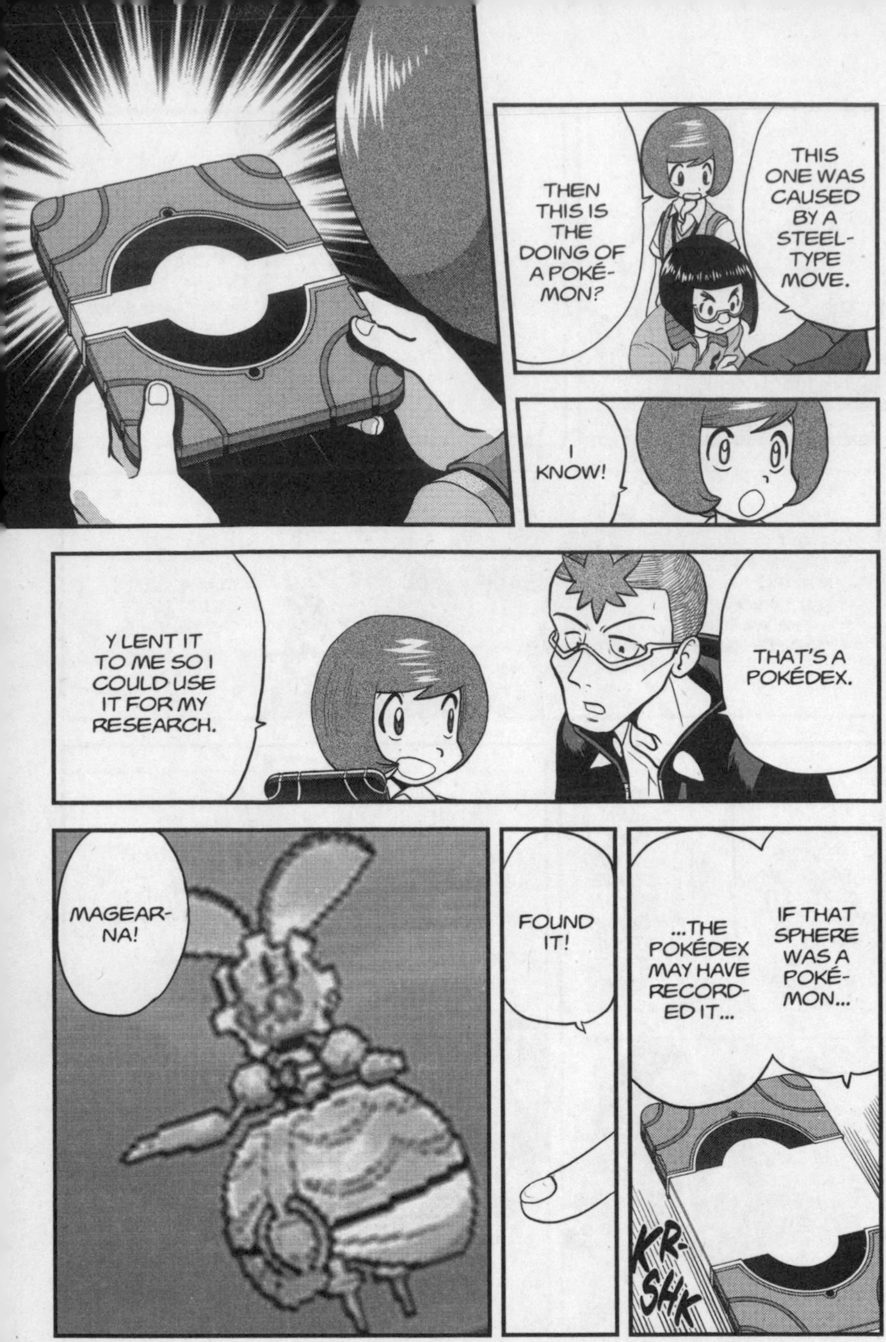
THIS ONE WAS CAUSED BY A STEEL-TYPE MOVE.
THEN THIS IS THE DOING OF A POKÉMON?
I KNOW!
THAT'S A POKÉDEX.
Y LENT IT TO ME SO I COULD USE IT FOR MY RESEARCH.
IF THAT SPHERE WAS A POKÉMON...
...THE POKÉDEX MAY HAVE RECORDED IT...
KR-SHK
FOUND IT!
MAGEARNA!

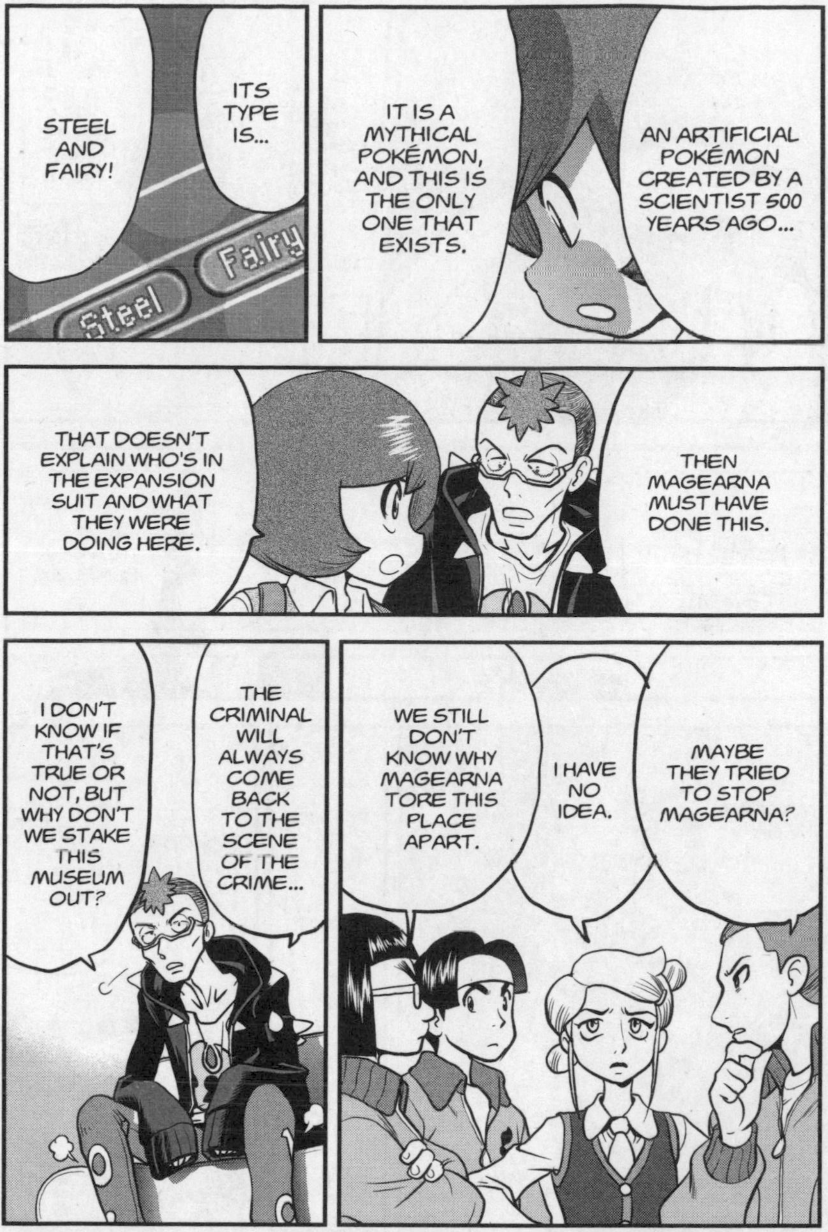
AN ARTIFICIAL POKÉMON CREATED BY A SCIENTIST 500 YEARS AGO...
IT IS A MYTHICAL POKÉMON, AND THIS IS THE ONLY ONE THAT EXISTS.
ITS TYPE IS...
STEEL AND FAIRY!
Fairy
Steel
THEN MAGEARNA MUST HAVE DONE THIS.
THAT DOESN'T EXPLAIN WHO'S IN THE EXPANSION SUIT AND WHAT THEY WERE DOING HERE.
MAYBE THEY TRIED TO STOP MAGEARNA?
I HAVE NO IDEA.
WE STILL DON'T KNOW WHY MAGEARNA TORE THIS PLACE APART.
THE CRIMINAL WILL ALWAYS COME BACK TO THE SCENE OF THE CRIME...
I DON'T KNOW IF THAT'S TRUE OR NOT, BUT WHY DON'T WE STAKE THIS MUSEUM OUT?

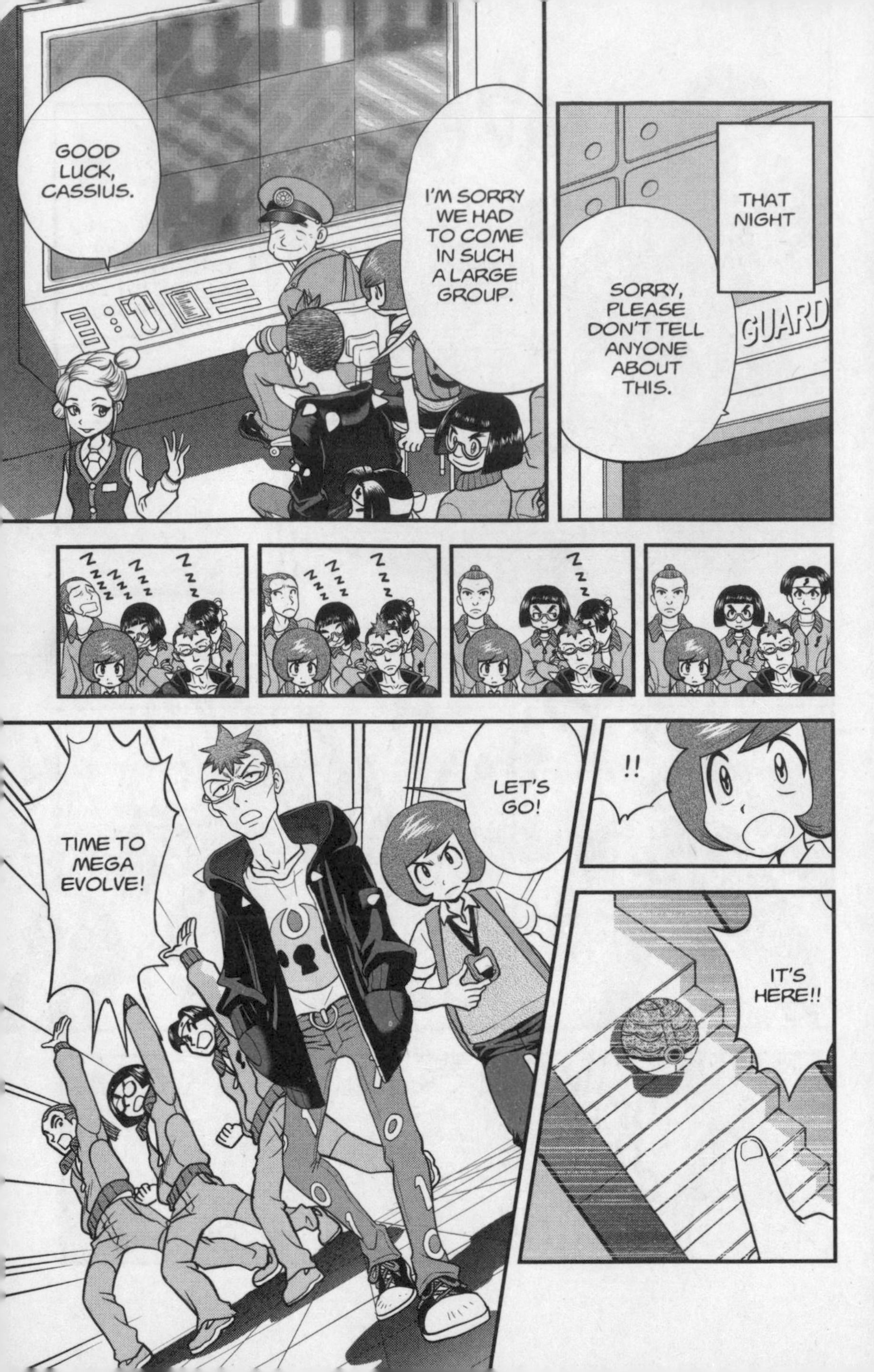
THAT NIGHT
SORRY, PLEASE DON'T TELL ANYONE ABOUT THIS.
GUARD
I'M SORRY WE HAD TO COME IN SUCH A LARGE GROUP.
GOOD LUCK, CASSIUS.
!!
IT'S HERE!!
LET'S GO!
TIME TO MEGA EVOLVE!

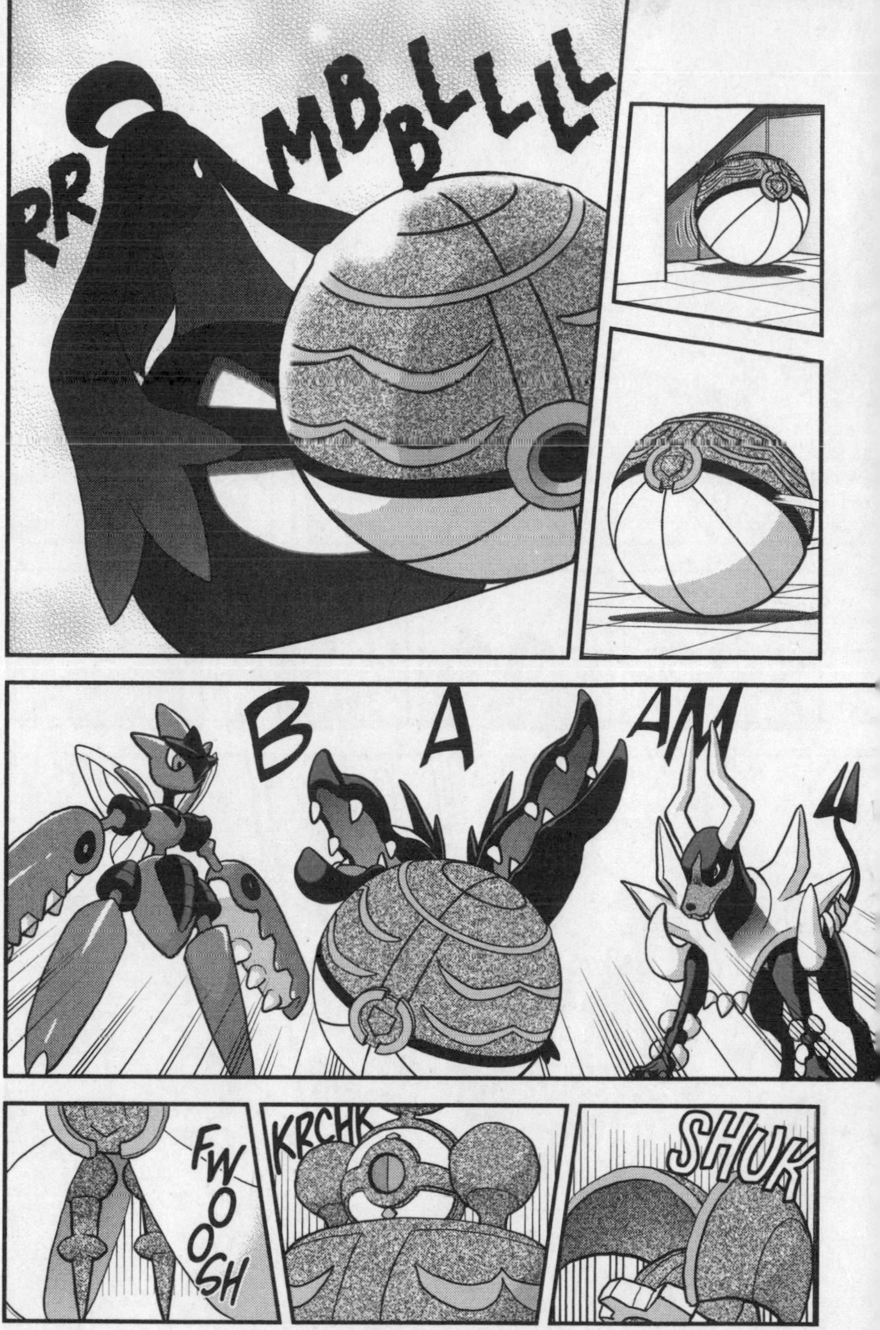
RRMBBLLLL
BAAM
SHUK
KRCHK
FWOOOSH

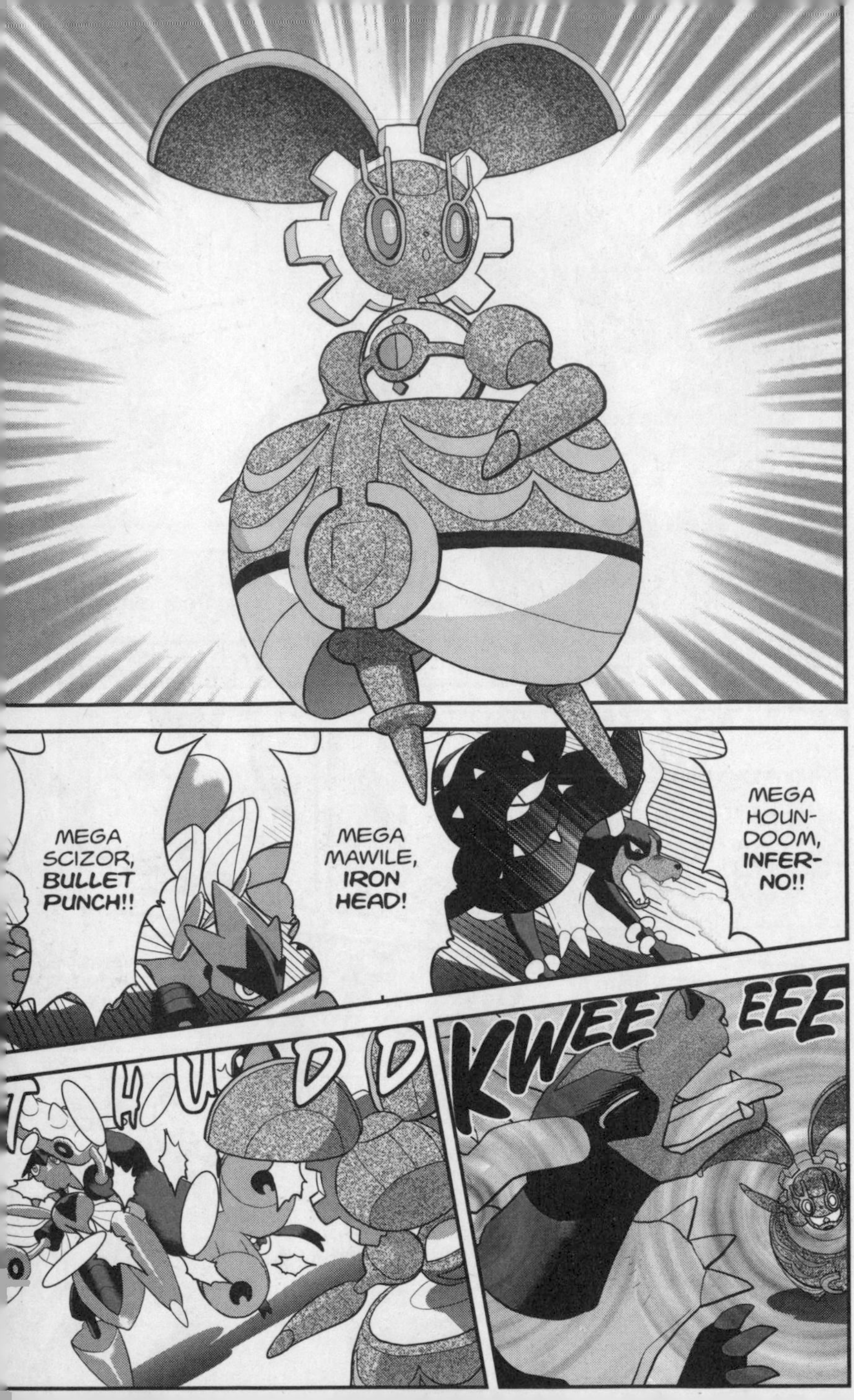
MEGA HOUN-DOOM, INFER-NO!!
MEGA MAWILE, IRON HEAD!
MEGA SCIZOR, BULLET PUNCH!!
KWEE EEE
THUDD

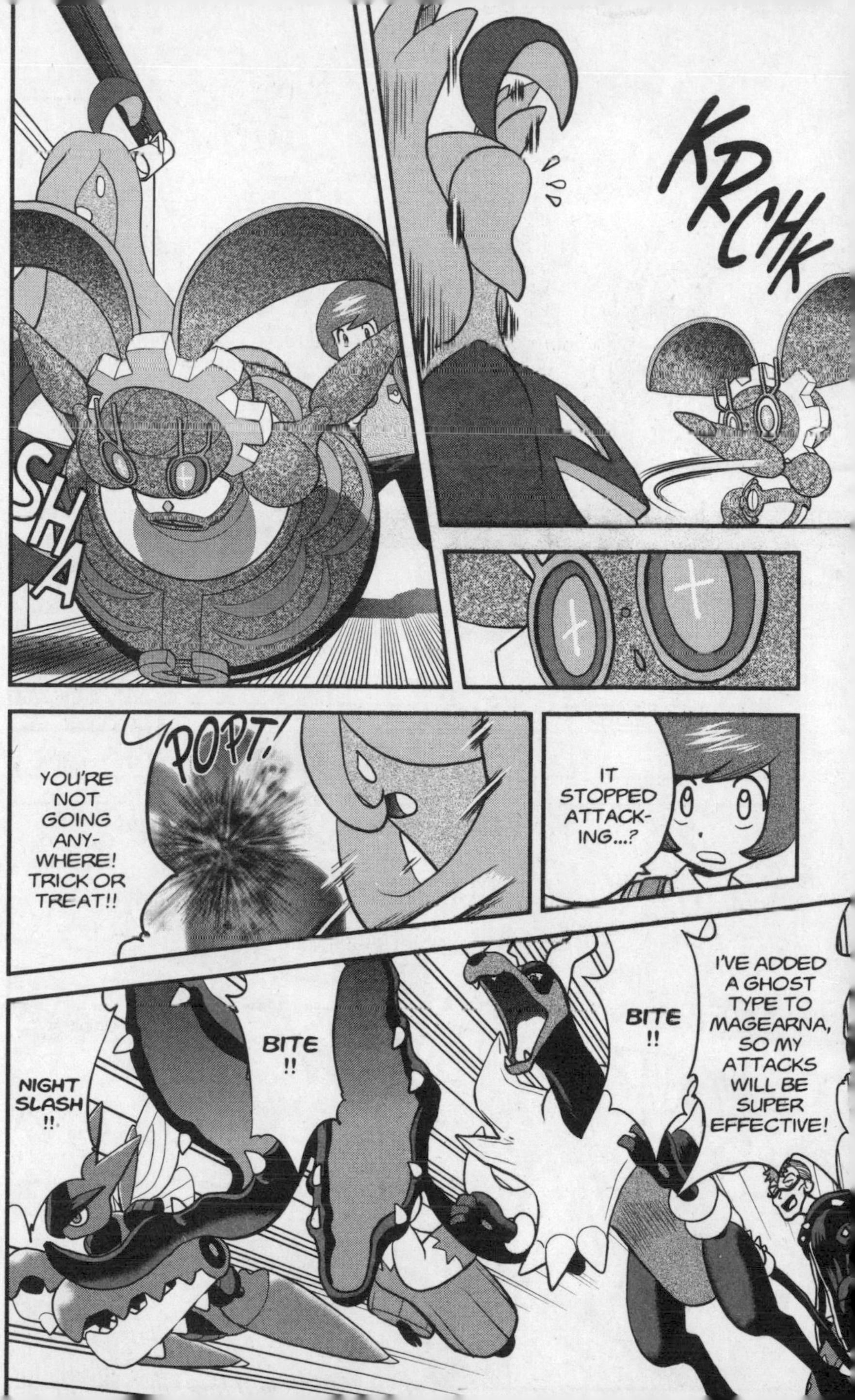
KRCHK
SHA
IT STOPPED ATTACKING...?
POPT!
YOU'RE NOT GOING ANYWHERE! TRICK OR TREAT!!
I'VE ADDED A GHOST TYPE TO MAGEARNA, SO MY ATTACKS WILL BE SUPER EFFECTIVE!
BITE!!
BITE!!
NIGHT SLASH!!

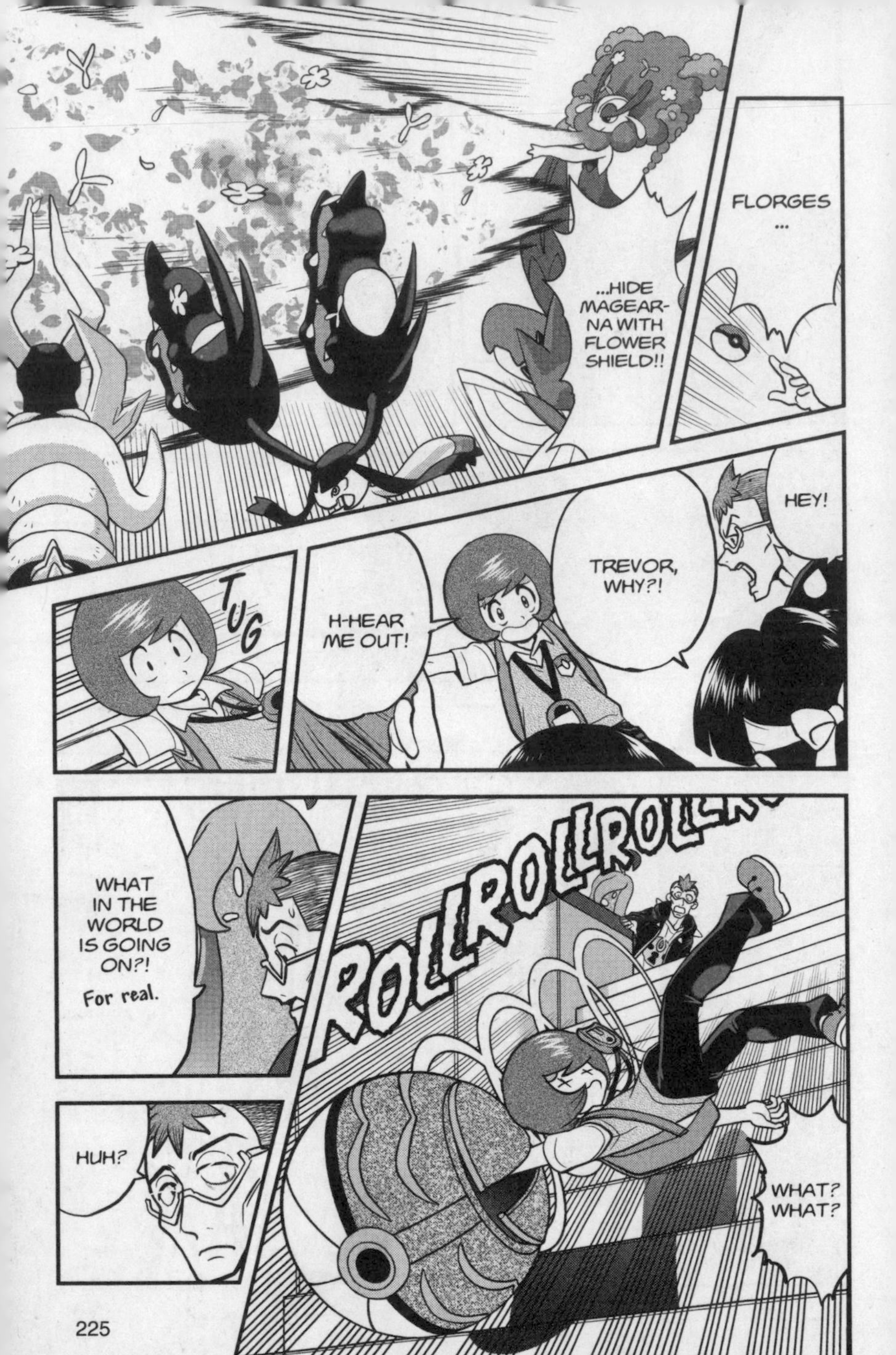
FLORGES ...
...HIDE MAGEARNA WITH FLOWER SHIELD!!
HEY!
TREVOR, WHY?!
H-HEAR ME OUT!
TUG
ROLLROLLROLL
WHAT? WHAT?
WHAT IN THE WORLD IS GOING ON?!
For real.
HUH?

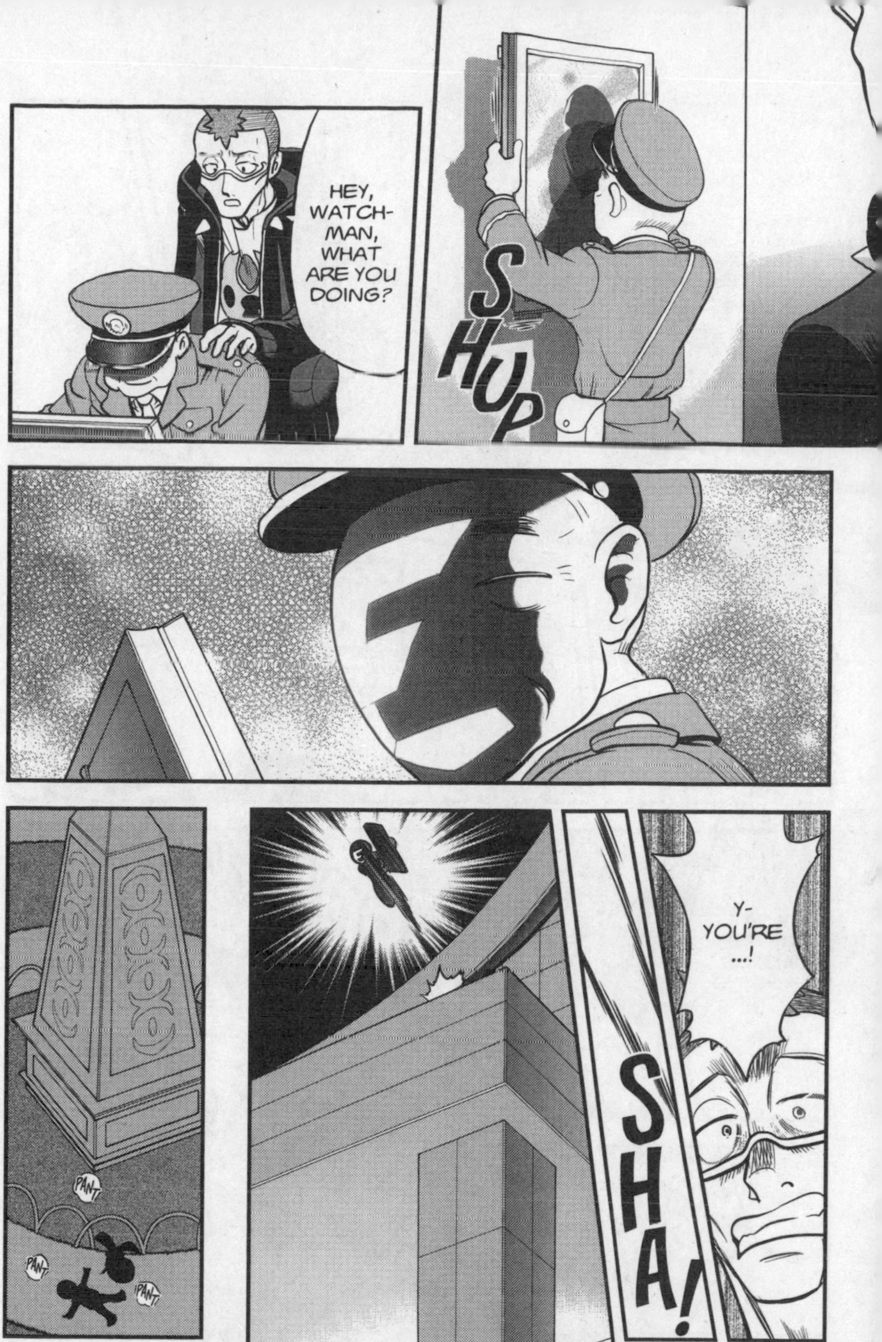
SHUP
HEY, WATCH-MAN, WHAT ARE YOU DOING?
Y-YOU'RE ...!
SHA!
PANT
PANT
PANT

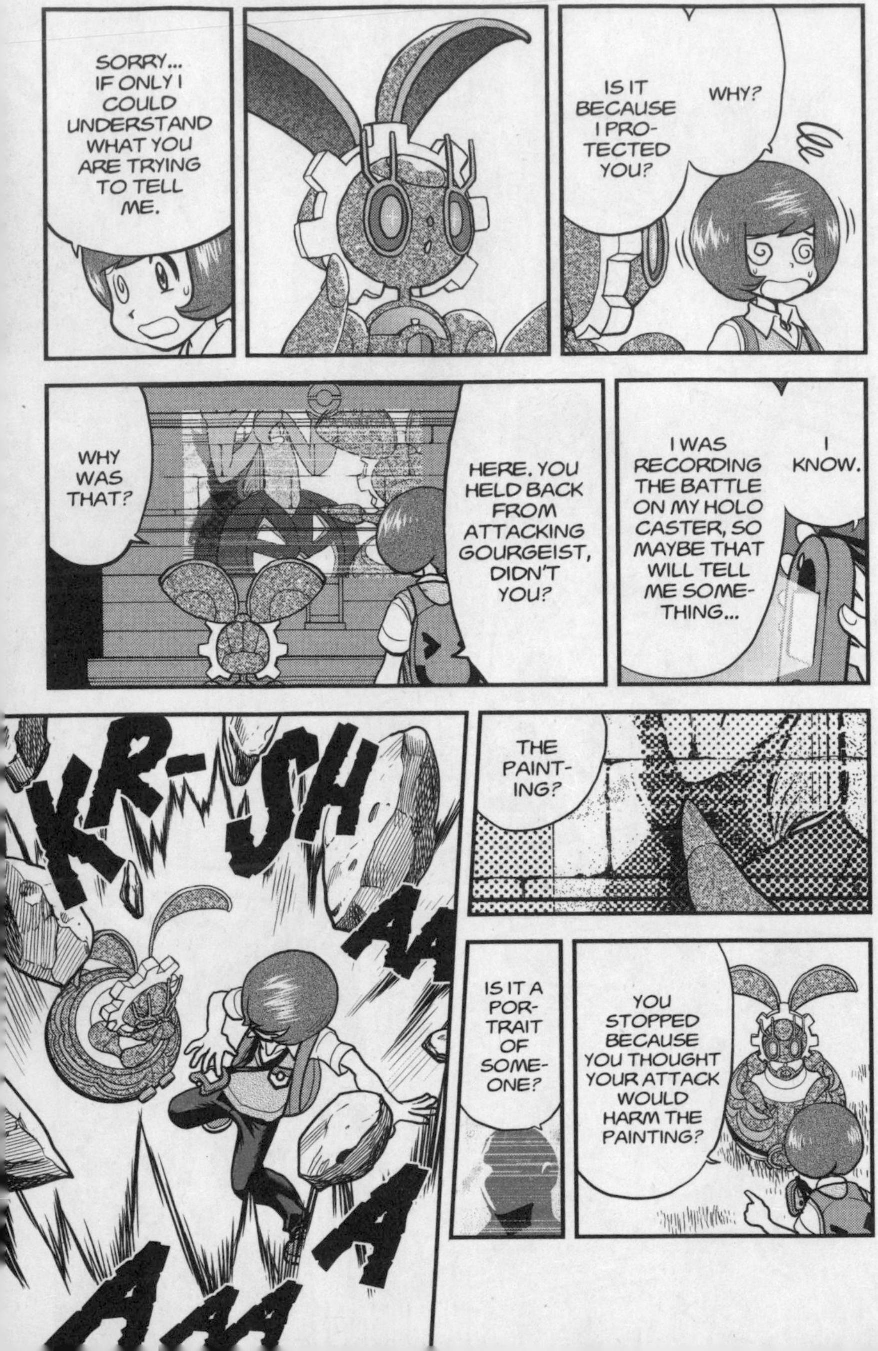
WHY?
IS IT BECAUSE I PRO-TECTED YOU?
SORRY... IF ONLY I COULD UNDERSTAND WHAT YOU ARE TRYING TO TELL ME.
I KNOW.
I WAS RECORDING THE BATTLE ON MY HOLO CASTER, SO MAYBE THAT WILL TELL ME SOME-THING...
HERE. YOU HELD BACK FROM ATTACKING GOURGEIST, DIDN'T YOU?
WHY WAS THAT?
THE PAINT-ING?
YOU STOPPED BECAUSE YOU THOUGHT YOUR ATTACK WOULD HARM THE PAINTING?
IS IT A POR-TRAIT OF SOME-ONE?
KR-SH
AAAAAAA

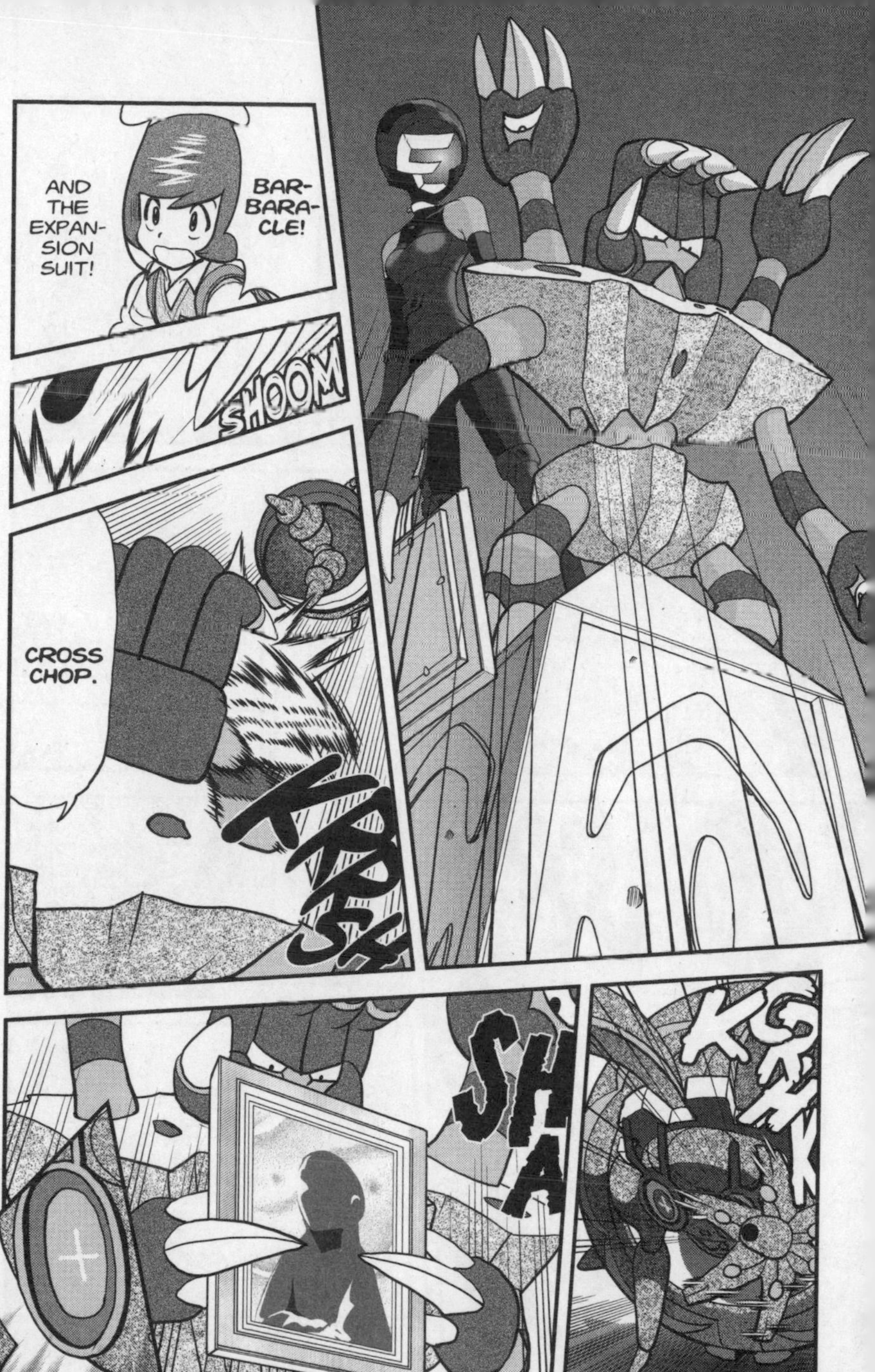
BAR-BARA-CLE!
AND THE EXPAN-SION SUIT!
SHOOM
CROSS CHOP.
KRRSH
KGRHK
SHA

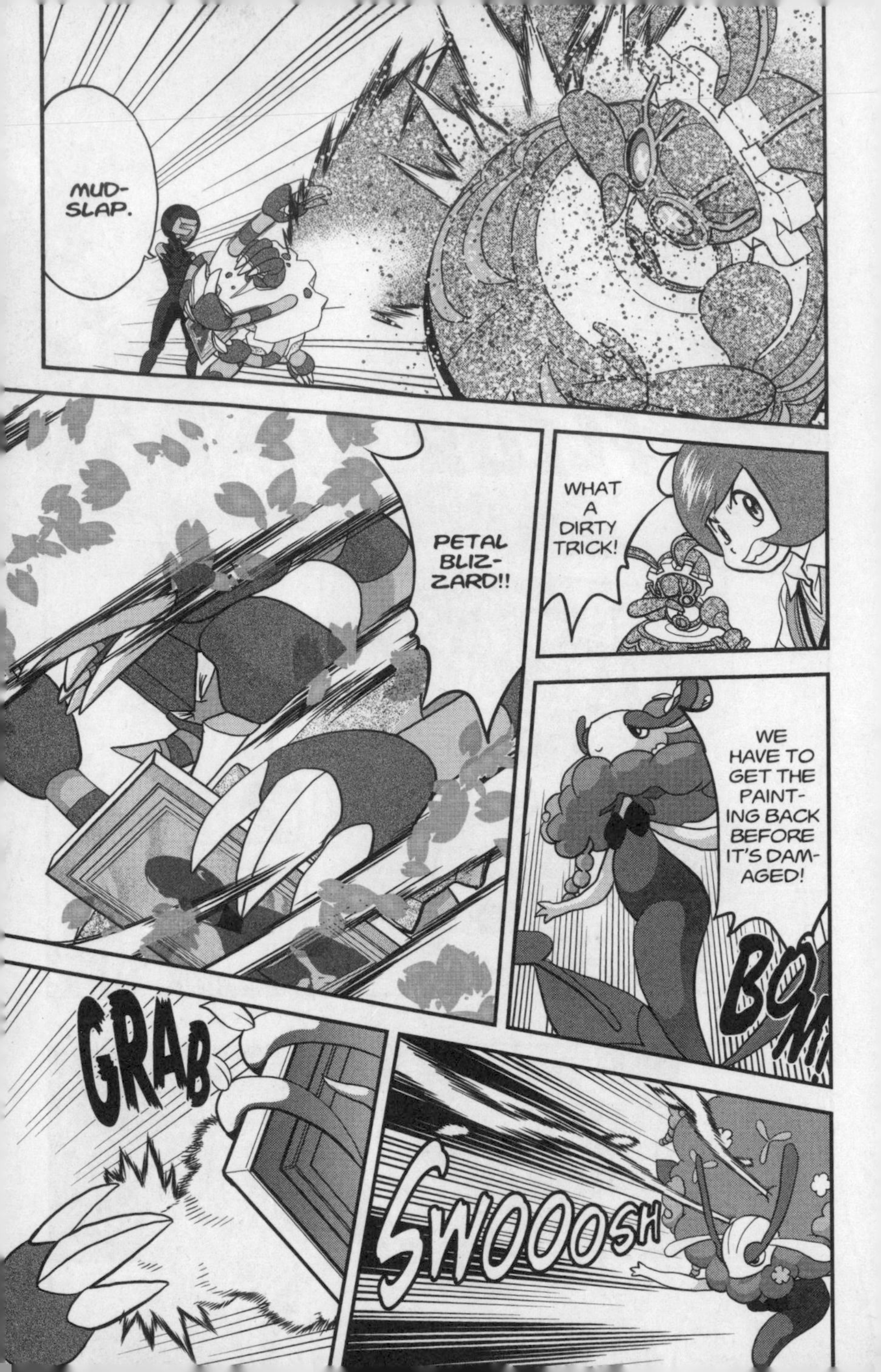
MUD-SLAP.
WHAT A DIRTY TRICK!
WE HAVE TO GET THE PAINTING BACK BEFORE IT'S DAMAGED!
PETAL BLIZZARD!!
SWOOOSH
GRAB

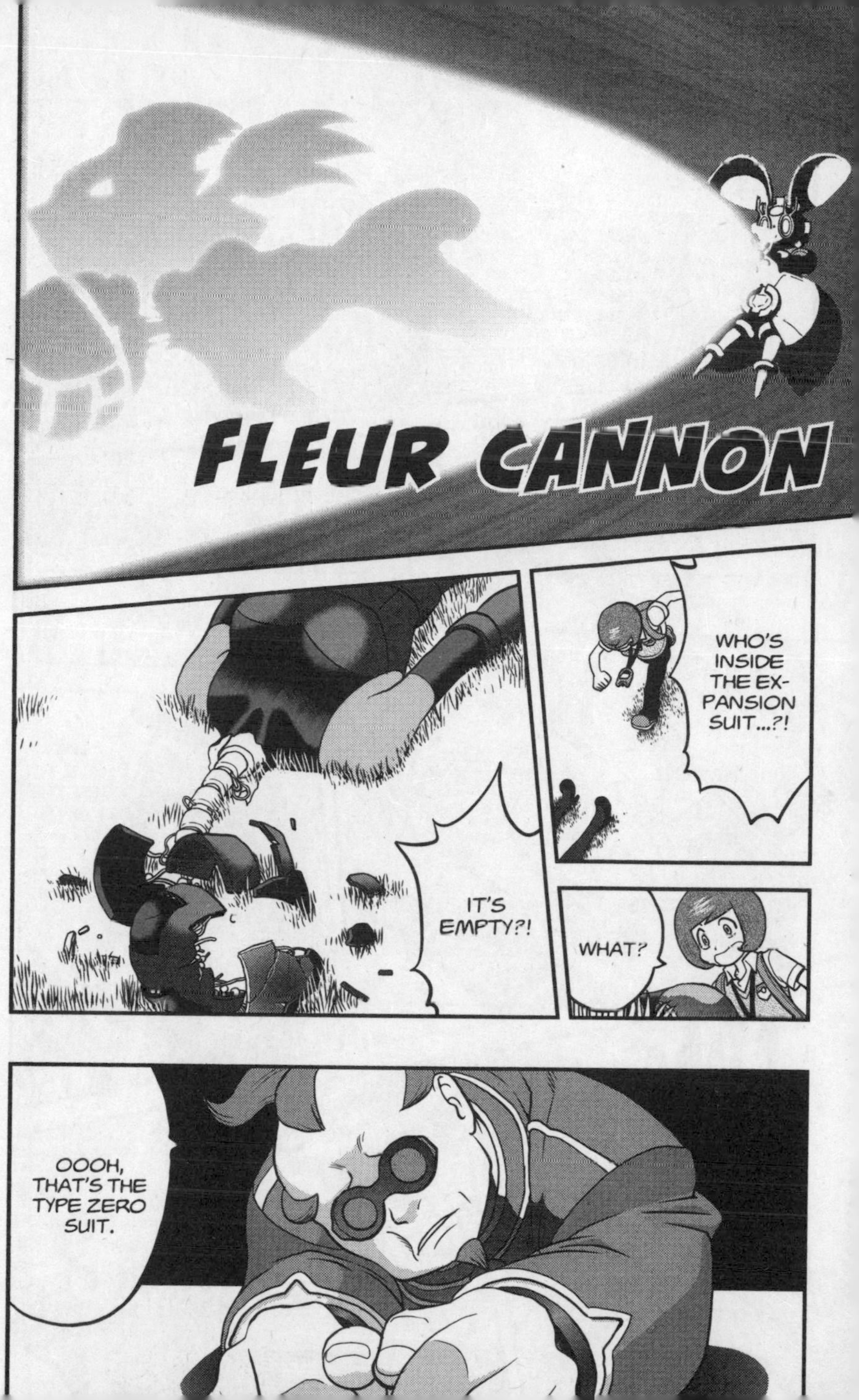
FLEUR CANNON
WHO'S INSIDE THE EX-PANSION SUIT...?!
WHAT?
IT'S EMPTY?!
OOOH, THAT'S THE TYPE ZERO SUIT.

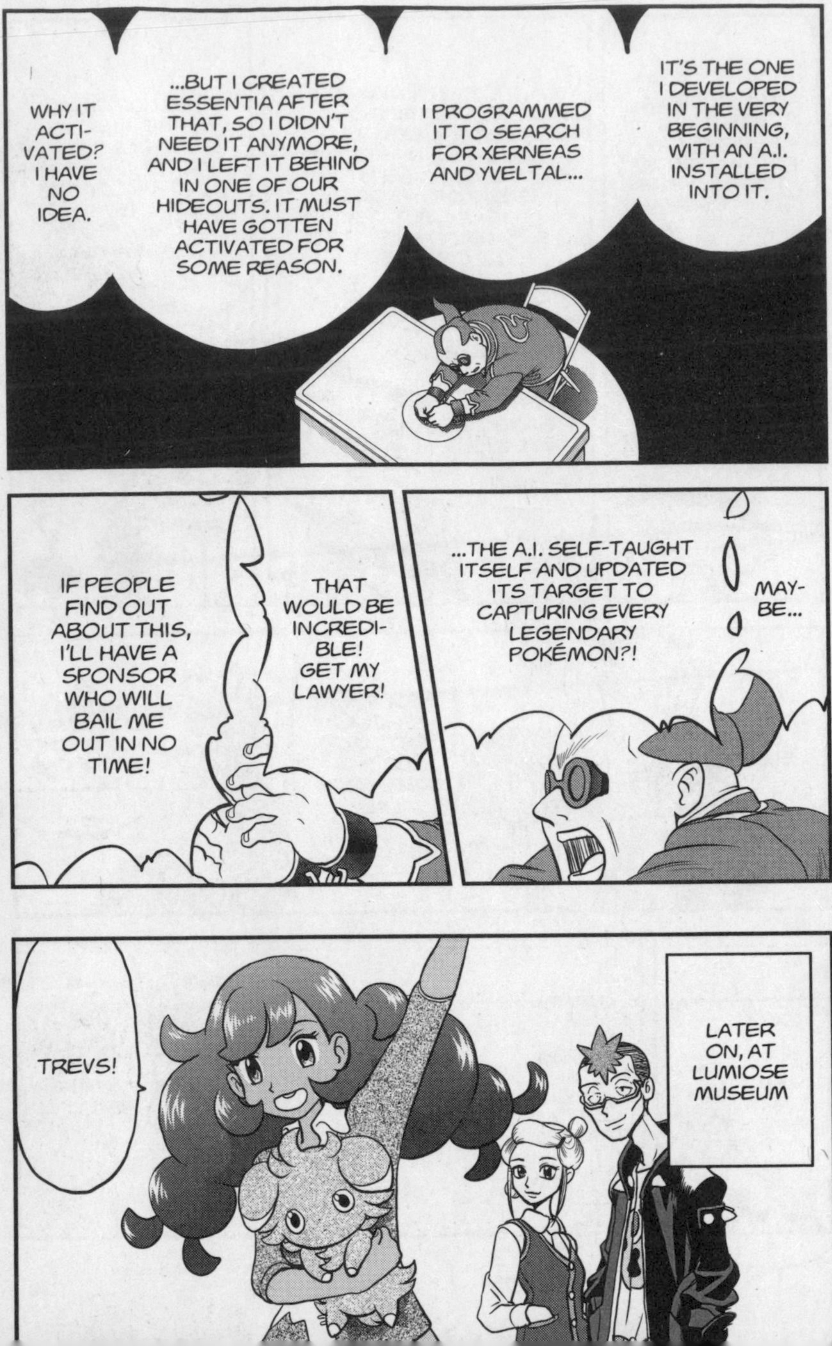
IT'S THE ONE I DEVELOPED IN THE VERY BEGINNING, WITH AN A.I. INSTALLED INTO IT.
I PROGRAMMED IT TO SEARCH FOR XERNEAS AND YVELTAL...
...BUT I CREATED ESSENTIA AFTER THAT, SO I DIDN'T NEED IT ANYMORE, AND I LEFT IT BEHIND IN ONE OF OUR HIDEOUTS. IT MUST HAVE GOTTEN ACTIVATED FOR SOME REASON.
WHY IT ACTI-VATED? I HAVE NO IDEA.
MAY-BE...
...THE A.I. SELF-TAUGHT ITSELF AND UPDATED ITS TARGET TO CAPTURING EVERY LEGENDARY POKÉMON?!
THAT WOULD BE INCREDI-BLE! GET MY LAWYER!
IF PEOPLE FIND OUT ABOUT THIS, I'LL HAVE A SPONSOR WHO WILL BAIL ME OUT IN NO TIME!
LATER ON, AT LUMIOSE MUSEUM
TREVS!

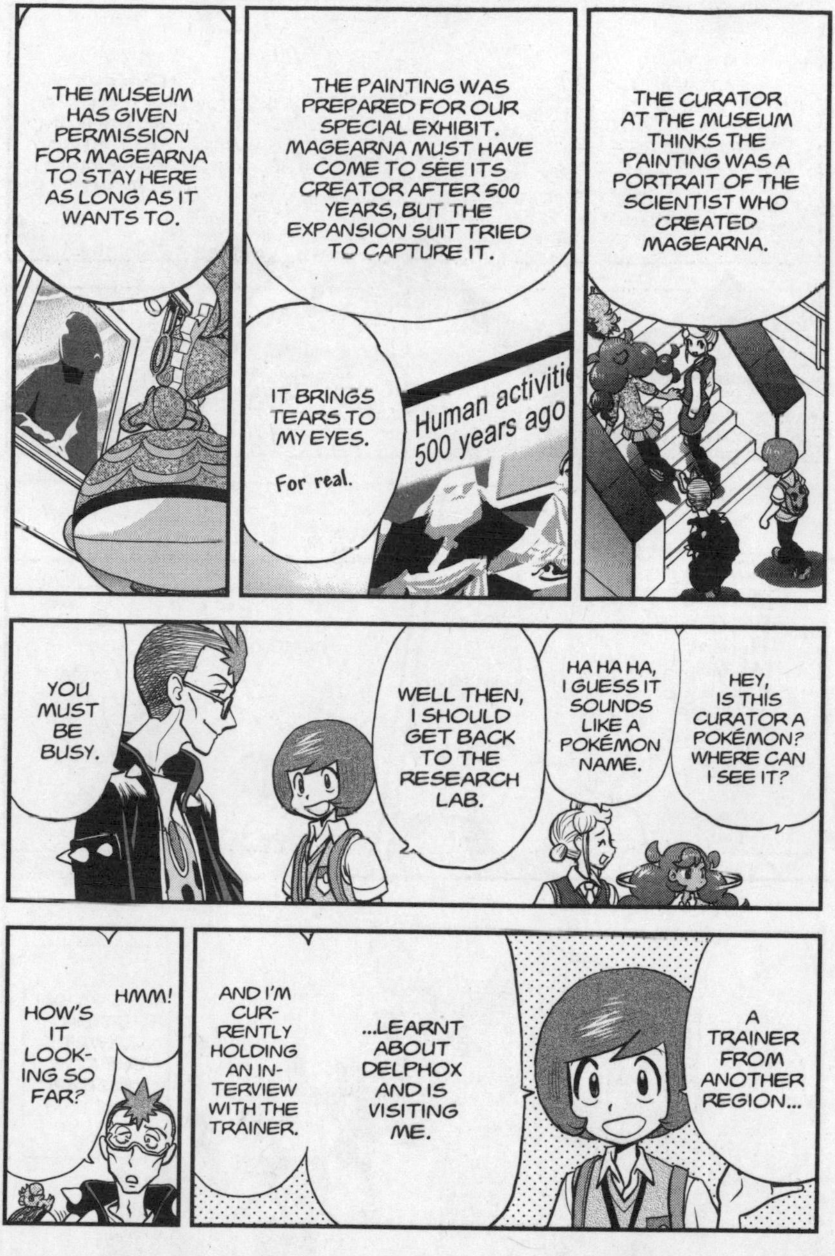
THE CURATOR AT THE MUSEUM THINKS THE PAINTING WAS A PORTRAIT OF THE SCIENTIST WHO CREATED MAGEARNA.
THE PAINTING WAS PREPARED FOR OUR SPECIAL EXHIBIT. MAGEARNA MUST HAVE COME TO SEE ITS CREATOR AFTER 500 YEARS, BUT THE EXPANSION SUIT TRIED TO CAPTURE IT.
IT BRINGS TEARS TO MY EYES.
For real.
Human activiti
500 years ago
THE MUSEUM HAS GIVEN PERMISSION FOR MAGEARNA TO STAY HERE AS LONG AS IT WANTS TO.
HEY, IS THIS CURATOR A POKÉMON? WHERE CAN I SEE IT?
HA HA HA, I GUESS IT SOUNDS LIKE A POKÉMON NAME.
WELL THEN, I SHOULD GET BACK TO THE RESEARCH LAB.
YOU MUST BE BUSY.
A TRAINER FROM ANOTHER REGION...
...LEARNT ABOUT DELPHOX AND IS VISITING ME.
AND I'M CUR-RENTLY HOLDING AN IN-TERVIEW WITH THE TRAINER.
HMM!
HOW'S IT LOOK-ING SO FAR?

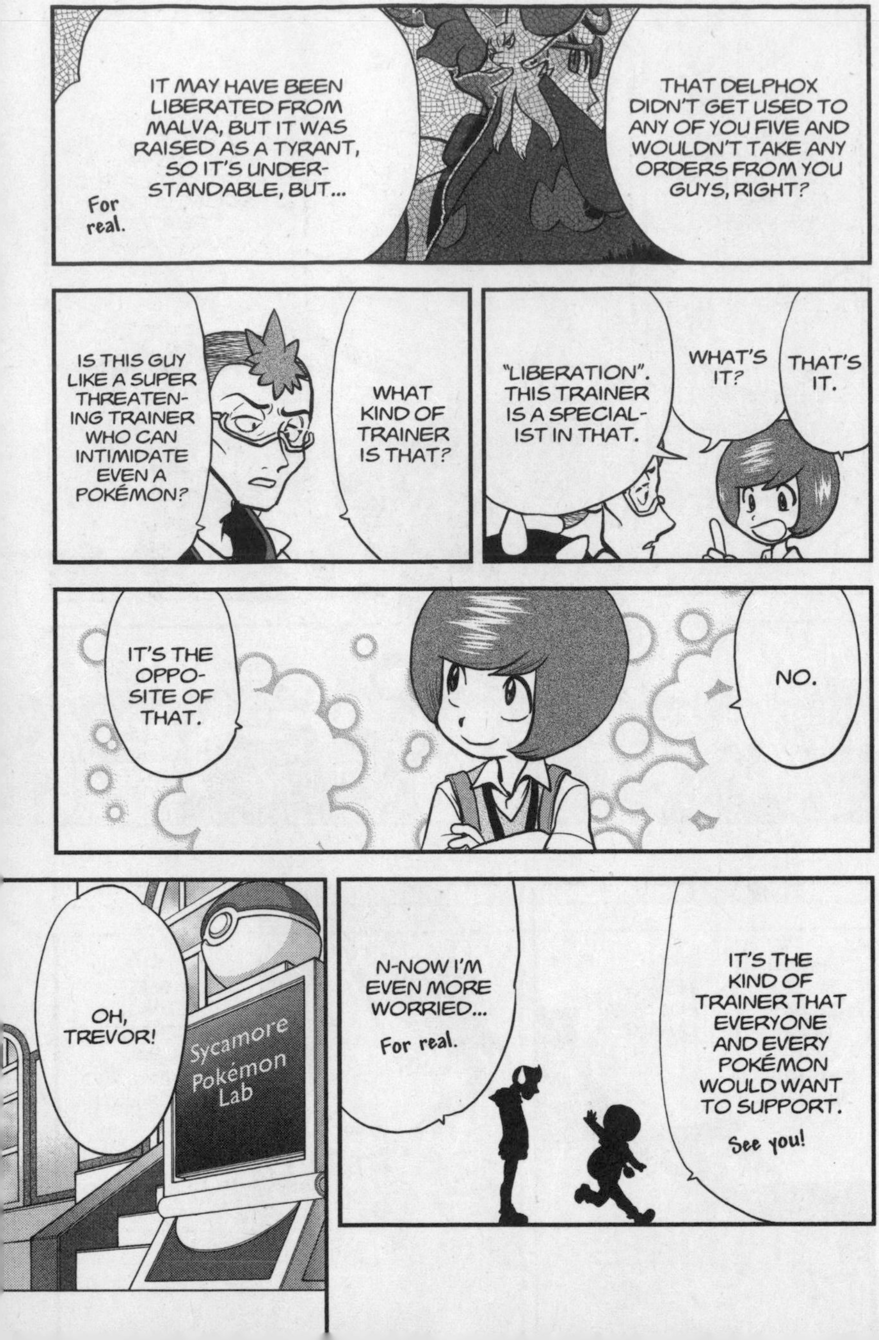
THAT DELPHOX DIDN'T GET USED TO ANY OF YOU FIVE AND WOULDN'T TAKE ANY ORDERS FROM YOU GUYS, RIGHT?
IT MAY HAVE BEEN LIBERATED FROM MALVA, BUT IT WAS RAISED AS A TYRANT, SO IT'S UNDER-STANDABLE, BUT...
For real.
THAT'S IT.
WHAT'S IT?
"LIBERATION". THIS TRAINER IS A SPECIAL-IST IN THAT.
WHAT KIND OF TRAINER IS THAT?
IS THIS GUY LIKE A SUPER THREATEN-ING TRAINER WHO CAN INTIMIDATE EVEN A POKÉMON?
NO.
IT'S THE OPPO-SITE OF THAT.
IT'S THE KIND OF TRAINER THAT EVERYONE AND EVERY POKÉMON WOULD WANT TO SUPPORT.
See you!
N-NOW I'M EVEN MORE WORRIED...
For real.
OH, TREVOR!
Sycamore Pokémon Lab

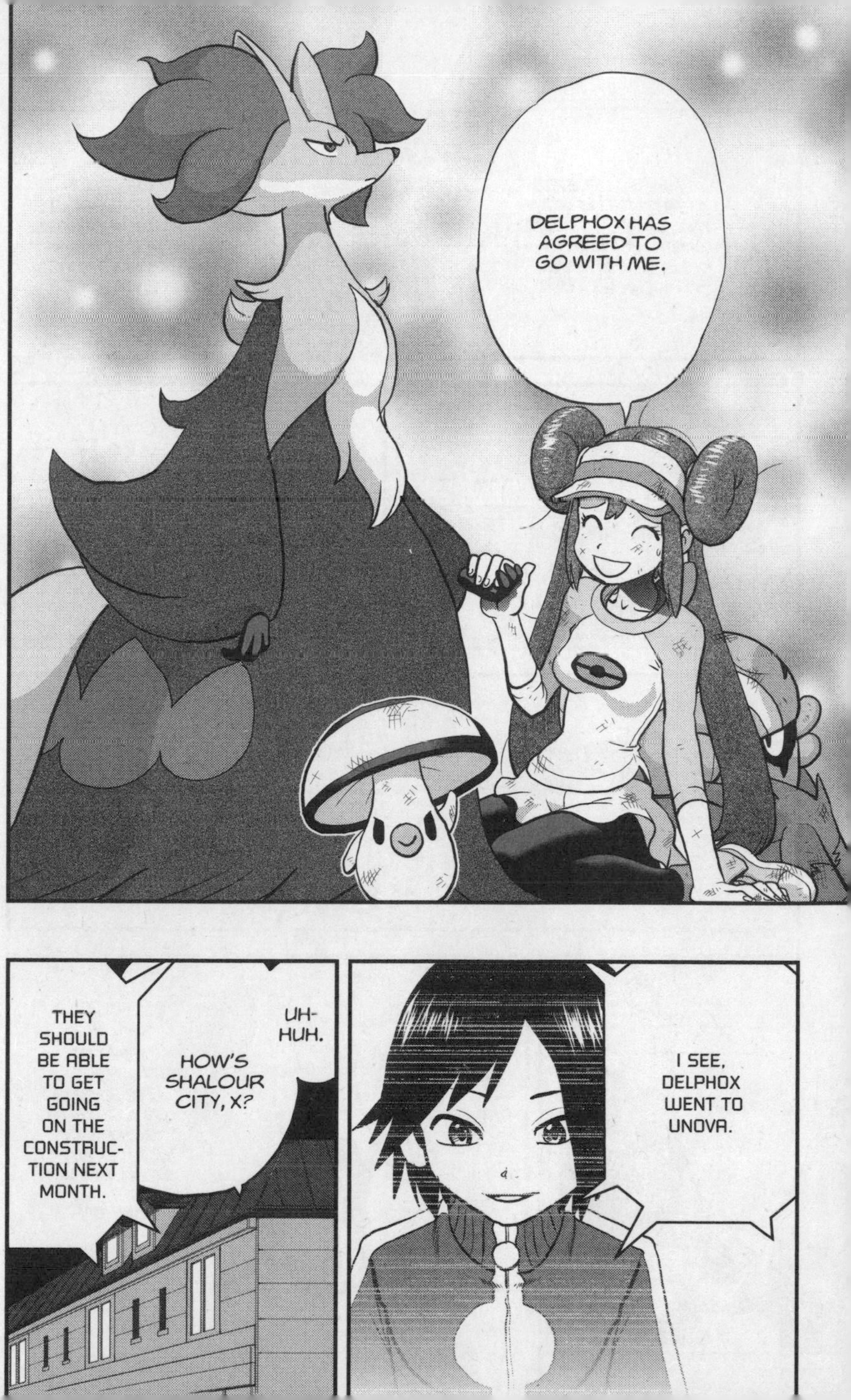
DELPHOX HAS AGREED TO GO WITH ME.
I SEE, DELPHOX WENT TO UNOVA.
UH-HUH.
HOW'S SHALOUR CITY, X?
THEY SHOULD BE ABLE TO GET GOING ON THE CONSTRUCTION NEXT MONTH.

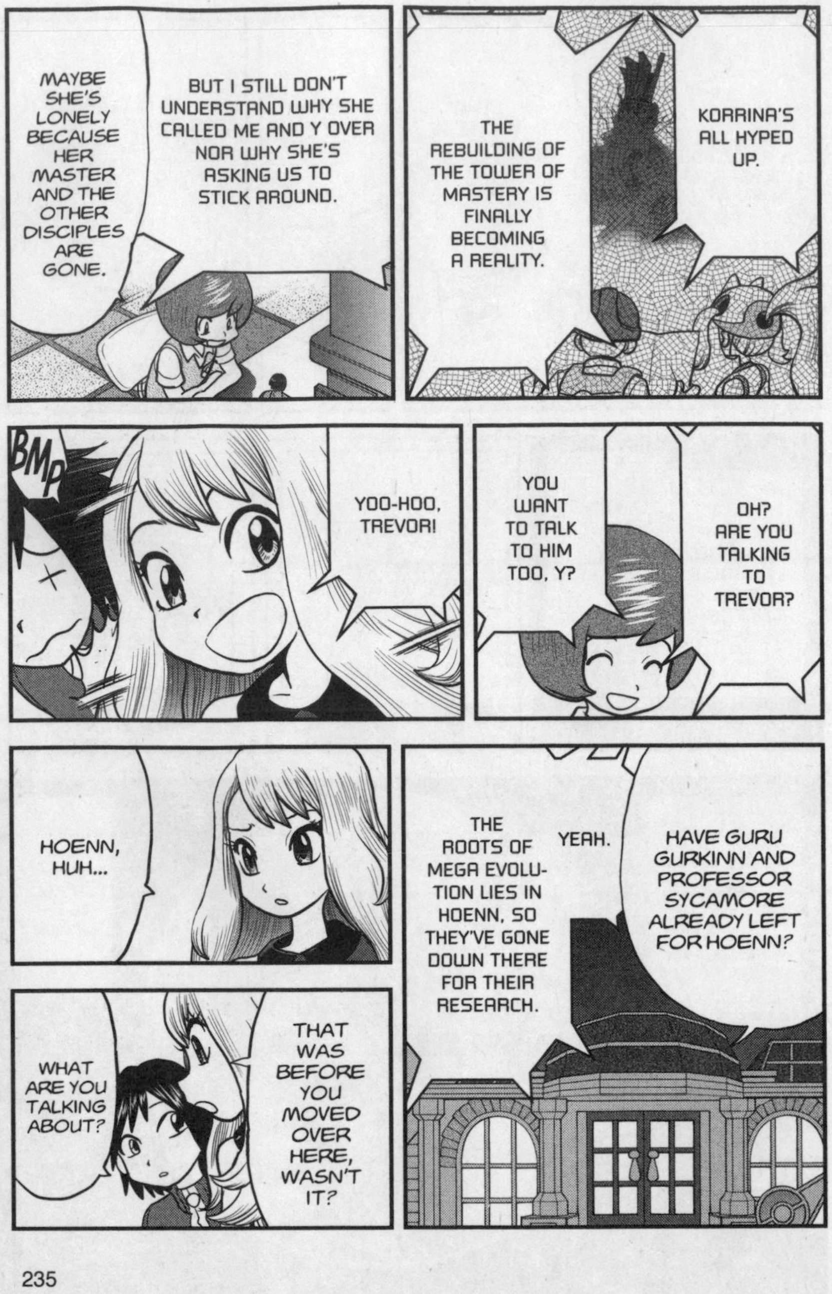
KORRINA'S ALL HYPED UP.
THE REBUILDING OF THE TOWER OF MASTERY IS FINALLY BECOMING A REALITY.
BUT I STILL DON'T UNDERSTAND WHY SHE CALLED ME AND Y OVER NOR WHY SHE'S ASKING US TO STICK AROUND.
MAYBE SHE'S LONELY BECAUSE HER MASTER AND THE OTHER DISCIPLES ARE GONE.
OH? ARE YOU TALKING TO TREVOR?
YOU WANT TO TALK TO HIM TOO, Y?
YOO-HOO, TREVOR!
BMP
HAVE GURU GURKINN AND PROFESSOR SYCAMORE ALREADY LEFT FOR HOENN?
YEAH.
THE ROOTS OF MEGA EVOLUTION LIES IN HOENN, SO THEY'VE GONE DOWN THERE FOR THEIR RESEARCH.
HOENN, HUH...
THAT WAS BEFORE YOU MOVED OVER HERE, WASN'T IT?
WHAT ARE YOU TALKING ABOUT?

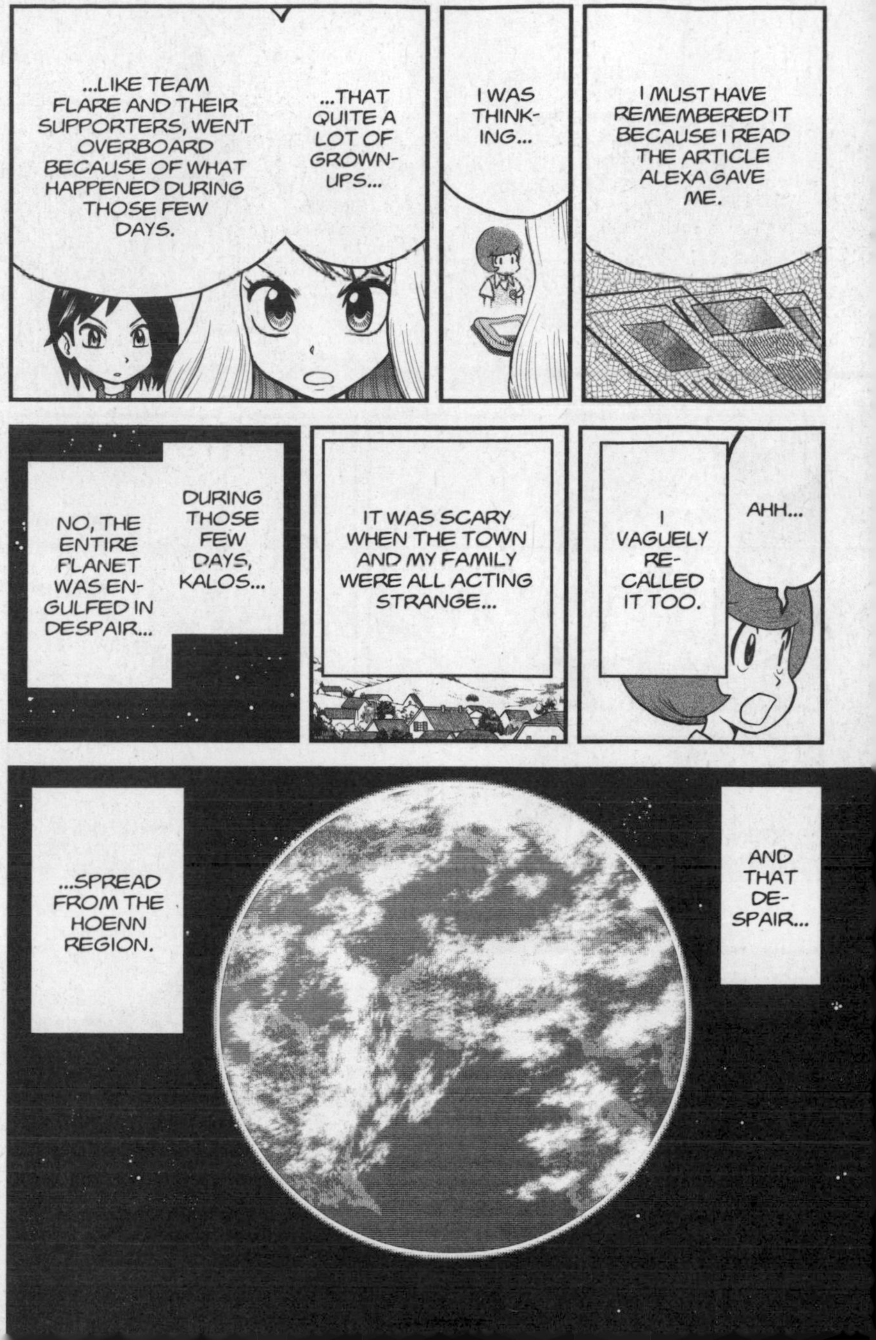
I MUST HAVE REMEMBERED IT BECAUSE I READ THE ARTICLE ALEXA GAVE ME.
I WAS THINKING...
...THAT QUITE A LOT OF GROWN-UPS...
...LIKE TEAM FLARE AND THEIR SUPPORTERS, WENT OVERBOARD BECAUSE OF WHAT HAPPENED DURING THOSE FEW DAYS.
AHH...
I VAGUELY RECALLED IT TOO.
IT WAS SCARY WHEN THE TOWN AND MY FAMILY WERE ALL ACTING STRANGE...
DURING THOSE FEW DAYS, KALOS...
NO, THE ENTIRE PLANET WAS ENGULFED IN DESPAIR...
AND THAT DESPAIR...
...SPREAD FROM THE HOENN REGION.

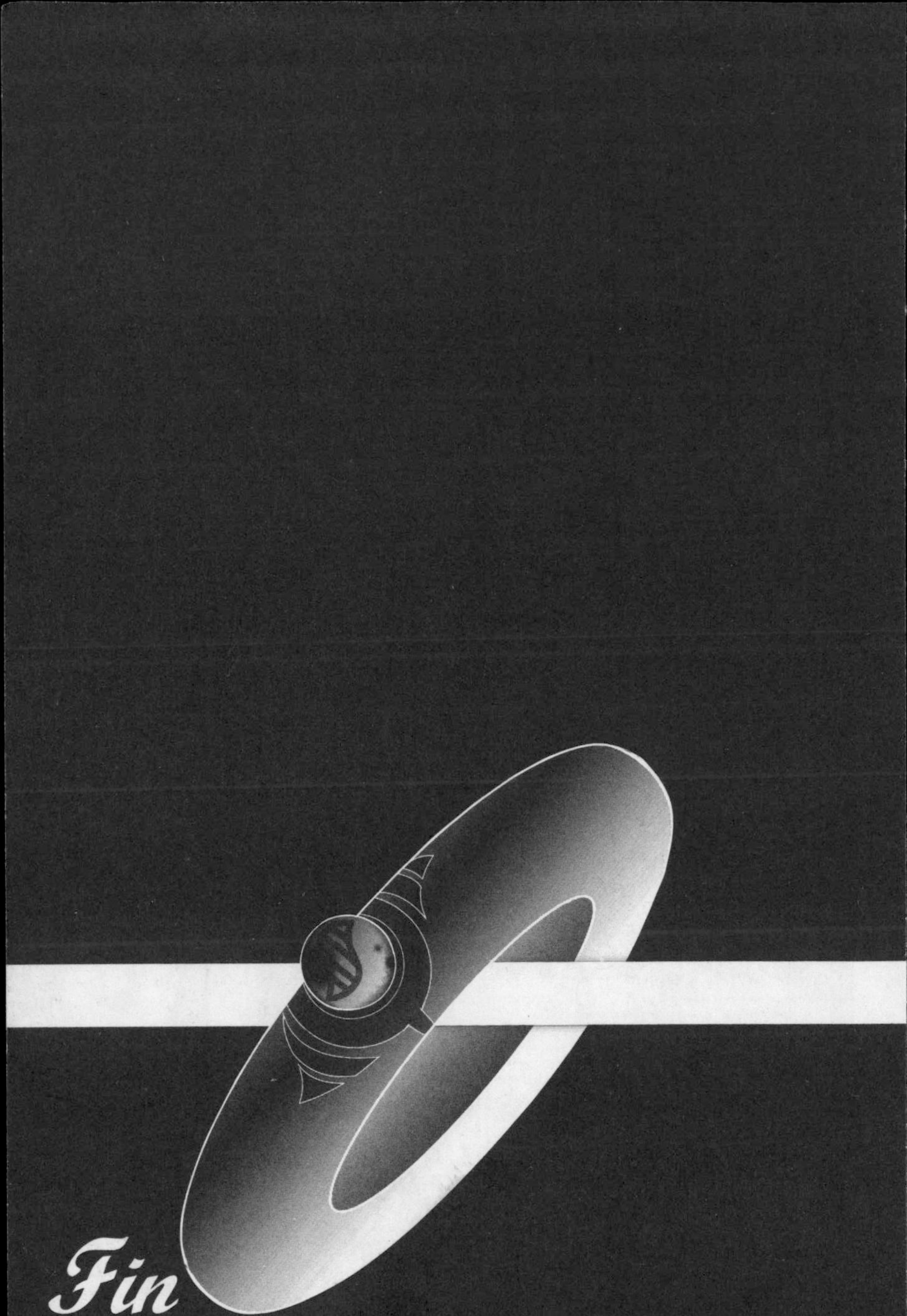
Fin

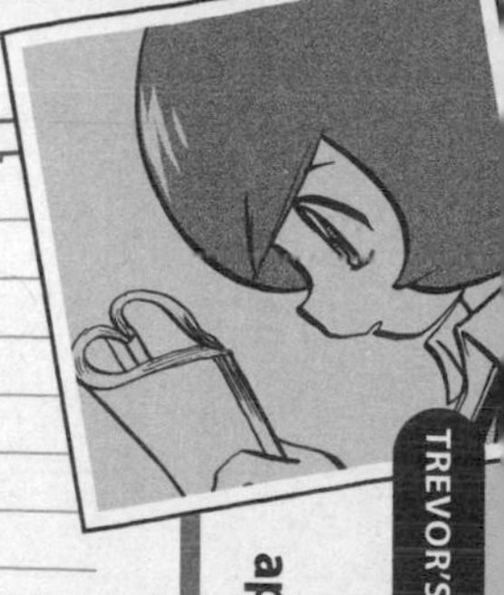

TREVOR'S REPORT 1

Observations on the variability in size and appearance of the Pokémon in the Kalos region

No.

Date

During the battle against Team Flare and over the course of our journey, I have been primarily concerned with Mega Evolution.

○Mega Evolution is a phenomenon in which a Pokémon transforms its shape and increases its power. In the Kalos region, however, we observed numerous other instances of Pokémon transforming, as well as variations in Pokémon's appearance unrelated to Mega Evolution.

○These variations are a notable feature of the Pokémon of Kalos.

○Differences range from power-ups to simple variations in markings, but I would like to enumerate them here and participate in further research on these phenomena

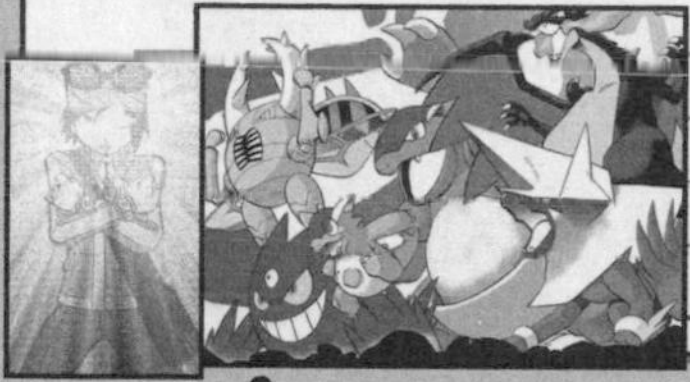

Mega Evolution

I was given many opportunities to observe this process because X is now able to wield Mega Evolution and has been adding Mega Evolving Pokémon to his team. The most remarkable Mega Evolutions I have observed are as follows…

● Two Types of Mega Evolution

I have determined that the same Pokémon holding different Mega Stones results in different Mega Evolutions. I observed this with Charizard and Mewtwo. I was especially surprised to discover that the same Mewtwo underwent two types of Mega Evolution during a single battle simply by switching the Mega Stone it was holding.

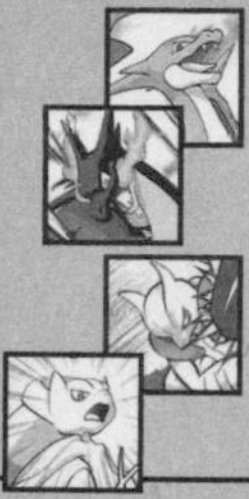

● Five Simultaneous Mega Evolutions

This was possible because X had obtained five Mega Stones. But the strain upon the Trainer wielding five at once is much higher than with just one.

Modes

Xerneas

I had the opportunity to observe this phenomenon at close range because Y captured Xerneas. Xerneas's horn can change color from a rainbow hue to blue. The scientific term for this variability is "Mode."

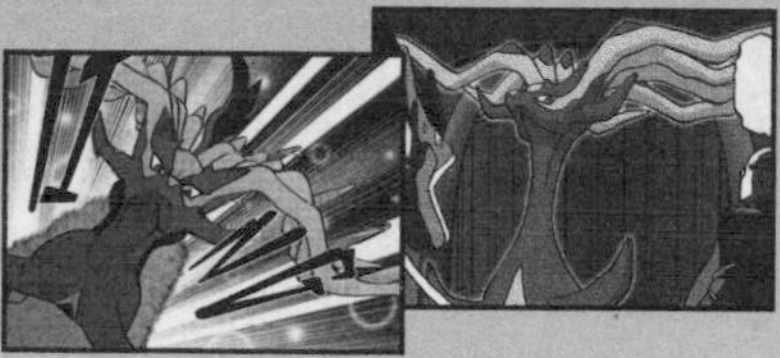

▲ The blue horn represents a dormant state and is called Neutral Mode. The rainbow horn represents a hostile state and is called Active Mode.

Different Trims

Furfrou

I asked Shauna—now a professional Furfrou groomer—to explain this. It turns out the differences in Furfrou's appearance are simply a matter of style and are created by a groomer through a skillful application of scissors.

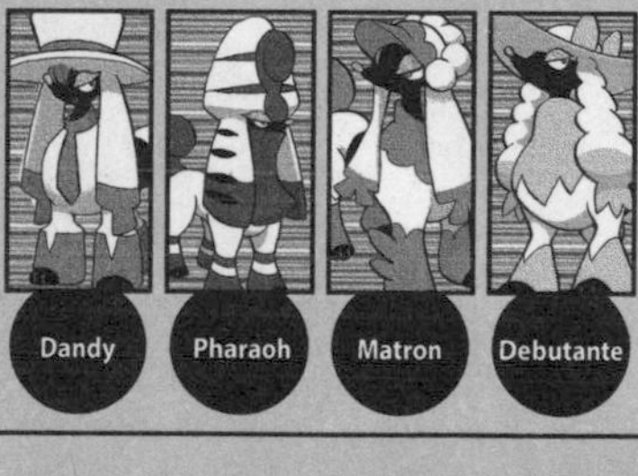
Debutante
Matron
Pharaoh
Dandy

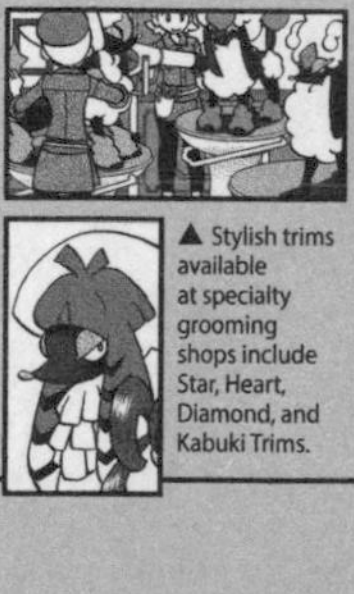

▲ Stylish trims available at specialty grooming shops include Star, Heart, Diamond, and Kabuki Trims.

Pattern Variations

Vivillon

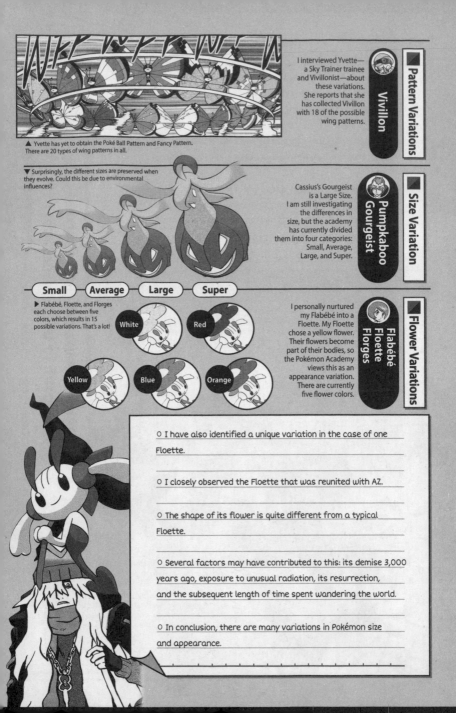

I interviewed Yvette—a Sky Trainer trainee and Vivillonist—about these variations. She reports that she has collected Vivillon with 18 of the possible wing patterns.

▲ Yvette has yet to obtain the Poké Ball Pattern and Fancy Pattern. There are 20 types of wing patterns in all.

Size Variation

Pumpkaboo Gourgeist

Cassius's Gourgeist is a Large Size. I am still investigating the differences in size, but the academy has currently divided them into four categories: Small, Average, Large, and Super.

▼ Surprisingly, the different sizes are preserved when they evolve. Could this be due to environmental influences?

Small
Average
Large
Super

Flower Variations

Flabébé Floette Florges

I personally nurtured my Flabébé into a Floette. My Floette chose a yellow flower. Their flowers become part of their bodies, so the Pokémon Academy views this as an appearance variation. There are currently five flower colors.

▶ Flabébé, Floette, and Florges each choose between five colors, which results in 15 possible variations. That's a lot!

White
Red
Yellow
Blue
Orange

○ I have also identified a unique variation in the case of one Floette.

○ I closely observed the Floette that was reunited with AZ.

○ The shape of its flower is quite different from a typical Floette.

○ Several factors may have contributed to this: its demise 3,000 years ago, exposure to unusual radiation, its resurrection, and the subsequent length of time spent wandering the world.

○ In conclusion, there are many variations in Pokémon size and appearance.

TREVOR'S REPORT 2

Observations on Zygarde's cell absorption and transformation

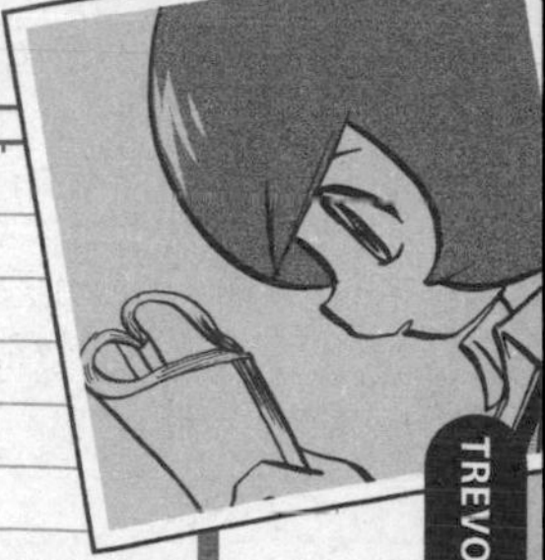

No.

Date

○ We've encountered Zygarde twice thus far: during the battle at the Anistar Sundial and during the final battle at Pokémon Village.

○ What intrigues me is Zygarde's absorption and dispersion behavior, which we witnessed right before it disappeared.

○ Since Zygarde is a Legendary Pokémon of equal or greater status as Yveltal and Xerneas, it likely harbors a secret we have yet to discover. I would like to use the data we've gathered thus far to investigate this possibility.

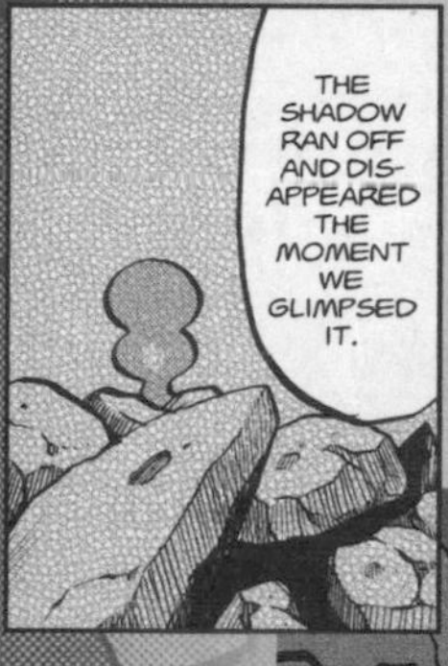

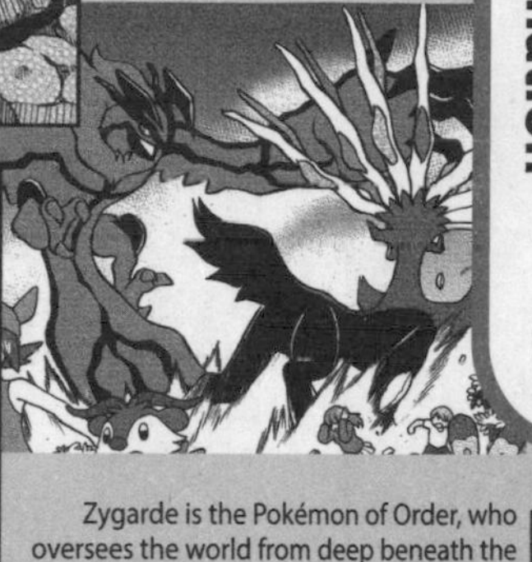

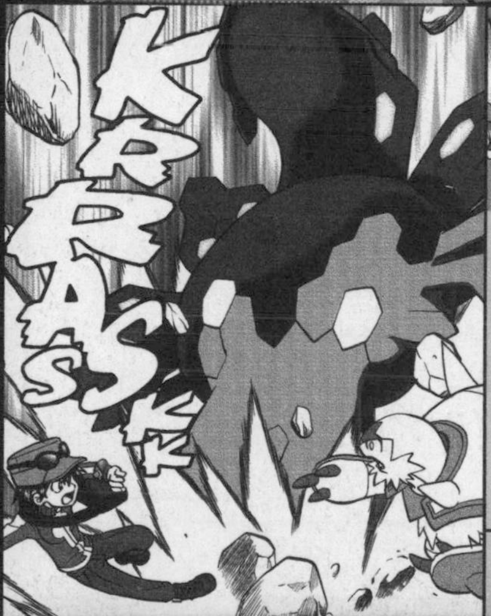

Zygarde Cells

Zygarde is said to have dispersed into little blobs after the battle at Pokémon Village. Our hypothesis is that Zygarde is actually a collective life-form composed of many cell-like units.

THE SHADOW RAN OFF AND DIS-APPEARED THE MOMENT WE GLIMPSED IT.

▶ The green shadow we saw, currently referred to as a Zygarde Cell.

▽ Come to think of it, Pokémon Village is a haven for hurt Pokémon. There might well have been a disruption in the ecosystem there that impacted them.

KRRASSK

The possibility of becoming something greater than the Overseer

Zygarde is the Pokémon of Order, who oversees the world from deep beneath the surface of the ground. When something disrupts the ecosystem, it rises out of its cave to wield its power and restore balance. That's what we've been told about Zygarde up till now. So what is the meaning of the absorption process we saw it undergo, in which it seemed to add more cells to its form? I suspect it was trying to become something more than an Overseer…

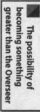

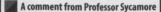
A comment from Professor Sycamore

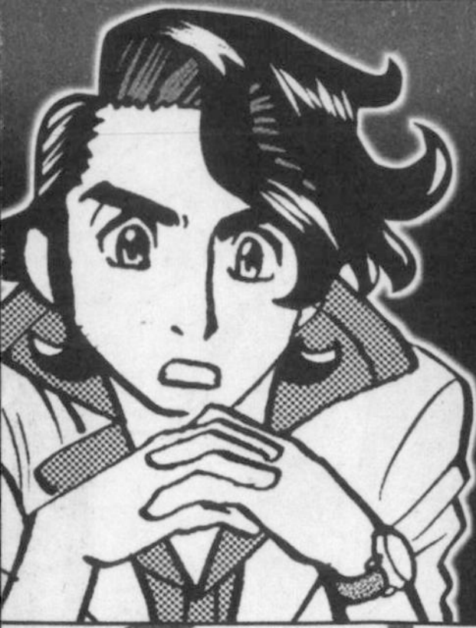

My colleagues, Professor Rowan of Sinnoh
and Professor Oak of Kanto, co-developed
the Pokédex. Through the vast network
of fellow Pokédex holders, I learned that a
green shadow was spotted in the region
where Professor Oak's cousin lives. I've sent
my two assistants to investigate it.

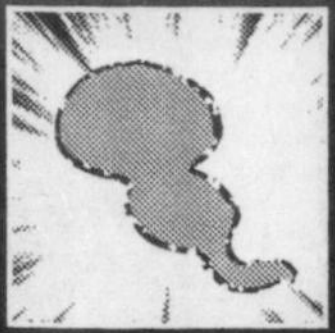

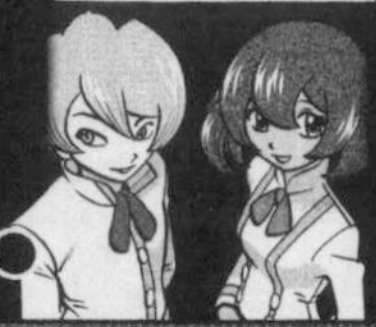

What are the tropical islands of the Alola region like?

The Alola region has a tropical climate and is rich in flora and
fauna. Colorful flowers bloom there throughout the year.
The weather is so warm and sunny that the inhabitants
usually dress lightly and enjoy lots of sunshine. Their region
is named after their word "Alola," which is used as a greeting
and is similar to "Hello" or "Have a nice day." Alola consists
of four natural islands and one artificial island.

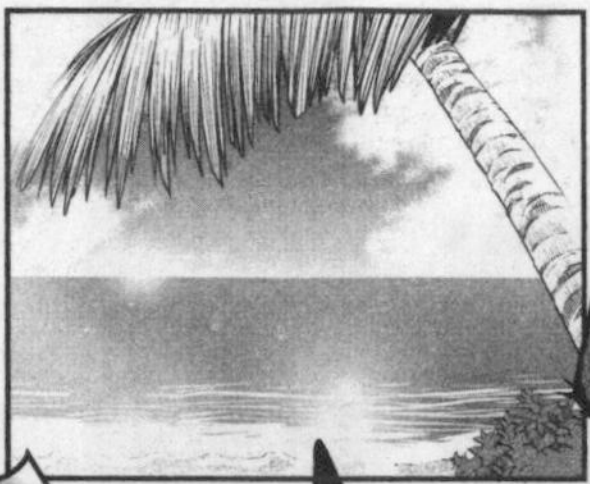

▲ If the spottings of the green shadows are verified sightings of Zygarde
Cells, and my hypothesis that Zygarde is attempting to become something
greater than an Overseer is correct…I wonder what its even more powerful
form will look like. I eagerly await a report from Sina and Dexio…

TREVOR'S REPORT 3

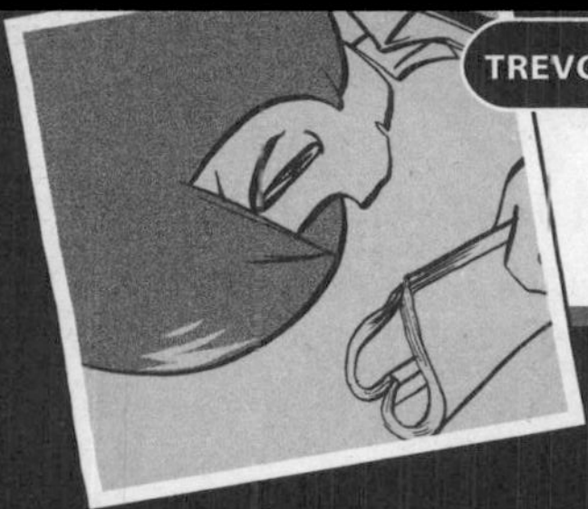

Expansion Suit Functions

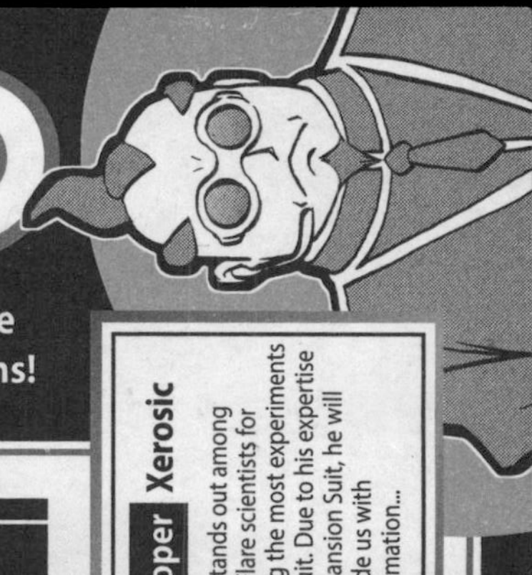

The Expansion Suit gathered attention again because of the Magearna incident. Let us take a look at its amazing functions!

Developer **Xerosic**

This man stands out among the Team Flare scientists for conducting the most experiments with the suit. Due to his expertise on the Expansion Suit, he will now provide us with some information...

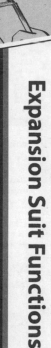

The woman inside the suit is called Essentia and has appeared in many battles

The black-clad Trainer who appeared before us numerous times during our battle against Team Flare. She turned out to be Emma wearing the special Expansion Suit provided to her by Xerosic. We also learned about the existence of the "Type Zero" prototype in the Magearna incident. This is an introduction of its functions as told to the police by Xerosic, the developer of the suit!

Essentia

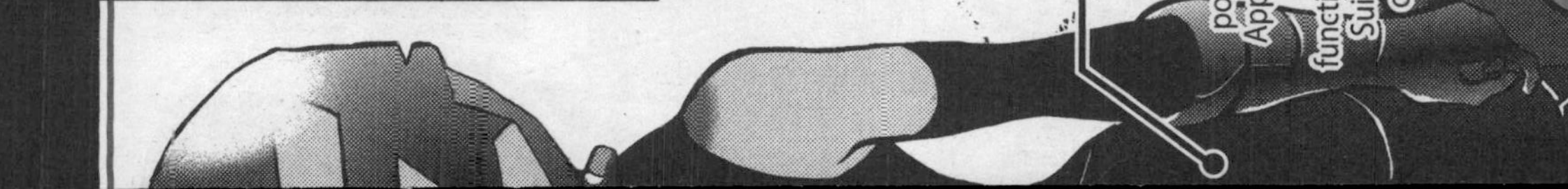

1 Trainer Enhancement Function

Essentia's moves are incredibly quick and powerful during battle. Apparently these moves are enhanced by the function of the Expansion Suit. The Expansion Suit can turn any ordinary Trainer into a super Trainer.

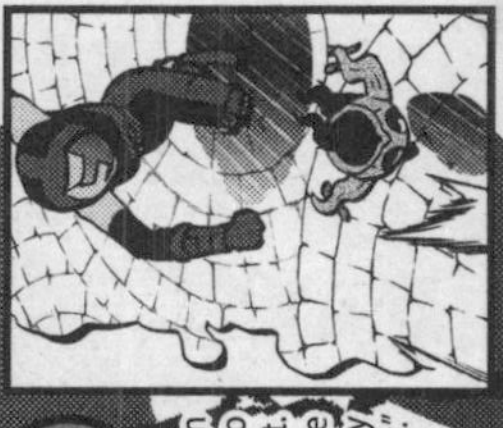

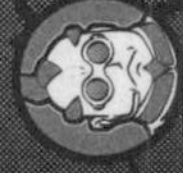

▷"As you can see, fire has no effect upon it. The suit can be deployed in any environment."

2 Poké Ball Jack Function

The Poké Ball Jack function enables the suit to seize control of other people's Poké Balls and Pokémon. The suit infects the Poké Ball with a virus that strengthens the Pokémon.

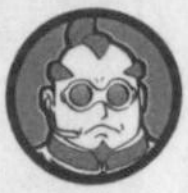

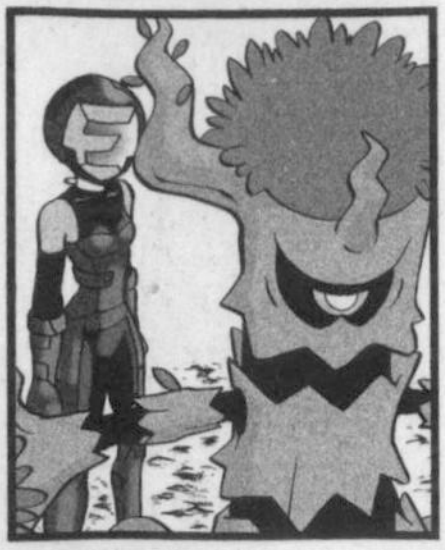

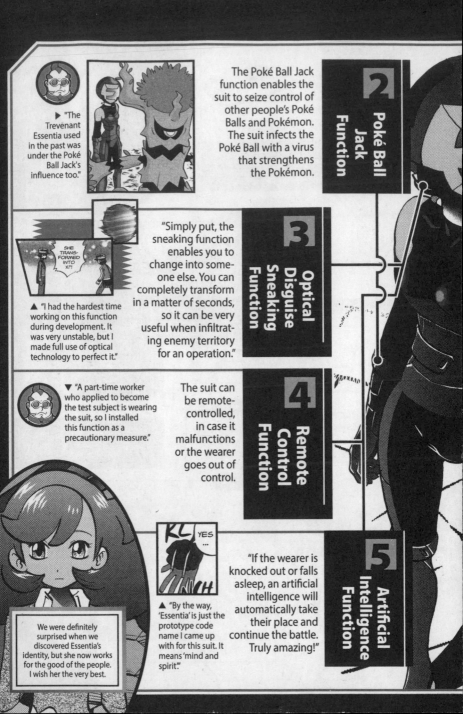

▶ "The Trevenant Essentia used in the past was under the Poké Ball Jack's influence too."

3 Optical Disguise Sneaking Function

"Simply put, the sneaking function enables you to change into some-one else. You can completely transform in a matter of seconds, so it can be very useful when infiltrat-ing enemy territory for an operation."

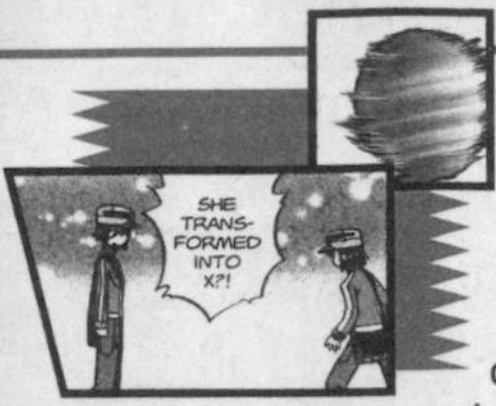

SHE TRANS-FORMED INTO X?!

▲ "I had the hardest time working on this function during development. It was very unstable, but I made full use of optical technology to perfect it."

4 Remote Control Function

The suit can be remote-controlled, in case it malfunctions or the wearer goes out of control.

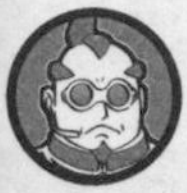

▼ "A part-time worker who applied to become the test subject is wearing the suit, so I installed this function as a precautionary measure."

5 Artificial Intelligence Function

"If the wearer is knocked out or falls asleep, an artificial intelligence will automatically take their place and continue the battle. Truly amazing!"

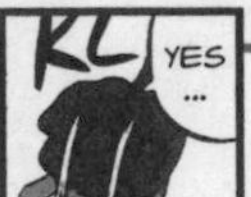

KLNCH
YES ...

▲ "By the way, 'Essentia' is just the prototype code name I came up with for this suit. It means 'mind and spirit.'"

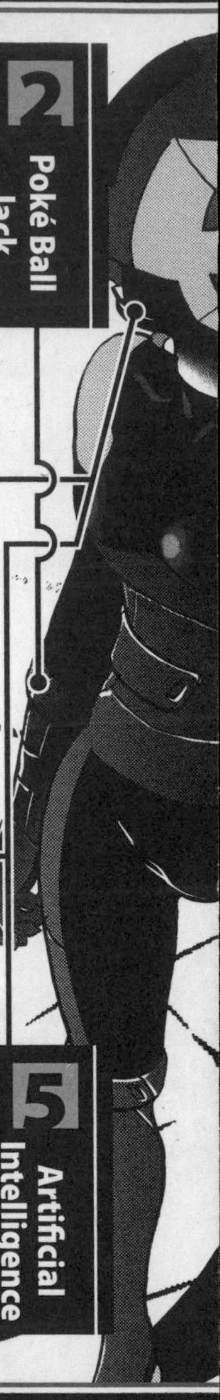

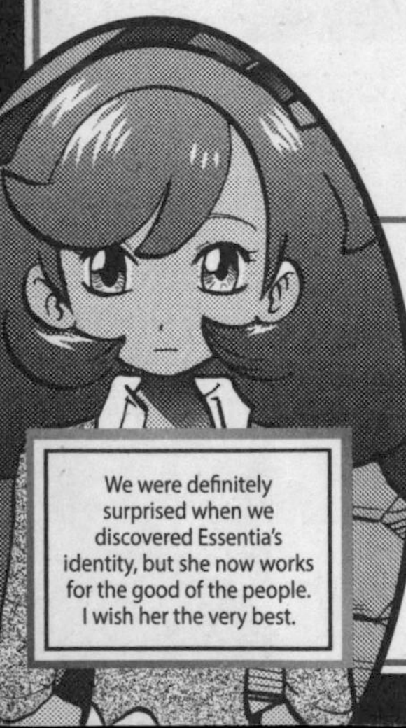

We were definitely surprised when we discovered Essentia's identity, but she now works for the good of the people. I wish her the very best.

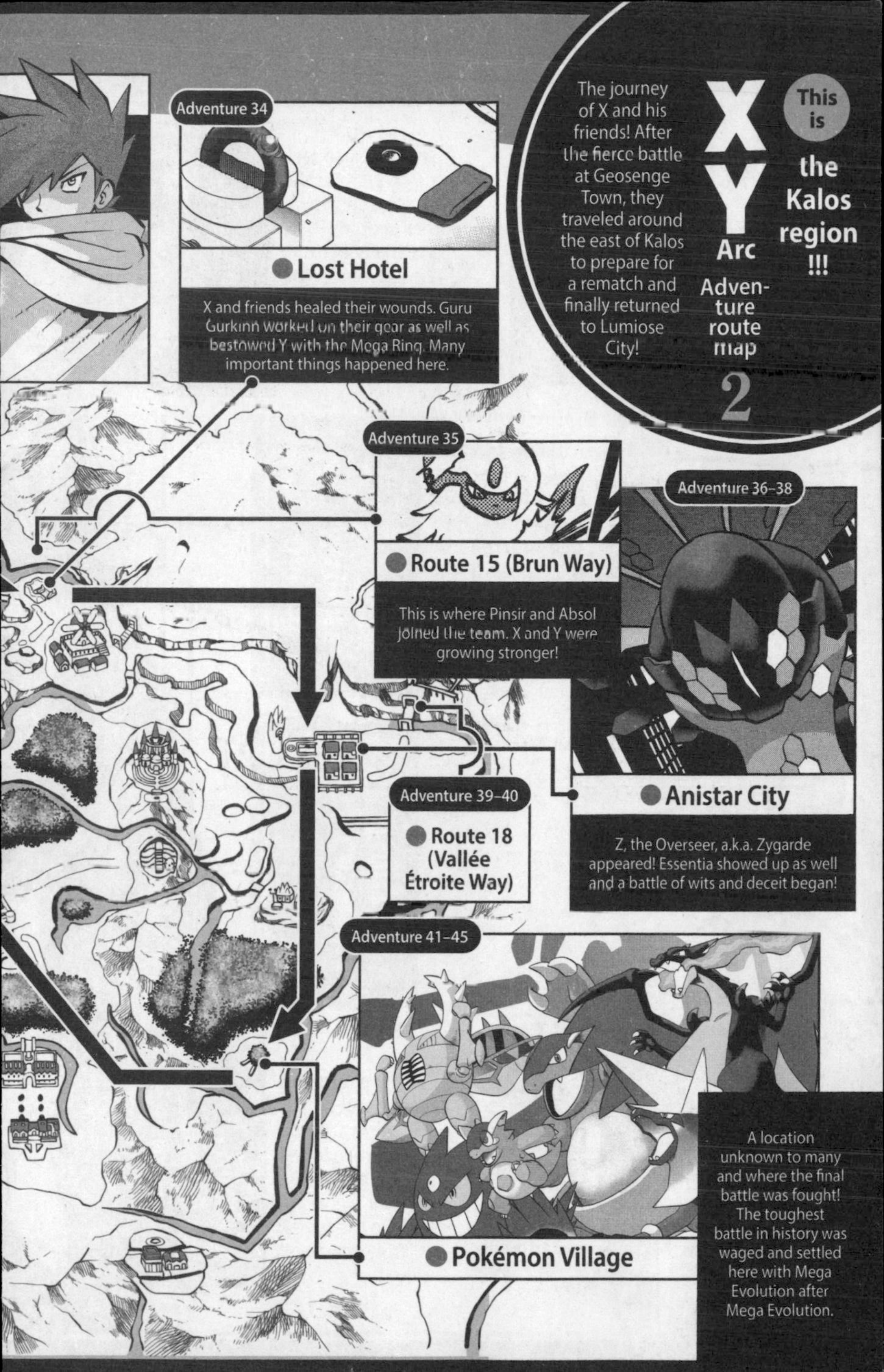
This is the Kalos region!!!
XY Arc
Adventure route map
2
The journey of X and his friends! After the fierce battle at Geosenge Town, they traveled around the east of Kalos to prepare for a rematch and finally returned to Lumiose City!
Adventure 34
Lost Hotel
X and friends healed their wounds. Guru Gurkinn worked on their gear as well as bestowed Y with the Mega Ring. Many important things happened here.
Adventure 35
Route 15 (Brun Way)
This is where Pinsir and Absol joined the team. X and Y were growing stronger!
Adventure 36–38
Anistar City
Z, the Overseer, a.k.a. Zygarde appeared! Essentia showed up as well and a battle of wits and deceit began!
Adventure 39–40
Route 18 (Vallée Étroite Way)
Adventure 41–45
Pokémon Village
A location unknown to many and where the final battle was fought! The toughest battle in history was waged and settled here with Mega Evolution after Mega Evolution.

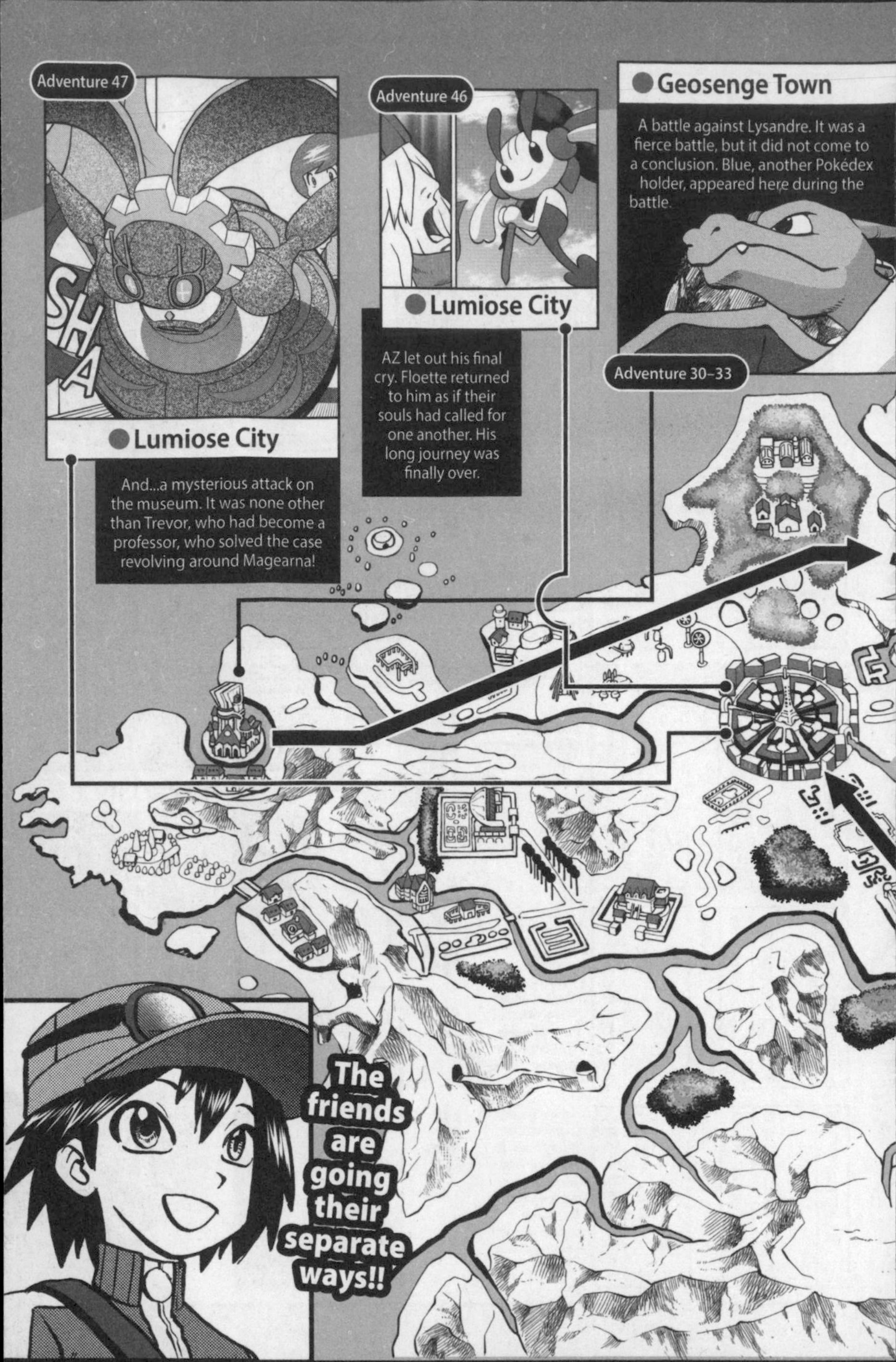
Geosenge Town
A battle against Lysandre. It was a fierce battle, but it did not come to a conclusion. Blue, another Pokédex holder, appeared here during the battle.
Adventure 30–33
Adventure 46
Lumiose City
AZ let out his final cry. Floette returned to him as if their souls had called for one another. His long journey was finally over.
Adventure 47
SHA
Lumiose City
And...a mysterious attack on the museum. It was none other than Trevor, who had become a professor, who solved the case revolving around Magearna!
The friends are going their separate ways!!

Kalos Region Pokédex Holders Pokémon Data

A complete edition of X and Y's Pokémon as of Adventure 47! Any stat that changes when they Mega Evolve is written after the ➡ mark!!

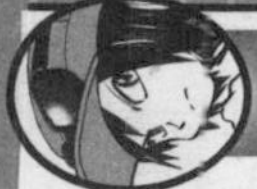

●X●

Kanga (Mega Kangaskhan) ♀

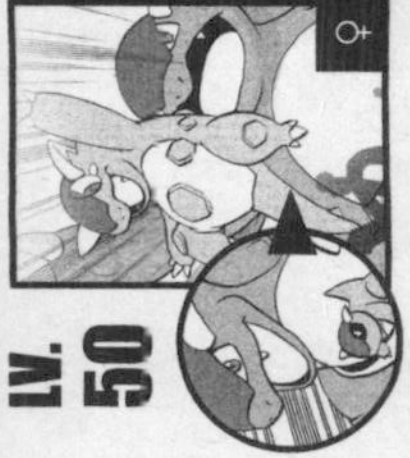

LV. 50

Nature: Bold.
Characteristic: Very finicky.
X's Pokémon who he has had with him since childhood. A strong and reliable partner!!

Category: Parent Pokémon
Type: Normal
Height: 7'03"
Weight: 176.4 lbs ➡ 220.5 lbs
Ability: Scrappy ➡ Parental Bond
National Pokédex: 115

Élec (Mega Manectric) ♂

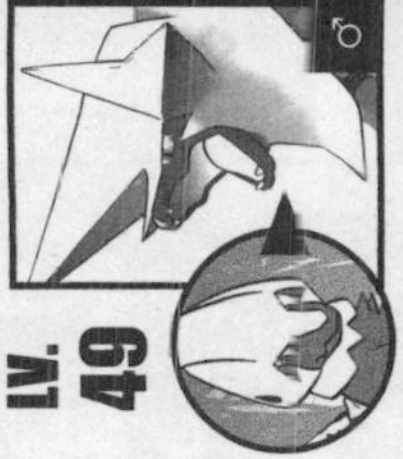

LV. 49

Nature: Naughty.
Characteristic: Mischievous.
A Pokémon with a powerful electric attack! It uses Wild Charge to attack its opponents.

Category: Discharge Pokémon
Type: Electric
Height: 4'11" ➡ 5'11"
Weight: 88.6 lbs ➡ 97.0 lbs
Ability: Lightning Rod ➡ Intimidate
National Pokédex: 310

Marisso (Chesnaught) ♂

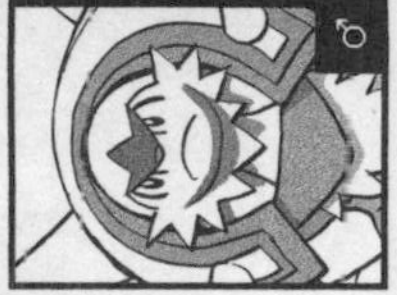

LV. 42

Nature: Hardy.
Characteristic: Somewhat stubborn. Its defense increased after evolving into Chesnaught. It can even withstand attacks from a powerful foe.

Category: Spiny Armor Pokémon
Type: Grass, Fighting
Height: 5'03"
Weight: 198.4 lbs
Ability: Overgrow
National Pokédex: 652

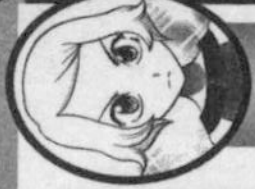

●Y●

Solsol (Absol) ♂

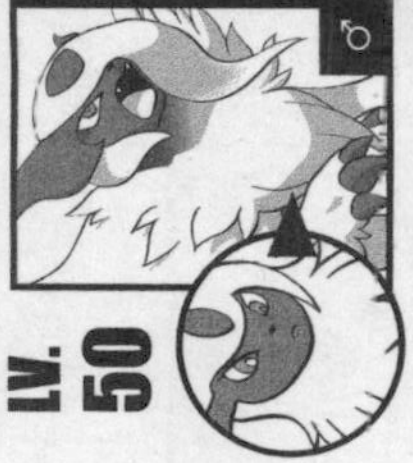

LV. 50

Nature: Adamant.
Characteristic: Often lost in thought.
A powerful Pokémon with an incredible ability to detect disasters!!

Category: Disaster Pokémon
Type: Dark
Height: 3'11"
Weight: 103.6 lbs ➡ 108.0 lbs
Ability: Super Luck ➡ Magic Bounce
National Pokédex: 359

Croaky (Greninja) ♂

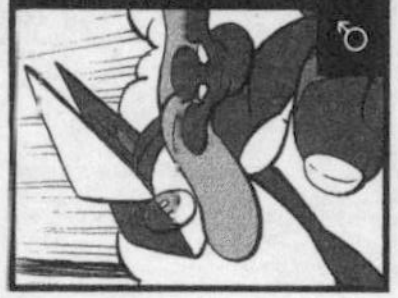

LV. 48

Nature: Careful.
Characteristic: Thoroughly cunning. A Pokémon that excels at ninja-like tactics. Its Water Shuriken fly at incredible speed.

Category: Ninja Pokémon
Type: Water, Dark
Height: 4'11"
Weight: 88.2 lbs
Ability: Battle Bond
National Pokédex: 658

Rhy-Rhy (Rhyhorn) ♂

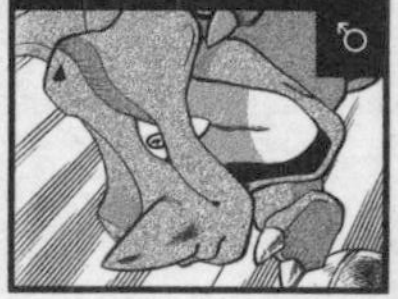

LV. 42

Nature: Bashful.
Characteristic: Sturdy body. It was originally a racing Rhyhorn but grew strong during the journey. X's tent was on its back.

Category: Spikes Pokémon
Type: Ground, Rock
Height: 3'03"
Weight: 253.5 lbs
Ability: Rock Head
National Pokédex: 111

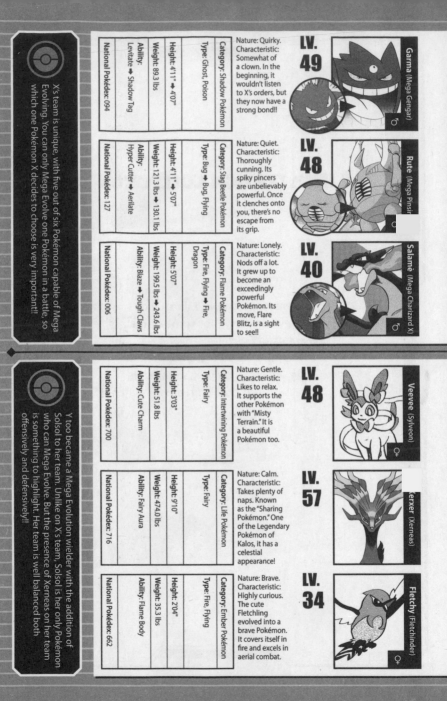

Garma (Mega Gengar) ♂

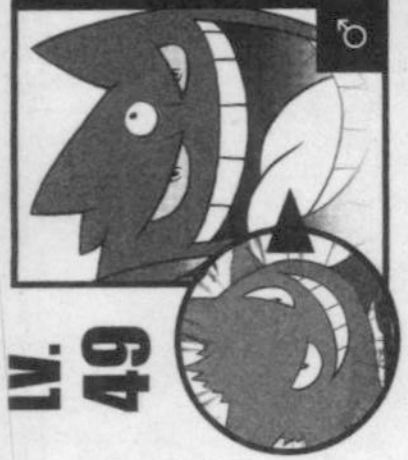

LV. 49

Nature: Quirky.
Characteristic: Somewhat of a clown. In the beginning, it wouldn't listen to X's orders, but they now have a strong bond!!

Category: Shadow Pokémon	
Type: Ghost, Poison	
Height: 4'11" ➡ 4'07"	
Weight: 89.3 lbs	
Ability: Levitate ➡ Shadow Tag	
National Pokédex: 094	

Rute (Mega Pinsir

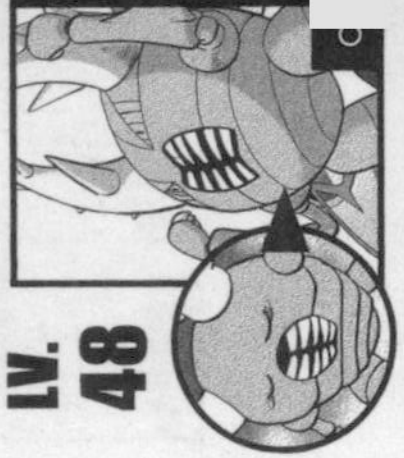

LV. 48

Nature: Quiet.
Characteristic: Thoroughly cunning. Its spiky pincers are unbelievably powerful. Once it clenches onto you, there's no escape from its grip.

Category: Stag Beetle Pokémon	
Type: Bug ➡ Bug, Flying	
Height: 4'11" ➡ 5'07"	
Weight: 121.3 lbs ➡ 130.1 lbs	
Ability: Hyper Cutter ➡ Aerilate	
National Pokédex: 127	

Salamè (Mega Charizard X) ♂

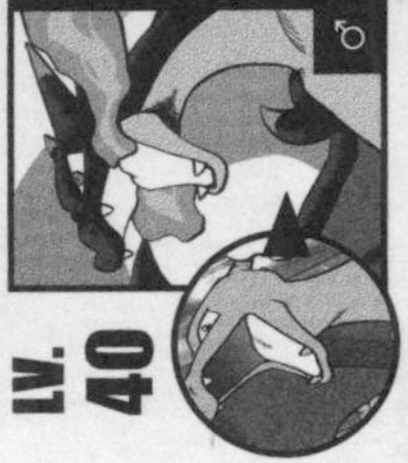

LV. 40

Nature: Lonely.
Characteristic: Nods off a lot. It grew up to become an exceedingly powerful Pokémon. Its move, Flare Blitz, is a sight to see!!

Category: Flame Pokémon	
Type: Fire, Flying ➡ Fire, Dragon	
Height: 5'07"	
Weight: 199.5 lbs ➡ 243.6 lbs	
Ability: Blaze ➡ Tough Claws	
National Pokédex: 006	

X's team is unique, with five out of six Pokémon capable of Mega Evolving. You can only Mega Evolve one Pokémon in a battle, so which one Pokémon X decides to choose is very important!!

Veevee (Sylveon) ♀

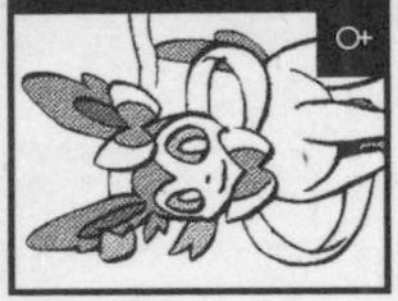

LV. 48

Nature: Gentle.
Characteristic: Likes to relax. It supports the other Pokémon with "Misty Terrain." It is a beautiful Pokémon too.

Category: Intertwining Pokémon	
Type: Fairy	
Height: 3'03"	
Weight: 51.8 lbs	
Ability: Cute Charm	
National Pokédex: 700	

erxer (Xerneas)

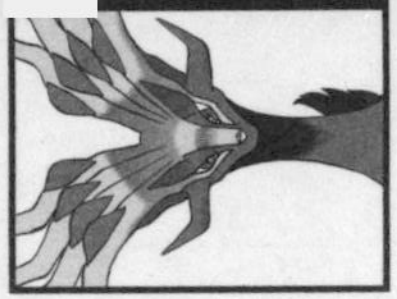

LV. 57

Nature: Calm.
Characteristic: Takes plenty of naps. Known as the "Sharing Pokémon." One of the Legendary Pokémon of Kalos, it has a celestial appearance!

Category: Life Pokémon	
Type: Fairy	
Height: 9'10"	
Weight: 474.0 lbs	
Ability: Fairy Aura	
National Pokédex: 716	

Fletchy (Fletchinder) ♀

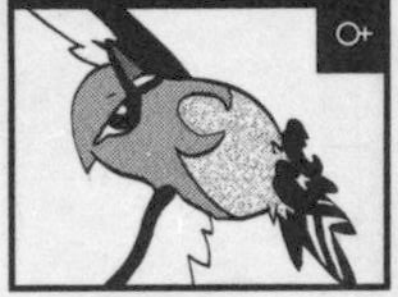

LV. 34

Nature: Brave.
Characteristic: Highly curious. The cute Fletchling evolved into a brave Pokémon. It covers itself in fire and excels in aerial combat.

Category: Ember Pokémon	
Type: Fire, Flying	
Height: 2'04"	
Weight: 35.3 lbs	
Ability: Flame Body	
National Pokédex: 662	

Y too became a Mega Evolution wielder with the addition of Solsol to her team. Unlike on X's team, Solsol is her only Pokémon who can Mega Evolve. But the presence of Xerneas on her team is something to highlight. Her team is well balanced both offensively and defensively!!

● ILLUSTRATION COLLECTION ●

Presenting title page illustrations
originally drawn for some of the
chapters of *Pokémon Adventures: X·Y*
when they were first published in
the Japanese children's magazine
Coro Coro Ichiban!

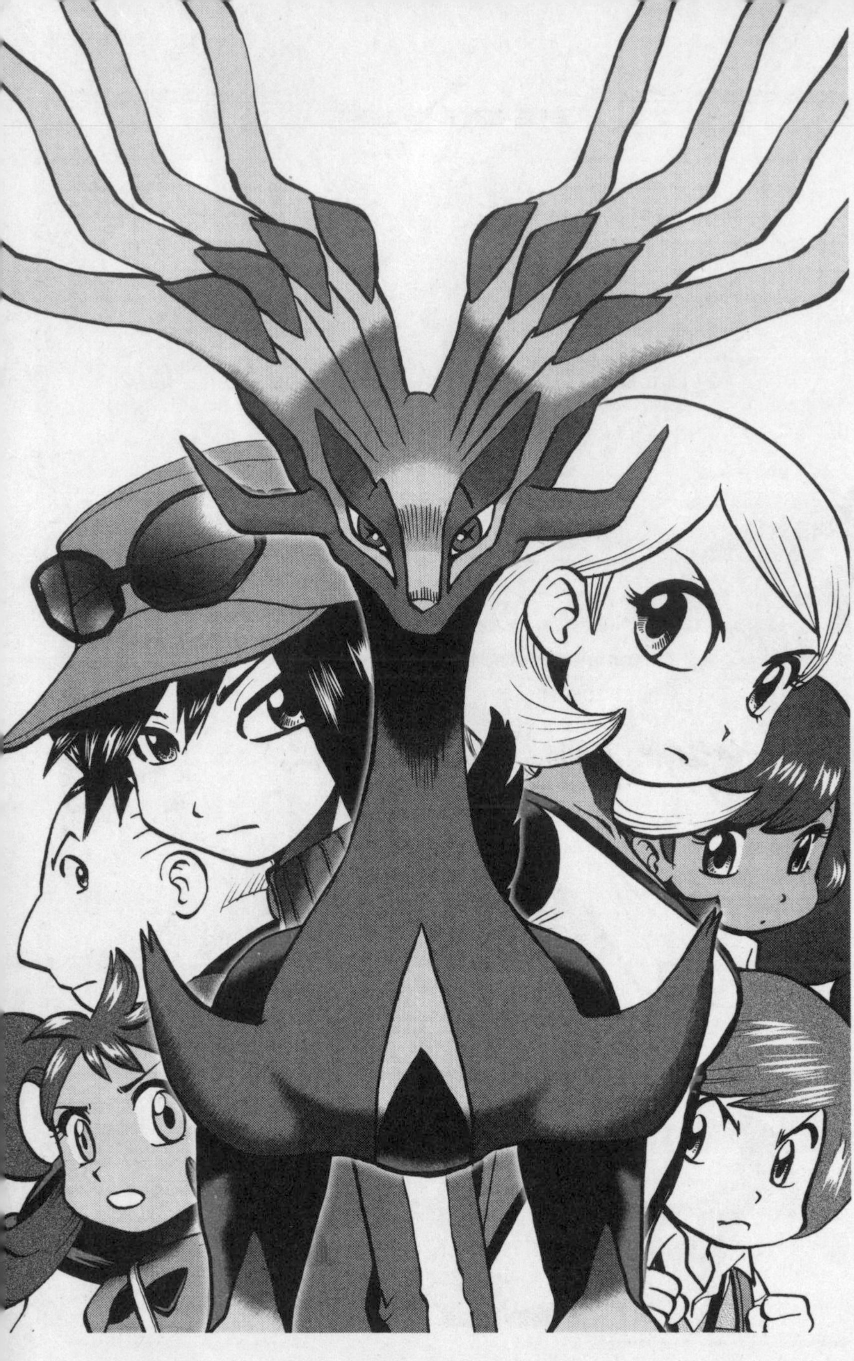

Adventure 33, *Coro Coro Ichiban!*, December 2015 Issue

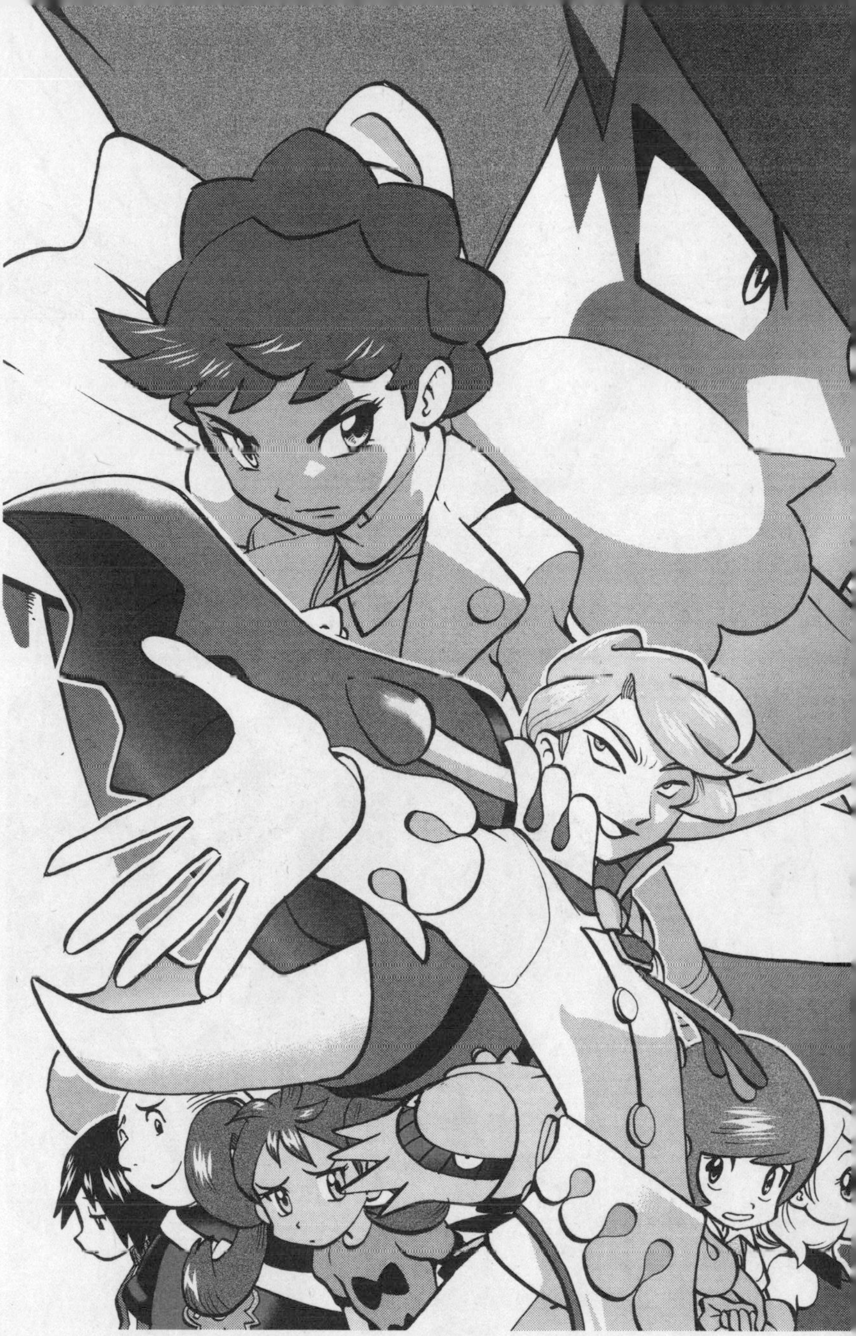

Adventure 34, *Coro Coro Ichiban!*, January 2016 Issue

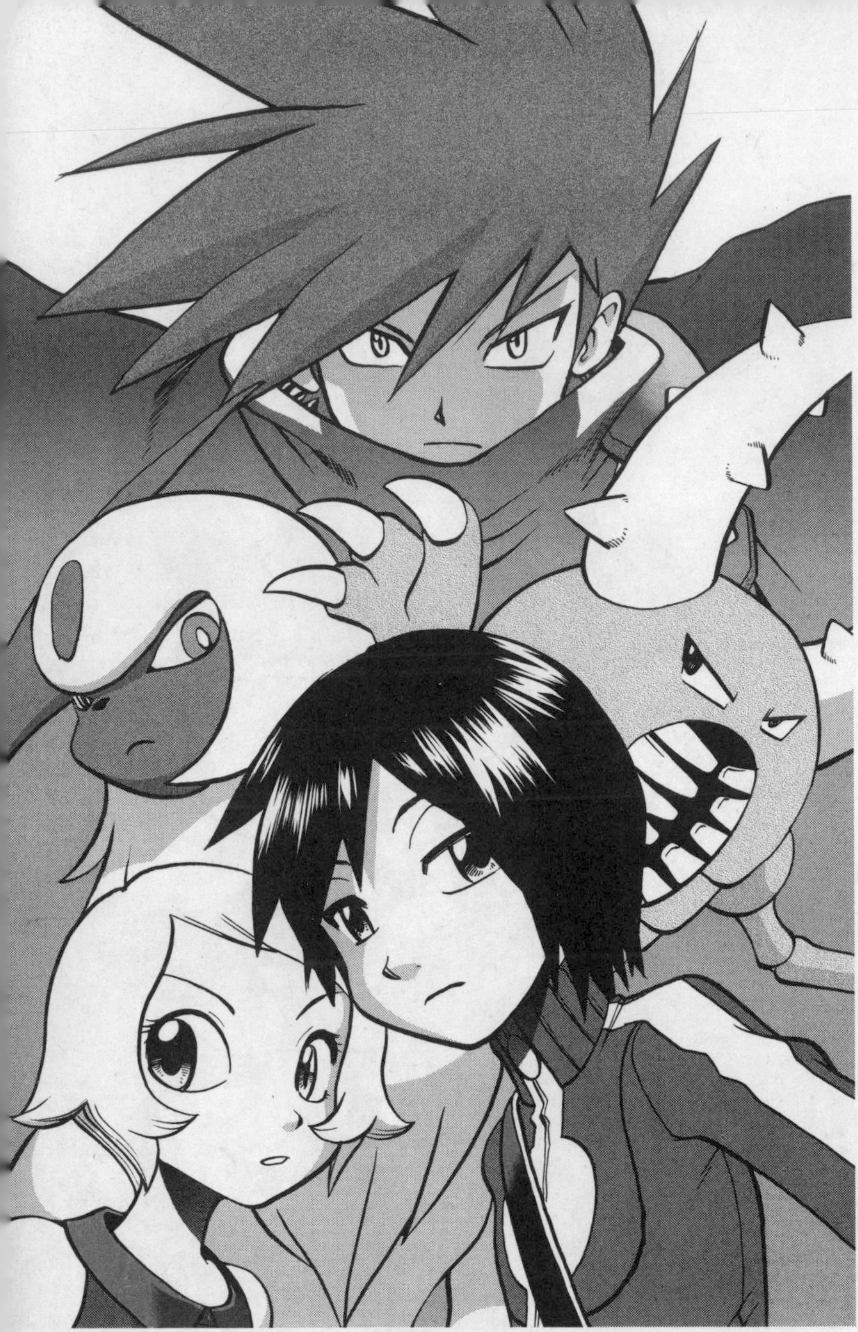

Adventure 35, *Coro Coro Ichiban!*, February 2016 Issue

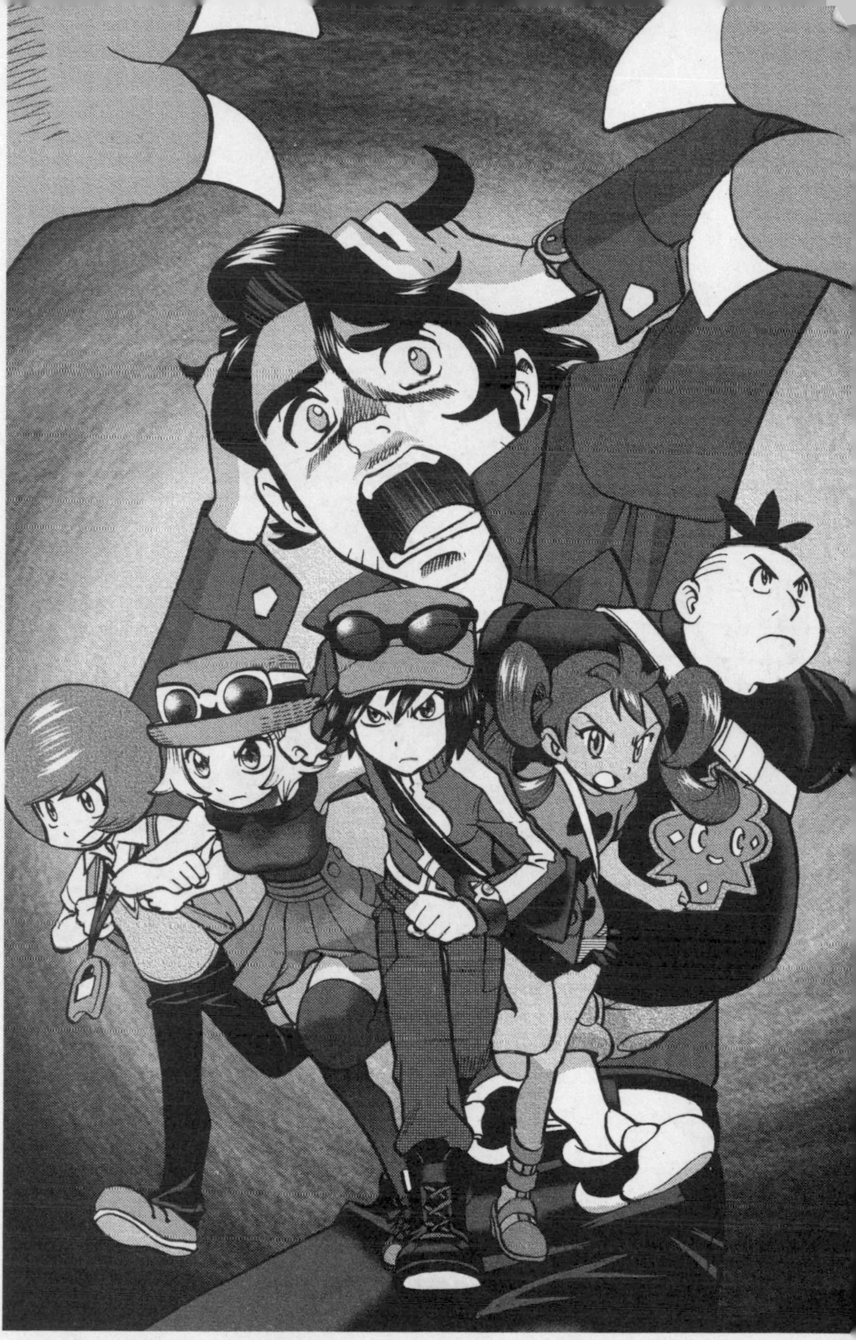

Adventure 36, *Coro Coro Ichiban!*, March 2016 Issue

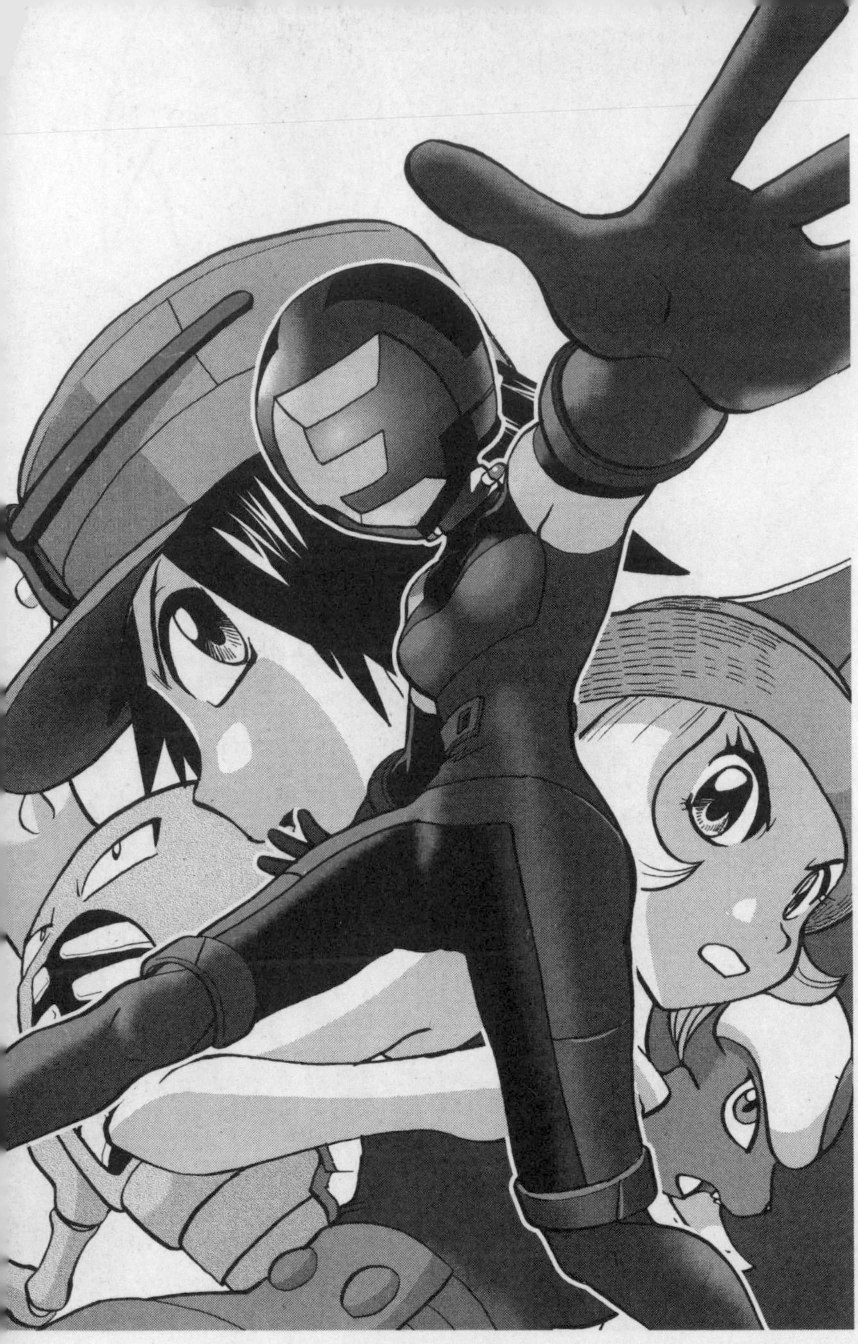

Adventure 37, *Coro Coro Ichiban!*, April 2016 Issue

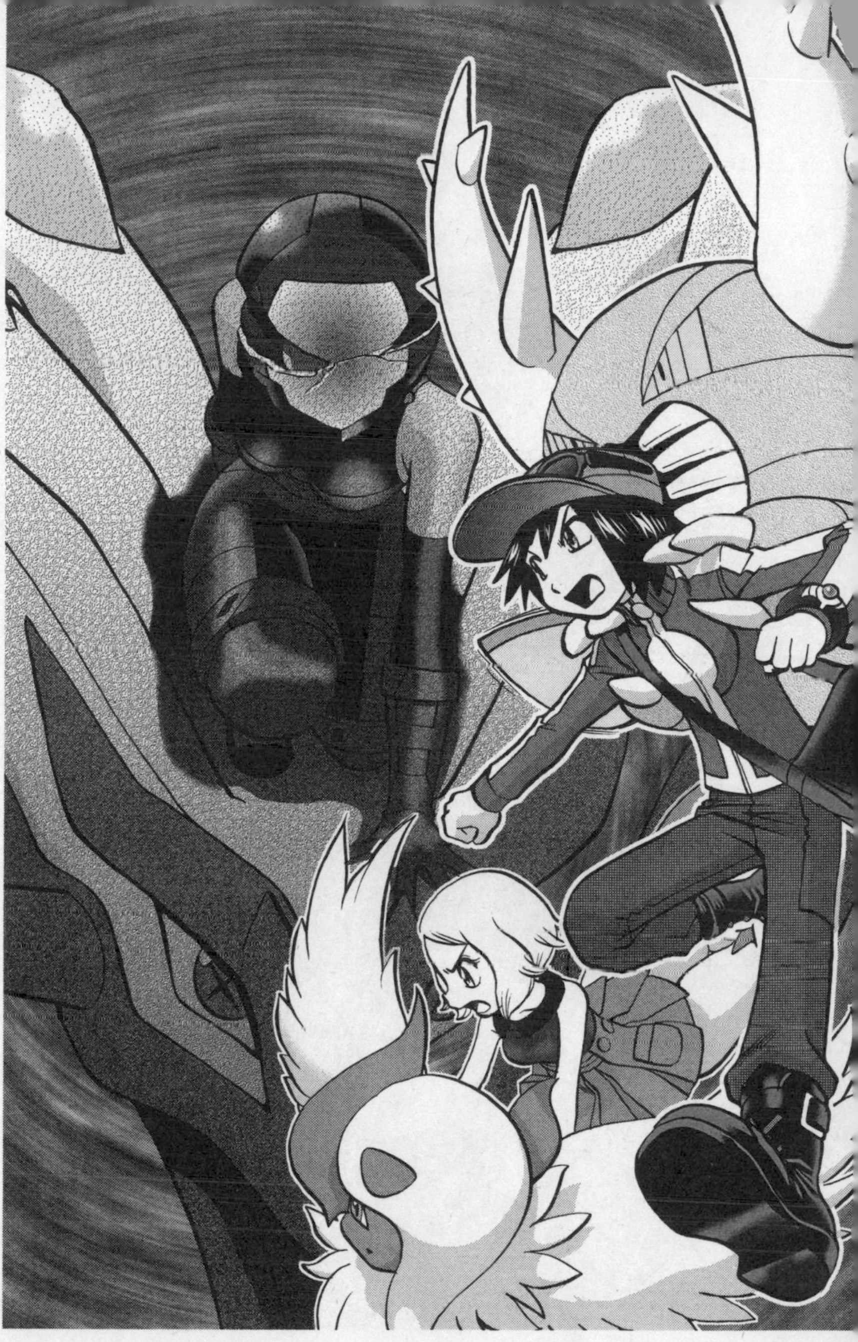

Adventure 38, *Coro Coro Ichiban!*, May 2016 Issue

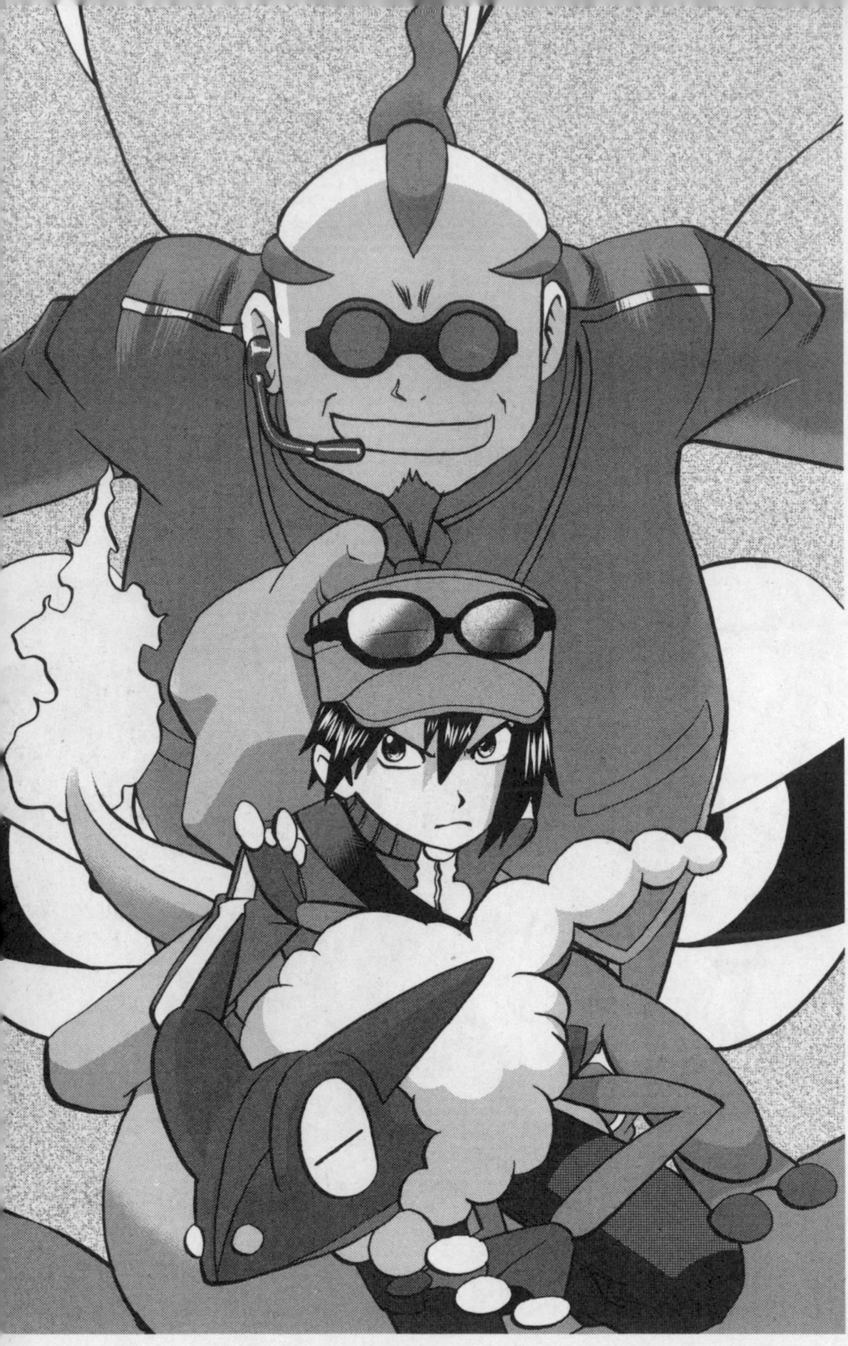

Adventure 39, *Coro Coro Ichiban!*, June 2016 Issue

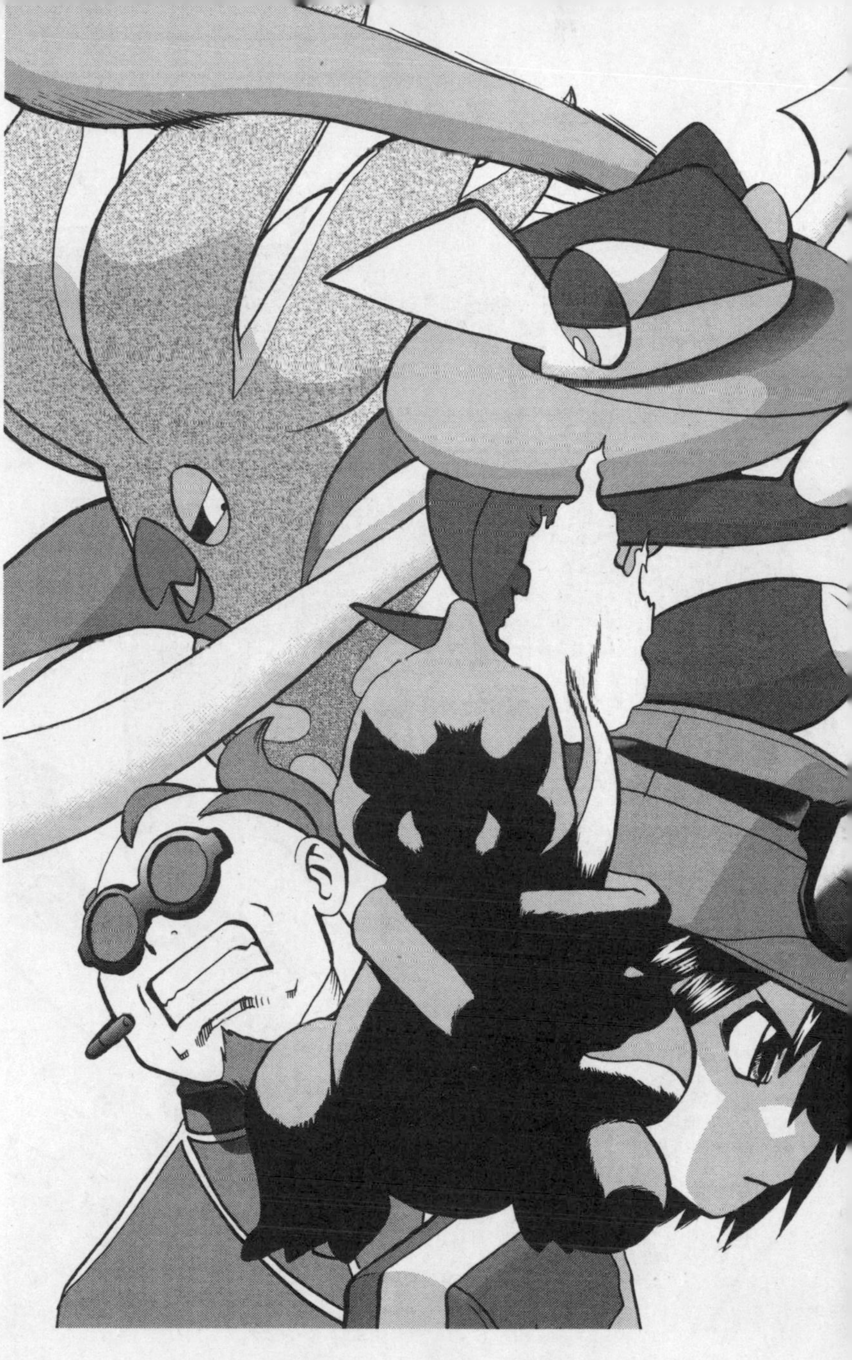

Adventure 40, *Coro Coro Ichiban!*, July 2016 Issue

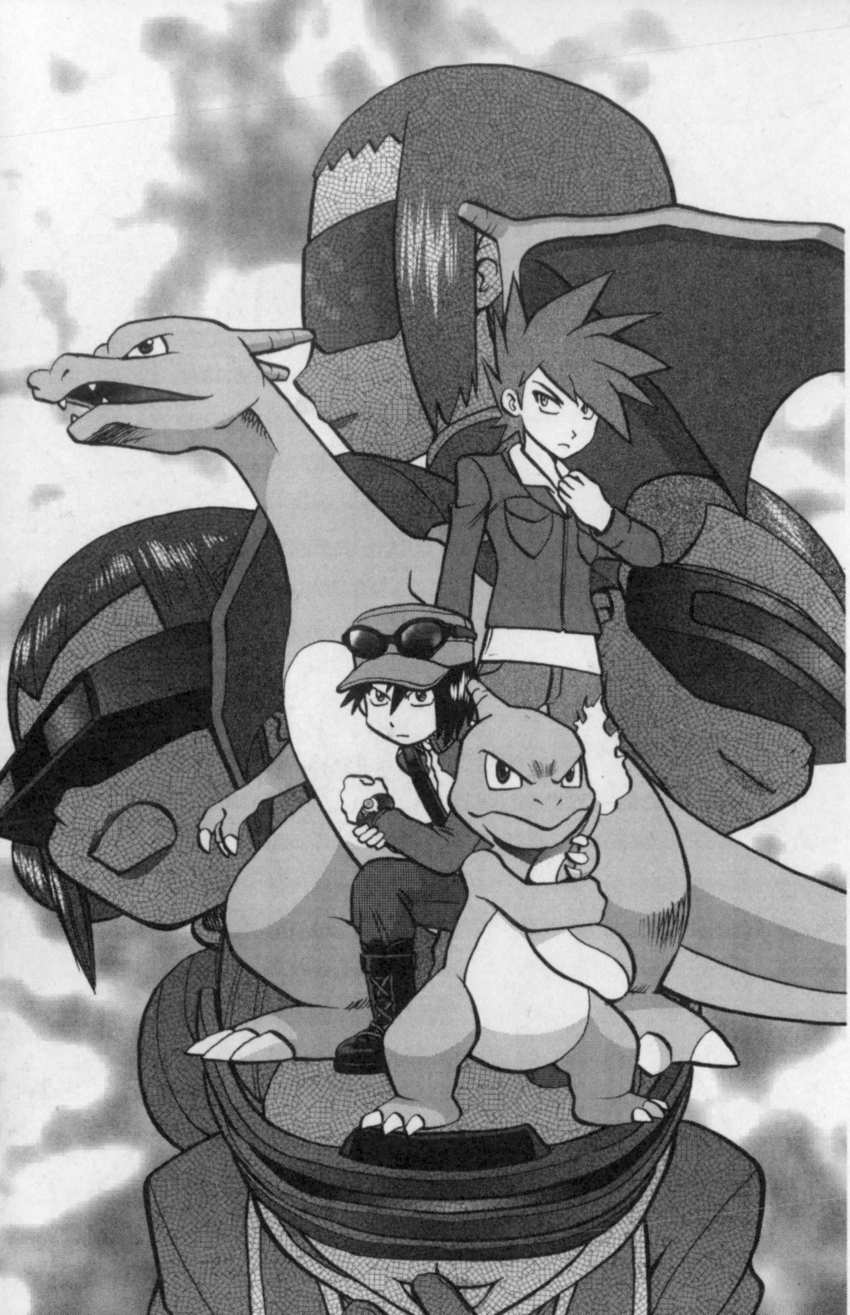

Adventure 41, *Coro Coro Ichiban!*, August 2016 Issue

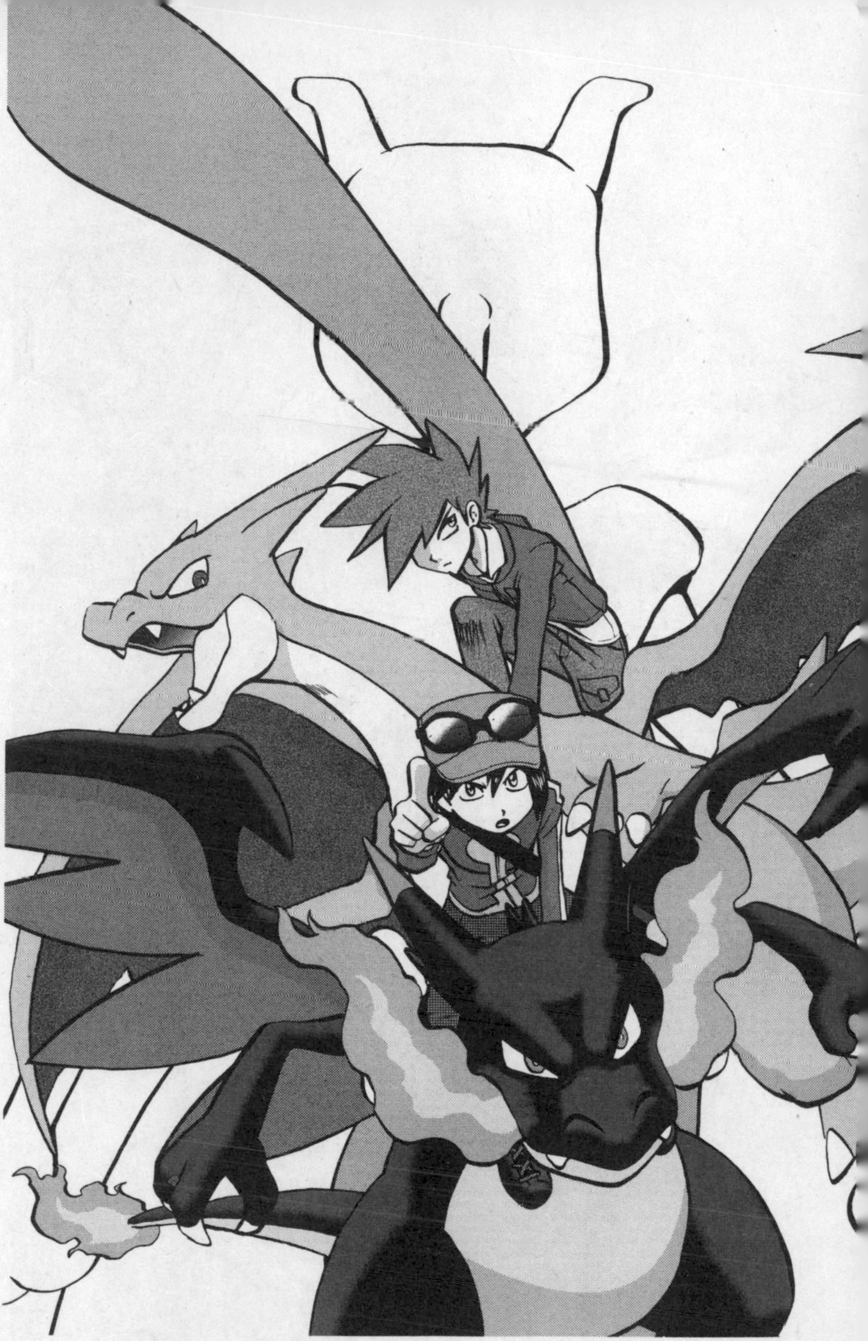

Adventure 42, *Coro Coro Ichiban!*, September 2016 Issue

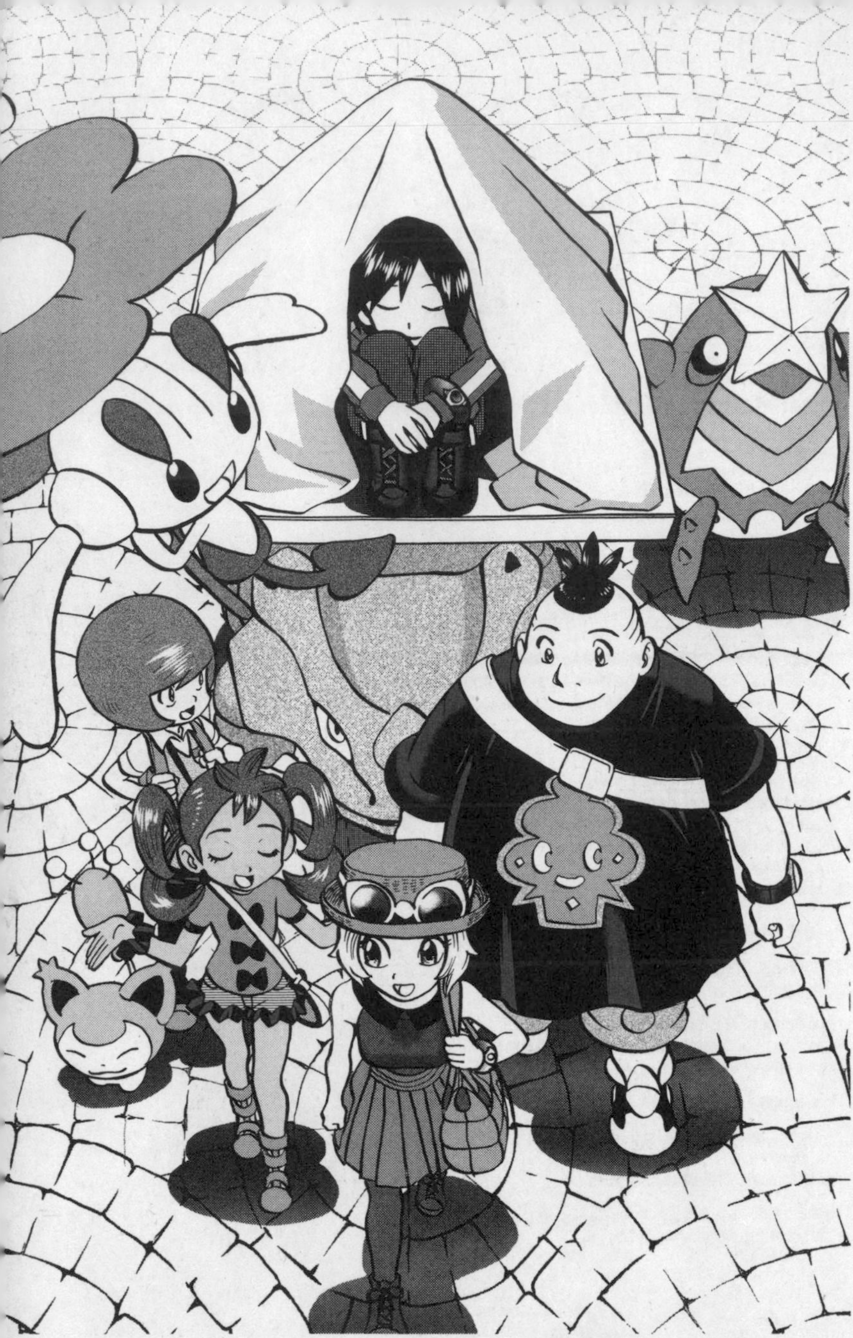

Adventure 46, *Coro Coro Ichiban!*, January 2017 Issue

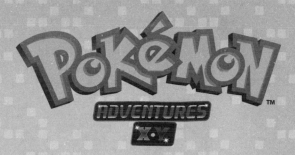

Pokémon ADVENTURES: X·Y
Volume 6
VIZ Media Edition

Story by HIDENORI KUSAKA
Art by SATOSHI YAMAMOTO

©2023 Pokémon.
©1995–2022 Nintendo / Creatures Inc. / GAME FREAK inc.
TM, ®, and character names are trademarks of Nintendo.
© 1997 Hidenori KUSAKA, Satoshi YAMAMOTO
All rights reserved.
Original Japanese edition published by SHOGAKUKAN.
English translation rights in the United States of America,
Canada, the United Kingdom, Ireland, Australia and New Zealand
arranged with SHOGAKUKAN.

Translation/Tetsuichiro Miyaki
English Adaptation/Bryant Turnage
Touch-Up & Lettering/Annaliese "Ace" Christman, Susan Daigle-Leach
Original Series Design/Shawn Carrico
Original Series Editor/Annette Roman
Graphic Novel Design/Alice Lewis
Graphic Novel Editor/Joel Enos

Special thanks to Trish Ledoux at The Pokémon Company International.

The stories, characters, and incidents mentioned
in this publication are entirely fictional.

Printed in Canada

Published by VIZ Media, LLC
P.O. Box 77010
San Francisco, CA 94107

10 9 8 7 6 5 4 3 2 1
First printing, September 2023

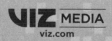
viz.com

PARENTAL ADVISORY
POKÉMON ADVENTURES: X·Y is
rated A and is suitable for readers
of all ages.

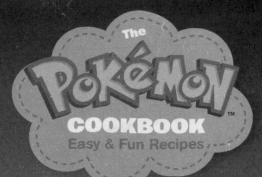

The Pokémon COOKBOOK
Easy & Fun Recipes

by **Maki Kudo**

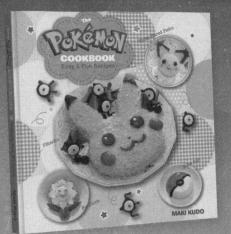

Create delicious dishes that look like your favorite Pokémon characters with more than 35 fun, easy recipes. Make a Poké Ball sushi roll, Pikachu ramen or mashed Meowth potatoes for your next party, weekend activity or powered-up lunch box.

viz.com

POKÉMON™

SWORD & SHIELD

Story by
Hidenori Kusaka

Art by
Satoshi Yamamoto

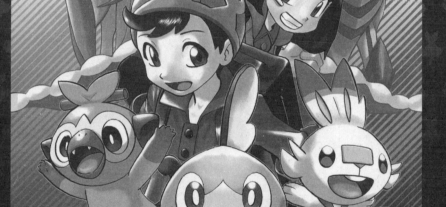

Awesome adventures inspired by the best-selling
Pokémon Sword & Shield video games
set in the Galar region!

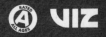

THE ART OF

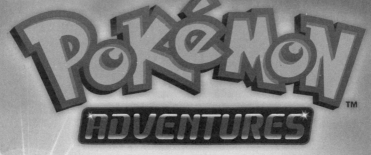

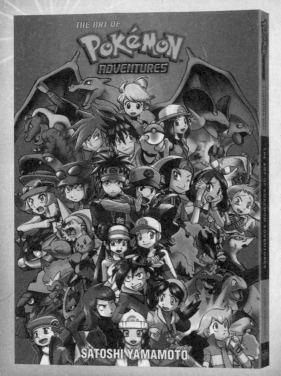

**STORY AND ART BY
Satoshi Yamamoto**

A collection of beautiful full-color art from the artist of the Pokémon Adventures graphic novel series! In addition to illustrations of your favorite Pokémon, this vibrant volume includes exclusive sketches and storyboards, four pull-out posters, and an exclusive manga side story!

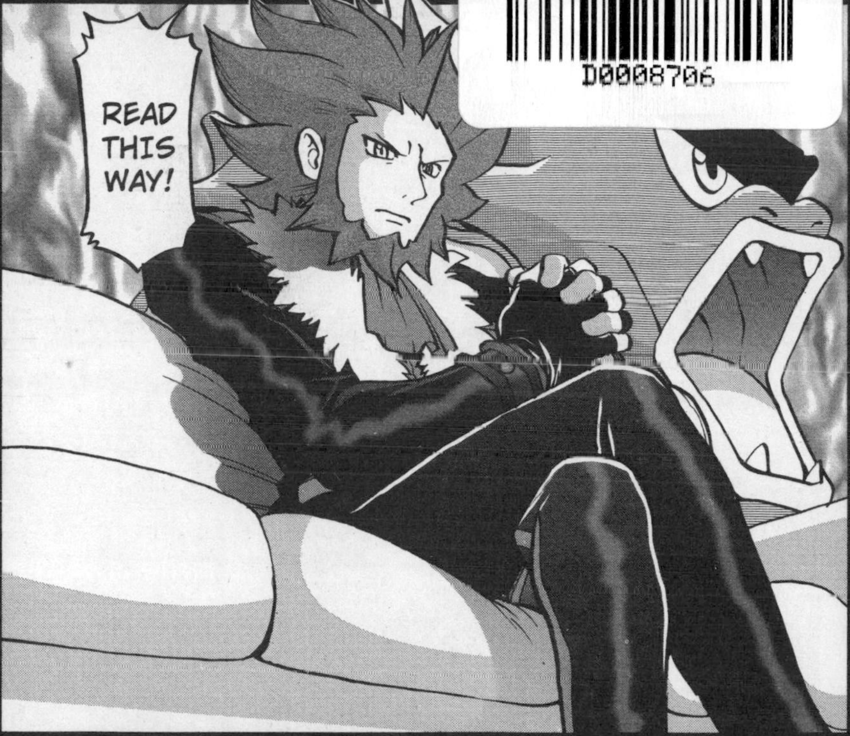
READ THIS WAY!

THIS IS THE END OF THIS GRAPHIC NOVEL!

To properly enjoy this VIZ Media graphic novel, please turn it around and begin reading from right to left.

This book has been printed in the original Japanese format in order to preserve the orientation of the original artwork.

Have fun with it!

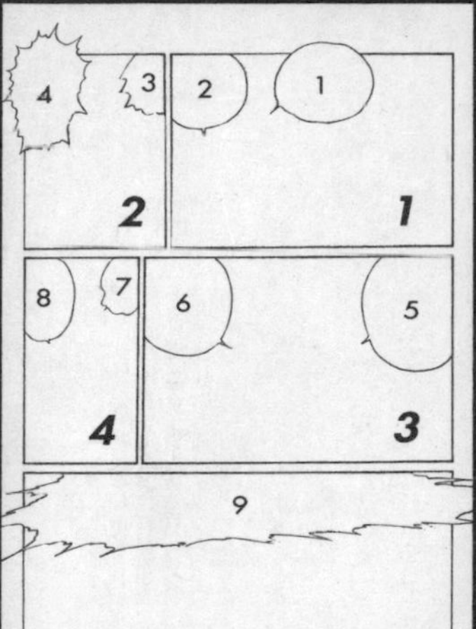

FOLLOW THE ACTION THIS WAY.